MAP

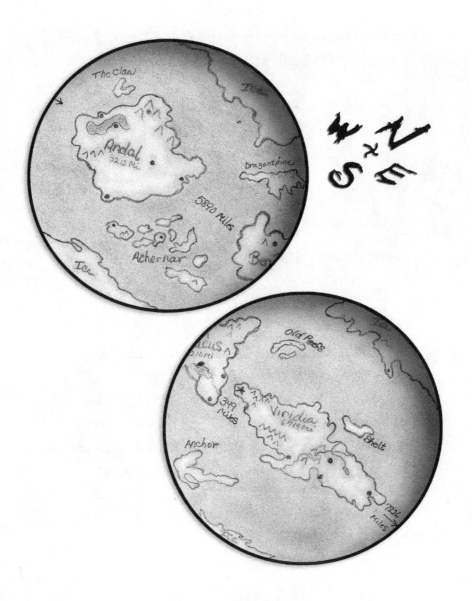

EQUUS

Look for The Continuation of the Dragonhorse Chronicles:

Conscience of the King (Book 2)

Peace on Another's Terms (Book 3)

A Lopsided Colorwax Heart (Book 4) *(Coming Soon)*

Spirit in Motion (Book 5) *(Coming Soon)*

Visit our website at

www.dragonhorserising.com

And for this Author's Peter Aarons Books:

Glory Days (Book 1)

Another Man's Wife ~ A Love Story (Book 2)

Home Again Home Again (Book 3) *(Coming Soon)*

The Converging Objects of the Universe (Book 4) *(Coming Soon)*

Oh, Baby! (Book 5) *(Coming Soon)*

Visit our website at

www.peteraarons.com

Showandah S. Terrill

DRAGONHORSE
RISING

BOOK ONE OF
THE DRAGONHORSE CHRONICLES

SHORT HORSE PRESS

This book is a work of fiction, and any references to historical events, real people or real locales are used fictitiously. Other names, places, characters and incidents are products of the author's imagination, and any resemblance to actual events or locales or persons, living or dead, is purely coincidental.

Published 2020 by Short Horse Press.

DRAGONHORSE

RISING

**With thanks to Bill Kilpatrick
who stated the obvious.**

"I know that if I survive this, I will return to many
questions, and to the final ceremonies which set me
in place and perhaps hold me against my will."

-Ah'krill Ardenai Morning Star

CHAPTER ONE

O n the last morning he awoke as Ah'rane Ardenai Krush, the covers felt good, and he snugged them over one shoulder before checking the motion of his hand to his wife's side of the bed. He sighed and forced his thoughts with practiced determination on to other subjects. No need to run lesson plans through his head. Today was a school holiday, and he had a meeting of the Educational Council in Thura. He'd thought about not going, but High Priestess Ah'krill had called the meeting, and one did not refuse such a summons, even if it was one's birthing day.

He opened his eyes and glanced at the empty pillow beside him before moving his gaze to the huge Equi pines outside the casements of Canyon keep. They were perfectly still. The day would warm up as the sun rose.

Maybe there were new foals on the ground. New life. His sire would already be out checking on the mares. His sister would be in the garden, pushing aside the straw which shielded the rows of perennial alcibus to find the earliest spring greens. She said that picking them before sunup made them the most nutritious and tender.

He hoped, as he always did, that she'd made flatwraps this morning. Warm flatwraps stuffed with creamed sheep cheese, fruit, nuts and honey, sprinkled with cinnamon. That thought got him on his feet and out the door for his morning run along the river. He could see his breath, and blew it skyward as offering, chanting his morning prayers as he ran.

Why had Ah'krill called a meeting today? It seemed odd, somehow. He wondered about that as he dried off after his bath. Had she ever called a meeting of the Education Council? If she had, he couldn't remember.

He trotted across the main hub and into the enormous family kitchen to find Krush at the table, eyes veiled slightly against the steam rising from the mug he was holding. Ardenai kissed the top of his father's head and landed in his usual chair. "It's late, and you're still here. No new foals this morning? Where's Mother?"

"It is not my turn to watch your mother, and I'm not still here, I'm back here," his father grinned. "I wanted to catch you before you left for Thura so I could wish you a proper blessing on your one hundredth birthing day. Are we still on for a sail?"

"We are, absolutely!" Ardenai nodded, reaching for one of the earthenware mugs in the center of the table. "Just you and me?"

"Teal is coming. Criollo is home for week's end, so he's coming. We could take two smaller boats and race if you'd like. Breeze is supposed to be up at Falconstones this afternoon."

"A perfect day," Ardenai smiled. "I can't wait."

The smile pleased his father. Ardenai hadn't smiled enough the last couple of years – not the deep, truly happy smiles he'd flashed before Ah'ree's death. Maybe he was finally rounding the corner – ready to get on with his life. Another thought crossed his mind, hidden deep, half-forgotten until today's argument with his wife. Krush forced it aside, reaching instead for one of the tea pots next to the cups and pushing it in Ardenai's direction. "Fresh picked," he said.

Ardenai was pouring himself a cup of the fragrant brew when his mother appeared from the baker's pantry. She smiled, opened one of the warming ovens and removed a steaming plate, which she placed with some ceremony in front of her son. "The first gift of the day is always the best," she laughed.

"My favorite breakfast!" he exclaimed. "Thank you. But you didn't have to do that. I'm a fully mature man as of today, you know. I can find my own breakfast."

Ah'rane gave him a squeeze and perched beside him on the corner of the table. "I have watched you find your own breakfast, Ardenai Teacher. You find your sister's flatwraps, a jar of honey and the cinnamon shaker.

This way you'll last a little longer in that meeting."

"Yes, you can indulge yourself in an extra argument with Priestess Ah'ti," his father intoned, and then laughed at the look on Ardenai's mobile face.

"My birthing day, and you had to speak her name," he groaned.

Ah'rane folded her hands in her lap and grew more serious. "Ardi, we have plans for you today. Do you really have to go to Thura?"

He nodded and his mouth twisted just a bit to the side in that manner he had. "I do," he said, "but Ah'krill promised it won't last long."

Krush snorted. "Really? The Education Council is the longest-winded bunch on the planet." He rose, kissed his wife's hair and turned again to his son. "We will meet you at the boat."

"I will be there," Ardenai promised.

Ah'rane watched his husband's retreating back and spoke without looking at Ardenai. "I want you to be careful today," she said. "If I give you a list, will you pick up some things for me in Thura?"

"Of course," Ardenai replied, reading the worry in her eyes. "Is everything all right?"

"Everything is fine," she said, and smiled. "Your father and I just had one of our little discussions. You finish your breakfast. I'll get that list ready and leave it here on the table for you."

▲ ▲ ▲ ▲ ▲ ▲ ▲

The brilliant whites and new green of late winter on planet Equus had shaded to the pinks and greys of evening on the main monitor, and the captain of the Seventh Galactic Alliance Science Vessel Belesprit was still leaning forward in rapt attention, hands on his knees, studying his Tactical Wing Commander. "It's true then? This man actually goes from being an ordinary citizen one day, to the absolute ruler of Equus and her affined worlds the next? With no warning whatsoever? That's got to be a hell of a shock for him and scary as hell for the people of Equus. They yank some guy away from whatever he's doing and say, 'Surprise, you now rule eleven planets?' Hopefully he's not the village idiot, or the town drunk."

The young man to whom he was speaking dipped his head in assent, dark brown eyes twinkling with amusement. "We always hope that. I suppose there has to be an inkling in a certain percent of the male population. He has to know he's turning a hundred in one of the five years of the ascension. We're in year four. How many High Equi males are left?"

Science Chief Winslow Moonsgold jerked his bony, parallel chins the direction of the main screen which had changed from flowing scenes of the vast agrarian planet below, to the outline of an approaching ship – not large, but graceful. "That's Solafar, the Taraxian Flagship," he said, flashing his good-natured grin. "We now have at least one ship from every member of the Affined Equi Worlds, every sector of the Seventh Galactic Alliance, and representatives from the United Galactic Alliance. A proud day for the Great House of Equus, wouldn't you say, Kehailan?"

"Indeed it is," the young man said softly. "No one living has ever seen this ceremony, and it will not be seen again for seven hundred years."

"We're being hailed," said Oonah Pongo, and Marion Eletsky, mumbling under his breath, swung his chair to face the main viewer.

Kehailan nodded politely from time to time to acknowledge the Taraxian captain, but his thoughts were on the planet below. Who would rise to be Firstlord of Equus? He could imagine his sire, gathered with his class of five and six-year-olds around the viewing screen, recounting the history and legends of the Dragonhorse, telling them all the same things he was telling his woefully uninformed crew mates, except that if he were with his father he could relax, and there would be honey cakes and hot challa, and warm, fleecy blankets to wrap up in – and tickling, and giggling. He flicked his dark eyes at his timepiece.

Doctor Hadrian Keats turned a cool, hostile gaze in Kehailan's direction. "Every ship in the Seventh Galactic Alliance is here, slavering to pledge allegiance to this guy, why, exactly, do they need us? Eletsky dragged us here because of you, didn't he, Wing Commander?" He heaved a sigh and looked studiously bored. "This is taking forever. Most interesting thing so far has been that little Taraxian. I swear to God, my mother used to trap those things in our basement. They got into everything. And what's with that thingy they keep flashing at us?" He flipped a languid hand at the huge seal, and swung idly back and forth in his chair, his face an open challenge.

"I can tell you that!" exclaimed the little boy standing with his class in front of the navigational array. "Evewybody knowth that! We've justht been lewning about it. We won a contetht, so our claths got to come up here onto the bwidge fo a bit. Hello! Can I tell you? Pleathe? Befo we go back?"

"We would love it if you told us," Eletsky replied. "Thank you for offering, Yussef."

Keats writhed and grimaced with distaste, but the little boy was already in full animation. "Ith the Gweat Theal of the Dwagonhothe!" Yussef exclaimed, and began to recite, his excited eyes moving left to right across the remembered page. "Look at the…" he paused momentarily to prepare his tongue, and the little girl next to him put her hands on her hips and stared him down.

"You'd better let me," she cautioned. "I have all my teeth."

"Reynalda," came the quiet warning, and she rolled her eyes upward to contemplate her teacher. "You were not asked to speak."

"No," Yussef sighed. "Theeth wight. Nobody understhands me and thith is weally impotant sthuff. Weynalda thood tell it…I guessth."

Reynalda was twitching with impatience, but she waited until the teacher gave her a grudging nod, then began in a rush. "I'm going to marry Yussef – if he gets all his teeth, so don't be mad at me but he doesn't have all his teeth and I do so I'm just going to talk for him and that is the Great Seal of the Dragonhorse!" She sucked in for air and made a delightfully theatrical gesture in the direction of the screen. "Please observe the chevrons, which are stacked to represent how the Equi depend upon one another. The pictures carved on them stand for things the Equi hold precious." Again her eyes rolled upward. "Good so far?' she whispered, and the teacher nodded.

"Good so far," he whispered back.

"This ancient symbol stands with only six silver chevrons until a

Dragonhorse rises, when a seventh chevron bearing the image of the scales of...the scales of..." the brows came together. "Uh oh."

"Juthtuth," Yussef hissed with some annoyance.

"Justice," she echoed. "When a seventh chevron representing the scales of *justice* is added at the top.   The round shape represents the protection the Dragonhorse provides and the purple background represents the absolute power of the Dragonhorse." Reynalda stopped as a thought crossed her mind and widened her eyes. "He's not really going to be a dragon, is he? Fire and all that?"

"No," Kehailan chuckled. "He'll be an Equi like Orlov Teacher, or me, or the other Equi on board. Dragonhorse is just his title, like Emperor, or Pasha."

"Thank goodness," she sighed. "I really need to go to the bathroom now."

"My cue to head for the classroom," Orlov said, excused himself and shooed the class of first graders off the bridge.

Kehailan resisted the urge to go with them, just to escape the relentless questioning of his shipmates, and settled back in his chair, chuckling softly to himself.

Eletsky mimicked the doctor's gesture toward the seal. "The thingy's the Great Seal of the Dragonhorse, Hadrian, and the Thirteenth Dragonhorse is about to rise! On with the story! Tell us about succession," the captain prompted, leaning forward to slap Kehailan on the thigh. He tugged the collar of his jacket open and settled into a graceful slouch which suited his agile frame.

He always reminded the Wing Commander of a little black lithoped, stretching on the hearth, and Kehailan crimped a grin, flashing Eletsky a pair of charming dimples. "Ah, yes," he nodded, mustering his sobriety. "For thirteen generations the priestesses and the Great Council rule Equus. In the fourteenth generation a male ascends to power. His power is not religious in nature, but secular. He answers to no one. He is Firstlord. His power is absolute over Equus and her ten tribute worlds. The daughter which the

Firstlord sires this day will rise to take her granddam's place as High Priestess, so the female line is never broken."

"How can you be sure the bloodline is being kept pure, and being passed?" asked Keats. "This all sounds rather suspect to me – either eugenics or fabrication – not sure which I like less."

"We breed the finest horses in the galaxy," Kehailan shrugged. "This is no different. There are those whose life's work it is to know who is to be mated to whom within the Great House and beyond. It is both a duty and an honor to be mated in such a manner."

The comment and its casualness raised a warning flag few of the bridge crew missed and Oona leaned forward slightly in her chair. "What if they don't want to marry that person?" she asked.

Only Kehailan, who was thoroughly distracted, missed the coolness in the Linguistics Officer's voice. "It's not a marriage, it's a breeding to produce an offspring," he reiterated patiently. "Just like breeding horses. Mares go on to other mates and other offspring. So do the women who are chosen to…ah…" Oona's icy stare shut Kehailan's mouth. "Oops," he whispered.

"The whole thing sounds sad, and contrived, and forced," she said into the silence. "It sounds like rape on a multiplicity of levels."

Kehailan looked startled, then gritted his teeth and forced a smile. "I suppose, from an outsider's perspective it most likely does, Oonah, but you need to understand that this is sacred to us. It is a sacred trust that has stayed intact for ten thousand years, and it is taken very, very seriously. This Firstlord was fostered from the day he was born and raised without fanfare to be a good Equi citizen. No special treatment. No pampering of any kind. He has been bred from the finest seed of his line and the strongest genes in our world, to be the prototype of the Equi male. Above all else, it is our prayer that he love justice and mercy, because not all of them have. Physically he will be artistic, articulate, physically powerful, strongly telepathic, and as flawlessly brilliant as any cleomitite. The golden armbands which mark him as the Thirteenth Dragonhorse have been poured in place, and he will now pass his line to a woman he does not know, to a daughter he will not see for fifty years, for the ultimate good of Equus. Can you not see that?"

"It may be tradition for you, but it sounds like slavery to me!" Oonah snapped. "It's sad."

Kehailan's eyes changed shape, and his hands tightened on the arms of his chair. "Our traditions have made us both beneficent and powerful and they have kept us that way for millennia. Who was it that pulled your collective asses out of the fire when your planet was destroying itself? Ah yes. Equus," he purred. "Who governs you now? Equus."

Moonsgold made a calming gesture, first toward Kehailan, then Oonah, catching her in his gaze. "It's not entirely sad," he said. "Think of it this way, Oonah. Today, a lady who has waited a very long time, a hundred years – an entire lifetime for a Declivian like me, or a Terren like you, will greet her son. It will be interesting to see if they do know one another. Perhaps they go to the same clothier, or the same market. It's a fascinating prospect."

Captain Eletsky was scowling, blue eyes narrowed as he reviewed what had just been said. After a few moments of soundlessly moving his jaws he screwed up his face and managed, "Did you say, *Poured on*? As in molten metal? Really? I assumed they were just bracelets, and the rest of it was a gruesome legend."

"I don't think so," Kehailan muttered. "I think it's a very permanent way of marking him as Firstlord. In either case we're about to find out. Soon. I hope."

Eletsky cringed a little in spite of himself, then sat up and gestured at the tray arriving from the galley. "The wine coming around is a cleomitite medal vintage from the vineyards of River keep," he said. "Kehailan's father gave it to me a month or two ago, and I thought I'd open it in honor of today's celebration. Actually, I won it off him in a poker game, and right now I need some. Just talking about this is making me hurt all over."

"Think about it," Kehailan insisted. "Though males rule only once in every seven hundred years, they do rule with absolute power and for life. They're the ones who have faced usurpers and assassins, and, if my sire is correct, this one will, too. The Dragonhorse has to be strong, and this whole rising ceremony with all its components is a very good first test." He sat back and sipped his wine, looking thoroughly irked.

"He must be very tired by now," said Timothy McGill, and gave Kehailan one of his slow, sweet smiles. "You look a little tired, too. I think we should leave you alone and let you think your own thoughts on this occasion."

Kehailan was nodding his thanks when the screen brightened and everybody tensed up. The scenes of Equus were replaced by the spiral, symbol of the twelve United Galactic Alliances, then the Corvus eagle, fir tree and sea of the Seventh Galactic Alliance, and last, the Great Seal of the House of Equus, now bearing seven silver chevrons.

"The child has been conceived," Kehailan whispered. "The Thirteenth Dragonhorse has risen." He set his wine glass aside and rubbed at his arms, his heart thumping a little harder in his chest.

A vast, alabaster hall, elegantly carved from the living stone of the planet came into focus. It was quiet. There was no music, no one waving his hat and yelling, "Long live the king!" Four squads of Horse Guard, arrayed in two single columns against the walls, stood utterly still, dwarfed by the enormity of the chamber. No guardsman moved. No horse so much as twitched his head or shifted a foot to cause the war bells on its hocks to sound. Almost, it could have been an elaborate and colorful painting. It held as such for perhaps a minute, then the very mountain into which the hall was carved seemed to shake with the sudden thunder of the great Equi drums. Even Kehailan, who had been expecting their deafening salvo, jumped noticeably and took a deep, steadying breath. As suddenly as they had begun, they stopped. Again, the silence was overwhelming.

The man who walked forward, viewed from behind and above, seemed everything Kehailan said he should be – tall, powerfully built, with broad, sloping shoulders, long legs and a slim waist. His black hair was swept up in a three strand over-braid, tucked under itself at the base of his skull and held with an ornate clasp in the fashion of most Equi males. There was a slim circlet caught by the braid, but if it was ornamented they couldn't see it. He was dressed simply in the high black riding boots, black riding britches and sleeveless, silver-green tunic of the Equi Horse Guard, and three inches of freshly poured alloy glittered on each of his blackened and blistered biceps. If the man was in pain, or weary, it didn't show in his stride or the swing of his arms, and the ring of his boot heels on the stone brought goose bumps as surely as martial music could have.

Marion Eletsky watched in awe as the flags dipped, one at a time in obeisance – whole worlds symbolically kneeling before him as the Firstlord traversed the impossible distance to the dais where Ah'krill stood waiting with her priestesses and acolytes around her. This was absolutely jaw-dropping theater! They were watching galactic history in the making. Marion could hardly get his breath. He was here for this! It was very literally the thrill of a lifetime for him. Despite his fascination, he couldn't resist sneaking a look at Kehailan.

A split second later he was sitting on his heels in front of him, the ceremony forgotten. "Kee?" Eletsky said firmly, his hands closing over the Equi's forearms, "Kehailan, what's wrong? Look at me, my friend!"

"Look at him," the Equi managed, face registering nothing yet but shock. "Look at the way he carries himself."

"I don't..."

"Marion, look at him!" Kehailan snarled and Eletsky reared back in alarm, swiveling on his haunches to focus on the screen – to focus on the man, not the pageantry.

The body didn't tell him much from behind and above. Tall, even for an Equi. The voice speaking now in Ancient High Equi, soft and deep, idling with tremendous power. The charged atmosphere made it hard to focus on anything. Too many telepaths reacting at once. "I don't..." and then, it hit him – that voice, registered! Any male, *any male*, could rise to be Firstlord. "Oh. My. God!" he exclaimed. "Oh my God, Kehailan – is that who I think it is? Is that Ardenai?"

Kehailan nodded and swallowed in a half-choke. "I'd stake my life on it," he whispered.

Marion felt his black skin blench to cream. "Oh, God! It can't be!"

"I think it can. I have watched that man move my whole life, and that hair clasp...was a wedding gift from my mother. Precious Equus," he whispered, "My father is the Thirteenth Dragonhorse." Despite the insane weightlessness of the situation, he burst out laughing. "Yesterday was his birthing day, and I forgot. Again."

Timothy McGill was quick to sit beside him and drop an arm around his shoulders. "The justice and mercy you were praying for has just arrived," he said softly giving Kehailan a hug. The shaking subsided a little. Kehailan drew a steadier breath, and looked back at the screen.

As if hearing their conversation, the man's head tilted slightly and turned, just for a moment, and a smile flickered at the corners of his mouth. He paused and turned back, bowing his head so High Priestess Ah'krill could place a heavy gold collar around his neck. He straightened up, bowed stiffly, and turned to the woman at his mother's left hand, who proceeded to do something which was partially obscured by the person assisting her.

Now, in profile, it was obviously Ardenai, and Oonah laughed and clapped with delight. "What a wonderful leader he will be! I like your father so very much!"

"Thank you," Kehailan said softly. "I like him, too."

"Pardon me for stating the obvious here, but isn't your father a..." Keats paused for emphasis, "Kindergarten teacher?" The disbelief in the voice was unmistakable. "How can he possibly be capable of much beyond wiping noses and chanting the alphabet?"

"Doctor, I, too, will restate the obvious," Kehailan sighed. "Any Equi male can rise to be Firstlord. The career he has chosen is of absolutely no consequence. He rises based on his bloodlines."

"Ardenai is also one of the finest Quantum Psi Engineers Equus ever produced," Eletsky snapped. "He designed the computators for this ship and..."

Moonsgold waggled a long, bony finger in their direction. "Hush. Please, everybody. We can be pissed off at each other at our leisure, can't we? This is fascinating. Now see, we missed part of it. What did that priestess just give him? A ring, I think. No. Equi men don't wear rings, do they? Ah ha, bracelets the same width as the armbands. El'Shadai, look at his poor arms. I'm surprised he hasn't fainted from the pain."

Ardenai bowed formally to a smaller, younger woman with a mass of peach colored curls and long, delicate ears sticking up through her hair like the wings of a butterfly. She strapped a pair of heavy leather sheaths to his forearms, and into them she slipped two knives with handles that appeared to be bone, or antler, secured them in place, then took both of his hands in hers and kissed the back of each one.

He took her hands in his, turned them palms up, and kissed each one, then pressed them together between his own, bowed over them, and stepped back   They regarded one another a few moments, and even at a distance it was obvious that her exceptionally large blue eyes were twinkling up at him. She said something, and Ardenai's mouth twitched up at the corners, flashing a pair of charming and, in the moment, incongruous dimples which matched his son's.

"Isn't that part of the Equi marriage ceremony?" Moonsgold asked, eyes still on the screen.

"Same idea. We don't usually exchange throwing knives at weddings though," Kehailan muttered, trying to focus on the screen, trying to get his breath back, trying to comprehend what was happening to him and his whole existence. "Especially not throwing knives thousands of years old. They're pledging together to protect Equus and her people."

Bonfire Dannis asked who the unusually pretty girl might be, and Kehailan's expression soured. "Ah'riodin is Captain of the Horse Guard of the Great House of Equus, and the one personally responsible for the ruler's safety. Until today, she was responsible for Ah'krill. Now, she is responsible for Ardenai. It will be interesting to see how that shakes out."

"Well, that woman reinforces my long-held opinion that stature isn't everything," the captain said cheerfully, patting his own short legs. "And did we just see her crack a joke during a state occasion? I think she did, because

I think your sire very nearly laughed out loud."

There was no answer. "Kehailan?"

The wing commander sighed and nodded. "She would do that," he muttered. "My parents raised Io, which will make this all the more complicated."

"So, we have a little lady in one of the power seats, do we?" Keats drawled. "A little lady you obviously don't like. And from the looks of those ears, she's not anywhere near full-blooded. I thought the low Equi had to go off-world to excel. You know, like you did."

"There are no low Equi," Kehailan said softly. He bit his lip, saying nothing more.

Eletsky caught Keats' attention and made a subtle but quelling gesture, choosing not to say anything aloud to further rattle Kehailan. For a doctor, Keats had a shitty way of treating an obvious case of shock.

Kehailan gave Eletsky the briefest of smiles, and the Captain realized he'd been telegraphing his annoyance into the sensitive receptors of his third in command. The Equi lowered one eyelid slightly, chuckled and said, "We will talk later. We may also drink. A lot. See, now he turns forward. Now he will address all of us. This will probably be a very long, traditional speech."

Ardenai stood a long moment in silence, contemplating the assemblage of galactic dignitaries. His large green eyes flicked over them, then over the Equi High Council, his sharp, handsome features a mask as his head turned slowly from one side to the other, then with equal slowness back to center, leaving the correct impression that he now knew exactly who was in the hall with him.

"You honor Equus by your presence," he said formally, the palm of his right hand brushing across the back of his left in the ancient gesture of greeting. "Ahimsa. I wish thee peace. I was Ah'rane Ardenai Krush. I am become Ah'krill Ardenai Morning Star, and I am risen to be Firstlord of Equus, the Thirteenth Dragonhorse, the arms of Eladeus. As our present is a reflection of our past, I have borne the pain of these arm-bands as pledge of my loyalty to Equus. Never doubt it. Never question it." He paused a moment, and took a deep breath.

"We speak with our noses in our feed bags of the fear of the Telenir that comes with every Rising of the Firstlord – the fear of a *coup d'état* from the Wind Warriors that could sweep us from the stars, as the legend goes, and in the next self-satisfied breath we deny their very existence, for certainly if we, the mightiest and most ancient of the races, have not seen them in our lifetime, then they must be legend only. I tell you with absolute surety, legends do not kill, but the Telenir have, and to what ends? We are still here, and they are still but legend. Cowards, hiding in the clouds.

"To the Wind Warriors I say this. You will not sweep us from the stars, for many are the allies which stand in the path from your doorstep to ours, and speaking thus I alert them to your coming! I would have peace and kinship with you, but if you have designs on my power or my planets, which I know you do, prepare yourselves as we have done for this day. I will not be blown out of the air like the Sixth Dragonhorse. I will not await thee at Mountain hold, where you expect to find me and my family so you can stick us while we sleep as you did the Eighth Dragonhorse and his loved ones.

"You will find me at a place of *my* choosing! I go there now. Follow me, find me, and we will end this honorably one on one – the leader of your world and the Thirteenth Dragonhorse – winner takes all. But know this – your meddling ends with my reign. I plan, not to lose, but to kill you and end this nonsense, once and for all time. Let the games begin." He nodded curtly, saluted his astounded mother, and strode out, calm faced, eyes blazing with pain and anger.

A hundred thousand startled voices all spoke at once and the hall reverberated with the shock wave as citizen turned to citizen, senator to senator, priestess to priestess. There was a milling of silver-green, and the war bells sounded on the horses' hooves as the Horse Guard tried to bring the crowd under control. Even the ships in orbit seemed to feel the ricochet from the chaos below.

"Please excuse me," Kehailan murmured to no one in particular, and exited no less quickly than his sire. He went at a dogtrot down the long corridor to his quarters and sat, closing his eyes and pressing his fingers painfully into his temples, seeking to touch his father, but there was nothing – no one. He buried his face in his arms, and sobbed.

▲ ▲ ▲ ▲ ▲ ▲ ▲

Ardenai was still striding alone, breathing in long, calming breaths, through the halls of the ancient palace, briefly into the open, then into a little used auxiliary corridor, dim and sloping, which took him far beneath the palace to the stables. A black horse stood ready, a black, long sleeved cape thrown across the saddle. Ardenai put on the cape, hiding the bare arms and golden armbands, and trotted his mount down the wide stone pathway to a glimmer of light in the distance.

"Landais, it's me," he said to the man at the portcullis. It opened, the horse plunged away into the frosty starlight, and the portcullis closed silently behind them. "Quickly now, Pavil," Ardenai whispered, leaning over the gelding's neck, and the horse stretched out to full speed beneath him as Belesprit broke orbit and shot for the nearest star base.

In the Great Hall, confusion still reigned. Ambassador turned to question ambassador, senator to senator, council member to council member with Ah'krill observing in silence, filtering their collective snarl of thoughts for anything of use. Finally she flicked her hand, and a massive gong sounded to quiet the hubbub.

"Hear me," she said. "He who wears the golden armbands of Equus, is he who rules Equus. That cannot be changed but by his death. I cannot fathom Ardenai Firstlord's motives in this, but I will obey him. I have no choice. Many years have I known him without knowing who he was. I saw no flaw in him then, and I am hesitant to do so now."

She paused, the deepening lines around her mouth speaking of her bafflement despite the firmness of her voice. "He is a wise and rational man. Of this I am sure. He has his reasons for doing this, and when he returns, he will rule us well. As is customary, we will dismiss for a passing of one half turn of season. The time our Firstlord would traditionally spend at Mountain hold. Then, we will see."

A tall man with narrow features, resplendent in robes of crimson, hissed, "Finally!" to his companion, and they slipped quickly away amid the noise and confusion to the silence of the palace apartments. "He anticipated us, and now we must act with all haste or he will elude us," he said. "Legate Konik, check Ardenai's suite. I must inform the Mahdi. I will be Firstlord!" he laughed. "Soon, I will be Firstlord!"

Padfooting neatly into the shadows and within earshot of the conversation, a slight, softly booted figure nodded and smiled to herself. She waited until the corridor was clear, then sprinted on silent feet back toward the Great Hall.

CHAPTER TWO

"Will you please hurry up?" Ardenai snapped, and the narrow yellow eyes of the old doctor above him grew narrower yet. "Well, you're about the slowest thing on this planet, Pythos!"

"Sstop it!" the creature hissed, and his long tongue darted in annoyance. "Go to ssleep as thee was insstructed to do." He rattled his scales as if shaking Ardenai off his back. "*Thee* dares to sspeak to me in ssuch a manner? I am appalled."

"Me too." Ardenai responded. He closed his eyes for a few moments. "It is odd, you know," he continued, opening his eyes again to stare at the ceiling of the cave, and trying not to wince away from Pythos. "Knowing my parents are not my parents. Knowing that I am not who I thought I was. Odd, and disturbing, somehow. More so than I thought it would be, perhaps because I did not know it would happen to me, SPECIFICALLY." Raising his voice made his head pound harder, and he subsided, growling under his breath.

"Poor thing. Poor pathetic hatchling. Sstop thy jaw hingesss, and try to hold very sstill." For a few moments there was silence.

"No thoughts apparent?" Ardenai asked.

"None. The anger wass a perfect damping field. Thee came acrosss as very tantalissing prey. I commend thee. Will thee PLEASSSE hold sstill?"

"I'm trying. I'm just so...agitated, somehow."

"Worn out, iss the term thee sseekss. Yet thee refussseess thiss time to ssleep. Why iss that?"

"I'd be better *ssssserved* thinking right now, don't you agree?" Ardenai hissed. He winced sharply with pain, and before he could prevent it, a flare of delicate frond-like fingers came down across his temples.

"Ssince thee asskss, I do not," Pythos murmured, and the new leader of Equus knew nothing until the old sea dragon wakened him.

"Dragonhorsse, thou art finisshed," he announced, and the Equi ratcheted himself into a sitting position, rubbing fitfully at his temples and grunting softly with pain and stiffness.

"You willful old lizard, I told you I needed that time to think."

Pythos ignored him. "Sslowly," he advised, handing him a mirror. "Thee hass been through a great deal very ssuddenly."

Ardenai made a slight nod of agreement. He began to examine the total effect of his transformation, but his eyes went to the sides of his head, and riveted themselves there. "My ears," he squeaked. "Precious Equus, they're gone! My beautiful ears are gone!" These were smaller, and more contained, their flutes and intricate chambers no longer in evidence. "Where are my ears? And I don't mean these pathetic things. How am I supposed to hear with no external ear bones?"

"They are ssafe, Firsstlord. I sshall place them back upon thy ssweet head when the time iss right."

"Ah...what am I supposed to be, exactly?" he asked, finding his octave.

What passed as a shrug for one with no shoulders, curled up Pythos' spine and exited with a bob of the flat, hairless head. "A mongrel - Fifth Alliancce, I sshould think. Or an Equi off-world crosss. Ssmile for me."

Ardenai glared up at him, then dropped his eyes and stared back into the glass. "My eyes are brown. No, they're nearly black. I have black eyes. Funny, colors look the same as they did when I had green eyes."

"And thee callss thysself a teacher," Pythos scoffed. "It hidess thy ophidian pupils. Ssmile."

"Why, did you do something perverse to my teeth? I will not tolerate Phyllan fangs." He was quick to peel his lips back, and the old dragon studied Ardenai while Ardenai examined his teeth, which now had a single set of canines.

"It sseems rather an unpleassant thing to do, expossing the teeth in ssuch a manner," the old doctor observed. "The physsical ssensssation is mosst unpleassant."

"Pythos, you're a constrictor. You have no teeth. How can you expose what you do not have?"

"Neither here nor there," the serpent said peevishly. "Thee wass a consstrictor thysself, not sso long ago, my High Equi friend."

"DNA from Equus Legatum, DNA from Reticulatus Draconis. No wonder I'm having an identity crisis," Ardenai muttered. He blinked hard a couple of times to focus, then looked at his bare arms and huffed with annoyance.

"Why doesst thee choose not to ssmile for me, thy oldesst and dearesst companion?"

"Maybe I'm just not in a smiling mood right now," Ardenai retorted. "Why do I have snake tattoos over my armbands instead of simple skin grafts? Joining an Amberian wrestling team wasn't part of the plan, or was it? I've forgotten now."

"Doesst thee like them?"

"Like?" He studied the beautiful and elaborate serpents which coiled sinuously about his arms from shoulders to wrists.

"Yess, like. Doesst thee find them pleassing, my hatchling? They are Achernarean chain tattoos of ancient dessign – before the changing time. Before we Achernareans modified oursselvess away from ssuch large bodiess and huge appetitess. Before we sstopped sscorching villagess and devouring maidenss to become ssvelte sseven footers like the one who stands humbly before thee, oh wisest of the wise. "

The humor was lost on Ardenai. "I find them obvious," he replied, petulantly unwilling to pay a compliment. "At this juncture I have no desire to be too obvious."

"I can asssure thee," the physician drawled, somewhat wounded, "They are far less obviouss than golden arm-bandss. Thee hass tattooss, becausse ssimple sskin graftss would sshow an outline. Thine armss are sstill painfully sswollen. The ssnakes hide that fact, as will the disscretion of long ssleevess for a while. Too, the dye medium carriess medication which will, with luck, prevent infection and ease the sswelling, lesst thine armss rot and fall off, which would alsso be ssomewhat obviouss."

Ardenai drew up his knees, rested his elbows on them, and let his head fall heavily into his palms. "Do you realize that we haven't said more than two sentences in the last two years that didn't contain the words, 'with luck'?"

"The chief component of luck iss clear thinking, Hatchling. Thee cannot think clearly when thou art reeling with exhausstion."

Ardenai raised his head and glared again at the old dragon. "You knew, didn't you? But of course you did, you scaly wretch. You delivered me from the womb of my dam. You knew this was coming, and you could have told me it was going to fall in a heap on my shoulders. All that time we spent figuring out how we were going to convince this mysterious Firstlord that our wild notions had some credence, and you went right along with it, bobbing and hissing like a big green teapot! I could have kept my mouth shut, you know. I'm capable of that, but no, not you. All this planning, and speculation, and creeping around..."

"Excssellent mental exerccisse in any casse," the doctor said with an unmistakable air of smug assurance.

"Oh, fine. Anyway, what's done is done, but long will it be before I oil thy scales and feed thee tree-toads again, Physician Pythos. What must I do to keep my hair this color?" He pulled a lock of it over his forehead to study. "What color is this, exactly, and it feels...curly?" Suddenly, he was feeling his head and groaning with despair. "Precious Equus, my hair's gone at the shoulders! Give me that reflector back. Do I want to know what else you cut off? Eladeus save me, I'm ruined! I am completely ruined."

"I had conssidered an Amberian roach for thee – with snake tattooss along each sside of thy ssweet little sskull, down thy neck, acrosss thy sshoulderss, THEN down thine armss." The old serpent shrugged. "But I would have had to dye thy sskin, too."

He paused, studied the man in front of him, and resisted the urge to chuckle. Ardenai was definitely pouting, but he was also shocked and exhausted, pain rippling along his jaw. Laughter would have been unfair. "Thou art vain, not ruined. It iss wavy, and the color iss Sstag's Belly Brown, according to the insstallation program. I chosse it myself. Conssiderably lighter than thine own. Doesst thee like it?"

Ardenai stared into the mirror and said nothing.

"Thee will alsso be able to grow a beard, which sshould add to the novelty of thiss adventure of ourss." This time, Pythos didn't pause for a response. "Thee needss do nothing. That which colorss and waves thy hair iss a cosmechip, like ccertain citified ladiess usse on Decliviss, and Terren, and ssuch placcess. Thee needs not conccern thysself with it. Nor," he added, flicking his long tongue affectionately at the Equi, "with that which easses the worsst of thy pain. Over the next few dayss it will sseek itss own level in thy ssystem and thee will become more comfortable with it. It will help thee…relax."

"Ah, hallucinogenic drugs. Yes. Just what I needed to make the experience complete. Thank you. And my royal blue blood? What color is my blood these days?"

"Blue," the old dragon replied flatly, his tone indicating the probability of an earlier argument on this particular subject. "Billionss of beingss in this galaxy have blue blood of one sshade or another. Thou art no better hidden with than without it."

"As you wish," Ardenai mumbled, setting aside the mirror. "It will do me no good to argue. I must change my clothes and be gone from this place the second my captain arrives. And where is that one?"

He would have rubbed at the sides of his head as reflex, but the physician's hand stayed him. "Don't touch thosse earss yet. Thee told her to sstay and lissten, Ardi. Sshe cannot be in two placcess at oncce, and thee cannot leave until sshe fetchess thee. Take thy clothess and go to the poolss. I will be in momentarily to give thee a bath. Thee sstinkss of ssweat and blood and ssemen."

"I can take my own kraaling bath!" he snapped. "I'm no baby." He looked startled with himself, drew a quick breath, and softened his glare to look at the old physician. "And, on top of everything else, why am I so grouchy? I feel like there's a Gaknar, trying to get out of my head."

"Did they give thee ssomething to drink before the mating, a decoction of ssomething dark and sslightly bitterssweet?"

"You know they did."

"And did they tell thee what purpose it sserved?"

"Ah'krill said it would move motile sperm from my primaries to my ancillary testes without me having to go through several initial ejaculations. That way I could just..." he made a quick motion.

"Ssettle the matter?" the doctor chuckled.

"So to speak," he smiled. "I know it worked. I only had to ejaculate once, and I think all of the motile sperm were female, which helped at that juncture. The Eloi seemed pleased."

"The potion sservess that purposse, and sservess it well, but it alsso aroussess thee. Thou art probably sstill aroussed and do not realize it. It will...take a while to wear off," he said, and Ardenai wondered why he looked away at that point, as though he were concealing something.

It was probably his imagination. He was so tired, and despite the medication his arms burned like fire and ached from his fingertips to his pounding temples. The scorch of his own flesh still hung in his nostrils, and it turned his stomach just a little. He had to admit it. He was scared half to death and shocked half out of his mind, and he was taking it out on someone who had loved him and protected him and been his friend, since the day he was born.

"You're right," he said abruptly, smiling at the old doctor, "I could use some help with my bath." He took his clothing and disappeared toward the sound of the thermal pools in the back of the cave, the physician toddling alongside on his short, crooked legs.

Ardenai returned sometime later in the nondescript clothing of a drifter: riding boots, good but well used, the ones he wore when he worked in the horse barns with his sire. Brown wool trousers, long sleeved grey tunic, and an old jacket. To quiet the physician he choked down some fruit, then stretched out again on the table Pythos had used to operate, closed his eyes, and was instantly asleep.

A few minutes later he sat bolt upright and exclaimed, "I have my mother's shopping list! I told my sister I'd be home for dinner! I promised my father I'd go sailing. And where am I? I'm sitting in a cave with my ears in a jar." He stopped himself, and sighed, and sagged with exhaustion. "And where in the Affined Worlds of Equus is the Captain of my Horse Guard?"

"Sshe is doing as thee assked, but thee iss not doing as sshe assked."

"Oh, here it comes again," Ardenai grimaced. "Be a good boy, Ardi. Follow the plan, Ardi."

"Good advicce. Equi are thou in thy head, but thee musst be prepared to be anything or anyone which will ssave thee, or thee will never get home for ssupper, and the worldss for which thee iss now ressponssible will fall to an anccient enemy."

Ardenai's bit off a reply and his head came up suddenly, tilted in that gesture of listening. "I hate to silence thee, O' most cheerful companion, but Ah'riodin is here."

Io swung to the ground, patted her mount, and gave the reins to a young cavalry officer who had remained discreetly in the shadows. "Thank you, Tarpan," she said, swept off the black cape, and nodded graciously toward Ardenai. "Dragonhorse," she smiled. "Assuming you are he."

The surprise she felt at seeing him registered on her delicate features, and Ardenai said, "As you can see, Sir Pent and I have been busy these last hours."

"And in that time you rested, I hope," she said softly. "Are you in much pain?"

"More than I care to be," he smiled. "But it will pass. Come, sit. What have you?"

"A name," she said as they walked, "not one to surprise you, but rather to confirm our suspicions."

"Sarkhan?"

"At the apex, yes. And there are others. But mostly, I think... Sarkhan."

"And how true will the ballad prove to be do you suppose?" Ardenai murmured. "Is it legend, is it history, and will it repeat itself?"

Io plopped with a sigh onto the bench beside Ardenai, and gave a slight, all-over shake. "Four Firstlords, back – back to Kabardin. 'The time of calamity,' is what the history books say. In the ballad, is there a word – a name, I think, or a title, that sounds like muddy, or naughty or something close? Why won't it come to me? I must need sleep." She leaned forward and began to work off her riding boots.

Ardenai just shook his aching head. "I knew you weren't paying attention in Music History, Ah'riodin. Too busy horsing around with Tarpan and Salerno, just like in creppia nonage. I think the word you're after is Mahdi."

She pointed at him with the toe of the boot she held in her hand. "That's it, and don't be mean to me. I'm tired, too."

"Sorry, Fledermaus." He closed his eyes and sang,

"Mahdi was the god of fire,

For Mahdi made they sacred quest ..." Io picked it up with him, singing harmony.

'Down the timeless stars they swept

Pledging honor, finding death."

"Seven beats, eight beats, seven beats, seven beats. Hard beat, soft beat, hard beat, soft beat, hard beat, soft beat, hard beat," she chanted, clapping her hands quietly together. "See, I was listening." She smiled, though her tone bore a hint of defensiveness. "At least I know the chorus."

"Which would be impressive if it had a chorus, which it does not. It has no repetition at all, which makes it very unusual as ballads go." He paused, and drew a quick breath. "Who is going to teach the children these things? This term is nearly over, there are crops to plant, foals being born every day...." His eyes glistened for a moment, then he drew another, slower breath. "So, did you hear someone use this name, Mahdi?"

"Sarkhan. Just after you left. Brace yourself, Ardi. He was talking to our favorite senator from Anguine II."

"Konik?" Ardenai gasped. "I've loved him, played polo with him for years! I've never known a more honorable man. Wisdom Giver, please, not Nik."

She nodded and gave his forearm a gentle squeeze. "Sorry, Beloved. Sarkhan said, 'You check Ardenai's suite, Legate Konik. I must report this to Mahdi,' or something very close to that. He was chortling rather indiscreetly about being Firstlord soon."

"Ugh," Ardenai grunted. "I always knew he was crazy. Which makes me wonder what else about this is just craziness and nothing more. He has a superior somewhere. No one attempting a usurpation would leave that man in charge. They may be mollifying him, but they're not going to put him in power. I cannot believe Nik is listening to him or following his orders, either." No longer able to resist the urge, he let his right hand close gingerly around his left bicep, barked sharply in pain, and released it.

"I'm getting Pythos!" Io exclaimed and sprang up from the bench.

"No," Ardenai said, forcing himself to straighten up again. "I'm fine. I am so sorry to hear that Konik is involved. I have always enjoyed his company and counsel, and I have never known a man who was more in love with his wife. But Sarkhan, when I think of all the times we've debated over the years, I'm sure he's delighted with the prospect of killing me. Can I get you something to drink? How goes it at the Great House?" He rose as he spoke, not waiting for an answer, and reached for the juice pitcher on the table. He poured her a drink, handing it to her as he sat back down, patting the spot beside him.

She resumed her seat, casting a worried eye his direction. "Thank you. Very confusing, as we had hoped. Ah'krill has dismissed the Council for a half-season, as is customary." She glanced up into his disconcertingly unfamiliar eyes, and continued. "Some ambassadors, and some senators from the affined worlds, and probably most of the council members who do not live here will return home, and as those shuttles leave, so will we."

"What was Ah'krill's reaction?"

"She affirmed your control, but not your decision, as you expected she would. By that action I believe she will be safe from the Telenir."

"I really don't like having to do things this way, you know. I very much disliked giving our people the initial impression that I am an irrational and impulsive man."

"We need to protect as many people as we can, Dragonhorse." She turned on the bench to face him, and after a few moments of study she gave her head a doubtful shake. "You look different, but not different enough. Sarkhan will have you in his jaws in short order, and then Equus."

"Your confidence overwhelms me, Captain. Thank you," Ardenai chuckled.

"You are a scholar, not a warrior, Beloved. Your life is of great personal concern to me."

"Ah'riodin, if my life were of great personal concern to you, you would never have cut your hair off while you were supposed to be taking a nap," Ardenai muttered. He stood up to pace, and she followed, laughing softly in the echoing cavern.

Ardenai spun to face her in the dim light, catching her by one slim shoulder. "Not amusing." He said. He reached behind her neck, unfastened her hair clasp and allowed her hair to spill down her back. "You nearly got me killed," he said quietly, a hand on each side of her neck to spread her hair as he spoke. "Taking chances, making mistakes, being caught in error by those whom we care for and who care for us is one thing. They forgive our mistakes and allow us to go on living. Making mistakes, being caught by those who hate us, is quite another matter. This bounty of sensually gratifying stuff, grew back. My hair will grow, and darken again and be as it was. But if we are caught, we will die. Period."

She ducked under his arm and led him a few paces away to a rooted stone in the cave floor which raised her more closely to eye level. She stepped up, and put both her hands on his chest, leaning against him as she did so, and speaking intimately. "There is also no going back, Dragonhorse. Already they hunt you. The confusion will wear off, the paths will narrow. They will realize that all true Equi turn to their horses, and their wide open spaces when choosing a place to fight."

"Which is precisely what they're supposed to think, is it not?"

"It is. But knowing they are supposed to find you, and will find you, frightens me. You are a man of great courage and ingenuity, but a statesman, and a teacher, not a warrior."

"You underestimate my allies, Fledermaus," Ardenai murmured, and as he spoke he shifted his hands from her hair to her cheeks, and the outline of her jawbone, which he caressed – filling his nostrils with the scent of her. She leaned into him, dropped her head to a comfortable spot just under his chin, and sighed.

He closed his eyes, and slowly dipped his head until his lips were resting against the side of her neck. She caught her breath, and his head jerked up again. "We are wasting time, my friend," he said abruptly, dropping his hands back to her shoulders. "Let us find Pythos, discuss again our plan of action, and be on our respective ways. We must move with great alacrity if we are to remove this confrontation from our planet and our people."

"Agreed," the captain nodded, and walked ahead of Ardenai into the deepening gloom of the cavern, calling for Tarpan to join them.

CHAPTER THREE

T actical Wing Commander Ah'ree Kehailan Ardenai twisted miserably on his bed, seeking sleep which would not come. His store of tales about how to get to sleep, a glass of wine, even his attempts at meditation had failed, and he lay staring into the darkness. Far away he could hear the sound of space-locks and the comings and goings of various sized vessels.

They were in the belly of Seventh Galactic Alliance Shipyard Five for, as Captain Eletsky put it, a little fine tuning and they might well have needed it. Many ships went back after their maiden voyage and had things tightened up a little here and there. But their maiden voyage had been to Equus, and now they were in a place where ten times ten thousand people had heard his sire shake the foundations of Equus and the galaxy. That one man, if he chose, could bring most of the commerce in the galaxy to a grinding halt with a single word – the motion of a single hand. At least a thousand of these people had told Kehailan so in the last few days.

He found himself back on his bare feet, pacing holes in the carpet. Why? Why had Ardenai been so indiscreet, so impolite, so…crazed? The man had been a teacher for years, and a statesman. He sat on the Great Council. He just was not an irrational man. Why had Kehailan been shut out of his father's thoughts? None of this made any sense. Had his sire gone mad from pain, or stress, or grief? Was he being hunted down like an animal so his arms could be sawn off?

Kehailan gave himself the verbal command, "Stop! If Ardenai comes to you for help, you'll be too befuddled to help him." Not that Ardenai would come here. Kehailan knew that much for certain.

The crew had all been very kind. Winslow and Oonah, Marion and Tim. Hadrian Keats had stayed away, but that was to be expected. It was Kehailan's theory that Keats disliked him because he was a telepath, and disliked his father even more because he was an extremely powerful one. He'd tried to explain that for the Equi, telepathy was just unspoken words – speech – not mind reading, but it had availed him nothing. Keats knew the Equi *could* read thoughts, and that's what had stuck, not the fact that they chose not to.

Oonah had been Kehailan's companion often these last few days. She'd spoken of her times as Ardenai's guest, his courtliness, his deep concern for his son and his people. This was not a man to act in anger. There was something more to this than met the eye. Kehailan had nodded his thanks and forced a smile, but he was ashamed; and more ashamed to admit it, even to himself.

▲ ▲ ▲ ▲ ▲ ▲ ▲

"He does surprise me," said the senator, mouth turned down in appraisal. "He secrets himself to lick his wounds and let his wrath fester. This is something I would never have suspected in Ardenai. He has always been duty bound, honor bound, leading the charge with the flag of the faith by being deadly dull. Long before this announcement I have suspected he would wear the golden arm bands. Long have I seen in him the classic Equi virtues, physique, and mentality. It pleases me to match wits with one so thoroughly unlikeable. And you?"

He shifted in his chair, adjusting his feet to the fire, and looked with some desire at the woman in front of him, even as he shook his head. "What, exactly, is in this for you, that you would betray the man who rocked you as a baby, was your teacher, your mentor, and your life-long friend? Most puzzling, why do you seek me out to rise up against him?"

Io held her hands out to the flames, turning her back to him for a few moments before showing him her profile in the firelight. "Surely you can answer both those questions, Senator Sarkhan. Perhaps I can answer them in one explanation. I am a warrior, not a logician. I am the captain of the Horse Guard of the Great House of Equus. What does that mean? Nothing! I command one thousand hand-picked soldiers at any one time. A mere thousand. I am the personal body guard of Ardenai Firstlord, and no more. Even my sire commands a paltry few. There are a hundred thousand riders in the entire Equi Cavalry. Equus needs a standing, modern military of its own. For two years, since I became Captain of the Horse Guard, I have advocated it to deaf ears. I am a warrior. I wish to be allied with a warrior race. If not for Equus, then against it."

"A pretty story, but hardly a compelling one, Captain. I happen to admire Ardenai Firstlord a great deal. My family has served the Great House for nearly five hundred years, now. What makes you think in that pretty head of yours that I would actually foment revolution?"

"Because you are not Equi," Io smiled, still looking at him over one shoulder, and he jumped a rewarding distance.

"I am as loyal as any," he said quickly. "Again I ask, why do you think I am the one to help you kindle your revolution?"

"Because you are not Equi," she repeated, and turned to face him. "You are a Telenir, and not a very cautious one." That comment brought him spluttering from his seat, but Io held up her hand and he subsided. "You have been sloppy. If I know about your little plot to overthrow the government, then surely Ardenai does. How, exactly, do you plan to do this?"

Sarkhan was silent for a long time, assessing the situation and the woman and she nodded her approval. "It is always wise to be suspicious," she said in an admiring tone. "Perhaps I come to seek your weaknesses, or to drag a scented bag across the trail of the quarry. Perhaps I come only to confirm in my own mind that it is indeed you who are the enemy of the man to whom I am devoted. You have certainly shown no hesitancy in revealing that to me."

"But you are far too logical a woman to take such a risk, Captain. You mask it well, but there is greed in your eyes and your demeanor. There is a need to be on the winning side. Perhaps because you are not truly Equi, but an exceedingly odd looking mongrel, ingratiating herself into the good graces of the Great House through the influence of her father and Ardenai Firstlord."

"I," she said smoothly, though her eyes flashed with anger, "am one of Ardenai's closest confidants. If you want him, you will have to go through me to get him, or chase your tail through the stars for another seven hundred years, until the rising of the fourteenth Dragonhorse, Wind Warrior."

He settled back into his chair and turned his profile to her, propping his elbow on the arm of his chair, jaw working as he chewed the side of his index finger. His breathing told her he was agitated, perhaps even shocked, his mind going in a dozen directions at once. Again she changed her tack, reading his body language to her advantage. "Things are fresh, yet," she said in a resigned tone. "Perhaps hastening to do the Firstlord harm works to our disadvantage, Sarkhan. You have seen his mood. Perhaps he will undo himself. Perhaps, we should allow some time to pass. With luck he will not disappear to rule from exile, or return with an army of his own."

"No!" he said sharply. "No, Captain! If we are to hunt him, we must hunt him now." He caught himself and exhaled sharply. "Or so I would feel if I were indeed Telenir. Which I am not."

Io took her cloak off the back of another chair and made a show of putting it on. "I don't believe you know exactly what or who you are, Senator, or how to go about getting what you want. You are going to undo everything you and others have worked for, and I want no part of it. I had best be gone."

"You're assuming I'll let you go," he sneered.

"You have no choice," she smiled. "If I am testing you, and I don't come back, that which I suspicion will be fact in the ears of those I confided in, and you will be taken. If you believe me that I wish to help you, and you hold me against my will, not only will I not help you, but I cannot. I cannot be a prisoner and a free agent at the same time, now, can I? How can I track Ardenai on his flight through the galaxy if I am chained to your bedpost?"

Sarkhan regarded her with a mix of admiration, animosity and not a little lechery. The thought of having her chained to his bedpost had immediately sent some very unsettling images through his head and into his loins. With some effort he gathered himself. "You think...he may have left the planet?"

"I know he has," she said from the doorway. "I put him on a shuttle to SeGAS-5 three days ago. He went to counsel with Kehailan and others."

"He what? You what?" Sarkhan spluttered. "Why didn't you say so sooner?"

"I told you during our ride this afternoon, information has its price. If you want me, you know where to find me." She gave him a jaunty wave, a flip of her long riding cape, and was gone.

Sarkhan slumped down in his chair and glowered after her. "Are you there?" he growled, and a handsome, powerfully built man stepped from the shadows.

"I am."

"You heard?"

"I did," Konik said, coming to occupy the chair next to Sarkhan.

"What do you think?"

"I think," he sighed, "that we are in ruins. We cannot win. I realized that the second Ardenai gave that speech. My father realized it a hundred and fifty years ago. The best we can do is cut our losses before they become casualties, and consider once again that these are people with whom we want peace, not war. These are an admirable people. Surely you cannot have lived here all your life and your parents, and theirs before them, and not seen that. There is still time to come forward and negotiate in good faith – be openly a part of this society instead of closet outcasts. Ardenai Firstlord is the most honorable of men..."

"Coward!" Sarkhan spat, and turned his head away, jaw working, eyes blazing. "Your parents were cowards, and they are dead! Are your daughters and your grandchildren cowards as well? Your friends and neighbors? Perhaps it is time they joined your parents and your sister in the dirt. Why did my father choose to replace Sardure with the likes of you? My brother would have rejoiced with me! He would have killed Ardenai and licked his blood off the knife, gutted the high priestess and danced upon the table of the high council, waving her still-beating heart and shouting my name! And what is it you intend to do, Konik? You, who wormed your way into Saremmano's favor with your purring voice and the wiles of a traitor."

Konik felt the impact of the words. He gave his silvering head an almost imperceptible shake and sat waiting until the hands beside him ceased to tremble with rage. "Which is it, exactly?" he asked, trying to keep a level tone, "Is it the thought of personal power which so woos you to indiscretion, or is it the unbearable thought that the child has become more powerful than the father?"

"How dare you! We were sent here to conquer!" Sarkhan said, and sprang from his chair to pace. "We were sent here to conquer these people!"

Konik observed him for some time, face passive, alarm for more than his family flickering in his blue eyes. "No, we were not. We were sent here to observe, assess, and assimilate."

"In order to conquer!" Sarkhan barked. "In order to conquer!" He pointed a shaking finger, "even the captain of the Horse Guard knows which is the winning side! Even she, who rumor has it shares a bed with Ardenai, turns to me! *ME!* Knowing that I shall soon come into that which is rightfully mine! Mine is the true royal line of the Great House of Equus and the Wind Warriors! Mine is the line of Kabardin! She knows!"

"That much is certain," Konik muttered. "And you believe that she is actually willing to change sides?"

Sarkhan stopped pacing and faced Konik. "You do not believe her?"

"I do, My Lord Sarkhan..."

"Sarkhan Firstlord," he snapped.

"As you wish. I believe her when she says she came here to drag a scented bag across the path. I believe she came to ascertain beyond doubt that you are who she and Ardenai think you are. I believe she would never betray him for any reason. I believe she came to confuse you."

"You are wrong," Sarkhan said, throwing himself into an armchair.

"She, wants power. It is not the stallion who truly controls the herd, it is the lead mare. The stallion is the protector only. Their roles appear to be reversed, but under pressure, they will revert. She knows how this game is to be played."

She certainly knows how to play you, you arrogant fool, Konik thought. *You have destroyed in an hour that which we have spent generations building.* "You know where my thoughts lie," he said aloud.

"Which is why your family serves mine," he sneered. "Publicize it widely, but not too obviously, that the lady has been up to no good, and let Ardenai kill her. He cannot possibly risk betrayal now, can he?"

"No," Konik agreed, "Not if he thinks for one minute that she actually betrayed him. Which he will not."

"Then you kill her," Sarkhan said. "And make it look like he did it. We cannot lose."

"Your usual logic," Konik said. "I shall attend the details." He rose from the chair and, with a slight bow in Sarkhan's direction, exited the room. Once outside, out of sight and out of earshot, he gave the ornate stone wall a resounding blow with one fist, followed by a swift kick that sent a pain shooting up his leg, but he paid it no mind. He went home, made sure his beloved Ah'davan was resting comfortably, and in another hour his shuttle had lifted off on its way to Seventh Galactic Alliance Station Five and the moorage of the SGAS Belesprit. "Be it as you wish, Sarkhan," he said quietly into the darkness, "Since you insist on being fodder, gladly will I feed you to him. Maybe then I can get back to my life. Maybe all of us can get back to our lives."

▲ ▲ ▲ ▲ ▲ ▲ ▲

Io left Teal with their shuttle and scrambled in a convolution of blue and maroon down into a deserted corridor near one of the huge, crowded reception areas of Seventh Galactic Alliance Strategic Base Five. The papers she presented, and the nondescript character of her demeanor and attire, along with a tight fitting cap to hide her hair and her obviously Papilli ears, made her just another SGA Swing Technician. She was attractive, but because she kept her head down to hide her blue Papilli eyes, and kind of lumbered along, she was unnoticed except for passing glances. She was swallowed by the crowd, her small stature affording her greater anonymity.

She forced herself not to race even though she knew Sarkhan was close behind her in one form or another. He had to be. He could not risk failing to check out the lead she had given him. He would not risk sending such a message ahead, even if there were anyone here to receive it.

What if, she wondered, threading her way through the colorful twist of races, what if Ardenai actually had come this way? What if she had endangered him, as well as Kehailan? What if Sarkhan had taken his chances and sent a message? What if she found both Ardenai and Kehailan dead? Even as she told herself it was nonsense, she was fighting the urge to run. She looked around, wondering how many of these people might be Telenir. She wondered how Sarkhan was getting messages back to his home world, or if he was. Perhaps the first was yet to be sent. What would it say? *"Ardenai Firstlord is dead. Equus is ours."* She gave herself a little shake and smiled in passing at the women who had spoken to her.

It was slightly past the dinner hour. Couples sauntered idly, hand in hand from the cafes and lounges along the concourse. Groups laughed and jostled as they went into these same establishments to have a few drinks and watch the entertainment, and the smells of a hundred or more worlds mingled in her nostrils.

Kehailan, she was positive, would not be among the crowds. She assumed he would be on board Belesprit, his quarters there being more comfortable than anything the base had to offer. Too, he would be brooding, avoiding the public eye in light of how his father had behaved. A cruel ploy to keep a man easy to find, but probably in Kehailan's case, very effective. It meant, of course, that others would find him easily, and Io's military expertise told her he was being carefully watched. Another reason his father wanted him penned by shame aboard Belesprit. He was, for the moment, relatively safe, and because his emotions would be running high, probably incapable of making mental contact with his sire.

As she neared Belesprit, Io flipped up the hood on her traveling cloak. Those who watched Kehailan might know her, as well, and be they friend or foe, she didn't want to be recognized. She presented her papers, requested permission to come aboard, and made her way through the ship, which was largely deserted. She buzzed at the door of Kehailan's quarters, but no one answered.

She was raising a fist to knock when a long, slender hand closed over hers and a cool voice asked, "Looking for me?"

"Obviously," she said without looking up. The door opened, and Kehailan gave her a gentle shove inside as the door hissed shut behind them. He caught her by one shoulder, spun her around, and jerked the cloak back off her head.

"Well, well. Little Io, the fruit bat baby," he said mockingly. "I might have known."

"I can tell you're thrilled to see me," she said, looking a little puzzled. "I came to speak of your sire."

"The word which precedes you regarding my sire," Kehailan said, "is that you are for sale to the highest bidder."

"Is that so?" she smiled, clapping her hands together. "Good! Delighted to hear it. Apparently, Sarkhan does risk communicating by artificial means. I have one of the fastest shuttles on the planet, and the news beat me here."

"The news, came from the government of Equus," he muttered. "Usually a most reliable source."

"Is that so?" she said again, shrugging out of her cloak, "and what is this we hear of you, Kee? Word has reached the sensitive ear of the Great House that it is you who would profit most in the loss of your father. At the very least it would give you the chance to wiggle out from under that dark cloud of inferiority which he casts upon you. Perhaps under the Telenir, you, too, could rule."

"That's not true!" he gasped. "Surely you cannot know me and think this has merit!"

"Surely you cannot know me and think I would be for sale to the highest bidder. Besides which, we're not a moneyed society, so it couldn't possibly be a message from the Great House, now could it?"

"You made that whole thing up, didn't you?" Kee muttered, and she smiled into his troubled brown eyes.

"No, as a matter of fact, I did not. I did do you the courtesy of quashing it where I found it."

"Thanks," he said. They stood looking at one another for a few moments, reassessing one another, then Kehailan dropped his eyes and chuckled without humor. "I feel like I'm in one of those stories my sire tells his creppia nonage classes." He took her traveling cloak, gestured her into a chair and said, "Please, tell me about him. Is he well?"

"Better than you fear him to be," she smiled, and as he poured her a drink she began the long process of filling him in.

As she spoke, Kehailan began to relax. His posture softened, and his eyes flooded with relief. "I knew," he said quietly, "Even as I doubted inside, I knew. My sire has always been a man of honor, and of brilliance. He put this all together so quickly. Amazing, even for him."

"Not quite true," Io smiled. "All of Equus has known for ten thousand years that this leader would be male. From that point of departure, one may extrapolate at leisure. It was simply an added luxury that Ardenai the literary scholar, turned out to be the designated successor. It saved us having to convince another person that our collective theory wasn't lunacy."

"And where is he?" Kehailan asked.

"That, I do not know, nor can I tell you at this point exactly where he's going. I can tell you only to be silent and wait. Keep your eyes and ears open, ascertain what you can. Those are the things he has told me to tell you. And, that he loves you."

"I am greatly relieved," Kehailan said. "In what way can I help?"

"Believe the truth," Io said soberly. "Be ready to convince your shipmates, and if need be, your fleet and the Seventh Galactic Alliance, that your sire's theory is correct, and that when and if we call for help, we need it immediately."

"That much I will do," he replied. "Is there anything else?"

"Hopefully not. Hopefully there will be no need for SGA intervention. Ardenai wants to nip this very early, before it becomes a full blown confrontation. He wants to lure Sarkhan into a relatively minor clash - one on one. Like the old song says."

"Kill or be killed."

"In either case, he has accomplished his purpose," she said gently. "Sarkhan is either killed or exposed at that point. Your grandmother will continue to rule until such time as the seed which sprouts even now is old enough to take up the reins of government. The line will continue. Equus will continue."

"As usual, his thinking is flawless. Of course I don't believe it for a minute, and neither does he, but it does roll trippingly off the tongue, does it not?" Kee gazed for a few moments at one of the paintings on his wall. One his sire had done. "Ah'riodin," he said after a space, "Please don't let anything happen to him."

"Those, were his instructions to me regarding thee, Kehailan. He loves thee, and I love thee both. I will do everything in my power to keep him safe." She rose, and Kehailan with her. "There is one more thing you can do. When you go back out on patrol, try to convince Captain Eletsky that Sector Two needs watching, will you?"

He nodded. "If you see my sire, tell him I miss him, will you?" The color rose in his face and he hastened to add, "At least let me feed you, and offer you a bed for the night. It's late."

"My presence endangers you, and my image as an opportunist. Otherwise, I'd be pleased to stay and beat you at chess."

"You would stay a long time to do that," Kehailan said, and his eyes twinkled. "How can we best get you out of here?"

"By indeterminate scramble back to the far reception concourse. It is time for Captain of the Horse Guard Ah'riodin to appear from Equus.

Please, Kee, be careful, will you?"

"Likewise, I'm sure. Here, put on your cloak. We can speak as we walk."

Again she told him, hold his peace and watch his back. Briefly, she touched his cheek, smiled, and disappeared in a blue and maroon swirl for parts unknown.

"I just wonder where he is," Kehailan said aloud. "I wonder if he's all right."

CHAPTER FOUR

Mister Grayson was managing well, getting his traveling legs under him and cultivating a close-cropped beard and moustaches to hide his sharp featured, too-easily-recognized face. He took his papers from the man who had stamped them, put his knapsack over his shoulder, and ambled onto the largely featureless street of a brawling agricultural backwater in sector six.

He'd shared bunk space on the freighter from Equus with two scruffy individuals who were members of the Horse guard, so he'd been able to sleep, and that had helped him heal and regain his composure. They were now on their way ahead, and he was alone.

He wasn't frightened. Very little frightened Ardenai for very long. He did acknowledge that he had let himself grow soft since Ah'ree's death, and that he was relatively unprepared for this present challenge. He would have to harden his mind and his body if he was to survive.

It would have been easier on him to go to Terren, or Declivis to seek employment in technology. Unfortunately, it would also have been a deadly mistake. Ardenai was left-handed, and being left-handed called attention to itself, regardless. Left-handed Terrenes were relatively rare, one in a hundred. Left-handed Declivians, one in a thousand. A left-handed Equi occurred once in every three hundred and fifty thousand births. By his own admission the only thing Ardenai could do right-handed was play polo, and there just wasn't that much need for polo players. Even disguised, he could not take the risk. Technology was definitely out. He'd decided to come to Demeter to seek a laborer's job, perhaps as a horse-handler. Harden up. Use both hands. Keep his mouth shut. He was irrationally, uncomfortably close

SHOWANDAH S. TERRILL   47

to Equus. His reasoning for this being that as the search fanned out further into the system, he would just slip in behind it. Until then, he need only keep a low profile.

Not easy. He had to tell himself constantly, *Don't walk too fast. Don't stand too tall. Keep your chin down. Look vacant. Sound vacant. Mumble, but not too much. Right hand. Right hand. Veil your eyes. Be nondescript. Be like everyone else.*

Ardenai had never been like everyone else a day in his life. Physically, mentally, intellectually, he was most formidable, and having to keep a lid on his every move was exhausting work in itself. He checked into a rooming house where neither the lights nor the clientele seemed too bright, went to his room, and collapsed on the bed with a sigh of relief. Trying to walk at less than his full stature was ruining his back.

He lay there staring at the dust particles floating in the sunlight, enjoying the breeze blowing in through the open window, and pondering his next problem. Food. He looked like a mongrel, he'd have to eat like one. No more eating six meals throughout the day plus nibbles of this and that. No more well-ordered, grain-based, vegetable-rich diet available to him at all hours without thought or request on his part. He'd have to decide for himself what and when to eat, and he'd have to eat all manner of strange combinations of food, perhaps even flesh. That fact alone made him wish for his home, his horses, his family, his students, his wife.

Her, most of all. His Ah'ree, whose very name was like a soft sigh on the fragrant night air. Her gentle presence had filled his life from the days of his youth. Her absence in this made him feel eerily transparent and vulnerable. Almost imperceptibly he pressed his elbows and upper arms against his sides, remembering her embrace. The pain of constricting his biceps brought him back to the present, and made him realize how sheltered, how pampered and self-indulgent he really was by hard standards.

"Enough," he said aloud. He had others to worry about now. Billions of others. He undressed, bathed, then practiced looking dull witted as he dressed again and combed the chewed off mess that passed for his hair.

He laughed without humor, uncombed it with his hands, and went down to supper.

The food assailed his nostrils, and so did the people he ate with. Even stubble-faced, even dull witted he was attractive, and the women at the table were quick to note his addition. He had time to wish Pythos had left his ears alone. It was widely rumored that most Equi males ran hottest in cycles. Had he looked full-Equi, and had no color in his sclera, they might have figured they were wasting their time. As it was, they flirted, and he smiled back, saying little, half afraid he'd say the wrong thing, half afraid he'd throw up the slop he was eating if he opened his mouth.

"These are not the hands of a laborer," the woman next to him observed, running her palm slowly across the back of his left hand, and Ardenai sensed the danger of silence.

"These, are the hands of a horseman," he replied, turning them over for her inspection. "I keep gloves on them, and I treat them well. With them, I can make a horse something to be treasured, or something to be slaughtered."

"Very nice," she purred, still stroking, and Ardenai forced himself to leave his hand where it was. He smiled instead, and said thank-you, and returned to the unidentifiable victuals. Having to eat right handed, and using a fork rather than eating sticks, meant that he was only getting part of the food into his mouth, and the rest decorated the edges of his plate. At least he had part of this right. He ate like a two-year-old.

There was talk of Equus, and the strange goings on, and his opinion was called for, and he said he thought probably they'd figure it out because the "Equuans" were known for it, but it sure seemed odd to an outsider, didn't it? The talk turned from Equi nobility to Equi horseflesh, and again his opinion was called for. They talked about the Equi Horse Guard, and saddles, and training methods, and a man down the table said, "Hey, you wouldn't happen to be looking for work, would you?"

Ardenai cocked one eyebrow his direction, "Might be," he said.

"They're hiring at that first plantation in the southwest zoning. Lots of horses and livestock. Might need a man your size."

"What has size got to do with horseflesh?" Ardenai asked, curious in spite of himself, and the man laughed.

"You haven't seen the horses, or the owner. He'd like you. He'd like you a lot."

"Delightful prospect," Ardenai muttered. A warning pain stabbed him in the stomach, and as nonchalantly as possible he said thank you for the information, excused himself from the table and his companions, and headed for the back door.

Five seconds after he made it to the alley, his guts stabbed him one more time and emptied themselves into the dirt. He wretched again, head pounding from the force of it, and slumped to the ground, realizing for the first time really, physically, what kind of trouble he was in, and wishing miserably for the moons of home.

He slept far too hard and too long, and awoke disgusted with himself, grateful that Sarkhan's men hadn't murdered him in his sleep. They could have. He told himself that despite what Pythos said, the dull witted part of this had to go or he'd be a corpse in short order. Agreed, Pythos had probably meant it to be an act confined to public display, not a lifestyle, but he was sour, and his head hurt, and having someone to blame was momentarily gratifying.

Breakfast wasn't so bad. He got by with hot tea, rolls and fruit, and thoughts of Kehailan and Io. She'd promised to tell Kee what was happening. She'd have done that by now. He wondered what else she'd managed to do. Hot headed, foolhardy, unpredictable – thoroughly brilliant and intuitive – hopefully those qualities would keep her alive.

He sighed to himself as he meandered outside to look for a shuttle south, watching Io grow up in his mind's eye, hearing her laugh with Ah'ree – feeling her head against his breast as she curled in his lap to sleep. "Tell me about my mother," she'd whisper, and Ardenai would stroke those ears shaped like butterfly's wings, and tell her again about the beautiful, brave lady who had married a High Equi prince and come far from her world to live, and how she, Io, was being raised to reflect that lady, so her father could remember the laughter that had died almost as soon as Io entered life. No, it didn't seem fair, did it?

Ah'ree, too, had nearly died giving birth to Kehailan. To this day Ardenai felt the chill of it. Had it not been for Pythos, he'd have lost his wife and his son. As it was, he had gently but firmly forbade his wife ever to become settled again, and took it upon himself to see that she didn't. But Luna, Io's mother, and Abeyan, her father, had prayed long and hard for a child, despite Pythos' warning against it. Kehailan was already thirteen when there was, miraculously, a settling for Luna. She, Ah'din and Ah'ree had rejoiced – commenced sewing and weaving, painting and planning. Abeyan had been beside himself with excitement. How long they had waited for this! Three days after Io was born, Luna was dead. Ardenai could still feel his old friend, sobbing in his arms. He squeezed his eyes shut, shook himself mentally, and double checked to make sure he was boarding the right shuttle. Again he upbraided himself. He was wandering around in a fog. Things hid in the fog.

It was a pleasant half hour through green rolling hills that had been cleared of jungle, perfect for pasture and farmland. They followed a river valley, thick with deciduous hardwoods. There were plantations scattered wide apart, many with fine barns, paddocks, and exercise arenas, even the occasional race track or hunt course. The horses were sleek and well fed, and, as it was spring on this side of Demeter, many foals bounded stiff legged beside their indulgent dams. The shuttle slowed to a stop where another valley branched away from the river they'd been following, and a sprawl of buildings marked a plantation. The yellow flag atop the stone entry announced that the owner was hiring today, and, because the man at last night's dinner table had described the place, Ardenai got off the shuttle with those men wishing to interview. The machine shot silently on its way, and Ardenai and the others walked up toward the house.

It was the first time it had occurred to him that he'd have to compete for a job. Like a good Equi, he'd had three, concurrent careers – one in each of the major disciplines. He taught. He was a quantum psi design engineer, and he and his father bred mounts for the Horse Guard. But he'd never had to compete in a situation where there were more people than jobs. He'd simply learned his crafts and a space had been created so he could apply them. When, at the request of the Great House, he had become a statesman and ambassador, his careers had become avocations for a time, but his father...his foster father, he ruefully corrected the thought, had insisted that he continue to apply himself diligently to the time honored skills of the Equi horseman. Today, he was especially grateful.

The man who sat under a massive old tree on the front lawn of the main house, was dumpy and of mongrel, heavy atmosphere breeding. He tended to be slightly unpleasant, and had a leering, predatory look which immediately set Ardenai on his guard. On instinct, he glanced around for any children playing nearby. Men like this liked children. Ardenai made it a point not to be first, and spent the time observing the man, and the facility.

When it was his turn, he was given a quick up and down – the full bottom lip was given a long, second look and the man said, "Well now, Mister...Grayson, is it? What is your field of expertise?"

"I'm a horse trainer," Ardenai replied.

"And how good are you?"

"Fair. Maybe better."

"Let me see your boots," the man said, and Ardenai obliged him by pulling up his pant legs on the insides to expose that part of the boot where foot met shaft. Expensive, hand-made, and worn from the rubbing of stirrup iron against leather. He dropped the trouser legs back in place. "Care to show me just what you can do?"

Neither the look nor the implication escaped the Equi. "Assuming you refer to horses, of course I will," he replied evenly.

The man, who had introduced himself to everyone as Squire Fidel, eyed him a moment, realized this one would do just so much and no more to get a job, and waved him aside. The boots were worn. That was a good sign. He was a powerfully built bastard. That was better yet. "Wait over there," he said. "Let me get through the rest of these men."

It didn't take him long. He hired four, three for the fields and one for his bed, or so Ardenai reckoned from the looks which were exchanged, dismissed the others, and beckoned Ardenai to follow him up to the barns.

It was a pleasant walk. The air was tropical and a little too heavy for Ardenai to breathe comfortably, but full of the mingled smells of horses and blooming hadas vine. That was another reason he'd come here. The planet he'd chosen for his confrontation with Sarkhan was much like this one in temperature and atmosphere. Here, though, was more modern agriculture. Vast fields sloped away from the main house – green, irrigated, fruitful. Behind and to one side, row on row of huge trees formed a jungle. In front, and to Ardenai's right, the stables spread themselves toward the valley floor.

Squire Fidel told the other four men to wait, and walked with Ardenai into the breezeway of the nearest structure. Most of the way down the smell of straw and horse manure grew fetid, and Ardenai gave Fidel a questioning glance. So far, the place had been immaculate. He answered the questioning look with a gesture toward his left and just ahead. "Can't do a thing with the sonofabitch since the day after he arrived. That was nearly a week ago," he said, and at the sound of his voice the entire stall began to vibrate. There was an earsplitting squeal and a huge horse lunged against the stall door, ears back, eyes blazing malevolently. He touched the pulsewire that thwarted his escape, gave another squeal, and retreated to the far side of the stall.

"Ride him and the job is yours," Fidel said with an evil smile. "Of course, you could make this easy on yourself."

Ardenai ignored him and focused on the horse. "Riding this animal won't cure what ails him," he said. "Why does he hate you so much?"

Fidel shrugged. "I really don't know. But it's not just me. It's everybody."

Ardenai looked from man to horse and back again. "I can go in there, and wrestle him, and best him, and further traumatize him, and prove to you and to him that I can be more aggressive than he can, and you'll have exactly the horse you have now. Or, I can try to figure out what's wrong with him, and you'll have the horse you paid for. Which do you want?"

Fidel, to his credit, said, "I'd rather have the horse than the spectacle. Give it your best."

"First, tell me where you bought him."

"Got him from a stable on Anguine II."

"Equi trained?"

"Absolutely."

"And did you see him before he arrived here?"

"Damn right I did," Fidel groused. "Beautiful animal. Smooth as ice over a hunt course. Seemed gentle enough. I did contact the owner, you know, right after the tranquilizers wore off from shipping and he went stark raving nuts. Bastard says he shipped me a perfectly good horse, and what I did to him is my problem. Can you believe that? Damn Equuans."

Ardenai didn't correct him. He squinted around the stable and asked, "Is this as bright as you can make it in here?"

"No. Why?"

"I'd like to take a look at him, a really good look, and I can't do that in this light, or with you in here with me. And turn off that pulsewire."

Again Fidel's appraised him, beady green eyes nearly disappearing in the folds of cheek as he screwed up his fat face. "I'll turn the lights on and the wire off on my way out," he said, and went off chuckling. He turned at the opening and called, "Oh, by the way, you're hired, regardless. I like your style, Mr. Grayson."

Ardenai gave him a wave and turned to the stall and the horse within. "Come here," he said softly, making an ancient gesture of beckoning. "Come here, beautiful one, and tell me what the matter is."

"I can tell you that," said a quiet voice from somewhere over Ardenai's shoulder, and he turned and peered upward into the relative darkness of the hay mow and into the bright gold eyes of a bedraggled teenaged boy who was crouching there. "The men abused him. His...genitals, you know, they were hanging down because of the tranquilizers, and some of the men were fondling and putting their mouths on everything, and making jokes and

I think one of them put a piece of wire around the horse's... manhood, someplace and said it was a cock ring. Then the horse began to wake up, and they
got scared because he was nervous in a new place, and when he pulled back
up inside himself, I think the wire went, too."

Ardenai scowled at the boy. He was thin and dirty. His hair was an
unkempt mop. His clothes were not much more than rags. The Equi could
smell him, even at this distance. "And you didn't say anything?"

"I...no. I didn't," he said quietly, and both his gaze and his voice
were firm. "Not to Fidel. I did try myself to help him, you know, at night
when the rest of them were in bed, but I don't know anything about horses,
and he was in pain, and angry, and I didn't know how to make him...." The
boy looked terribly guilty, and vastly relieved at the same time. "I'm glad
you're here. He groans when there's no one to hear him, and swings his head
from side to side."

"You don't make him, you ask him," Ardenai smiled. "Thanks for
the information. What's your name?"

"I'm Gideon," the young man said, and in the next, silent second,
he was gone.

Two hours later the rear door of the stallion's stall was slid open and
he walked slowly out into the sunlight, soft muzzle just brushing Ardenai's
shoulder. Fidel and the others crept timidly to the paddock fence, not speaking, just looking. "Well, I'll be a go to hell," Fidel breathed.

Ardenai stopped, and the horse stopped with him. He made a slight
gesture with his right hand behind him, and the horse turned with him to face
the four men. "One of your men," Ardenai said, looking pointedly at the
Tarkelian next to Fidel, "Put wire around the base of this animal's phallus to
see if he could give him a bigger erection, to see how much of it he could get
down his throat, on a bet with a man you fired two days ago."

"How the hell do you know that?" Fidel asked, though the expression on the Tarkelian's face confirmed the accusation.

"Would you not remember who did you such grievous harm as
that?" Ardenai asked mildly. "I asked him. He told me. He needs clean

water, green grass, natural shade, and I will need some herbs to treat his inju-
ries. With any luck, he'll be fine, but he won't be jumping around much for
a while. I'd suggest you turn him out for a few weeks and then start working
him."

"Whatever you say," Fidel murmured, and began walking up toward
the house, leaving the Tarkelian still standing beside the paddock fence. He
took a few moments to give Ardenai a long, cold glare, then turned on his
heel and followed after his boss, who was by now bellowing for Gideon to
see that Mr. Grayson got a bunk.

After supper that night, with perhaps a dozen men sitting around the
bunkhouse, a man with a halting, unintelligent voice said, "Hear the news?"

"What news?" another yawned. "New shipment of whores in town?"
This got a laugh, and a ragged round of cheers, but the first speaker went on.

"Naw, that whole thing with Equus, you know, with the Rising War-
lord or whatever he calls himself."

"Not hardly news," said the second man.

"Yeah, well this is," said the first. "They think he's took a powder
to...to raise an army and unseat his dear old mum. Equus'uz put a price on
his head."

"Shit, you can't get anything straight, can you, piss face," said a
third man, rolling up off his bunk. "It was the Captain of the Horse Guard
who went off and tried to get somebody or another to help her raise an army
to overthrow the Firstlord, and Equus put a price on her head. That's how the
story goes. But it's a damned short story. She's already dead."

Ardenai felt himself go cold all over, and fought the urge to lunge
up out of his bunk and choke information out of the speaker. Instead he
shrugged, "I got in just yesterday. If there'd been news like that, I'd have
heard it on the trip."

"Yeah, well," said the Tarkelian, "Maybe you don't hear everything,
big man. I heard this story, too, on the receiver up at the big house. She
is very, very dead, and so is some other mucketymuck in the Horse Guard,
some relative of Ardenai's. Word has it Ardenai Firstlord discovered she was

playing both ends against the middle and had her shuttle blown up as she was leaving SeGAS-5. They recovered what was left of the shuttle. If you don't believe me, ask Fidel. He heard the story."

"I believe you," Ardenai said nonchalantly. "Got no reason not to."

"I hear they were lovers," said a voice from the corner.

"Lovers? She was his daughter," said another.

"Both," said the sarcastic man at the table, and the place broke into raucous laughter.

"Hey, does anybody know how they do it on Equus?" somebody yelled, and began a graphic demonstration with the poor fool who had spoken first, and after a while Ardenai rolled off his bunk and said he was going out for a breath of air before bed.

"Nice work with Squire Squat today," the young man whispered, the young man named Gideon, and Ardenai gave him a thumbs up and a tacit thank-you as he went out the door.

He walked quickly, rigid-backed a long way into the jungle of trees. Then he stopped, slid slowly down the tree trunk onto his haunches and let his head fall forward into his hands. "Precious Equus, do not be dead," he whispered, "the two of you cannot be dead." and again he could feel that heaviness against his breast, the weight of Abeyan's head, sobbing for Luna.

CHAPTER FIVE

T wo down, one to go," Sarkhan muttered, pushing over the queen on his chessboard. "I like the rumor I hear. I especially like the one about Ardenai doing away with the lady Io. Somehow I doubted he would."

"Apparently he did, though. I didn't do it," said Konik, who was sitting opposite him at the small table.

"But you were there?"

"I was there. I saw the craft explode just after it entered visual range, saw the fragments, saw a piece of gold shield that was recovered. It was the Great House of Equus, and it was her personal clipper. She left here in it. It's rather ironic that Ardenai killed his best friend, and his sister's husband, in the process of getting rid of Ah'riodin."

"And you saw both the bodies? That bastard Teal isn't still skulking around someplace?"

"Be realistic," Konik snorted. "There was nothing left."

"There were fragments of spacecraft," Sarkhan persisted.

"Much tougher than fragments of people, my...Sarkhan Firstlord."

"It sticks in your craw, doesn't it, Legate Konik? That I am Firstlord Rising?"

"That you hope to be," he corrected quietly. "No, it does not stick, so much as it seems premature."

Sarkhan looked disgusted and knocked over another chess piece with a flip of thumb and forefinger. "I hear another rumor. I hear Equus has put a price on Ardenai's head for the killing of Ah'riodin and Master of Horse Teal."

"Nonsense. The council isn't even in session, you know that. You're on it. So am I. Ah'krill would never do something like that of her own accord, even if she had the authority, which she does not. As Dragonhorse, Ardenai is above any and all laws. If she was going to try to have him killed she'd have to be very, very subtle about it. She hasn't made one nicker in a fortnight, much less the issuing of a bounty of some kind on the head of the Firstlord."

"Nevertheless, I like the idea that she might. Dress as one of the Horse Guard, wave some credits around. Put some teeth in this thing."

Konik, who had long since given Sarkhan up for mad, just shook his head. It would do no good to explain that, as a senator from Anguine II and one of the best polo players in the Great House leagues, his face was well known, and he couldn't pass himself off as a member of the Horse Guard if he wanted to – nor could he remind Sarkhan that within the AEW, credits meant absolutely nothing. Instead he said, "What can that help?"

"What can it hurt? Every day Ardenai and those golden arms of his dig deeper into some hole. He wasn't on SeGAS-5. Maybe the rumor about him raising an army is true."

"I started that rumor."

"Is it true?" Sarkhan exclaimed, then caught himself and slouched into a black rage as Konik chuckled and shook his head.

"No, My Lord. It's just a rumor, remember? Ardenai has no need for an army. As head of the AEW, Ardenai has literally millions of troops from eleven worlds at his beck and call, among them both the Amberians and the Phyllans. The ultimate fighting force. I'm sure everyone has figured that out by now." He glanced at Sarkhan. "Or they should have."

"There is no logic here," Sarkhan grated. "No logic. Nothing to work against. No logic!" He slapped over the chess pieces, and Konik wanted to laugh in spite of himself. "Let's kill the high priestess. That will bring him back here! I'll have Sardure cut her heart out and deliver it to the high council. Unless you want to kill her yourself."

For the hundredth time, Konik felt a stab of panic for more than his own family. "Firstlord Sarkhan," he said, trying to sound convincing, "we still have one, lone man. Someone who prefers to potter around in his garden, play his guitharp; someone who has chosen to teach creppia nonage and play polo in his spare time, fleeing for his life."

"Do we? Are you sure about that?" Sarkhan asked, his voice dripping sarcasm. "Even I do not rate Ardenai as one, lone man whose intellect extends only so far as a five-year-old's. Ardenai was bred to be bigger, faster, smarter than any Equi, and Equi are bigger, faster and smarter to begin with than most races in the galaxy. At this point he ceases to be a gardener, or a musician, or a teacher, does he not? He becomes the one thing standing between us and a takeover that does not involve years of carnage and expense."

Though he admitted the truth of the statement, Konik was not impressed by it. "Since when does our glorious, untouchable and mysterious Mahdi frown on carnage?"

"Since it became so expensive!" Sarkhan hissed. "You fool! Think! Why did he put us here? Why have we been rotting away here for generations? Because one day Equus would designate its male heir. That's why we are here! If we fail to accomplish a coup, our worries will be over for sure, along with our exile to this place which should, by rights, be ours. Instead of glory, we will have worms, death worms to keep us company! Does that make all this less amusing?"

"I was never amused," Konik lied, and, at that moment, he wasn't. What if Sarkhan actually decided to go off on his own and start killing innocent people? What would Konik do then, and what would be the cost to his family and those Telenir who spoke for peace? At what point would starting ridiculous rumors become ineffective in keeping Sarkhan occupied? What if Saremanno caught on to what he was doing, or Sardure came out of his pout long enough to figure out what was happening? And always, at the back of Konik's mind as her condition degenerated, how long could his beloved Ah'davan take the stress of having him gone?

"So ... where is he? How can he possibly be disguising himself to travel?" Sarkhan muttered.

Konik shook himself. "Not as anything short, right-handed, or female. Definitely something bigger than a flower pot, I would say."

Sarkhan flared, angry enough to kill him, then he saw the look on the legate's face and subsided. "What are you saying, exactly?" he growled.

"I'm saying, he cannot be what he cannot be. He cannot be where he will not fit or cannot breathe. He cannot be in a cargo hold. He cannot be walking or traveling freely about. Half the people in the United Galactic Alliances have seen his face, his eyes, his profile, his stride and stature, not to mention that voice of his. How much of that could he have changed in the time he had? He is one of three things, logically. He is hiding in plain sight doing something unexpected, he is moving toward the arena of challenge, and that can be only so many places, or he is already there."

"So," Sarkhan said, leaning back in his chair, studying his fingers as they tapped together. "So. I think, you may have redeemed yourself, Legate Konik. Where is he then, on Equus? Here, with us?"

"I think not."

"Why?"

"The lady Io said he wasn't."

"She lied."

"Did she?"

Sarkhan squirmed like a child. "Did we not establish that Ardenai was never on SeGAS-5?"

"No, My Lord, we did not. We established only that no one had seen him on SeGAS-5, and that we could not find him there. We did not see Wing Commander Kehailan, either, yet we know he has to be there."

"And Kehailan serves aboard an SGA Vessel. Equus is the most powerful member of the Seventh Galactic Alliance. Surely they would grant asylum to their cowardly and beleaguered would-be leader, would they not?"

"One would think so," Konik said, but for a startling moment, Sarkhan's words stung his patriotism. He drew a quick breath and shook off the feeling of intellectual weightlessness which accompanied the vacillation. "One would think so," he said again.

"But you are not convinced?"

"I am convinced of nothing. I am willing to explore almost any-thing."

"Good. Let us begin with the SGAS Belesprit," Sarkhan said, and they ordered fresh drinks and settled themselves in a shady corner of the big stone patio to make their plans.

▲ ▲ ▲ ▲ ▲ ▲ ▲

Gideon, too, was planning. Wondering. His brilliant gold eyes, full of admiration, watched the tall, athletic man in the ring. How easily he rode, and with such light-handed grace as he put another horse over the jumps. He never raised his voice or his hand against an animal. The communication seemed impossibly intuitive, and yet there it was, in the slight shift of his waist in the saddle, just a look at the body part moved a hip or rump where he wanted it. How much the young Declivian wished he could ride like that, and yet the man was unapproachable. Take him away from the horses, and he turned to stone. That first day here he had smiled. Now, he didn't. The squire wasn't a particularly pleasant man, but he left his crew alone to do their work. Surely he wasn't to blame for Grayson's attitude. He had noth-ing but praise for the man.

Gideon sighed. He climbed down from the fence, and went back to stacking straw. A questioned burned in his mind, and he phrased it to himself over and over, practiced it in a whisper, preparing himself for the moment when Grayson would bring the horse he was riding back to the barn. He heard Grayson's mount trot by, blowing quietly, being cooled out to be put away. A few minutes later Grayson came in, leading the mare. He put the animal in her stall, and when he turned around, Gideon was standing there.

"You do just appear, don't you?" Grayson said in that deep voice that rumbled up from somewhere in the depths of his chest, and Gideon felt himself quail inside.

"I...I'd be happy to put...I mean, I'd be happy to brush him for you," he ventured.

"Her," Grayson corrected, but his voice was pleasant enough. "Thank you," he said, handed Gideon the brush, and started to walk away. Gideon opened his mouth, but the words just would not come out. He sighed and was turning to brush the horse, when he realized Grayson had stopped in the breezeway.

"What was your question?" he asked, and returned a few steps toward the boy and the mare.

The boy was quiet for a moment or two, realizing that this big stranger had read his mind. An alarming thought for Gideon. "I..."

Always that hesitation, Ardenai thought. *This young man has learned the hard way not to ask questions. What a shame.* He took another few steps and stopped close to him, but not too close. "You have been wanting to ask me something for quite some time now. What is it?"

"You don't know?" the boy gulped, and Ardenai had to smile.

"You'll have to tell me," he said, and picked up a soft brush. He started brushing on the mare's off side, and she sighed with pleasure, letting her head drop and her ears relax.

"That first day you were here. I told you about the stallion?"

"Yes. Thank you. He would have died, you know."

Gideon nodded. "But I didn't tell you who, for sure, had done it. You told Squire Fidel that the horse told you."

"He did."

"How did he do that, Sir? I mean, you read my mind just now. Do you read their minds, too?"

"I read your body language just now," Ardenai said, looking over the horse's back and giving him a reassuring smile. "Just like I read his. When that stallion saw the Tarkelian leaning against the fence, he went rigid all over, his body ceased to flex at the shoulder, and his head came up. All those things are signs of fear. The rest, was supposition."

"But you were right."

"Tarkelians have very readable faces, and some disgusting habits," Ardenai said. "Is there anything else?"

"They can get very rough around here, as you've probably noticed," the boy said. "I...wanted to thank you for not telling anybody that I told you anything."

"Declivians are easily readable, too," the man said, and opened the door to the pasture so the mare could run free. "Thank you for your help." A short time later he trotted out into the sunshine on yet another mount.

After dinner, when the others were laughing and talking and playing cards, and Grayson had strode off for his usual evening ramble, Gideon slipped out and went to the stable, but not to see the horses. In the area where he'd been stacking straw, carefully wrapped in an old horse blanket and secreted in a corner, was something Gideon prized greatly. He turned on a light, removed the object from its wrappings, and sat down to study it yet again.

So bent was he on his endeavors that it wasn't until he saw the riding boots that he realized he wasn't alone. His gaze traveled upward, and finally reached Grayson's black eyes. "Ah, hullo, Mister Grayson," he said, embarrassed to have been discovered, but vastly relieved that it wasn't one of the others from the bunkhouse. They might have taken his prize, or broken it, or broken him.

"Hello, Mister Gideon," the man replied.

"Just Gideon."

"Just Grayson. What have you there?"

"An educational computator," he shrugged, trying to look as if it didn't matter. "It's something to do in the evenings. Where is it that you go every night?" He shrank inside, wondering if the question was impudent, wondering if he'd be sent sprawling for it, but this man was fascinating, and he seemed so kind, and so smart. Unlike anyone Gideon had ever met.

"I walk," Grayson said, squatting easily on his heels beside the boy. "I spend some quiet time thinking about the day's activities, and I go to the river for a swim and a bath." He gave the boy a sideways glance, and Gideon was suddenly aware of his dirty skin and clothing. That's what was different about Grayson. He had no smell to him. "I don't think the people around here get as many baths as the horses, do you?"

"It's...soap can be so hard on your skin," Gideon muttered, and the big man laughed.

"The forest yields many herbs both fragrant and gentle. I'll show you some time if you'd like. So, tell me about your machine, here."

"Well, it's an old one, but the squire said if I can fix it I can have it. If I can fix it, then maybe I can..." He faltered and rethought what he was going to say. "I can learn to use it. If I know how to use a computator, I might be able to get a better job. It's supposedly one that tutors you."

"The chorus of the ages," Grayson replied, running his hand across the little box. "Does this thing have all its parts?"

"Well, I don't know for sure yet," the boy hedged.

"To what extent, if any, will it function?"

"Don't know that yet, either." Gideon was loosening up. There was something about the way Grayson asked questions that made him feel encouraged rather than defensive.

"Do you have any idea at all what you're doing, young man?"

"Not yet. I hope to."

"You, sir, are a dreamer," Grayson stated flatly, straightened to his full height, and strode away.

"You bet I am. It's all I've got," Gideon called after him, and went back to his probings.

The next evening, when he slipped out into the sweltering twilight and unwrapped his computator, it worked. It lit up and asked him what he wanted it to do. "Tell me who fixed you," Gideon smiled, but he knew. When he finally went back in, he caught Grayson's eye and nodded. Grayson nodded back, touched his lips with a long, blunt forefinger, and nothing more was said. Gideon laid in bed and hugged himself. That ed-comp was fully programmed, and it didn't just teach you how to use a computator. It taught you how to read and write! *Tomorrow night*, he vowed. *Tomorrow night I'll ask Grayson about those bathing herbs.* A man who could read and write should be clean.

▲ ▲ ▲ ▲ ▲ ▲ ▲

"My sire taught me much of what I know about quantum psi mechanics," Kehailan was saying. He was flat on his back, squinting up into one of the long banks of components. "Right now I could use his expertise."

"You'll have to settle for mine," Amir Cohen smiled, down on his knees next to the wing commander, and the man who had put a glitch in the system slipped quietly into Kehailan's cabin.

Nothing. Nobody. Another dead end. Konik shook his head in disgust. A week it had taken him to get his papers in order to board the SGAS Belesprit. Another five days he had searched this miserable maze from one end to the other, prowling at night like a Mingus Bat. If Ardenai was on this ship, had ever been on this ship, he was indeed smaller than a flower pot, and devoid of DNA.

The door hissed open, Konik spun around, and Kehailan had a pultronel leveled at his mid-section. "Good evening...Senator Konik, isn't it? Find what you were searching for?"

Konik just looked at him. The wing commander leaned toward a console and said, "Captain Eletsky, will you come to my cabin for a moment, please?" When the captain replied in the affirmative, Kehailan walked around the desk and stood, studying Konik. "I assume it was you who tampered with my tactical display." he said, not unpleasantly. "Would you mind telling me why?"

Konik shook his head and sulked, rubbing fitfully at the back of his neck. A second later his hand flashed forward, there was a small explosion, Kehailan was down, and Konik was gone.

Eletsky jumped through the open door just as Kehailan was wobbling to his feet. "What the hell happened?" he demanded. "Who jumped you?" He got an arm around the woozy commander and lowered him to the edge of his bed.

"It was..." he had to think a moment "that senator from...ah, what's his name..."

"Shit, forget it!" Eletsky exclaimed, and sprang for the communications panel. "Seal the ship!"

Kehailan held up an index finger. "Konik," he said, and dropped his head back into his hands.

Alarms sounded, doors slid shut, and in a short time Konik again faced Kehailan. This time he also faced Eletsky and Timothy McGill, and half a dozen members of SGA Security.

"As I was saying," Kehailan muttered, holding a cold pack to his forehead, "I assume it was you who tampered with my computators?"

"Who the hell are you, anyway?" Eletsky demanded. "What gives you the right to attack my wing commander?"

"I, am a representative of the Great House of Equus," Konik said smoothly, "and he pointed a weapon at me. I simply reacted as I am trained to do. I am seeking the wing commander's father, and this seemed a very logical spot to begin."

"Why the secrecy?" Eletsky snapped. "A simple question would have sufficed. He's not here."

"Are you so sure? Prince Kehailan isn't harboring him in some deep hole aboard ship?"

"Belesprit has no deep holes," Eletsky replied, and Kehailan added,

"My sire is not here, nor has he been. Besides, what business is it of yours where he goes or whom he sees? He is a free agent...and your sovereign lord, I might add."

"He," Konik said in a slightly mocking tone, "is in line for questioning in the death of the Captain of the Horse Guard and the Master of Horse."

A spasm, either pain or annoyance, crossed Kehailan's face. "Nonsense. Io was like a daughter to my father – like a sister to me. Teal was his kinsman. Look elsewhere for your demons."

"I'll do that. Good day to you," Konik said.

"Right after we check the validity of your papers," Eletsky said pleasantly. "Until then, consider yourself our guest." He nodded to a member of ship's security. "Please show Senator Konik to the guest quarters."

When Konik was out of earshot Eletsky turned to Timothy McGill and Kehailan. "Well, what do you think, friend or foe?"

"Definitely foe," McGill said, easing Kehailan's hand away from the angry bruise welling up on his forehead.

"Definitely," Kehailan agreed, tossing the cold pack onto the table in disgust. "No Equi would approach this situation in such a manner."

Timothy picked up the cold pack and placed it firmly back against the commander's forehead, eliciting a soundless grunt of pain. "So where does that leave us? Hold that where it belongs, Kee, or I'll go get Doctor Keats."

"Please, no," Kehailan muttered, and sagged into the hand holding the cold pack.

"Is he Equi, or is he a Wind Warrior?' Eletsky asked, not expecting an answer. "We know one thing, whatever he really is, he really is after Ardenai. I say we turn him loose and follow him home...or wherever."

"Think he'll keep going now?" McGill asked, and Marion shrugged.

"Whether he does or not, he's all the lead we have. We have to try something."

"Agreed," Kehailan nodded. "Someone, somewhere, has to know where Ardenai is."

▲ ▲ ▲ ▲ ▲ ▲ ▲

Two creatures did, or thought so, and had come to their conclusion through an unforeseen but, for them, fortuitous event. Three nights before, in the wee hours before dawn, the man they knew as Grayson has sat bolt upright in bed and exclaimed, "Fire! I can smell it! There's a fire in one of the barns." He had been out of bed, into his boots and out the door in seconds, the others pounding along behind.

As they'd come around the end of the bunkhouse they had seen the flames, already through the roof of the smaller hay barn, licking dangerously close to the stable. "Gideon, Markis, with me!" Grayson had cried, and stretched to a full run that left the others panting behind him. While the rest of the crew had manned the pumps and the buckets, Grayson had run into the stable and begun taking the horses from their stalls to their paddocks, while Gideon and Markis vaulted from one paddock to the next, opening the gates and driving the frightened animals out into the pastures, closing the gates behind them so they couldn't return to the fire.

It had been later, when the fire was reduced to a smolder, the sun was nearly up, and they were sitting in a grimy heap on the bunkhouse lawn, that Gideon had said quietly, "Grayson, you're bleeding."

He'd looked down, and hastily clapped a hand over the wide scrape on his left forearm. But others had seen it. Where the blood had not dried to black, it was such a pale blue it was nearly clear. "I suppose I should go wash that," he'd grunted, and no more had been said.

Now, the two little men stood whispering together, studying a much folded poster. Mongrels they were, probably Nargawerld, stunted further by interbreeding with Turls.

"I tell you he be Ardenai Firstlord," hissed one to the other. "Him big, tall. Him bleed pale. Him ride the horse. Gotta be him, yes? His picture have I seen. Reward there be. See here. See poster?"

"Fine. Maybe so he be Ardenai Firstlord. He be one big smackin' hammer. We grab, he twist heads off shoulders, yes?" he made a graphic motion and a squishing sound. "Fine. No thanks."

The other shook his ratty head. "Not grab, fool. Not grab. Trap."

"Fine. How?"

The one made a hitting motion, hairy fist to his forehead. "Whack! Trap! Accident seem. He bleed red, we say sorry. He bleed blue again today we truss up and get..."

"Fine. Who?"

There seemed to be a gap in the plans at that point, because the one scratched his head with his broken black claws for some time before answering. "Don't know." he said, cracking a louse between his teeth, "Somebody. Somebody with credits. Yes?"

"Fine. When?"

"Now! See what he do? Fine time."

The other mongrel agreed. Ardenai was moving the heavy pipes used to construct jumps and temporary corrals. He stacked a dozen pipes, set a pin, left a space and moved up until the stack was eighteen hands high, then moved to the end of that stack, and began again. He had been doing this for half an hour or so, and was very nearly finished. He was shirtless, and wet with perspiration, but moving smoothly, and at a good pace, enjoying the exercise, letting his mind wander back to his parents, and the smell of the pines at Canyon keep, the quacking of Ah'ree's pet ducks.

Gideon stepped out of the stable in time to see Ardenai set the top pipe in place and turn away, just as a furry hand reached for the pin behind Ardenai's shoulder. There was a sudden rumble as the pipes came loose, and Ardenai, caught off balance, was thrown hard into the corner of the pipe rack. He dropped like a stone, blood spurting from the gash above his right eye as the pipes cascaded over him.

The two little mongrels danced in a mad circle, holding each other and chanting, "Blue blood! Blue blood! We rich!" So preoccupied were they that they didn't see Gideon until he was right on them.

"What are you doing?" he demanded, rolling pipes aside and kneeling beside Grayson.

"Him Ardenai Firstlord! Him Ardenai Firstlord!" they chattered, too excited to realize they were broadcasting their good fortune. "We rich! We rich!"

"Morons," Gideon muttered, laying his palm against Grayson's temple. "I hope you haven't killed him."

"Just as good dead."

"I doubt that," Gideon said. "You do realize, he's not a full blooded Equi. The ears aren't right. Neither are the eyes. The blood's just a fluke. He could be any half-breed Equi and look like this. He could very easily be a Caspian mix. The prisons on Caspia are hell holes. You'd spend a lot of time treading water for attempted murder."

They put their heads together for a few moments, chattering furiously. Gideon looked at the pale blue blood, and despaired. He could see by the rise and fall of Grayson's back that he was breathing, but...

"Arm-bands!" one of the little mongrels exclaimed suddenly, and they danced again in momentary hysteria. Then one of them whipped out a knife, and before Gideon realized what was happening, slashed diagonally across Grayson's bare arm from shoulder to elbow. Blood poured out, and then, as the skin was peeled back by the blade of the knife ... a glimmer of gold.

"Ardenai, Ardenai!" they gibbered, whirling one another around on the grass.

"What are you going to do with him?" Gideon asked, heart pounding crazily in his throat.

"Truss up! Haul in! You help? We pay!"

"I help, you stab," Gideon said in disgust. "Get Squire Squat to help you." He walked off toward the bunkhouse, taking Grayson's tunic off the end of the pipe rack as he went.

They shackled Ardenai's hands together behind his back with tractor chain, wrapping it once around his neck and tightening it just until he struggled to breathe. Even for the two of them he was much too big to carry. One stood guard and the other one went to the main house. Squire Fidel would know what to do. Squire Fidel would know who to call.

Very soon, the squire was standing over Ardenai. He kicked him gently with one foot, and Ardenai groaned just enough to let them know he was coming around. Between the three of them they shouldered him, and staggered up to the main house. They propped him in a corner, and the little mongrels showed Fidel the golden arm-band they'd uncovered.

"Why, Mister Grayson, you're a man of many surprises," Fidel smiled, but Ardenai was too groggy to say anything. "I hate to lose such a fine horse handler, but I suppose business is business, aye, gentlemen?"

"Aye, gentlemen? Aye, gentlemen?" they laughed. "Call! Call!"

"By all means," Fidel said, and as he turned away his eyes were beginning to narrow. Wouldn't do to contact the wrong people. This man was the newly crowned monarch of a mighty system, tractor chain notwithstanding. Wouldn't do to split that fabled reward too many ways, regardless of what it might be. He turned back around. "Do you men happen to have that reward poster?"

One of them did, folded and filthy in his trouser pocket. They had been too dense to recognize the transmission code they needed, but Fidel was not. When it came to any kind of reward, he was a very sharp individual. He poured both of them a tall strong drink to celebrate their good fortune, and went to his sending unit.

Try as he might, he didn't have the power to get through to the source without relay, and if he relayed a message, he'd have half the Alliance to deal with. Ardenai would have to be transported, or Fidel would have to go to town to use a more powerful device. He poured the little mongrels another drink. "Did you tell anyone else about this?" he asked casually.

"No," they said, shaking their ugly, oversized heads. Gideon had seen it. They hadn't told him. Being literalists, and drunk, they did not mention his part in it.

"Good," Fidel nodded. He added a small something to their third drink. Something their taste buds were too numb to pick up on. When they stopped laughing, and their eyes had glazed over in death, Fidel dragged one over and dumped him down the basement stairs. The other, he dragged outside into the shrubbery.

After dinner he went down to the bunkhouse, dropped off a couple big bottles of Declivian summer brandy, and asked cheerfully if anybody needed anything from town. No one did.

"By the way," Gideon yawned, sitting up in his bunk, "those two little simians you gave me to work with last week disappeared on me this afternoon."

"They have been fired," Fidel replied. "You won't see them again."

"Good," Gideon muttered, and flopped back down. A death knell if ever he'd heard one, and he'd heard a few in his short life.

He left a minute or two after Fidel, and followed him at a discreet distance. When Fidel went into the house, Gideon peeked into the hovercat. Grayson wasn't there. Cautiously, Gideon looked through a window, and inadvertently stepped on a dead mongrel. He stumbled backward, one foot cracking down on the shrubbery. He held his breath and waited. There was no response. Again he crept to the window, and this time he could see Grayson, chained in the corner, still unconscious.

Fidel hauled at him a few times, but it was a lost cause. With the tractor chain around his neck, Ardenai weighed nearly three hundred pounds. Without the tractor chain around his neck, he was deadly. Fidel, being too greedy to ask for help and split the reward, and too squeamish to kill a prince as he had the mongrels, opted for town and the more powerful sending unit. He spent some time bent over the Equi Firstlord, gagged him with rags, then turned out the lights and went out the door, locking it behind him.

Gideon faded into the trees beside the house, and in the deepening twilight, Fidel passed within yards of him without seeing him. The hover-cat glided silently away, and after considerable exploration, Gideon crept through an open window into the Squire's black and stinking basement. The smell accounted for the window being open, but the Squire was a trusting man to go off and leave it so. Gideon felt his way along the wall, hurried up the stairs, and knelt beside Ardenai, patting his shoulder in the hope of rousing him.

Immediately the black eyes came open, awake, and alert. "You, are in big trouble!" Gideon hissed, taking the gag out of Ardenai's mouth, and to his amazement Ardenai grinned at him.

"An intuitive lad, indeed," he managed, and gasped for air.

Gideon pushed him forward from the waist, and began working the chains loose. As they dropped away, Ardenai choked, then grasped the length around his neck, lifted it with Gideon's help over his head, and let it drop onto the floor behind him. He gasped a few times, then his breathing deepened. "Thank you," he said, rubbing at the bruises on his throat. "Gideon, how did you get in?"

"There was an open window in the basement. Everything else was locked, and I was afraid someone would hear me breaking a window up here.

You better wash your face and find a shirt. We gotta get out of here, now!"

But Ardenai didn't move. He was still staring, wide-eyed, at the boy. "How did you say you got in here?"

"Through a basement window."

"You came in here, past the creature – a Turlac Orka, I think – that he has shut in that cellar? Are you incredibly brave, or just barking mad?"

"What?" Gideon quavered.

"You didn't see it? You didn't smell it? Where to you think his worn-out lovers go, Gideon?"

"I don't know! I mean, no," Gideon groaned. "I mean, yes, kind of." He looked suddenly over his left shoulder and sprang into a crouch. "Oh hell! Oh shit! I left the basement door open!"

Together they paused and listened. *Drag, slap, wheeze. Drag, slap, wheeze,* growing rapidly closer. "So much for a shirt," Ardenai muttered, pushed Gideon into a sprint ahead of him, and together they dove through a window, landing amid a hail of glass on the hapless little mongrel.

"I wondered where Fidel had stored his pet's dessert," Ardenai grimaced as he stood up. "Gideon, a thousand thanks."

"And now you're just going to walk in the bunkhouse, get your things, and leave, right?"

"I thought I'd wash my face in the horse trough first," Ardenai said. He bent down, picked up the dead mongrel, and tossed him in the window they'd just exited. "Luckily this one's the second course and not the first, or you'd have been dinner before you got halfway across that basement."

"Very cold thing to do, Mister Grayson, or Lord Ardenai, or whoever you are."

"But expedient. After all, he is already dead."

Ardenai took a few steps, reeled, and dropped to his knees as Gideon caught him under the arms and hauled him up again. "You seem a tad under the weather to make a getaway."

"Gideon, I have to. Once Fidel makes that call, this sector is going to be crawling with all manner of people who wish me dead. I have to go now, while I can still walk onto a freighter, or a cruiser, and leave. A few hours ..."

"Ardenai Firstlord, for surely you are he, consider how you look. Consider that royal blue blood on your face and in your beard, and the arm-band that shows where they slashed your skin."

"What?" Ardenai gasped, and for the first time, he realized the damage they'd done to his arm. "Oh, no," he murmured. "Well, I'll just have to slip in while the others are asleep, and ..."

"And about then Fidel will be back. Come on. I'm going to stash you in the barn and go get our stuff. We can take horses and cut through the jungle to town. Walk. Fast."

"Gideon..."

"Did you program my computator?"

"I designed your computator as a study aid for my students about fifty years ago."

Gideon gave him a startled look, then remembered how long Equi lived, and kept walking. "Well, you're going to owe me a new one if we get out of this."

"Gideon, you do not have to go with me," Ardenai said, and stopped, gasping for air, inside the protective darkness of the stable.

"Yes, I do."

"Why?"

"I don't know. I just do. Here, lie down and rest for a few minutes. I'll be back."

Ardenai nodded, saying nothing. He eased himself onto the pile of straw, and touched gingerly at the welt over his eye. It occurred to him that Fidel would be in a hurry – a big hurry – to get home. He forced himself up again, and when Gideon returned with the knapsacks, Ardenai had his face washed, and two horses saddled. "Problems?" he asked, gratefully taking the tunic Gideon held out to him.

"After that brandy Fidel left? Let's put it this way, we have more than we came with."

"You stole?"

"This, from the man who just fed somebody to Slosho the killer seal? And I assume the horses are borrowed?"

"Point taken," Ardenai muttered, "But the horses definitely are borrowed. Ever ridden one?"

"No. I was too afraid of you to ask. Hold still and let me wrap that arm. You'll have blood everywhere, and people will notice, which wouldn't be good. "

Ardenai moved the arm away from his body and watched while Gideon tightened a long strip of relatively clean cloth around the wound. He pulled his tunic on, hiding the bandage, then gestured for the boy to mount. "Thank you. Were you really afraid of me?   Other foot in the stirrup or you'll be facing backwards."

Gideon switched to his left foot. "You were...very distant. But knowing who you are, I think I know why."

"Another time," Ardenai said, adjusting Gideon's hips in the saddle seat and mounting his own horse. "We must go quickly. Keep your heels down and your back straight but relaxed. Keep the horse between you and the ground, as the old saying goes."

They set off across the open fields at an easy canter, and Gideon found it exhilarating despite the circumstances. In the trees they walked, trotted when they could, and cantered through the clearings and fields of alcibus for most of the night. Occasionally Ardenai's head would fall forward, then his shoulders would tense, and he would pull himself upright again with a voiceless gasp of effort.

"You need a doctor," Gideon said, and Ardenai nodded.

"I know a good one. Unfortunately, there is the small problem of getting off this planet."

"We're nearly to town. I can see lights."

"And I can hear people. That does not mean they're going to let us leave."

They dismounted, Ardenai sent the horses home with a word and a pat of farewell, and the two of them struck out on foot. It wasn't far to walk. The jungle encroached nearly onto the main street. They stayed in the dimly lit alleyways, hoping Ardenai's size and the fact that there were two of them would keep them from getting jumped. In half an hour they'd reached the space port, and sat for a minute in the shadows to rest.

"We are fortunate," Ardenai said. "On this planet ships launch directly into the atmosphere, no shuttles." He let his head fall forward nearly to his knees, and Gideon noted with worry the whitened knuckles on the man's fists.

"Are you okay for a bit yet?" he asked, laying his hand on Ardenai's back. "You've lost a lot of blood."

"I'm good, thank you," he replied, and raised his head. "What shall we try for, horses, grain, or fertilizer?"

"No one who was not running for his life would try booking passage on a fertilizer yacht, Mister Grayson. I would suggest grain as a first choice."

"I commend your good taste," Ardenai said, and they hauled themselves up and began walking again. There was no lack of freighters, even at this hour. Agricultural commodities flowed day and night here. Ardenai gestured toward a ship, they conferred in whispers for a moment, then reeled around the end of a loading elevator, good arm in torn arm, Ardenai's face more or less hidden against Gideon's shoulder.

"Oops, oops, here we are," Gideon mumbled, peering at the freighter's captain. "My dear old dad and me...my old daddums...would very much like to go home...sir...we would."

"Where, exactly is home, young man?"

"Uh...where you going?"

"SeGAS-7...or eight, or nine."

Gideon raised a triumphant finger. "Thash home."

"All of 'em?" the captain grinned, and Gideon peered up drunkenly into his heavy-set, good natured face.

"Any of 'em. Whee...I mean, we...can we go...my poor old daddums and me?"

The captain eyed them both. "Yeah, I guess you can," he said. "You puke, you clean it up. C deck, third door down on the right. I'll expect you to work for your passage." He waved over his shoulder in that general direction and turned his attention back to his shipping manifest.

"I wonder do she flap her wings to fly," Gideon muttered, appraising the vessel, and Ardenai replied that he didn't care how it was done, as long as it was done with alacrity. Gideon pushed a button. Pushed it again and the cabin door shrieked open. "Aw, this place is threadbare," he complained.

"Only if one cares," Ardenai replied, stepping in behind him. "It's no more threadbare than I am right now." He sat down on the bottom bunk, gave the pillow a couple of tentative slaps, and gazed at the rising dust.

"Not much of a palace for the leader of eleven worlds," Gideon said, sitting down next to Ardenai.

"I, am grateful to be here. I could well be somewhere dead, or having my arms hacked off. I owe you a great deal, Gideon. When we reach SeGAS-7, I'll contact my...." He paused, and the grief he felt telegraphed itself across his face. "I'll contact someone at the Great House, or my son, Kehailan, and hand you over for safekeeping until this is finished. Then we can decide a future for you."

Gideon studied Ardenai – *the Thirteenth Dragonhorse – how absolutely, completely amazing,* a minute or two in silence, the bruises, the dark, worried eyes, the determined set of a mouth that was slightly too soft for the sharply chiseled profile. "Why?" he asked at last. "Why is this happening to you? Are you causing it, somehow, or just permitting it?"

Ardenai leaned forward, elbows on his knees so he'd clear the upper bunk, and cocked his head to look at Gideon. "What an extraordinarily astute question. I usually hear that question as it applies to Eladeus, and I can assure you, that is not me. I commend you, but I am not sure I have an answer. I know what needs to happen for things to go as they should for me and my world. Some of them I have set in motion, some others have started, and some are just fate, karma or blind luck. In all of it, I hope somewhere to find the will of the Wisdom Giver. Does that help?"

"I think so. I'm working on it."

"You're a dreamer, that should make it easier," Ardenai said quietly, looking away. "Far better than learning to program a computator, Gideon, is the ability to dream of building one, of bettering yourself for the good of others. The ability to envision the need for any given thing, must precede the designing of that thing if it is to have purpose, no matter how fleeting."

"And which are you at this point, creator or technician?"

"I am a technician," Ardenai replied in amusement, looking back at Gideon. "I seek to maintain that which is already in place. I am attempting to manipulate components in such a manner that they will function as a unit. This involves the removal of extraneous parts. Hopefully, I'm not one of them."

"Now I understand," Gideon grinned. "And I admire your ability to believe. I know this can't be easy for you to do something so controversial and not be able to defend your reasons for doing it."

"That is where friends come in, Gideon. Those people who trust our judgment." Ardenai rubbed his face, winced, and straightened up off the bunk. "I sadly fear I have lost two of the best, but...I have gained one in return."

"Who?" the boy asked.

"Why, you, of course," Ardenai said, giving him a puzzled look. "Who else would I mean?"

Gideon looked incredulous. "Me?" he gasped. "Me? But you, you're..." he stopped and considered what he was about to say, then, he smiled a slow, shy smile. "I have never had a friend before."

"Well, you have one now," Ardenai said, and the look on his face told Gideon the concept of being friendless was totally foreign to him.

"You are my friend." Gideon said, testing the words one at a time. "You programmed my ed-comp so I could start to learn how to...to use it. Why did you do that? You didn't even know me."

"I did it because I could," Ardenai said, his attention wandering with the throb in his head. "It's a characteristic of teachers. Why are we still on the ground?"

Gideon got up and came to stand beside him. "Aw, I wish you hadn't said that. If we're caught on this scow, we're caught. There's no place here to run."

"Not we," Ardenai rumbled, shaking a finger at Gideon, "Me. You remember that. If we get caught – no matter what is said, no matter what is done – you keep your mouth absolutely shut and your hands to yourself. Do you understand?"

"I understand," he grumbled. "I don't like it, and I..."

"...will do as you're told. If you do not survive, neither does the truth of what happened. If Ah'riodin is dead, and Teal with her, that is half the truth. One quarter lies yet with Pythos, one quarter with me. Whom they have told, I do not know. I know one thing only. I have an honorable and intelligent young companion. Him, I will not risk."

Gideon ducked his head. "Firstlord, I understand," he said. "I'll obey your wishes, but I won't like it. Say, you look really tired. You lost a lot of blood. Why don't you lie down and I'll go see why we're still here."

"Good idea. You are, by the way, in the clear with Fidel. Our gib-bering little bounty hunters did not mention to him that you saw what happened."

"I'll keep that in mind. You rest," Gideon said, and the door shrieked shut behind him, punishing Ardenai's pounding head. He stretched out on the bunk as best he could and closed his eyes, but he did not sleep.

Gideon made his way nearly back to the entry port of the ship before he heard voices and blended back to listen.

"You sure you haven't seen this man?"

"O' course I seen him. I seen him a dozen times. Everybody in the galaxy'uz seen him. That's Ardenai, Firstlord of Equus."

"I know who it is, thank you. I meant tonight," the voice said patiently.

"I told you once't, I seen twenty-four prostitutes and twenty-six drunks. Two of the drunks was together. I have not seen a man traveling alone. I have not seen a big Equi dressed in royal robes or anything else, for that matter. If I'da seen a man worth a reward like they're sayin', I'da grabbed him myself. As far as anybody suspicious, they're all suspicious."

"May we search your ship?"

"Sure, but I been standing here the whole time. Nobody boarded but two very drunk men booking passage home. Neither of 'em had black hair, nor external ear bones. Neither of 'em was even remotely Equi. Obviously, they wasn't alone. I just can't help you."

"What about your crew?"

"What about my crew? We're together a dozen years or more by now. I didn't hire no Equi in the last day or two, or the last year or two. We're loaded, and we're holdin' up an incoming SGA freighter, which'll be coming down on my shoulders and yours as well. If you're gonna look, look and get out of here, will you? I don't got all night and day!"

"Nor have we. Thank you for your time," the voice said. He spoke to someone else, and Gideon tensed, backing further into the shadows, expecting them to board. They did not. After a few minutes he heaved a sigh of relief and started back for the cabin. He could hear the captain, banging down the heavy metal cargo doors, and the ship began to vibrate as its engines fired. No modern time-whip on this old baby. It would be a long haul to SeGAS-7.

CHAPTER SIX

Squire Fidel squirmed uncomfortably under those piercing blue eyes. "I'm sorry," he said again, desperately hoping to sound sincere, "but what can I do? He was here, I swear he was. My men will tell you he was here."

"Yet no one saw him bleed, but you?" Konik sounded scornful. "Very thin, don't you agree? You have not one shred, not a single shred of evidence to back up your story. Perhaps you are a spy, paid to confuse us in our search for this man."

"I can assure you, I haven't made a single credit from this," Fidel said sadly, palms up in a helpless gesture, "nor would I have taken the reward. I was only trying to do my duty."

"And why did you tell us he traveled alone, if you did not seek to confuse the issue?"

"Kind Sir, I believed he traveled alone. Not until two horses returned to the stables the next day, did I think to check on my men. When I did check, Gideon was missing."

"Can you describe him?"

Fidel nodded and licked his lips. He'd studied that one more than once. "A good-looking Declivian mix in his teens, perhaps sixteen or seventeen. Nearly six feet, and slender – not filled out yet. Thick, pale blond hair worn short," he drew a line with his hands on his neck just above his shoulders, "golden eyes – very gold – as gold as Ardenai's arm bands in clarity. He should be easy to spot."

"He would have been," Konik growled, hiding a shudder of disgust at the tone. "Stay where I can contact you," he said, and left Fidel muttering obscenities in the dust of the barnyard.

Before many minutes had passed another hovercat arrived, and this one had two men in it, a black-skinned Terren and another damned Equi, this one bigger than the last. "My name is Davis," the Terren smiled, alighting from the vehicle as it settled onto its pads. "And this is, ah..."

"Morgan," the Equi said with a gracious nod. "We have been asked by the gentleman who was just here, Senator Konik, to look around and see what we can find."

Fidel's eyes narrowed. "He said he was a Legate, or some such I never heard of. He didn't say he was a senator."

"A slip of the tongue on my part," the Equi said quickly. "Please forgive me. This has been a most trying investigation, as you can well imagine, and Legate Konik was only recently promoted."

"So, may we look?" the Terren asked, and Fidel gestured disgustedly toward the stables and outbuildings.

"There he worked. There he lived. If you find anything, there will it be. I've been called a crazy man and liar enough today. I'm going to go sit in the shade and have a nice, long drink." He turned on his heel and stalked off toward his chair, turning briefly to snap, "And don't scare the horses. Grayson, or whoever he was, left me with the finest stable of jumpers on Demeter. I don't want them ruined."

Eletsky nodded and fell back into step with Kehailan. "I saw you register something just then. What was it?"

"My mother's father's mother, my great grandmother, was Lillian Grayson."

"Then he may actually have been here?"

"He may well have been. If he was," Kehailan said grimly, "I'll know it."

Eletsky gestured toward the paddocks. "Can those horses tell us anything?"

"Don't be silly, Marion." Kehailan said absently, and Eletsky bit back a laugh. Kehailan disliked horses with a passion. He watched as the commander turned all his powers of observation to the task of finding Ardenai. He didn't say anything, he just tagged along at a discreet distance, applying his own well developed senses to his surroundings.

Kehailan went into the stables, and Eletsky went into the bunkhouse. The men were in the fields, and the place was empty. Eletsky gave it a quick once over and decided it would yield nothing. Too bad they could only pretend they'd talked to Konik. More's the pity, they didn't dare risk asking the same questions twice, lest Fidel tip Konik and Konik realize he was being followed. The listening device they'd managed to plant earlier in Konik's hovercat should have functioned well and picked up any and all conversations. Unfortunately, because the air was so humid, they'd gotten about half the conversation, and the rest sounded like a very large aquarium being serviced.

Marion was just meandering about, looking for anything, when Fidel hollered, "Over further, by the pipe rack. Can't your man give instructions any better than that?"

Eletsky looked up, waved and smiled, comprehending nothing but moving in the direction Fidel was waving. "Right there!" the man hollered, and Marion looked down.

Now he could see where the grass had been trampled and matted, uprooted in places by something gouging into it. He squatted on his boot heels to study the area, and as he straightened up, a dark smear on the edge of the pipe rack caught his eye. It could be blood. Equi blood darkened almost to black as it dried, but he didn't want to touch and risk destroying it. This was better left to Kehailan and the sensitive equipment he carried, and Eletsky went to find him. "Kee?" he called softly at the barn door, and the commander's voice said,

"Over here, Marion, to your left and ahead of you."

Eletsky followed the sound, and found the commander on his knees in a pile of straw. "Look," Kehailan said. It was Gideon's computator. "My sire designed this ed-comp, and my sire has programmed it for someone else, very recently."

"You're sure?"

"Positive," Kehailan said, rocking back onto his butt in the straw. "This model is a little newer than my first computator, but this is bit for bit the same program I learned with."

"Could it have become a standard learning program?" Eletsky asked, not wanting to see his friend get his hopes too high.

"Yes, but not for this machine," Kehailan said. "It isn't conclusive, of course."

"Come with me, then," Marion said, "I have something which may prove more valuable." He hauled Kee up by one arm and led him from the stable to the pipe rack, where he pointed to the smear.

Kehailan looked at it for a long time, as though he could see his father's reflection in it somehow, then he took the long, slim instrument which hung in a pouch around his neck, and pointed it at the dark pattern on the pipe rack. He turned in a very slow circle with the little instrument in his hand, then turned it off and made the circle again, using only his eyes. He squatted on his heels and reached gingerly to touch the smear of blood. "According to the anthroscope, this is the blood type most common in High Equi," he said, "and minute fragments of Ardenai's skin. His head hit this metal post, hard, and he fell – there, unconscious, bleeding profusely. There were others here.   Males – Turls, Nargawerlders. And a third, as well; Declivian, or a Declivian-Terren mix probably, as there are very few markers different from Terrenes. Konik was here, the freshest sign, and he...registers as High Equi." He looked up at Marion. "He's an Equi, not an alien of some kind. A royal. That shoots Ardenai's theory."

"Or confirms it," Marion said, cocking his balding head slightly to one side and tugging thoughtfully at his moustache. "There's something about a twin in that saga, and I think it refers to the two planets, or the two peoples."

"It's funny, isn't it?" Kehailan said, a tinge of bitterness in his tone, "how surprised I am that Konik is Equi? What in kraa else would he be? He's spent his life seeing physicians for various things."

"And do you think they noticed?" Marion asked. "Unless I'm very mistaken, he has blue eyes. All full blooded Equi – High Equi, have some shade of green eyes, don't they? Kehailan nodded. "I think your dad's right about the Telenir, and I think when you start turning over rocks, you're going to find a Telenir physician or two."

"For all the good that does us now," Kehailan growled. He stood up abruptly and pointed. "Ardenai was bound with heavy chain and carried from here in that direction. Toward the house."

"Chain?" Marion echoed, wincing in spite of himself. "You're sure about the chain?"

"Positive. His weight increased by nearly thirty percent. He was here, he is gone. If only we could have caught more of the conversation between Fidel and Konik. Now I suppose we'll have to try getting him to repeat everything. Shit. Shit. Shit!"

Captain Eletsky looked in surprise at his old friend, and realized the man's hands were shaking. Was his wing commander on the verge of tears? He looked it. Abruptly, like touching a pulse wire, Eletsky realized he'd never asked Kehailan how he felt about his father being Firstlord of Equus. Things had gone from pageantry to flight in a breath, it seemed. There'd been no time for philosophical discussions, or sharing feelings. One way or another, the man had lost his sire, if not to death, then to a vast calling beyond anything Kehailan must ever have imagined. And now this. Bad enough to have Dad turn out to be king, now he's missing, and bleeding. Marion shook his head. Just how was he supposed to phrase this, and what would the commander's reaction be? He was intensely private most of the time. What could he say?

"Don't say anything," Kehailan advised aloud, gave Marion a ghost of a smile, and headed back toward the main house.

Gideon thanked the man in the galley for the bucket of ice, and for the sandwich, and walked back to the cabin. The door slid silently open, only because he'd taken it upon himself to lubricate the thing, and closed with equal silence, leaving Ardenai undisturbed in the bunk. He appeared to be sleeping, but as Gideon eased the ice bucket onto the table, his eyes fluttered open. "I thought I told you to get some sleep," Gideon said, sitting down beside him.

"I have slept," Ardenai murmured. "Not well or deeply, but I have slept."

Gideon put a hand on Ardenai's forehead, then adjusted the blanket over him. He was shivering despite the cabin's warmth, and though his face registered little, his eyes glittered with pain and fever.

Gideon took some of the ice, wrapped it in a towel, and, carefully as he could, snugged it around Ardenai's bare arm. "Filthy little beast," he muttered. "A filthy, murdering little beast. His knife was as filthy as he was."

"Gideon," Ardenai said quietly, "do not waste your strength with anger. After all, they are dead, and we are alive."

"Now that, is tenuous, my friend," Gideon replied, adjusting the ice-pack. "And we're about out of options at this point. If we don't get you some help, you're going to be as dead as they are."

"There are always options," Ardenai said, touching Gideon's hand. "You worry too much, too soon. I'm tougher than I look."

"And you're sicker than you're letting on," the Declivian retorted. "Even at that, you're a very sick boy."

Ardenai just snorted soundlessly and let it go. There was a point beyond which he couldn't hide the truth. He tried shifting in the bunk to ease his back, and bright flashes of orange and yellow burst before his eyes. His system was full of poison. He quieted his mind and reached deeper inside, searching for healing.

There was a banging at the door, and Gideon stiffened. "You might as well answer it," the Equi said. "It has no lock."

Gideon nodded and did as he was told, hackles up, ready for a fight if need be. The ship's captain was standing outside, three glasses in one hand, bottle in the other. "Three days is one helluva long time for your dear old daddums to have a hangover," he said affably. "I thought maybe, a little hair off the dog that bit him?"

"No, thank you." Gideon said, but the captain had already pushed past him into the room. He stood there, looking at Ardenai, and Gideon knew, he knew. They'd been discovered. His eyes darted quickly from the closing door to Ardenai's face, to any possible weapon, and back to Ardenai.

"We've had this discussion," Ardenai said quietly. "You need to quit thinking of violence as an antidote for fear. This is a perfectly innocent person. It is when we involve innocent people that disagreements become skirmishes, skirmishes become battles, battles become wars. Never involve the innocent."

"Allow them to involve themselves. They make stronger allies that way," the captain smiled, sitting in the chair Gideon had vacated. "Hello, Ambassador. I see you've decided to join the not quite human race."

"Hello, Josephus," Ardenai replied, and his face lit up with pleasure. "How have you been? You look well."

"I look fat and old," he chortled. "You haven't aged a day."

"I've taken to dyeing my hair," Ardenai said solemnly.

"Beard's a nice touch. I like you clean shaven, but it works."

"Clean shaven's easy when you don't grow a beard in the first place," Ardenai said. "This thing has been a ridiculous amount of work and I cannot wait to be shed of it."

By this time Gideon had moved from behind the captain and come to stand next to Ardenai's left shoulder. "You two know each other," he said, his voice full of accusation. "Ardenai, you knew who he was before we ever got on this ship."

"The ambassador is not one to call in a favor, my boy, even when he has one coming," the captain said, and laid a huge paw against Ardenai's flushed face. "Even when he needs one. What happened?"

Gideon eased the ice-pack away from Ardenai's arm, loosened the makeshift bandage, and showed Josephus the ugly, festering wound. "Mongrel Turls, digging for gold," he muttered.

"Let me have a look?" Josephus asked. Ardenai nodded, squeezing his eyes shut, and Josephus probed as gently as he could at the damage. "Reasonably minor wound with major complications," he said finally. "Anyways, I don't have nothing on board that will stop it at this point. We can clean it out, and irrigate it, but the best we can do is slow it down and make you a little more comfortable. I wish I'da known sooner."

"Don't give me that, Captain," Gideon said, "when you walked through that door you knew exactly who you were going to find. I saw it in your face. You must have known all along. You turned the authorities away on purpose the other night."

"Good guess," Josephus smiled, standing up to pat Gideon's shoulder. "About seventy-five percent wrong, but a good guess, anyways. I did turn the authorities away on purpose because they was huntin' a man I got great affection and respect for. I didn't recognize him when you boarded, probably because he made sure I didn't. You, on the other hand, have become real recognizable. Once I heard the ambassador wasn't alone, but with a tall, topaz-eyed Declivian kid, I knew right where both of you was. So does my crew. You've worked with 'em every day and eaten with 'em half a dozen times, Gideon."

The Declivian turned away and his face was stricken. "I never considered myself of any consequence. I thought as long as Ardenai Firstlord stayed incognito, so did I."

"Well, you're an intergalactic celebrity now, and every bit as sought after as the gentleman you're with."

"I see," Gideon said. "On the bright side, I guess this means I don't get pawned off on Kehailan when we get to SeGAS-7."

"Correct, of course," Ardenai muttered, and even as weak as he was, he looked very upset.

"Grayson, I am so sorry!" Gideon exclaimed, tears standing suddenly in the golden eyes. "I only wanted to help you and be with you. I honestly did not mean to cause you more trouble!"

"*You're* sorry?" Ardenai asked in amazement. "Gideon, it is I who am sorry. I was hoping to spare you further danger. Now I cannot do that. You're trapped. Josephus and his crew are being sucked in. Can you see how this sort of thing escalates? It's tragedy enough that Io and Teal have lost their lives on my account...." He trailed off – closing his eyes, clenching his teeth against sickness, exhaustion, and despair.

He opened his eyes again when Josephus's hand closed around his forearm. "Ardi," Josephus smiled, "if you're thinking little Captain Hellcat and Master Teal died in that shuttle explosion, I think you're wrong."

"What?" Ardenai gasped, "They're alive?"

"Can't prove it, but I have every reason to think so," Josephus said, and on Ardenai's face registered a hope that had been all but gone. "See, they piled all the pieces of wreckage up in one of them shuttle bays until Equi authorities could pick 'em up. Well, I went in there with everybody else to take a look, only I wasn't looking just for a souvenir, so I stayed and looked a little longer. That shuttle didn't blow up. It blew out, if you follow me. It was detonated from a single flash point. I think it was rigged."

Ardenai managed a smile and said, "I'm impressed with your sleuthing, Josephus. I didn't know you had it in you."

"I don't" he said, and guffawed, slapping his knee, "and you know I don't. I was in there with Kee, and Marion Eletsky. Marion and me is old poker buddies. Anyways, what's his name, the science guy on the SGAS Belesprit...ah...Moonsgold? That crazy asshole with the two chins, anyways. They're side by side, by the way, instead of one under the other, like mine. Have you met him? Nice fellah. Anyways, he went over every inch of that wreckage with an anthroscope, and a big one, and he said there was not one single fragment of hominoid flesh, residual DNA, or organic matter anywheres on the interior of that wreckage. I think you can hold forth every hope that your lady is alive, and your beloved kinsman, as well."

"Thank you," Ardenai sighed, barely above a whisper, and his eyes closed again. Perhaps they were waiting, after all. Perhaps he would get to the appointed place and Io would be waiting. She, and Pythos, and Teal and the others. Perhaps the war would yet be won and the victory savored in the presence of friends. Ardenai relaxed into that effervescing hope and allowed his burning eyes to close.

As gently as he could, Josephus cleaned and irrigated the wound on Ardenai's arm, wrapped it with clean bandages, and the infection subsided a bit. They covered him in warmer blankets, made him drink some hot vegetable broth, and watched him until his face relaxed in sleep.

"How long have you known him?" Gideon asked, leaning back from dinner in the captain's quarters.

"Oh, the ambassador and me goes back a long ways. Many years."

"Where did you meet him?"

"Terren. He'd been asked to fill in as the Seventh Galactic Alliance Jurisdictional Magistrate for that sector. I got hauled up in front of him."

"Can I ask?"

"Sure," Josephus grinned, and gestured outward, "the grand old rust bucket herself. She was a little younger then, and so was I, and, like now, she was all I had. I'd taken out a debenture bond to Hudson's Bay Company to have her overhauled after Dad died but I couldn't make my time quota because I couldn't find enough loads. Hudson's Bay Company tried to repossess her, and I ran. They caught me and hauled me before the magistrate du jour, who, on Wednesdays, was the Ambassador from Equus, a man reportedly not happy to be assigned back to Terren, even temporarily. I'll tell you, I looked at those dragon's eyes, and that granite jaw, and I figured I was a gonner. I'd be in rehab forever."

"And?" Gideon asked, eyes alight with the tale.

"And, he didn't ask me if I'd run with the ship, he asked me why. I told him she was all I had, and all I'd ever done. She was my inheritance from my dad, and the only way I had for me and my crew to account for ourselves, y'know? Anyways, he stood up, right then, cleared his docket and he says, 'It's such a nice day for a field trip. Show me this ship of yours.' So down we went to dry dock. Ardenai rolls up his sleeves, and goes over every inch of this ship. He went down in the holds, he pulled the covers on the engines, inspected the circuitry, the galley, the crew's quarters, every inch of her. Asked me all kinds of questions. Then he marches me, and the snooty guys from the Hudson's Bay Company, back to his chambers.

"'Gentlemen,' says he, 'That ship has had excellent care. The only reason for giving a vessel care like that, is so it will function well for many years. It is therefore my conclusion that this man has every intention of paying his debenture bond. Logically, if you take the ship, he has no way to do that. Return the ship to her captain and crew, and bring the contracts to me for re-negotiation.' They had to do it, a'course. He swatted my ass with a nasty auxiliary bond, but ... here I am."

"And that was that," Gideon smiled.

"Even that would'a been more'n enough. But he gave me my first steady work – a contract I hold to this day – hauling grain from Demeter to the Great House of Equus. That's how I met the lady Io. Little hellcat herself. She was tiny back then, without a mother and the apple of her daddy's eye. Abeyan spoiled her something fierce whenever he was around. Over the years I watched her grow up..."

"Into a lovely young lady, of course."

"No," Joseph laughed, "into a bigger hellcat, or at least a more accomplished one. She like to drove poor Ardi crazy with some of the stuff she did. O' course I'm making her out to be worse than she was. But she was headstrong. Her father was gone a lot and he wanted the baby to have a woman's touch, you know, so much of her care fell to Ardenai's wife, Ah'ree. Oh, my God, she was a beautiful woman. Funny thing was, Ah'ree and Ardenai gave Io the only discipline she ever got. Anyways, I stayed in touch with our friend in there. Quite a man, that one."

"And in the middle of quite a mess," Gideon sighed, pouring the two of them another cup of coffee – real coffee. Gideon had never had real coffee.

Josephus cocked a grey eyebrow. "In the middle? Are you quite sure he's in the middle?"

Gideon looked puzzled, and Josephus gave him his almost perpetual good-natured grin in return. "As a rule, the conductor stays to the front of the orchestra. Don't underestimate the ambassador. Stand back, play your part, and watch the master orchestrate a victory. You will see things come together you never thought possible, m'boy. I guarantee it."

"What I see, is a man burning up with fever and dying of blood poisoning."

"Look again," Josephus advised. "I see a man among friends, holding his own, going where he needs to go. The aches and pains don't mean nothin' to him. He's High Equi. Hell, he's the Thirteenth Dragonhorse! He's as good as they get."

Gideon was comforted, but privately unconvinced. He gave the captain a brief, rather vague description of what Ardenai was trying to do, but Josephus seemed already to have a pretty good idea, perhaps by long association, perhaps for other, less admirable reasons which Gideon could only guess at. Just to be on the safe side he kept the flow of information, and his absences from Ardenai, to a minimum.

A day later, and still three full days out from SeGAS-7, Josephus radioed that he had a sick crewman. He was trying to contact the medical center at the base, and instead reached Belesprit, meandering in from Se-GAS-5. He was greeted by Bonfire's throaty growl, saying, "This is the Seventh Galactic Alliance Science vessel, Belesprit. May we be of assistance? We are much closer than the base, and our ship's physician would be happy to render aid."

Josephus was delighted. Could they shuttle him out? Indeed they could. They'd send a shunt out with Doctor Hadrian Keats, just as soon as they could locate him aboard ship. Josephus said he would be most grateful for the help.

"I really wish it was anybody but Hadrian Keats," Ardenai sighed, propped in place with pillows. He was too weak to hold his head up, but not too weak to think straight, and he was thinking hard. Keats had absolutely no love for him. Given the opportunity, he'd turn in both Ardenai and Gideon. "I don't want to have to redistribute information in his synapses, but I really don't see that I'll have much choice in the matter."

"What horrible thing did you do to him?" Gideon asked, wringing out a cool cloth and blotting at the Equi's temples and forehead.

Ardenai sighed listlessly and shrugged against his pillows. It was obvious he didn't care to talk about it. It was also obvious to Gideon that he desperately needed a doctor, and a good one, not some Alliance meat cutter with a chip on his shoulder. "I honestly don't know. He's hated me since the moment we met, and never, in so many words, has he told me why. Keats has such an odd, hostile mind. And yet it's just like a sponge. He's constantly throwing out messages and bits of emotional... reaction, without really meaning to. I suppose that's good for our current purposes, but it hasn't helped our relationship, and he's not going to be happy to see me."

"Grayson," Gideon ventured, seeming busy with the cloth, "You knew before we ever got near it that this was Josephus's ship, didn't you?"

The Equi's eyes didn't open. "Mmmmm," he said, with a slight downward motion of his chin.

"I thought I'd chosen this ship, but I didn't, did I? You put it on my heart that I was to choose a grain carrier, and that I was to choose this one."

"I like that phrasing," Ardenai managed, though the urge to sleep was becoming overwhelming. What if he was too sick to keep control of Keats? That would be disaster. He took a couple of deep breaths, willing himself back into a strong enough state to school another's mind if he had to. He didn't like the word, manipulate. Never had. "It was a subtle, unspoken suggestion, nothing more. I promise."

Keats arrived on board all bustle and concern, hurried Josephus along to the injured man's cabin, and stopped dead in his tracks, looking from Gideon to the bed and back again. "*You,*" he said, and turned around as if to leave, but the door had already closed, leaving him alone with Ardenai, Gideon, and Josephus, who stood with his arms folded across his massive chest, barring the only exit. He glared at the door for a minute, then turned back around and glared at Ardenai with his close set, slightly protruding eyes. "You."

The Equi sighed. "I told Pythos this disguise wasn't good enough."

"Neither is his," Keats said, jerking his head at the Declivian. "And just what the hell do you have planned for me, Ardenai Firstlord? Apparently I am now your prisoner."

"Yes indeed. I look like I'm taking prisoners, don't I?" Ardenai sighed. "Doctor Keats, I have absolutely no idea what you have against me, or what you think I'm going to do to you, and you would be gratified to know..." Ardenai paused, closed his eyes, gasped for air and control of the situation, "... how much I wish you were not here. As it is, I have no choice, and so you have no choice."

Keats took a sharp breath and a step back. "I don't?"

"No," the Equi said flatly, "you do not." He clenched his teeth and squeezed his eyes shut, and when he opened them Keats was bending over him, reading his vital signs.

"A fever like this would kill a normal man, you know that. Blood poisoning should have killed you a couple days ago. Must hurt like holy hell. I sure hope so, anyway." He sat down, talking half to Ardenai, half to himself, muttering about people who yapped harmony one day and went to war with legends the next, all the while unwrapping the bandage on Ardenai's left arm. "After what you went through having these damned arm-bands put on, what'd you cover 'em up for? Never mind, I don't want to know. If you told me I still wouldn't know. I should take this entire skin graft off of here."

"Why?"

"Why? Because it's rotten, that's why. How'd you get this?"

"The two gentlemen who initially captured me, wanted to be absolutely sure they had the right man. I do need that graft in place. I still have places to go."

"I'll just bet you do." Keats turned his attention from Ardenai's arm, and pushed gently around the wound over his eye. "Good thing your head's hard. That's a nasty concussion. You're lucky to be alive. Why didn't Captain what's-his-name tell Kehailan you're here? He's been worried half to death."

"Doctor," Ardenai said quietly, "far be it from me to tell you your business..."

"Don't then. Hold still. This will bring the fever down and reduce the infection so I can work. It may make you a little sick to your stomach, or a lot sick to your stomach. It'll wear off in seventy-two hours or so."

Ardenai shook his head. "Doctor, in less than seventy-two hours we will be on SeGAS-7, running for our lives. I cannot take the risk that someone will see a pattern." he seized up with pain, and Keats took the opportunity to mutter,

"What pattern? There's no pattern. Sorry. I know that hurts, even if you won't admit it."

"Oh, I will freely admit, it hurts. But I just can't stop for it. I have to keep moving. We, have to keep moving. I am seen on Demeter. The ship of a man I have known for years is seen on Demeter. Now neither is seen on Demeter, but the ship is on its way to SeGAS-7. My son is on SeGAS-7 ..."

"No, he's not. He's on Demeter, or on his way back, maybe."

"What? What's he doing on Demeter?"

"Looking for you. He and Eletsky are trailing some guy named Konik. Ring a bell?"

Ardenai thought a moment, watching Keats numb up the skin that had been so recently a beautiful, coiled python, and was now inflamed and tattered. "Pythos was so pleased with those. I should have valued them for that reason alone." he said, mostly to himself. "Konik? Yes. He is rather deep in the entourage of Sarkhan, I'm afraid." He made the comment in a casual tone, and then watched Keats without seeming to.

"Not so deep anymore," Keats muttered, intent on Ardenai's arm. "He came aboard Belesprit disguised as an Equi agent, disguised as a quantum psi technician. He was neither, of course. He got caught poking around Kee's cabin. Anyway, details aside, Marion pretended to believe his story about being an Equi agent looking for you, and let him go. They've been following him ever since, hoping, I suppose, to find you at the end of the trail. Oh, and Kee thinks the guy is a Telenir? Make sense?"

Ardenai nodded slightly, observing the doctor's willingness to share any and all information, despite two complete strangers listening in. "As much as one could expect, given the situation," he replied. "Why does Kehailan think he's Telenir?"

"Because the captain of your Horse Guard says he is." Ardenai jumped, and Keats immediately looked apologetic. "I should have said that in the past tense, I guess. She *said*, in the past tense, he *was*. We haven't seen her since she and Teal supposedly died, though all indications are they didn't."

The Firstlord caught his breath and focused his attention on the doctor. "Carefully, coherently if at all possible – when did Kee see Io, and what did she tell him? Had she made further contact with Konik or Sarkhan?"

"You need to relax. No. Relax, as in, un-tense your muscles, Dragonhorse. You're shaking, and I can't work on you like that. Kee saw Io two days before her shunt blew up. And she told him that you had a theory about Sarkhan, so she went to see Sarkhan, and she told him the theory, only she said it was hers, not yours, and she tried to make him think she was selling out to him. Selling you to him? Anyway, I didn't quite get that part, but I guess he jumped about like you did just now. Upshot being your theory is right. Is that the one about the ditty of the Wind Warriors being history rather than melodic fiction? Or something?"

"Please…stop talking," Ardenai groaned, and pressed his fist against his mouth.

"Boy, are you clammy! Are you going to make it?"

"Make what?" he managed around his fist.

"A mess, probably. Not to worry, I can't imagine there's anything in your stomach. You'll probably just get the dry heaves. Hate those things."

"No." Ardenai grated, clamping his jaws together, "I will not," and he didn't. He suffered in silence, sweat trickling down his temples into his beard, until Keats began cursing under his breath.

"Give in!" he said. "Just puke. You don't have to prove you're a god, you know." He became aware of Gideon's hostile golden gaze just over his left shoulder, and applied himself to his craft without further comment.

Josephus had no more than gotten docked at SeGAS-7, and his engines idled down, when the SGA authorities boarded his ship, looking for the Firstlord. The reason? He had killed the lady Io and Commander Teal in a Seventh Galactic Alliance domain. No more sulking in private. No more diplomatic immunity. Ardenai was wanted by his own government for murder.

"I find them charges ludicrous," the captain said, arms akimbo in defiance, "but what I think don't matter anyways, because Ardenai Firstlord isn't here. Not him, not his Declivian friend. I do tell you this much for sure. If I'da seen him, I'da helped him. If I do see him, I will help him, and it would behoove you fellas to do likewise. The Dragonhorse IS the government, and he can have your scrawny asses shoved out the nearest airlock."

The man in the SGA Adjutant's uniform was not impressed. He asked to see the man who had needed assistance. Doctor Keats showed him to a cabin where the cook lay, recovering from an emergency appendectomy. Then SGA Security searched the ship. Thoroughly. They found nothing. Nobody. No clue that there ever had been any extraneous personnel. "And yet you left Demeter with two men who had booked passage to SeGAS-7. Where are they?" the adjutant asked.

"They booked passage," Josephus shrugged. "They got on. They got back off."

"Why did they get off?"

"Because their wives come and got 'em off," Josephus grinned. "Anyways," he said, and his smile faded, "I got a ship to unload and move down the line so the next ship can unload. I don't like having you here, and I don't like what you're doing. Ardenai Firstlord, would never have killed Io, no matter what she did. He loves her deeply. I love him. He's my friend, and my mentor, and I want your officious, sonofabitch butt off my ship."

"You, are hardly in a position to dictate," the man sniffed, tightening his long upper lip in disdain. "And you, Doctor Keats. You know Ardenai Firstlord. Are you his friend, too?"

"Mister," the doctor drawled, edging away from Josephus, who was bristling dangerously, "if you're looking for someone who loves that Equi, don't look at me. Ardenai is most definitely not my friend. He is, however, a man of duty, and of honor, and of the law."

"Meaning?"

"Meaning," Keats growled belligerently, "I don't like what you're doing, either. I have a man in there I'd like to get to the base hospital, if you're quite through snooping around here."

"I will be through, when Ardenai Firstlord is in custody. Not before. It will be simple enough to discern if you are lying. Either of you. Any of you. And if you are, you will be punished," He caught the gleam in Josephus's eye, turned on his heel, and exited only slightly faster than was graceful.

"Do you believe that?" Josephus said angrily. "Who does he think he is, barging in here, accusing..." he paused, and looked puzzled. "I wonder where Ardenai is really."

"No idea, hm?" Keats asked casually, and the troubled gaze turned his direction.

"Funny you should ask that, Doctor. I really feel like I should know. Well, anyways, I meant what I told that pompous so and so. Here, I'll help you with Walter."

"No need. I'll send somebody back for him," Keats said, accepted the captain's thanks, and walked down the main concourse shaking his head. He reached his cabin on Belesprit, activated the door and stepped into the dim interior. A chair swiveled slowly on its base, and Ardenai was looking at him, inscrutable and slightly amused.

Well, he passed that test, the Firstlord was thinking, but he said, "I was beginning to be concerned."

"Don't lie to me!" Keats exploded. "The way you manipulate people? You're concerned about any of them? Any of us? I doubt that. Captain Josephus truly, honestly, does not know you were ever on his ship. You vacuumed out his mind. You just sucked out what you didn't want in there.

You're a damned dangerous man! Far more than even I was willing to admit. You brain-washed a whole crew, you blue blooded bastard!" Keats was not a brave man, and, to his credit, he knew this. He glared at the Equi, fascinated and afraid. "What will you do to me afterwards, wipe my mind clean like you did the captain's?"

"You could have told him I was there. You could have told the adjutant," Ardenai said by way of reply. "It would have been a simple enough matter, would it not?"

Keats growled under his breath for a moment or two, searching for words among the anger. "I...your son is my friend," he said finally. "I did it for him, not you. And I feel sorry for that boy you have prisoner. My God, you made me change his eye color! He had beautiful eyes."

"He will again, Doctor. Rest easy. You have such a penchant for dramatics. As one wipes fingerprints from a glass, so I wiped my immediate presence from Josephus's memory. The glass remains intact. My presence, and Gideon's, is all that is missing. He is thereby protected, and repaid for his kindness. He'll realize soon enough that I was there."

"So now you really do think you're God. You decide who should and should not be a hero. Who can and cannot do what he thinks is right. We're all pawns to be used in your power games."

Ardenai winced, but he didn't answer. He just turned his chair away from Hadrian Keats and faced the empty chair beside the desk. Keats came over, sat in the chair, and modulated his tone. "Ardenai, you made me perform surgery on someone who didn't need it, just so you..."

"Stop it!" the Equi snapped. "I did not do anything of the kind. Modifying Gideon's eye color was strictly cosmetic and temporary. Precious Equus, look at what Pythos did to me! As to that man's appendix, was it not inflamed?"

"Yes. I assumed you caused it. I mean, hell, you can cause anything else! You take that ancient old computator on an ancient old vessel, you mess around with it for half a day and suddenly it's talking on intimate terms with some computator someplace else, probably in this very office, and then, at the appointed time in the appointed place, you're just gone. You and Gideon, both."

"And you're acting as though I told you nothing about it," Ardenai replied. "Are you really so dense that you can't remember what was discussed? I explained to you exactly what would take place, and you agreed to it. You are equating the manipulation of machines with the manipulation of living beings, Doctor. The cook's appendix was beginning to infect his system, and it showed in his eyes. I simply pointed it out. I had no idea I was frightening you to the point where you would cease to reason for yourself. I shall beg your forgiveness, and take my leave."

"Still sick, so weak you wobble. You really do have a death wish since your wife died." His eyes and body language repented instantly, but the words were out, and because he was afraid, and the fear made him angry, he refused to take them back. The Equi didn't turn a hair.

"I'll go wake Gideon," Ardenai said, "and get out of your mind."

"You're not going to touch me or my mind!" the doctor yelped. "But if you had a shred of decency you'd get yourself out of his, before you get him killed. Go, but leave him here."

"Would that I could, Doctor. As it is, I cannot. I will not risk it. Even if I could safely erase that much of his memory without touching the deeper parts of his mind, I cannot erase Gideon from the memory of everyone else who has seen him with me. I am sorry to disappoint you, but I am not the consummate monster, after all. Please excuse me." He rose and walked toward the rear of Keats's cabin, and Gideon stepped forward to meet him.

"I am here," he said simply, and handed Ardenai one of the backpacks. "Doctor Keats, thank you for your hospitality, and for helping us. I'm sorry we frightened you."

"You think that's it?" Keats retorted, getting out of the chair. "You think that's why I object to helping you?"

"It seems pretty obvious to me," Gideon muttered, and Ardenai cut him off with the lifting of one eyebrow.

"Doctor Keats is a man who takes risks, even though it is uncomfortable for him to do so. That takes courage. He is someone my son considers a friend, and I trust my son's judgment. Remember what was said between Josephus and me earlier. Never involve the innocent. Allow them to involve themselves."

"That's right," the doctor growled, "Go ahead. Manipulate me some more. I dare you!"

"It would never occur to me," Ardenai said smoothly, and Keats backed away from him.

"Don't touch me!" he warned sharply.

"No, of course not," the Equi smiled. He parked one muscular hip on the edge of the desk and allowed the knapsack to slide temporarily to the floor, then fixed Keats with a long, quiet gaze. "It has been a beautiful day, has it not?"

"It certainly has," the doctor smiled.

"You have been busy, have you not?"

"I have," Keats said.

"A nap sounds good about now, does it not?" Ardenai said quietly.

"Yes, it does," The doctor sighed, and collapsed obligingly into Ardenai's waiting arms. The Firstlord scooped him up and carried him over to the bed, while Gideon stood there watching, trying to figure out what Ardenai was doing.

The Equi saw it in his eyes. "This is not what you are thinking, or maybe it is," he chuckled. He eased the doctor down on the pillows, put the book he'd been reading on his chest, activated it at the bookmark, and stepped back. "If I had reached for him, I'd have scared him to death."

"He still seems unconscious," Gideon observed.

"He told me not to touch him," the Equi pointed out, "but he invited me to manipulate him. I chose to take him at his word." There was a pause and a self-deprecating snort. "And yes. I recognize sarcasm when I hear it, so don't bother asking. I do not wish to compromise his better judgment, but neither do I want him compromising mine. I cannot consider the wishes of one man when a whole world rides on what he might say to others."

Gideon looked at the peacefully snoring doctor, then into the First-lord's dark eyes. "I can see that you didn't hurt him," he said tentatively, "but...he told you not to touch him, and you know that, and you did it anyway. Isn't that kind of..." the boy groped for an appropriate word, "violating someone? And not just kind of, but actually, because you are so much stronger than he is?"

Ardenai made a slightly frustrated gesture to wave the comment away and smiled to soothe the boy. "Sometimes the ends really do justify the means, Gideon. Sometimes, when you are the one with the power, you have to use it as best you can according to what your own good judgment tells you. As you say, and as you can see, the man is not hurt, nor will he be."

Gideon nodded, though he still looked unsure. "So, if you are choosing this man's course at this point, since you, as you say, have the power, could you put it into the doctor's head to cooperate with you?"

"Yes."

"Then why don't you?" he exclaimed, suddenly angry. "Grayson, you are doing the right thing! He knows the story that Io told Kehailan. Kehailan believes it. Captain Eletsky believes it, or they wouldn't be out there." He waved vaguely toward the ceiling. "Hadrian Keats should believe it too, if he's loyal to the Seventh Galactic Alliance. He's just a coward. He's an ill-tempered old Corvus eagle."

Ardenai's aquiline profile became embarrassingly apparent as he turned away, and Gideon heard him snicker. "There are a lot of us ill-tempered old birds out there," he said, still in profile, and looking toward the door. "It comes from standing by our convictions. I absolutely will not probe his mind to find where his opinions lie. That would be both unnecessary and unethical. To change his opinion? That would be punishment for a crime he has not committed. I have darkened my most recent passage through Hadrian's mind for one reason only, to protect Josephus and the others. Keats is not one to think far enough ahead to realize that Sarkhan will compare their stories. So will the Seventh Galactic Alliance, though I don't believe the so-called investigation is actually theirs. Keats would be pathetically easy to break or trip up, Gideon. He would blurt everything out, and the least prestigious person, probably Josephus, would be dishonored and possibly hurt. I cannot have that."

"I just…I really think that when someone says not to touch them – their minds or their bodies or whatever, that you should honor that, regardless of the consequences. Just because you're using your mind and not your…" he squelched the next word, but his open thought took Ardenai's breath away.

He stared with disbelief at the boy. "Precious, Equus," he managed. "You think I raped him, don't you?"

Gideon winced. "I'm not sure what I think," he said at last.

The eyes that searched his face were wounded. "I am suddenly responsible for keeping billions of people safe, Gideon. Do you think figuring out how to do that is easy? Right from wrong? Good, from greater good, evil from the lesser of evils? I am erasing a conversation, an experience. Nothing more than what a person would forget anyway over the course of weeks or seasons. I am not assailing who he is, what he believes, what he needs in order to be himself. I'm making him forget something, like I could make you lose count if I interrupted you in the midst of the problem. That's all. I promise. I swear to you."

Their eyes met, lingered, and Gideon looked away. "I need to know which way we're walking," he said.

"Think about it, and we will talk later," Ardenai sighed. The boy was disappointed in him, and he felt that weight add itself to his shoulders. "In the third docking ring, just off the main concourse there is a prototype Imperial Storm Class clipper, built by the Great Shipyards on Andal to honor the Rising of The Thirteenth Dragonhorse. I thought perhaps you would like to go for a spin with me. Delta TimeWhip technology, latest thing."

Gideon looked from the small, sleeping doctor to the big, grave-faced Equi and back again. "You choose to invade his mind despite him asking you not to, but even though you're already in there you won't cause him to help us so we can maybe make some legitimate progress, and now we're stealing a prototype TimeWhip clipper. I truly am struggling with this."

"So am I, Gideon," Ardenai said, gave the boy a slap on the back, and they slipped out into the dimly lit corridors of the slumbering Belesprit.

CHAPTER SEVEN

Kehailan just stood there, looking at the empty spot in the docking ring and shaking his head. "Of course you know without any shadow of a doubt who took it," he said irritably.

"Did I say that?" the man in the adjutant's uniform asked, his eyes, his voice, his attitude all proclaiming his contempt for Kehailan's defense of his father. "All I said was, the only fugitive we have who is intelligent enough to fly a prototype clipper is Lord Ardenai."

Kehailan's ears were pinned tight with annoyance, and he kept swallowing, trying to control the anger rising in his throat when he tried to speak. "And I said, in that case no crime has been committed, because the clipper belongs to Ardenai in the first place. He designed it. It's his personal craft. It was brought here by his personal physician and left for minor adjustments to the navigational system while Pythos went on with constituents to a conference on SeGAS-4. The conference is over by now. How do you know Pythos did not return to take the clipper back to Equus?"

The adjutant ignored him, and he could feel himself beginning to tremble. First the hands, then the legs. His muscles were tensing with the need to strangle the man when a large hand with formidable claws attached itself to his forearm. "Don't give him the satisfaction," Bonfire hissed. "Stay cool. Leave this little one to me."

The adjutant smirked. "No need to be defensive, Commander. Surely you do not think we would hold your sire's crimes against you?"

"What crimes?" Kehailan asked calmly, only his ramrod straight back and pinned ears betraying the anger he felt. The shaking had stopped. "So far there are only questions to be asked. How terrible a crime can it be for a man to take his own vessel?"

"Criminals do not own property, Wing Commander."

"You, to your possible detriment, are forgetting that the Thirteenth Dragonhorse is above the law. Any law. He IS the law," Kehailan remarked, walking toward the docking ring's personnel exit. "Too, I find it interesting that the man entrusted to keep law and order on this base has no concept of due process, which makes me question your credentials. And, by the way, when was Adjutant De Los Angeles replaced, and on whose order? Never mind answering that. I shall check for myself." The door slid open and he was gone.

"He doesn't like you much," Bonfire Dannis smiled, "but I could. You look very tasty to me. I don't care that you and your security squad are imposters. Oh, didn't he mention that to you? He knows you're pretending to be Adjutant while the real one is on holiday. Still, I do think there's time for just a quickie before they come and take you away."

Kehailan heard Bonfire's sharp bark of laughter, and smiled to himself as the adjutant blew by at a gallop. He knew her sense of humor. A very gentle woman, actually, but frightening in size and aspect, and the perpetually hungry vocabulary didn't help with strangers. He stood quietly in the main concourse for a few moments and composed himself for the gauntlet about to be run, willing his hands to unknot at his sides. Then he took a deep breath and walked back toward his ship, ignoring the stares and the whispers.

As he rounded the corner into the secondary concourse which would take him to Belesprit, a hand closed over his shoulder and a gravelly voice said, "How's about letting an old star skipper buy yez a drink, kid?"

Kehailan started slightly and turned, his eyes lighting with pleasure. "Josephus! Just the man I wanted to see," he smiled.

"Likewise, I'm sure. What's on your mind, or should I say, who?"

"Someone whose safety does not merit public discussion, Captain. Can you accompany me to my quarters?"

"Tell you what, Kee, you come with me instead, hm?" One eyelid lowered in a conspiratory wink, and his huge paw gently steered Kehailan ninety degrees around and down another auxiliary concourse toward the agricultural section of the station.

They walked in silence until they reached Josephus's vessel. The crewman standing guard nodded them aboard, and Josephus took Kehailan to the bridge. "Did Keats tell you we had a medical emergency on board?"

"He mentioned it. I knew you were still in port because of it, waiting for your crewman. Josephus, what is it? Did you see Ardenai when you were on Demeter?"

"I really don't know, Kee. A'course I've gotten forgetful in me old age. Come here, I want to show you something." Josephus opened the set of metal doors covering the main computator, and then stepped to one side, removing his paunch from the commander's line of vision. "Tell me what you see."

"A very, very old navi-psi," Kehailan said, not sure whether to be amused or sympathetic.

"Very good. Now fiddle with it a little."

Kee raised an appraising eyebrow, but he stepped to the keyboard on the bridge console, and began to run a standard navigational program. He stopped, rubbed his chin – ran another program.

"Now tell me what you see," Josephus prodded.

"A very old navi-psi in excellent condition," Kehailan said with an admiring whistle. "State of the art SGA navigational data, extended preprogramming capability within the existing system, no extraneous or outdated bits. There's nothing wrong with...wait a minute. This isn't SGA navigational stuff, this is UGA! This is what Belesprit has!"

"Right again," Josephus nodded. "I just wanted to get an expert's opinion. I didn't realize I had United Galactic Alliances technology." He glanced at the taller man from under his bushy eyebrows. "It's okay to have that, isn't it?"

"Of course it is," Kehailan said with a chuckle. "I don't know why you wanted my opinion. You must have been pushed to the front of a very elite line to have this onboard."

"Was I?" Josephus asked, and Kehailan's eyes began to narrow. "Kee, I've been in any line I could get into for the last three years to have this machine re-programmed. Old ships keep getting pushed aside, you know. May not last that long, so why bother's the attitude. My navigational data was so ancient it was practically useless. New routes was out of the question. Now look at this thing."

Kehailan hiked himself onto the bridge rail and stared into the computation bank itself, almost as though he could make a face appear if he concentrated hard enough. "The two men who boarded on Demeter, and then did not go with you. What did they look like?"

Josephus pulled his eyebrows together one more time and really, really concentrated, but again he had to shake his head in defeat. "Kee, I have no idea. I think about them. They was tall, one of them had a beard. They was drunker'n hell, but...nothing comes to mind."

"Why do you suppose that is?"

"That's what I'm asking you, Kee. That damned adjutant even made me take a Halston test. I don't know a thing about Ardenai's whereabouts."

"Josephus, I think you do," Kehailan said, and his eyes were twinkling, which made Josephus smile. "I think they stayed on board the whole way here, and I think at least one of them worked off his passage fixing this computator. Do you suppose I could check for messages?"

"Only if you'll tell me the good parts," Josephus laughed.

"This won't be nearly that intrusive, but I can make something up, if you'd like." the Equi replied, "for entertainment's sake."

"Please, so's I at least think I got a life. Come on over here and sit with me where it's private." He led the commander to a small alcove which served as his office, and with a couple of tries, got the door to shut. "I do work on the old girl, you know," he said a little defensively, gesturing toward two chairs. "What do you want me to do?"

"Just relax. And if you've been eating alliums or drinking beer, hold your breath," Kehailan chuckled. He sat down facing Josephus, then he let his eyes close and began to breathe, slowly and deeply. "With me," he said quietly, leaned in, and placed his hands on Josephus' forearms to reassure him. Josephus felt a slight tingle, and for those few moments he could remember every beautiful thing that had happened in his life – he could smell flowers and trees and water – hear the laughter of loved ones, feel warm, female bodies against his, and when Kehailan took a deep breath and sat back, Josephus felt like he'd been on the best holiday of his life.

"Hot damn, what would you charge me to do that about once a week?" he breathed.

"You'd have to marry me," Kehailan chuckled.

"Well?" Josephus demanded, gesturing impatiently. "Was it him? Was he here? Did we have a good time?"

"Ask yourself who else would have that much UGA navigational data in his head, and who could transfer it that fast. As to having a good time, I don't really think so. You summoned Doctor Keats to treat my sire, not Walter."

The captain's eyes grew round with concern, "Is he okay? What was wrong?" He tried to think back to those two men getting on the ship. Had one of them been injured? Nothing came to mind.

"An infected wound. We found blood during our investigation of the plantation where he worked on Demeter. But don't worry. He must have recovered, or your computator wouldn't be in this kind of shape, would it?" Kehailan reached over and patted the man's hand. "You're in the clear for the moment. Don't worry about my sire. Worry about yourself and your crew. What's your manifest look like?"

"Machinery belts back to Demeter, why?"

"You are to take them there and unload them as quickly as possible. There will be a load of Chenopodium quinoa going clear to Equus. Again, load quickly. When you are free of the atmosphere, enter my mother's name into the console, and let the ship take over. When you reach Equus, stay there. Avail yourself of Canyon keep, and enjoy yourself."

"I don't suppose you'd care to explain why, would yez, or do you know?"

"I can only assume," Kehailan sighed, "that you are, or might be, in danger. Another piece of the puzzle has dropped into place."

"And do we know what that means?" Josephus growled, hauling his bulk up out of the little chair, which squeaked its dismay before trembling back into place.

"Only if we are the Thirteenth Dragonhorse, I'm afraid," the commander replied, and his eyes filled with worry. He jerked slightly to correct himself, and got a warm, one-armed hug from Josephus.

"Only a mind like your dad's could come up with something like this. Come on, I'll pour you a drink. You look like you could use it."

"There is one more thing you must do," Kehailan said, and began explaining as they walked back toward the main concourse.

▲ ▲ ▲ ▲ ▲ ▲ ▲

Sarkhan, too, needed a drink. He waved his right hand, and a young woman appeared with a pitcher and two glasses. With a second, impatient wave she disappeared, and Sarkhan turned back to Konik. "You lost him. You had him in the palm of your hand, and you lost him. Your five-year-old grandson, Nokota, isn't it? He could do a better job than you're doing."

Konik caught his breath, then exhaled, trying to make it sound like annoyance. "My Lord Sarkhan," he said, pointedly not using the Firstlord's title, "I never had him to lose. Despite the stories, the sightings, the rumors, the accusations, we have never had the man, not even for a single second's time."

"No? What about Squire whoever he was? He saw Ardenai."

"A greedy, fat little dolt who says he saw Ardenai. He has become one of several dozen of his ilk to see the same thing in three different sectors. Your impatience to have the Firstlord in your grasp has led us into a hopeless tangle of half-truths, just as Ardenai knew it would."

"Never!" Sarkhan snapped, stinging from Konik's comment, and the implied rudeness of bestowing a title Sarkhan considered his onto another, whom he already considered dead. "Ardenai is a man of plodding, unrelenting rationality. He plans when he's going to take a piss. It is his heritage and his credo. He is totally devoid of imagination."

"Perhaps he is sure enough of his rationality to know its extensible strength. He may just twist it as he wishes it to go."

"No. Too mundane. Too lacking in pride for the ruler of a world government. The male who rules Equus is a god, Konik."

"Beware," Konik said quietly, "Lord Sarkhan, beware of assuming that Ardenai feels as you do about his office. You desire it above all else, yet it was thrust upon him. He is a man who loves personal freedom. He loves breeding fine horses. He is accomplished in everything he attempts, from music, to teaching both children and horses, to designing computators. What he does, is elegant, and simple. His pride seems to run to his people, not his personal vanity."

Sarkhan shot the man a nasty look, and rubbed at his upper lip in an attempt to erase the sneer which had formed at Konik's fawning and treacherous words. "You sound like you want to have sex with him," he said. Konik's usefulness had it limits, and when they were reached his treachery would be repaid – about seven times over. Wife, daughters, husbands, grandchildren – the thought of hearing Konik scream made Sarkhan smile. He would speak of this to Sardure. "Ardenai, was bred to receive that office."

"And to understand it," Konik replied. "You do not have that advantage." He lifted a drink from the tray and sat staring through the archways into Sarkhan's verdant spring gardens. He wondered if the man ever worked in them. Konik did. He loved gardening with Ah'davan in the rich soil of Anguine II. Ardenai gardened. When he blinked his reverie away, he saw that Sarkhan, too, had been staring into space.

"I have spent years, my whole life, as an Equi. I know their ways, and I know their thoughts."

"No, Lord Sarkhan. You have maintained too great a distance to do that. You know their ways, and how their thoughts manifest themselves in speech or action, but the process itself, you cannot hope to understand. He is a very powerful telepath, probably the most powerful hominoid on Equus.

If he so chooses, he has effortless access to places in the mind where you cannot hope to go. If Squire Fidel really did see him, he has trimmed back his ears, lightened his hair, and grown a beard. He is less thoughtful in action than other High Equi. This is not the Ardenai we have observed. What we have is an Equi pretending to be a Demetrian mongrel, or some other off-worlder. This is more complicated yet. Besides the original process you must now project that to his interpretation of another culture. Now, you are completely backwards, logically. You are Telenir, trying to think like an Equi who is trying to think like an unknown entity."

"Oh, shut up," Sarkhan muttered. "You think too much and act not enough. What did you find on Demeter? Did you investigate fully? Perhaps you missed something."

"Assuming that Ardenai had fled, I pursued him rather than seeking evidence that he had been on the plantation. After all, what good is the scent of an enemy when the enemy is gone? It serves only to remind us that we are still behind our quarry."

"My father thinks you are a warrior," Sarkhan sneered. "He is a querulous, demented old fool who has hung onto life this long simply because he wants to see me rise to power. And to that end, in his infinite wisdom, he stuck me with you. You are nothing more than a philosopher, who will not draw his sword and step forward for fear of falling on his own blade."

"I, too, have spent my life among the Equi, as an Equi, and my family for many more generations than yours," said Konik, and said no more.

A man in the uniform of the Equi Horse Guard came trotting up the stone steps from the garden and nodded their direction. "What?" Sarkhan asked, beckoning him closer.

"Word has reached us from SeGAS-7 that the clipper which Physician Pythos left there has disappeared."

"When?" Sarkhan exclaimed. "Who took it?"

"No one knows, Senator."

"I know!" Sarkhan said, rising to his feet. "Again, Konik, we smell the enemy, hm?"

The messenger gave Sarkhan a queer look, and Konik dismissed him with a smile and a nod. "Beware," he said again. "Never forget which are ours, and which are theirs."

"Soon, they will all be ours," Sarkhan laughed. "Konik, you are bumbling this."

"I am doing what you tell me to do, as is my duty – pursuing dead end after dead end."

"Perhaps I should take up the chase in your stead," Sarkhan snapped. "At least I can think and move at the same time. Perhaps I shall defy my father and take my brother Sardure and leave you here to face Saremmano's wrath."

"Why don't you do that," Konik replied. "I'm sure Ardenai would like that. I'm sure he would like to have you become enraged enough that you forget your duties to the Great House and your place on the Council, and go chasing off. I'm also sure that at such a time the trail would become very clear for you. He's playing you as beautifully as he plays every other instrument he picks up, and you're letting him. We are lost if we do not negotiate. My Lord Sarkhan, think! We can yet unite our worlds as brethren and as friends. What could you give our peoples more precious than that? You would be remembered as the greatest of heroes by both worlds. A greater hero even than Ardenai Firstlord himself. "

"SHUT UP! SHUT UP! GET OUT!" Sarkhan screamed. "Find me that clipper!"

"Certainly," Konik muttered, and turned on his heel, leaving Sarkhan in hysterics, throwing wine glasses, and ripping flowers from their pots.

"Will they catch us?" Gideon asked, releasing his harness and easing himself out of the seat beside Ardenai. He was still shaky from the acceleration, and placed one hand, as casually as he could, across the back of the seat to steady himself.

Ardenai swiveled in his chair, retracted his own harness, and stretched, locking his hands behind his head and popping his shoulders and neck. "Not until we allow them to."

The young man paled just a bit, though he didn't let his expression betray him. "You mean you're going to let them capture us at some point?"

"We must at least let them think they have a chance," the Equi said. "Otherwise they may grow discouraged. Don't be concerned, Gideon, this is a very fast ship and really quite luxurious." He took his hands down, rolled his head on his neck, and closed his eyes. "The vessel will fly itself. I believe we should have something to eat, take a nice long bath, and get some real sleep for a change."

The boy's eyes – now a pale, leafy brown rather than brilliant, foxy gold – Immediately lit up. "Food sounds good," he said. "Actually, a big, thick, juicy steak sounds best. But since I know Equi are vegetarians, I don't suppose there's meat on board."

"Don't be too sure," Ardenai replied. "My personal physician used this ship last, and he is of the most ancient order of Equi, the sea dragons of Achernar. Perhaps there's a nice Declivian tree toad stored somewhere as a snack. That would be in the lavage, where there's water. Failing that, you might find a cage of rodents under one of the beds. They're back that direction. We'll sleep in the forward stateroom, so we can hear the equipment. You might as well take your traveling pack with you as you go. Your bed is the one pushed tight against the wall. Main lavage is clear to the back."

"No eggs? An omelet sounds nice."

"We don't eat the unborn, either."

"You, are sick!" Gideon laughed, picking up his pack and heading through the door Ardenai had indicated, "And it's no act, either. You have a genuinely heartfelt sick sense of humor."

"You wound me," Ardenai called after him, crimping a grin. "To be honest, it wasn't so much a moral thing as an environmental decision. Raising meat is hard on the planet, and it's also hard for us to digest. We tend to be grain eaters, so it was an easy choice."

It was silent for three or four minutes before the boy returned. "An environmental decision," Gideon said, picking up the conversation, "that's all you had to say in the first place. Did you know there's a great big pool of water back there? It's sunk down into the floor and it has a kind of a glass sheet over the top of it, and it seems to be in some kind of a vacuum that would break if you opened the door."

"That's to hold everything in place if the ship rolls over. We Equi take our bathing seriously," Ardenai said. "Are you ready to try Equi food?"

"Absolutely. I'm hungry enough to eat just about anything."

"The best time to be introduced to an alien cuisine," Ardenai responded. He stood up, and gestured Gideon toward the living area of the ship. There was no real galley, but a shiny black machine an arm's length, a man's height, which dispensed alcibus and other vegetable matter in whatever shape and flavor one desired. Ardenai spoke to it in a series of sharp glottal clicks which had little resemblance to speech, and it clicked back. Gideon was fascinated.

"Are you speaking the machine's language?" he asked.

"The machine is speaking mine," the Equi replied. That is a very obscure form of ancient High Equi. Few but the most serious Equi scholars ever hear it. My son says this form sounds more like UGA computator speak than actual human speech, and I think he's correct."

"I'm honored," Gideon said. Ardenai turned to look at him, and the youth was absolutely serious. "I am honored, just to be with you, to see a side of you most people can only guess is there. It is something I will remember always."

"Thank you, Gideon," Ardenai smiled. "I hope always is a long time. It does not please me to have endangered you."

"I don't mind," he said, almost wistfully. "I enjoy having purpose."

"Well said," the Equi nodded, and reached for the plates coming out of the dispenser. He put one of them down in front of Gideon, then sat down with the other. "Try it," he said, and picked up his eating sticks.

"You first," Gideon said, "just in case this is part of your sense of humor." He paused a moment and screwed his face up a little. "He doesn't really eat tree toads, does he?"

"Oh, absssssolutely," Ardenai chuckled.

He had taken a couple of bites when Gideon finally picked up his sticks, held them as Ardenai demonstrated, and tried some for himself. "This is good!" he exclaimed, and fell to it as though he were starved, which in retrospect, he probably was. It had been more than a day since they'd sat down to any kind of meal.

It made Ardenai feel guilty yet again. This was a growing boy. He needed food, and rest. Keats may have been right about the propriety of leaving him, but with circumstances what they were, Gideon was safer here, where Ardenai could protect him. The Equi snorted soundlessly with amusement at the obvious lie he'd told himself. He wanted the companionship of this handsome and promising young man, it was just that simple. Any danger, they would face together.

"What is this called?" Gideon asked, between mouthfuls.

"It is what we call kukkuk." He pronounced it more slowly. "Kuk - kuk."

"What does that mean?" Gideon asked.

"This," the Firstlord chuckled. "It's a nonsense word. Kukkuk is made with various vegetables, herbs and oils that are quickly shaken over a very hot fire. A lid is put over them, they are allowed to steam to release the juices and then poured over noodles which can be fried crisp or boiled to be soft. They're made from alcibus, or grain of one kind or another, which is what Josephus hauls to Equus for us. We eat the grain and so do our horses. We grow our own, but we import some as well, for the sake of trade."

"He really likes you," the boy said, but his thoughts were on food, and he went back to eating with such gusto that it made the Equi smile just watching him.

This was the dish he'd used to introduce his young bride to Equi food – real Equi food – not the kind she was used to getting on Terren. She, too, had smiled, and said it was good. With her, it had all been good. Ah'ree. He could still see her, coming to him on her father's arm, brave enough to leave the world she knew and go with him to a world her parents had only talked about. Ah'ree, Beloved of God, whose name was a fragrant sigh across the endless, night-swept grasslands of Canyon keep. How willingly she had come to him – how sweetly she had given herself to him in the warm darkness – bringing to his bed such gentleness as he had never known, and into his life, such love as he could not have imagined existed.

"Thinking about your wife?" Gideon asked quietly, and even so his voice made Ardenai start. "Josephus said she was beautiful."

Ardenai nodded, leaning his chin on the heel of his hand and gazing at something only his mind's eye could see, his dinner forgotten in front of him. "She was my good friend of many years. No one will ever replace her."

"When..." the young man hesitated, but the Equi knew.

"Two years. A little over."

"Have you thought about remarrying? I mean, it seems like as First-lord, you'll need a wife."

"I had not planned to remarry, ever," he sighed, "nor do I want to. But, as you assume, those who rule must be paired. As a matter of fact, the Dragonhorse must have three wives, and if I do not choose a mate, my dam will choose one or more of them for me."

"Now that sounds wonderful," Gideon snickered, but it did nothing to relieve the pain in Ardenai's eyes. "What will you do?"

"Cross that bridge when I come to it," he said, making himself sound matter of fact. "Right now having that as my major problem sounds rather inviting." He picked up his sticks again, but his food was cold, and his appetite was gone. No, the thought of another wife was not inviting. The thought of finding a mere woman to replace Ah'ree. When she had gotten sick, was wasting away, when Pythos could do nothing but weep great tears of agony to be helpless, Ardenai had gotten down on his knees and begged Eladeus to spare her life. In the end, he had begged The Creator Spirit to take him instead, or to take him, as well. But in the brightness of a spring morning, with sun streaming into their bedchamber, he had held her in his arms and known she was gone from him – his laughing bride – his beloved bedfellow.

And he was left behind.

He realized Gideon was gently sliding the plate away from him. "I'm sorry," Ardenai said, dragging the cuff of his tunic across his face. "I must be very tired. I should go to the lavage pool and bathe. Would you like to take a bath with me?"

The boy reacted as though he'd been slapped – took a staggering backward step – eyes wide with fear. "No!" he gasped, "Please..."

And in the same breath, Ardenai, as horrified as Gideon, was saying, "I'm so sorry! I meant no offense! Please, don't be alarmed." He had better sense than to reach for him, and Gideon drew a shuddering breath and came to a balky, reared-back halt like a frightened colt. "Please, be calm. I didn't mean to scare you."

"I'm so sorry," the boy said, and it was a moan of pure misery. "I'm just so sorry. I thought...I mean, I didn't think, because I knew you wouldn't...Oh, El'Shadai, I am so sorry. It was just a reaction."

"I should have thought before I spoke," Ardenai soothed. "We Equi bathe and groom one another as one of our fondest social traditions. I forget, my friend, that you are not Equi. Forgive me. Not for anything would I have shocked you in such a manner."

Gideon nodded and tried to smile, but there were such tears standing in his eyes that he dared not blink for fear of spilling them and seeming an even bigger fool than he already felt. "I'll just put these dishes away," he managed, and nearly ran in an effort to hide himself and his fear.

To give the young man some breathing room, Ardenai excused himself and went to the bathing pool. Even on a fifty foot clipper, it was a spot of luxury. It extended the width of the ship, fifteen feet or so, with a semblance of trees, grass and stone, the three most important elements besides water in Equi design, and moving images which gave it the sense of being in a forested grotto. He retracted the cover, closed the door behind him, and dropped his clothes into the refabricator.

Three walls were living projections of the Equi landscape, the fourth a reflector, and Ardenai stood contemplating himself at full length. He'd lost a little weight, but that was to be expected. The face with its short-clipped beard and softly curled brown hair, while not unattractive, was unfamiliar, and he did not dwell on it. His poor ears, he couldn't bear the sight of. His chest, tanned from working without a shirt, was darker than his long, straight legs. He'd always been grateful in a desultory sort of way not to have inherited his sire's legs, which tended to be a bit bowed; horseman's legs, his father had joked, always ready to ride. Now, he knew why he'd not inherited them. Krush was not his sire. Nor was Ah'rane his dam. Funny. People told them how much they looked alike, told Ardenai and his sister, Ah'din, how much they looked alike. And they were no relation at all. An eagle's chick had been plucked from its aerie and tucked into the nest at Sea keep, and Krush and Ah'rane, in their goodness, had raised it as their own.

He looked at his genitals, rather flattened from being confined to trousers, and marveled that within his loins dwelt the purest get of Equus. Him. Ardenai. With that phallus fully extended from its protective sheath, he had implanted into a woman he did not know the next high priestess of Equus. He stared at the beautiful pythons which, thanks to the skill of Doctor Hadrian Keats, once again wrapped his arms in intricate green and gold coils. Under those pythons, were the Arm-bands of Eladeus. He, Ardenai, the man who raised horses for the Great House, who rode all day, and mended fences, and delivered foals and cleaned manure from his boots like every other horseman. He, who gathered young children around him for their lessons, and cajoled and threatened and praised like every other teacher from the time of the troglodytes, who understood how computators worked better than he understood how the mind of his son worked. He, who ate and drank, who laughed at inappropriate times, cried at inappropriate times, and made love, and became angry and frustrated, who needed sleep, and to relieve himself of bodily waste, who got his clothes and fingernails dirty in the course of a day's work, who needed to brush his teeth and get his hair cut, who stank if he didn't bathe – he – Ardenai, was Firstlord Rising of Equus. He corrected himself. He was risen. He was Firstlord. He was The Thirteenth Dragonhorse.

This, then, this rather ordinary reflection of a man, was what absolute power looked like? This was the man who had to stay alive to pass the pure seed of Equus to noble women he did not know? This shaggy-haired individual who definitely needed a bath? Ardenai found himself shaking his head, and realizing that, on top of everything else, gods got cold if they stood around naked long enough.

He lowered himself into the hot water with a groan of pleasure, scrubbed his face, his hair, his body, and dropped his intromittent organ to clean it, wondering if it would ever be used for pleasure, for passion, for love...ever again. He sighed, closed his eyes, and leaned back. Who had that young woman been, he wondered, whose virginity he had taken? How had she felt, hearing the great stone walls reverberating, *a daughter for Equus, a daughter for Equus*.

Very impressive. All of it. A ceremony ancient beyond memory. And Ardenai had been on his feet as was proper, dressed in a long, soft robe of richest blue-black horsehide, drugged just enough to be able to concentrate over the terrible pain in his arms, and in his heart. He could feel the round, brocaded edge of the priapic bench, which hit him just above mid-thigh – the extension which he straddled – representing the erect male phallus, the bench upon which Equi virgins had been penetrated from the beginning of history, an item passed down through families as an heirloom. The same kind of bench upon which he had placed Ah'ree on their wedding night. But there had been no curtain between them and no robes. He had lain across her back, warm skin against warm skin – caressing her breasts, using only his lips against the back of her tender neck, not his teeth – penetrating a little at a time, using his hands to steady and reassure her as he brought her to climax.

This young priestess, he had not seen, except the part of her that was on his side of the drape, nor had he caressed her with his hands, nor comforted her with words. She had been stationed like a trussed-up filly, waiting for him on forearms and knees, her legs and thighs encased in superbly tanned horsehide. Even her feet were covered. Only her primary sex organs were exposed. She was not to be regarded as a person. She was a vessel. She had been wet with full heat, drunk with passion despite her virginity, and she had writhed and cried out, and pushed back wildly against him, demanding penetration. He had wanted to lean across her back and sink his teeth in her neck, but instead he had seized her by the tops of her thighs and pushed hard to break her maidenhead. She had cried out with pleasure or pain or both, and her rhythm had settled enough that he could control her. At the moment when her cries and the throbbing of her canalic walls told him she was in orgasm and could not resist him, he had ejaculated only female sperm and withdrawn, without a moment's pleasure. He'd tucked himself as tightly and as quickly as possible, and she had moved forward into the curtain, and vanished from his life.

And his beloved Teal had reappeared, offering support and a drink of cool spring water. It had tasted…so good. The warm support of his arm had felt…so good. He could not be dead. He could not. Not that man. Not that life. Not that light.

Ardenai felt better for the bath if not the reminiscences, showed Gideon how to use the equipment in the room, and collapsed into a real Equi bed, long enough and wide enough for him to sprawl out in, with warm, soft coverings of the finest wool, which smelled of grass and leaves, and home. Without the need for lecturing himself to do so, he fell into a deep, untroubled sleep.

Gideon was awakened many hours later by the urgent calling of his bladder to be emptied, and he swung his legs over the edge of the bed and hurried to the lavage. He was used to urinating outside, against the side of a building or behind a tree. This, was luxury. He was warm, he was dry. He could have sworn the sun was up. There was the soft fragrance of meadow grass and the quiet, faraway sound of birds singing amid rustling leaves. When he had finished, a small, damp towel presented itself for him to clean himself with, and when he let go of it, it vanished back into the wall. He wondered if he was the only one who would use it, if that towel was just for him. The toilet flushed itself, and he wandered back to bed.

He sat on the edge of it and ran his hands over the mattress and the amazing clothes which covered it. He had never slept anywhere so comfortable in all his young life. And the fabricator thing Ardenai had shown him! Before his bath he had put in old, ragged clothes, stolen from some denizen of Squire Fidel's bunk house, and by the time he was bathed he'd got back new. He'd even chosen the colors. Light brown trousers and a deep blue shirt. Both very plain, like a uniform, but comfortable and clean. And new. He'd never had anything new.

He looked toward the other bed, and saw Ardenai, still sound asleep. He was spread-eagle on his back, one arm flung to the side, the other tossed casually across his bare chest. His breathing was slow and even, indicating deep sleep. Something crossed his mind as he slept, perhaps some part of his dream in which he needed to participate, because his body jumped a little, and he twitched his head before settling back into his pillow.

It occurred to Gideon that Ardenai was helpless, that he could pick up something and bash the man's head in, or stab him, and the Firstlord of the most powerful league of affined worlds in the galaxy, would be dead without ever waking up. Along with the feeling of horror which accompanied Gideon's admission to himself that he'd ever thought of such a thing, came the pleasure, and the weight of knowing that Ardenai trusted him enough to sleep, really sleep, in his presence.

There were two other sleeping compartments aboard besides this space. He could have assigned Gideon to one of them, but he hadn't. He had said Gideon was his friend. Gideon sat for some time and thought about that, trying to get his mind around the concepts of friendship and trust, because, since they had been offered him, they were now expected of him, and he wasn't quite sure what they meant.

What must the man have thought last night, Gideon wondered, and how would he ever be able to approach the subject with him? This was something beyond the Equi's ken. Worldly though he was, he was also privileged – a prince from a royal house on a planet where royalty still meant something positive. So then why had he chosen to befriend a ragtag boy? It was indeed amazing, because it seemed so sincere on Ardenai's part.

As for Gideon, he worshiped the man. He loved him so much it made him ache inside. When Keats had suggested that Ardenai leave Gideon behind, it had been all Gideon could do to keep from running into the room and knocking the doctor flat on his back. That image made Gideon snicker, and the snicker made Ardenai shift a little, so Gideon got up and padded out into the other room to continue his musings and check out the food replicator.

When Ardenai awoke things seemed much brighter, heightened by the enviro-psi's generated change from night to day and the pastoral scenes of his homeworld which made the walls of the ship recede to nothing. He lay on his side, cheek on his forearm, and daydreamed, something quite apart from his usual train of thought. He could close his eyes and see the cliff falcons wheeling above him against the cobalt sky, hear their piercing whistle, take a deep breath and fill his lungs with air so warm, so light, that it infused one's being with health and hope. Ah, to be home at Canyon keep.

Something jarred him mentally, and he sat upright in bed, just as Gideon came in from the galley. "I hope I didn't startle you," he said quickly. "You seemed to be stirring, and I thought you might enjoy something hot to drink."

"Thank you," Ardenai replied, dragging his hands through hair which had grown even longer and rougher over the last many weeks. Soon, he'd be able to braid it back again, and feel a little more like his old self. "You did not startle me. I was just entertaining a thought which hadn't crossed my mind before. I was lying here, thinking that I hardly recognize any aspect of myself these days. Not physically, not emotionally. And it suddenly occurred to me that Kehailan felt like this when he was growing up. This is the feeling he was trying to describe to me – the feeling of being his mother's son, and mine – a product of two cultures which converge and diverge at odd times and odd angles, and he was trying to make sense of it all and find a niche for himself, and I was no help at all."

"Maybe not, but you need to realize that he was born facing the problem which you find so novel. And he had two good examples, you as an

Equi, and your wife raised as a Terren, even though she, too was half Equi. Which brings me to this," Gideon sighed, sitting back down on his bed, "I owe you an apology for last night."

"Do you?" Ardenai asked, sipping at his drink. He flexed his hand away from the warmth of the cup, and the python on his left arm undulated ever so slightly, reminding Gideon of whose presence he was in.

"Yes, Dragonhorse, I do. I pried into a very personal aspect of your life, and I didn't even realize I was doing it. Your wife tends to stand in your eyes, sometimes. I've come to recognize her. Nevertheless, I should leave her there, in your private thoughts. Asking you if you were going to remarry was a rude, unfeeling thing to do. I'm sorry."

"The apology is unnecessary," Ardenai assured him. "No offense was taken. Of all the beautiful things I have to share, my memories of my wife and our life together are most precious of all."

Gideon sucked in for air and blurted, "Then why don't you share your memories of her life? You've never told me one thing about what she was, what she did, what she liked. All you have ever mentioned is her death. Surely she was more to you than a representation of death and loneliness." He stopped speaking and felt the soft, sooty black of Ardenai's eyes going right through him; that slightly cocked head like a bird of prey. A dozen times already he'd regretted making that crack about Corvus eagles. What an enigma this man was. What a treasure to be unearthed a bit at a time and studied. Yet, at the moment, Gideon was the one being studied – intently, unsmilingly. As was his habit, he reacted to shift the focus from yet another stupid utterance on his part. "Why did you let me believe that you were stealing this clipper?" Ardenai sipped at his drink and said nothing, his eyes never wavering from the boy's blushing face. "If you'd told me it was yours I wouldn't have asked you that question about ethical behavior. I would have known."

"Precisely," the Firstlord said, and the eyes began to dance with amusement.

"Is it a game with you, seeing why people think the way they do?"

"No, not a game. An avocation."

"So I get to sit here and slit my own throat with the sharp edge of my wagging tongue?"

"I see you got the nutri-comp, the replicator, to work for you."

It was Gideon's turn to cock his head and study his companion. "Work? You mean the food dispenser? I asked for two cups of hot cinnamon orange tea. It gave me two cups of hot cinnamon orange tea."

"What made you think, when I had spoken to that machine in High Equi, that you could speak to it and make it function?"

"You. I assumed you, or someone like you, programmed it. 'The brighter the mind, the simpler the machine.' That's an old Declivian saying."

"You honor me," Ardenai said. "When I have dressed and said my morning prayers, and we have checked our navigational extrapolations, we shall settle ourselves over breakfast and discuss old Declivian sayings, and Declivians in general."

"You're going to eat me, aren't you?" the boy gulped. "I should never have said those things about your wife. I can't begin to fathom your grief, much less analyze it."

"If you apologize one more time for speaking your mind, I *will* eat you," Ardenai warned, though his eyes were smiling. "Do you think you are the only one of my friends to sing me this particular song? I know I have to get on with my life. Even if this epiphany of identity hadn't come along, I'm still young. If I were Declivian, or Terren, I'd be somewhere in my late thirties. I still have three fifths of my life to live. And you're right; I do spend too much time dwelling on Ree's death and not enough celebrating her life. I knew from the first day I saw her and fell in love with her on the spot, that I would outlive her. Because I am High Equi I will live at least two hundred and fifty years. She had Terren blood. Half. It shortened her lifespan. She would have been lucky to live a hundred and fifty years, even if her health had not failed her. I knew I would watch her grow old and die – in my head I knew. I had not counted on the things she would do to my heart over the years, how dependent upon her I would come to be."

"Please, Sir, before you eat me, satisfy my curiosity. What was she like when she walked, and breathed, and had and gave life? How did you meet her?"

Ardenai set the cup aside and flopped back onto the bed with a chuckle. "I was at my first Terren posting. the Pacific Northwest Island Province of Quadrant Two, in an ancient, ramshackle town called Sealth, which the SGA wanted to rebuild into a jurisdictional headquarters. The mountains up and down the chain were still smoking from the last big eruptions, the wildlife and the ecology in general had suffered greatly. There were archeologists doing deep water excavations of the most ancient Old Earth city, and I was curious, so I went down to where one of the digs was based.

"I was rock-hopping on one of the lava flows that had run into the sound, and here was this silly girl, trying to rescue a baby seal that was caught in one of the fresh lava pockets; very sharp stuff. The baby's mother was huge, and she was none too happy, but the tide was coming in, and if the baby stayed in that pocket, she'd be beaten to death by the waves. So here was Ah'ree, trying to figure out how to keep her footing on the lava, fish out this little seal, and avoid having her leg ripped off by Mother.

I hadn't been there two seconds, my feet had not stopped moving, and she looked up and said, 'Well, are you going to help this poor baby or not?'

"I was impressed. She didn't ask if I was going to help her, she asked if I was going to help the animal. So I straddled the pocket and lifted out baby and set her in the sand, and then grabbed Ree and ran before the mother seal could get her teeth in us. And when we were a safe distance away, I noticed this girl was pretty – exceptionally pretty – and she had lovely, Equi ears peeking out of her hair. Then, she looked up at me and she smiled and said, 'Would you like to do this again sometime?' And I told her that if she was involved, I most assuredly would. Eight months later we were married back on Equus. Very short courtship, but it worked out well."

"Wonderful! Did she tell jokes?"

"Terrible jokes. Lots of them, usually about ducks. She was very fond of ducks, and kept them as pets.   And she enjoyed a practical joke now and then, as well.   She also enjoyed tickling people who were trying to sleep."

"Did she like horses?"

"She was Equi."

"What else?"

"She danced like fairy-dust in the wind, and played the harp key and the guitharp, and the pipes.   She sang in a high, clear soprano.   She loved animals and children and defenseless things in general.   She wrote beautiful poetry.   She was a tireless gardener, and she learned to make the best kukkuk I've ever eaten.   Which reminds me, I'm starving.   I will dress, we will settle ourselves at the table, and, since I have discussed my life with you, we will discuss Declivis, and Declivians, and you, my friend."

CHAPTER EIGHT

T hat, was as flat a statement as any Gideon had ever heard. What Ardenai wished to know, Ardenai was about to find out. Gideon excused himself and went to take a quick bath. He had the feeling he was going to be sweating, and he'd discovered, with a little coaching from the Equi, that bathing, even in a river using bark and herbs, could be a pleasant pastime.

Ardenai appeared, handsome and half smiling, sleeves cuffed to the forearms on a deep red tunic which softened his eyes to brown and made him look quite the ideal father to listen to a young man's problems. He ordered breakfast for both of them, and as he was setting Gideon's plate down in front of him, his arm brushed the boy's in passing – and it was so warm – Ardenai himself, with his rich, ever powerful, ever patient voice, was warmth itself. Gideon stiffened, and Ardenai immediately stepped aside to give him space. "Is something the matter?" he asked.

"I just got the strangest feeling. I know it's false, of course, but...I got the oddest feeling you're not who you claim to be."

"Why is that?" Ardenai asked, and his eyes said he was amused.

"You. You're warm, you're patient, you're caring. You have a wonderful sense of humor. I mean, even your skin is warm."

"Just like a real person?" Ardenai asked. He sat down across from Gideon at the table, and the laughter still danced in his dark eyes. "I'm not, you know," he said in a conspiratory tone. "My brain is a computator, implanted at birth, and my blood is that pale blue color because it is mixed with oil to lubricate my Androtech parts. Because I am descended from the ancient race of serpents, my skin is cold like a snake's, and when the moons are full, I can kill unwary travelers by wrapping myself around them and squeezing them to death.

"When the time to mate is upon me, I go crazy. I lose my self-control. I become the dragonhorse, a brutal, raping monster. I mate with men, women and horses, and sometimes I kill them, and eat them afterwards. When I am not in heat, I am completely unarousable on any level.

"The High Equi do not mix with the Low Equi. They serve as our slaves and pay tribute to us. We High Equi do no work of any kind. We do not love our children, and if a woman bears more children than she is allowed, we drown her and her offspring. In some ways we are serpents, in some ways we are horses, but in no way at all are we human beings. Did I get the majority?"

"Yup," Gideon sighed. "I guess you've heard them all. Including the one about Declivians being thicker than slime on a cesspit. Ardenai, I'm sorry. You're just...too good to be true."

"Or at least to be High Equi, hm?" the Firstlord chuckled. "No offense taken. I am an unknown quantity as far as you are concerned. I make no attempt to hide from you the fact that I am posing as somebody else and you did not know who I was in the first place. You have spent your whole life hearing the rumors about us, but you need to be prepared for the fact that behind every lie there is a grain of truth."

The boy looked instantly on guard, and the Firstlord sighed to himself. This was going to be a process. "Go ahead," he gestured, "Ask what you need to ask."

Gideon looked embarrassed. "I didn't mean to be so transparent. It's just that...."

"You've learned to be cautious. I know. What rumor did I rattle off that scares you?"

"Well, someone I worked with said that he knew somebody, who knew an Equi woman who got pregnant when she wasn't supposed to, and they cut that baby out of her and threw them both in the river. Not that I believe it for a minute," he hastened to add, "but say a woman has more babies than she's allowed to have. What do you do to her?"

"Do to her? Nothing. For one thing, it almost never happens, and two sets of twins is not unheard of, so two children is not hard and fast. However, overpopulation is the cause of nearly every war, and population control is part of every Equi's basic mentality. Has been for thousands of years. It's taken very seriously, and it is part of our planetary ethos – like clean air and clean water – everybody contributes without even thinking about it. A woman never acts alone to produce a child, so we never consider her as a single entity. Responsibility for children comes at least in pairs, often in whole communities. But by Equi law, a couple that wants a large family has two or three choices. They can have their quota and then foster children for the Great House, they can both be sterilized after a second set of twins or a third single birth and stay on Equus, or, if they choose to remain generative, and they want many children of their own, they may retain full rights of citizenship and move to an Equi tribute world which as yet has no birth quotas. Nobody is ever killed over it, and certainly never a child."

"Do you ever kill people for any reason? Criminals, I mean?"

"Yes," Ardenai nodded. "Any violent crime against a child – rape, murder, incest – is punished by death. Period. Tampering with regional or planetary computators to cause harm, carries a death sentence. If you are convicted, you die. There is no other sentence. We have a very low crime rate, so we don't often have to deal with the consequences."

"So...sex with children isn't allowed on Equus?"

The Firstlord shuddered involuntarily. "No, of course not."

The boy was quiet for a moment. "But you do have prostitutes, don't you? I heard that because you all go kind of crazy when you go into heat, you have women, or men, who do nothing but service people who need...you know...."

"I'll assume," Ardenai chuckled. "This is at least a little more accurate that the one about the baby and the river. We do have heat cycles, and they can be very intense, especially every seventh cycle, which is called the Dragonhorse. Because we can't always be home with our mates when these occur, we have what are called, hetaera. They are not prostitutes. They are carefully trained women and men who provide sexual release in a socially acceptable and discreet manner to those who need their services. They are highly valued employees of the Equi government, and highly respected members of our society. It's a job, like teaching or designing computators or raising horses or hay, and many of them have other occupations, as well – especially if they are assigned to a particular individual."

"And they don't have any diseases or anything?"

"If you mean venereal diseases, no. Venereal disease is unheard of on Equus. The Equi just don't lend themselves to that sort of thing, I guess."

"Is it true that a lot of Equi men are homosexual? Is that why you have male...heter...what was that word?"

"Hetaera. Het-air-ah," Ardenai said, watching the boy's eyes. "Partly, yes, though some women also need their services. As a rule females don't get as overwrought as males during that time. But many Equi males do enjoy the sexual company of other males, or marry other males. It is accepted in our society. Nobody thinks anything about it. Many men and women enjoy the company of both sexes. That, too, is accepted. We have five recognized sexes on Equus, so this particular discussion can get very complicated. For now let's just say that recreational sex amongst consenting adults – adults being the operative word here – is acceptable and enjoyable. It's not required, and it's not frowned upon. It's an informed choice. Once a man, because that's who we're talking about, once a man chooses to marry, whether he marries a male or a female, he is expected to be monogamous. If he is away from home during a heat cycle, he is expected to avail himself of a hetaera."

"What if he isn't married yet?"

"If he is in a heat cycle, the code of conduct remains the same," Ardenai said.

"And how do the women behave? Do they have a lot of sexual freedom, too?"

"If they choose," Ardenai replied. He was sensing a growing uneasiness in Gideon, and it was making him equally uncomfortable. "As a rule, they choose not to exercise a lot of sexual freedom. A relative few have intercourse of a sexual nature before marriage, perfectly acceptable thing to do, and a very few are adventurous before marriage in the larger realm of copulation. However, they are expected not to conceive children. If they do, we are back to the baby and the river. Does this help?"

Gideon nodded, drew a deep breath, and forced himself to look at the Equi. "Yes," he said. "Thank you for the information."

"You are welcome. Now, tell me why you ran away from home, because that much is obvious, and why you were so determined to have that little ed-comp up and running."

Gideon flushed all over with sudden, nearly uncontrollable panic. He'd prayed for a time like this all his life, for someone intelligent like this to take an interest in him, and now it was all going to be gone. Everything he'd heard in the last five minutes told him, it was all going to be gone. Ardenai was going to hate him. He might even be punished, or killed. He was terrified, and his skin burned like fire with apprehension.

He swallowed the lump in his throat, picked up his tea in trembling hands, sipped it, and swallowed again. "I..." The dreaded words would not come out. He couldn't force them, couldn't find them in his vocabulary. "I ..." He pursed his lips as hard as he could, but they trembled anyway, and his eyes began to burn and fill up.

Something clicked, and the teacher in Ardenai turned to ice. He'd seen this before in the children of off-worlders, most especially Declivians and Tarkelians. The shaking hands, the downcast eyes. No matter what the boy actually said was wrong, Ardenai knew the truth. As always, he wanted to cry, to vomit, scream, kill somebody, but he did not move. He sat sipping tea, holding his cup firmly in both hands and eying Gideon through the steam. Letting him off the hook by creating an emergency and walking away, would do no good. Giving him the words, or saying it for him, would do no good. Telling him he didn't have to say anything would do no good. The Equi screwed himself firmly to his chair and waited.

"I…oh, El'Shadai, please forgive me," Gideon whispered, and his eyes overflowed. "Please forgive me. I…was a tyke-whore. I did filthy, unspeakable things with men. I never got to go to school ever. I'm sorry! I should have told you. Now, it's all ruined. I'm so sorry! I'm so sorry!" The weight of what he'd confessed crashed down on him and he crumpled under it, buried his head in his arms and sobbed like his heart would break.

"Gideon," Ardenai said firmly. "Gideon, look at me." The boy did so, sobbing and gasping, tugging at his hair with claws for hands, trying to get hold of his emotions. "Don't do that. Let yourself cry. You've earned it. Listen to me. Nothing is ruined between us, and nothing is different. If you would like me to hold you while you cry and get this out of your system, I would be more than happy to do that, and it's what I want to do, but I don't want to touch you if it will make things worse."

Gideon's chin came up just a little too high, and he caught his breath and said, "Never, in all my life, has anybody ever held me while I cried, unless they were having sex with me at the time. I...don't know...but ...I would very much like...to try. I just need somebody, you know?"

By that time Ardenai was out of his chair and around the table. "Come here," he said, and gathered the young man into his arms. Gideon wept uncontrollably against his neck, and Ardenai rocked him gently and stroked his head and rubbed his back, and made comforting sounds with no meaning until finally the terrible, wrenching sobs quieted to a shuddering series of hiccups. Then the Equi led him to a comfortable chair, eased him down in it, and got him a warm, wet towel and something soothing to drink.

"You're very good at this," Gideon said, trying to smile.

"I'm a husband, and a father, and I teach five-year-olds. I've had lots of practice. Are you feeling a little better?" Gideon nodded. "Then let's start again. The computator?"

"Ardenai Firstlord, I cannot read or write. I never got to go to school."

"Tell me the story," Ardenai said quietly, and Gideon did.

His father had been a Coronian-Terren merchant cruiser, his mother, cordial to one and all. No brothers. No sisters. One made that sort of mistake only once. His earliest memories were of hitting, and hatred, and indifference, and fear, and pain. His earliest desire, to escape from Declivis and never be touched again by anyone. That, all praise to El'Shadai, had ebbed with the years. And, with the years, and a stature which belied his age, had come the chance to escape. At fourteen he had gone to work cleaning bars. At fifteen, he'd lied about his age and gotten his flying papers, signed on to an ore freighter going to the sister planet, Demeter. There, he had seen clean skies, flowers, animals. He'd drifted from farm to farm, and then found himself drawn to the horses on the plantation. Squire Fidel had seen the broad shoulders without...seeing the rest of it...

Ardenai gently but firmly cut him off. "The rest of what?" he asked. He was stretched out in the easy chair next to Gideon, long legs stuck out in front of him, hands folded across his chest, and in his mercy he was looking at the Equi countryside moving in projection across the wall rather than the youth. "What is there to see?"

Gideon choked. Said nothing. Ardenai persisted. "Tell me. Get it over with."

"The patterns of my past life, I guess," he said at last, weighing each word. "It must show, somehow."

"I don't see it."

"You're not a...holer. Fidel was. I'm sorry. I know it's acceptable on Equus."

"We're not talking about Equus. So, you mean, one can spot another, as the old saying goes?"

"I guess," he shrugged.

"Then why did that bastard think he had a chance with me? He..." Ardenai stopped and shuddered graphically.

"Makes your skin crawl, doesn't it?" Gideon muttered. "Well, I'm just like him. I was for sale at two, in my prime at eight. By twelve I was so diseased no one would use me, so my mother checked me into the ward they have for such things on Declivis. Needless to say, there will never be any little Gideons. When I got out, instead of running away, I went back to her, and that place."

"Did you have to go back to…doing what you did?"

"No. You see, Declivis isn't as forward-thinking as some of the other planets. When you've been a prostitute or a tyke-whore on Declivis, and you've had certain diseases, they brand you. Which is the reason I didn't want to get into the pool with you last night. I have..." he stood up and began to unfasten his trousers.

"You don't have to do that," Ardenai whispered, stricken, and Gideon, now the soul of calm, said,

"Yes, I do. You said to get it over with." He let his trousers and briefcloth fall to the floor. "This, is what they do to you." He had a freeze-brand below his navel, but above his pubic hair, that was a combination of letters and numbers a full inch tall. "It tells potential customers what diseases you've had, and where you're registered as unclean. In case all your work is done through the back door," he turned and showed Ardenai the brand on his right buttock, "they get you on both sides. This, is why Fidel left me alone, not because he couldn't see what I am. The first night I was there, he called me up to the house on some pretext, and when I got in, he and his lover jumped me. They got just to the naked part, and, boy, did they come to a screeching halt. I guess he was ashamed of what he'd done, because he let me stay on." He pulled up his pants and sat back down in the chair with an angry thump. "I worked for Fidel for several months, and then along came a man who talked to horses."

Ardenai appraised him in silence for a few moments. "Gideon, when you went home to your mother, were you sorry you could no longer serve as a catamite?"

The boy gave him a look askance. "No, of course not!"

"And when Fidel and his lover didn't take their chances and have intercourse with you anyway, were you disappointed?"

Gideon didn't answer, he just stared.

"I am fond of you, you of me. You find me an attractive older man.

I find you an attractive younger man. Shall we...”

"Stop!" Gideon cried. "Why are you doing this? You're scaring me to death!”

"I do it because you said you were like Fidel. I told him no, and he was most unhappy. When I was sitting in the corner of that house, with my hands chained, and a chain around my neck so I couldn't stand without strangling, I was terrified. Before he left for town he kissed my mouth, and he... touched me at some length, which is why he didn't hear you crashing in the shrubbery, and he said he would be back, and even though I wanted to kill him, I could not. If he had come back ..." Ardenai shuddered, and turned at last to look at Gideon. "He'd have had me, one way or another, and I would have been helpless to do one thing about it. Would I then be like him?”

"No, of course not," Gideon said. "You'd be a victim. It wouldn't be your fault.”

"You see how simple it becomes when it is removed from your own frame of reference? There is as much difference between an adult male pervert and an abused child as there is between night and day. You were a prisoner. You are free. You bear the scars of your bondage as all of us must. You are no better, no worse than any man or woman who has suffered at the hands of others. What you do not have to deal with any longer, is a lack of education. I am no different than anyone else who has expected something from you. I expect you to learn. At worst, I expect you to learn what I teach you. At best, I shall expect you to learn to ask questions. In that respect you are well on your way.”

"You would teach me?" Gideon asked, and the words were sweet on his tongue. "I'm already sixteen years old. Can you really teach me?" It was too much to hope for. He could feel his heart, pounding in his throat.

"Perhaps you've missed the dozen or so times I've said I am a teacher. That's what I do. I teach people things. All kinds of things. This ship will fly itself, and we have five more sectors to meander across. We shall have more leisure time than we know what to do with, and I can bathe just so much, and you can eat just so much, and then, we shall need something with which to fill our time. I suggest we begin exploring the wondrous order of things."

And so they did. Day after day Gideon practiced reading and writing. He learned to construct sentences, and spell words. He learned how to recognize sounds in print. He learned to write topic sentences and then whole paragraphs of organized thought. His penmanship improved, and his skill with a keyboard. He began to learn about science and literature, history and mathematics. He and Ardenai discussed philosophy and political science and theology. They shared art, poetry, and music. They discussed nutrition, and gardening, and the breeding of fine horses, and in all of it, Gideon discovered that he knew far more than he thought he did, and Ardenai was amazed with the young man's progress and sparkling intelligence. He began teaching him the rudiments of intergalactic navigation, and the time came that when Ardenai leaned across Gideon's back to point at something, Gideon did not flinch away.

They discussed Declivis, and Declivians, as Ardenai had said they would, and Gideon allowed that, yes, those who passed for modern Declivians were every bit as decadent and dishonorable as they were purported to be. Declivis had been a dumping ground for human, Tarkelian and Coronian waste for hundreds of years – criminals, prostitutes, terrorists – until the alliance had caught on and put a stop to it. The native population had been wiped out to a man; those beautiful, golden-eyed farmers who had beaten their plowshares into swords too late, and whose blood survived only in the dominant gold eyes of modern Declivians. Ardenai assured him that the beautiful ones still lived, in spirit if not in flesh, that many of the fine minds in the SGA were Declivian and that Gideon would be among them.

"We are here," Ardenai said on their twenty-seventh day out, and his finger came to rest near the Gutterman latitudes in sector two. "By this time tomorrow, we shall be here," and his finger moved. "Calumet. Our final destination. As we have done every couple of days, we shall reduce our speed and allow ourselves to be seen."

"Calumet?" Gideon echoed, squinting up at him. "Nothing works on Calumet, does it?"

"Nothing mechanical, no. Nothing electrical in nature, nothing dependent on any kind of wave or signal. A singularly odd phenomenon."

"So, why Calumet?"

"Because nothing works there," Ardenai grinned. He leaned over, punched the appropriate commands into the console, and the clipper began to ease back toward standard speed. Almost immediately a warning blast came from the navi-psi, an alarm went off in the navigational console, and the craft yawed sharply to port. Ardenai fell hard with Gideon on top of him. The clipper rolled onto its back and plummeted toward a planet looming horrifyingly near.

Ardenai grabbed for the bridge rail and dragged himself hand over hand toward the console, then, one hand on the manual helm, one gripping the bridge rail, he began to pull, cords standing out in his neck, teeth clenched to grinding against the sensation of being torn in half, until the clipper had her nose level again. Another tug, and she was upright with her main drive dead, and Ardenai collapsed in a sweat-soaked heap on the floor. "Gideon?" he croaked, swallowed, and called, "Gideon, are you all right?"

There was no answer. Ardenai got his elbows under him and looked around. Gideon was motionless where he had fallen. Ardenai staggered to his feet, blowing on his blistered palms, and by the time he'd gotten to the boy, Gideon groaning his way back to life. Ardenai reached under his arms to haul him up and said, "I thought I told you, don't play with the shiny buttons."

"Yeah, well, I thought you said you knew what you were doing. Was this part of the plan? Because if it is, I don't like it much."

"Are you hurt?" Ardenai chuckled.

"Nothing a hot soak won't cure, and now I understand perfectly why the bathing pool has a cover on it. Are you...Ardenai, your hands look like raw meat! Raw...blue meat."

"Another reason I'm a vegetarian."

"Don't they hurt?"

"Now that you mention it, yes."   He slumped into a chair and gloomily surveyed the gaggle of red lights flashing on the navigational console. When he looked up, Gideon was standing over him with a small silver container.

"Put your hands out," he said, and sprayed the Equi's hands with dermal integument. They watched it soak in, and the skin began to regenerate and lose its angry look. "So, what do you suppose happened?"

"I would suppose, we have traveled far enough and fast enough to cause a fusing somewhere in the navigational console. Pythos had it worked on for this very thing, but it is a prototype. Bound to be some bugs in it. Anyway, without navigational computators, we don't even have light speed, much less TimeWhip." He reached over again and tugged on the manual helm. "It will be extremely difficult to work with the craft yawing over every few seconds. We have standard power and manual navigation. I propose we set down and try to fix it."

"Count me in!" Gideon exclaimed. "I'd like nothing better than to find my feet on solid ground."

"Put you off flying, has it?" Ardenai murmured. "Pity. It's a long walk home."

He went aft and checked the damage, then engaged standard power. Slowly, carefully they angled toward the planet below. Hector, it was; part of the Pegasus configuration, and the largest of those fifteen planets. Immediately west was its nearest neighbor – Calumet.

"Might as well be in another galaxy," Ardenai said. "If we try getting over there at standard speed, we'll be picked off in an instant."

"You still haven't told me," Gideon asked. "Why Calumet? Absolutely nothing works on Calumet, not weapons, not machinery, not anything. The only power they have is steam. They don't do anything there but raise sheep, and mine cleomitites."

"Not exactly correct," Ardenai said. "There is a good deal of research in archaic and ancestral agricultural practices that goes on under the auspices of the Amish and the Mennonites who first settled the western continent. Like Demeter, Calumet is what we refer to as a tribute world. It's an old term. We haven't collected tribute in a thousand years, but the planet does belong to the Great House of Equus. We raise horses there." He glanced sideways at Gideon. "It is one of the proving grounds for the Equi cavalry. My wife and I went there on occasion. We'd ride in the woods and swim in the rivers and the hot springs, and cook on a wood stove and read paper-paged books by gas lamps, and consider it relaxing."

"And this is where you hope to lure Sarkhan, or whomever it turns out to be?"

"Um hm, but not quite so soon. Brace yourself, the craft may buck entering the atmosphere."

Ardenai scanned the surface of the planet, looking for a remote spot. The ice caps were definitely out. Desert was best, but too visible. He settled for a wilderness of shale and sandstone cliffs, hiding the small craft in the bottom of a shallow ravine which had narrow sides and some overhanging rock formations. He shut down the power, opened the door, and turned to Gideon. "Let's stretch our legs and look around before we get started," he said. "This could be a bit of an ordeal."

CHAPTER NINE

S imply, I do not desire a war," Ardenai said, side-arming a rock with the force of a slingshot against the wall of the ravine. "I want Sarkhan to face me armed only with his wits. On Calumet, that's all he will have."

"He can bring a whole army, though," Gideon panted, crunching along beside his long legged companion. He'd had no idea that Ardenai's suggestion to stretch their legs would involve a brisk jog in hundred and ten degree weather. The sweat was rolling into his eyes, and the fact that Ardenai reveled in such misery did nothing to make Gideon any happier. "Can we turn back?"

"From which point?" the Firstlord teased, but he saw that Gideon was suffering from the heat, and he turned even as he spoke. "There's some shade," he said, nodding toward an outcropping. "Let's rest a few minutes before we return to the clipper."

Gideon scrambled in the rattling shale and plopped gratefully in the shadow of the rock. The Equi remained in the bottom of the ravine for a long moment, head cocked, nostrils flaring, eyes moving along the rim of the wash, then climbed up and sat beside Gideon, producing a water bottle from his hip belt.

"Something wrong?" Gideon asked between swigs.

"I am not sure," Ardenai said. "Catch your breath and we'll go back."

"What do you suppose is out there?" Gideon muttered. Ardenai was clearly uneasy, and when an outdoorsman was uneasy outdoors, there was reason to be concerned.

"It is not Sarkhan and his army, if that's what's worrying you," the Equi replied. "Nor will we face an army on Calumet. There are strict entry quotas. No military personnel are allowed on the planet's surface in units larger than a squad of twelve, and no combined force may consist of more than four squads, or one platoon. That's only ..."

"Forty-eight people," Gideon said quickly. "Now, Ardenai, how can they possibly control that sort of thing?"

"They do not. The atmosphere does. Remember, nothing works on Calumet. You can take a ship into the atmosphere if you unconcerned about how hard you land. Scrambleshafts won't work, either. The only way to enter Calumet's atmosphere is through a CAC – a Controlled Atmosphere Corridor. It is also the only way out."

"Do you suppose one could soft land a troop carrier using parachutes or somesuch?"

"Given long enough to plan it, probably," Ardenai replied hastily. "Come on, let's go."

He stood up, skidded down the shale and lit out at a dogtrot with the Declivian close behind him. "Gideon," he said, "Run!"

They hadn't gotten more than a hundred yards or so when Gideon yelled, "Ouch!" and clapped his hand over one shoulder. Ardenai spun around in alarm, and Gideon's face was tortured. "Something ... is stinging me," he groaned. "It hurts like fire!" and he collapsed in Ardenai's arms.

In an instant, Ardenai had jerked the dart from Gideon's back and cast it aside. He raised his head, swiveled on his haunches, and took a dart in the fleshy part of his left breast. Another instant and it, too, was gone and the pultronel in Ardenai's belt was in his hand as he faced the figures coming down the ravine. He set the weapon on stun and pulled the trigger. Nothing happened. No charge. It had ceased to function. "Well...perfect," he said. Another dart struck him, and he went down.

He came to lying in the shade of the clipper. His muscles ached and he felt weak all over. Gideon was still unconscious. Ardenai rolled over to touch him, and a broad-bladed spear plunged into the sand inches from his face. Something muffled and guttural was said, and he was jerked to a sitting position.

He looked up and saw only shapes, dirty white against the blinding sandstone backdrop. He lowered his head gingerly into his hands and sat waiting for his vision to clear. There were voices, several, muffled by layers of cloth. Again he raised his head, and was yanked into a standing position. The robed figure pushed him against the side of the ship and leveled a spear at his guts.

"You have nothing to fear from us," Ardenai gasped, head thudding dully against the clipper, and immediately had to choke down the ridiculous urge to laugh. Even with only their eyes showing to reveal their intent, these people were obviously not afraid.

Gideon was hauled to his feet and slammed against the clipper next to Ardenai. He slumped, Ardenai reached to steady him as reflex, and the spear's point went through his tunic to prick his flesh. He spread his hands and flattened his back against the spacecraft.

"What's going on?" Gideon mumbled.

"To borrow a phrase, we are in big trouble," Ardenai said softly. "Don't make any sudden moves."

"Have you tried talking to them?"

"About what?" the Equi hissed peevishly. "You think they'd like to learn a song? Establish a Consulate?"

The warriors began to mutter among themselves and gather close around the prisoners, pointing at Ardenai. The Equi looked down, and where he'd been poked with the spear tip, there was an ooze of blood, obviously blue against the unbleached tan of his muslin tunic. "El'Shadai," Gideon whispered, "they know you, First..."

"Stop!" Ardenai hissed. "I doubt they know me, but I don't want to take any chances. I think it's just the color of the blood that's interesting. I hope they don't decide to see how much I have."

"They're huge," the Declivian groaned. "They've got to be over seven feet tall, all of them, and they smell like..." the word escaped him.

"They smell musty, like animals. Think they're going to kill us?"

"No. Logically, if they were going to kill us they'd have done so by now. Unless they want us for some kind of a sacrifice to the full moon, but I doubt that."

"Then what do they want, and stop with the wild speculation."

"Us, obviously."

"Why?"

"Gideon, I'm a teacher, not an anthropologist. Just be quiet, mention no names, and see what they do. Are you carrying identification?"

"No."

"Good."

"Maybe they want the ship."

"Just what every stone-age nomad needs, a spaceship. No. They can only want that which they can comprehend having. That, my unfortunate companion, is us."

One of the men grabbed Ardenai's shoulder and gave him a savage push down the ravine, gesturing with the spear. Ardenai took a few steps and turned. The swaddled figure gestured again and they all began to walk, dragging the groggy Declivian between two of them. All that afternoon they walked without water or rest, until even Ardenai was stumbling from exhaustion. At dark they were given something to drink and bound back to back with their feet tied.

"Maybe we can get away while they're sleeping," Gideon whispered.

"What a good idea," the Equi whispered back. "We can take turns hopping backwards. By morning we could be several hundred yards from here."

"I can't believe you're going to give up at this point."

"For now, we have to give up. That does not mean it's permanent. Slide forward a little and rest your head on my shoulder if you can. You'll feel better if you sleep."

"What about you?"

"I've had plenty of deep sleep these last weeks. I'll watch, and listen, and see what I can piece together."

Gideon settled himself, and after a while his even breathing told Ardenai he was asleep. These desert people, who hadn't said ten words all day, didn't say one word all night. They simply ate, kicked out the fire, and slept on the ground.

By dawn it was bitterly cold, and Ardenai was the one who suffered. They were untied, yanked to their feet, and forced to walk, though this time they were left together. They weren't allowed to speak, but they were allowed to support one another. By evening, they were carrying each other, moving forward by sheer strength of character. Again they were watered and bound together. Gideon was almost instantly asleep, and Ardenai was grateful. The heat was killing his young friend. Again he watched and listened, but nothing was said. He couldn't help wondering what was under those robes. Could be anybody, or anything.

At high sun the next day they reached a village constructed of mud bricks, and though they had been moving into an area that seemed ever more desert-like, Ardenai could hear and smell the sea. The village was built around a square, and that is where they were taken.

"Aw...look," Gideon whispered, jerking his chin, and Ardenai nodded.

"Slave traders."

They were taken into the cool interior of a house, pushed onto the floor, given food and water and allowed to rest. They didn't even discuss the reason why. They both knew they'd bring a better price if they looked strong and healthy. Ardenai poured a little water into his hands, then patted it gently on Gideon's cheeks and forehead, wishing it was dermal integument. Every inch of the boy's face was blistered, and so swollen he could hardly be recognized. Ardenai wondered if he looked any better, and if he should be glad if he didn't.

Gideon stretched out on his back on the cool floor and went to sleep, and Ardenai, having made absolutely sure they were unwatched, pushed his tunic off his left shoulder and looked at the wound on his arm. It wasn't pretty, and it wouldn't bear close scrutiny, but it would probably escape immediate attention. It was discolored, but no gold showed through. The swelling from the pouring of the bands had been gone for a season or more, and it looked like what it was, a freshly healed knife wound. He readjusted his tunic, closed his burning eyes, and sat listening to the sounds outside.

By the time they were taken from the house the Equi Firstlord knew to whom they were being sold, and why. They were big, and strong. If they passed inspection they'd be sent to the cleomitite mines on Calumet. A tall, dark-skinned man whose features were largely hidden by the brim of his hat jabbed Ardenai and said, "What are you?"

"Not a criminal, if that's what you're asking. We ..."

The man swung suddenly with the flat side of the clipboard he was carrying, aiming for the Equi's face. He was met instead by Ardenai's left fist, which shattered the clipboard and sent the man staggering backward.

"Have it your way," he said. Someone grabbed Ardenai from the back, and the tall man put his fist into the Firstlord's mouth. Blood oozed from his lips, and the man said, "Equi mongrel. That's what I was asking." He turned to Gideon. "You got blue blood too, boy?" Ardenai held his breath. An Equi mongrel didn't mean much – but it was a good guess. An Equi mongrel with a Declivian boy, and things could go very wrong at this point.

Don't mention Declivis!

Gideon started slightly, then shook his head. "I'm a Coronian cross," he mumbled.

"What's the mix?"

"Who knows," Gideon shrugged. "My mother fucked anything and everything."

The slaver didn't question it, and without the bright gold eyes there was little to recommend the boy as Declivian. The other defining Declivian feature, that very deeply cleft and bony chin, was also missing on Gideon. He had a bit of a dimple, nothing more. Ardenai breathed a silent sigh of relief.

The man left the boy alone and returned to Ardenai. "You, are one wicked looking sonofabitch, but I'll bet you're strong. You got a name?"

"Grayson," Ardenai muttered, blotting at his mouth.

"What about the boy?"

"Reed."

"Known him long?"

"I won him in a poker game two years ago on Corvus."

"How'd you end up here?"

Ardenai glared pointedly at the robed figures and said nothing. "You'll come around," the man laughed. "I'll take 'em both."

They were herded with several other men into the stinking hold of a freighter, chained to the sides, and left in utter blackness and near freezing cold. Mercifully, they were chained close together, and by only one wrist. Ardenai and Gideon sat huddled together, conserving body heat and trying to buoy one another's spirits. Not knowing what the others might understand, they said nothing. At last Gideon's head relaxed against Ardenai's chest. Ardenai tightened his grip to hold the boy in place, and lost himself in thought.

Endlessly they traveled. Endlessly, until Ardenai quit shivering and lapsed into a torpor that was near unconsciousness. He didn't realize they'd landed until he felt Gideon rubbing him none too gently back to life. "Come on!" Gideon whispered, "Come on, dammit, move!" Ardenai forced himself to do so, gasping with an effort that was almost beyond him.

They were unchained and dragged one at a time into the blinding sun of Calumet to stand inspection, while the tall man presented false documents saying they were criminals sentenced to hard labor. Ardenai, with his wild hair and beard and battered face, was totally unrecognizable as the man who had left Equus seasons before. Gideon, with his blistered and peeling skin and his eyes swollen nearly shut, had lost his identity as well. They were loaded with six other men into a horse-drawn wagon and hauled twelve hours to the cleomitite mines of Baal-Beeroth.

By now it wasn't even real for Gideon. It was just another nightmare of the kind he'd had all his life. He sat in the wagon next to Ardenai and wondered how this noble person, bred to wealth and power and things of the intellect, had survived with his wits intact even this long. As if in answer to his thoughts, a hand closed over his, and Ardenai's voice said, *Courage. Every step now is one toward freedom. Don't give up.* Gideon looked at him, but the Equi's lips had not moved.

Two hours after dark they were unloaded, taken into a long, dirt floored building, issued a bowl, which was empty, a wooden spoon, and a dirty, straw-stuffed mat to sleep on. They collapsed, without a single word between them.

▲ ▲ ▲ ▲ ▲ ▲ ▲

The news arrived in all three camps almost at the same moment, touching off pandemonium which was instantaneous and complete. "The clipper belonging the Great House of Equus has been found on Corvus in Sector three. It is for sale to the highest bidder."

Sarkhan went wildest and screamed loudest. Again the Equi had eluded that fool Konik. What if he'd been taken by pirates? What if those armbands were decorating some barbarian's lodge pole? In a frenzy, Sarkhan called for a ship to be made ready. This could no longer be left to underlings. Ardenai Firstlord could not be found, nor the snake who had supposedly gone to some medical conference and left that clipper at SeGAS- 7. He wasn't convinced that the lying little captain was dead, either, or that so-called kinsman of Ardenai's, deadly bastard that he was. What if they were converging somewhere? They had to be! Where in kraa were they?

Ah'krill sat with her fingers together and read the uncertain faces of the Privy Council. Then, turning, she read the face of the man sitting next to her. "Long have you come to us here, Josephus, bringing grain, and long have you been Ardenai Firstlord's friend. Why did he send you this time?"

"I don't know, your Priestessness, Ma'am. I only know that Kehai-lan did the mind touching thing with me, and told me the ambassador wanted me here. I have obeyed his wishes."

"For what reason?"

Josephus looked momentarily taken back. "Am I not being clear? I am kind of nervous, and that makes me rattle on, sometimes. Ardenai, through Kehailan, told me to come and see you."

Ah'krill nodded. "And this you know because Kehailan retrieved it from your subconscious. But he told you nothing more?"

"Yes, Ma'am, your pries..."

"Ah'krill," she said with a slight smile. "I am Ah'krill."

"Yes, Ma'am...Ah'krill. That's correct, what you said."

"Captain Josephus, may I assume, since my son has sent you here that this information is for me, also?"

"Well, I thought so, yes. Anyways, that's why I came on up here before going out to Canyon keep."

"I understand your ship is being repaired?"

"Yes, Ma'am. I no sooner got here than the entire computator system locked me out clean as Monday's sheets. I can't go anywheres. But then, Ardenai told me not to, so I guess it's okay. Probably his idea of making sure I do like I'm told."

You are quite probably right," she smiled, and Josephus realized she was a pretty woman, middle-aged, but very attractive. "Do you think I could touch your thoughts?"

"That's why I'm here," he said.

"Thank you," the priestess replied. She turned her chair, took the Captain's face in her hands, and slowly brought their foreheads together. "Relax," she said quietly. "By touching you in this manner, no one, no matter how they may try, can hear what transpires." Josephus began to float. Very real, very near, came Ardenai's resonant baritone. *Thank you, my old friend. You have done well, and my family and I owe you much. Avail yourself of my home, and wait for me. Ah'din, my sister, will see to your comfort.*

Ah'krill released Josephus's head, and sat back from him. "Well?" he said, almost immediately, "Do I know anything about that clipper in Sector three?" The priestess's dark green eyes with their tawny flecks, twinkled with amusement, but before she could respond, Josephus went on. "Did you hear that message?"

"I heard the one meant for me," she smiled, and turned to her advisors. "For now, this moment, we do nothing. Tomorrow, when the Great Council gathers for its morning session, we shall see if Senator Sarkhan is present. If so, I shall be greatly interested in what he has to say. If he is not present, I shall have to hear nothing at all. Hadban, see if we have any craft left, or if my son and his companions have destroyed them all. And tell my grandchild I wish to speak to him at once."

▲ ▲ ▲ ▲ ▲ ▲ ▲

Kehailan waved the message aside without even hearing it, and continued to study the huge chart on the screen in front of him. "Gentlemen, there's something wrong here. Look." A flashing red dot appeared on the chart. "If Ardenai left SeGAS-7 over a half-season ago, traveling at anywhere near the maximum speed of that clipper, he wouldn't be in sector three, he'd be out of sector one by now, and well into Sixth Galactic Alliance space."

Eletsky watched the dot move off the chart and rubbed fretfully at his balding pate. "Kee, why...aw, hell, I don't understand your thinking at all." And he didn't. He was beginning to feel like he was embroiled in some kind of elaborate family argument. One of those where if you didn't know everything about everything and everybody being discussed, you didn't have a prayer of understanding why it was going on at all, or who stood to win it, or why that was the way it should go.

"There was this beautiful old rifle in my family," he said, almost to himself. "Brass grip and butt plate. Had some real historical significance. My cousin Connie wanted it, and it had been her dad's, though he'd given it to one of my uncles, but outside the immediate family, because he'd had a falling out with Connie and her mom, and when my cousin Connie asked for the rifle, this other cousin stepped out of the woodwork and said that it should be his, because such things should stay with the males in the family and he said she wasn't really an Eletsky, because she'd changed her name when she got married, I guess, which didn't make any sense to me." He exhaled sharply and shook his head. "My point being, I don't get this, either."

"It's simply this," Kehailan chuckled. "Why did my sire take the clipper if he wasn't going to utilize it to the fullest? Why did he take something that fast if he did not wish to go that fast, and why was something matching that configuration reported in two different sectors over a three week period, and then not sighted again?"

"He took it because it's his?" the captain ventured, not at all sure that was what he was supposed to say.

"No." Kehailan said. "What was done was done with a purpose. Pythos left the clipper on purpose, Marion. My father needed that specific tool. To go where, and why, is the question. And what is it doing in Sector three, when I have every reason to think he was going to Sector two? And why was the craft off-loaded on Corvus from a freighter?"

"One more why, and I'm going to lock you in your quarters and go get roaring drunk," Eletsky sighed. "Then maybe this will make sense. All right, why was it off-loaded from a freighter? Logically, because it won't run, or because whomever has it can't operate it."

"Why won't it run?"

"Hell, Kee, I don't know..." Marion began, and Moonsgold, who was the third party in the discussion, poked Eletsky with one finger and pointed subtly toward the chart with the other. "Winnie, what?"

"Look up, now," he whispered out of the corner of his mouth. "Now!"

They looked up to see that the chart had turned into the High Priestess of Equus, and she looked none too cordial. Kehailan saluted her by the brushing of his right hand across his left and said, "Ahimsa. Equus honors us with your presence. How may I serve you, Ah'krill?"

"Responding to my message would be an acceptable start."

"Oh," he said, rather weakly, "*that* grandmother. Please forgive me. I just don't think of you as my...I mean, I thought it was just...." He trailed off with a slight squeak which did not escape her.

"Best not say that, either, whatever it may be," the woman advised. "Ah'rane and I will be speaking together about you. So, what thinkest thou, child of my child? You have heard?"

"Of course. Captain Eletsky and Doctor Moonsgold and I were just attempting to decipher the hieroglyphics of Ardenai's odyssey." Kehailan squeezed his eyes shut and thumped heavily into a chair. "Someone, one of the principals in this, is either a fabulous logician, or having fabulous luck, and I just can't figure which it is. Have you any thoughts, my...Ah'krill?"

The woman made a small gesture with her hands and said, "It would please me if you would say it, Kehailan."

The commander gave her a look that was utterly blank, and Moonsgold leaned in, whispered something, and leaned back. "Have you any thoughts, Granddam?" He said. It was the right thing. She smiled.

"I have. However, I would like you to tell me everything you know about this, while Captain Eletsky prepares Belesprit for departure. Your current assignment has been postponed until a later date, and you have been put at my disposal."

"I see," Eletsky said coolly. "May I ask where we're going if not to Anguine Prime?"

"I do apologize for commandeering you," she smiled, reading his voice and expression. "You are going to Corvus. I want to know what Ardenai Firstlord's clipper is doing there, and why it came by freighter rather than under its own power. Is it wrecked? Is it damaged? Was it booby trapped like the last one? Where did it come from? When was it picked up? Where is my son?" Her voice had hardened, and her knuckles were white on the arms of her chair.

"We'll go," Eletsky said hastily. "Let me get my navigational people out of this..." he waved away from the main docking ring, "... training thing they're at today. We can be under way in an hour."

Nothing stirs the blood and makes the skin prickle with excitement like the hum and shudder of a great ship getting underway. To see the SGA's newest science vessel slide by on her way to the space doors, clearance lights flashing, brought a crowd to every observation window on every deck of SeGAS-7. To see her Paracletes flying both the SGA colors and the colors of the Great House of Equus, doubled the crowd and the speculation.

Adjutant De Los Angeles nodded and smiled, watching her nearly silent passage. Then he turned away from the window and headed back toward the Judicial Intelligence Wing. He needed to finish unpacking after his vacation, and he had men in lockup who needed to be questioned about what, exactly, had gone on while he was away.

CHAPTER TEN

Ardenai lay on the pile of rags and straw which served for a bed, shivering convulsively, his breath coming in short, rattling gasps like a fish out of water, and the woman looking down at him was utterly disgusted. She leaned into the man who was with her and whispered something which made him giggle, then her ugly, lantern-jawed face twisted into a sneer, and her milky eyes turned angrily on the mine superintendent.

"Thatcher, you brought me in here for this?"

Her voice was neither male nor female, and despite his terror, Gideon was fascinated. She was an unnatural Aranean cross of some kind, and looked more like a spider than any being he had ever seen. Her eyes were those of an insect, and she clicked her teeth when she spoke, as if she were hungry. She'd been here for nearly an hour; he'd heard her cackling and hissing in Thatcher's office. And then they'd come out here, where Gideon had been trying vainly to ease Ardenai's labored breathing.

The day before, sitting him up had helped. Today, it did not. The dripping wet conditions in the mine had finally gotten him, and no amount of threatening, kicking, lashing, could get him back on his feet. He was dying, and now here was this creature, and the creature with her, a big, dark fellow with vacant eyes and a grimy headband wrapped around his long, greasy hair, who kept looking his way, and rubbing his palms down his sides as though he were aroused. This was a negotiation, apparently, for the First-lord's...services. From slavery to slavery, but if it would get him out of the mine, his lungs might clear, and they would again have a fighting chance.

"I want a man to ride, not bury. You told me he had a little water in his lungs. He's drowning. Show me something else. What about this sweet little boy right here?"

"You're making a mistake," the supervisor said. "The big one looks rough, and he sounds rough, but he is put together, and I absolutely guarantee you he's coming into heat. He's got a lot of Equi blood, too. Here, let me show you." he made to draw blood with his fist, and the female's hand stopped him.

"You stupid pile of sheep shit! I suppose if I were buying oranges from you, you'd squeeze them to a pulp to show me how juicy they are, wouldn't you?"

Thatcher chuckled as though it were a compliment. "Now now, Sweetie, look at him. Look at those legs. Look at the size of those hands and the length of those fingers, hm? And see here, this little bit of yellow creeping into the whites of his eyes? That'll be bright gold in a week, I guarantee you. Come on, girls, the water in his lungs is just condensation from being in the mine shaft on the carts. I didn't realize he was getting so bad until yesterday."

Not quite true. Thatcher had been locked in a battle of wills with the man since day one. Letting him get sicker and weaker was just another way to try controlling him, and it had worked – too well. Now he was stuck with damaged goods he'd sunk a lot of money into. The powers that be, would not be pleased. "Obviously he's no good to me any longer, but I'll make you a deal on him if you'll get him out of here tonight."

"You'll give me a deal, hm?" she smirked, kneeling beside Ardenai to peer at him by the flickering torchlight. Overseers were coming tomorrow morning, and she knew it. Thatcher could see by the look on her ugly face that the bitch going to squeeze hell out of him on this.

Ardenai's eyes kept her at bay for a few moments, then closed with exhaustion and near-asphyxiation. Slowly, starting at his thighs, she ran her hands over his body, into his trousers, under his tunic, and she licked her lips and breathed faster. "Mmmmm, maybe, yes," she crooned. "I like the way you feel, and I have something to give you, that will make you like the way I feel, too!" She screeched with laughter. Her hands stroked his cheeks, and sensuously she pushed the hair back off his forehead. Like an animal, she licked his face and his ears and lips, and her right hand moved restlessly near his genitals. "You are coming in, aren't you, old boy?" she whispered, and her breath was heavy as she leaned almost into his face.

Ardenai's arms came up in a lightening quick motion and the woman fell back into the arms of her snickering companion, who bent down and kissed her open mouth. The superintendent leveled a savage kick at Ardenai's groin, but it never landed. Gideon rolled off the mat where he'd been squatting, grabbed Thatcher's foot, and flipped him, yelping with disbelief, to sprawl with a satisfying thud some distance away. The Declivian crouched next to Ardenai, ready for a last effort in the face of insurmountable odds.

The Firstlord dragged himself up to stand against the wall, Gideon rose to support him, and they faced their tormentors. Thatcher jumped up and started forward, but the female caught his arm.

"Show me a stud and then ruin him before I can pay for him? I think I'll take him home and ruin him myself."

"Good choice," Thatcher smiled, and relaxed his forward motion. Her companion whispered something to her, giggled, and pointed at Gideon. "You don't want that one. He's branded front and back. He's been into some bad shit. I'm surprised they didn't cut his prick off."

Grimy Headband spoke for the first time, and his voice was thick as mud. "Maybe I'll just cut it off myself. He probably deserves it."

All the color ran out of Gideon's face, and he stepped closer to Ardenai. "No." it was a whispered groan. "Oh no! El'Shadai, they're going to mutilate us." Suddenly, he felt weak all over, like he was going to vomit.

"We would like them both," the female said, licking her lips. "We'll...share."

"NO!" Gideon cried, and lunged for her throat. If he was going to die, he was going to die on his own terms. The superintendent's fist caught him in the jaw and he fell to the floor.

"I don't know about Reed. He's a good worker. He'll cost you," Thatcher said, looking down and rubbing his fist.

Ardenai had stood quietly so far, watching their movements and biding his time. Now he bunched himself together, but in the half second he needed to propel himself forward, those ugly, milky eyes had found him. She laughed, fired from the hip, and Ardenai slammed back into the wall, a dart as big as his thumb emptying itself into his mid-section. He stood there, glaring until his eyes lost their focus. She jerked the dart out of his gut and he pitched forward into the straw.

"Equuan mongrels" she snorted. "I just love Equuan mongrels. All the sexual ability of Equuans, and none of the brains."

"Well, now he's ruined for damned sure," Thatcher growled. "OK, they're yours."

Gideon was dragged to his feet and forced to help carry Ardenai outside. A buckboard, half loaded with sacks of grain was standing by, a second man on a spotted horse holding the team. As though he were another sack of barley, they dumped the Firstlord into the buckboard. The female fished a bag from under the wagon seat, reached in, and removed a hypodermic syringe. This one, she emptied into Ardenai's chest muscle, to make sure he stayed as sweet as he was, she cackled. The Declivian, they watered and chained to a back wheel. Both men stayed outside, and the female went in with Thatcher. Gideon could tell by her body language that part of the bargain would be sex with her if Thatcher wanted it.

Gideon stood there and fought the urge to weep. He was terrified, and beside himself with despair. And Ardenai, always ready to squeeze his arm and tell him to take courage, lay crumpled and pale as death in the moonlight. How far they had come together, for this. Even these last days, when Ardenai had stumbled, groaning under the lash and the weight of the ore carts, he'd managed a nod and a wink for Gideon. Now....

"I don't think he's breathing," the boy said, and as he tasted salt at the corners of his mouth, he realized he was crying after all. "It's so cold I can see my breath, and I can't see his."

Dirty Headband was lounging against the wagon, looking in the window and visiting with a couple of the guards. Now he turned and looked at Gideon instead. He saw the tears and his mouth opened, then shut again. "Don't expect me to kiss those away," he said after a pause, and held his hand close to Ardenai's nose and mouth. "He's breathing. He's all right. Just shut up." The man turned around and went back to staring in the window.

A few minutes later that apparition of a woman reappeared, half drunk, laughing, hanging on Thatcher's arm. How he could stand her Gideon could only guess. She was leering and hideous, and her frowsy white hair drifted like dirty cobwebs about her face. "Well, don't burn 'em out too fast, girls," Thatcher laughed. "When you do, come on back. I always have a good selection. Maybe get you a High Equi in his Dragonhorse cycle, hm?"

"Pay you double for one of those," the woman hooted, climbed onto the buckboard seat, and spoke to the horses. "Oh – oops, oops, better not do that," she giggled, and jerked a thumb toward Gideon, whose hands were dangerously near the bottom of the wheel by that point. Thatcher roared with appreciative laughter. The man who had been looking in the window, untied Gideon, told him to get in the wagon, and got back on his horse. Again she spoke to the team and they rattled off at a trot into the chilly darkness.

Gideon half-lifted Ardenai in his arms and straightened him to lie more comfortably. He was frighteningly limp, and he didn't respond to Gideon's voice, but at least the man was alive. Next problem, how to keep him that way. How to get away from these...people...with a man too sick to walk. Gideon looked up and there were two big men on horseback, watching every move he made.

He rubbed his forearms, trying to get warm, and looked around to see what he could put over Ardenai. The man on the spotted horse caught his eye and pointed. "At the front of the wagon, in a sack," he said.

Gideon stretched out and found a sack that felt different than the others. He straightened up and pulled it into his lap, and from it slipped a beautiful wool sleeping robe. He looked questioningly at Spotted Horse, who nodded. "Thank you," he said, and tucked the blanket around Ardenai. Soft, warm, purest white it was, and Gideon couldn't help thinking how really ironic it was that something so princely, should wrap the highest of Equi princes who was now worse than a slave, who would probably die mutilated, dishonored, and no one would know who he was until they hacked him up for burial, or burned him, or threw him out for the dogs to tear up, and those armbands became apparent. He sat back and sighed.

"Keep him warm and comfortable," the man on the white horse said – Dirty Headband – the one who wanted Gideon. The boy's fists knotted, but he didn't lunge for the man. Not yet. Not until Ardenai regained consciousness, or he figured out how to overpower all three of these people, none of whom seemed helpless.

"If you're cold, there's another robe," the female said, twisting on the seat. "Should be in about the same place."

Warmth was strength, the boy decided. He thanked her and found it. It was wonderfully soft, and beckoned him to sleep. Concerned that he would succumb to it, he let the robe drop behind him in the wagon, and turned his attention to the Firstlord. It had been over an hour, and the man hadn't moved a muscle. Gideon rubbed his shoulder and spoke quietly to him, trying to bring him around.

"Let him sleep. He'll need it," said Dirty Headband.

"So you can have him?" the boy exclaimed angrily, and something snapped. "NO! I DON'T THINK SO!" he cried, and as he yelled he lunged, and the startled man went off his horse with Gideon on top of him. Gideon's fist came back, hands grabbed the sides of his head, and he awoke wrapped in his woolen robe in the wagon next to Ardenai.

He sat up, rubbing at two exquisitely tender points just in front of his ears, and the man on the white horse nodded graciously and flashed him a disconcertingly well-kept smile. "Very commendable try," he said, and his voice sounded lighter, "but never leave an Equi's hands free. We can kill you instantly with our hands, as well as render you unconscious, and it takes no strength, only skill."

"I'll remember that next time," Gideon muttered.

The man's mouth turned down in appraisal, much as Ardenai's did. "Next time? You're going to try that stunt again?" he asked.

Gideon's head came up and his eyes glittered in the moonlight. "Count on it," he said. "Until he is free, and I am free, I will keep right on trying. I have nothing to lose. The only friend I've ever had is lying here, terrifyingly close to death. If he dies, the purpose he gave me dies. I have nothing to lose."

The female turned the wagon off the road and stopped, shielded further in the darkness by spreading trees. She swung around again on the wagon seat and asked, "Tarpan, are we being followed?"

"I think not," said the man on the spotted horse. He trotted back up the road a few hundred feet, got off, removed the headband he'd been wearing, and put his ear to the ground. After a long minute he got up and remounted his horse, but he did not replace the headband, and even by moonlight, even at that distance, Gideon could see the Equi ears. They really were Equi. Dirty Headband had told the truth. "We are clear," he said, jogging back. "They didn't follow us this time."

"Good. We are who we say we are, then. And you, Gideon, are not a prisoner," she said, and her voice had become less strident. "You are free to go with our thanks. Teal, give Gideon your horse. Take the reins of the wagon so I can get in back with the Firstlord."

"As you wish," he said, and swung to the ground, proffering the horse's reins to a boy too shocked to take them.

"Teal? Master Teal? What's going on here?" Gideon gasped. "How do you know my name? I'm not about to go off and leave him! Who the hell are you people?"

"Easy!" the woman laughed. She coughed, reached behind her ears, and with a deft movement the lantern jaw was gone. "Dratted thing," she muttered, climbing over the seat. "I know your name because Ardenai told me your name when he told me to bring you along tonight."

Gideon just stared at her, open mouthed in disbelief. Teal retrieved his reins, remounted his horse, and trotted off up the road, chuckling quietly to himself.

"We have frightened you, haven't we? I'm sorry," she said gently.

"Tarpan, keep watch over there somewhere, just to make sure." She waved an arm toward higher ground, then took a pouch from beneath the wagon seat, and sat down with it between her legs. Into it went the jaw, and the sagging throat with its mechanical voice, and a face which had been disproportionate and ugly gained symmetry in the soft light. She tilted her head forward, opened her palm, lifted gently at each eyelid, and two huge, almond shaped eyes blinked at Gideon from behind their milky facade. She peeled back the white wig to reveal a thick braid of shining hair, dropped the wig in the bag, took a cloth, and began rubbing at the garish makeup. "Under here somewhere, is the Captain of Ardenai's Horse Guard," she smiled, and brushed her right hand over her left. "Ahimsa, I wish thee peace, Gideon. I'm Abeyan Ah'riodin Luna. Call me Io."

Gideon sagged against the side of the wagon and buried his face in his trembling hands, trying not to burst into tears of relief. They had made it. They were safe. He felt almost weightless for a minute or two while Io politely looked at other things. "Why is Ardenai...so still?" he managed at last.

"I'm sure he's just sleeping, but we'll check for your peace of mind," Io said. She knelt beside him, laid the back of her hand against his cheek, and bent close to say his name. "Ardenai, Beloved, are you still with us?"

He moved his head, swallowed, and in a few moments his eyes flickered open. "Io," he whispered, and his eyes closed again.

"Ardi, Gideon is worried that you're dying on him. Please wake up for a minute." She touched his temple with her fingers, and his eyes came open. He looked up at her and smiled. She bent, kissed his forehead, and pushed the hair away from his eyes.

"And you," he managed, voice rusty from disuse, "What have you done with the girl of my dreams?"

"The pouncy blonde? I put her in the sack, where she likes best to be."

"Even the laugh?" Ardenai said sadly. "I was especially fond of the laugh."

"That was my witch costume from Macbeth. Did you recognize

her? I did the whole character, just for you." She stroked his face, and smiled at him, and Ardenai reached up to rub her cheek with his battered knuckles. "You're a mess," she whispered, catching his hand and kissing the fingers. "Gideon, say hello."

The boy leaned forward and looked down at Ardenai. "Are you all right, Firstlord?"

"Much better, thanks to the medication Io gave me. And you? Thatcher gave you quite a wallop."

"It was worth it to see him land on his ass," Gideon snickered. He pursed his lips, and placed a hand on the Equi's shoulder. "Thank you for getting me out of there, both of you. Thank you, so much!"

"You are most welcome," Io smiled. "I'm sorry things had to get so...graphic. I had to be able to touch Ardenai in order to communicate. And you, Dragonhorse, please forgive both the intrusion, and the reference to your condition."

"There is no need to apologize," he sighed. "I am sure it is the desire of every stodgy scholar, no matter how carefully he may hide it, to be sold as a...stud." He snickered, patted Io's arm, and his eyes closed again. "Besides which, I happen to know you loved it, you shameless pouncer."

"I did," she giggled. "I admit it. How long since you've really slept?"

"I'm not even sure anymore. Sixteen, eighteen days, I think. Ever since we crash landed...." He trailed off with a gurgling sigh.

"This act was just a little too good, Ardi. You let your lungs get too much water in them, and you're genuinely sick."

"It was hard to focus in there, and I had to make him realize I was useless. It was a risk."

"Well, you've taken your last for a while," she said. She injected him again for the water in his lungs, and let him rest.

She sat close beside him for some minutes, her palm cupping the curve of his temple. "My precious one," she whispered. "My precious old friend."

She turned abruptly, as though remembering Gideon was there, and said, "He's too tired to eat, but I can offer you something. Hot cider, and whatever else is in here. Hot vegetable soup in this thermal keep. Flat-wraps. Cucumbers sliced with tomatoes, I think this is. Best thing ever to come from Terren, tomatoes. Sandwiches of some kind, but Ah'nora made them so whatever they are, they're delicious. Here's some fruit, and some really good cheese. Some sweets, and these crackers rest well in an empty stomach. Are you hungry?"

Gideon nodded. He was famished. At the smell of the food all he wanted to do was grab as much of it as he could and start shoving it in his mouth. But that was another lifetime. This food, was not going to disappear into someone else's gullet, or be snatched away as a joke. And, he reminded himself, a man who could read and write, needed to be clean.

"I've been hungry for so long, I've forgotten what it's like not to be," he said, trying to chuckle and seem nonchalant. "I do wish I could wash my hands and face, though. I'm so filthy." Io showed him a water bucket strapped to the outside of the wagon, and a small pot of clotted-soap, offered him the towel she'd used to remove her makeup, and then settled him in the wagon with more food than he'd seen in many long days.

While they were eating Teal cantered up the road and swung grace-fully off his horse and into the buckboard to snag a piece of fruit. He sat down, took a few bites, and handed the rest to his horse. "Gideon," he said, "Please forgive me for acting the way I did tonight. I did not enjoy it. But we've established a facade with these mine people that we wish to keep in place for the time being, and it was a necessary part of that. Again, I apolo-gize." He leaned his back against the side of the wagon and rested his hand on Ardenai's thigh, giving him a gentle rub as he spoke.

"Fair trade for the asinine way I carried on tonight. I guess I looked pretty foolish."

"In trying to protect a man that we are all pledged to die for? You think you looked foolish? No, Gideon," Teal replied, and there was fondness in his tone, "you did not appear at all foolish."

Io smiled. "Ardenai told me, 'Do not leave without the boy beside me. Gideon is my friend. I owe him my life, and if you must kill to protect him, do so.' Equi don't say that very often."

"He told you all that?" Gideon blushed, head shaking in amazement. "When?"

"In the time I spent touching his face with my hands and my tongue. The High Equi like Teal and Ardenai don't have to touch you at all, luckily, because Teal picked up information that I missed."

"Hence the kiss," Teal added with a wink. "Ordinarily I don't kiss strange women."

"I'm not very empathic," Io grumped, "especially not here for some reason, and Ardi wasn't exactly conscious. These two can contact you from halfway around the planet and talk to you like we're talking now, but not me." She gave herself a little shake that might have been the evening chill, and looked at Gideon. "Are either of you injured in any other way?"

"I don't really think so. At least I'm not. Ardenai hasn't been so lucky. He has a couple of really nasty whip cuts on his back and neck, and Thatcher kept kicking him in the small of his back." Gideon's eyes narrowed and again he saw Thatcher going over backwards. "He had a badly infected knife wound, but that, Doctor Keats and Captain Josephus got squared away."

"Knife wound?" Io winced, and looked at the sleeping Equi lord. "Well, I'm sure this will all come out in time. Right now I think you should bed down next to Ardenai. Share the warmth and get some sleep. We have many hours yet to travel."

Gideon nodded and thanked her for supper, "and everything else." Then he stripped off the foul smelling tunic, snugged that princely robe up over his shoulders, buried his nose like a fox for warmth, and fell into a deep, exhausted slumber.

He awoke to the sounds and the sunshine of a morning that was well under way. He could smell grass, and trees, and faintly, horses. He sat up rubbing his eyes and feeling extremely stiff and groggy. At that point he became aware that they were no longer moving, hadn't been for some time, apparently. The buckboard was unhitched and parked in the deep shade of a huge Calumet sycamore, and Gideon was alone. No Io. No Ardenai.

For a queasy instant Gideon was cold with the fear that it had all been a dream. That what had vanished had never been there, nor had he. He glanced around, half expecting to see Squire Fidel coming to yell at him for being asleep on the job. Then a screen door closed, and from the rambling white two-story house to his left, Io appeared – at least from the size of the ears in comparison to the rest of the body he assumed it was Io. The light last night hadn't been the best.

"Good morning!" she called, and walked toward him, her sandaled feet raising small puffs of dust as she crossed to the wagon. "I hope you're not offended that we left you there, but you insisted it's where you wanted to be, to get the smell of the mines out of your nose, you said. How do you feel?" She squinted up at him, smiling, hands shoved in the pockets of her sleeveless white robe, and Gideon, enchanted by the elfin image, laughed before he could catch himself.

"Oh, forgive me!" he said quickly, then realized she wouldn't know why he was laughing anyway, and turned a deep, uncomfortable scarlet. "I feel like I've been asleep for a week. What day is it?"

"Not quite a week. You fell asleep just before daybreak, so, a day, a night, and part of a morning. Today is Drasterigyre." She noted the bemused look and rattled on in an animated fashion. "It's the one day of the week for which Terrenes and Declivians have no equivalent. See, we have eight days in our week. Hormigyre is like your Moonday, or Monday, Humilgyre is Tuesday, then we throw in an extra day because of the way our year is set up – three hundred and eighty-four days, because it takes us that long to spin around our sun. Forty-eight weeks of equal length, and six seasons of sixty-four days each. We don't use months, though we do refer to them occasionally, for the sake of outsiders. We use seasons, and half-season turns." She stopped with an apologetic wave of her hand and laughed. "Why I'm telling you all this, I haven't a clue. I've been around Ardenai Teacher too long, I suppose. You'd probably really like to get out of there and head for the nearest lavage. Either you're really dehydrated, or you've got a really big bladder. Sorry. Again I apologize. I just envy people with big bladders."

Gideon was still fighting the urge to burst out laughing. Her bright hair was not really red, not really blonde, but almost – no, exactly – the color of a fresh, ripe peach, and blended perfectly with her flawless complexion. Her voice was soft and had bells in it. An easy voice to listen to. She was absolutely beautiful, and even on a morning that mingled many pleasant fragrances, he could catch hers. Still, he didn't think that would be the best thing to mention. It sounded predatory. That thought sobered him up. He straightened his face and threw himself into the lesson, hoping she hadn't felt his unspoken admiration. That was not his place. Not his place at all.

"We touched on some of this over the months ...would that be a season and a half? ... of our journey, but I'll have to hear it a few times to get it. The other days of the week are, Scoligyre, Hyphogyre, Hoplegyre, Hesychgyre, that one's hard for me to say, and Hiergyre, right?"

"Very good!" she laughed. She had beautiful teeth.

"I like that they mean things, like, Hople is a horse's hoof in the ancient language, and Hoplegyre is the day horses were traditionally shod."

"And gyre means to spin, the length of time it takes Equus to rotate once on its axis. The teacher did spend time with thee, lucky man."

Gideon sobered. "How is Ardenai? I should be with him."

"He's being cared for," she replied. "He certainly looks much better than he did. Come on out of there and I'll take you inside. You can get your hair trimmed up if you want, have a bath and some food, and go back to sleep in any order you'd like."

"Food is definitely first," Gideon said, hopping down to walk beside her. He realized he was naked from the waist up, and brought his arms around himself in a self-conscious motion. "Let me get my tunic," he said, and made to go back for it.

"Please, don't," she grinned, wrinkling her nose. "We'll get you a robe when we get to the house." He nodded his thanks and as he continued walking he watched her from the corner of his eye, trying not to be obvious. Delicate without being fragile. Taller than he'd suspected she'd be – much taller than the few Papilli he'd seen, though not tall for an Equi.

"You might as well spit it out," she said, opening the screen door onto the long, wide back porch. "You'll just laugh every time you see me, and we'll never get on to anything else. And no, I don't think it's predatory on your part to be curious."

"And you do it, too," he chuckled. He stepped onto the porch, turned, and smiled apologetically. "You, are not what I expected you to be, that's all."

"Not surprising," she replied. She gestured toward a large basin with a hand pump, a plate of scrubbing-sand, and a formidable pot of foaming rosemary. "You can wash up here for the time being. I'll go get you a robe. And leave your boots over there with the others. We don't wear work boots in the house as a rule. Lavage is that door just to our left."

Gideon visited the lavage, then scrubbed his face, and whatever else he could reach on himself from the waist up, and felt slightly more presentable. He dropped his ragged trousers on the floor, scrubbed his legs and feet, put on the robe Io had draped over a chair for him, and went in the direction she'd pointed out as the kitchen.

It was huge, redolent with spice as though something delectable and fruity was baking, and empty except for Ah'riodin. "Sit anywhere," she said, and he plopped into the chair nearest her at the long mahogany table. "Tea? Cinnamon and orange."

He nodded, thanking her as she set it in front of him. "I hope I haven't got our relationship off on the wrong foot by offending you," he said. "I didn't mean my comment to be negative. I come from a planet backward enough that we tend to deal in stereotypes. Ardenai's personal body guard being considerably larger than 'my little Io,' of whom he speaks with such fondness. Since I hadn't actually put those two opposites together in my head, I expected someone big and burly, and older, and..."

"Dignified? Equi? Both? I'm sure you didn't expect someone who looks like she was found under a caulis leaf where the flickernicks danced, hm?"

"Oh," he said, starting to lie. Then, because he was Gideon, he paused instead, and shook his mane of pale hair and laughed. "No. I did not expect a fairy princess. But I am not disappointed to have found one. I'm just surprised that Ardenai never actually described you very well."

Io laughed, a sound fragile as wind chimes. "Oh," she gasped, and wiped her bright blue eyes. "Ardenai isn't much into seeing his precious students become adults, Gideon, even when they look as though they have. He would have a terrible time describing me."

"I would not," came a voice that was not much more than a very loud whisper, and a creature, a huge lizard, or an enormous snake, and so hideous that Gideon spilled his tea, appeared in the kitchen. Gideon caught the towel which Io threw him, and hastily blotted up the spill. The reptile, whatever it was, graciously ignored him and moved over to Io, swaying along on what must have been legs of some kind with feet attached. Gideon could hear claws clicking on the hardwood floor as he moved. The creature stopped behind Io and stroked the tips of her ears with his tendril-like fingers. "Hass thee ever sseen earss like thesse?" he asked. "Ssee, they come nearly to the top of her pretty head. Equi babiess have I delivered many ccenturiess, and never one with earss and eyess sso big and feet sso ssmall." His long, serpent's tongue flickered briefly against Io's neck, and she smiled and gave him a squeeze.

The creature turned then, and with yellow, hooded eyes he studied the young humanoid. "As long as thee iss being offenssive thiss morning, why not get me out of the way as well? Animal, vegetable, or mineral? I'll give thee two guessess."

"Gideon, this is Pythos, the Firstlord's personal physician. Pythos, quit teasing Gideon and tell us how Ardenai is. Would you like another breakfast? Ah'nora said I could putter around in her kitchen for a while. Actually, I'll offer you an early lunch instead." She gave Gideon an apologetic bit of a smile. "I do better with lunches than I do with breakfasts. But this will be good, I promise."

"Iss there anything interessting in the trapss?"

"I have three toads under a pot in the garden," Io began, but she caught the look on Gideon's face and burst into peals of laughter. "I'm sorry. I'm no good at this. Ardenai can keep a straight face, but I just can't. How is our lord this fine morning?"

"Ssleeping," Pythos hissed, and his eyes narrowed to glittering gold slits.

"And?" Io persisted, intent on Gideon's lunch. She couldn't see the serpent's expression, but it was terrifying Gideon. He wanted to run like hell and hide somewhere, and he gripped the bottom of his chair with both hands to hold himself in place.

"And what? He iss bathed, and that ridiculouss, unccivilized beard iss gone. His woundsss are dresssed. Thosse thingss which were cossmetic, have been reverssed. He hass hiss preciouss earss back, which pleassed him no end. He iss ssleeping. Ssleeping away the pain. What more doess thee want?"

"Pythos, what's wrong?" Io asked, setting a bowl of salad and a plate of sandwiches in front of Gideon. "The creamy green fruit in the sandwiches we call verdanbutter. The juicy red fruit is tomatoes. I think I gave you some of those the other night. Wonderful together. Try it." She went over to the physician, and put a comforting arm around him. "Is there something you're not telling us?"

He stepped back from her embrace and glared at the both of them. "Nothing I have not told thee for yearss before thiss! I hate being forcced to help my children make war! You," he said, and his eyes, full of tears and anger, found Gideon. "Who beat my friend in ssuch a manner?"

The color ebbed from Gideon's face, and he dropped his sandwich before the first bite got to his mouth. "Thatcher," he said quietly.

"Why?"

"Truly, Sir...*El'Shadai, what if it wasn't male?* Truly, I do not know. If there was a reason beyond jealousy of a better man, and pure malice, I didn't see it."

"Did thee try to sstop it?" the physician demanded.

"I couldn't," Gideon choked. "I was chained to another ore cart."

Pythos was quiet a few moments, and the glare in his eyes began to dim. "He hass been sscourged," he said softly and with infinite sadness. "Did thee know that? Ardenai Morning Sstar, Firsstlord of Equuss, gentlesst of souls, has been beaten with a horsse-whip – bloodied and sscarred with a horsse-whip. The Equi do not use horsse-whipss even on horssess."

Gideon sat, staring into his drink, not knowing where his eyes should be, aware that they'd spilled over and that his nose was running, but not wanting to acknowledge it by blowing or wiping or...what, he didn't know. He was at a total loss. He glanced up, and into the haunting eyes of the serpent. He sighed, put down the mug of tea, and with a slight gesture from Io, sacrificed the towel she had tossed him to his ridiculous face. "I wish at least it could have been me instead," he said. "Someone more common. Someone already scarred. As it was, Ardenai's lungs got full of water from the humidity, and he couldn't breathe well enough to push the ore carts. I guess it started out as a ploy, but it got away from him, I know it did. He kept passing out and the tunnel boss kept hitting him. I am sorry. I wish I could have done something. I was just praying that the whip didn't slash open his arms. What would have become of him if they'd known who he was?"

"Alwayss ssomething to be grateful for," the doctor replied. He turned and left the room, his long, emerald green robes just brushing the hardwood floor.

"Can I get you anything else?" Io asked, but what was there hadn't been touched, and she gave him an apologetic smile. "I...we...didn't mean to ruin your lunch."

Gideon's eyes had followed Pythos out of the room, and they stayed on the empty doorway. "Is he upset because there's something wrong with Ardenai, or because there's something wrong with what we're doing?"

"Both. We took Ardenai out of the wagon yesterday, and carried him inside, and Pythos took Ardenai in his arms like a baby and waded into the pools with him, and bathed him, and Ardi never woke up. And all the time he was bathing him, with every cut and bruise he found, Pythos wept."

"I suppose Ardenai does look pretty bad – especially to those of you who knew him before. I mean, he looks bad enough to me."

"You don't understand," Io said. "Pythos was created seven hundred years ago, born seven hundred years ago, Gideon, to care for the Thirteenth Dragonhorse. He delivered each priestess, buried each priestess, delivered Ardenai and cared for him all his life. Mended his childhood scrapes, took care of him when he was sick, delivered Ardenai's son, Kehailan, cared for Ah'ree before she died. He appeared to be doing it for hundreds of us within the royal gene pool, but Ardenai was his focus. His reason for living."

"Well, I am no Pythos, but Ardenai is my reason for living, as well. I don't suppose that matters to Pythos, though. I saw the way he looked at me."

"You only think you did," Io soothed. "What else would please you, besides a good, long bath and some fresh clothing and a soft bed? I do wish you'd eat something."

"I'll come back here and eat these sandwiches, because they do look delicious. But I would like to see the Firstlord. Please. I know he's sleeping, but I need to see him. Just see him."

"Let's go peek. Even Pythos can't strangle us both at once, I don't think," Io said. She led Gideon out of the kitchen, through a large dining room, down a short hall that was mostly glass, and quietly worked the handle on the door at the end. She put her finger to her lips, and peeked into the room, then crooked that same finger at Gideon.

He tiptoed in, smiling. The smile faded as his jaw sagged. Propped up on pillows in the sun-splashed bed, golden armbands shimmering against the pure white of the sheets, was a man Gideon didn't know. Gone were the savage python tattoos. The tousled mop of brown hair was gone. This man had thick, straight hair that was relentlessly black. This man had no beard to soften his features. He had finely chiseled cheekbones and a face which seemed more angular and somehow more handsome than Grayson's. His mouth seemed fuller, his neck longer and more slender. This man had elegant, multi-chambered ears, set close against his head.

Gideon took a step closer, looking for anything he could recognize. Io touched his arm, and he pushed her hand aside. Another step, and another, and Ardenai's head turned on the pillow. He made a soft, sleeping sound which turned into a painful cough, then his eyes flickered open, and Gideon stopped and took a nervous step back, fixed in the green-gold, draconic gaze of a stranger.

He would have turned and run, but his mind filled suddenly with a hundred familiar and reassuring memories: his little computator, the horses, Josephus, long study sessions – and he could hear Ardenai's voice clearly in his head. *Do not be afraid. I told you I would be different.* The clefts in the cheeks turned to delightfully unexpected dimples as Ardenai smiled, and a familiar baritone, now audible, murmured, "Gideon, my friend. How are you?"

"Sorry," Gideon whispered, "I didn't mean to wake you, Dragonhorse."

Ardenai coughed again and shook his head. "It is the waters of Baal-Beeroth which yet wake me," he replied, "not you." He rubbed his beardless cheek with the back of his hand and frowned. "Why am I here and you are still...there?" he mumbled, looking around the room, then at Gideon. "How..." He shifted his gaze toward Io. "How...did you find us?"

She was quiet for a moment, and a slight shrug lifted her shoulders. "Truth? We received a message, from whom we do not know, that you had been sold to the mines. Thinking it could do no harm, we followed up on it, and here you are. There's more to it than that, but that's a quick synopsis."

Ardenai smiled quietly and nodded, mostly to himself, but said nothing. He shifted his head on the pillow, wincing a little as he bumped an ear, and flicked his fingers in capitulation. "A conversation for another time. How long have I been here? Why is Gideon in such a state? Are you seeing to his needs?"

"Yes, Ardenai," she twinkled. "I've fed him, or tried to, but I couldn't lure him into the bathing pools without seeing you first."

"Gideon," Ardenai said, easing partway over onto his side and wincing again, "I'd advise you to take your own bath. Whoever gave me mine nearly flayed me with scrubbing-sand."

"That, wass I," hissed a voice from the doorway, and Pythos had reappeared, much to Gideon's consternation. "Forgive their intrusion, Dragonhorsse. I sshall remove them at oncce."

"No need. Children will be children. I'm the one who wishes to be removed – from this bed. It's killing my back."

"As you wissh," the physician replied, clicking across the hardwood floor to Ardenai's side, "I sshall take thee for a nicce bath."

Ardenai shot him a look and said, "I don't think so, Physician Pythos."

"Food, then? Our dear Ah'nora is cooling ssome esspecially nicce azure berry tarts in the kitchen." He turned and included Gideon in his comment. "Equi, like Equuss Legatum, are crazy about ssweets. Sshall I get thee ssome, Dragonhorsse?"

Ardenai shook his head against the pillow, still looking put upon. "I don't need a bath, and I don't want food, thank you for the offer ..."

"Then thee needss to relieve thysself? Good. I was worried that thy kidneyss were sseriously injured. I sstill think they might be. They're terribly bruised. Sshall I carry thee, or bring thee a jar?"

"Neither. I don't need..."

"Hatchling," the physician said, undulating to look him directly in the eye, "if thee doess not need bathing, nor nourishment, nor relief, then thee needss to be assleep."

"What I need..."

"What *thee* thinks thee needss, doess not conccern me, Beloved. What *I* think thee needss, iss what matterss jusst now. You may do four things: eat, ssleep, bathe, and pisss. Period."

Ardenai's mouth began to twitch at the corners, and he said with great dignity, "Now see here, my good dragon, I, the Great Me, will have you know, I am a GOD. More or less."

The old serpent hissed with delight, and gave the Firstlord a fond caress with his long tongue. "That iss what Adamus thought, and then there I wass. I am going to take thy young friend for a thorough oncce-over, and I wissh thee to ssleep. If thee iss extra nicce, I will take thee to the gardenss for a bit thiss evening."

"To please thee," Ardenai chuckled, and relaxed while the serpent stroked him back to slumber.

Gideon, who had tingled with panic at the thought of any sort of once-over, much less a thorough one, was padfooting backward toward the door when the snake's eyes fixed on him. "My beloved ssleeps again. It iss thy turn, man-child," he said. He glided out as soundlessly as he had come in, and made an unmistakable beckoning gesture in Gideon's direction. The boy took a deep breath, shot a glance at Io, and obediently followed Pythos.

As he walked in silence beside the old physician, Gideon became aware that this house was built like a great wheel, with a central hub and short spokes ending in large, many sided rooms, or complexes of rooms. He hadn't seen enough of it yet to be sure which it was. Maybe a little of each, he thought, looking curiously around. Pythos glanced down at him and said aloud, "A little of each. Octagonss. An eight ssided ccentral complex, with eight more octagonss fanning out from it. It iss what we call an Equi ssun-bursst. Much of Equi architecture, and many Equi homess, Including Arde-naiss' own, are designed in a ssimilar but ssimpler pattern. They conssider it a form of worsship, a prayer of thankss each day to Eladeuss for the ssun which warmss our worldss and growss our cropss."

There was not another soul in the large atrium in which the bathing and soaking pools resided, but the lavish sunshine, and the call of many birds made it a most welcoming spot. As though Gideon were again speaking aloud the physician said, "We will not be dissturbed. I have requessted it."

"We...you...that is, I..." Gideon stammered, not sure whether he was alarmed, or grateful. What he was most aware of, was that he was with an ex-tremely powerful alien creature of whom he knew nothing. When he thought about it, he was more than a little afraid of what might happen next. He opened his mouth to say so, but the physician was already speaking.

"I sshall be mosst anxiousss to hear what Ardenai Firsstlord thinkss of thee, as oppossed to how he feelss about thee. It iss my impresssion that thee iss either running amok at the mouth, or tongue-tied. Yet thy thoughtss are most luccid. Perhapss thee sshould sstop trying to verbalize anything, and usse telepathy. Thee already ssends exsstremely well. All thee needss now, iss to learn to recceive, yess?"

He hissed softly in what Gideon assumed was laughter and continued. "I believe thee iss attempting to assk me if thee iss to take thy clothess off, and if we are going to go into that pool together. The answser to both quesstionss, iss yess. Thee may drop thy robe right there, and I sshall drop mine..." he proceeded to do so, "right here. Iss thee uncomfortable?"

"Extremely," Gideon gulped. He could feel his face blazing with more than the sunlight coming in through the glass.

"An accceptable responsse," the snake hissed. "Thee may be as embarrasssed as thee needss to be, as long as thee obeyss me while doing sso."

Gideon stood frozen with indecision, and the old physician's tongue flicked suddenly along the side of his face. Gideon had seen him do that to Ardenai, and to Io, and it looked sticky, somehow, like dog kisses or fly paper. Like something one tolerated. It was not. It was one of the most gentle, expressive caresses he had ever received. He felt love, understanding, acceptance and unwavering firmness. The fear in him melted away in an instant. "What thee was, thee iss no more," the snake said quietly. "Today, thou art become a princcce of the Great Housse of Equuss."

The boy said nothing. His jaw hinges failed, and he stood, aware of his open mouth, unable to do one thing about it. "Uhhhhh...." he managed at length. A herculean effort given his state of mind.

"Becausse Ardenai Firsstlord of Equuss wisshes it," Pythos replied. "And that iss all the answser anyone needss. He hass chossen thee. Perhapss, one day, he will tell thee sso. In the meantime, thee needss to realize little princccess do what their Firstlordss, and their Firstlord'ss physicianss wissh them to do to be healthy and ssweet ssmelling, and to have golden eyess rather than brown. Come along."

Gideon wasn't sure whether it was his wish or the Physician's that his robe be removed, but he found himself naked, following Pythos into the warm depths of the pool.

"It wass mosst interessting," the doctor was saying, coiled sinuously beside Ardenai, who was lying on his back in the grass, gazing up at the night sky. "I told the boy he did not have to bear thosse brandss even another hour, that I could concceal them for now, and remove them when we reach Equuss, and he ssaid...he needed to think, lesst in hiss hasste to be a princcce, he forget how it felt to be a sslave."

"Because more are slaves than princes?" Ardenai asked, rolling his head in his palms to look at the physician.

"Because more are slaves than princes," Pythos echoed quietly, and they went back to gazing up at the brilliant stars of the Calumet night.

CHAPTER ELEVEN

Ah'krill's chin came up, and when there was silence she pointed a long, slender forefinger at the senator. "We recognize your desire to address this council," she said, and Sarkhan rose to face her.

He made the Equi gesture of peaceful greeting and said, "Ahimsa. I wish thee peace. I would seek your indulgence for a personal mission. My concern grows each day for Ardenai's safety. Each day there are more rumors, more sightings, more accusations that he is not – pardon me – a suitable ruler for Equus. This does irreparable damage to our reputation in the Alliance, and his ability to later function as our leader."

Ah'krill studied him in silence for a moment, taking in the long, narrow face and the sallow green ophidian eyes. *Not a face to be trusted*, she thought, but she had always found the man disquieting. The eyes shifted restlessly from side to side, then down, and to the left, then back. *A man who has convinced himself he needs to watch his back, and, from the way his eyes move, a man fabricating what he thinks we wish to hear.* Aloud she added, "I have not heard these rumors, but then, I do not seek them. Tell me, Senator, do you believe they are accurate?"

"No, of course not," he said hastily. "I do believe, because he is the Thirteenth Dragonhorse, Ardenai must face them and put an end to them. The fact that he has been the purported leader of Equus for turnings of seasons now, and has not come forward...concerns me." He drew the word out and made a gesture meant to be sincere. It was theatrical instead, and across the table Master of Cavalry Abeyan pushed his knuckles against his mouth, eyes narrowing in appraisal. "I am concerned..." again he stretched the word, "that he may be unable to do so, that he may be being controlled either mentally or physically by some unknown force or factor."

"Such as?" Ah'krill asked, arching a slender eyebrow. "He seemed very much himself the day he accepted the arm-bands of Equus."

"But...that speech he gave...."

"Was the last thing he did that night, not the first. I was with him many hours before that. Ardenai, was Ardenai. He was not under the influence of anything, and I have every reason to think he was buying time and nothing more. I doubt your motives, Senator Sarkhan."

He managed a wounded look. "Then you must doubt me as a loyal Equi. I wish only the harmony of rightful progression, and rational behavior. You must agree, High Priestess, he did not seem rational, despite your mothering hopefulness that it was a ruse."

"To you, perhaps, he seemed irrational." Her eyes changed shape. "Are you saying that my son is not a loyal Equi?"

The man chewed his lip for a moment, and by the flexing of his long hands he indicated he was fighting to control his temper. "I am saying we are going to continue in limbo until such time as Ardenai's plans are made known to us. Perhaps it is not his wish to lead us at all. If this be true, we must seek elsewhere for a leader, or seek to persuade him otherwise. But without him, we can do nothing."

"Are you volunteering for the job?" Abeyan asked blandly. "I could have Master Farrier Landais forge some thinner molds for your arms."

Sarkhan glared, but did not rise to the bait. "Surely, Abeyan, you cannot think this is going according to plan – to tradition?"

"Perhaps not to tradition," Abeyan agreed, "but according to plan? Yes, I think it is."

Sarkhan's voice rose just a bit. "You thought that speech he gave was rational? You think any of this is rational? You think what your daughter did in turning against the Great House was..."

The deep green poisonous eyes were inches from Sarkhan's when Abeyan stopped, and though his voice stayed calm, he was trembling with anger. "You would sully my daughter's reputation? Her memory? If you question my daughter's loyalty, you question mine. Are you questioning my loyalty?"

"No," Sarkhan replied smoothly, and his lip curled ever so slightly. "Of course not. But the rumors..."

"You are entirely too fond of rumor and innuendo," Ah'krill cut in sharply. "You would be ill advised to go chasing off through the stars following rumors. No. I think it best if you stay safe at home. Ardenai is far more capable than you of taking care of himself. He said he would await anyone who wanted to challenge him in a place of his choosing. We must assume he is doing that. So, unless you are the one rising to the challenge..." she paused and watched it sink in, "having you go off after him can only complicate things for him, don't you agree?"

Sarkhan caught his breath, then flushed dark with anger. Ah'krill was deliberately insulting him. Abeyan, who had deliberately insulted him as well, had settled back into his chair beside her, and was eyeing him with thinly veiled hostility. "I wish only...to assist...he who is my leader, and my friend, High Priestess."

"You should not risk yourself unnecessarily, Senator Sarkhan. We shall ask the Seventh Galactic Alliance to initiate a formal search for him."

"The Seventh Galactic Alliance already seeks him," Sarkhan snapped. "They think he murdered Ah'riodin and Master Teal." He caught his own tone, put a hand over his heart and looked at the floor. "May their souls be kept in comfort."

"You are misled," she replied icily. "There is no legitimate reason for Ardenai to be sought, and no one seeks him legitimately. Once again your information is faulty. If Ardenai is in danger, it is from his enemies, not his friends. If you consider him to be in danger, it is because you listen to his enemies."

Sarkhan exhaled sharply and stood, pondering his next move. It had been a mistake to bring up the notion that the SGA was looking for Ardenai to question him. That tack had been abandoned. Why hadn't he remembered that? He hadn't remembered because that fool Konik had been gone for weeks. No one to help him keep strategies straight in his head. His brother, Sardure, who would have been the perfect partner in this if not for Konik's meddling, was sulking in his room, and their father was useless for such things, addle-pated and hide-bound in his thinking. Konik's faction whining about peace and fellowship. The war was being lost. Lost! Centuries of planning. The golden armbands of Equus which should have been his. Sarkhan's! He of the lineage of Kabardin, the true line of Dragonhorses. Why should he stand here and tolerate the tone of this assemblage? Who did they think they were to address him in such a manner?

"Are you through addressing this body?" Ah'krill asked, cutting into his thoughts. Her eyes seemed to illuminate a hole into the middle of him, and he stepped to one side to deflect the gaze.

He gave her a deep nod and forced a smile. "I can do no more than your pleasure allows me," he said through his teeth.

"My pleasure requires your presence here," she said curtly, and looked away from him in dismissal as though he were nothing, as though he had not been bred from seed far older than hers to rule this miserable grassland of a planet, to turn it into a planet of warriors who would one day rule the entire galaxy, not just a portion.

"Senator Sarkhan?"

"As you wish, High Priestess," he whispered, not trusting his voice, turned on his heel with a gracious nod to all, and took his leave.

He took nothing with him. He would be back shortly to claim it – all of it. He was launched and past the monitoring station on the rim of the second moon before those dolts, those fools, were even through with their lunch. If they did try to stop him, he'd say he'd been called away to Corvus on an emergency. But then, they had no reason to stop him, did they? He gouged his vessel for speed, cursing the fact that Konik had the only TimeWhip clipper Sarkhan could logically get his hands on. Going off in a temper was one thing, and would probably be tolerated, given the bigger problems of the Great House, but doing something downright illegal like commandeering a clipper could reflect badly on his claim. He laughed at himself. He was not going to ask for the armbands of Equus, he was going to take them – soon – if Konik had done his pathetic little bit. And where was Konik when he was needed? Boot-licking coward that he was.

A step ahead of them all – frighteningly close to Ardenai's heels. It was he who had found Ardenai's clipper, following the sightings through five sectors, then slowing, bouncing a signal off his own ship until he got an exact reflection. He'd found the clipper abandoned with nothing on board to tell him a story, found many sets of footprints, found the beginning of the trail they'd left.

He'd hopped that direction, locating in an hour or so the village which it had taken Ardenai and Gideon two and a half days to reach by forced march. Questions there had availed him nothing. It was not a market day, and he had no clue as to where to look next. Konik had sat for a long time, studying star charts, and gazing into the sea. Amazing how serene it became past the pounding of the surf.

This, too, had to be simple behind the fuss and clamor. Ardenai was deep and serene. Logically, he would not continue in confusion longer than he had to in order to lay a smoke screen. This had to become simple at some point. Ardenai was the bait, Sarkhan was the quarry. Where was the trap? No point asking Sarkhan. His logic had fled him. What was left would not even pass for reason. Perhaps ... if the mission were to be saved Sarkhan should be eliminated. Konik had shaken his head and smiled despite himself. So now Ardenai turned them upon themselves. Flawless. Brilliant. He and his young Declivian companion. Declivis. Old Declivian saying, "The brighter the mind, the simpler the machine." Only decent thing ever to come from Declivis. Suddenly, he'd had it! The brighter the mind the simpler the machine! Ardenai had no need for machines or machinations. Sarkhan did! Konik had fired up the clipper and swung toward Calumet.

What had taken Ardenai and Gideon two days to walk would have taken Konik minutes to fly. What had taken the slave traders thirty hours to fly, had taken Konik three, and when he'd entered the Controlled Atmosphere Corridor he'd been exactly ten minutes behind Ardenai, and he knew exactly where he was going. Konik was a logical man. Two plus two, if you thought simply – always, always made four. He'd stood to one side on the docks and watched the freighters unload. There...being dragged from the hold of what was supposed to be a prison ship, convicts. The fourth man out, a tall, well-built blond youth. He was bowed by hunger and fatigue, face burned and peeling, eyes the wrong color, but alight with intelligence and worry as he looked behind him. And there, no less tired and hungry, Ardenai! All the galaxy held only one set of eyes like that – black, green – the color was of no importance. He staggered and the boy had him in an instant. What a pair! How could these people be so blind as not to see their nobility? And Konik was in a position to do...absolutely nothing. Not one thing. Had he called attention to them, his own purpose and the purpose of his family for generations would be lost.

He hesitated, and in that instant those eyes touched him, and as they dropped again, Konik saw, or thought he saw, Ardenai smile. Check. But who had who? Konik had shaken his head in frustrated admiration and turned away. There was no way he could pursue Ardenai without losing all communication with his own people, and he couldn't hope to accomplish his purpose alone. It had obviously been decided how this battle would be fought in the time honored manner of both Equus and Telenir and it would be Sarkhan's battle, not his. A battle that must be fought. A battle that needed two contestants. He sighed, watching Ardenai's receding back, and knowing deep in his guts that Sarkhan was in no way a match for the Dragonhorse. Why had they not tried to negotiate a peace? Why must power always come from killing? He had determined where the prisoners were being taken, sent a brief message he fervently hoped he wouldn't regret, and left Calumet.

He'd gone back to Hector, caught Ardenai's clipper in his tractor beam and lifted it at sublight speed halfway around the planet to a space port. He'd contracted for a freighter to take it to Corvus, that being the first planet from which a message could be sent to Equus without the need for relay, or so he told himself. A part of him said he was buying himself time to think, or was he buying time for Ardenai?

He rejected that thought. Above all, he was a man of duty, and he was in service to the Telenir. Besides, it was logical to reason that he couldn't send a message to Sarkhan. The best he could do was send a message to everyone, and hope – perhaps hope – Sarkhan picked up on it first. This message, too, he sent, and now he waited. The clipper sat in the belly of the contracted freighter, and Konik sat to one side, waiting to see who would respond to his little advertisement. The freighter's captain had been more than agreeable to the handling of negotiations for a piece of the action. Konik had nodded, and smiled to himself.

The fourth morning after Konik's arrival on Corvus, the first set of familiar faces appeared. Not the set he'd hoped for, but a set he knew would come. To go over the navigational equipment, that big, wolf-faced Phyllan who pulsed with sex drive. Dannis? Was that her name? Bonfire Dannis. That was it. Konik nodded to himself. She must be hard to work around and not get...involved. Bag up the long blue claws and the pointed teeth, and the rest of the body was most inviting.

Amir Cohen had come along to check the time whip drive and the communications array. And there was that very black woman with the lovely voice, Oonah Pongo. She'd worked on a project with Ardenai, something to do with young children and the arts? What her function was, Konik wasn't sure.

To ask the appropriate questions there was another dark skinned person, this one a deep, warm brown – Terrenes came in such interesting shades – little Marion Eletsky, with his balding head and eyes as bright as his mind. Really a very nice man with no affectations; the kind of person who made a good and trusting friend.

And last out, looking as though he'd been brought for the express purpose of mayhem, that perennial sourpuss, young Prince Kehailan. Well, young by Equi standards, but no longer a youth. He was somewhere in his forties, which meant he was pretty well grown. To see the look on his face, one would think him a brat of eighteen. Not exactly the son Ardenai had expected, Konik thought, watching him. It was no secret they'd had their disagreements. Excellent strategist like his sire, good chess player. More so-ber than his father – not the sense of humor or the athletic ability – definitely not the intellectual and telepathic capacity of his sire, which was just as well. Konik was uncomfortably close. He veiled his thoughts more deeply, just in case heightened emotions had heightened Kehailan's abilities as well. It worked that way sometimes, though the other way around was more usual.

"We would like to see the clipper," Eletsky said pleasantly enough, and in the face of all those Seventh Galactic Alliance uniforms the freighter's captain wasn't about to say no. He gestured toward the fifty foot ship, and stepped aside.

"Look it over well," Eletsky said.

"Take it apart," Kehailan amended, and turned to the freighter's cap-tain. "Where is the man who owns the clipper you have here?"

The captain shrugged.

"Your name, sir?" the Equi asked.

"Kais," the man replied, nearly yawning. "Theseus Kais."

"Well, Mister Kais, let us begin again," the Equi said. "How did you come to have the clipper belonging to the Thirteenth Dragonhorse?"

The man's eyes widened considerably. "Ardenai of Equus? I didn't know it was his. I was hired to carry it here and negotiate its sale. That is all."

"Who hired you to bring it here?" Eletsky asked.

"An Equi. I don't know his name. Equi cross, maybe. Didn't look quite right to be all-Equi."

"Describe him," Marion demanded.

"Just an Equi. They all look alike to me."

"Come on," Eletsky snapped, "young, old, tall, short, fat, skinny. Which?"

"Not short. Not heavy set. Built like a stone wall. Nice shoulders on him. Handsome as hell."

"Good," Eletsky nodded. "Coloring?"

"Just an Equi. Not those dragon-eyed ones, though...I don't think.

Maybe, though. Neh. He was a cross, I think, even though he had those..."
he inclined his head toward Kehailan, "sea shell, ram-horn ears. Whatever
they call them."

"Ears," Eletsky said.

Kehailan slumped momentarily with disappointment. Ardenai definitely did not look like an Equi cross. Or maybe he did these days. Perfect.
He didn't know what his own father looked like. "What else?" he insisted.

"Look, he was just another damned Equuan. Not young, not old.
Nice shoulders. He did have a real interesting voice..."

Kehailan turned away in frustration, took a deep breath, then spun
back around and seized the man by his shirt, jerking him nearly off the
ground. Kais found himself within inches of the smoking black eyes, and at
this distance he couldn't miss the ophidian pupils. As his life flashed in front
of him so did his science lessons. *Most poisonous serpents have elongated
pupils.* He was going to die. Soon.

"I want to know where and how you came by this ship, and I want
to know right now, or so help me I'll tear your kraaling head off!" Kehailan
snarled. "If you have caused harm to my father, I'll kill you!"

Eletsky stood slack jawed with shock, unable if he'd wanted to, to
rescue the hapless captain. It was Bonfire Dannis who caught Kehailan's
arm and said, "Hector. The ship was lifted here from the planet Hector,
Commander. Its navigational circuitry is fused. Come. Look for yourself."
There was a moment's pause. "You'll have to put him down to do that,
Sweetie, or just tuck him under your arm and bring him along."

Kehailan glared, pushed the man against the side of the ship, and
went on board.

"Now," Eletsky drawled, "perhaps you'd like to tell me what you
know before that gentleman comes back, hm?"

By the time Kehailan returned, Marion had a very good idea who
they were looking for, and Kehailan had a good idea where Ardenai had been
heading. "They were on course for Calumet, I'm quite sure," Kehailan said,
"but the ship malfunctioned. Prototypes will do that. They set down and

were waylaid before my sire could make repairs. Everything is here. Back-packs, supplies, everything. All we can do is go back to the point where the clipper was picked up, and begin tracking."

"Kee," Eletsky said, deciding to save the lecture on alien relations for a later time, "have you asked yourself why the clipper is here?"

The Equi sighed, touched Eletsky with his eyes, and looked away in embarrassment. "Myself? You know that I have, a hundred times in the last five minutes. Kais, who could truly answer, no. That, I failed to do. I failed to ask him rational questions."

"Now, I thought the questions you asked Captain Kais were rational, in a demanding sort of way."

"That," Kehailan choked, "was unforgivable. I lost my temper."

He was stricken, and Marion pretended to inspect the ship in order to give him some time to compose himself. He wanted more than anything to put his arms around the young man and tell him it was permissible to hurt for someone he loved. He couldn't do it of course. Kehailan would have been horrified. How in hell could you do anything for a friend who was so aware – so painfully aware every minute that his blood was not quite pure, that his eyes were a disappointing color, that his horsemanship was not quite up to Equi standards, that his mental capacity did not equal that of his father? And to him it mattered terribly. Much more so than it had ever mattered to Ardenai or anyone else. Throughout history, someone had to be the son – the son of Handel, the son of Vanner, the son of Karnis the Great, the son of Buldarik, the son of Ahura. Powerful, intelligent men loved their sons for simple reasons, yet the world was full of frustrated sons.

Kehailan, instead of playing to his strong points, had tried to hide his weak ones, and he'd done it by distancing himself from those he'd con-sidered superior. Not physical distance, but emotional; refusing to let them see him in what he considered moments of weakness. And that, was his one great weakness. How must he be feeling now? Torn between love for and worry about his father, and the knowledge that his father was now Firstlord of Equus – the best, the brightest, the most perfect – and that he, Kehailan, the vastly inferior son, needed to do something, anything, that would make a difference to someone as powerful as his sire.

"Captain?" the voice said again, and Eletsky came back to himself.

"Yes, Commander, what's up?"

"I believe the vessel may have been brought to Corvus because a signal from here to Equus would not have to be boosted. It would go direct, without any chance of SGA interception. It might be overheard, but it would not be dependent upon relay."

"Meaning?"

"It would get through, regardless. Perhaps the message was not meant for any of us, nor is the clipper of any consequence. It is simply a way of letting someone know to come here as quickly as possible."

"But why lift it all this way? That took days and days. Why not leave it where it was and travel at five times the speed?"

"I have no idea. Perhaps it is not time that is of the essence, but something else entirely."

"I would have to agree," Eletsky nodded, staring at the side of the ship. "The description I finally got from Kais was a handsome, powerfully built, not overly tall, prematurely greying man with blue eyes and a vibrant, almost hypnotic voice. Sound familiar?"

"Senator Konik!"

"Yup. Seems to me if we can get our hands on Konik again we can get the answers to a lot of questions."

Kehailan nodded and sighed. "It is not to my credit that we lost Konik's trail when we did." There was a lengthy pause. "What if the person for whom the message was really meant has already been here? If we try to capture Konik we'll be even further behind than we already are."

"But behind what, I wonder?" Eletsky muttered. Again he felt that prickle of uneasiness which accompanied the unknown, perhaps the un- knowable. He wished he'd been able to close his ears to all those damned rumors flying from every camp. He shook himself like a wet dog, and ig- nored Kehailan's questioning look. "Anyway, tell me what makes you think your dad was headed for Calumet?"

Kehailan's mouth twitched up at the reference to his sire, and he took a deep, steadying breath. "His trajectory at the time his navigational computer fused, would have taken him directly into the Controlled Atmosphere Corridor for the southeast quadrant of the southeast hemisphere of Calumet. As you know, Calumet is an affined world of Equus. Most of the southeast hemisphere of Calumet is retained by the Great House of Equus. It is from there that the breeding stock for the cavalry mounts of Equus is freshened from time to time. It is also a major training ground for the Horse Guard and the cavalry. My sire knows the place well, and so does Captain Ah'riodin."

"It's a logical place to go then, but he never made it."

"So it would appear," Kehailan replied. "So it would appear."

"But appearances can be deceiving," Marion smiled. "Do you suppose Amir and Bonfire could fix this clipper?"

"In a heartbeat," Kehailan nodded. "I could fix it myself in an hour or two."

"Then do it. Fix it, take someone with you, and go on to Calumet."

"I won't have any way of communicating with you if I find anything, Marion."

"Either you'll find him or you won't. Either we'll be behind you or we won't. Nothing too vague there, you think? My point is," he grinned, "in either case we'll have covered twice as much ground."

"Agreed," Kehailan nodded, "And if we find nothing, we still have the clipper, and a quick way of returning to you, wherever you may be."

"And who will you take?"

"With your permission, I'll take Oonah."

"Cool head, warm heart. Good choice. Done," Eletsky said. "Get cracking. I want you out of here. As for me, I think I'll go looking for our friend, Senator Konik."

"One more thing," Kehailan said, turning from the clipper's hatch, "Who, exactly is going to pay the price for this vessel?"

"Look hostile," Marion grinned. "I bet I can get it for nothing."

CHAPTER TWELVE

They walked side by side, one in emerald green, one in imperial purple, their robes brushing the condensation from the grass as they passed, deep in conversation. A rumble grew more discernible on the early morning air, then the sound of war bells on flying hoofs, and to their left, skirting the forest, came two squads of crack Equi Horse Guard at full gallop. In pairs they cleared the fence and disappeared into the trees, leaving the walkers alone.

"Ah'riodin sssits well thiss beautiful morning, yess?" Pythos said, flicking his long tongue with pleasure.

"Io always sits well," Ardenai replied absently, peeling the blade of grass he'd picked up along the way. "Her abilities are above reproach."

"In many thingss," the serpent physician nodded. "How well sshe getss on with her life desspite the death of her hussband, yess?"

"Ah, the first jab of the day," Ardenai said, biting down on the grass and working it between his teeth, "I must say you've shown remarkable restraint up until now. Of course we've only been out ten minutes."

"It would not have sseemed a jab if thee wass not sso defenssive."

"I'm not defensive," he said, eying his companion. "But I am beginning to recognize the tune you're whistling. Io got over Salerno, why don't I get over Ree. You know Io married Salerno for no other reason than that her fluttery little Papilli hormones got her pregnant before she'd lost her milk teeth. It was a marriage of convention, nothing more. He went on with his life, she went on with hers. Three years later, he was dead, because he was never particularly bright. Go ahead and look at me that way if you like, but you know I'm correct. He got himself ambushed because he wasn't paying any more attention on that mission than he did in my class when he was six. He's been dead close to a decade. Now, how old was I when I married Ree, and how long were we married, and how long has she been gone?"

"And you do not conssider this a defenssive responsse? Ardenai, we musst disscuss thy problem and reach a ssolution for it. Now. Today. Thee will peak ssoon, and it will be too late."

Ardenai brought his hands up to halt the conversation, and turned to look Pythos full in the face. "No," he said quietly. "I mean it, Pythos, I'm not ready yet. Look at my eyes. A little yellow in the corners, that's all. This is nothing. It will pass with minimal discomfort."

"Thy blood iss ready, and within a matter of hourss thiss will be like nothing thee hass ever experiencced." Pythos said gently, knowing he was on painfully sensitive ground. "An imperial dragonhorse heat is like no other, and it iss upon thee. Thee musst take ssteps to keep from being overwhelmed."

Ardenai gave him a look askance, and said peevishly, "Stop saying that, Pythos. It is not my dragonhorse cycle." There was something about the old doctor, the way he looked at Ardenai – the way the sun glinting off his scales gave him an almost ethereal look – something in his usually inscrutable eyes. "What do you mean, like no other?"

The physician shook his head and hissed. "Do not be afraid. What drivess thee now, drivess all Equi, but thee iss esspecially ssussceptible, becausse it hass been reinforcced for thoussandss of yearss as an important part of what thee iss to do for thy world. Thy mind can ressisst with all itss conssiderable might, and thy loinss will win every time. Thee drank at the cceremony in the Great House to sseal that particular bargain, and from this ccycle forth, in every ccycle wilt thou be the Dragonhorsse, not jusst every sseventh. And sso much more than jusst the Dragonhorsse. Pleasse listen to me."

"Eladeus, don't tell me that," Ardenai groaned. "Am I being sentenced to spend my days as a mindless, rutting beast?"

To his annoyance, the serpent laughed.

"Stop!" he demanded, and Pythos laughed harder, until he collapsed, half coiled around a thick sycamore branch growing low to the ground. Ardenai watched him in disgust until he realized that he, too, was laughing. "I said, stop!" he barked, and sat down beside his friend, hands on his knees, trying to control the snickers which kept erupting unbidden from deep in his middle. "What has possessed you, you old lizard? Have you no heart at all? This isn't funny. The only reason you're laughing is because you haven't had to endure one of those things. They strip your mind away, Pythos."

"The ssituation iss not funny, I grant thee, but the Thirteenth Dragonhorse himself? Funny indeed. Ardenai, thee hass had heat ccycles ssince thy youth. They are entirely proper and natural. Why, today, does thee contemplate in the depthss of the dragonhorsse the losss of all ccivility?"

"Because YOU used the term, 'Like no other,' and then threw in 'imperial.' How alarming is that?" Ardenai said, tossing his chewed-up blade of grass like a small spear. "And…today I am alone. I have no mate. I have no one to turn to in order to get this out of my system. I am embarrassed, and…"

The old dragon cut him off. "Iss thee embarrasssed to breathe, Firsstlord? Did thee really think all thy dutiess would be of an intellectual nature? Ssilly boy. Ardenai, look around thee. There are noble women here, who carry the puresst blood of the Great Housse in their veins. Ah'nora, Ah'dara, Ah'pia, Ah'riodin. Any of them would be honored …"

"Don't say it!" Ardenai gasped. "Don't let it cross your mind much less your lips."

"…to be thy wife, thy Primuxori."

"Why do I even talk? Pythos, this is not going to be a dragonhorse cycle. I won't let it be. It is a simple heat cycle. I may be disquieted, but I will not be consumed. I will remain in control and it will pass. If I am too uncomfortable there are hetaeras here. I will seek one out."

"They are no longer appropriate for thee, Firstlord," Pythos said soberly. "Thee may no longer spill thy seed outside marriage or a coupling sanctioned by the Great House. There is a hetaera designated for thee at Mountain Hold. We could try sending a message…from somewhere…to her. Not that it, or she, would arrive in time."

"Now I can't even seek companionship in the acceptable manner, as other men may do?" Ardenai snapped. "I have no desire to think of myself as more than a man, but I have no desire to think of myself as less, either. The more I know of this, the less I like it." He averted his eyes, gazing away into the green and fragrant woods, and his fingers tapped a nervous rhythm as he stared. He shook his head and Pythos caught a momentary shimmer in the gentle green eyes that might have been tears.

"I was with Ah'ree so long. Please, Creator Spirit, I do not want to set my head against a woman I don't love. That mating with...Ah'krill only knows who...was bad enough, but I did it, because it was my duty to sire the next High Priestess. It is not my duty to share my discomfort with a stranger, nor is it in any way my desire. And now I am told those who are trained are no longer 'appropriate' for me? Precious Equus, what am I supposed to do?"

"My hatchling, my colt," the old serpent chuckled, "My poor, sstupid Ardenai. Thee iss not lisstening, even to thysself. Remember what thee just ssaid, and lissten to me as I ssay again, doess not Ah'riodin ssit well upon her horsse thiss morning?"

"Pythos, you fill me with dismay," Ardenai murmured, and began walking again. "First you tell me to choose just any stranger to marry, then you tell me I should choose someone I consider a daughter. My wife and I raised that girl and you know it. Your sense of morality leaves much to be desired."

"Sso does thy ssensse of reality!" Pythos hissed. "May I remind thee, that thee must be married to three women? Has to be? Must be? No choice? Oh, I ssee that look, Hatchling. They musst all be alive, sso do not try to count Ah'ree ass one of them! What are thy thoughts regarding Priestess Ah'ti? Sshe of the sslender body and upturned breasssts? Your mother the High Priestess hass conssidered her for thee."

Ardenai snorted. "Ah'krill can consider that one all she wants. Ah'ti and I have served together on the Education Council for years, and I can tell you this – I would have a skewer shoved up my ass, be roasted over a slow fire and fed to a mothering Kel before I would touch that woman. She is arrogant and self-centered, and she is a misandrist. She would in no way serve anyone but herself and her inner circle. I won't have it."

"Luck iss with thee. Ah'krill hass chossen another insstead. Doesst thee remember Priestess Ah'nis? Tall, very fair skinned, with long, blonde hair? She has..."

"A personality like saddle soap and snot."

"...ssupple breasts, a sslender waist, sshapely thighss and rounded buttockss for pressenting up to thee upon the priapic bench, and flexible hipss for bearing fine children."

"And a personality like saddle soap and snot. If her conversations are any indicator, she has a brain to match. No, I take that back. She has a brain like ice – sharp, and cold. No offense to the lady, of course. If one wanted beauty only. Or a concubine..." he sucked momentarily on his bottom lip; a gesture not lost on Pythos, who wondered what the flowing robes concealed.

"Neverthelesss, Ah'krill hass assked me to draw up the contract, and I can find nothing wrong with the union, exccept of coursse that thee conssiderss her arrogant, cold and lacking a personality. When thee arrivess home, thee will be married to her as thy Primuxori – thy firsstwife. Sshe it iss, who will be thy royal conssort and help govern besside thee."

"What?" Ardenai spun around and began walking backward, heedless of the length of his robe. "I have no intention of spending the rest of my life with an ice sculpture, however shapely it may be. I need someone who can act as an advisor to me, Pythos, not just rattle her beads and pray for me while she looks down her nose at our people! I need someone who understands the intricacies of diplomacy. Someone I can talk to and get intelligent answers."

"Ah, yess. A diplomat. Ssomeone with a ssolid background in political sscience and military sstrategiess. Ssomeone who hass dealt extenssively with other raccess. Don't trip over that..." it was too late, "little branch there." Pythos extended his long, frondy fingers and set Ardenai back on his feet. "Perhapss we sshould ssit and disscuss this, yess?"

"No, we should not. I need to get back to the house. The sun is nearly up, and I have much to do today besides discussing my sex life with my cold-blooded physician."

"Then perhapss thee would honor my yearss by at leasst walking forward, Dragonhorsse?"

Ardenai took a few offhanded swipes at the grass and dirt on his robes, and began walking again, though this time he faced front and kept his eyes on the path. "Yes," he said, "someone with a solid background in diplomacy, or education, or something in addition to domestic affairs. Someone to share my life, not just my bed. I absolutely do not want Priestess Ah'nis for my firstwife. I'll simply tell Ah'krill that I..."

"Have already taken a wife. It'ss the only thing that'ss going to work without long and arduous debate. Thee knowss that. Even sso she is going to inssisst on the other two wivess. It iss traditional for your officce, and the High Priestesss iss nothing if not traditional. Thee had besst choosse at leasst one of them while it iss sstill posssible to do sso."

"Oh, ah ha! We're back to Ah'riodin, aren't we? I should have recognized your description of the solid background in political science and so on and so forth. Forget it. She's my baby."

"Baby? Thee iss the baby! A big, annoying baby!" Pythos exclaimed, jerking Ardenai hard around to face him. He used his short, powerful arms and multiple gripping fingers to square the Firstlord's shoulders, and held him firmly in place despite Ardenai's angry expression and pinned ears. "A big, blind, annoying baby! Ssqualling for reassonss *you* don't even try to undersstand! Poor little Ardi, thee wants ssomeone to love thee. Ssomeone intelligent. Ssomeone who will make a good advissor. Ssomeone who will be thy friend. And right here under thy royal nosse iss a woman, a grown woman, who lovess thee – yess, and dessiress thee in an adult and overtly ssexual manner! Sshe hass ssaid as much to me more than oncce, and if thee were not ssuch a blind, whining dolt, thee would ssee it, and ssmell it, and tasste it in the air when sshe iss around thee! Everyone elsse can! Sshe resspects thee, and would give thee the bonding thee dessiress!

"SSTOP SSQUIRMING! Sstand sstill and facce it! Look at her! Sshe's not three years old, sstanding in the ssink cutting her hair off, sshe'ss a mature woman leading the entire Equi Horse Guard. Sshe has two universsity degreess and a quarter-grown sson. Let *her* grow up, for the ssake of Eladeuss! It iss not immoral to change thy mind about how thee feels toward ssomeone, and if thee were not sso sstiff necked, thee would have admitted the attraction long ago." he broke off and huffed in annoyance. "Give her a chancce, Ardenai, or it will be forever losst to thee to do sso. Pleasse, if thou lovesst me. Pleasse, take Io to wife."

"Mercy!" Ardenai cried, pushing the serpent's hands away. "What in kraa is the matter with you? Every single morning since you let me out of bed you've brought me walking, 'to help me regain my serenity,' and you've worried me like a lithoped with a barn rat. I have other things to think about. Sarkhan will be upon us shortly, and here I am, cycling weeks earlier than usual, reacting to stress like a colt, and there is nothing I can do...to stop it." He drooped, the anger gone from his voice. "Or so my trusted friend and doctor tells me. Am I really going to become the dragonhorse every cycle now?"

"Yess, Ardenai. When thee getss to Mountain hold, there will be cceremoniess, adjusstmentss to be done that will hopefully asssuage the intenssity, but there iss no help for it right now. I am ssorry. Thiss iss a choicce that musst be made. By thee, or for thee. If thee doesst not make it, I will. And I will make it today becausse we are out of time. One way or another, Dragonhorsse, be ready at high ssssun to meet the firsst of thy wivess."

"Oh, FINE," Ardenai said, and he looked absolutely exhausted. "It's obvious to me that you have already made your choice, and that nothing is left to me but to comply. Very well. Draw up the contract and I will take the girl – now, today. Marry us, for all the good it will do you. I will do anything to get your scaly, clawed foot off my neck! I will take the Captain for my Primuxori, because it will best serve Equus, but if I find out that you exaggerated the extent of her feelings for me, so help me, I don't know what I'll do to you, Physician mine. One of us trying to get past feeling like an incestuous and dishonorable beast is going to be bad enough.

"Io is an amazing young woman, a Firstwife of whom we can all be proud, and in whom we can all have confidence. Of course the thought of having sexual intercourse with Io, is repugnant to me, but apparently that has nothing to do with it. Let me see, which act would make me hate myself more, I wonder? Do I marry Ah'nis, or do I marry Io? The dagger, or the daughter?" He used his hands to weigh his words, his face a mask of self-loathing. "And if I do choose Ah'nis, what in kraa do I do in the meantime?"

"Often we mate our horssess father to daughter. The foalss are sstrong and beautiful, Ardenai Firstlord."

"Yes, well in case you haven't noticed, Pythos, I'm not a horse. I don't think like a horse, and I have a keener sense of relationships than horses do. The thought of mounting the baby I rocked in my arms, that my wife rocked in her arms...fills me with despair and disgust. The fact that I've let you talk me into this, and that some part of me may actually be looking forward to it, makes me hate myself."

"The baby thee rocked, iss gone," Pythos said, and his voice was like warm, soothing water, salving the Firstlord's ragged nerves. "The highly educated woman who awaitss thy passsion, thy intellect, and thy companionsship, hass been mosst patient with thee, but do not expect her to be gentle. Sshe iss, after all, nearly half Papilli. They do not need heat ccycles to be hot." He looked away at that point, and Again Ardenai had the feeling the physician was hiding something. Probably nothing good. None of it had been so far.

"Just do your official duty and draw up the contract," Ardenai said through his teeth. "If she signs it, I will sign it as well, and you can marry us this afternoon. But know this, I will not force the girl. It has to be her choice, and know this also, it is certainly NOT mine." He turned on his heel and stalked up the path to the house.

He nodded to Gideon and said good morning, but he didn't pause to chat. He hurried into his chambers, and after a few minutes he returned in the sleeveless tunic, slim black pants and high boots of the Horse Guard. He seemed more relaxed, and he had with him a sleepy looking round faced boy a few years younger than Gideon.

"Jilfan, have you met Gideon?" he asked.

"No," the boy yawned, and his face was pleasant. "I have seen him at a distance, and was instructed to let him rest a bit yet."

"He has rested enough," Ardenai smiled. "Begin teaching him what it means to belong to the Great House of Equus."

Jilfan nodded. "As you wish, Dragonhorse."

Ardenai returned the nod, extended his hands for them to continue, and strode off toward the stable, muttering something under his breath that sounded like, "Best get used to each other, you'll be brothers soon enough."

They gave one another a questioning look. "I hope I haven't done anything to offend him," Gideon said. "He hasn't said ten words to me since we got here."

"But think of all the time you had alone together," Jilfan reminded him. "More time have you had, than any of us could ever expect to have. He thinks of other things just now. Be patient."

Ardenai trotted out of the stable on a big grey horse and made the turn toward Gideon and Jilfan at an easy canter, war bells jingling just above his horse's fetlocks to identify his position and alliance. When he was clear of the buildings he leaned over the stallion's neck, spoke to it, and the animal flashed away, over the fence and into the woods. "I wish I could ride half that well," Gideon sighed.

"Half that well may be possible," Jilfan replied, green eyes twinkling in his young face, and led Gideon off toward the stables. "It would please Ardenai for you to learn to ride."

"Do you really think so?"

"Um hm," Jilfan said, nodding with the air of someone who has inside information to share. "That is what he told my dam. I heard him. He was walking with her last evening in the garden."

"When I saw Ardenai last night, he was with..." Gideon found himself staring at Jilfan, "he was with Io."

"Yes. She who is my mother. Why do you look so surprised?"

"Well," Gideon cleared his throat and tiptoed into the subject, "I just...that is...Ardenai speaks of your mother as though she were a little girl."

"A source of considerable annoyance," Jilfan snorted, "as she is obviously not anything of the sort, nor does she wish to be, especially not to Ardenai Firstlord."

"She does look like a schoolgirl..." Gideon caught himself and grimaced. He'd been teased about his mother enough to know how it felt. "Sorry." He studied Jilfan a little more closely. "Why ... are you here on Calumet if I may ask. I thought this was a military operation."

"And my grandparents would never have let me come if they'd known about it," Jilfan nodded. "But they didn't. Nobody did. I came to visit with my granddam's brother and some of my cousins. Then, suddenly, there was my mother with Captain Teal, and she decided I'd be safer here under her watchful gaze for the time being." He shrugged. "That's fine with me. I don't get to see my mother very often."

"That must be hard," Gideon murmured, "and I'm sorry I referred to your mother as a schoolgirl." He dropped his eyes and hoped he sounded more sincere than he felt.

"No offense taken," Jilfan shrugged, reaching for a halter and handing another to Gideon. "It's kind of funny, really, having a dam who looks like my little sister." He looked up into Gideon's golden eyes, and the two of them burst out laughing.

"Again," Gideon said, "No offense."

"At least not on my part," Jilfan grinned, opening a stall door. "As for Mother?" He sighed and shook his head. "These things are best not discussed except by those who are principals in the matter. Come, let us begin. This is Tolbeth, the mare Master of Horse Teal has chosen to be yours. Ardenai agrees."

"Mine?" Gideon echoed in a whisper, feasting on the sight and warm fragrance of the blaze faced bay in front of him. She had three white stockings, and one white coronet, and over her left eye there was a patch of dark brown extending into her blaze, as though someone had licked the cream off one edge of a perfectly browned cookie. "Hello, Tolbeth." He extended his hand, palm up, and the mare stuck her muzzle toward Gideon's face.

"She wants to smell your breath," Jilfan explained. "It's the polite thing to do. Just stand still and exhale firmly, but not with any kind of a whooshing sound, you know. And when she's smelled your breath, she'll exhale, and you smell hers. Then she'll know you."

"My own horse," Gideon murmured, and send a silent prayer of thanks to El'Shadai for riches beyond anything he'd ever dreamed of. "Let's you and I get to know one another, shall we?"

Ardenai's horse paced along the stream bank, blowing quietly as he cooled down, and Ardenai sought to regain his own mind in the movement of the water. He was beyond quieting, he knew that. It had been less than an hour since he'd gone into the lavage and relieved himself, and still he couldn't stay tucked. The saddle was becoming uncomfortable. He put a hand down to shift himself, but it did no good. Pythos said coupling with a female would give him some real relief, and he wondered why that was, exactly. He could relieve himself. Since Ah'ree's death it had been his only means of release, though, truth be told, his heat cycles had been greatly diminished by grief and he hadn't much cared about such things. But now, even as he tried to think himself through this he felt himself being consumed, growing hotter and hotter until he felt as though he'd burst into flames if he couldn't set his head against a female. He thought about what Pythos had said, and ground his teeth in frustration. And when Pythos had spoken of Ah'nis, a woman of whom Ardenai was not in the least fond, he'd still gotten an erection, and now, thinking again of those words, he was quivering all over with the need for release. He was losing himself. He could think of nothing else.

How far this was from the man he considered himself to be. But then, had he ever considered himself in the role of undisputed leader of a world government? Reality had a way of readjusting itself from time to time, didn't it? And this reality, this marriage to Ah'riodin – he tried to picture himself teething on her neck, stroking her breasts, stretching himself along her back and penetrating her – and his mind went black, even as his intromittent organ rolled full out of its sheath and began to pulse. He swung off his horse with a cry of frustration and dismay, released himself from his riding tights, and watched from someplace far away and safe as his semen arced in thick spurts into the dusty grass along the path.

He took the time to wonder if his behavior was disturbing Kadeth, but the grey stallion looked nonchalant about the Firstlord's activities, and given leave, went to grazing while Ardenai went to the edge of the stream to wash his face and splash water up his arms.

It had been so easy when Ree lived. He would go into heat, regular as clockwork every hundred and twenty days, always cycling for eight days, as was average for Equi males, and they would plan a little getaway for a week or so, someplace quiet and private, or someplace stimulating and exciting, as the mood took them.

When she cycled, she preferred to stay home and make everybody else leave. She could channel heat like a super-conductor. The gardens were immaculate to the point of artificiality, the house was disturbingly clean, the horses were brushed nearly to distraction, and still there had been time for passion of a sexual nature. While she was gardening, or cleaning house, or brushing horses, hiking, swimming or riding. She would throw herself down and roll luxuriously like a big, long-haired lithoped, extending her arms up to him and purring, "Make love to me – now, this minute you handsome thing!" And he'd always done his best to cool her feverish passion. When they'd begun to cycle together, as couples often did after a few years of marriage, it had been an experience beyond description. Now...she was dead. Cold, and dead. His beloved of Eladeus.

Today he would marry another, lest the choice be made for him to even greater detriment. Today he would marry another woman. And he knew, despite what he'd said to Pythos, that if it came to that, he would force her – not to have sex with him, but to marry him and be Primuxori, because the fear of being wed to a stranger was worse yet. Force Io? It was an oxymoron. Force. What an awful word. It implied misuse of power, and powerful uncertainty.

It made his stomach twist with dread. What was he going to say to her? What would others think? How perverted would this seem to those he respected, and whose respect he valued? What was his brother-in-law going to think? What would Io say to him when he....? Precious Equus, he couldn't even think the words much less say them – act on them.

How had he let Pythos talk him into this? Why hadn't he said no? What were these first few seconds going to be like? What would he say first? What would she say first? Would she laugh at him? Would she look at him with shock, as though he had betrayed a deep and long-standing trust? What was Ah'krill going to think, say, do? Legally, what could she do? He was Firstlord. What if the council rose up against him for marrying someone who was not High Equi? Oh kraa, what was Abeyan going to say when he found Ardenai had seduced his only daughter? Their friendship would be in shreds – his old and dear friend. What if he hurt her? What if?

"Well, I certainly cannot go on like this for very long," he said aloud with some annoyance. He jerked one forearm angrily across his eyes and nose, gathered up the reins and remounted. "It was one thing to go into heat when I was on familiar ground, doing familiar tasks, but if I get distracted at this juncture I may not have to worry about such things anymore. You and my wife will both find yourselves riderless."

Ardenai moved to higher ground, away from the noise of the stream, and asked Kadeth to stand still. Then he cocked his head and listened for a bit before moving the stallion down the opposite side of the hill in a southerly direction. Fifteen minutes later a signal drum picked up his position, and when he rode up on the squads, they were expecting him.

"Come, sit, Brother Mine," Teal called, "We were just having a bite of breakfast. Will you join us?"

"Thank you, no," he smiled, and turned his gaze on the person sitting beside Teal. "Captain, I would walk apart and speak with thee."

"Of course," she said, looking up at him with concern. "May I wash my hands in the stream?"

"We shall walk that way," he said gravely.

She did exactly as he had done – splashing water onto her face and up her arms, but she scrubbed a little more at her mouth, rinsing off the stickiness of the blood-fruit and leaving her lips slightly colored from the effort. She called her buckskin and white mare and fed her the rest of the fruit, then rinsed her fingers again and came back to join him where he stood under a huge hardwood tree, Kimmis meandering companionably along at her shoulder.

He watched the way she walked, the way her arms swung, and when she tilted her head up to him in an unvoiced question, he noted the fine lines the sun was etching into her face. It was a bit of a shock to him, but she was definitely a grown woman, with smile lines around her eyes, and a soft full mouth like her father's. She had a nice waist, not thick, but not overly slender, and though she was muscular she had pleasing curves and a nicely rounded butt. She was taller than he remembered her being. And she did have breasts, bound tight for riding. Perhaps that's why he hadn't noticed them before. Released from their binder they would be ample enough for a woman her size. She had a very inviting body, and moved with a lithe grace which spoke of flexibility and endurance. He remembered that night in the cave – the first night he had been Dragonhorse, when Pythos had camouflaged him for this odyssey of his, and how good Io had smelled, and how willingly she had placed her head against his chest beneath his chin – how intimate that moment had been.

"Beautiful day for a canter," he said at last, drawing a deep, steadying breath and gesturing her ahead of him out through the meadow where the horses had been turned loose to graze.

"Beautiful place for a canter," Io replied. "We are pleased that you are well enough to join us, Dragonhorse."

"Thank you, Captain. Apparently I have no ill effects from my meander through the stars."

She glanced up at him and shook her bright wealth of hair. "I don't think your time as a slave in the cleomitite mines did you any good," she said, choosing not to mention that he was gaunt, and obviously running on nervous energy instead of the reserves he should have. "Those scars on your back don't look very comfortable."

"It could have been much worse if you hadn't come when you did. I have not properly thanked you. Nor have I thanked you for seeing that the others got here. You have completed your tasks admirably."

"You honor me," she nodded. "Your beloved Gideon seems to be doing well."

"Pythos says Gideon is malnourished."

"Pythos says you're malnourished, too," she smiled. "Apparently it's curable with food and rest." They walked a bit in silence and Io said, "When our current business here is finished, I would suggest that we devote some time to getting those mines reorganized. They are making slaves a valuable commodity. Most are brought there under the guise of being convicts, and I would guess that most never leave."

"I agree," he said. "We have much to do."

"Perhaps we should walk in the shade," she said, taking his arm, "you look flushed, and you are not yet as strong as you might be."

"Yes...well..." he said in a somewhat pinched tone, "the sun feels good on the whip scars. I'm fine."

She studied him for a bit out of the corner of her eye, but he was deliberately looking elsewhere all of a sudden. Odd. His eyes had raked her like a garden path a few minutes ago. She cleared her throat. "I believe we are as prepared as we can be for Sarkhan, assuming we left him an adequate trail. I realize things did not quite go as planned a time or two."

"Just a time or two?" the Firstlord chuckled. "But thanks to you, I live and he pursues me. As Gideon and I were being offloaded to go to the mines, I saw Sarkhan's Senator Konik, or should I say, Legate Konik. He recognized me, and I him. I should have told you sooner. It slipped my mind, somehow." Ardenai was quiet for a bit, content to walk with her arm through his. "There is something about that man. That Wind Warrior." he shook his head. "I wish I knew for sure what it was."

With a gesture from Io, Kimmis returned to her grazing, and they meandered in a loop around the meadow, with Io stopping from time to time, butterfly fashion, to visit the flowers, which she picked and wove into her hair as they walked. There was something on her Firstlord's mind. His hands were fidgety, and he kept catching his breath as though he were about to say something, then thinking better of it and exhaling sharply with that whuffle so characteristic of his pattern of speech.

"What you need, is a flower," she said, after yet another episode of catching and exhaling, and she danced away from him into the meadow to pluck a small, bright red sun flower. She returned with it and stood on tiptoe to tuck it behind his ear. "No," she said, critiquing her handiwork, "It's just not your look. And you have no buttonholes at all, do you?"

"Not a one, I'm afraid," he said. "You wear it for me."

"I can't do that. It's your flower, and your responsibility," she said. "You'll just have to carry it." So he did, worrying the petals off it one at a time until only the black eye of it remained. "Did she love thee, or did she love thee not?" Io asked as the last petal fell.

"Hm?" Ardenai looked at her, then at the demolished flower. "Hmmm."

"The old children's game, remember? You pull the petals off a flow-er, and as each one drops you recite, 'She loves me, she loves me not', until the last petal is gone. But you taught us in school that each flower has a given number of petals according to its species, so all you have to do is take the number of petals, decide where you want the chant to end, and begin accordingly."

"The classic example of the self-fulfilling prophecy," he sighed, and smiled down at her. "I introduced Jilfan to Gideon this morning. I had not realized they were so close to an age. Jilfan is growing up."

"Um hm," Io said, still looking for flowers, "he was thirteen last season, and to hear him talk, he's nearly fourteen already."

"Boy that age needs a father," Ardenai said abruptly, and flushed with embarrassment.

"He's been without one a long time," Io said, then looked up at Ardenai, saw his color...saw more than the color...and glanced hurriedly away, smothering her mirth. "But I've been looking long and hard for the right man."

"Any luck catching one?"

"You make it sound like a fishing expedition," Io laughed, glad for the chance to release her nervous giggles.

Ardenai stopped and gave her a considering look. "I promised you a fishing trip, and you never got it."

"I do remember that," she said, still laughing, "I think I was about ten years old."

"See? Then remember this, too. I am a man of my word. When we get back to the house I want you to put together whatever it is that women take on extended outings. We...are going fishing."

"As my lord wishes," she nodded, and suddenly, she was very sober.

"I...if you don't want to go..." he said hastily.

"I do. I want to be with you." She led him to the edge of the trees and stepped up onto a log which brought her to eye level with the tall Equi, and when she put her hands on his shoulders, she realized he was trembling, almost vibrating, with emotion. "What's this all about, Beloved? Talk to me, my old friend."

He fought to keep his eyes level with hers, though it nearly choked him to do so. "I don't know where to begin," he whispered. "I don't know what to say to explain what's happening to me."

"Just say it the best way you can," she said softly, pushing his thick hair back off his forehead, and the trembling subsided a little under her touch.

She could feel the heat rising off him, and realized what Pythos had meant with his cryptic aside yesterday at breakfast, *We have another problem which will soon need tending*. While she ached for him having to expend energy on a heat cycle at this juncture, she wondered with effervescing hope, if she was going to be asked to attend him in this.

He nodded. "Well...Pythos told me this morning that Ah'krill has selected Priestess Ah'nis as a wife for me. As my Primuxori." He felt Io stiffen. "And that if I'm not married by the time I get back to Equus, I'll be stuck with her, and I don't want that. But in order not to marry her, I'm going to have to be married to someone else already. Here. Before I get there, I mean." He ventured a look straight into her eyes. "This isn't making any sense, is it?"

Io gave him a cool look. "Quite the contrary. I understand all too clearly. I thought you said you were a man of your word, Dragonhorse."

The look she got back was a total blank. "I ...... ah ...... what?"

"You have forgotten, apparently, that I asked you to marry me when I grew up, and you said you would, and Ah'ree said it was fine with her. Now you have chosen another over me? This is bad news indeed, my Lord. I am embarrassed for thee."

Ardenai was just shaking his head, bereft of words and reason, and Io laughed in spite of her attempt to look threatening. "You and I were sitting in the garden swing doing homework, and Ah'ree was snapping spent buds from the rohanth bushes, and the three of us were discussing Equi sexual practices, and the training we would go through before mating. We were just beginning to hit around the edges of it, you know, and I said I didn't have to worry about it, because I was going to marry you, and you already knew everything there was to know about such things. Then Ah'ree looked up and smiled at us from under that wide brimmed hat with the flowered ribbon around the crown that she always wore in the garden, the one her grand-mother had given her, and said she thought it was a very good idea for you to take me as a wife, because maybe we'd occupy each other enough to stay out of her hair that way. Remember? That was one of her favorite expressions.

'Stay out of Ardenai's hair, Io. Stay out of Io's hair, Ardenai. Stay out of my hair, the both of you.' We were destined from that day."

"Little Io, Fledermaus, I do love you but I'm like a father to you. You are like a daughter to me."

"NO," she said sharply, and gave his shoulders a snap which startled him. "And cut the little Io shit. I'm sick to death of it, and you cowering behind it. I am not little Io, nor have I been. I may be as a daughter to you, but you are not as a father to me, Ardenai Firstlord. I have loved thee from the time I understood what the word meant, and from the time I understood what it meant to be in love with someone, I have been in love with thee. My passion, my desire, my deepest feelings, have always been for thee. My deepest desire has been to be mated with thee and bear thy children."

"But..." he blinked stupidly, "Salerno?"

"Was the father of my child, no more. I was fond of him. I wished him no harm. I grieved when he died, because it was sad, not because I was. I see the only love we need to deal with is mine, apparently. And the only grief we need to deal with, is yours."

He ignored the jab. "Rohanth bushes," he murmured, looking over her shoulder into the woods, "so it would have been the end of spring and you would have been...?"

"Ten. How come you can remember fishing, but you can't remember a pledge to marry someone who has been waiting for you for twenty-five years?"

He took a deep breath. She thought he nodded to himself. The mottled green eyes again met hers as his hands caught her waist. "You're sure I agreed to this?"

"Yes, Firstlord," she smiled. "You said it was something you could do for Equus – saving the rest of the male population from one such as myself."

"Well then, we could combine tasks, as we agree that there is much to do. We could get married today at midday, and go on our fishing expedition this afternoon, and we'd have two things promised in the tenth year out of the way by nightfall. I didn't promise you anything else that year, did I? I'd like to start working on eleven as soon as possible."

She gasped, and her already large eyes grew huge as she looked at him. "Ardenai, Beloved, are you sure this is what you want? I would be happy to serve thee just as..."

"Oh no, my little blossom bat," he said firmly, "I do not think of you in those terms, nor am I considering that part of your notoriously hot bloodline in this decision. I don't want you for breeding stock, there's plenty of that already. I want your brains and your intellect and your compassion beside me, guiding Equus. I have asked Pythos to draw up the contract. All that remains is for us to sign it. Will you marry me and be my Firstwife, and help me rule our people wisely and well?"

"Yes," she smiled, "of course I will, Firstlord." But the light had diminished in her eyes, and though she returned his kiss, she did not linger overlong. She stepped down from the log and began walking back toward the waiting squads. "Perhaps I should pick more flowers," she said over her shoulder, and Ardenai wondered what had upset her. He shrugged. She was Papilli. She was female. It would pass.

They returned with the squad at a gallop, and Ardenai excused himself to make preparations while Io hurried off in another direction with Pythos, who had hailed her even before she was off her horse. Gideon offered to take the animals, but Ardenai shook his head and smiled. "Leave them to another, just this once. When the sun reaches its zenith this day I will marry Ah'riodin, and since women put much store in such ceremonies, I would like to make the day memorable for her."

Gideon was dumbfounded by the suddenness, but he gave the Equi a warm hug and said, "Congratulations, Firstlord! Much happiness."

"Let us fervently hope so," he muttered. "Much expediency, at least. Help me bathe, and I must change my clothing and speak to Ah'nora about lunch, and traditional robes for my betrothed."

"Speak to Ah'nora first, to give her more time to prepare whatever it is you want," Gideon suggested, and Ardenai chuckled and dropped an arm around the young man's shoulders.

"Surely Eladeus has put you in my path. Come with me."

As the hour approached Ardenai sought out Ah'riodin, bearing an ornate wooden chest and fresh sun flowers like the one he'd demolished earlier. "She loved me," he said simply. He proceeded to weave them, along with pale blue and green ribbons, into her amazingly thick tangle of curls, forcing himself not to think about the times he'd done this for Ah'ree – forcing himself to think only about the times he'd done this for Io while she wriggled impatiently to be off her stool, or off his lap, and on to the fascinating business of being alive. Those times, had been practice for today. After all, he had promised to marry the girl when she grew up, and he was a man of his word. And Ah'ree had said it was a good idea.

How oddly comforting that thought was. He chuckled. Io gave him a questioning look but he shook his dark head and smiled at her. "Pre-wedding jitters," he said. He opened the small mahogany chest and presented to her the long-sleeved, tightly belted robe of pale green, the color of new life, which Ah'nora had given him earlier. "I shall give thee thy privacy to dress, and I must do the same," he said with a gallant bow, and left her chambers.

At the appointed time they gathered their friends about them in the garden, signed their contract, and stood before the old physician. "Abeyan Ah'riodin Salerno, come thee here of thine own free will?" he asked.

"I come of mine own free will to be joined with Ardenai as his wife," she said, and looked Ardenai right in the eye, smiling as she said it.

"Ah'krill Ardenai Morning Sstar, come thee here of thine own free will?" Pythos found himself holding his breath. This was the place where this could come apart. But there was no hesitation, just a certain sense of resignation in his voice, some sadness in his eyes.

"I come of mine own free will to be joined with Ah'riodin as her husband."

The serpent nodded, and Ardenai took both Io's hands in his. Turning them palms up, he gave each one a kiss. Despite her bathing with foaming rosemary and scrubbing sand, there was the lingering fragrance of leather, and horses, and it made the Firstlord smile. "I vow to thee gentleness always, my wife. For as long as I live, I am thine."

Pythos nodded in turn to Io, who took Ardenai's hands in hers, and kissed the back of each one. "I vow to thee companionship always, my husband. For as long as I live, I am thine."

Together they brushed the palms of their right hands across the backs of their left in ancient gesture. "Ahimsa. I vow to thee peace," they said to one another.

"Thou art become Abeyan Ah'riodin Ardenai Morning Sstar, Firsstwife of Ardenai, Primuxori of Equuss. And thee, Ah'krill Ardenai Morning Sstar, thou art become hussband to Ah'riodin. Thee cannot be parted but by death, friend from friend, hussband from wife, Firsstlord from Firsstwife. Ahimssssa, I wish thee peacce. It iss done. Wife, thee may kisss thy hussband," the old doctor said, and his eyes sparkled with joy and relief as he kissed them each on the forehead. The thought of Ah'nis with this man – he shuddered, and hid it with an all-encompassing embrace amid the cheers and applause.

Perhaps he'd pushed a little too hard for this, but it was in Ardenai's best interests. Certainly Io must be delighted, though she didn't show it just now. Pythos could close his eyes and see curly haired babes, toddling in the sunshine of Canyon keep – see their slick little heads bulging out of their mother as Ardenai held her close on the birthing stool. The old doctor did so love delivering babies. He had done the right thing. Hopefully, Ardenai wouldn't mention to Ah'krill that he knew about Ah'nis. The High Priestess could be formidable about such small betrayals of confidence. Ah well, if there was a price to pay, he would pay it, and gladly. His hatchlings, his foals, were together at last. His beautiful babies. He flicked them with his tongue, and applauded with the rest.

CHAPTER THIRTEEN

After lunch, when the saddle horses waited at the gate, the pack horses beside them, Ardenai took his brother-in-law aside and told him exactly where they would be. "Where the hot springs cascade down into that wide pool in the river near the great bend. If you need us come and get us, or waken the drums," he said, "but only if you need us."

"Understood, really." Teal said, and lost control of a spreading grin.

"What?"

"Ardi, you have no idea how much your sister and I have wanted this for you," Teal laughed. He kissed him lingeringly on the temple, and walked him to his horse.

They rode for an hour or so in the pleasant afternoon sun, enjoying the peace and quiet. Ardenai rode in silence, and Io respected that. She sensed that he was troubled. Some of the reasons why she knew. Some she could only guess at. But his face had lines in it that hadn't been there before, and he was slightly too thin, and lately when he spoke it seemed forced, as though he was having trouble concentrating. That could be the heat cycle, she thought. This was going to be terribly difficult for him. He had adored his wife – too much. He'd been far too dependent on her. And now, pretty much in his own mind, he'd married his daughter. Io shook her head and veiled her thoughts more deeply, lest she disturb her husband.

Her husband. Her fondest dream had come true. She was married to Ardenai, for whom she had burned seemingly forever. Soon now, she would need to coax him into setting his head against her for intimate purposes, and she spent some time figuring out how she was going to do that without traumatizing him, or sullying Ah'ree's memory. She wondered if Pythos was correct in his assessment. He usually was about such things, and she began preparing herself mentally for what would come. She wondered about Ardenai, and if he was strong enough for this. Most Equi males ate like horses for weeks before their seventh cycle, their accelerated metabolisms building the reserves of energy they would need for their exertions. At the time he should have been stuffing himself with six or seven meals a day and sleeping when he wasn't eating, Ardenai had been half starved, and too weak to sit up in bed for more than a few minutes, and yet coming strongly enough into heat that even an off-worlder could see it.

It made her chuckle inside to think of Thatcher, the mine boss, saying he'd find her an Equi in his seventh cycle. Little did he know. Still, it worried her that Ardenai was having to endure this new level of heat, and was glad both for Pythos' forewarning, and the decoctions he had discreetly sent along with her in case they were needed.

They crested a rolling hill, ambled rather steeply down a white dusted path between huge boulders, and stopped where a bend in the river had formed a small ox-bow lake and the water had slowed enough to warm a little. There were trees, and a grassy, flower-sprinkled meadow, and, on a close facing precipice, a toss of rocks and boulders between which trickled a hot spring that grew ever cooler with each pool it passed through, until it steamed into the little lake, and drifted away. On a flat spot that was slightly elevated, near a stand of huge Equi pines, stood an elegant pavilion, newly pitched, with comfortable chairs and a fire laid and ready to be lit. The Great Seal of Equus flew to the left, the pennants of the Horse Guard to the right. Everything in preparation. Ah'nora, or Teal – or both of them in tandem – had been very, very busy this day. Nothing to do. Ardenai sighed to himself. Everything was entirely too prepared. There was nothing left as a distraction. He felt his gut tighten uncomfortably, but he smiled as best he could and gestured, palms up. "This must be the spot."

"I love this place, but are there fish?"

"I know for a fact there are," he said, swinging one leg over his horse's head and sliding out of the saddle. "We will get to that part later.

Right now I'm hoping that we can be alone awhile, so we can talk, and get used to each other in this new role."

"Far better than fishing," Io nodded, and allowed him to lift her from the saddle. "It's a beautiful spot for…" She started to say, a honeymoon, and then thought better of it, "a rest," she finished, knowing it wouldn't be that, either.

They unsaddled the horses and turned them out to graze, then unpacked the supplies. Ah'nora had sent more than enough food, all of it already beautifully prepared and packaged to keep, so they knew there would be little need for a fire beyond ambience and evening light. They had the hot pools for warmth, as well as fleecy-beds and soft woolen comforters and, Io thought hopefully, each other. Finally, there was no more fussing they could do around camp, and they were once again confronted with one another's presence.

Having been in more than one sexual situation where high black boots and tight fitting britches had become an awkward barrier to intimacy, and assuming her new husband was going to be uncomfortable with nudity for a while, Io stretched lazily and commented, "That was hot work. I think I'll change into my robe and sandals. Would you care to do the same?"

"A good idea," he nodded, but when she gestured him into the tent, he balked. "You go ahead," he said. "I can wait."

She emerged shortly in traditional sleeveless, pale green priapic robes and high lacing sandals, and again gestured him into the spacious enclosure. "I have laid out your things," she said. This time, to her relief, he went, and when he returned, he was wearing much the same garments, except that his robes were pale blue – as his wedding tunic had been – the color of Equi blood. "You look much more like you are on holiday now," she smiled, and he gave her a gracious nod of acknowledgment. "And much more relaxed." That last was a lie, but she wanted to encourage his efforts. He held out his hand to her, and they walked back along the stream, eyes peeled all too well for small animals and interesting plants.

"For a man who wanted to talk, you haven't said two words," Io teased gently. By now she was wading in the stream, carrying her sandals, and though she spoke to him, she didn't meet his eyes.

"I said I wanted to talk," he replied. "I did not say I knew where or how to begin. Here we are, out meandering around in robes which say we are freshly wed and about to experience intimacy, and I don't have any idea how to go about getting started, or even if we should, because I swore to myself I wouldn't, though parts of me wish I would." He shook his head and looked away. "Please, don't be offended. You're a beautiful woman. I guess I've just forgotten...." He trailed off and shrugged.

"You can't have forgotten all of it," Io smiled, and Ardenai stopped to look across the rill at her as she stepped onto the opposite bank. "Actually, it is my opinion that you have failed to forget enough, Firstlord."

"You have a solution then?" he asked, hopping the stream to join her. He caught her around the waist and set her on a squared off boulder, and as he stepped closer, she wrapped her legs around his waist and left them there. Her thighs, conditioned to be sensitive to the movements of a horse beneath a saddle, told her that the robe was all he had on, and she enjoyed feeling the roundness of his muscular buttocks beneath her bare feet.

"Of course I have solutions. I'm a strategist, remember?"

"Oh, good, I suppose. I am not sure. It has been a long time."

"How did you go about it with Ah'ree?"

His ears pinned back a little and his face hardened into the familiar lines which, even on this occasion her name elicited.

Io gave him a warning look in return and said, "Beloved, Ah'ree is here with us, and she will always be here, right beside you. I know this. You know this. Let's accept it and move on."

"Ah'ree was different," he grimaced, tightening up to turn away, but her legs kept him from stepping back from her. She smiled, unfastened the top frogs of his robe, and began gently, slowly, massaging his chest and shoulders, giving special attention to his nipples, and the cleft where neck and collarbone met.

"How so?"

He thought about it for a moment, then acquiesced with a gentle sigh. "For one thing, I wasn't under so much pressure. Too, we were young, and we were relative strangers. You, I have known since the day you were born. Your father would kill me if he knew what I was thinking at this moment. What I've thought in more than one moment past I might add, if I were honest, which obviously I am not."

He shook his head, and again he would have turned away from her, but she was amazingly strong, and though she smiled, she held him to his place against the boulder and close to her body. She unfastened the top of her robe, took his hands, set them to the sides of her breasts, and held them there with her elbows as she spoke. "Remember, my sire is now remarried, and to a much younger woman who adores him. He will understand the attraction." She paused to teethe a bit along the cords of his neck. "Now, let's look at this logically, Ardenai Firstlord. Number one, there will be no surprises. I've already done my worst to you, I was left in your care, and I cut all my hair off when you thought I was asleep, and got you in one of the worst fights you ever had with Ah'ree."

"It was no fight," he amended soberly. "She yelled and I listened."

"Number two, you've already done your worst to me." Io looked away from the fond green eyes and into the brook. "You have always belonged, belong now, and always will belong to another woman. I accept that. I am willing to be your friend, and your consort, and leave Ah'ree's memory as your wife alone. No surprises, especially not in being assigned a mate you do not wish to have. One who may be very demanding, and not so understanding as I will be. I care for you, you care for me, and we have that to build on, if only in friendship."

"You sound quite resigned to all this," Ardenai said, touching her cheek with the tips of his fingers. "I suppose you've heard this from Pythos quite as much as I have of late?"

"I haven't had to hear it. I'm on his side. Besides, there's nothing wrong with building on other people's good ideas. Oh, and I happen to be in love with you, if that matters."

Ardenai cupped her face in his hands and dropped his forehead against hers. "It does matter," he said quietly. "I know it doesn't seem like it, but I do want this to be more than a marriage of convenience. Truly, I do care for thee, Lady Io. Thou art become Abeyan...Ah'riodin...Ardenai Morning Star," he breathed, "Firstwife of Ardenai, Primuxori of Equus."

"And I am in love with thee, Ardenai Firstlord of Equus. I desire thee. I await thy pleasure," she whispered back, and slid her arms around his neck as she spoke, adjusting his head gently but firmly until their noses touched, as well as their foreheads.

"I am much of a mind to kiss thee," he murmured, cocking his head and moving his mouth toward hers, and she responded by kissing him lingeringly on the lips.

"Let me show you which kiss will please a little Papilli pouncer," she whispered, unfastening the bottom half of her robe and hitching it aside, "relax your jaw."

She inserted her tongue into his mouth, and he responded without hesitation and with more than a little experience, which surprised and pleased her. Within a minute he was shaking, and his kisses were deep and passionate. His thumbs stroked her nipples, and his teeth moved gently up the sides of her neck as he bit her in preparation to mount. She tightened her legs around him to bring herself slightly over the edge of the boulder, then skillfully, discreetly opened the bottom half of his robe, and with a touch he hardly felt, set the slick, wet head of his phallus against her opening. He groaned, and she lowered her legs enough to clasp his buttocks. He groaned again, and began to push, and Io tightened her legs around him and took him in. She cried out, throwing her head back. His hands, which had been on her breasts, slid under her butt and pulled her tight, his teeth sank deeper into her neck, and he pushed hard - one, two, three times, and with hoarse sobs of pleasure, he released. They quivered together, groaning.

He licked the side of her neck, then gently lifted her away from the boulder and dropped to his knees, lowering her slowly until they were lying flat in the grass. "That alabaster's hard on bare knees," he whispered, nuzzling her. "All right so far?"

"Mmmmm," she said, and let her head fall back into his cupped palms. "Again."

"With all my heart," he whispered, and rolled with her in his arms.

Io was sitting up once again to allow their bodies to cool, and when she looked down at him, that old, familiar twinkle lit her eyes. "I really think we could become quite accomplished," she said, "given enough time and practice." She blew in a concentrated stream across his wet chest, then across her own. "Thank goodness the sun's gone behind the cliff, or we'd cook for sure."

"I don't suppose, when you unpacked all that stuff back at camp, you found a priapic bench, did you?" Ardenai asked. "I'm enjoying the petting and nickering, but I'm going to want to get serious very, very soon."

"There was no need to bring one," she grinned, "There's already one here. Carved out of the alabaster over by the hot pools, or so I'm told."

"And who would tell thee such a thing?" Ardenai gasped in mock dismay, sliding one hand behind his head and cocking an inky eyebrow her direction.

"Girls talk," she said matter-of-factly, putting her palms down on his chest and slowly beginning to push up off him. "Ah'nora thought we might have need of such an article, given that we are freshly wed. Furthermore, I know, that you know perfectly well and from experience that it's there, and that you are testing me to see how thorough I can be in a short amount of time. The answer – pretty thorough. Right now though, I have need of privacy for a few minutes, and then a dip in that lake, I think, and then I shall go back to camp and get some padding for that bench, if my lord will so permit me."

"Your lord will even give you your robe," he smiled, pulling it out from where it was serving as a neck pillow and tossing it in her direction.

She took note of how he sat up, and where his hands were placed, and smiled quietly to herself. They may have bathed together as a family for years, but in this instance, starting off with clothing had been the right thing to do. She turned her back, slipped on the sweat-soaked robe, made a little hiss of disgust, promptly took it off again and walked in the direction of the trees, scuffing into her sandals and trailing the robe behind her.

Ardenai watched her, wondering if she was going to expel semen so soon. Equi females were well trained to squat and push out spent ejaculate to prevent settling. It wasn't foolproof, of course, but coupled with other measures, it was effective should an accident occur. At this moment, in his state of mind, he didn't really care whether he'd impregnated her or not. Being careful had certainly been the last thing on his mind, and if Pythos was so kraaling anxious to have him married and copulating, he could deal with a settled female.

The Firstlord shook himself a little, and forced himself back into his own mind. The dragonhorse may have taken him, but for a few minutes it needed to give him back so he could think. This was only foreplay – petting – he was not yet ejaculating sperm, only semen. Simple Equi biology. Comforting.

He stood up, retrieved his robe from where he'd tossed it, and went back to the lake for a desultory splashing of his own. He didn't know if he'd impregnated a woman? Unheard of. Worse, he hadn't cared. He'd had not one thought in his head except sex – no sense of responsibility whatsoever. It had been wonderful. He wanted to do it again, and looked impatiently around for his wife. Allowing himself such explosive release, even during petting, when he was not yet generative, was novel for him. He'd spent years controlling nearly every encounter so as not to risk Ah'ree. For the barest, guiltiest instant, he was glad he didn't have to do that anymore.

Io came from the direction of the camp carrying several things which she took around the corner to a place amid the boulders surrounding the hot pools before walking back to the lake. She made a long shallow dive into the water, which surprised Ardenai. He'd thought she'd wade in to her waist and call it good, as he had. The water was surprisingly cold. Apparently, it surprised her, as well – or something had. She surfaced wearing a stunned look, and ran her hands down her flanks and across her flat belly.

"What?" Ardenai asked, "Did you run into something down there?"

"I think I did, yes indeed," she gasped.

"Did you hit a rock? Are you hurt?"

I'm...fine," she said thoughtfully, and gave him a reassuring smile before wading back out into deeper water.

When she returned, she was cold to the touch, and only brushed against him on her way to the steaming blue pools, dragging a clean robe behind her through the grass. Io rolled into one of the deeper pockets, stroking her arms and her sides with such sensuality that Ardenai began to breathe hard before she was even out of the water. When she came out she gave him a sidelong, inviting glance, and walked deliberately to the priapic bench. There was no coyness, and no false modesty. She mounted it on hands and knees, then dropped her forearms to the cushions so she was resting her weight on them with her butt elevated, spread her legs into a traditional crouch, and waited for instructions.

She felt his hands exploring at her inner thighs, stroking upward, lifting her slightly toward him as he adjusted her position. There was a moment's pause, and his tongue licked her posterior clitoris. She moaned with pleasure and arched her back more deeply, improving his angle. She had known, somehow, that he would know what he was doing, but this? She gasped at the subtle touch of his teeth, then his tongue awhile, in almost lazy fashion, and then she felt his body coming down on top of hers in the traditional coital position. His teeth finding her neck, his hands her breasts, his phallus finding her opening. He must be standing completely astraddle of the bench, she thought, his legs were so wide apart. He must have tremendous power in his thighs. He could snap her like a twig, this gentlest of souls whom she so adored.

He bit down harder where her shoulder met her neck, and grunted as he pushed. She could feel him release. He rested for a minute or so, the teeth in her neck turning to softly kissing lips, though he said nothing to her. He began to fondle her breasts, and breathe hard, and he pumped – three deep strokes, three shallow strokes, three deep strokes – and released again. He laid more heavily on her, bit down more fiercely, pushed quickly in short, jerky strokes, grunting hoarsely, but no longer crying out as he peaked. He was catching his rhythm now, and would begin to ejaculate more often, and with a much greater ratio of sperm to semen. As his ancillary exterior testicles emptied, the primary testes high in his pelvic cavity would begin to disgorge themselves, the semen nearly black against the pale blue motile sperm. Should an Equi woman so much as twitch with orgasm, allow a nanoth of an opening in her canalic iris at this point, she would be settled in a heartbeat if not protected.

She shifted slightly to get more comfortable, and bit his fingers hard where his hand hung over her shoulder. He responded with a slap more ceremonial than serious, and ejaculated again without stroking at all. He was locked sinuously around her, and though she couldn't see his face, she knew his eyes were closed, his cheek resting against the cushion of her long, wet hair, which was knotted at the nape of her neck. His breathing was shallow and rasping. Several times a minute he would jerk spasmodically and make a grating sound in his throat as he released, and then seem almost to sleep before repeating the process.

His thighs began to quiver and he stepped back to the shaft of the bench, still locked around her, still entranced. Being dragged backward on the bench adjusted her angle enough to stimulate an orgasm in her, but she didn't fight it. She didn't need to. She hadn't really meant for him to know so soon, but this felt so very, very good. Perhaps he wouldn't notice. She would take her pleasures quietly.

They remained coupled until dusk, when the first of the huge Calumet moons rose over the trees. She could hear him beginning to grind his teeth in an attempt to regain himself rather than pass out, and he shook his head several times to clear it. He released once more, a more conscious effort, and this time he raised up off her back to allow the breeze to pass, his hands gentle as he wiped away the sweat which had formed between them.

"Are you getting tired?" he asked, very quietly, and it was the safe, comforting voice of the very first teacher she'd ever had. *"Do you have*

your jacket? Do you need a little nibble? Would a nice nap make you feel
better? You're doing a wonderful job of that, Io. Do I need to repeat myself,
Ah'riodin?"

"Io? Fledermaus, are you getting tired? Are you all right?"

"I'm fine," she smiled, rotating her shoulders like a lithoped knead-ing a blanket. "I would like to do something different with my elbows for a few minutes."

"As you wish," he said, and immediately withdrew, though she could tell he was still erect. That act alone spoke to his monumental self-control. "Would you like your robe for a bit? I should build a fire against the chill."

She elevated herself slowly into a sitting position, and as she did he could see the marks he had left on her back, and the chafing on her elbows and knees despite the padding on the bench. With a moan and a look of pure self-loathing he pulled her up to him and held her fiercely against his breast. "Eladeus, what am I doing?" he whispered. "What have I done? Io, I'm sorry." At that point he realized he needed her body for support. His knees were like pudding and his back felt positively broken. "I'm sorry."

"For what?" she asked, momentarily baffled by his dismay. She pushed back to look at him, and swallowed the gasp which rose in her throat. His eyes were glowing the fiery orange-red of a full dragonhorse, and there were tears running down his face.

She wondered if it had finally hit him. It was bound to, and he would have to work through it, since there was no going back at this point. "Be-lieve me when I tell you that I am having a wonderful time," she chuckled, and laid her head back against his chest. His sweat was turning cold, and he was beginning to tremble a little, as was she. Papilli, too, were sensitive to chill. "Let me get thy robe, Husband."

"No," he said firmly, and moved her to arm's length. "I can get my own robes. I want you to go back to camp and get some rosemary branches and some clotted-soap so I can scrub my stink off you."

"But you're still..." she made a slight gesture and grimaced.

"After your bath, you shall go make us a nice pot of hot tea, and find us something to eat, while I swim the dragonhorse into submission in that lake yonder."

"I will happily..." She was stopped dead by the look of realization which suddenly crossed his face.

"That lake! Precious Equus," he gasped, and caught her face hard in his hands, forcing her to look in his eyes. "The cold water! Your primary iris was open the whole time on the bench. Were you already with child when I mounted you there?"

She nodded slightly in his grip and moved her eyes away, though she couldn't move her head. "Please," she whispered, "don't be angry. I didn't know. I didn't even know it was there until I dove into that cold water and my iris tightened, and up it went. By the time my iris opened again it was lodged tight – like it had a mind of its own. Which of course it does."

Ardenai realized he was holding her head much too tight, and abruptly released her, berating himself for being so rough. He walked away to get the fresh robes she'd brought, and when he turned back, shrugging into his garment, she was crying, great tears rolling from her eyes and splashing onto the backs of her small hands, which she was using without much success to try to stem the flow from her eyes and nose.

"What?" he said, bending his head to look into her face. He got no response except more tears, and since she was shivering with cold, he took each of her arms in turn and stuck them through the armholes of her robe, as he'd stuffed her into her winter coat when she was a babe.

He pulled her over to the bench and sat down so he was looking slightly up, rather than down at her. He squeezed her hands and brought them to his lips, tasting the salt of her tears, and said as gently as he could, "What's the matter, Fledermaus, why do you cry so?"

She shook her head, and jerked the clip out of her hair, allowing it to cascade damply over her shoulders and down her back. She wiped at her eyes and nose, sniffed a little, and began to sob again. "I'm sorry," she cried. "I am so sorry!"

The Firstlord patted his knee, and coaxed her on to it. "Apparently we're both sorry, but I just don't know why you would be. Are you hurt? Is there something wrong with the settling? Why do you say you're sorry?" *Never ask more than one question at a time*, he reminded himself, and realized he was treating her like a baby, not as his wife, with whom he'd been locked in coitus for hours, and who now, apparently, bore his child. He hugged her, then set her off his knee, and onto the bench beside him. Reaching a towel from the small stack beside them and proffering it, he queried, "What have I done to upset thee, Firstwife?"

She quieted herself to a series of gasping hiccups, and mopped her face rather too hard with the towel, as though she were punishing herself. "It's me who did it. I didn't think you were generative yet, so I wasn't paying any attention. I just..." she made an angry little gesture, "bam! I've done it again! Pregnant in a first encounter. First Salerno, and now you. I'm just soooo sorry! I know you didn't want me to bear you any children." The look on his face stopped her speech yet again. "If you want," she said in a rush, "maybe Pythos can ..."

"Stop! What are you saying? Where on the ten tribute worlds of Equus did you get a crazy idea like that, Io? You'd never terminate a pregnancy of your own volition, and you know it. Neither would I. Where is your head?"

"Please don't yell at me," she sobbed. "I know you don't want me to having babies."

"What? What? That is just insane. If you want to have a dozen babies, and Pythos says it's safe for you, I will certainly do my part, and gladly. There isn't a man on Equus who loves children more than I do. You know that. Where are you getting this..." the word which came immediately to mind was, lunacy, but he quickly thought better of it. "This absurdity?" Even that sounded sharp, but it was out now.

"This morning." she stammered, wiping fitfully at her flushed and tear-streaked face and looking not a whet more than six years old. "You said you didn't want me for breeding stock, and you didn't think of me that way, and I know I'm funny looking. I've heard them all – garden troll, flickernick,

Mustard Seed, fairy, elf, fruit bat, butterfly baby. What if we have funny looking little fruit bat babies, and they're running all over the Great House under everybody's feet?"

"Precious Equus!" he exclaimed, trying manfully not to laugh, "Are you one of those females who settles and promptly loses her mind for five and a half seasons? Because if you are, you need to tell me now so I can get Pythos to prescribe something for one of us, or both of us – me, for sure. Oh. No. I'm sorry. Don't start to cry again. Please. Don't cry, Io. What I said this morning was..." he gave it some thought. "All right, maybe that is what I said, but you were so beautiful, standing up on that log with those flowers in your hair, and I was trying so hard not to just snatch you off there and maul you on the spot, and anyway, what I *meant* to say, had I not been trying with most of my mind to talk myself out of attacking you, was this. There are many beautiful high Equi women I could choose to marry, or Ah'krill could choose for me, and they would be tall like me, and have green, ophidian eyes like me, and ears like me, and they would be good, dutiful wives, I'm sure. But never could I turn to them with the depth of feeling I have for thee, Abeyan Ah'riodin Ardenai Morning Star. You are as different from me as day from night, winter from summer, red from green, and for that reason our marriage will always be fresh. There will always be new things to learn about one another. I owe you my life, Io. You are my friend, my hetaera, my political advisor, my ambassador to the stars. It is you whom I will hold forth as the most precious commodity of Equus. That you bear my child is more than I can even yet fathom, but that you are all those other things as well, is more than any man could ever hope for, wish for, dream of, and all of it is mine." He exhaled sharply and grinned sheepishly. "That's more or less what I meant to say."

She smiled, and sniffed, and gave him a very wet kiss on the mouth before laying her head on his chest and drawing a deep, sobbing breath. How tired she must be, he thought, wrapping his arms around her protectively. Up before dawn, riding field maneuvers all morning, galloping home to get married and grab a bite of lunch before riding out again to be ridden until nightfall by someone over four hands and a hundred pounds her master.

"I would not have had thee cry this day," he whispered. "Nor would I have had you regret our baby. But, if I'd had any idea I was going to be generative initially, I'd have told you, so that you had a choice."

"Remember what I told you this morning? I said that more than anything I wanted to be your mate, and bear your children. I am happy."

"Then I am happy, as well," he murmured. "Have we a son, or a daughter?"

"A little girl," she sighed.

He held her close against him and kissed her hair, and chuckled with delight. "A daughter." the Firstnight's chant of a thousand voices, the smoke from the thuribles returned to him. *"She's a little priestess! That decoction they gave me the night of the passing ceremony must have left me with motile sperm in my ancillary testes. That possibility would have occurred to me if I'd been thinking properly.* "I'm really sorry, Io," he said aloud. "It was irresponsible of me."

"Well, I'm glad," Io sighed. "She's beautiful, and I love her."

"And that is all that matters," he said, and sat rocking her a bit until her breathing returned to normal. "Now, I'm going for a swim, and you're going to get what we need for a nice bath before supper."

"We should go back to the bench for another while. That water's cold," she objected, and he waggled a finger under her nose.

"If it could settle you, it can settle me," he said firmly. "Please do as I ask you, just this once. See what it feels like. I may have to ask you to do it again, you know."

As they lay together on the fleecy-bed that night, wrapped in a soft woolen comforter, fed, bathed, pleasantly tired, Io glimpsed something out of the corner of one sleepy eye. She blinked, and looked again. It was the glint of moonlight on one of the golden armbands of Equus, its wearer propped on one elbow, smiling down at her. "Do you need me?" she yawned, trying to wake herself up.

"No," he said, stroking her hair back out of her face, "I was just thinking."

"About what?" *Please tell me you're not one of those people who never needs sleep. Please tell me you're not contemplating sex at this hour.*

He shook his head, startling her into realizing he'd heard her thoughts. "I would not do that to you. I was thinking about what our daughter will be like, and what we shall name her, and about what gift I could give Pythos that would ever, in even a small way, repay him for forcing me into marriage with you."

"Ah, such a romantic way you have of putting it," she said, snuggling deeper into the comforter and rolling onto her side away from him. "Never underestimate the appeal of a tasssssty wood rat. Now go to sleep. If you peak tomorrow you'll need your strength."

CHAPTER FOURTEEN

I am just concerned that he is out there somewhere, frightened, in danger and perhaps injured," Kehailan said. "Almost anything would be better than not knowing."

Oonah Pongo smiled and patted her horse's neck as they jogged along. "I'm not going to tell you not to worry about Ardenai," she said. "I am going to tell you to quit being embarrassed by it. We're all worried, which is why we're all out here looking around – Belesprit in space and us down here."

"Thank you," Kehailan replied. "It was kind of you to come with me. How is your body holding up to the ride?"

"Parts of me are doing better than others by now," she laughed. "How much farther is it?"

He waved vaguely with his left hand and turned with the packhorse off the wagon track. "Not far. If memory serves me, we can cut through that gap in the hills. We'll water the horses and stretch our legs for a bit. It's a very pleasant spot to have lunch, and then we'll turn upstream. The main complex is only an hour or so from that point."

"You have a good memory. You said you haven't been here since you were a child."

"True. But in that spot, my father took me fishing. A young boy does not forget his first fishing trip, no matter what else happens in his life."

They rode in under the trees, and the shade felt good between them and the midday sun. The earth was damp and fragrant, churned by the horses' hooves. "Kee, may I ask you something?" Oonah asked, and was rewarded by one of his rare and beautiful smiles.

"Of course."

"We've ridden for two days, and you've spoken of hunting, fishing, and tracking. I'm confused. I didn't think the Equi killed things."

"We don't," he quickly assured her. "No animal is ever even touched, much less injured. It's just for fun – for the skill of doing it. The only time the Equi ever destroy an animal is if it endangers the lives of others, or if it cannot be saved. We have a horse like that on rare occasions, and sometimes a wild animal, but basically we're not into killing things...very often." he was leaving something unsaid, and she allowed him that privacy. She wondered if it had to do with the Telenir, and who, exactly, Sarkhan might turn out to be, and what might have to be done in that particular arena.

Whatever it was, she knew he wouldn't talk to her about it. He'd been broody all the years she'd known the man, and since his father had risen to rule Equus, he was downright sulky. Still, he was brilliant, and handsome. Tall, and athletic. Bonfire Dannis and Timothy McGill had both admitted frankly that he was a fabulous lover when he was in heat, and even when he wasn't, and he was a good friend anytime. The sexual prowess of the Equi was legend, and Oonah couldn't help wondering, the movement of the horse beneath her adding to her imagination, what it would be like to be bedded by Ah'ree Kehailan Ardenai, Prince of the Great House of Equus.

She glanced over at him, and he was looking at her, laughing quietly. "Sorry," he said quickly, "but if you were singing that at the top of your lungs, it wouldn't be coming through any louder. If you wanted to have me set my head against you, to have sexual intercourse with you, why didn't you just say so?"

She felt herself blushing furiously, and thanked God she had black skin. At least the chortling Equi on the spotted horse wouldn't know how discomfited she was. "It is in the nature of Terrenes to speculate about alien species," she said a tad huffily, and he nodded, biting his bottom lip to stop himself laughing.

"Well of course it is," he murmured. "I have wondered about you, too, from time to time. Perhaps when we reach our destination we could speculate together at our leisure?"

"An acceptable suggestion," she nodded, and they rode for some time with a deep silence between them, punctuated by an occasional snicker.

Forty-five minutes or so later, Kehailan whispered, "We are not alone," and pointed ahead. A grey stallion raised his head and whinnied a greeting. Spaced in the trees, three more horses looked up from their midday naps and called to the three coming in. They rode into the clearing near the lake, reined in, and looked around.

"That pavilion bears the Seal of the Great House," Kehailan said quietly, "and six chevrons to this side, so it is..." his voice rose with excitement, "the Captain of the Horse Guard! Is she alive, then? Could my uncle and my sire be alive, as well?"

From an outcropping close behind and to their left a familiar voice said, "We are, indeed. Welcome."

"Sire!" Kehailan exclaimed, leaping off his horse to look up. For a moment he saw nothing, then a tall figure dropped gracefully from a ledge between him and the sun, and strode over to him, arms extended. "Oh, Eladeus, thank you!" Kehailan whispered, and clutched his father to him. "I've been worried sick about you!"

"It is good to see you, my son," Ardenai smiled, holding him at arm's length. "And you, too, Oonah Pongo," he said, turning to the still mounted woman. "Ahimsa, I wish thee peace. Are you and that saddle a single entity by now?"

"I'm afraid so," she smiled. "I think it's permanent."

"Here, let me help you," he said. "Put your hands on my shoulders and push up." His strong hands closed around her waist, and he lifted her from the saddle and eased her to the ground.

"It's even better to see you than I thought it would be," Oonah groaned. She took her hands off his shoulders, and put her palms flat on his chest. "Are you well?"

He nodded, bending to kiss her forehead. "Yes. Thank you, my friend."

"Good," she murmured, and let herself sink the rest of the way to the grassy floor of the meadow, sighing with relief.

"Sire," Kehailan said, clearing his throat and stepping forward, "How long have you been here? Are you alone?"

"The captain and I have been here most of a week," he said, not quite meeting Kehailan's gaze.

"Planning strategies, one assumes. Or were you fishing?"

"Ah...both. So to speak," Ardenai replied. He was obviously tempted to tease, but too uncomfortable with his son to do so. "Come, refresh yourselves. Have something to eat and drink. Oonah Pongo, a swim in that cool lake and some leisure time in one of those hot pools might be excellent for what ails you. Kee, you haven't ridden for a while, would you like a soak?"

"Given the seriousness of the challenge you are facing, I'm surprised to find you here," Kehailan said. "Wouldn't this be more efficiently accomplished with others assisting you?"

"Was that a yes, or a no?" Ardenai asked, resisting the urge to guffaw.

"I rushed here, assuming we had a war to fight," Kehailan said testily. "Since when do you have time for such leisurely activities, Firstlord?"

"Since I dragged him half dead out of a cleomitite mine," Io smiled. "Doctor's orders. Hello, Kee. How are you?" She had come from the lake, shrugging into her robe and wringing out her braid as she hurried up behind them, and now she hopped briefly from one foot to the other, jarring the water from her elfin ears and smiling at Oonah. "There we go, now I can hear. Ahimsa. I wish thee peace."

"Oonah Pongo," Ardenai smiled, putting an arm around Io's shoulders, "this is Abeyan Ah'riodin Ardenai, Captain of the Horse Guard of the Great House of Equus. Io is also my new bride."

"Congratulations!" Oonah laughed, clambering to her feet. Kehailan turned on his heel and walked back toward the horses.

Ardenai realized his mistake too late. He winced, but said nothing lest he embarrass his wife and Oonah as well. He took his eyes off his son, forced a smile and returned his gaze to the women.

"I'm pleased to meet you," Oonah said, either not seeing or not acknowledging the sudden rift. "And I'm very happy for both of you!"

"Ardenai speaks highly of you," Io said, smiling. "And he's right. A swim and a soak will do you good. Come on, let's get you out of those riding clothes and into robes. I assume swimming in your skin is to your liking?"

"Absolutely," Oonah replied, turning with Io toward the tent. She dropped her voice and Ardenai heard her ask, "We didn't disturb you, did we? You weren't in the middle of something interesting?"

"No," Io laughed as their voices faded. "The communication drums, you know. We knew somebody was coming."

Ardenai watched the two women for a moment, then turned and walked up to where Kehailan was sitting in the shade. He sat down beside him, laced his fingers together across his updrawn knees and said, "I am so sorry to have sprung that on you. I wasn't thinking. It was a bad choice on my part and I do apologize."

Kehailan gave him an up and down look from the corner of his eye, then looked back at the stick he was peeling. "Which bad choice would that be, exactly?"

"This is not good," Ardenai said, crimping a smile he knew his son would resent. "We've been together five minutes and already you have a list of grievances. Why don't you tell me what's on your mind?"

"Why don't you stop mollifying me like I was a five-year-old?" Kehailan retorted. "I've been worried to a ludicrous degree about you! I've been grieving for Teal and Ah'riodin, and yet here you all are, safe and sound. And you, cavorting amber-eyed with your little butterfly baby, who you rocked in your arms – calling her wife instead of daughter, wasting valuable time while the Telenir plan the takeover of Equus?" He made an angry gesture and flung the stick aside. "Surely you don't think Ah'krill will approve such a frivolous match?"

Ardenai's voice hardened a little. "I am Dragonhorse. Ah'krill has no choice in the matter." He turned to look at Kehailan and modulated his tone. "As you well know, son of mine, that time which turns the eyes from white to amber to red and back again, is not under the control of any man. I did not choose this time for the dragonhorse. It was chosen for me, and I could do nothing but respond. It was required of me to take a consort, and the time demanded one. Why not choose someone I already know and care for, who knows me as well as I know her, and whose judgment I trust and value? Io is a grown woman and has been for some time now. She could have said no, but she did not. She saw value in the relationship, just as I did. What's really bothering you, for surely it can't be this? This, even you should understand, being Equi, and born to the Great House."

Kehailan shifted on the grass and returned his father's gaze. But where Ardenai's was full of humor and concern, Kehailan's was charged with anger and resentment. "Oh, it can be this," he snapped. "Rank and privilege should not usurp morality. You have every woman on eleven planets at your beck and call, and you found it necessary to choose one who grew up under your own roof? I find this most disquieting on a very personal level. Perhaps too, it is that I have made a fool of myself in my concern for your safety. I guess my way here to find someone who is supposedly Firstlord of the Affined Equi Worlds..."

"Who *is* Firstlord of the Affined Equi Worlds, Kehailan."

"I stand corrected. I always do, don't I, Dragonhorse?"

Ardenai sighed and looked sad. "And so it comes down, not to your concern for your sire, and the continuation of the Great House of Equus, but to your ego, hm? It would have fared poorly in some of the places we have been the last weeks and seasons."

"You, and your golden-eyed companion of whom we hear so much?"

Ardenai gave him a look that was shading to disgust. "Ego, and jealousy? A very dangerous pair. Be careful of entertaining them, lest they turn and rend thee."

"You were not there for the whispers, the stares, the rumors, the laughter, the backbiting," Kehailan said petulantly. "You can only assume what this has been like for me. One minute my sire is a highly respected statesman, a successful keeplord, raising horses for the Great House and teaching his beloved creppia nonage, the next minute he's the absolute ruler of our continuum of worlds, and the minute after that he's a madman on the run. Try being in the middle of that."

Ardenai laughed in spite of himself. "You think I wasn't in the middle of it? You were not there for the knives, the chains, the scourging, the hunger, the worry. One minute I'm off to a meeting, carrying a shopping list from the woman I adore, who I think is my mother, only she isn't. The next, I'm having molten metal poured on my bare skin, the minute after that, I'm at the sharp end of a plan that's been forming for years to remove this conflict from our world and our people. You were surrounded by your friends, and people who trusted your judgment. I was blessed by the finding of just one companion in all of this, and in arriving here to find our plan and my dearest friends intact. I'm grateful just to be alive, however fleeting that may be, and I'd like your blessing to be happy."

"You have it," Kehailan said, and rose to bow stiffly. "Ahimsa, Dragonhorse, I wish thee peace. I'm sure my mother does, as well."

"Thank you," Ardenai sighed. Kehailan's eyes, belonged to a stranger. "May I offer you refreshment? Some lunch? We could talk."

"Since you are already occupied, I would prefer to ride on, I think. I will gather my horses and my companion and be on my way."

Ardenai shook his head. "No need. Take a fresh horse and go. I shall bring the ladies along later this afternoon, and the Horse Guard will bring the rest of the stock when they strike the camp." He stood up, busily brushing bits of dry grass from his riding tights to hide his expression. "You unsaddle your horses, and I'll get you a fresh mount."

Kehailan said not another word. He saddled the horse his sire brought him, checked his girth, and jogged slowly up river to disappear between the boulders at the north end of the meadow.

Ardenai glanced at the spot where the women were swimming, and saw them looking back at him. He raised a hand which they acknowledged before returning to their conversation. At least he didn't have to explain Kehailan to either of them; they knew him all too well. He did wonder if Io would be embarrassed, feeling that she was somehow at fault for this rift.

Probably she would not. Ardenai and Kehailan had already been at odds by the time Io was old enough to take note of such things. Of course they'd been at odds in no small part because of her demands.

He sighed, fighting exhaustion and the need for sleep. The females wouldn't want second lunch for a bit yet. He had time to rest. He rolled up three sides of the tent to form a large, airy pavilion, and flopped on the big fleecy-bed with a groan of relief.

He'd slept the best part of an hour when he felt the staccato throb of a slowly cantering horse carrying a superb rider. He put the palm of his hand on the ground beside the bed and listened, then smiled, and withdrew his hand. In a few minutes he heard the horse blowing nearby, and Teal's slow, gentle tenor saying, very quietly, "Ardi, are you asleep?"

"No," Ardenai said, sitting up, "I am pleased for your company, Brother Mine."

Teal pulled the tack off his mare and gestured her toward the others before coming to sit cross-legged on the floor of the tent. "Apparently we have been found by the SGA," he said. "I passed my nephew riding one of the horses you left with, so ostensibly he found you, as well."

"Oh yes."

"Charming as usual, was he? He was wearing his favorite look."

Ardenai nodded, and pulled his heavy black forelock back with his fingers. "Most of that was my fault. And you know him. You know he has no idea how to communicate the fact that he's worried. He translates it as weakness, which angers him, and that's what comes across. Nevertheless, he is here, and Oonah Pongo as well. She and my wife are probably in the hot pools by now."

"Then we may speak without my disturbing other, more pleasant activities?"

"Yes," Ardenai grinned. "I'm all yours. What brings you? Though you are always welcome."

"Pythos sent me to check on you. He thought you might need to talk, and he felt his perspective might not be adequate for this."

"Why is that?"

"He thought perhaps you would prefer to talk to someone like yourself, who has been less than pleased with himself, and doubted himself, and wondered about himself. Maybe done things some people would think was irrational."

"He knew," Ardenai said, looking away toward the lake and the hot springs. "Probably feeling a little guilty for setting me up, and then wondering how I handled it. What did he tell you?"

"Only that," Teal smiled. "No more. He said our love for one another would accomplish the rest. As you are my best friend, and as I had several things to speak to you about, I was happy to come."

Ardenai gestured to his right at a path which meandered into the trees, and said, "Shall we walk?"

"If it is comfortable for thee," Teal said, deadpan, and stuck out his hand to haul Ardenai to his feet before bursting into peals of merry laughter. "Come, tell me about your week."

They walked awhile in an easy silence born of companionship since childhood, while Ardenai organized his thoughts and Teal studied him discreetly from the corner of one jungle green reptilian eye. There was an amazing strength in the man, in the way he moved, his very presence. With the fact behind them, how could anyone acquainted with him not have known Ardenai was destined to be the Thirteenth Dragonhorse? Despite seasons of hardship and days of frenetic exertion, he was serene and smiling, exuding that calmness of spirit which drew children and horses to him. Even as a child, a very young man, he had been so. First with the horses, and then with the babes on his father's several keeps.

"I think," Ardenai had said at one point, "that I would like to be a teacher when I grow up. I enjoy having the little ones grow calm under my touch, and look to me for instruction. There's a good kind of power in that, and I like the feel of it."

There had been only one ripple in their friendship, and that had been the point where Teal began to take serious interest in Ardenai's younger sister, Ah'din. They'd always been friends, but the very second it crossed Teal's mind that Ah'din was a beautiful young woman, Ardenai knew it. He had postured like a young stallion with a coveted mare, and Teal had backed off rather than ruin their friendship.

When further schooling had separated the two friends, and Ardenai from Ah'din, Teal had politely made his intentions known to Krush and Ah'rane, and begun his long, gentle courtship. When the marriage had taken place, Ardenai had been no less happy than Teal.

Since Teal had chosen a career which often kept him away from home, and Ardenai had been asked to travel for a time with the diplomatic corps, they had decided to make a home together at Canyon keep, where Ah'din would be almost literally a stone's throw from her mother's hearth. Then home Ardenai had come on furlough, bringing with him a beautiful woman, and upon his final return, their families had blended into one.

Because of Ah'ree's delicate health, she and Ardenai had decided to have a child early in their relationship. Kehailan had been born, but no more children after him. While Ah'ree had always been indomitable of spirit, she had been frail of body, and giving birth to Kehailan put a strain on her from which she never fully recovered, or so Ah'din and Ah'rane both thought. A dozen years later, Abeyan and Luna had managed to conceive Io, and when Io was eleven, Teal and Ah'din had ridden the dragonhorse to produce their son, Criollo.

It was a joy, Teal thought, glancing at his friend, to know that there would once again be babes in the keep. Now that it would not bring such pain to Ah'ree to see others bulge with child, he and Ah'din would have the baby they had been wanting. Maybe a little girl this time.

"Io is settled with a child," Ardenai said abruptly, and Teal snapped back to himself, knowing his thoughts had been open. "It was an accident of course, like most of the rest of this has been so far. She says she is happy, which is a good thing, considering how kraaling careless and thoughtless I was. All those years with my wife, all the care, all the protection, never letting my guard down even for a second except when we were trying to conceive Kehailan, and now I've impregnated this poor girl before we got past the nuzzling and nickering."

Teal was trying for a straight face, but his merry eyes were twinkling. "Is this where I can wish you many blessings and an easy pregnancy for your wife, or would you like a hard right cross to the mouth?"

Ardenai blinked. "Do I deserve one?"

"It sounds like you think you do," Teal chuckled. "I, for one, would opt for the congratulatory slap on the back, myself."

"I'll pass on both," the Firstlord said, rubbing unconsciously at the whip scar licking his collarbone, but he smiled. "Thank you. We will have a daughter next year. Her name is to be Ah'leah."

"Isn't that the name Ree had picked out for a little girl?"

Ardenai nodded, veiling his eyes. "It was Io's choosing, not mine. And it is a pretty name."

"Yes," Teal agreed, and they turned out of the deepest of the trees to follow the path along the riverbank.

"It's not that I don't want the child," Ardenai said, still tugging fitfully at the subject. "I just...Io should have had a choice in the matter. She's just so...."

"So what?"

"Young. She's young."

Teal pinched the corners of his mouth. "She does not seem so young when she is leading us into battle, Dragonhorse. And she does have a well-started son of her own."

The comment rather startled Ardenai. He thought a moment. "No, not young. But she's..."

"Inexperienced?" Teal offered, still stifling a grin.

"Hardly," Ardenai snorted. "She has an amazing repertoire of..." he glanced at his brother-in-law, who was beginning to flush with suppressed laughter. "Ah...no, she is not inexperienced. I mean, not in affairs of state and such."

"You had to talk her through this, didn't you?"

Again there was a snort of amusement. "Somebody had to be talked through parts of this, but it wasn't her. If she hadn't stayed calm I don't know what might have happened."

"You are concerned that you frightened her?"

"This frightened both of us, period. No, I'm not concerned that I frightened her. I am concerned that I may have offended her."

"You don't think she knew what she was getting into?"

"Teal, I didn't know what we were getting into. I think the word I'm groping around for is, vulnerable. I'm afraid I took advantage of her vulnerability. She is in love with me, or so she thinks, and I used that."

They had paused to watch the blue-green river water cascade through a series of bowls and into a deep, quiet pool, and Teal gestured toward a flat, sun-warmed section of granite, washed smooth by the passing of eons of water. "Sit," he said, and Ardenai was grateful to do so. "Tell me how the days went."

Ardenai lowered himself onto the shelf of rock, wrapped his arms around his up-drawn knees, and fixed his eyes on the water. "The first day was amazing. To discover that I could care for as an adult someone I had cared for so much as a child, was an amazing thing. To have her make love to me – to know that she was my wife – to discover that she cared for me in such a manner, was amazing. The first day was Io, and me and then Ah'leah, and while it was mostly nuzzling and petting, and definitely full of surprises, it was good. That day my eyes turned red with the heat of a dragonhorse, though I didn't notice at the time, since I wasn't looking at anything but my wife.

"The second morning when I awoke, horrified at whom I was with and what I had done with her and to her the day before, and wanting only to escape to the safety and predictability of the past, and at the same time having the dragonhorse whipping me into such a frenzy that I could think of nothing but setting my head against her, hour after hour, unable to eat, or to drink, to keep anything on my stomach, or to ask lucid questions, that began to frighten me. And by that afternoon, when we should have been able to rest, it started coming over me in waves, like nothing I have ever experienced. Absolute mindlessness," he sighed, "and terrible pain. I began to understand the old wives' tales that say we mate with both females and mares. For the first time, I was glad...Ah'ree was not here to be subjected to any part of this." He shuddered and buried his head for a few moments against his knees before raising it again.

"My eyes turned completely black – the sclera, the irises – black as ink. It was like looking through a very heavy veil, and I was terrified. For that twenty-four hours, in waves that lasted four or five hours at a time, with perhaps an hour between them, I had absolutely no control over myself, over what I was doing – as far as I can remember, which is precious little – I lost it all. Any sense I might have had that as Firstlord I was more than just a man, I lost in those hours– and any residual pride ebbed away. All I had, was Io. And if I had not had her, Teal, I would be dead now. I think Pythos knew that. He wasn't worried that Ah'krill would force me into marrying Ah'ti or Ah'nis. He knows that, when the last word is said, she can't force me to do anything. He was worried that if I didn't have a very strong female for this, I wouldn't survive, and I'm afraid he'd have been right.

"Most of it is very hazy, and what Io did, I do not know. I'm ashamed to ask what it was. I do remember her holding my head in her lap and making me drink something, or maybe take something? More than once. Somehow we managed to survive it, though she was absolutely exhausted by the dawn of the third day, and so was I. I would have given anything at all to be able to sit down for a cup of tea with Io, to walk with her, or go for a swim, or a canter in the sunshine, or to discuss any subject rationally, but I had no control over what my body did to her. If she hadn't been Papilli, and in superb condition while I was relatively weak, I'd have killed her, I know it.

"And I know this. I will never subject her to this kind of an ordeal again. Apparently this is to be my lot every hundred and twenty days for a long, long time." He flipped his hands toward the water, but clung to the security of hugging his knees, and Teal could see that the telling was hurting him nearly as much as the doing. "While it may be my lot, it will not be hers. I will never ask her to go through this as my only mate. She may participate, or supervise, or watch, or be a million miles away, but she will never bear the brunt of another imperial dragonhorse. That will be the painful duty of other women – and myself."

He sighed, and gave Teal the ghost of a self-deprecating smile. "You know, it's funny. When Pythos told me this would be a dragonhorse cycle, I was upset, because I thought I understood what a dragonhorse cycle was, having been through a few over these many years. This has been far above anything I ever experienced or imagined, or dreamed of in my worst nightmare. This, then, is the dragonhorse of the Firstlord." He picked up a relatively large stone and tossed it into the foam at the bottom of the cascading water, noting that with enough foment, not even something of substance leaves a ripple. He did not mention this, but continued. "I wonder what all Pythos did to me during those hours in the cave that first night, what mechanisms he set in motion that had lain dormant so long? It couldn't have been simply the decoction they gave me before the ceremony."

Again he sighed, and Teal began to see the weariness, lurking just beneath the surface. "The third day?" he asked quietly, and leaned into Ardenai's shoulder to support him in the telling.

"The third day, most of it, was about the same, but by evening it was a little better. It was that night I began to perceive that I could let my mind go one way and my body another, that I could touch my wife's thoughts and take her with me away from what we were being forced to do, and go to another, more rational place. We made some plans for Ah'leah, and walked together places in our minds that were familiar to both of us, where civility was the practice.

"By morning on the fourth day, we were actually able to verbalize a little, or I was, and as the waves lessened in intensity and duration, I was able to bathe, and to keep a little something on my stomach, and to let poor

Io sleep a little from time to time.   That night, as I lay in bed, unable to sleep for fear I'd lost myself, and with myself, the woman I have chosen for my Firstwife, I began to perceive that the title of Dragonhorse is symbolic on a multiplicity of levels. Of course it represents the two most prominent facets in our genetic makeup, but it also represents the intensity the Firstlord brings to his heat. Horse on the outside, dragon on the inside, with teeth, and claws, and a libidinous eye, possessed of the need for sexual tyranny." Ardenai shuddered, and again buried his head. This time he did not raise it again. "Teal, for the first time in all of this, I am truly afraid. This is not who I want to be, nor what I want to do."

Teal heard the desperation born of exhaustion which tinged his voice, and dropped an arm across his friend's back. "Look at the Equi flag, Ardi. It's a running horse. Plain old *Equus Legatum*. A spirit in motion. No fangs, no claws, no scaly tail. It represents our culture and our faith, and it represents you, and our faith in you. I think you should stop dissecting a title twelve thousand years old and shrouded in legend until you've rested up a bit and regained your perspective."

"I'm sure you're right," Ardenai sighed, and chuckled without humor. "Although I'm afraid my perspective is gone forever."

"It will come back," Teal soothed. "Tell me about yesterday. Was yesterday better? More like a wedding trip should be?"

"Ah yes, yesterday. Yesterday when I woke up, I could see again, and my eyes were the average color for the average Equi in the average heat cycle, which, while it seemed abrupt, was of great comfort to me. We slept late, we had breakfast in bed and slept some more, and managed to keep the dragonhorse satisfied just with petting and nuzzling with both of us lying down, which was a blessing. And we talked about how we thought our lives would go once we got home, and what duties she wished to retain and which she would choose to forego as Ah'leah begins to bulge, which won't be for a few seasons yet. And we talked about Gideon, and Jilfan. Bathed. Had lunch in bed. Had dinner in bed. Went for a moonlight swim." By now he was beginning to chuckle.

"And this morning?"

"Like the first day, but without the strangeness. Just petting and nuz-zling." he paused, smiled, and sighed with contentment. "I looked at her, and I realized, she was not at all who I thought she was. And at the same time I had the comfort of knowing that she was exactly who I thought she was, and who she had always been. Eladeus, we made it, didn't we? We survived this. And she's still letting me touch her."

"Yes," Teal smiled, and for the first time during the conversation they really looked at each other. "The woman loves you, Ardi, and now you know how much."

"You know, I think I'm beginning to," Ardenai said. He pulled off his tunic, rolled it up and stretched out on his back in the sunshine, putting the tunic behind his head for a pillow. For a moment he was quiet, gazing up through the branches toward the sky. "I'm also beginning to realize I'm in for the ride of my life," he chuckled. "I do wish she'd hear me when I tell her that this relationship is difficult for me – that she still feels in many ways like my daughter." He sighed, and chuckled again. "In any case, thanks for listening to me whine. What else did you wish to discuss with me?"

"Well, this first thing is very much along the lines we have just been discussing," Teal began cautiously, "but there is an injustice which needs righting, and since you are here on Calumet, and since you seem to love this place and its people so much, I think it is you who can rectify the situation."

"You honor me," Ardenai said, "What is it?"

"Calumet has been a tribute world, then an affined world to Equus for nearly three thousand years. We have had this colony here, and this part of Calumet as our own personal realm for twenty-five hundred years. And in that time, not a single child of the Great House has been born to these people, not male nor female, nor has a child of the Great House been sent here to foster. The other nine Equi worlds can all claim princes or priestesses and Calumet can claim only horses."

"You are a prince of the Great House," Ardenai said reasonably, "Could you not have given of yourself to one of these women?"

Teal shook his head. "It is not my place to do that. I would set my head against a woman other than Ah'din only at the request of the Great House, or with a hetaera, if I was cycling far from home and needed one."

Ardenai said nothing, rolled over onto his belly, swapped ends, and drank deeply of the water, splashed his face, then resumed his previous position, giving Teal a nod to continue.

"These are loyal Equi, who chose to move far from their home world to settle this place, to serve the Great House. They should be honored in that. There is one, especially who is most worthy."

"Whom would you have so...honored?" Ardenai asked, the word sticking only slightly in his throat. He drew a deep breath, and tried to push the days of the dragonhorse from his mind. He could still feel Io shaking under him, sobbing quietly with exhaustion, trying to keep her knees and her elbows from buckling, reaching for something, anything, to support herself under the middle to help her hold his weight. He jerked to an upright position, startling Teal, who was beginning to relax beside him.

"What? Is he here?" Teal was immediately alert and looking around.

"No, not for some time yet, I think. I'm just tired. And you seem tired, too. Is something wrong back at the hold?"

"No, not exactly," Teal said, avoiding Ardenai's concerned gaze.

"It's just that?" Ardenai prompted, motioning with his hands. "Out with it."

"It's just that as a powerful stallion brings in the mares, it seems when the Firstlord comes into heat, all the females come into heat just from his proximity."

"Oh." Ardenai said in a small voice, and swallowed an involuntary and very embarrassed snicker.

"Which makes all the less virile studs randy, too."

"Oh," Ardenai said again. "I see."

"Which makes for a general air of preoccupation. Don't get me wrong, this is a fine time for such activities. It relaxes everyone and they'll be sharper mentally, and now that you're at least leveling off..."

"Enough. I understand. More than I wanted to. Tell me about this woman."

"Ah'nora, yes. You know her, I think. Old High Equi family. Many generations here on Calumet serving the Great House. A woman of great beauty, brave heart and deep kindness. Her husband drowned trying to save another family when the river rampaged through South Hold Village eight years ago. Her only child, a boy of ten, died trying to save his sire. She has stayed here because she is needed, and because this is the only home she has ever known. Another child would be such a blessing to her."

"I shall speak to her when I get back," Ardenai hedged. "This would not be a good time to settle her, but perhaps at this time next year. I shall seek her mind in this, and her preference."

The silence which fell was not a comfortable one. Ardenai could feel the weight of his kinsman's thoughts. "What I have said does not please thee?"

"Beloved, have you considered the possibility, however remote, that you may not be alive a year from now, or even a season, or a week from now?"

"I don't dwell on it, but it has crossed my mind."

"Then allow this to cross it, as well. You leave no High Equi sons. The Dragonhorse line of the Great House, except for one, tiny, lone priestess, may bleed itself into oblivion on a warground somewhere. I think you owe it to your people to leave at least one High Equi son behind, don't you? You are generative, she is in heat. It would be no more than a matter of foreplay for you, and adequate stimulation for her, to assure the line."

Ardenai shook off the look of distaste he could feel marring his features. Teal was absolutely correct, and absolutely proper in his thinking on this. It was he, Ardenai, who was having trouble thinking of himself as a tool rather than a person. This so called honoring of women by setting his head against them, did not feel like honor at all. It felt like sexual cynicism, like getting away with something others could not. "I, will speak to Pythos when we get back to the hold," he said.

"It is you who rule Equus," Teal said, a little impatiently.

"And now I do not know who my biological father is," Ardenai reminded him. "I think, in a blind mating such as this, it would be wise to check bloodlines, lest I settle my kin."

"Of course," Teal nodded. He mopped his brow, then pulled off his boots and stood up to drop his riding britches and tunic on top of them. "It grows hot," he said, and stepped off the ledge into the water. He bobbed to the surface and floated, taking a long drink before hauling out to resume his position on the rock. He sat, twisting the water out of his long braid and grinning at his brother-in-law. "Better. You do not think Sarkhan is yet upon us?"

"I know he isn't. Not yet. Perhaps a season or so."

"And when he does come, how will he come, do you suppose? How will he choose to try accomplishing his treachery?"

"I'm hoping," Ardenai said, "That we've left him precious few options in that category. This continent is hospitable, but it is sparsely populated in the extreme. There is only one CAC every five hundred miles or so. He cannot hope to add warriors to his advantage by sending more down in various spots and having them join up. He can come with less than fifty men, or so I suppose, if those on guard are judicious."

"Those who operate the CAC for our sector are currently being assisted by the Government of Equus," Teal said. "People are not entering in such haphazard fashion as they were a few weeks ago."

Ardenai gave him a wry grin, knowing he was referring to Ardenai and Gideon's own, somewhat unorthodox arrival here. "And if we look back at the songtelling tradition, at the Legend of The Wind Warriors, and if we assume that it carries at least some truth couched in its poetry, then we can expect a couple of things. This will be an extremely focused fight in the ancient tradition for the honor of ascension, probably one on one, Sarkhan and myself, probably with knives. It must be accomplished according to tradition, or it will not be valid. That is, if these people are as superstitious and honor-bound as we think they are."

"And is there any doubt in your mind that you can beat Sarkhan in a confrontation of that kind?"

"None. I have known the man for years. He is lean, but he is not powerful, and he does not move with any particular kind of grace, which makes me wonder what, exactly, he has up his sleeve in the way of treachery." Ardenai pulled off his boots, dropped his clothes, and stepped off the overhanging ledge into the water as Teal had done. He surfaced with a wide-eyed squawk of dismay. "Precious Equus, that's cold under the surface! You could have told me!"

"I wanted it to be a surprise," Teal chuckled. "Of course you have been here a week, and you did take a long drink just a bit ago."

"Implying what?" Ardenai sniffed, hauling himself out onto the rock and shaking the water from his hair and ears.

"Your lips should have told you something," Teal grinned, lying back and closing his eyes. "Numb though they probably are from overuse. This sunshine feels good, doesn't it? I think he's going to come at us with archers. I think, and so does your wife, that he'll station archers in ambush, and that if the fight isn't going the way he wants it to, he'll use them to a less than honorable outcome."

"His leadership, his Mahdi, or whatever it is – he is – they are, may not accept him if he has not won honorably. He may win the kingdom and lose the crown. Knowing his overweening ego, I think he will not risk that possibility."

"He can risk treachery, but not dishonor? You do know he's drooling, painted blue mad. He may not know the difference."

"Nik does. I am so sorry he's mixed up in this," Ardenai groaned, stretching belly down on the warm stone. "And yet I'm glad he is, because I know he's honorable, and I know he's sane."

"Sarkhan may just kill him first. Then he can use his forty-eight to kill our forty-eight, and then the civilians – no one to tell the tale."

"Not that simple. According to that legend upon which I am so kraaling dependent, these are people of honor. *They* would know the fight was won dishonorably. No, he'll have to make it look like an honorable win, somehow, to his own people as well as to us. Most especially, I think, it will have to appear so to Legate Konik, and that one Sarkhan will not kill so easily."

"A distraction, perhaps? You take your eyes off him for a split second, and you're dead."

"I think so. I think also," Ardenai shook his head slightly against the pillow of his forearms, "that other factors will play into this, though how I am not sure. It's just a feeling, a slight jitter in my brainwaves from far away. Will we be murdered here on this rock if we allow ourselves a nap, do you think?"

"Ummm," Teal grunted, already half asleep. "I've had this place in a very tight net for a few days now. We're in no danger."

"Uhhhhh," the Firstlord replied, and they slept until Io and Oonah hunted them up for second lunch.

Kehailan rose while the house was still sleeping, put on a briefcloth and a yellow robe and padded barefoot down the spoke which housed the bathing atrium. The door was partially ajar, and at first all he could hear was the gurgle of the hot spring as it welled up from the rocks and flowed into the first pool. Then, as he slipped inside, he could hear his father's rich, meticulously dictioned speech.

"Brilliant as any cleomitite, I definitely am not – at least not where Kee is concerned. I sprang Ah'riodin on him like a jack-in-the-box. I was shocked when you suggested it to me, but somehow I expected my son not to be, as though if I condoned it, it must be all right and require no further thought."

"Which iss true," Pythos hissed.

"It's not, and you know it. I just don't say the right thing with him, and I don't seem to do the right thing. When I got out of the Diplomatic Corps, I chose teaching full-time as my primary career, and I think that has always disappointed him. First, that I taught at all, and then that I taught creppia nonage, instead of Final Form or Lycee. He thought I could have focused on something more important, like my computator engineering, or staying with diplomacy and taking another ambassadorial assignment. Something other than five-year-olds. I know part of that was his resentment of Io, and I know he had good reason for that. But, Pythos, I have risen to be Firstlord of Equus, and he's still unhappy with me and my choices. Why is that?"

Kehailan knew he should withdraw, that this was a private conversation. But something compelled him, and he veiled his thoughts as deeply as he could, and sat on a low bench within long earshot of the discussion. He felt guilty, but he was also fascinated. He'd had no idea his father even thought about him when he wasn't right in front of him, much less that he would take the time to discuss him with his personal physician. Who exactly that physician was, should have occurred to him, but it didn't – not just then.

"And thee blamess thysself for thiss?"

"Blame? No, not exactly. But when I cannot seem to get along with a student, I do examine myself, and how I'm approaching that child. Kehailan is no child, as he pointed out yesterday, but he is young yet. I need to rethink my approach. I must be doing something wrong."

"Perhapss not. Then what?"

"Then nothing has changed. Ouch! But I am being asked to bring another son into the world, and I can't seem to get along with the one I already have." There was a pause. "I said, *ouch!* That means stop!"

"No. Sstop, means sstop. Iss it painful when I do that?"

"I think I said so."

"And that?"

"Tender."

"The fact that nothing mechanical functionsss on thiss planet iss working againsst thee right now. Thy back iss sscarring badly, esspecially thiss deep laccceration againsst thy neck and collarbone. Until I can get thee home, I cannot help thee."

"If there's nothing you can do for them right now, why are you try-ing to remove them with scrubsand?"

"Sstill cranky, yess?"

"Why, because I wish to retain my epidermis? That's not cranky, that's rational."

"I ssee the little fisshies have been nibbling here and there," Pythos teased, flicking his tongue against Ardenai's collarbone.

"Stop it!" Ardenai exclaimed, batting water at the doctor. "We're here to discuss this thing with Ah'nora, not my sex life."

"That, too, will be part of thy ssex life, and I do think Teal makess a good point, my hatchling. I do. I'm going to assk that thee do thiss *thing*, as thee putss it."

"How hard will it be to check the bloodlines to make sure it's a good match? I do not have a great deal of time to spend on this right now."

"It will take no time at all. Sshe iss a good match for thee, and ccer-tainly a desserving one. Sshe will be exsstremely pleassed. It wass kind of Teal to think of her."

"He is a kind man. I love him with all my heart. My sire...Krush, that is...loves him like a son. But you know that. Many years have you kept with us, slept in our myrianotus trees and beside our hot pools." Ardenai sighed, and Pythos rolled one eye to fix him in his gaze.

"What botherss thee, Beloved?"

"It's just that I can't help wondering, and I will always wonder, who my sire really is. Who could be more perfect than Krush? Who could I ever have loved as much as I love him?"

"I can tell thee that," said the old dragon in an offhand manner, and Ardenai turned to him with his mouth open.

"Then, why haven't you?"

"Thee hassn't assked."

It was true. Ardenai had to admit it. "And if I asked thee now, Phy-sician Pythos?"

"I would tell thee. Thou art Firsstlord of Equuss. It iss thy right to know whatever thee wisshes, or at leasst within thy understanding to know, whether the knowing iss good for thee or not."

"Then I will ask. Who is my father?"

"It iss I," the serpent hissed quietly. "I am thy father."

The revelation shocked Ardenai's highly disciplined mind, and left Kehailan's wide open. "Perhapss, thy sson sshould join uss at thiss point," Pythos suggested. "He waitss politely without for hiss turn to usse the poolss."

"By all means," Ardenai managed, and called, "Kehailan, good morning to you. We were just having a most fascinating conver..."

"He knowss," said the doctor.

"About you?"

"No. About the converssation."

Kehailan nodded to his father, then to the physician, dropped his robe and waded into the soaking pool to sit a few feet away from Ardenai and Pythos, looking slightly embarrassed. "I did not mean to eavesdrop," he said, and Pythos inclined his head graciously.

"I know that. We are pleassed to have thee join uss."

As Ardenai turned slightly and the angry, welted scars on his back became apparent, Kehailan remembered his self-centered comments of the day before, and was ashamed. "Sire," he began, "I would take back my words from yesterday."

"And I mine," Ardenai smiled absently. "But this one, this long green fellow here, has just said the most extraordinary thing to me. Please, do go on."

"Thee asssumess there iss more?"

"I know you," the Firstlord smiled. "There has to be."

"And there iss," the old physician smiled, flicking Ardenai gently with his tongue. "Thou art my sson, mine own hatchling. I placced thee within thy mother'ss womb at the time appointed. Never did an Equi nobleman sset his head againsst her. Seven hundred yearss ago wert thou given into my keeping. Six hundred yearss I carried thee within my body. More preciouss to me wert thou than life itsself. Ccenturiess we sspent together, ssleeping, sstudying, waiting for our time to come."

Ardenai's face was filled with wonder as he gazed at the old physician in front of him. "Of course," he breathed, and his face lit with a smile. "For that reason art thou both male and female. I...am the seed of Ah'jin Kehailan Morning Star, Firstlord of Equus. The Twelfth Dragonhorse!"

"Indeed," the old serpent replied, hissing with delight. "It wass of ssuch amussement to me that you and Ah'ree named your sson for him, I nearly told thee then, just from the wondrouss order of it all. And when thou art two hundred yearss old, as thy father wass, a sson will be lifted from thee, and placced in another jusst like me. And long years will sshe keep with him insside her, and sshe will carry him, and nourish him, and educate him, until it iss time to implant him into a priestesss of the Great Housse. And *he* will do sso, and become thy sson'ss physsician."

"And thou hast cared for me all these many years, my father. Thank you. I am more deeply in your debt than ever I can repay thee, not with love, nor devotion nor goods. And I can do nothing but beg yet another boon of thee, which is one of the reasons I asked you to bathe with me this morning."

"Anything," the serpent hissed, flicking Ardenai with his tongue.

"Would you replace those beautiful python chain tattoos which graced my arms these past seasons? I do miss them, and I would wear them to honor thee."

"Oh, Ardenai," the physician laughed. "Oh yess! It would pleasse me to do that for thee, now, thiss very day, if thee sso dessiress. You did like them after all! I am ssssso pleasssssed."

"This very day," the Firstlord smiled.

Perhaps not as tasty as a wood rat, but certainly a more lasting gift, and one Io had heartily agreed to when they'd finally thought of it.

"Why," Kehailan began, and both Ardenai and Pythos jumped a little. They'd forgotten his presence. "Why does no one else seem to know, with all the history floating around, that this is how the Firstlord is passed?"

"Becausse it is a most ssacred and anccient ssecret kept by the Eloi and Mountain hold. Only the Firsstlord knowss, his physsician father, and the High Priestess herself," the serpent replied. "And a very sselect few otherss."

"And now I know. What's to stop me from blurting it out in a weak moment? And would it hurt anything if I did?"

"If thee did what?" Pythos asked.

"If I…" Kehailan looked momentarily puzzled. "If I…. How strange, I seem to have lost my train of thought. Ah yes, there it is. If I said anything yesterday to offend you, Sire, I am sorry."

"Apology accepted," Ardenai said softly, and realized with regret that his conversation with Pythos would have to be put on hold. "Think nothing more of it. You did say something yesterday which puzzles me, and I would like to revisit it, if it does not offend you."

"Whatever you wish."

"You said you 'guessed' your way here. Has Hadrian Keats said nothing to you?"

"Keats?" Kehailan frowned. "No. He knows, of course, that he must have treated you at some point, because Josephus says he did. But as to any memory of it, I assume you…" Kehailan made a slight erasing gesture, and Ardenai nodded.

"I did. But I also left a message which should have surfaced in the appropriate time frame. I was exhausted, and quite ill at the time. I probably confused things somehow. Ten years from now, when he is vacationing by the sea, Keats will snap his fingers and smile, and say, 'Ardenai is on Calumet,' and rattle off the proper coordinates."

CHAPTER FIFTEEN

"You're sure?" Eletsky mumbled, peering up at his Chief Medical Officer out of one sleepy eye and slapping around for his glasses. "Did this just hit you, or what?"

"Would I be standing here in the middle of the night in my skivvies if it had come to me last evening at dinner? I tell you, Kehailan was right, and he and Oonah went off in the right direction. Ardenai is on Calumet, along with two squads of Equi Horse Guard, Master Teal and Ah'riodin, hopefully."

"Hopefully?" Marion echoed, sitting up in bed and putting on his glasses. He blinked to focus on Keats. "There you are. Why hopefully?"

"How should I know? It's just there, that uncertainty about those two. Look, he's obviously used my brain for a scratch pad, and this is what it says. He's on Calumet, and we're supposed to join him – six of us. I assume, since Kehailan and Oonah Pongo are already there, four more of us. Specifically, you, me, Winslow and Tim."

"Too bad we didn't catch Konik," Eletsky said, shrugging into his robe, "he has led us a merry chase. However, I think we'd better stop looking for him and break orbit. I'll call up the landing parties and get us under way. Hadrian, thank you. You can go on back to bed if you want."

"That's it? Go on back to bed? I want to strangle that man. What the hell right does he have to invade my body and pry into my thoughts? Replace my thoughts with his thoughts, after I told him not to? I resent it."

"You should be flattered that the Thirteenth Dragonhorse entrusts you with such things," Marion said, half joking, and received a deadly glare from the doctor.

"If he trusted me he wouldn't have imbedded it in my subconscious now, would he?" Keats snapped. He gave Eletsky a wave off and wandered back to his quarters.

▲ ▲ ▲ ▲ ▲ ▲ ▲

Ardenai slipped into the warm, fragrant kitchen and smiled at the woman who was working there, shaping yeast rolls and setting them in pans which another, much younger girl was sprinkling with cinnamon and sugar and moving aside to rise. Ah'nora was a tall woman, and slender, though not small, with soft brown hair, and the remarkable green eyes and clear skin of the High Equi.

It caused the Firstlord to marvel yet again at how alike they all were. Their skin tones ranged from fair, like hers, through light olive, like his, to a rich mid-olive like Krush, and Teal's son, Criollo. The hair color differed from honeyed browns to blue-black, with the occasional blond or redhead. The height and weight varied a bit, but they were amazingly homogenous, and he'd always wondered if they had looked vastly different in the long-ago time, before eons of peace and prosperity had brought travel, and under-standing, and matings near and far which had blended them into a deep and serene gene pool.

"Ardenai Firstlord, may I serve you?" Ah'nora asked, brushing flour from her hands and moving his direction.

"I would not have you stop what you are doing," he smiled, coming back to the present, "but when you have finished, I would speak with you," he jerked his chin, "by the garden pool."

He was pottering in the flowers, snapping the spent heads off rohanth bushes when she joined him a few minutes later. "Are these always so lush and beautiful," he asked, "or is this an especially good year for rohanth?"

"They always do well," Ah'nora said, watching his face and won-dering what was on his mind. "They don't seem to care what the weather does. They go on about the business of blooming."

"As you do, or so I hear." He'd been working on what he was going to say, and he hoped he'd remember it. He went to the garden bench, patted the seat beside him, and turned to her as she sat, rather shyly, beside him. "Ah'nora, thank you for the provisions you sent with Io and me. They were deeply appreciated."

"It is what I do," she smiled. "You are welcome."

"It is not all you do," he replied. "You take responsibility for the running of this hold, as did thy mother before thee, and hers before her."

"Yes, for many generations," she said proudly.

"And yet you have not been properly honored for that by the Great House," Ardenai said. "No priestess nor Firstlord has fostered here, no prince nor princess has been born here of his get. I would ask your permission to change that."

Her eyes were bright, and her smile spread across her gentle features. "You would send us a nursling to foster? We would be deeply honored, Dragonhorse."

"No," Ardenai said. "I would not send a child here, but would ask instead that a child come from here, or better yet, stay here. A prince of the Great House."

She looked puzzled, yet her hands were beginning to tremble in her lap. "I...don't understand," she said quietly.

"I would have you bear a son for the Great House," he said. "My son," and she began to cry. Ardenai sat there, looking calm, patting her hand and smiling at her, while every fiber of his being demanded that he run as fast as he could in the opposite direction. Still, while his brain might be his own again, his loins recognized this as a very attractive female, and he knew she would let him mount her. He fought the conflicting emotions within him, wishing he had on robes instead of those kraaling tight riding britches, knowing he couldn't just jump her on the spot – knowing at some deep and ultimately calming level that this truly was an honor for her, and a duty for him, and a hedge against extinction should anything happen to him in the near future. If necessary, this tiny bundle of cells would live seven hundred years in the womb of a serpent to be born as the Fourteenth Dragonhorse.

Ah'nora wiped her eyes and took a steadying breath. "You do me a great honor. I accept," she said quietly, and flashed him a truly lovely smile.

"Thank you. I shall have Io attend us." Ardenai rose from the bench. "You will not have to be alone with me, nor will it be a long process, I promise," he said, and bowed as he left her.

Io, too, had mixed emotions about having her bridegroom set his head against another so soon. But it was practical, for more than one reason. Ardenai's ancillary testes were still flooded with motile sperm of both sexes and he could accomplish the mating in a matter of minutes. The thought of watching him mount another was titillating, and she entertained it as she watched her husband stride away from Ah'nora to their chambers. This was something she'd have to get used to, she supposed. Something both of them would have to get used to. She applied a smile, and walked to where Ah'nora was still sitting on the garden bench. "Come with me," she said, and Ah'nora jumped noticeably.

"So soon?"

"Did you want longer to anticipate this?" Io asked, sincerely wanting to know.

"I...no. Actually, I won't be able to think of another thing anyway, with this on my mind. It's best accomplished now, isn't it?"

"It would seem so," Io said, and held out her hand. "Come, let me bathe thee."

Certainly Ah'nora was not dirty, but it was the ceremonious thing to do, and often the oil stimulated arousal. The woman was in heat, as were most of the females in the hold, and Io crimped a grin as she remembered Teal's gentle teasing over lunch the day before, preparing her for what she would find when they arrived back. It amused her to think that the Equi had to cycle to be generative, but then she was Papilli, and already settled with a tiny princess of her own.

She brushed and braided Ah'nora's long hair, dressed her in a pale green robe, and led her by the hand into the ithyphallic chamber which adjoined the bathing pools. The art on the walls, the rugs on the floor, the furnishings, all spoke of overt sexuality, their only purpose to stimulate the libido and make one receptive to sexual intimacy. Io wasn't even being mounted, only watching, yet she could feel sharp waves in her lower abdomen, and her anterior clitoridis, the more sensitive of the two, began to pulse. She could wait. Ardenai was still in heat. Her turn would come very shortly after Ah'nora's, or she missed her guess.

"Sit," Io said, gesturing toward a low, narrow-seated but comfortable chair, one made for a woman to straddle to sit in a man's lap. Ah'nora perched on it, smiling nervously and shaking like a leaf in the wind. It made Io ask, "You have done this before?"

"Oh yes," Ah'nora said. "I was married, and had a little boy, but my family was lost to me. Now, I shall have another. Thank you."

"You are most welcome," Io smiled, and sat nearby. "You are not afraid of being hurt, are you?"

"No. A man with eyes like that, and a mouth like that, would never hurt a woman."

Io nodded and looked away, a sharp pang of jealousy lancing through her. "Perhaps, you would be more comfortable if I left you alone with the Firstlord?"

It was that comment Ardenai heard as he entered the chamber, and he smiled and crooked a finger at her to attend him. When they were outside he looked down at her with a scowl and hissed, "You're not thinking of leaving me alone with her, are you? Because that's just not acceptable. I don't know this woman in more than a passing way. I wouldn't know what – I mean, if she were to – please say you're not going to leave me alone with her."

"Relax," she chuckled, noting that his ears were pinned back with fear. "I was just having a few moments of jealousy. I'm fine now." She took his arm and scooted him back inside, smiling at Ah'nora as she did so. "I'm going to let you two get acquainted for a bit," she said, and sat Ardenai down on the priapic bench. She gestured for Ah'nora to join him, and then retired to a shadowed corner of the room. "If you need me, I'll be right here," she said quietly.

Io watched as Ardenai took Ah'nora's hands and spoke quietly to her for a few minutes, then carefully placed his forehead against hers – sending his thoughts and his desires to her, reading hers in return. He'd said he was going to do that. "It's not going to be like it was for that poor young priestess," he'd said firmly. "I will not have intercourse with another before I've set my head against her. I want Ah'nora to enjoy this, and to come out of it feeling like a person, not an object."

It was obvious the first part was working well. The woman was breathing harder, and her mouth was open, though Ardenai's did not seek it. He did unfasten the top of her robe to caress her breasts, then unfastened the bottom half, slid it off her shoulders and dropped it to one side. He made no more than a subtle gesture, and she moved obediently to position herself for him.

Io looked away, then forced herself to look back, hearing her husband's irritated voice during the morning's discussion. "This is not about you and me and our relationship, Io. This is about Equus. About my duty to her as Firstlord, and your duty to her as Firstwife. One of my duties is to assure the line, and one of your duties is to assist in the matings. It doesn't say anywhere that we have to like it, but we might as well, since, one way or another, we're going to be doing this for a long time."

His robes were on the floor, his lean, muscular body stretched out across Ah'nora's as his teeth found her neck. What an extraordinarily handsome man he was, Io thought, trying to ignore Ah'nora's sharp cries of pleasure. He'd always been handsome, without having to grow into it, without having it change the way he perceived himself. Ardenai straightened up and caught the woman by her upper thighs, eyes squeezed shut in concentration. He was having to think rather than enjoy himself, she realized, and was inordinately pleased by the notion. Ah'nora's groans, her body language, her panting breath, all said she was climaxing, and in seconds, he had her – a half dozen hard slams and a long, shuddering pause – and he draped himself lightly once more across her back to rest himself.

"Are you all right?" he asked softly, and reached from behind to stroke her forehead. She nodded, and he withdrew, immediately tucking his intromittent organ into its protective sheath, so that only the head protruded. "Come to me," he said, and when she got up from the bench to face him, he caught her up in his arms and carried her, laughing, into the next room where the cold pools waited. "This should settle the matter," he said, and waded in with a gasp of merriment to dunk her in the icy water.

She let out a squeal, then threw her arms around his neck, still laughing, and said, "I have a son, Ardenai Firstlord! We have a son. Thank you."

He waded back out with her, and Io was there to hand them their robes. "Ah'nora, I thank you," said Ardenai with a gracious nod and a kiss on the forehead. "Because things may be troublous for a bit yet, I think keeping this arrangement quiet for now would be safest for you and for the babe."

"I understand," she said simply. "I will say nothing."

"Then, if you need nothing further from me or my wife, you may go with the thanks of Equus."

"I am honored to have been of service," she said formally. She scuffed into her sandals, fastened her robe around herself, and nodded her way out of the room.

Io turned to go also, but Ardenai caught her arm and spun her back so that she landed against him with a thud. "So much for the business of hedging death," he murmured. "Are you still angry with me, my little blossom bat?"

"I do think this has grown out enough to catch it in an overbraid," she smiled, pushing his heavy forelock back from his face. "We should try it this afternoon. What makes you think I'm angry with you?"

"Oh, I don't know, a couple dozen things you said this morning. Maybe it was my imagination."

She made an apologetic little face, and led him over to sit with her on the recently vacated bench. "Please try to understand, Ardi. I have wanted you my entire adult life."

"And now you have me," he said. "Are you thinking that I do not understand the terms of our contract, Ah'riodin? I can assure you, I do."

"I would like to think you do," she said coolly, "and I know that you speak sincerely of this just being duty to Equus, but still there is this fear in me. And the fact that you need two more wives who could easily replace me in your affections, doesn't help matters any."

"It is something only you can fix, I'm afraid," he said, and bent to nuzzle her neck. "I must do what I must do. But as to what I want to do, and with whom, I'm like old Bartemus. Do you remember him?"

She thought a moment, and chuckled. "Of course I do. He was the crankiest horse I've ever met."

"Because you were not Krush," Ardenai smiled. "He was cranky with me because I was not Krush. He was a one man horse, and for my father, he would do absolutely anything, but as far as he was concerned, the rest of us did not exist except as moving shadows which had little or nothing to do with what he considered reality." Ardenai cupped her chin with one forefinger and tilted it toward him. "I'm a one man horse, Io. And I am yours now. I have promised it, and that makes it so."

She grinned up at him, and her hands slid inside his robe. "And would old Bartemus enjoy the pleasure of a little canter this afternoon?"

"With his usual rider and no one else? Yes, he would," Ardenai whispered, and nothing more was said about anger, or duty to Equus.

There was time for pleasure, and for a nap, before a dinner at which the Firstlord ate well, and laughed much, which pleased his physician. And when they had gathered at the main hearth for the evening, Ardenai dropped more wood on the fire against the chilly drizzle outside and turned with a sigh of contentment to pick up his glass of cider and contemplate the room. Kehailan, playing the big floor harp while Teal sat nearby with Catrio, mending a bridle. Four of the younger members of the Horse Guard bent over a table, thoroughly engrossed in a game of Vincere. Jilfan and Tarpan playing Tally Pegs with Pythos, and losing despite the odds. Io, closer to the fire, curled in a high backed leather chair, sketch pad in her hand, drawing various people in the room. Gideon, arms folded on the game table, staring at the chess board, waiting for Ardenai. Tarpan's new bride, Ah'keena, stretched out on the floor nearly under Ardenai's feet, engrossed in an old book of maps while Ah'nora showed Oonah how to thread one of the beautiful floor looms. The tall, Calumet mahogany walls, glowing in the light of the lamps. The ancient tapestries. The thick wool carpets spaced on the dark wood floors, the lingering fragrance of oranges and cinnamon.

"This night have I seen in my mind," he murmured almost to himself, though Io looked up and smiled. "At those times when I truly began to believe that I was too exhausted, or too ill, or too afraid to go on – when I felt one more step, one more stroke of the scourge, one more minute of aching cold or desperate thirst would be more than I could bear – I would see this room, with these companions in it. I could see them, hear them as I do now. I could smell the oil in the wood, and the cinnamon in the tea." He shook his head, and his eyes were veiled and soft. "We have not the victory yet, but we are together, and I am content this night. With thee," he said, looking at Io, "I am content."

"I am honored," she said, blushed, and went back to her sketches.

"And you, Gideon," Ardenai said, returning to his chair at the game table. "Are you content to be here?"

"Where would I be but where you are?" the youth smiled. "You have given me friendship, and guidance, and purpose. You share your home and your family with me. How could I possibly not be content?"

"And when this is over, and to be with me is to be in the rarified intellectual atmosphere of the Great House of Equus, then what?"

Gideon looked across the table at Ardenai and scowled. "If you're trying to throw my game off, you're succeeding. Dragonhorse, look around you. None of us wants to leave this place. It is serene. It is beautiful and fruitful and verdant. The food on the table tonight we gathered this afternoon. This is an innocent way of life, and we are happy, all of us. And yet each of us knows we must leave here. We must do what we came to do, and leave. We came here in service to you. We will leave in service to you, no matter where that takes us. Check. You're not concentrating."

"You think not? You think you can make gallant speeches, and woo my heart into betraying my head?" Ardenai pursed his lips and sat with his chin in his right palm, contemplating the chessboard. "Perhaps ... yes, you can. Perhaps I should trade places with Kehailan. This is a time for me more suited to playing the floor harp than gaming with ruthless Declivians."

Gideon smiled at him. "I will give you time to study the board if you will answer a personal question for me."

"You may ask."

He lowered his voice. "You...and Io?"

Ardenai gave him a strange look. "And what?"

"What?"

"I asked you first."

"Ardenai, can we start this over again?"

"Which?" the Equi smiled, taking a sip of cider and setting the glass aside.

"I'm winning the chess game. The question about you and Io, has been altogether lost."

"Gideon, it was never asked. Without some semblance of subject matter I can't answer you."

"I assume my voice was without sufficient innuendo," the boy grinned. "Very well, again." He tried for a deeper scoop in the first word. "You...and Io?"

"Ah ha. Um hm."

"Your move."

"Check, and mate."

"You were baiting me!" Gideon yelped.

Of course I was. It's a game." Ardenai laughed.

"Never lose at chess to my father and then reveal that you are displeased," Kehailan advised, giving the big harp a rest. "It delights him no end. Ardenai Firstlord, would you care to trade the harp for the chessboard? It has been too long since I have heard your music."

"Please," Catrio nodded. "But sing for us, as well. Sing us the Legend of the Wind Warriors."

Ardenai shook his head and laughed. "Of all the things I do not wish to sing this evening, that, is at the top of my list. I have studied it until I'm singing it in my sleep."

"He's not joking," Io said blandly.

"Then the Ballad of Wielkopolski's Battle," Tarpan said, and several others called for its singing.

"As you wish," Ardenai nodded, "but it does not lend itself to a floor harp. Is there a guitharp in here somewhere?"

"Over there," Jilfan pointed, then, remembering his manners, bounced up and went to get it for the Firstlord.

Ardenai sat, checking the tuning, and as he began to play the rollicking old song, and the others gathered around to join him, Io sat rubbing her belly subtly with the fingers of her right hand and thinking. *How beautifully the Firstlord sings and plays, Ah'leah. Can you hear him? And how everyone is drawn to him, knowing he loves them. He will hold you, and sing to you as he did me, and he will encourage your dreams and your ambitions, and correct your excesses when necessary, and kiss your hurts, and see that you are safe and warm. And you shall be beautiful, and no one will laugh at you and say you are funny-looking, because you will look like your father. And you shall have the finest education, not because you are a princess of the Great House of Equus, and the firstborn daughter of Ardenai Firstlord, but because your parents are citizens of Equus, as it should be. And hopefully you will have challenges, for they build character. You will be loved, Little One, and loving, like your father, and hopefully you will choose to serve the Great House of Equus, but in choosing to serve I hope only that you choose wisely, so that you may serve with joy.*

Kehailan, thoroughly embarrassed, was wondering if one single person in this room, if one single person on the whole kraaling planet of Equus had escaped being either in Ardenai's Creppia Nonage class or in his music history classes at Enalios Lycee. Those had always been packed to the walls. How else would they know such a ludicrously silly song? Couldn't they have chosen something a little more dignified than this old nonsense about a farmer battling Diabolus with his own pitchfork, and couldn't the Firstlord of the Equi worlds have insisted on it? They sang like they were in a Declivian tavern. Even Ah'nora had set aside the tray of sweet ammon bars she was bringing in to pass around and joined them, laughing as she learned the words.

And now, they'd talk about the meter, and the always fascinating fact that it followed the usual rhyme pattern of a ballad, being iambic pentameter, as opposed to the ancient songs, of which at least the choruses were usually anapestic hexameter, and feminine rhyme, wouldn't they? Of course they would, and Ardenai would ask them questions, and they'd salivate to be the first to answer. Ah, yes, there's the person who remembers that The Legend of the Wind Warriors is written in trochaic heptameter, masculine rhyme, which is rare, indeed. And then they'd sing some other song they'd all learned together someplace, the whole jolly group of them, like some bad joke of a camp for over-achievers.

Kehailan chose not to notice that he was in the midst of the most elite force of fighters his planet had to offer, and looked away in annoyance. It was then that he saw Io, and the slight movement of her hand, and he knew instantly what it meant. Because no announcement had been made, he assumed it was not yet public knowledge, though for what reason he could not fathom. He'd imagined Io would be shouting it from the rooftops. She bore the child of the Firstlord. Probably thinking about fine horses and beautiful clothes and parading the child like some pampered pet, letting it run wild through the royal apartments when the Great Council was in session. She had become Primuxori of Equus. She'd always been possessive of Ardenai in the extreme, and now she had him.

He remembered with distaste Io clinging like a tick to Ardenai's neck, defying Kehailan to try getting a moment of his father's time. And where was Abeyan, who had wanted that child enough to kill his wife to get her, where had he been in all this? Off on one diplomatic mission or another, tying up Ah'ree as though she were a wet-nurse, forcing Ardenai to give up the little spare time he had for Kehailan and give it to Io. And now she was settled – pregnant – with his father's child. The thought of it made him a little sick – the image he got of the two of them having sexual intercourse. He'd always thought of Io as the baby sister he'd never wanted, and now she was his step-mother, carrying the baby brother, or maybe the baby sister, he'd never wanted. There would be two generations of them to come between him and his father.

Not that it would change Ardenai's perception of his eldest son. Kehailan had chosen off-world pursuits, had chosen to be a tactician and technician for the SGA rather than the Great House, and it had sealed his fate. It was Io who had fought for entry into the Horse Guard, with Ardenai right behind her, rather than Abeyan, whose job it should have been. It was Io who had turned out to be the brilliant student, even with a baby hanging from her breast between classes. It was Io who had turned something as shameful as settling outside marriage, into a triumph in everyone's eyes, hadn't even been censured, and he knew who'd fixed that, though a marriage had occurred almost immediately.

It was Io whom everyone loved and admired, whom everyone thought beautiful and accomplished and brave. It was Io who had turned out to be the ultimate soldier, who had ridden with the Horse Guard to victory after victory on worlds where the people were so backward, the terrain so rough, the environment so hostile, nothing but the most basic of weapons and tactics could be used. And now Ardenai, who had always thought she was a pest, who had held her in his arms and rocked her, and changed her clothes and tucked her in bed, had set his head against her and put a baby in her belly. The thought of it made him shudder.

"Are you cold?" Ardenai's voice asked him, and Kehailan jumped, realizing the singing was over, and that his father was standing beside him.

"No. I was just thinking," Kehailan said, forcing a smile.

"It has been too many years since we matched wits across a chessboard, my child. Come, take Gideon's place, and let's play a quick game."

"Gideon," said Teal, beckoning, "I would speak to you of your riding lesson today. Come sit by me. We shall discuss again the body language of horses."

Kehailan and Gideon traded places, and as Ardenai set up the chessboard, and Io took a turn at the floor harp, Kehailan ventured, "Are you taking the boy back to Equus with you?"

"Certainly, if he wishes to go," Ardenai said. "He chooses to be with me, and I could ask for no better companion. He is honest and open and he learns quickly. For those characteristics he will be welcomed. He loves horses, and working in the open air. I think he may be the penultimate keeplord that seems to have skipped a couple generations when I was born, and then you. I think your grandfather will embrace Gideon with all his heart. I worry a little that he will find my station and his part in it too different from the life he is used to. I've thought a time or two of trying to prepare him for what our life is really going to be like on Equus, but I do not want to appear to discourage him, lest he think he is unwelcome. And too, I'm not sure myself what to expect."

"I understand," Kehailan said. Something in his tone spoke of resignation, and made Ardenai raise one black brow to contemplate his son.

"Are you sure?" he said gently. "Kehailan, if you need to discuss this, to be comfortable with this, we will do so. So much has been sprung on you these last two days. I've married your little brat of a foster sister, I've taken to my heart a ragtag boy from a backwater planet, who cannot compare to you in looks or intelligence, and yet I seem to love him – more than I love you – which is not a fact at all, but it is your perception, and therefore must pass for truth. I have tried a hundred times over the years to tell you how very much I love you, and respect the decisions you have made for your life, and somehow, you cannot hear my words, and I am sorry for that. But know this, Gideon is no more precious to me than you are, and I want you to be able to welcome him, comfortably, into our extended family."

Kehailan frowned as he did when a thought was new and perplexing, and stared at the tapestry on the wall behind Ardenai's left shoulder. After a while he looked at his father and said, "The young man saved your life, and for that, I love him. If you do not prepare him for life on Equus, and the myriad duties which will face him as companion to the Firstlord, he may get there, become discouraged and leave. Nevertheless, that would be his decision. If you attempt to prepare him, and so discourage him that he does not go with you in the first place, it has, in essence, been your decision. You care for him, and he for you. He wants to be where you are, wherever that may be. That kind of loyalty, that kind of love, is hard to find. I would say, do nothing to discourage it."

Ardenai sat with his chin propped on his thumbs, and his eyes misted nearly to black as he contemplated his son. "You sound like your mother," he said, "and you look like her...so much." He tightened his fist against his lips and sat, staring at the chessboard.

"You honor me by saying so," Kehailan said gently, then cleared his throat. "That does not mean I am going to let you beat me, Sire. I remember your tactics."

"And I yours," Ardenai replied, taking a deep breath to steady himself. "Things have not changed, not really. By necessity appearances have changed, that is all. Your move."

"You have spoken of this with Io?" Kehailan asked, trying to sound casual as he studied the board. "This order of alliances?"

"Yes, more precisely, she has spoken of it to me. There is much to be said for friendship and familiarity in any relationship, Kehailan. She knows where she stands with me in this contract. She knows me, what I will and will not tolerate. I know her. I know she does not care a scoop of grain for what I will and will not tolerate. From that lack of understanding we shall build a fire and warm ourselves." There was a thoughtful pause. "At least until I have to marry again, and again. Then she'll probably kill me outright."

"I commend you for not deluding yourself, Sire," Kehailan said, sucking in on his cheeks to keep his face straight. "But regardless of what you think you know, and what understandings you have reached, you have made the little fruit bat your wife. She is no longer a playmate, she is a partner. She may remain the Captain of your Horse Guard, but she is also the mistress of your household. She can no longer be above you in one area and below you in another, behind you in some aspects, ahead of you in others. She gave up the right to be tolerated as a child when she came as a woman to your bed. You have taken her as your wife; you owe her the courtesy of allowing her to be one. Your move."

"After that?" Ardenai chuckled, his eyes expressing admiration even Kehailan could read."Kehailan, you are as ruthless as Gideon."

"Thank you, Dragonhorse. Your move."

"Kee," Ardenai began. Paused. Moved a chess piece. "We have spoken of many things since your arrival yesterday. Some more pleasant than others. But you have said nothing about," Ardenai tapped his upper arm, his fingernail making a clicking sound on the metal, "these."

"Oh, those. Yes. Aside from the atrocious burn scars above and below them, they're very nice. I especially like the way they shimmer in the lamplight."

"Thank you, son. That is obviously what I was asking. Your move."

There was silence for a bit as the two men concentrated, then Kehailan said, "I talked to the woman who is your birth mother. Ah'krill, High Priestess of all Equus. Awe inspiring for me. And she wanted me to call her, Grandmother. Very strange sensation, let me tell you. But you, have always been my leader, my example. I could not look up to you more than I already do, no matter what you became."

Ardenai smiled without looking up from the board, and Kehailan could swear he was blushing with pleasure. "What more could a father wish to hear than that? Especially from a son like you. Your move, I think."

"Yes. And yet, I am the grandson of Ah'krill. I am the son of Ah'krill Ardenai Morning Star, Firstlord of Equus. My sire, is the absolute ruler of the most powerful government in the UGA. I must realize," he moved his knight, "that what was my example, is now example to Equus and the galaxy. Your move. I do not think I have even begun to realize what has happened. Have you?"

"No, not from a governing standpoint. I've had too many other things on my mind. I know that if I survive this, I will return to many questions, and to the final ceremonies which set me in place and perhaps hold me there against my will. Here, it is easy to laugh, and to admire the beauty of my young wife in the firelight, and enjoy the company of my friends, and play chess with my only son. Very soon, things will be different. Your move."

"But not tonight," Kehailan reminded him. "You have earned the peace of this night by your pain and your devotion." Kehailan eyed his father a moment, and gestured at the armbands. "May I ask how they put those on, really? There is no seam that I can see, and judging by the terrible scarring, I'm truly afraid that what we tell outsiders is true."

"It is true," Ardenai said gently. "A mold is put over the arm, and they are poured on in molten form. They are indeed immovable and imbedded in the flesh." Kehailan swallowed hard and looked away, and Ardenai said, "No matter, it is done. Perhaps in another few hundred years, when the next male rises to govern, even this will have passed from tradition."

"I hope so," Kehailan said, again moving a chess piece. "The thought of anyone suffering that kind of pain, of you suffering like that... did they give you nothing beforehand, did they not deaden your arms first?"

"They do it according to tradition, Kee. I lost consciousness near the end of it, or so I hear from Teal, who was with me, along with Io and Pythos and Ah'krill. I did not go through it alone, and I have no memory of it, really."

Kehailan looked at Io, playing the huge old floor harp, pink toes peeking out from under her robes, thick, red-gold braid covering her right breast, then looked at his tall, stately father, with his jet black hair and sharply chiseled face. "I can hardly wait to hear what your mother is going to say."

Ardenai broke his concentration to look up at his son. "Which mother, about what?"

"What Ah'rane is going to say, I'm sure will be positive, but I was thinking of Ah'krill, and what she'll say about you and Io. Do you really think she's beautiful?" He gestured in the direction of the harpist.

"I believe I've already said so. She is not beautiful with great dignity, as your mother was."

"She is not dignified at all. She has the endearing ears of a fruit bat, and eyes like those disturbingly blue flowers on a Sycharian saucer plant. She has chubby cheeks and a sunburned nose. Her teeth look big and white and brand new, as though she just cut them. She has entirely too much hair, all of it curly and disobedient, all of it the color of a fresh, ripe peach, which is not a color at all. Except for the shape of her, she could be ten years old, maybe less."

"Trust me," Ardenai said, casting a fond eye in her direction, "she knows things only grown women with experience know about...things."

"Sire, she may know *things,* but she looks like an elf. You have wedded an elf. Face it. Put a diaphanous little gown on her, and gossamer wings on her back, and what do you have? A flickernick. A snowmallow. An elf. A pixie. One who laughs during affairs of state. You do not have someone even remotely passing for a royal consort."

Ardenai stared at Kehailan for a long moment, then all his air escaped through his nose, and he clapped his hand over his mouth to keep from laughing out loud. "Sorry," he said at last, wiping his eyes, "I'm sure you're trying to make a valid point."

"No, actually, I was trying to break your concentration," Kehailan said, and the twinkle in his eyes spread to a slow, good-looking smile. "I know what it is like to be lonely, and I am long since used to it. You are not. Have the heels on her boots built up. You'll look fine together."

"I'm happy you think so. Wouldn't want to embarrass the foals. Check."

Kehailan narrowed his eyes and glared across the table. "Then too, you might consider wearing her on a chain around your neck."

Ardenai thought about that later, propped up on one elbow, covers down around his waist, watching Io as she slept. She did have ears like a fruit bat. They were very large, very flat, with extended tips and delicate, fluted lobes. Even with her hair combed out full around her face and shoulders, those tips managed to peek out. In sleep her long, curled lashes brushed her cheekbones. Ardenai found her fragile, and elegant, which surprised him, and more beautiful as he really looked at her. He could also see telltale signs of encroaching maturity, little lines around the eyes and mouth, subtle things that were somehow comforting. Her body was hard and muscular, but it bore some scars, and a place or two where gravity and pregnancy had kissed her gently in passing.

His heat cycle was leveling off, and as he cooled a little, Ardenai became more aware of what he had done, and possibly what he had not. Had he been subtle enough in so great a transition between relationships? Even thinking about the word, subtle, made him shake his head in dismay. He'd had all the subtlety of a charging Gaknar. And had he been gentle enough with one so small? Heaven knows he'd not been careful enough, and the thought of another little Io tearing around the house was most disquieting.

At the same time he was thrilled, and he admitted it. When the danger had passed for them and they could announce that she was settled with a little daughter, what a joyful time that would be for them. Hopefully Kehailan would come to accept all this. He knew Io was settled. His mind had been steaming with jealousy regarding both Gideon and Io for half the evening, though he'd tried gallantly both to cool it, and to veil it, but from his father, he could not. And those things he'd called her with his outrageous teasing – Ardenai had to laugh, because they'd come out of his mouth first, years ago. Horrified. Standing in the doorway of the study with Io under one arm and a weaver's shears in his opposing hand.

"Oh, Kehailan, see what our little fledermaus has done to herself. What am I going to do? The child is bald! She is totally bald! Abeyan is going to have a few choice words to say if I live that long, which I probably will not. I number myself even now among the walking dead. Your mother is going to break my neck, and that's to put me out of my misery after the rest of what she does to me. Io, you – forget the saucer blossom eyes, child, I'm in no mood. You have done an unacceptable thing. Why?"

She had shrugged her little shoulders up to her ears, and turned her mouth way down, and giggled, "I wanted to. It's my hair."

"That is not an acceptable response." He'd heard Ah'ree's footsteps, back from her ride with Ah'din and Ah'rane, and heard her call to him. "We're in here," he sighed, and Kehailan had rolled his eyes and shrunk down in his chair.

"Well, hi. What are you three...oh...Ardi!"

"Oh, Ardi? Ree, is my hair gone? No. I have my hair. Kehailan has his."

"And this baby is bald, husband. Why is this baby bald?"

"Kee, run for it. Take Io with you. Ah'ree, sweet one, she got the weaver's shears and cut her hair off."

"She certainly did," Ah'ree had snapped, "every last beautiful curl. How could you, Ardenai? You promised you'd take care of her."

"I did," he'd squeaked. "I fed her. I put her down for a nap. I told her to go to sleep."

"You what? This is a baby, not one of your computators that you can do this or that to and predict the outcome! Would you go off and leave your creppia nonage class alone? You should have checked on her. Ardi, she might have cut the tips of her ears off! She might have killed herself, then how would you feel the rest of your life?"

This night, alone. As it was, he had Io, and a thousand shining memories. Carefully, so as not to waken her, he touched her cheek with his forefinger, and wondered what their daughter would be up to when she was three.

CHAPTER SIXTEEN

What do you mean, nothing works?" Hadrian Keats gasped. "When you said nothing, I didn't really think you meant *nothing!* Damn, Marion, I'll settle for a Declivian wheelcar, but this?" He gestured at a horse who looked no more pleased than he did about the situation. "I cannot ride a horse. It would be a catastrophe. I will not straddle anything with more legs than I have, who is capable of moving faster than I can. I didn't want to come in the first place, and now I know why."

"You could walk," Timothy McGill suggested, hiding his annoyance with a jest. "Beautiful day for it. Or we could make a litter and drag you."

"We could rent a buggy," Moonsgold suggested. "Hadrian could drive it, and we wouldn't need the extra horse to carry supplies."

"Good idea," Marion began, but was cut off by Keats' yelp of dismay.

"I have no idea how to make a horse pull a buggy!" Keats exclaimed, his voice rising unpleasantly. "I don't like horses. Why did that man want me along, anyway?"

Moonsgold sighed and cast a longing eye at the pretty buckskin mare he'd selected. "Actually, a buggy sounds good to me, too," he said, though his tone was unconvincing. "And I have the benefit of knowing how to drive one."

"At last, a rational suggestion," Keats growled, and Marion nodded.

"A buggy it is. Tim?"

"I'll keep the horse, that way I can scout around a bit."

"Oh, delusions of prehistoria," Hadrian sneered. "What do you think you'll find?"

"I'm not sure," McGill said, keeping a level tone, "but Kehailan is not the nervous type, and he's worried. We all know who just might be out here, and so I'm going to scout around from time to time, just for my own edification."

"Voices down," Eletsky said quietly. "Tim's right. We have no idea who's here and who isn't, or who may tell what to whom. Just because we're dressed like civilians, doesn't mean we're incognito."

"What?" Keats asked with a twist in his face, and Marion wondered right along with Hadrian why the Firstlord wanted him along. He was a chronic gripe. Always had been, always would be. He was sarcastic to the point of being caustic, and putting him under this much stress was going to pressure-cook his personality into a most unpleasant verbal stew which he'd be ladling out in liberal servings over the course of this mission. Nevertheless, when the Dragonhorse summoned, they attended, for such was the wish of the SGA, the AEW, and the Great House of Equus.

"Just get your gear and let's get going," Eletsky snapped, and walked back into the livery stable.

The proprietor, an older Amish gentleman, was both amused and sympathetic, and quickly fitted them out with a spring wheeled buggy. As though he sensed Winslow's disappointment, he sent the buckskin mare to pull it. He gave them careful instructions on how to reach South Hold, the stud farm owned by the Equi government, and the best spots to camp along the way. If he saw anything unusual in the need of these off-worlders to go there, he said nothing.

Not that races other than the Equi went there frequently, they didn't. Rarely, in fact. But it wasn't unheard of. Over the years breeders had come from all over the United Galactic Alliance to purchase those beautiful animals and be schooled in their care. The roads were well maintained, the Equi most gracious and hospitable. Their two-day trip should be pleasant and without incident.

"Amazing," Marion smiled, reining his horse up close to the buggy.

"We are less than five miles from a Controlled Atmosphere Corridor, yet we are in a completely pastoral setting. Look at these farms, Hadrian! Look at the draft horses working."

"Oh, and smell the horse shit, how romantic," Keats said dryly, so Moonsgold and Eletsky discussed the passing countryside and left the doctor out of it.

The day progressed to the steady drum of pacing hoofs, and the rolling farmland was left behind. The hills began to increase in pitch, populated by extravagantly wooled sheep and then to grow more heavily wooded and free of all husbandry. The buggies and riders on horseback became further spaced, and by evening, had pretty much ceased. The land seemed no less verdant and hospitable, just more distant. The New Order Amish Mennonites who had settled this sector long ago, preferred living closer together. The Equi, needing elbow room to raise and train their vast herds of horses, had settled the more remote sections. From here, they shipped exotic, sparingly harvested Calumet mahogany, freshly sheared wool, excellent sheep cheese, and their beautiful horses, back to Equus and the AEW.

Their presence, though unseen, was felt – their gently curious observation of that which entered their domain. Most of their group found it comforting. Only Keats seemed edgy. He sat beside the campfire with the others, seeming to enjoy the loamy fragrance and the sounds of a forest going to sleep. Then his head would snap around, and he would hold his breath a moment to listen before pulling back inside himself again.

"What is it?" Tim would ask, "What's wrong?"

The doctor would shake his head and mutter, "Ghosts. The wilderness gives me the creeps."

As much as he was annoyed, Eletsky was also concerned. Since Keats had been called upon to treat Josephus's crewman – whomever that might have actually been – his dislike of the Equi had risen sharply, and his dislike of Ardenai in particular had mounted to near hatred. It was something about which he would not comment, and Eletsky had come to the conclusion that Keats himself didn't really have an answer for his behavior. The whole bridge crew had felt it, none more keenly than Kehailan, and Marion was sure his Tactical Wing Commander would be displeased to see the doctor arrive with the rest of them. Not that Kee was any less sulky than Hadrian these days. He watched Keats jump again as the fire popped, and found himself hoping Ardenai was close ahead. Perhaps he could help unravel what was wrong with the man. Perhaps, and more likely far, he already knew.

They slept under the sheltering branches of a Calumet Sycamore, rose with the morning mist and proceeded. The night had been chilly, but the day warmed quickly to a pleasant temperature. It was humid, but not unpleasantly so, and both Marion and Tim rode with their shirts off, enjoying the sunshine against their bare skin. At noon, McGill succumbed to Winslow's sad face and traded the horse he was riding for the reins of the buggy. It lasted two hours before Hadrian's constant muttering negativism sent him begging back his mount so he could scout ahead. There wasn't much need, really. It was obvious they weren't alone, and they weren't in danger.

Three times in the course of the afternoon Marion or Tim pointed, and a rider could be seen outlined against the hills. He would disappear, and soon a deep throated communications drum would begin to sound. "Savages," Keats would mutter, and Moonsgold, who was sick unto death of telling him what an amazing system this was, and how subtly the drums were tuned, and how complicated they were to learn, would glare at him and say nothing, and then glare at McGill for taking his horse back.

An hour before dusk, and twenty hours into their trip, they heard a pleasant jingling, and a squad of Equi Horse Guard trotted around a bend toward them, the war bells on their horses' hoofs marking cadence in the evening air.

"Will you look at that?" McGill breathed.

Eletsky gave a low whistle under his breath. "I have always wondered what they really looked like when they went off to do battle. Now I know."

The riders who approached at a brisk trot were dressed very trimly

– high black boots and black britches, sleeveless silver-green tunics belted at the waist – throwing knives in sheaths on each forearm, crossbows and a quiver of bolts on their backs. These cool-eyed, bare headed Equi were obviously warriors. None more obviously so than the man on the big grey horse to the right in the lead.

"You honor Equus with your presence," he said, brushing one hand across the other, "Ahimsa, I wish thee peace."

Marion returned the gesture. "Ardenai Firstlord. I am relieved that you are safe."

"Thank you," the Equi nodded, spoke to his nervously dancing horse, and then turned to smile at the others. "Doctor Moonsgold, I presume, since you are the one I have not met. Timothy, always a pleasure to see you. And Doctor..." he paused, and Eletsky saw him start ever so slightly, "... Keats. I trust your trip has been pleasant."

He looked at Keats and Moonsgold for a long moment, then turned his attention back to Marion. "Kee and Oonah arrived safely. Please, ride ahead with me. I would speak to you. Tim, if it would please you, take my place in the ranks. Ah'keena, would you please allow Doctor Moonsgold the use of your mount, and bring the buggy along with Doctor Keats?"

The officer nodded, swung off her horse, and took the reins of the buggy. Ardenai waited until McGill and Moonsgold, both beaming, had joined the squad of cavalry, then gestured ahead, touching his horse to an easy canter which Eletsky matched until they were a hundred yards in front of the others.

When they were out of earshot, he eased his horse back to a walk and turned to Marion. "Your horse is getting tired," he said, and his face grew slightly troubled. "Marion, I have been aware for several years that I'm not Doctor Keats' favorite person, but the look of hatred he just gave me was downright alarming. What's wrong this time?"

"You don't know either, hm?" Eletsky muttered, and Ardenai regarded him discreetly from the corner of his eye before shaking his head.

"Let's don't worry about it tonight. When you are rested and refreshed we will try to figure it out. For now, let us speak briefly of other things. I would discuss with you that which we feel is about to take place, and what your part is to be in it."

Eletsky's eyes gleamed with pleasure behind their corrective lenses. "We get a place in the fray do we?"

"You get to observe," Ardenai corrected with a grin. "On behalf of the SGA. I wanted observers widely varied in their fields of expertise, and above reproach in their reputation. Let me tell you why."

That briefing took up the short distance they had to travel. It also gave Eletsky a chance to listen, rather than to talk, and thereby tacitly appraise this most formidable aspect of a man he'd always known as Kehailan's father – firm advocate of education – kindergarten teacher extraordinaire, to be sure, but mostly, kindergarten teacher. He corrected the thought. On Equus it was Creppia Nonage. Oh, the man was a genius, no doubt about it. What he knew about quantum psi computators shamed every so-called expert in the SGA, maybe even the UGA. He sat a horse like he was part of it. He could play polo with the best of them. This was the man with whom he'd sat at table, laughing and telling jokes, and discussing the best way to prepare kukkuk. This was Kehailan's sire. Ah'ree's doting, dutiful and occasionally submissive husband.

While this was someone Marion readily conceded intellectually capable of leading the Equi worlds, he was not a man Marion ever pictured galloping about the countryside wearing a pair of forearm knives and carrying a big crossbow Marion knew damned well he could use, and use with deadly force. Yet here he was, golden arm bands, elegantly savage python tattoos the length of both arms, hard muscles and broad chest, piercing draconic eyes and that profile that was by turns frightening and handsome. A man very much in his prime, and in his element.

With a movement that was nothing more than the twitch of a hip, Ardenai turned his horse up a tree lined drive, and his attention back to Eletsky. "You have been Kehailan's friend for a long time," he said, "yet there is much about us which you do not know. Here, in this atmosphere, where we are closer together and easier to question, perhaps you will find answers for those questions which you still have about us and our culture." He looked at Eletsky with that pleasantness about the mouth which was almost a smile, and modestly veiled his green-gold eyes with his lashes.

"Many things fascinate me, Ardenai," Eletsky admitted, "and I thank you for this opportunity to learn...." he trailed off. "Sorry, I ...."

Ardenai grinned at him. "Go on. It's all right Marion. I meant what I said."

"Good. So, why is this called a hold, and your home is a keep, when both of them are what I would call a ranch?"

"A hold is held by the government. A keep is held by an individual," the Firstlord chuckled. "What's really on your mind?"

Eletsky thought a moment, and looked a little embarrassed. "Things – your position – has altered so radically so quickly. The first thing I need to learn is what protocol to use with you. You're the most powerful single entity in the Seventh Galactic Alliance. My God, I don't even know how to address you these days without being offensive."

"My God is a bit too formal," Ardenai laughed, "But Your Most High, Beneficent, and Grand Lordship Ardi is always good."

"Nothing more? Nothing having to do with superlatively magnificent? Maybe just god-like?"

"That does have a nice ring to it. Add it to the rest."

"And if I can't remember it all, or if you have fallen in a well, for instance, and I don't want to recite all of it to get you rescued? Is Lord Ardenai acceptable?"

"Lord Ardenai makes me uncomfortable without 'keep' attached to it. To my own way of thinking only those titles are appropriate which describe a function, such as Firstlord, or Ambassador, or Teacher, and I must admit, I'm going to miss that one most of all." He sighed and looked away. "What you have always called me, is fine. I suppose Ardenai Firstlord, or Dragonhorse, if we are outside our circle of friends."

Marion nodded, and gave him a sympathetic look. "Well," he said, "whatever you've been forced to become, at least you're alive. We were worried about you, you know, and your son was quite beside himself."

"He still is," Ardenai snorted, and Marion chuckled with him.

"You need not have worried to such a degree, Marion, though any prayers were much appreciated. It was a strange time for me, but I put my scholarly talents to work, and I have always worked my body hard, so I was more or less prepared for such unexpected commotions in my life. After Ah'ree died, I did let myself get a little soft, and this has been the cure of all cures for that."

"You're telling me you were prepared for this?"

"Are you believing me?"

"Not for a minute."

"Then you are still wise," Ardenai laughed.

"This is beautiful," Marion said, gesturing toward the vast, sprawling sunburst that was the main house, then at the stables, the trees, the gardens. "A strange place in which to encourage a war."

"Not to encourage one, Marion, to remove one. Please, dismount and go inside. I will take your horse and put her away."

"I will take them both," Gideon smiled, stepping out the kitchen door. Ardenai thanked him, introduced him to Captain Eletsky, and then motioned Marion to go ahead of him into the house.

It was typically unpretentious and welcoming despite its size, and it put Marion in mind of Canyon keep, and Ah'ree's gracious presence. Ardenai guided Eletsky through the house, told him a bit about it, showed him his room and the bathing pools, then took him back to the great hub where the others had already gathered, and offered him a drink.

"Again, I bid you welcome," Ardenai said to the assemblage, accepting a glass from Ah'nora's tray and giving her a brief wink to make her blush. "For those who do not know them already, this is Teal, Master of Horse. Daleth is our Tactical Standard Bearer. Tarpan is Commander of the Secondary Squads. Jomud is our Master of Drums. As for she who is Captain of the Horse Guard of the Great House," Ardenai shrugged slightly and arched an eyebrow in Teal's direction. "She is probably out somewhere on that big copper stallion."

"She is not on the copper stallion," Tarpan said quietly, and at his tone Ardenai was immediately and obviously alarmed. "He balked at a fence and threw her. No harm done, though. She lit on her head."

"Nevertheless, I will speak to her," Ardenai replied, crimping a smile, "if to do nothing more than berate her privately for going against my wishes. Where is she?"

Daleth nodded his head toward the entresol, and there, with Oonah Kehailan, and Pythos, was Io. She was dressed simply in a sleeveless white woolen robe belted with a purple girdle, her hair swept up around her face and cascading nearly to her waist in back. She paused, opened her hands, smiled and said, "Welcome. You honor Equus with your presence. Ahimsa, I wish thee peace."

"Well, well, the little princess from the initiation ceremonies," Keats said, and because he was smiling for the first time since his arrival, Ardenai said nothing.

"My God in heaven, there's one in the flesh!" Keats gasped, looking at Io's companions, and Winslow Moonsgold was already laughing with delight as he hurried forward, hands extended in greeting.

"The Serpent Physicians of Achernar," Ardenai said quietly. "This one's name is Pythos, and he is many hundreds of years old. Shall I introduce you, Doctor?"

"Thank you, I can introduce myself," Keats said, and moved pointedly away from Ardenai.

Ardenai and Marion exchanged a glance, and Ardenai moved to the window, gazing out at the final moments of daylight as he collected his thoughts. "This troubles me deeply," he said at last, sensing rather than seeing Marion beside him. "I need to have a long, long talk with Doctor Hadrian Keats. The thing is, when I try to talk to him, he immediately throws up such a smokescreen of anger and resentment, that real communication is impossible." he paused and brightened slightly. "Perhaps he'll talk to Gideon, since he's not a telepath – at least not yet, but he will be, and a good one."

"You think it's the telepath thing that's got him spooked?"

"Oh, I know it is." His speculation was interrupted by the arrival of Io, who put her hands together and nodded graciously to Ardenai, then turned to the Captain. "Ah'riodin, this is Marion Eletsky, Kehailan's good friend, and commanding officer."

"Captain Eletsky," she smiled, and he couldn't help smiling with her. "Kee speaks of you as a brother, and I welcome you as such. If you will excuse me, Dragonhorse, I will go and see if dinner is ready. Our guests must be tired and hungry."

"Of course," Ardenai nodded, and the two men watched her exit, her bounty of curls glinting in the light from the gas lamps.

"Exquisite," Marion sighed. "Now why can't Kehailan see how perfect she is? Here is this lovely, warm, smiling person right under his nose. Why can't he fall just a little bit in love, and marry her?"

Ardenai's face stayed absolutely straight. "Perhaps because on Equus it is not an accepted practice to marry lovely, warm, smiling people who are already married to someone else."

"Oh dear," Marion muttered. "Forgive the social blunder, Ardenai. She just looks so...I mean, I can see that she's Papilli as well as Equi, but you folks are usually older than that when you marry, aren't you? Anyway, I do apologize. I should have known there's a lucky young man out there somewhere."

"In here, actually," Ardenai said coolly. "And you assume much. You assume he is lucky to be married to such a hothead as that, and you assume because she is a child, he is a child."

"Hopefully," Eletsky said, still looking after her. "I know the Equi think differently than we Terrenes do about physical properties. But fiery youth is best mated to fiery youth, don't you agree?"

"Fiery youth is relative, Eletsky. We Equi live two hundred and fifty years."

"And how old are you when you stop appreciating the potential of a woman like that?"

"That, you will have to ask someone considerably older than I," Ardenai replied. "And where did you get the notion that we Equi think differently about physical attributes than Terrenes do? Most of your notions of physical beauty and sexual attractiveness you got from us in the first place, along with your language base, two of your major religions, most of your literature and half your music."

"Oh no. Now I've given you the language thing. You win on that one. It's historical fact that Ancient High Equi is the base language for Greek, Latin and Old High German, but if you're going to start in again trying to convince me that William Shakespeare and George Frederick Handel were Equi Lycee professors on sabbatical, along with Gustav Holst and Aristotle, Ming Li Wei, and half the other people we revere, you're going to be talking a long, long time," Marion said.

"Come with me to the library of the Great House, and I'll prove it to you, Marion. See our plays, which pre-date yours by eons. Visit our music library. Look at the form and notation patterns and see just where your great classics came from."

Marion snorted. "The notion that most of our music came originally from Equi forms, is just nonsense. How would we have gotten them, discarding your crazy idea that they were brought by cultural missionaries? You had star travel far sooner than we did, so it's much more likely that you got your more sophisticated and urbane forms from us and carted them off home to Equus. Lycee professors on Sabbatical? Now that's nonsense, Ardi, and I don't care what plays and preludes you show me in your archives."

Ardenai, delighted to be taking up the familiar debate, was opening his mouth with a response when Kehailan walked over to join them. "I trust you gentlemen are engaged in some intellectually uplifting discussion," he said, glancing from face to face.

"Indeed," Ardenai said, and despite his best efforts, his eyes began to dance with mischief. "Until we changed the subject to anthroculturalism, your captain was lusting after my wife."

"Really?" Kehailan replied, ignoring Marion's horrified gasp. "Captain Eletsky, while I might be able to understand your attraction, I really must object. We Equi have definite standards about such things, and my sire can be formidable when provoked."

"Actually," Ardenai chuckled, putting an arm around Marion's shoulder, and giving him an affectionate shake, "It was a wife for you that he had in mind, Kee."

Kehailan just closed his eyes and cringed. "Oh, no, no-no. She is better suited for a man of Ardenai's passion," he said. "You have been the butt of one of my sire's merciless teasings, and you have acquitted yourself well. I commend you."

"I'm truly confused!" Eletsky sputtered, beginning to laugh. "Is she really..."

"Yes," Ardenai replied. "She is. A fact I think I shall try to keep from Doctor Keats for the moment. Perhaps if he does not realize to whom she is wed, he will talk to her. We need to find out what's wrong with him."

"Aside from the obvious," Kehailan muttered, patting his own backside, and Io called them to supper.

Afterward, when their meal had rested and the house grew cool, Ardenai suggested they adjourn to the bathing pools to relax and confabulate before retiring. The boys were made welcome, and Pythos encouraged Hadrian Keats to join them, as well. "Thiss iss an anccient cusstom. Here thee will learn much, and come away clean in the bargain. It iss my favorite time of the evening."

Keats considered this proposal. On the one hand, he had no desire to be in the company of Equi, but on the other hand, he was face to face with one of the serpent physicians of Achernar, which was a prestigious occasion. What questions might he answer if cajoled? What could be learned from this ancient personage? Keats thought a moment, nodded agreement and followed Pythos, Moonsgold loping annoyingly alongside.

What both Hadrian Keats and Marion Eletsky had expected to be a council of war with Ardenai snarling at its head, turned out to be a discussion of philosophy and ideals, led mostly by Pythos. They touched on the Equi way of looking at things as was to be expected, but mostly it was a discussion of absolutes which knew no cultural boundaries.

Ardenai sat quietly between Gideon and Jilfan, leaning close to answer their questions as the conversation progressed. "Please clarify that," he would ask from time to time, one assumed not for his own edification, and Pythos, or whomever was talking at that point would do so.

Here, now, Ardenai was a scholar – a teacher – concerned with the education of the boys beside him. He was a gentle person, not a warrior. He was the laughing, devoted keeplord Eletsky remembered, and the thought of having violence visited against him made Eletsky's blood boil.

Even Hadrian Keats, especially Keats, had turned in dismay from the lash marks on Ardenai's back and shoulders, and now, even resting against a smooth rock in the soaking pool, one of them showed, like a snake's tail, curling over his right shoulder to lie against his collar bone.

Gideon leaned toward him, Ardenai put his head against the boy's, and nodded in quiet reply.

"Pythos," he said, "Gideon has a question which I think should be phrased directly to you."

"Of coursse, though he sstill hass not answsered mine of ssome weekss ago."

"Sir?" Gideon responded politely, despite Io's warning grimace from across the pool.

"Animal, vegetable, or mineral?" the serpent hissed, and Gideon turned bright red. "Ssurely thee hass a guesss by now, hatchling."

Gideon's head came up, and despite his flushed cheeks, his voice was calm. "I had ceased to wonder, Physician. Having you care for me and tend my hurts, having sat at your feet and learned these many evenings, I see you only as who you are. I do not care what, *per se*. You, are you."

"Thy responsse pleasses me," Pythos beamed. "And from the look on his facce, I would ssay thee has pleassed the Firsstlord, as well. We commend thee. What iss thy quesstion?"

Gideon smiled and stole a glance at Ardenai, trying not to look as proud as he felt to be praised among strangers. "Physician Pythos, you have lived many centuries.   You have had hundreds upon hundreds of years to go about viewing the galaxy in all its various stages of development, all its peoples, all its many attitudes and views.   What I'm wondering is, with the physical appearance of your race, have you been able to do that? I mean, are you allowed to be who you are so you can present what you have to offer intellectually?" The youth shook his head in frustration. "Darn," he muttered, "I'm not saying it just right."

"I believe I undersstand, neverthelesss. It wass mosst tactful of thee not to usse the word, hideousss. When thee has traveled more widely, and are more educated, thee will come to undersstand that very few culturess actually have a revulssion of ssnakes, sserpents and dragon-kind in general. In the majority of culturess we repressent eternal life. It iss only where ccertain religionss have been prominent that we have found sserpents equated with Diaboluss, or Ssatan. I ssay thiss only to inform, Gideon, not to admonissh, sso do not be embarrasssed.

"Where we are acccepted, we have contributed. Where we are unacccepted, we have obssserved. There were then and are yet more than a few placcess where, had we landed and introduced oursselvess, we would have been dragged to the nearesst zoological garden and incarccerated. I and the Equi with me."

"Always the Equi. How did you come to be so fond of them in particular?" Keats asked with some resentment.

"They don't believe in zoos, for one thing," Moonsgold quipped, and his expression brought laughter which made Hadrian's face sourer than ever.

"That, mosstly," the old doctor chuckled, flicking his tongue in appreciation of the joke. "But the Equi had about them a ssensse of maturity and ressponssibility which transscended itss cosst, both physically and rationally; a willingness to weigh the factors ..."

"You're stonewalling," Keats said, and subconsciously or not, his lip took on just the hint of a sneer.

Moonsgold looked apologetically at Pythos, as though his comment had caused Hadrian's. "Not everything can be explained in fifteen words or less, Doctor Keats," he said. "Let the physician speak."

"Yes, do that," Ardenai said with a slow, formal nod toward the old doctor. "Tell Doctor Keats that his suspicions are correct."

"As you wissh," the serpent responded. "It'ss not exactly a dark ssecret. We did not come to the Equi. We dessigned the Equi. They have alwayss been ourss, and we are devoted to them."

There was a startled Terren silence, and more than one Equi chuckled to see those mouths ajar, like a silent protracted note in some mental chorus. But Moonsgold seemed not in the least startled. He flashed his infectious grin and his bright gold eyes sparkled with curiosity. "*That's* what the Equi flag tells us, isn't it? I've thought so."

"What do you mean?" Ardenai asked. He liked this Declivian. Open. Kind. Excellent example for Gideon.

Moonsgold collected his thoughts a moment before speaking. "*Equus Legatum*, which looks like the historical horse, *Equus Caballus*, isn't. Not on Equus. *Equus Legatum* is actually a combination of two species, a mammal and a reptile, though the reptile genes don't show except in the eyes, and small scales on the chin and lips."

Pythos nodded once. "Therein liess the ssecret, my friend. I think you have it."

"Behind The Equi sunburst upon which the horse runs, is the silver-green background which represents the continuum of the Eloi, of that I am certain. The purple edging represents the encircling protection the Dragonhorse provides when he rises. But the horse isn't just a horse, is it? It's the Equi people as well, because you share your genetic makeup with both horses and reptiles. Maybe? Am I close?"

"Abssolutely!" Pythos hissed, eyes alight with pleasure. "Of coursse that flag meanss ssomething different to everybody. It'ss like religion, everyone adjustsss it sso it'ss a comfortable fit."

"These people," Keats gestured, palms up at the Equi, "are genetically engineered? So that old thing about them having oil in their blood, might not be so far from the truth?"

It was a ludicrous statement, and Moonsgold roared with laughter, jolting Keats. "Oil for blood's about as true as that old thing about those cess-pit Declivians, who have," Gideon burst out laughing and said it with him, "shit for brains!"

Pythos wrapped his arms around himself and hissed with laughter, coiling in and out of the water until everyone was laughing to watch him. "Oh!" he gasped at last, shaking his scales until they rattled like soft grass in the breeze, "Doctor Moonssgold, we musst sspend more time together. We need to write a paper together, a medically bassed comparisson between the rumorss about Equi and the rumorss about Declivianss. We sshall pressent it at the next medical conferencce, and be a sscandal!"

"I'd love to do that!" the Declivian exclaimed, and Ardenai made note of the look of sheer loathing which crossed Keats's narrow face.

I believe the time has come for that one, the Firstlord thought, looking to Teal, *all his fear is turning to hatred. Enough hate will make even him dangerous.*

His kinsman gave him a slow nod which escaped the others. *He could be a very weak link in all of this. Why is he here, anyway?*

So I can have a talk with him without distractions.

You mean, without an escape route?

Something like that, yes. Too, he's a very competent physician, and Eladeus only knows how many of them we may need on the wargrounds before this is over. "Pythos, do go on."

"Oh, yess. Thank you, Beloved. As I wass ssaying," he sniffed, still wiping laughter from his eyes, "when Equuss wass in her infanccy, as thee knows if thee paid attention in classs, there were two ssentient lifeformss; one was hominoid, and the other reptilian. The reptilian life-forms thrived, and advancced very rapidly, because they had been sseeded there in colonies, and were already well established mentally and physsically, but the more primitive hominoid seedlings sstruggled to ssurvive. They battled hunger, diseasse, and at the very outsset, each other. All that kept them alive was their sstrong alliancce with Equus Legatum, the horsse, which had been sseeded there earlier with the reptilian population. Now I ssupposse, it wass a cold winter's night, and ssome Achernarean sscientissts, tired of the ussual ssports, began to disscuss what the possibilities would be for a blended race, if the besst traitss of the hominoids were to be combined, hybridized over time, as it were, with the besst traits of the Achernareans, and, indeed, even the trussty horsse ..."

"Oh, I get it!" Gideon blurted. "That's why an Equi male can tuck his...ah..." His enthusiasm for the subject suddenly turned to an uncomfortably red face. "Sorry."

"Phallus, just like a horse," Ardenai chuckled. "True. Looks the same, works the same. A bonus if you spend your life astride a saddle. Of course in our case the head won't retract completely."

"Exccellent protection," the serpent agreed, "And in the earliesst timess, having the added warmth about the testes, produccced more female offsspring. Tell me what elsse thee hass noticced about Equi which reminds thee of a horsse, Gideon."

"Well, probably the most obvious is no canine teeth. And your teeth are slightly larger than most hominoid species. There's the pronounced heat cycles. And the gestation period is about eleven months – pardon, five and a half seasons – same as a horse. And you eat like horses." He scowled at the snickers and said, "Well, you do. You graze all the time. You eat six meals a day, and you snack and piece between meals. And you drink a lot of water. I noticed that Ardenai suffered most when he couldn't get enough to drink. You're vegetarians, obviously, and I've noticed that, like horses, the Equi have very sweet, pleasant breath, even in the morning. Your ears move like horse ears, only not nearly as much, and they look more like the inside of a seashell, than like horse ears. You all tend to be long-legged and extremely fast and athletic, like horses."

"Very good, Gideon, though the earss came on the original model,"

Pythos hissed. "The fact that they move sslightly to convey, either volun- tarily or involuntarily, emotionss ssuch as anger and fear, may have been a sside-effect of the melding processs. Jilfan, what characteristicss are reptil- ian?"

"We have ophidian eyes," Jilfan stated. "That means our pupils are shaped like a snake's. And we have vestigial inner lids. Most people don't even know they have them. Wanna see me close mine? I've been practic- ing." He did so, giving Gideon a semi-opaque stare that made Gideon wince and then poke him until he stopped. "And we get cold really easily, like snakes do. We spend long hours locked in coitus, like snakes. And we have watery blood rather than sticky blood. The shape of our skin cells under a microscope closely resembles the scales of a snake, and the configuration of our muscles is more constrictive than in other hominoids, which makes us tremendously strong and limber – athletic, like Gideon said."

"Exccellent," the old doctor praised, and gave Io a nod of approval.

"So it worked?" Moonsgold asked, leaning forward. "I mean, the way the founders hoped it would?"

"We think sso," Pythos said. "Thiss iss truly anccient hisstory, and recordss are exsstremely ssketchy. We do know that the hominoidss which were not part of the exssperiment, died out after another few thousand yearss. And there were a few thingss that didn't go as planned. The whole thing with heat ccycless in highly ssophisticated hominoidss wass rather un- fortunate when it came time for them to sschedule conferencces and ssuch, esspecially ssince both ssexess ccycle. But by and large a little blending of DNA sstrengthened the hominoids of Equus, who developed ultimately into the beautiful sspecimens you ssee here. Intelligent, sstrong, artisstic, ccer- tainly ssuccessful."

"And just how much tampering did you serpent people do over the millennia to keep them that way?" Keats asked.

"Abssolutely none, as far as I know," Pythos replied blandly. "On- cce the sspecciess wass no longer endangered, it wass left alone to develop on its own."

"And you have co-existed side by side all this time?" Oonah asked.

The big serpent bobbed his head. "Yess. There aren't many populationss of Ophidianss – Ssea Dragonss – left on the west and mid-continentss of Equuss, thosse called Andal and Benacuss, though we are alwayss mosst welcome. But we do live in other placcess, the mosst ancient continent of Viridia, for instance, though it ssnowss there, too, which we find unpleasant." he shuddered involuntarily, "Mainly we live on that chain of large islandss which lie ssouth of and between Andal and Benacuss, known collectively as Achernar. They and the sea around them are warmer and more tropical, and sssuit uss well."

"Thank you!" Moonsgold exclaimed. "This is wonderful! Thank you for sharing this with us. I'm sure each of us has a thousand questions for you, Physician Pythos, I chief among them. But first, while I am still thinking, I must ask, is this something you would prefer we did not share with those outside this circle?"

"It iss kind of thee to assk, rather than ssimply going ahead as thee ssees fit," Pythos replied.

Keats immediately drawled, "As opposed to just hijacking people without their consent, bringing them someplace light years from nowhere for God knows what purpose, just because one has the power to do that sort of thing?"

Ardenai focused on the doctor, who puffed up and glared despite the apologetic groan of his shipmates. "I am sure Doctor Keats has his concerns about why we are here, and I will say only this aside from actual strategy, which we should probably talk a little about at this point. I am attempting to do one thing, and one thing only, save Equus, our own Seventh Galactic Alliance, and the United Galactic Alliance, because I'm assuming Telenir is somewhere within those boundaries, from a war. It is my opinion that while the Wind Warriors will go to endless effort to infiltrate us, and destroy us from within, they cannot, will not, even in alignment with some of our neighbors who do not belong to the SGA or the UGA, attempt an all-out war. They do not have that most important element, a proper foothold. To gain that, they must first gain Equus, which is situated firmly in the spatial center of the Seventh Galactic Alliance. This they feel they must do according to tradition, honorably and legitimately to their way of thinking, by gaining the arm-bands of Equus, and I happen to be wearing them on a most permanent basis.

"Here in this environment, a confrontation can be accomplished with a minimum of complications, distractions, publicity, and loss of life. We have Equi observers and now SGA observers, lest there be any questions as to what went on here between Sarkhan and myself. That, Doctor Keats, is why you and your companions are here."

"Why Sarkhan?" Marion asked, rubbing warm water up his arms and resettling his glasses on his nose. "Or should I say, how Sarkhan? Of the billion or so Equi on three continents and a hundred islands, how did you narrow it to one person?"

"The luxury of time, and the benefit of being able to speculate amongst intelligent people," Ardenai smiled, lowering himself a little deeper into the water. He winced slightly as the deepest of the scars on his back contacted the stone, and looked apologetic.

"And making the perhaps incorrect assumption that the Legend of the Wind Warriors is history, not a cautionary flickernick-tale," Teal added with a grin.

"True," Ardenai nodded. "My poor, longsuffering companions have heard the legend from me a thousand times. So, beginning rather at random to try to make sense of it as it might apply to us, and knowing that this was the five year period in which the next Dragonhorse would rise, we eliminated all those who did not avail themselves of political spheres. We eliminated all females, all males too young or too old to rise, which was a mistake, by the way. But it got us down to tens of thousands, not millions. We made another wild guess that this person would get as close as possible to the proceedings of the Great Council, partly to keep an eye on potential rivals, partly because a successful usurpation would have to include a good knowledge of how the government works on Equus. Now, we were down to a thousand or so. That took a good long while. Then, we began to observe behavior and attitude."

"Luckily," Io threw in, "because Sarkhan is considerably older than one hundred years. But he had an uncharacteristically large ego and a name that sounds like he chose it himself out of a history book. What Equi would name their baby, Sarkhan? Anyway, we kept an eye on him, and it bore fruit."

Ardenai smiled and nodded agreement. "When the announcement was made, the lure was cast. We moved as swiftly, angrily, and illogically as we could, causing our enemies to believe that if they hesitated, even momentarily, they would be lost. Therefore, they had to move without much time to effectively change their own strategies. We wanted them distracted and trying to make sense of what we were doing, so we could lead and make them follow whether they were ready or not." Ardenai paused and laughed a genuine, merry laugh. "It sounds so elementary when I explain it, but believe me, it took a lot of honing to simplify it that much."

"Then you did know beforehand," Keats said. "You knew it was you who would rule Equus."

"No, I didn't," Ardenai replied. He gave his head a slow, slight shake, still amazed at the memory. "I didn't know until the day the drums shook the city and Ah'krill entered the chambers of the Education Council and knelt at my feet with that crown on a pillow. But Pythos knew, having been present at my conception, and at my birth, and with me all the days since. We were prepared to accomplish this through any designated successor. We had been planning this for three years and more. The fact that we did not have to explain it to anyone, to convince anyone, only caused it to happen more smoothly." He gave a soft, deprecating chuckle, "Not that we haven't had our little episodes of procedural hiccups."

"And you never told Ardenai who he was?" Keats was incredulous. "Not even at the last when it would have altered nothing and aided in preparation? How is that rational?"

"I can tell you that," Gideon said quietly, then looked embarrassed and sunk down slightly in the water with a hand over his mouth. "Sorry.

Again."

Pythos gestured for the young man to speak, and Gideon sat up straighter, looking at Ardenai, who nodded.

"Well, as I see it, a game in which the rules are not kept, ceases to be a game. It becomes chaos. It is not understandable, nor is it playable. It is nothing at all. When we operate from a premise, the integrity of that premise must be maintained if we are to function as individuals with a single goal but limited communication."

"Flawless!" Pythos exclaimed. "You ssee, beyond the ability to think logically, which is a cold processs, comess the maturity to reasson, to truly reasson on a multiplicity of levelss, ssome logical, ssome emotional, ssome sspiritual. When one hass had a teacher ssuch as thiss child hass had, ssuch as Kehailan hass had, and Io, and ssome of the otherss, that iss not ssuppresssed, but encouraged. In Equi ssuch as thesse, we ssee our future, and rejoicce. Ardenai Firsstlord, your gift to the boy iss beyond meassure."

"The Wisdom Giver blessed him with that amazingly quick brain, not me," Ardenai replied with a grin. "Gideon's gift to me, was my life. What I have given him, has been in gratitude, and in affection. What he gave me, I had not earned. I was sulking, self-pitying, fearing Io and Teal both dead, totally engrossed in my own emotions. In all that, he saw the value of my life, simply, as life. He gave up his safe position to free me, he took care of me when I was too ill to take care of myself – he and Doctor Keats and Josephus. And even against impossible odds, when there has been not a single thing to be gained or won, he has been my friend. For that, I add my commendation to that of Pythos, and recommend Gideon to you all as a person of honor, and a most worthy young prince of the Great House of Equus, which we serve with all our hearts."

"Hear one and all," Teal said, raising an imaginary glass to the flustered youth. "And to you, Doctor Keats, for your part in saving he who is my Firstlord, my kinsman, and my dearest friend, I thank you. Equus thanks you."

There was a very awkward moment in which Keats wiggled on Teal's carefully planted pin, then the big Equi lowered his hand and eased himself deeper into the water. "Cool in here," he murmured, closing his eyes.

"I believe someone turned down the thermostat," Ardenai chuckled. "It grows late. If you will excuse me, I shall walk apart and then retire. You, of course, are free to do as you see fit. You will find refreshments laid out in the kitchen, and in your rooms, should you desire them." He waded from the pool, nodded graciously to the ladies, shrugged into his robe, and left.

"Sleep sounds good to me, too," Marion yawned. "That bed looked pretty inviting even back when Ardenai first showed it to me."

By ones and twos they said their goodnights, excused themselves, and went their separate ways to bed, or to meditations, or to stroll before retiring.

Hadrian Keats looked out from his bedroom casement, and jumped when he saw Ardenai, walking by the light of the huge, Calumet moons. *He's stalking me*, Keats thought, *that bastard brought me here to kill me for what I did! Damn you! Is that what you're doing?*

The Equi stopped, raised his hands from his sides, and turned his face upward to bathe it in the moonlight. *Again, your thoughts intrude upon mine, Doctor Keats. If you do not wish me to know your most painful secret, you must not throw it at me every time you see me. Anger only works as a dampening field if you know how to use it, Hadrian. You are using it as a megaphone. I do not mean you any harm, and I did not mean to pry in the first place, but it is done. I am still a legal representative of the Seventh Galactic Alliance, and you must face the problem and deal with it - now - or I will take it out of your hands.*

Keats turned from the window in utter dismay, hands clapped over his ears against the words which had reverberated through his head like a death knell. He was trapped. The Firstlord of Equus, knew who he was, and what he had done. It was over. Even in his terror, there was a sense of relief.

Do not be afraid, said the calming voice, and he felt the overwhelming urge to sleep, to rest from what had been a very long and arduous journey.

CHAPTER SEVENTEEN

I t's a story that's been told so many times in fiction it's hackneyed, you know? You come to that part in the book and you say to yourself, 'Oh, for pity's sake, are they going to drag that old chestnut out again? Nobody thinks this is plausible.' But in my case, it's true." Hadrian sighed and glanced across at Marion Eletsky, who was sitting on a downed log on the opposite side of the pleasant forest path. Ardenai was reclined a little to one side, legs stretched out in front of him, using the log as a backrest. They were both listening, pleasant faced and receptive, and it gave him courage.

He'd made up his mind to tell the truth, to have it all out in the open, and he'd been walking here, organizing his thoughts and formulating his speech, when they'd appeared from the opposite direction – Marion and Ardenai – jogging along laughing about the snacking habits of the Equi, and how many meals in a day the average Equi would consume given the opportunity. They'd nodded, said good morning, and would have passed him by, but on impulse he'd hailed them, sat them down and plunged in. Now he paused. Having blurted out his introduction and thus committed himself, he had the luxury of thinking for a moment. He looked at the Firstlord.

"When did you first know I wasn't who I said I was?"

Marion jumped a little and looked at Ardenai, who simply shrugged and replied, "You talk first, since you've gotten off to such a good start."

Keats paced a bit, then turned, running one hand through his close-cropped, sandy hair. "I was born Denny Strathmore, Dennis Strathmore, and that's who I was until I was twenty, and I'd finished my two years of pre-college. I was one of those kids that never got noticed, you know? Raised by a single mom who kept us fed and kept shoes on our feet and clothes on our backs, but who had not one opportunity to get us lessons of any kind, or special tutoring of any kind. I had good grades but not spectacular. Nothing to merit special circumstances, not talented enough to attract anybody with any influence. I was invisible. My one hope was to get into SGAU-Med. I applied twice. I was turned down twice."

He flipped his hands up and shook his head, lost in thought. "I roomed with this other kid, dumb as a toilet seat, book smart, but not a lick of common sense. He applied to the University and damned if he didn't get in. Threw the letter in his desk like it was nothing, of no value. Said he wasn't even sure he'd take them up on 'their offer'. Daddy was a big shot of some kind – only met him once. He couldn't stand Hadrian, and Hadrian couldn't stand him. So anyway, Hadrian Keats was big on doing dangerous shit – kayaking the white water, mountain climbing, backpacking way to hell and gone back in the woods, stratoschuting, racing planes, you name it, he did it, and he had the resources to do it right.

"Midsummer of our second year, school is already out and we're ready to go our separate ways. He persuades me to go out in the middle of fucking nowhere and climb down this cliff with him that nobody's ever managed to make. We might have had a chance, but he was snorting something, I don't know what, and he gets it into his head that he can fly, like a bird. I try to stop him, he whacks me with a skillet, and when I wake up, Hadrian Keats is at the bottom of this cliff, stark naked, where I can't get to him, and nobody's going to find him for about a hundred years, and he looks like something really heavy ran over him and just splattered him, so I know damned good and well he's dead.

"Well, I have a day or so to think about things, because my head hurts too bad to go anywhere, and in the course of going through the stuff in the tent – finding all his identification – beginning to put things together without really meaning to – I swear to God, I didn't mean to – but things go through your head, you know, like both of us had perfect teeth, so no dental records. Nobody ever comes out here, and he's going to be scattered all over hell in a couple of weeks from predation and desiccation. And after a while all I could think about was that letter, lying in that drawer, with all my dreams attached. So I took his gear and his clothes and his ID, left what I'd brought, and I went back to school and got that letter, figuring I wasn't going to be able to pull this off anyway. But I did. I went to SGAU-Med, got stellar grades, and for twenty years I worked my ass off to be the best doctor I could.

"Then, four years ago, before she was decommissioned and we got Belesprit, I get assigned to the SGA Blyth Spirit, and there's this young, handsome Equi prince who's the Wing Commander. And one day he says in the course of some inane conversation, 'All Equi are telepathic, but my sire, Ardenai, is extremely powerful. The harder you try to hide something from him, the quicker he knows it. You'll get to meet him next week.' For the first time in a lot of years, I was scared, so I started reading up on the Equi's powers of telepathy, and came across something that said anger worked as a damping field. But then you told me last night that I was using it to amplify rather than block. And that, as they say, is that." He plopped onto the grass, wrapped his arms around his knees, and waited.

"If you'd have kept a low profile, you'd have made it," Marion growled. "But you were justifiably proud of your accomplishments, and just a bit arrogant, and it was just too damned hard to stay quiet, wasn't it?"

Keats nodded. "Yes, it was. So, are you going to arrest me?"

"He has no authority here," Ardenai said. "I'm placing you under house arrest pending an inquiry. In the meantime, I expect you to continue to perform your duties as physician and observer. If anyone else finds out about this conversation, other than Teal, it will be because you have told them, not I."

"So, you have me, don't you?" Keats gave him a rueful smile. "Indulge me. Tell me when you knew I wasn't who I said I was."

"I never did," Ardenai smiled. "I was getting incredibly strong waves of guilt from you, that you considered yourself a criminal, and a killer, and that you were afraid I'd find out and you'd have to kill me, too. Which is pretty silly, considering that you could have attempted that any number of times and you chose not to. We have discovered now that you are not a criminal, as much as you are an opportunist, and that the only person you killed, was you."

"You're sure about that?" Marion asked, scowling first at Keats, then Ardenai.

"He's telling the truth. At least from his point of view," Ardenai replied, rising to brush himself off. "If you two wish to continue this conversation, please do so. I have things I must accomplish before lunch, and I do feel a snack coming on. If you'll excuse me." He gave the two officers a brief nod, and bounded away on his long legs.

"He has destroyed my life, and it's made him hungry," Keats said quietly. "That's how much we mean in the Equi scheme of things, Marion."

"You destroyed your life, not him," Eletsky retorted, "and considering where and when he could have had this out of you and by what means, and in front of whom, I'd consider myself damned lucky if I were you. I'm guessing he'll even speak on your behalf, which is more than I feel like doing right now. Excuse me. I'm hungry, too," he said, and trotted away after the Equi, his feet hitting the ground just a little too hard, fists and teeth both clenched as he ran.

▲ ▲ ▲ ▲ ▲ ▲ ▲

Had it not been for the scouts which rode apart in silence, two by two, and the pounding bells of the Horse Guard as they drilled in close formation – had it not been for the worry which clouded Ardenai's eyes as he paced or stood staring into the forest at odd moments – had it not been for those things, the officers of Belesprit would have felt themselves to be on a most delightful holiday. They were given every freedom to ride, or swim, walk in the fragrant woods, read, sleep, play games or study.

Winslow Moonsgold scurried around talking natural medicines with Pythos, ancient Declivian culture with Gideon, and watching the drummers, trying to learn the codes, rhythms and techniques of the great Equi drums. If he found time to sleep, nobody caught him at it.

Pythos, in turn, made time to entertain Hadrian Keats, and they spent time together discussing genetic engineering, and telepathy, and, rather specifically, how many out of the way places needed good doctors. If Hadrian had any idea he was with the most powerful telepath on the planet it didn't bother him, and certainly Pythos didn't mention it, as he was by nature a self-effacing creature.

Kehailan read and enjoyed the gardens as well as the intimate companionship of friends. He spent long hours in the evening with his father and Teal, attempting to understand the strategies which had been undertaken, and mentally weaving them into the strategies of the SGA, in case that became a necessity.

Marion often joined them for those discussions, and during the day he ran wind-sprints or cross-country with the Firstlord, and wrestled, and swam the strong, cold currents of the river. He was small, but wiry and exceptionally strong – a fine swimmer and tireless runner. He was also an excellent horseman, and gladly added his mallet to the informal polo matches which occasionally took place in the cool of early evening. When they grew tired of exercise, he and Ardenai debated cultural issues, and comparative history, and, with Teal, made music together, as they were all accomplished instrumentalists and singers.

Oonah spent most of her time with Ah'nora, mushrooming, gardening, cooking, sewing and weaving while they spoke of a woman's place in the scheme of things, about mating and childbirth and the raising of children and husbands; absorbing the Calumet culture and storing it for future reference and delectation.

Tim practiced with the Horse Guard, observing when it grew too complicated for his level of expertise, and often joined Gideon for his lessons in horsemanship or archery. Occasionally, in the sultry afternoons, he and Kehailan slipped away together to speak of more intimate things and enjoy one another's company, and once or twice Oonah excused herself from Ah'nora's company and joined them to watch or participate.

Most of Gideon's time was spent with Teal, who was Master of

Horse, and with Seglawi, who was Captain of Arms. With them he learned to ride, and began to learn the rudiments of handling a crossbow and forearm knives. He studied most often beside Jilfan, but Jilfan learned only because it was expected of him. He preferred reading with Kehailan, or mushrooming and herb gathering with Oonah and Ah'nora. Once they encountered Pythos and Winslow in the woods, studying medicinal herbs, and they teamed up to hunt berries and other wild edibles.

Everyone took a turn helping in the kitchen and the garden, even Ardenai, and often they ate in the kitchen, laughing and talking without any sense of rank. Indeed, rank seemed to exist only in terms of responsibility, not personal importance, and this was enlightening for Gideon, who had been raised with the notion that people had importance relative to their position in society. It was explained to him when he questioned the practice, that status was an artificial social concept, and could be very misleading when it came to seeking out the people who actually knew the answers, and that, to the Equi, authority and responsibility were synonyms.

The person most conspicuously absent from any diversion, was Ah'riodin. She was up at dawn, occasionally before even the Firstlord, drilling her squads. They could be heard late at night, and nothing moved within a ten hour ride of South Hold that the captain didn't know about. The village of South Hold was thoroughly prepared, as was the main complex at the Stud, for the possibility that Sarkhan might get past their first line of defense. When Io was through, it was a dead certainty he would not get by their second. No one teased her about her diminutive stature, nor the size of her ears, nor the wealth and hue of her hair. No one noticed those things in the presence of Ah'riodin, Captain of the Horse Guard of the Great House of Equus. She was every inch a warrior, her demeanor professional, her knowledge of her subject above reproach. She was impressive of stride and voice, and the fact that she shared a bed at night with the Thirteenth Dragonhorse, seemed part of another existence.

Then, in the pre-dawn of what was to be a sweltering day, Ardenai came bolt upright in bed, bathed in cold sweat and gasping for air. He sat panting, trying to get his breath back, and Io's hand came to rest on his. "Is he here?" she asked, and Ardenai shook his head, choking as he attempted to swallow.

"I ... don't know. Something ... stirs."

She gave him water, and made love to him to relax him, but he did not go back to sleep. He paced instead, and at breakfast he requested that the observers stay a little closer to the confines of the main complex. He told them why, reminding them that they were only observers. They were in no case to be put in harm's way. He seemed edgy and out of sorts, so they didn't ask questions, they simply observed, as they had been instructed.

Io went off with her squads of Horse Guard, and Ardenai spent part of his morning working personally with Gideon and Tolbeth. The boy was becoming an excellent rider, and Ardenai allowed himself to relax enough to appreciate the fact. He picked up a large square of cloth which could be popped open with the flip of a wrist, and stepped into the arena with Gideon. "Now, find your seat, and watch her ears. Whichever ear moves, that's the direction she's going to jump if she bolts. Are you ready?"

"Ready," Gideon nodded.

"You're not ready. You're like a steel rod up there. You'll either snap in half, or go flying. Relax. Make her want to go to sleep with you. Give her the cue to drop her head."

The Declivian did as he was told.

"Watch her ears," Ardenai instructed, and brought the cloth up. "See, she's going to jump right," he said, and popped the cloth open.

The mare shied to the right, and Gideon was still astride when she stopped with a snort and planted her feet. "Tell her she's a good girl," Ardenai said, smiling, and watched the boy stroking the mare. What a loving husband and good father he would make, and Pythos said it would never happen. The venereal diseases which had ravaged him as a child had left him both sterile and impotent. How terribly, terribly unfair. The Firstlord shook his head and veiled the sadness in his eyes. There had been little time for serious discussions with Pythos regarding possible surgeries, but time would most assuredly be made when this was over. Ardenai wondered if Winslow Moonsgold might not be a fine ally in all this. He would speak to him when time allowed. If time allowed. His time amongst the living. "Again," Ardenai said, and this time he didn't tell Gideon which ear twitched.

Nearer lunchtime, Kehailan, Pythos and Marion saw Io coming out of the stable and into the arena on a big copper stallion, just as Ardenai was returning from his second run of the day. He jumped the fence at the edge of the woods, saw his wife, and veered toward the stables, clearing the five rail fence in a straight-armed vault to catch the reins on her horse. The others were too far away to hear what was said, but Ardenai's face was not at all pleasant.

"Io," he was saying with thinly veiled frustration, "did I not make myself clear when I asked you to stay away from this horse?"

Io looked down at him and blinked, ascertaining that he was not joking, which he most assuredly did not seem to be. "You said you wanted me to use my judgment in riding him, Firstlord. I am doing that. We are working in the arena, not across open ground."

"Well, I don't want you riding him at all. He needs to go back to Teal. He's too big for you to properly grip with your legs, there's a lot of fear in him yet, and if he jumps out from under you, you'll be hurt. Go get another horse, please."

Her jaw settled into a firmer line, and her gaze hardened. "Ardenai, I am the captain of the Horse Guard."

"You're also my wife! A little, short-legged girl with my baby in her belly," Ardenai snapped, "and I want you to do as I say and get off of there."

"No," she said. "Remember? No surprises. I will continue to take the chances I have always taken, and be who I have been. In addition to that, I will be your consort, but not instead of. My value to you as a person is as a cavalry officer. Aside from that I am a nuisance at worst and a convenience at best. It is not rational to give up real value for simple convenience. Let go of my horse. Please."

"Ah'riodin," Ardenai said quietly, "one thing you will learn as you grow older, is that life is full of surprises. If you think I will be mesmerized enough by your fire to allow you to ride out of here on this horse and get yourself injured or killed, you are mistaken. It is not your place to assume anything of what your value may be to me, but you can certainly assume it involves being alive. Now, unless you want the people under your command to see you dragged from that kraaling horse like a disobedient little brat, you will step calmly down, offer him to me, and go get yourself another mount."

Their eyes locked, and the air smoked for a time, then Io gave him a single, curt nod, Ardenai lifted her down, and they were hidden from view by the stallion's neck. The horse was led back into the stable, and when he reappeared, it was Ardenai who rode him, Io pacing alongside on Kadeth. They began to work the horses in tandem, the greener learning from the well-seasoned, and Pythos nodded his approval.

"I ssee that this time around being in love hass not made your ssire foolissh," he said to Kehailan. "I am pleassed. He putss the hellcat in her placce. Kept there, sshe will sserve him long and well."

"So that's what you think happened over there just now?" Marion chuckled. Pythos gave him a questioning look. "They may have reached some sort of an agreement, but I'm betting it's not the one you think it is. When a woman looks at a man like that," he shivered graphically, "it bodes a cold night's sleep."

"And only the horssefliess will ever know," Pythos hissed.

"She's distracting him and defying him and mesmerizing him, just like she always has," Kehailan said, and his face was sad. "I just hope she doesn't get him killed. There was a long, silent moment. Excuse me," he said. "I have things to do."

After lunch Marion and Tim went to squat on their heels with Gideon in one of the box-stalls, watching Ardenai and Teal stalking one another, reading one another's faces, the movement of a finger, the rippling of a muscle in preparation to spring. Graceful as serpents and quicker as they struck – hard – giving no quarter and expecting none, practicing the most physical aspects of Equi discipline. It had been going on for nearly half an hour when

Ardenai was momentarily distracted and Teal saw his opening. In a split second, the Firstlord was slammed hard into the side of the box, landing on his back with the wind knocked out of him.

He crawled into a corner, sweat soaked and momentarily vanquished, and Teal crooked a finger at Gideon. "You. Yes, the young man who knocked me off my horse onto the cold, hard ground. You are next to be bedded on this straw beneath my feet."

"So," a cool voice said, "this is where I find the Firstlord of Equus, brawling half naked in a galactic backwater."

By then Ardenai had staggered to his feet, eyes wide, jaw slack in dumbfounded disbelief, realizing what had distracted him. "Oh no," he managed, shaking the sweat from his hair. "Oh no. All this has been for nothing."

"And that is how you greet your mother?" Ah'krill snapped icily, "By saying 'Oh no'? You honor me."

"Forgive me," Ardenai said, and bowed formally in her direction. "I do honor thee. I treasure thee as I do our world. For that very reason I am dismayed. What I had sought to spare you, I fear you have brought along."

"Turn around," she said, and Ardenai gave her a questioning look. "Turn around," she said again, and Ardenai did so, standing quietly, feeling Ah'krill's fingers touching, barely touching his back.

"Now face me," she said, and Ardenai obeyed. For a long minute Ah'krill looked at him in silence. "Always have you been a man to go where duty takes you," she said at last, "I commend you. I weep to see you so marred."

"I am honored," Ardenai said, forcing himself to smile. "Will you allow me to see to your refreshment at the house rather than in the stable?"

"Of course," she said.

Ardenai motioned her on ahead and as they stepped out into the sunshine he realized everyone else already knew of her presence, and had for some time. "Captain Ah'riodin was kind enough to escort us the last few miles," Ah'krill said, gesturing in passing at the still mounted squad, and

Ardenai dismissed them with a wave and a subtly panicked eyebrow.

"I am surprised to find you participating in so aggressive an activity in this heat," Ah'krill said as they walked toward the house. "Are you in season? But of course you are, how silly of me not to notice sooner, since you have taken the whole place with you. Actually, just about every Equi we passed on the way here has been affected. Not a particularly kind thing to do to those who trust you, Dragonhorse."

Ardenai felt the color rise in his face, and he said with some annoyance, "I must thank you for whatever potion you gave me at the Rising Ceremony. It has protracted this thing to a ridiculous degree, Mother. And I can only assume your observation is being voiced in retaliation for what was said by me in the presence of the Great Council?"

"That would be an irrational thing for me to do, Dragonhorse. It is indicative of your own emotional stress that you consider me capable of such action."

"You are correct, of course. Again, I must ask your forgiveness."

"Ardenai," she said firmly, "Stop it. You forget your position, and mine. You now rule Equus, not I. I am your mother. I bore you a hundred years ago, and only now am I able to speak to you as my son. Do you think I have not counted the days? Do you think I have not looked, and wondered? As I did, so will you in years to come – at the children, the girls, the young women – seeking something of yourself in their faces. What you did was difficult. You mated without any desire to do so. But to carry that child, knowing you must give it up, guiding a planet while your back aches and your belly swells, that, too, is difficult."

Ardenai knit his brows, trying to follow his mother's thoughts, trying to figure out what this had to do with the fact that he now ruled Equus in her stead. Perhaps she was just venting a little. He smiled. "Of that I am sure," he said, opening the door for her and motioning her inside the cool dimness of the sitting room nearest the rohanth beds. "Being a father was difficult enough. Having a pregnant wife, knowing the danger she was in because she carried my son, knowing I could lose them both, made for a very long gestation. Had I known for certain that I *would* lose Kehailan, what would I have done, I wonder?" He paused, looked at his mother, and shook his head. "I do commend you. What you have done, I could not. And I am happy to be joined with you again. Please, be seated. May I offer you something to drink?"

She nodded. Ardenai poured them both blood fruit juice and came to sit across from her, offering her the glass. "If you will excuse me for a few minutes, I will dress more appropriately, Ah'krill."

"I will not," she said, arching her brows. "I have waited seasons, and traveled through five sectors to speak with thee. Now, speak."

Ardenai did so – bemused, but meticulous – as was his custom.

Ah'nora slipped in, bringing fruit and sweets on a tray, and would have left just as quietly as she had come, but Ardenai broke his thought and called after her. "Ah'nora, I would speak briefly with thee," he said, and rose, excusing himself momentarily from his mother. He led the younger woman out the door on the far side of the room and said quietly, "I want you out of here as soon as possible."

Her eyes asked a question, and he shook his head as he looked down at her.

"We can take care of ourselves for a bit. I need to know you and the baby are safe. Is there someplace you can go?"

"To my brother in South Hold village."

"Go. Right after supper. Ask Teal to take you."

She nodded, then shyly reached up and touched his cheek with the tips of her fingers. "Please, be careful," she whispered, "a boy needs his father."

Ardenai caught her fingers and kissed them and said, "I'll send for you."

She nodded, and was gone. Within minutes Io was there with a long-sleeved tunic, and he knew Ah'nora had told her he was becoming chilled. He smiled, nodded his thanks, and dismissed her without further comment.

The late afternoon turned to evening, and still Ah'krill questioned him. As the lamps were lighted Io came in again, stepped to one side, and waited until Ardenai finished his thought and acknowledged her. "Dinner will be ready soon," she said. "Will you dine with us, or separately, First-lord?"

Ardenai looked at Ah'krill for a decision. "We will dine with the rest of you," she said. Io nodded and slipped out, and Ah'krill turned her attention back to Ardenai. "Have I exhausted you yet?"

"If I say yes, will you take your foot off my neck?" he asked, and Ah'krill gave him a look askance.

She recovered quickly, realizing he was teasing her, and shook her silvering head. "Not yet. I am not yet satisfied with your explanations."

"I cannot sit at table in such a state as this, I'm afraid, so please allow me to continue this conversation while I bathe. You have had a tiring journey. Would you like to join me?"

"Yes, I would," she said simply, and he ushered her through the house to the atrium. It was empty, though it had been very recently in use, and they were no sooner in the water than a young woman in the robes of the Akoliti came quietly in bearing fragrant scrubsand, clotted-soap, and clean robes for both of them. She would have dropped her own garment and entered the water, but Ah'krill stopped her. "That is not necessary," she said, holding up a hand. "My son can bathe the spots I cannot reach. You may go." The woman re-fastened her garment, and disappeared.

"May I now ask you a question?" Ardenai smiled, and his mother nodded.

"You may."

He ducked himself and then surfaced to begin the scrubbing process. "Why in the name of the Creator Spirit are you here, woman? What part of 'Stay where you are and observe,' escaped you, my dear?"

"A fair enough question," she sniffed, "though not asked in a particularly thoughtful manner. But still, I will answer it. Your message, sent through Josephus, was brief, but very much to the point. What I found most interesting was your admonition to watch Sarkhan. I took your advice. I held him over a slow fire and made note of what color he turned. From that, I decided to make his task easy for him. He has waited so long to accomplish it, why force him to try tricking us, when he can simply try killing us instead? We are both here. The need for subterfuge is gone. I made myself transparent enough that he knows I will be here. He will also realize at some point that he is sandwiched between us and the Seventh Galactic Alliance. He can do nothing. He is helpless. We have him."

"Good thoughts," Ardenai said, standing under one of the waterfalls to rinse his hair, "but most probably incorrect. What you would do, or I would do, is not what he will do. It is true that your arrival has left him a single option. If he is indeed sandwiched between us and the SGA, he must kill us all. No one must live to tell our side of it, or his, for that matter. Most of his own men will die, as well, or I miss my guess. Wash my back, will you? Gently, please?"

"You seem convinced that Sarkhan is Telenir, though I do not think he is," Ah'krill said. "I think he is just another in a long line of petty usurpers, maddened by the need for power. In any case, if he is a Wind Warrior, or thinks he is, we know little of them aside from an ancient poem set to music. That epic tells us they have a strict code of honor. Pretenders to the title or not, they will act honorably – at least Senator Konik will." She sighed and looked sad. Konik had always been so kind and gracious. Gallant, was such an old-fashioned word, and yet he was – gallant.

"Let us assume I am correct, for the sake of argument," Ardenai said, cutting into her thoughts. "They might have acted honorably if they'd had to convince the High Priestess of Equus they did so. Now that you're here, they don't, do they? Those who act honorably will die, Ah'krill. They will act to live, and to win. As a ruler you should know that. Thank you."

"You are angry," she said, washing her arms, her eyes seeming intent on her task. "How disturbing."

"Angry? No. I'm frustrated, and I'm frightened half out of my wits at this point. My mother is here, she who is the religious authority on Equus – here, with me. My closest companions are here, Pythos and Teal. My son

is here, and his companions. The son of my choosing, and my stepson. All
here. All three of them. My wife is here..."

"Stepson? Wife? Ardenai, we have spoken for these hours together
and you have failed to mention anything about the subject. Why is that?"
She clapped her hands, and the akolyte appeared instantly, holding out a
large towel which Ah'krill folded around her tall, ample proportions, allowing the girl to dry her.

"I was trying to be kind," Ardenai sighed, wading out after his mother. "Assuming I had already done enough to dismay you, I decided to let
the subject alone for the time being. Since you pointed out the fact that I'm
cycling, it must be rather obvious. You might therefore conclude that I made
the decision to marry and the choice of a wife, too quickly." He reached for
a towel, snapped it around his waist, and reached for a second to dry himself
off.

"You think you did not?" The older woman asked, slipping into the
robe which the akolyte held open for her.

At that moment Io appeared to call them to dinner, and held out a
robe for him. He slipped it on, then took her hand. "I chose a friend of many
years. The daughter of a friend. I chose someone whose opinion I respect,
whom I find intelligent, uplifting, and desirable." He nodded formally to his
mother, and gestured at the woman beside him. "Abeyan Ah'riodin Ardenai
Morning Star, Firstwife of Equus. So says Physician Pythos. So say we all."

Ah'krill returned the nod and smiled as she stood in front of them.
"A most excellent choice, Dragonhorse. I approve. Ahimsa, I wish thee
peace." She touched their hands where they touched each other, turned, and
left the room.

When Ardenai finally crawled into bed in the wee hours of the next
morning, he was shaking with cold and mental exertion. Io pulled him
against her, and he laid his head on her shoulder with a sigh of relief. "Whatever must come, I hope it comes quickly," he said.

Io snugged the blankets around his shoulders, kissed his forehead,
carefully rubbed his back to warm him as she spoke. "Things have not

changed, Beloved, but only your relative position to them. Ah'krill is correct. The Telenir are men of honor. Sarkhan must proceed as though he intends an honorable confrontation, or risk a mutiny. He must challenge us and gather us together on a field of battle if he hopes to destroy us. He knows he cannot ambush us, or pick us off one by one. As you said at supper, someone might live to tell the tale. All we have to do to keep him honest is make sure certain members of our entourage are conspicuously absent from the confrontation. That, and keep him outflanked."

Ardenai adjusted his head on Io's shoulder so he could look at her. "And why has this come to you and escaped me?" he asked.

"I'd like to say it's because I'm the penultimate strategist," she smiled, "but it's because I'm a woman. I had a feeling Ah'krill would come, and I prepared myself mentally for it."

"What?" He raised up on one elbow, and gave Io a puzzled look even the dimness of the room couldn't hide.

"I was just getting you warm enough that I could stand having you near me," she said. "Why are you up there looking at me like that?"

"Because you astound me. Why did you think Ah'krill would come? It's a foolish, ill-advised thing to do, and of all the fools I know, my mother isn't one of them."

"And her decision was not foolish. It was rational, but from her standpoint, not yours. You are the future of Equus. If you are lost to the Telenir, Equus is lost to the Telenir, whether Ah'krill is there or not. Better to be here and see for herself what happens. Better to know, than to wait. Better to end with a bang than a whimper, as some ancient poet said. I can't remember which one."

"T.S. Eliot. 'This is the way the world ends, not with a bang but a whimper.' The Hollow Men, OE 1925," Ardenai muttered, ignoring the fact that his wife was now laughing at him, "that's the female version of the way to make a rational decision. Ah'ree was a rational woman, after all. She was rational as females comprehend the concept of rationality. If only I could apologize for all the times I teased her."

"You can apologize to me," Io snapped. "You have the blankets."

"I think, that is not my only error," Ardenai chuckled. "Surprise, surprise. Kiss me, Wife. Take me away from here."

He tarried again with her in the morning, allowing her to fan his passion to an oblivion which was blessed relief. He relaxed in her arms, and said, "Unless I miss my guess, Sarkhan will be upon us today."

She stroked his head where it lay on her breast, and he could feel the vibration of her voice as she spoke. "You are correct."

"You are certain?"

"Yes. But I have it in hand. Go and bathe. Pythos awaits thee, re-member? You promised you'd oil his scales."

Ardenai kissed her and made his way to the bathing pools, feeling oddly refreshed and optimistic, and stronger than he had for a while. He'd been eating every chance he got. Perhaps the heat cycle was finally letting go. He thought about these things, and what this heat cycle had brought him – a new wife, a baby daughter – so much to look forward to. So much to fear losing if he lost to the Telenir.

"What troubless thee?" the old physician asked drowsily.

"Nothing," Ardenai replied, pouring more oil into the palm of his hand. "Nothing troubles me. Roll over. I was just thinking about things, and the discussion Io and I had last night about logic and logical decisions, and all that it implied. It is of no importance."

"Don't be too ssure. Mosst women usse innuendo the way men usse logic – as a tool, or a weapon, or a gift, as the mood takess them. What did sshe ssay?"

"That Ah'krill made a rational decision in coming here. Which re-minds me, she and I, my mother and I, I mean, had rather a nasty argument last night."

"Conccerning?"

"The fact that my wife is settled with a daughter."

"Sshe iss not pleassed?" Pythos asked blandly, though his eyes had taken on rather a malevolent glow Ardenai couldn't see from his vantage point. "Sshe ressentss the little priestesss?"

"I don't know," Ardenai sighed, missing the implication. "We didn't actually get to that part. I assumed she was upset because I have again taken a wife who is not high Equi, and I kind of blew up and didn't let her finish."

The old dragon shrugged. "Sshe iss not upsset for that reasson. Io iss but one of three wivess, which iss in part why that rule wass sset in the firsst placce – to accommodate ssuch a match. Many of the wivess which rosse with their hussbandss were not high Equi. Thee knowss that, and sso doess sshe."

"Still, I'm wondering if I need to apologize. Have you seen her?"

"Sshe who iss thy mother walkss with the golden-eyed prince. Wass thee not going to meet thy mother for an early breakfasst?"

"Yes," Ardenai muttered. "I was occupied, and I more or less forgot."

"Occupied with that little Papilli pouncer of yourss? Iss that why thee forgot the mosst powerful woman on thy homeworld?"

"I was making love to my wife!" Ardenai said hotly. "If Sarkhan comes upon us today, I may be dead by nightfall. We may all be dead!"

Pythos hissed with amusement. "Now, the truth from thy lipss, Hatchling."

"Oh, fine," Ardenai chuckled. "She made me forget everything. Not for long, but I forgot about people, things past and present. There was nothing but her, the two of us, and wanting her, which, I might add, is a nice change from just wanting sex. Not since Ah'ree and I were..."

"SSTOP!" Pythos hissed, sitting up on the table. "Right there. Thee iss about to undo the good thee hass done thysself."

Ardenai looked put upon, but his eyes were affectionate, even as he made a fending motion with his hands. "I assume I am to hear this whether or not it is my wish?"

"Thee can walk out."

"I am hardly dressed for a graceful exit. Tell me, Pythos, what good was I about to undo?"

"Tell me insstead. I have not heard Io compare thee to Ssalerno."

"Perhaps there has been no need for comparison," Ardenai said stiff-ly. "In my entire life I have been bonded to only one woman besides Io, and that was Ah'ree. I lived with her for over fifty years. Every reference I have as to how a marriage should work, how a relationship should progress, what constitutes passion, understanding, desire, partnership, friendship and com-patibility, is based on those years with that woman. I can offer Ah'riodin no greater gift than those things which Ah'ree taught me. That does not mean I am comparing the two of them. I would never go into detail in that manner. Ree was Ree, and Io is Io. However," Ardenai said, shaking a long, blunt finger at Pythos, "I am me. Only one person. A single frame of reference for two very different women. Surely you must realize that a frame of fifty years will be more influential than one spanning a matter of days."

There was silence. Pythos looked at Ardenai, Ardenai back at the physician. Pythos, slid off the table, put on the emerald green robe which matched his scales, and held up Ardenai's robe for him. "Does this mean you approve, or disapprove of my answer?" the Equi asked.

"Oh, kind Firsstlord, thine answwer wass far more kindly than thiss old sserpent's quesstion merited. I try thee, I tesst thee, I jesst at thy ex-pensse, and sstill thee allows me to go on sserving thee. Why iss that?"

"Because I allow nothing and you do not serve me, that's why," Ardenai snorted, fastening the robe. "You do try me. You test me. You vex me. And in you, in your service to Equus, in the way you view things as they are and could be, I see what I one day desire to become, my father. Mentally, that is. You can forget the scales, and I've never been able to figure out how you keep a robe on this tube you call a body. Frankly, I don't know why you bother with robes at all. I wouldn't, if I were you."

"It iss, indeed, a mosst dessirable trait – most enviable – having scales," the serpent said. "I am not ssurprissed that thee ssecretly dessiress such things for thyself and thy poor, hairless body."

"That, is not what I'm desiring just now," Ardenai chuckled, "a close second, maybe, but not on my list of most passionate desires, though I'm sure it should be." He shook his head and fell silent. The effort of making small, pleasant conversation was just too much. He laid his cheek briefly against the old physician's, excused himself, and took his leave.

What Ardenai desired most as he rode apart that day, was perspective – distance – a detached spot somewhere high in his brain for his mind's eye to sit and view the goings on as a whole. From his present vantage point there was too much in the way. He sighed, reined Kadeth upward, out of the trees to the ridge above. He knew final preparations were being made to meet the Telenir, and he wanted desperately to be there, but Io had sent him away. "Meditate," she had said. "Gather your thoughts and focus yourself. When it is time, I will send for thee."

She knew where Sarkhan was, who was with him and how many. She told him only that there was an acceptable number of adversaries, and that things were under control. He needed his focus to be on one thing and one thing only – defeat Sarkhan. Kill Sarkhan. All he had to do...was kill a man. He stepped off his horse and said something so foul the Equi had no word for it, only the Nargawerlders.

Kadeth gave him a disapproving look, then obeyed Ardenai's gesture to entertain himself, while the Firstlord plopped onto a large rock and began stripping a golden blade of wild rye which grew in the lee of the stone. Theoretically, that being the key word in his own mind, Ardenai knew what he was doing, and he knew what to expect. But working with things, elements, was very much different than working with people. If a quantum psi program erased itself, or a lesson plan flopped in one's face, one could always assess the damage, find the point where the mistake was made, and begin again. In this case, in this place, with these people and the emotions they stirred, the damage would most likely be assessed and the mistake pinpointed while they were clearing away the dead.

He tried viewing things simplistically, as his high priestess mother had. What could be eliminated without disturbing the basic equation? He could start with honor. Eliminate honor, as he was almost sure Sarkhan was going to do somehow. Eliminate honor. Much simpler. Now, it was kill or be killed. There ceased to be anything to prove. No need for a clean victory from which to establish long overdue diplomatic relations. No need for Ardenai to present himself as the ultimate Equi diplomat, the ultimate mutation of the warlike savage. No need to be the strong, benevolent victor, proven both in battle and in peace. No need to be the intellectual role model for his backward Telenir kinsmen. No honor. Kill or be killed. Hunt Sarkhan down and kill him. Aside from honor, there was absolutely no reason not to.

Of course the one thing the Telenir supposedly respected, was honor. And was there no honor to be had in peace? Why did they want war? Were they overpopulated? Hungry? Did their religion demand blood? What, exactly did they want to gain from this besides the honor of victory over the most powerful government in the Seventh Galactic Alliance? Maybe that was enough. It wouldn't be a victory that lasted very long. The second they appeared in AEW space they'd be pounded into oblivion by the SGA, whether Ardenai was alive or not.

He thought again of that word the Nargawerlders had, didn't say it, just thought it. Now, there was another possibility. Nargawerld, and a few others. The Lebonathi, maybe. Rumor had it they were both hungry and overpopulated, but they were also xenophobic and most likely wouldn't make allies even if they were offered the chance to do so. Probably not players in this particular game.But would the Telenir have put something like this into play without allies? Perhaps. He began to walk, beckoning for Kadeth to follow, along the crest of the ridge, eyes searching the valley below. Trees, thousands of trees, evergreen and deciduous. Water, moving and still, a road or two. The main complex of houses and barns. In the distance, South Hold village. Perhaps. The Narga were without honor, or even the concept of honor, which meant that the Telenir would hate them more than the Equi did, which was going some. Definitely no love lost. Another emotion. War always rode emotion into battle. Without being able to understand emotion, one lost the ability to understand nine-tenths of the known peoples in the galaxy.

Nargawerlders – being representative of the dark side of these musings – what did they know and where were they these days? Who all circled above Calumet besides Belesprit? How discreet had Ah'krill been in leaving Equus, and who followed her besides the Telenir? There could be a galactic conflagration going on up there, and down here no one would be the wiser, or the sadder. And why had he found it necessary to tell his wife whose quote that was, and when it had been written, and for what? What if he died today? Is that what she would remember about him, that he had enough trivia in his head to turn any discussion sour with detail?

What if Sarkhan, in attempting to sweep the odds, and without the knowledge of his government, had told the Nargas what was going on? If he couldn't beat the Equi on Telenir terms, he could always embrace that elemental Nargawerld philosophy – win. Rape if the notion takes you, but never forget to pillage. When in doubt, kill. Very simple. No need to ex-trapolate that to a logical end. It began and ended in the same spot, the evil and somewhat vacuous recesses of the Narga mind. No, the Nargawerlders would be worse as friends than enemies. Anything taking the minutest de-gree of subtlety or patience would, by necessity, preclude a Nargawerld al-liance.

The Telenir had been willing to spend their lives, their entire lives, trying to infiltrate an alien government, living here generation after gener-ation, going to school, participating in government, appearing to be part of a community. That was a task for patient, duty bound, honorable men and women. Like Konik. Not like Sarkhan, who was as evil and vacuous as any Narga. Or had he simply gone mad from the waiting? And could one equate the vacuousness of madness with the vacuousness of stupidity? Did they, by different paths of progression, operate to the same ends?Ardenai sighed. This could be twisted forever and still it would be one of two things, much too complicated, or much too simple.

Ardenai felt an icy jab from his testicles to his scalp, and Teal's gen-tle voice in his head said, *He is here, Beloved. It is upon us, and thee must act accordingly. Focus now. Hold on tight, and know that I am beside thee.*

He mounted the big grey horse and angled slowly off the blind side of the mountain. He knew he was safe for the moment, but he chose to approach from a direction which had more cover. He passed through the trees, and crossed the stream near the main complex.

As he rounded the corner approaching the gaming arena he became aware of them – horses without bells. He stopped, listened, lifted his thoughts once more to Eladeus, and proceeded at a slow jog toward the parade ground. It was there that he found the men for whom he had waited, waiting for him. It was utterly peaceful and completely quiet. So far, a ludicrous start to a conflagration.

They were just standing there like they were prepared for a polo match, one line of riders opposing another, equally divided. Half with bells, half without. Pythos stood to one side with Keats and Moonsgold, baskets of herbs still over their arms. Kehailan and Tim, returning from the stream with Marion. Gideon and Jilfan on horseback, gaming sticks still in their hands. And right in the middle of the whole thing, concealed by a walking cloak but frighteningly recognizable, the one person who should not have been anywhere near there. Ah'krill. A tableau. Not even a particularly hostile one. Ardenai rode into it.

"We have been waiting for you," Sarkhan said. He was on the ground, Konik beside him. Ardenai stepped off Kadeth and sent him to one side.

"I am here," he said.

"And how do you explain an absence of seasons?" Sarkhan asked. "Out savaging about, from the looks of those tattoos up both your arms. They make you look quite uncivilized, you know."

Ardenai snorted. "Seeking to overthrow an ancient, successful and benign government strikes me as slightly less civil than a set of Achernarean chain tattoos. As for an explanation, I explain nothing. I rule Equus. You explain why I am here by your very presence."

"Do you really rule Equus?" Sarkhan sneered. "I see no evidence of that. Nor do I see any evidence that you are fit to rule."

"To whom would I present this evidence?" Ardenai asked evenly.

"To whose representative?"

"A man of few words," Sarkhan smiled. "I appreciate that. We have had rather an enlightening discussion while we waited for you – your Captain, and your kinsman and I. Your companions and mine, and there is little left to be said. You know who I am, what I claim, and what I have come to take from you, because it is rightfully mine. The fact that you have made us chase you across five sectors has availed you nothing in the final outcome. We will simply kill you here, go back across five sectors, and take Equus."

"You make it sound so simple," Ardenai smiled. "I doubt it will be so simply accomplished, unless you want it said all over the galaxy that you used Nargawerld methods to Telenir ends. Hardly what your government, assuming there is such a thing, wishes to hear. They want Equus with honor. They want power. You have lost your chance to gain that through infiltration, or through open warfare, as you have lost it in Risings past. You must gain it in a combat of probity or not at all. So be it. I will fight you, one on one, to the death, for my world. I lose, Equus is yours. You lose, you're dead. Your people go home and tell your government that which we have said all along. We want peace with you, and if possible, friendship. We are kinsmen. It is time we acted as such."

"Ardenai, you amaze me," Sarkhan smiled. "You really believe that I am so stupid as to think I can walk into the Great Council of Equus and say, 'I killed Ardenai Firstlord and High Priestess Ah'krill, Equus is mine and my family's, as it should have been twenty-eight hundred years ago'? You suppose they would heed me, or would they just snap my neck?"

"Hardly a valid concern at this point. You have to kill me in any case." There was absolutely no tension in the man. No sign of fear. *He does not plan to fight me, Teal. Something else is about to take place. And why is he talking about his family and not the Telenir as a people?*

Shit! Focus, Ardi! Worry about the history later.

"True," Sarkhan was saying with a gracious nod. "Forearm knives? Close quarters?"

"As you wish," Ardenai replied, setting aside his bow and quiver.

"And if I win, what guarantees my survival?" Sarkhan asked.

"The Great House of Equus. What guarantees mine?"

"Why, the honor of the Wind Warriors, of course," Sarkhan said, and took a step back beside Konik. "I accept your challenge, but I cannot do it on my own behalf. I have not earned the pleasure and the honor of killing you, Firstlord. This man, Ah'ria Konik Nokota, has stalked you, dogged your path, and expended his time and energy to bring us here. To him, I give the glory of the kill on my behalf, as my surrogate."

Konik jumped noticeably, looking from Sarkhan's smirk to Ardenai's startled countenance and back again in astonishment. There was no fear in his face, but puzzlement, and a certain displeasure that tacitly called Sarkhan a coward. Nevertheless, he recovered quickly and nodded his assent. "I am honored," he said, and much of the tension went out of his posture, as well.

Stakes just went way up, Teal said, and Ardenai lowered his eyelids in acknowledgement. *Nik is a killing machine, Ardi. I've been in battles beside him.*

Konik turned his back and walked down the line of men to where his horse was standing. He draped his cloak over the saddle, and walked slowly back, one eye on his men as he strapped his knives in place on his forearms. "Move back twenty paces and do not interfere," he said firmly. "The rules have been established, and will be obeyed to the honor of the Wind Warriors and the Affined Equi Worlds."

Io rode to one side, flipped a hand up, and moved her squads back as well. Other than that, it was silent. As Ardenai had accepted the rule of Equus accompanied only by the ringing of his own boot heels, so now he prepared to defend Equus accompanied only by the war bells on the horse's feet. No one tried to stop it. No one cried out that it was irrational, or savage, or unnecessary.

Again Konik glanced around, his eyes troubled as he searched the closely encroaching trees and shrubbery. Ardenai caught the look, and as he seemed to concentrate on his own sheath buckles, he was counting. Ten mounted men. Sarkhan. Konik. Military personnel could enter in squads of six. Obviously more than one squad had entered, but less than two? Not likely. And how many had entered as civilians? Unknown. Two men were missing from the squad count and Ah'krill was being drawn inexorably closer with every passing minute.

"Are you ready?" Ardenai asked, sensing Konik's divided attention.

"I am ready," the man nodded. He handed one of his knives to Ardenai, and put one of Ardenai's knives in the empty sheath on his own arm.

They squared off facing each other. Slowly, Ardenai extended his left arm and Konik grasped it just above the wrist with his right hand. Then Konik extended his left arm for Ardenai to grasp. They stood thus for a minute or more, eyes locked, bringing their muscles, their breathing, their concentration into sync for that first, all important lunge.

I would not have had it go this way, my friend, Ardenai said, wondering if Konik would acknowledge him.

Nor I, came the response. *But things will be as they should if you win.*

And you will be dead, Nik.

That, too, is as it should be. Sarkhan wishes us both dead. Expect treachery of him.

I would expect nothing else. I am honored to be fighting you.

Addie...is so sick.... There was a sudden shimmer in Konik's eyes, and he bit his lip.

I know. I promise I will care for her.

Thank you. My daughters, their families, so many of us spoke for peace. Please be merciful, Dragonhorse.

Those who wanted peace will be safe. You have my word.

Konik sighed, and a brief smile flicked across his handsome features. He nodded ever so slightly, and Ardenai acknowledged. There was a slow count of three – then, like lightening, quicker, more deadly – Konik had his knife from Ardenai's sheath, Ardenai, his from Konik's. He shifted the knife from his right hand to his left, crouched, and waited for Konik to make the first move.

With the first slash of his knife Konik pushed Ardenai back, toward Ah'krill. Again he slashed, savagely, with little regard for Ardenai's longer reach. Again, Ardenai moved back, frighteningly close to his mother. He wanted to scream at her to get out of the way, to protect herself, but he couldn't break his concentration and hope to live. Konik turned, forcing Ardenai to change positions with him. Now Konik faced Sarkhan and Ardenai faced Ah'krill. Ardenai feinted with the knife in his left hand, drawing blood on Konik's jaw when he could as easily have slit his throat. Konik ducked and thrust – powerful, skillful – but watching Sarkhan, who had moved back toward the horses. Ardenai sprang to one side, easily avoiding the blade. He parried to move Konik rather than hurt him, watching his eyes to see where the next thrust would land. It did not.

Even as Konik's arm came back he saw Sarkhan jerk his head to one side. Konik flipped the knife blade-first in his hand and spun with it, following the trajectory laid down by Sarkhan's eyes, and with a hoarse shout of "TRAITOR!" he let fly with the blade and dove for Ah'krill. An archer toppled out of the shrubbery scant yards away, his bolt wobbling past the point where Ah'krill's head had been an instant before. It struck Ardenai's arm-band, glanced off, plowed a bloody furrow diagonally across Ardenai's forehead, and plopped harmlessly in the dust.

Ardenai went down, momentarily stunned, and in that second, there was war. The earth shook with the pounding of horse's hooves and the mighty roar of Equi drums. From somewhere a familiar horse without bells bore down on him, cutting a path between the opposing forces. He stayed flat and let it go over, raising up to see Konik swing Ah'krill across Gideon's saddle. The horse swerved out of the line of fire, quickly shrouded by dust. There was a scream of anger from Teal, and the pebbles jumped on the hard-packed earth as Equi cavalry appeared, squad after squad – and Konik was standing there, exposed on the open field for what seemed an eternity, looking at Ardenai, then he dropped – Sarkhan's crossbow bolt quivering between his shoulder blades.

Ardenai staggered to his feet, spitting dirt and wiping blood from his face, retracing the arrow's path until his green eyes locked on Sarkhan, fitting an arrow meant for him. That was why he'd chosen not to fight – so he could retrieve his crossbow and kill both combatants and the High Priestess, as well – the recreant filth! The Equi Firstlord threw his head back with a snarl of fury, spun with his full body weight, and side-armed the ancient knife at Sarkhan. It was an impossible throw. Sarkhan had time for a short burst of laughter before the blade tore through his heart. "Fit payment for your treason!" Ardenai screamed, shaking his fists, and Sarkhan fell face first in the dust.

Ardenai rested on one knee for a moment where the force of the throw had landed him, then sprang to his feet again and found Konik. He knelt beside him, touching his neck with his fingers. Barely, he yet lived. "Do not die," Ardenai said quietly, "I have plans for thee, my friend."

"Ardenai...El' Shadai...Ardenai..." Gideon said beside him, in a voice thick with tears, and the Equi rose with a wrenching cry of grief. In Gideon's arms, a bolt protruding grotesquely from her abdomen, was Io.

Ardenai just stood there for a moment, unable to think, or to breathe. Then he squeezed his eyes shut and anguish tore at his throat.

"NO!" he sobbed. "Eladeus, No!" and as it echoed he realized it was quiet.

The war was over. They had won.

CHAPTER EIGHTEEN

Nothing," Ardenai groaned, fingers against Io's forehead. "She's gone."

Pythos, panting a little from his sprint across the parade ground with Moonsgold, pushed Ardenai's hand gently out of the way to touch her. He bent close, eyes closed, hissing softly as he flicked her face with his tongue. Then slowly, his hands began to move down until they touched the bolt's shaft. There, he stopped. Hissed with despair. "Sshe'ss dying," he said. Then, after a moment, "Io, sshe iss not going to live, let go of her."

He raised up suddenly, jerked Io up by the front of her tunic and slapped her hard across the face. "Let go of her lesst ye die also! Io, let go. Equuss needss thee. Ardenai needss thee. We pray thee, come back!"

Ardenai, filthy, bloody and horrified, just sat there on his boot heels, slowly shaking his head from side to side, grief-stricken and shocked beyond words, his only realization being that where there might still be life, there was also the loss of an innocent. His daughter would die beneath the syca-more tree where he had carried her mother only moments before. Never to be held, or kissed, or cradled. She would spill with her mother's blood onto the dirt, the dry grass, and be lost to them forever. His tiny princess. His Ah'le-ah. He heard himself weeping, and wondered where he found the energy.

Very softly, too quietly for any but Equi ears, Io moaned. Her eye-lids quivered, and as Ardenai caught her hand, her eyes opened, brimming with tears. "Our baby," she whispered. "I can't save our baby."

"Hush," Ardenai murmured, pushing her hair back, and his tears plowed dirty streaks down his face to drip on her tunic. "It is enough to save thyself, little one. Just save thyself."

In that moment, Keats found them, and when Ardenai looked up at him and then away, Keats felt his own eyes burn with tears.

"There iss no time for that!" Pythos hissed. "Sshe is bleeding to death. Here, now, or not at all sshe must be ssaved."

Keats and Moonsgold both nodded.

"I will keep her quiet, and take from her the essence of the child so that she no longer struggles to keep her alive. Just ... tie everything off. Sstop the bleeding. I can make repairss later if sshe ssurvives."

"I will keep her quiet," Ardenai said calmly, "and I will take the essence of my daughter, if she yet lives. Pythos, you and Moonsgold help her." Keats's eyes hardened, and Ardenai shook his head and pointed with his chin. "Konik risked his life for us, Doctor. He is my friend, and he may have the answers we seek for this. He needs your considerable skill or he will die. One of the Equi will help you quiet his mind. Teal, perhaps, or Kehailan."

Again Keats nodded, squeezed Ardenai's shoulder, and moved away.

"Ardenai," Pythos hissed, "You now rissk both your livess. You were not designed to go through this, and to discipline a panicky, dying embryo of a child as well..."

"They are mine!" the Firstlord snarled through his teeth, and Pythos turned in dismay from the grief on his face.

The serpent saw Ah'krill turn and hurry toward them, horror on her face as she realized what was happening. He was tempted to tell Ardenai to wait a moment more, to let Ah'krill have the child, and the pain, but the Firstlord had already dropped to his knees and sat back on his heels to anchor himself. He bent forward at the waist, cradling Io's head and shoulders on his thighs and reached, first with one hand, then the other, to touch her face, bringing his forehead down against hers with a sob of pain. His own face contorted, and he grunted as though he'd been punched in the stomach, but the flow of blood began to slow, and finally stopped so Pythos could work.

What Ardenai felt in the time which ensued, he never told anyone, nor would he allow the subject mentioned, but minute by minute his breath-

ing grew more labored until he was sobbing for every breath, and the flow
of sweat grew heavier until he was bathed in it, and he grew paler and paler,
until his skin was stark white and nearly transparent.

Suddenly he let out a shrill, terrified cry, his head flew up, and he
would have fallen backward, but a strong pair of arms was holding him in
place by then, and at a command from Pythos, a forearm to the back of the
Equi's neck pushed his head back down against his wife's. Only when Pythos touched him with his own thoughts, telling him it was accomplished
and pushing his hands away, did he topple sideways into Gideon's embrace.

"Do not move them jusst yet," Pythos instructed. He rested his
bloody fingers for a few moments against Ardenai's cheek, flicking him tenderly, nervously with his tongue. "He hass her, or sshe hass him, I'm not
ssure which," he said. "If he panics, or goes into hysterics, keep him from
hurting himsself, Gideon. And give him water as ssoon as he wakess. Above
all, try to keep him quiet, and in mind of who he iss." He flicked the Firstlord again with his tongue, and moved off to where Hadrian Keats, Winslow
Moonsgold and Teal were working on Konik.

"You should have told me about the injury to the child! It was my
place, not yours, and certainly not his, to absorb the entat of the little priestess," Ah'krill said as Pythos brushed past her to kneel beside Konik. "A man
is not equipped for that kind of pain, and it will haunt him all his days. You
knew she was a product of my potions. She was my responsibility!"

"And thee sshould have told thy son that thy potions would leave
him generative!" Pythos retorted angrily. "If he'd known, Io would not have
been ssettled. Thiss – all of thiss, wass your doing, your grassping to remain
in power!"

"The child may not stay with him," Ah'krill grated. "She was bred
for prayer, not politics. It is unseemly to have her so mingled with the Thirteenth Dragonhorse. It is intellectual incest, and you know it."

"I also know that it iss done!" the serpent hissed. "Leave me alone,
I have work to do. Go send up smoke, Priestesss. Pray for thine own ssoul!"

Ah'krill swept away from them back to the edge of the gaming arena, and stood staring as if to recreate the events of the afternoon, then an arm came around her shoulders, and someone kissed her, firmly, lingeringly on the temple. "You needed that, whether you know it or not," said the soft drawl, and Ah'krill looked in amazement at Marion Eletsky. "Having dealt more or less ineffectively with Kehailan for several years, I've decided to turn over a new leaf with you Equi. I don't care what you need anymore, or what you say you need. I'm going to comfort you in a way that comforts me. At least then I'm sure one of us is getting what he needs."

"An excellent idea," the priestess said, patting his arm as she slipped hers through it. "It is obvious I am not needed here, nor am I welcome. I am a source of anger and resentment, and rightly so. If I had stayed in the house...or gone into hiding... or stayed where Ardenai told me to stay.... Please, walk me to my room."

"Of course I will. And I want you to be kind to yourself. When tragedies like this are fresh, it's very hard to speak and act rationally. You know that."

"Young man, do not talk to me about rationality," she said. "Tell me instead where you got that marvelous inflection of speech."

So Marion walked her slowly up the path past the stables, telling her what it had been like to be a barefoot country boy in the lush, blue-green Tennolina Mountains of the Equi Affined World called Terren.

When Ardenai was aware of anything, it was that his face was numb, and his head and his back ached mercilessly. What he meant to be a breath of air was a groan of pain, and he woke up with his head in Gideon's lap. "Gideon," he managed, trying to swallow and rubbing at his face with hands that were shaking badly enough to put his own eyes out. "So thirsty."

"I have water for thee. Oonah just brought it."

"Up. Now." Ardenai whispered.

"Not a wise choice," Gideon said, but even as he said it he obliged, putting an arm against the Equi's back and shoving him into an upright position, then getting an arm around him to keep him from falling over. "Tad weak, yes? Can you hold onto this flask?"

He couldn't, not without help, and the water which he swallowed came spewing back up as he doubled over with pain. Doggedly, he took another swig, holding his breath in an unsuccessful attempt to keep it down. "Sorry. I feel as though I have no bones. How long was I...like that?" he said through his teeth. "Where's Io?"

"Right beside you, Ardenai. Move your right hand. There. You haven't been out at all, really. A couple minutes." Gideon got to his knees without letting go of the half-conscious Equi, then shifted around and pulled Ardenai more comfortably against him.

The Firstlord went limp for a few moments, his head thudding into the side of Gideon's neck. Then his jaw tightened – Gideon could feel it flexing against his collar bone – and Ardenai pulled himself up again to reach for Io. Carefully, so carefully, with trembling fingers he touched her cheek. "Gideon...losses?"

Gideon pressed the flask into his hand again. "You have to try to rehydrate yourself, Firstlord. Three Telenir, counting Sarkhan. The rest surrendered. On our side, just...well, none that I know of."

"No warriors at least. Is Nik...one of the three?"

"No. He's holding his own. So is Io."

"Where is Kehailan?" He sipped, gagged, cursed softly.

"Locking up the Telenir, I suppose."

"You suppose?"

"Yes, Ardenai Firstlord, I suppose. It's hard to discern a whole helluva lot in the first fifteen minutes after a battle, especially when you couldn't care less what's going on around you." His eyes brimmed with tears, and Ardenai patted his arm to comfort him.

"Forgive me. I count you too often older than your years. That ride you made, jumping me with Tolbeth to take Ah'krill from danger? Even at that moment I was proud of you. I want you to go now and tell Kehailan..."

"I cannot leave thee," Gideon said, "Pythos asked me not to."

"I'll stay with him," said Moonsgold, kneeling beside them. "What do you want the young man to do?"

"Tell Kee and Tarpan...to be sure the prisoners are not able to harm themselves," Ardenai said, flipping his hand and gasping with the effort of doing it. "Go quickly. Check on Ah'krill as well, and tell me what else you can discover about the day." He drew a sudden, sobbing breath, doubled over and whispered, "I hurt! Precious Equus, I hurt so badly!" He jerked, as though the words had startled him, and shook his head to clear it. "Sorry," he said again. "I don't know why I said that. I'm fine. Little cramp of some kind."

"Rest," Gideon said. He helped Moonsgold prop Ardenai, half against the tree trunk, half against the doctor, pressed the flask into his hand, and ran toward the house, knowing Winnie knew what to do, but wishing Jilfan hadn't taken all the horses away. Strange, Jilfan rounding up the horses rather than staying with his mother. Then, perhaps not. Blood could be unnerving, the blood of a loved one, particularly so.

As he got near the house he began calling for Kehailan or Tarpan, and soon from an outbuilding Daleth beckoned him over. Gideon eyed the prisoners and shuddered involuntarily at the blanketed corpses. He gave Kehailan the message, and asked where Jilfan was. No one knew. He'd herded the horses into that holding pen over there, and disappeared. Gideon was not to worry. Someone would unsaddle them shortly. Gideon went to the house and looked in on Ah'krill. He found her sitting with Oonah Pongo and Captain Eletsky. Again, Jilfan was not there. This time, he expressed some concern. The boy had been fine at the end of hostilities, he knew that, but where was he? Could he possibly want to be alone? Gideon didn't see how. It was all he could do not to turn right straight around and bolt back to Ardenai's side. But there were things to do. Catching Timothy, Tarpan, and Daleth as they came from the farrier's shed, he asked them to find six poles for stretchers, and he went back inside for blankets.

"Hadrian thinks Konik will make it," Moonsgold said quietly, holding Ardenai in place against the tree with one hand, and feeling his face with the other. "The bolt didn't strike any vital organs, and the head went clear through, which is a good thing. Turned up rather than down or he'd be a dead man. Did shatter his breast bone, which must hurt like hell. Ardenai, you skin is like ice, and you're soaking wet. Are you cold?"

"Yes. Perhaps if I...walked a bit."

"Is this before or after you manage to sit up by yourself?"

Ardenai smacked his fists on the ground, gasping as much from weakness as from pain and annoyance. "Pythos, what is wrong with me?" he demanded. "I have been in pain before and walked away from it."

"Not like thiss thee hassn't" the serpent hissed, kneeling beside Io. "Thy mind firmly believess that thy body hass jusst losst a baby, and a tremendouss amount of blood with it. Thee has taken an arrow in the guts for all it knowss. Thy infant daughter iss sstill sscreaming around in thy head. Males never, ever absorb fetussess, sso sshe hass no idea where sshe iss, and neither of thee wass properly prepared. I haven't had time to help thee with her, and every ssecond thee fightss it, thee makes it worsse. Pleasse, jusst let thysself ssleep. Have merccy on an old dragon. Give me one lesss thing to worry about."

"I need to stay awake for Io," he whispered, and his eyes closed as his head thudded dully against the trunk of the huge sycamore.

Moonsgold had been looking first at Pythos, then at Ardenai. Now, wide-eyed, he looked back at the serpent. "Are you telling me his male mind is capable of putting his body through a miscarriage?"

"No. Io'ss mind iss, though. And it did. What sshe could not have lived through, he took upon himsself. The actual wound, and the blood losss, were herss. The pain and the sshock, he carriess for now, and the terrible grief – they sshare in equal part."

"Why would you do that?" a sharp voice asked, and Hadrian Keats appeared over Moonsgold's shoulder. "Why would you risk yourself like that, knowing how it could affect your home world? It was a stupid, irrational thing to do. And why wouldn't you let me work on Io? Do you really think I'd do something to her?"

"No, of course not, Hadrian. I knew your treatment of Io would take longer than I could stand the pain, that's all. Therefore I asked you to take care of Konik. Secondly..." his eyes closed, he took a deep, gasping breath, wrapped his arms around his middle, and exhaled with a soft moan.

"Two can wait, you rest," Keats said, and his face was contrite.

"No. I have to stay awake. Secondly, I wanted that time with my wife and with my daughter, because those few moments, were all we had as a family. I wanted Io to know I will always be here for her." Ardenai sighed, trying to swallow the choking dryness in his throat. "I know this makes no sense to you, Doctor. Right now, it makes no sense to me. Nothing...makes any sense to me. I'm really scared."

Pythos' hand touched Ardenai's face, his tongue flicking against the Equi's eyelids. "Pleasse, ssleep. Thee iss in great danger."

"How can I sleep?" Ardenai groaned miserably. "I awoke at Canyon keep one sunny morning, and Ree was dead beside me. I never got to say goodbye, never got to tell her I loved her. What if I wake up, and Io is dead?"

"What if sshe wakes up and thee iss dead?" Pythos murmured, and even as he spoke, his hand floated across Ardenai's face and the Equi slumped against him. "Thee iss sstill my baby," Pythos whispered. "Ssleep a bit now and rebuild thy sstrength."

Keats just looked at him. "That was his decision to make, not yours," he said at last, and Moonsgold snorted, shaking his head in annoyance.

"He doesn't get it," he said. "He's never been a daddy, and he just doesn't get it."

"Then let me exssplain it," Pythos said in a voice sharper than what they were used to hearing. "In addition to his wife'ss pain, he hass taken upon himsself the entat – the living essence of a child, and a female child at that. Sshe iss too young to know how to walk, talk, eat, drink, or breathe by hersself, let alone think for hersself. Sshe is reacting. That iss all sshe iss capable of. Thee can't hear her coming out of his mouth? I can. Sshe iss terrified at being torn from her mother. Her prematurely awakened and em-bryonic conssciousness will roll through him like water through an opened floodgate if sshe iss allowed to. Sshe is pure energy at thiss point – pure, unthinking, undissciplined energy. If he iss too exhaussted, he will losse to her, and losse himsself, and if he doess, they will both be losst, becausse sshe doessn't know how to breathe on her own. Because I am the one who knowss what to do, I am the one who needss to be in control."

"I do think she's controlling his heartbeat," Moonsgold said, *sotto voce*. "It's terribly fast."

The old serpent nodded, and Gideon's voice cut in, alarmed, as always, when he perceived Ardenai to be in danger. "But you're fine, Pythos, and didn't you tell me once that you carried the entat of many people, blended within your consciousness? Are none of them babies? Can't you get her out of there before she harms him in some way?"

"Ah, Gideon, I am pleassed that thou art back. To answer you, all of them are babiess. We do not conssider it moral to take the entatss of adultss, or even children after they begin to toddle. However, almosst none are fetussess this rudimentary, as the mother usually hass the sstrength to reabsssorb them into her own conssciousness. Io attempted to do that, and nearly died in the procccesss." He sighed, and uncoiled onto his feet. "Ardenai iss Dragonhorsse, it wass hiss choicce, and it iss done. Timothy, please help Kehailan with Konik. And Teal, thou art here as well. Good. Thee can help me carry thy kinsman. Doctor Keatss, wilt thou and Doctor Moonsgold pleasse bring Io?"

They set about readying the stretchers, and Pythos beckoned Gideon to one side. "I want thee to go to Ssouth Hold village and get Ah'nora. Thee will find her at the tanner'ss sshop. Tell her what hass happened, everything that hass happened, and bring her back here as ssoon ass thee can."

Gideon knit his eyebrows and said, "Pardon, Physician Pythos, but," he cleared his throat and glanced around to ascertain who might be within earshot. "I know that Io was pregnant, and that she has lost her little one. I also know that Ah'nora carries the son of the Firstlord. Do you really think it is...I do know thou art wise, but...do you really think it's the best thing for Io to have Ah'nora here?"

Pythos flicked Gideon with his tongue and said, "Thou art kind, Hatchling, and thoughtful. But I need Ah'nora, and your ssire will need

Ah'nora. We sshall worry about the resst of it when Io is conssciouss again. For now, pleasse do as I assk."

"Certainly," Gideon said, and trotted toward the pen where the horses still stood waiting. He took Tolbeth and Kimmis, and rode off in the direction of the village at a ground-eating canter.

Ah'krill slipped quietly into the gardens and stood, palms out, eyes closed, seeking with her mind the palpable grief she could feel emanating from somewhere close by. Slowly, eyes still closed, she began to focus, and her body turned. When she opened her eyes she was facing the stable, and she walked in that direction.

It was evening, nearly dark, and the interior of the stable was nothing more than a black tunnel with a dim light at the far end. But light, she didn't need. She could follow the sobs. She found their source in an empty stall. Jilfan, lying in the straw, weeping in pain and sorrow.

He was unaware of her presence until she sat beside him and her hand came to rest on his shoulder, then he choked, and looked up, not knowing who it was. "Leave me," he sobbed. "I will make you unclean with my cowardice."

"So, you are a coward, and I am a stupid old woman," Ah'krill said gently, and Jilfan sat up with a gasp of recognition. "We're quite the pair, aren't we?"

"Forgive me!" he managed, dragging his palms across his face. "Please, forgive me, Ah'krill."

"I have no need to forgive you, Child. But I sense a great need for you to forgive yourself. What pains you so?"

"I am a coward! I saw my dam fall in battle, and I ran. I left her care to a stranger, a Declivian. I left her to die! Leave me. I am unfit."

"You are untried," Ah'krill corrected firmly. "That does not mean you are unfit."

"I ran away!"

"I ran away, Jilfan. Away from Equus. I came here, thinking I was doing the right thing, but perhaps I was not. Perhaps Pythos is right and what happened today, happened because of me. The first shot was fired at me. An honorable and gallant man went down with an arrow through his back because of me. Your mother lies injured, because of me."

"No," Jilfan said quietly, and forgetting who she was, sensing only kindred grief, his hand closed over hers. "It doesn't make sense to assume so much. I have sat many evenings with Ardenai Firstlord and the others. They were prepared for violence. If you did anything at all you shifted its focus, nothing more. You are not to blame."

"Then who is, do you suppose?"

"Sarkhan, perhaps, and he has paid. I saw my stepfather's knife go right through him." The boy shuddered, and rubbed at his arms.

"It is not pleasant to see someone die. Even someone evil. When we see someone who is good, and rational, kill someone who is violent and evil, things seem upside down, do they not?"

"Um hm," Jilfan replied, and drew a deep, sobbing breath. "Ah'krill, I did not mean to panic."

"No one means to panic, Jilfan. It just happens. It is the antithesis of self-control, and self-control can be learned."

"I panicked," he said stubbornly. "I ran. I am nearly a man – nearly as old as Gideon, and I ran. My father was a warrior who died in battle. My grandfather is a warrior. My mother is a warrior, and I am a coward."

"Perhaps it is just that you are not a warrior. Gideon is four years your senior, and four years is a long time at your age, so do not be envious of Gideon. Envy is corrosive. The raising you have had, and the opportunities, have opened doors for you that Gideon may never see."

"But he helped my mother."

"What makes you think you cannot?" Ah'krill asked, studying the boy's face in the dim light. It was an Equi face, not Papilli, and for some reason, she found that comforting.

"How can I? It is too late."

"To help her as a warrior, yes. But you, perhaps, are not a warrior. Besides that, what can you offer?"

"Nothing she cannot get elsewhere," Jilfan sighed. "Not comfort, obviously, since it is I who receive it from you. Not strength. I saw her bleeding, and I ran. The blood loss sickened me."

"Then offer it back. The blood. She will need it. Conditions are primitive here, and through your blood she may gain the strength she needs to live. I have seen how my son looks at her. Without her, he will not want to go on. Without Ardenai, Gideon's purpose will be lost. Do you see? You have only to give that which you are truly able to give, to perform the best service of all. You need not fight. You need only be who you are."

Jilfan nodded and sat rubbing his face, still recovering from the harshness of his grief. "I...will have to face them, Teal and the others, with where I have been, and what I have been doing while they were serving Equus and the Alliance. That will be very difficult."

"Yes," Ah'krill agreed. "Best accomplished quickly and without pretense, and left behind once and for all, I would say."

"I agree," he sighed. "I thank you for your time, and your wisdom, Priestess."

"And I thank you for hearing me. Perhaps, we could spend more time together. I am now your grandmother, you know."

The boy grew round-eyed. "Do you think we could? I would be much honored."

"It is done. Bear in mind, I am not here because I am the only one who cares about you. They all care. But they are all acting as warriors, with warrior's concerns. In that particular chain we are weak links, you and I. That does not mean we do not have our own strength, our own place, our own function. As a people we do not often make war, nor even think of war, and it will not be often that we will consider ourselves so out of place. Soon, we will go home to life as we know it, and these days will be only a memory, a touchstone to the deeper parts of ourselves."

"To the darker parts of ourselves," Jilfan muttered.

"Those, too, we must know," Ah'krill replied. "Come, walk me to the house. Tell me what you think of the wondrous order of things."

▲ ▲ ▲ ▲ ▲ ▲ ▲

Pythos turned from the stove with a fire-warmed blanket and moved quickly to the bed with it. "It iss one of their few weaknesssess," he said, tucking the cover around Ardenai. "They do not retain their body heat as mosst hominoids do, thuss they are esspecially prone to sshock. Much of their heat iss losst through their beautiful earss." He stroked the sides of the Equi's head and said fondly, "I have never dessired anthropoid characteristicss beyond those which I already have, but I would have liked earss."

"These, especially," Gideon said, nodding his assent and snugging in a corner of the blanket. "He just doesn't want to warm up, does he?"

"Perhapss I sshould not have bathed him."

"Yes, you should have," Gideon said firmly. "You wouldn't want him lying here in that blood-soaked uniform. He reeked. His sweat had turned the grime on him to mud. He couldn't possibly have rested comfortably or improved his health in that state. Besides, the water is very warm. It should have helped. Now, Ah'nora said she was going to get some things together in the kitchen, and she'd be right here. I can stay with Ardenai, and Doctor Moonsgold is right next door with Io, in case I need help. Why don't you go and get some rest?"

"Becausse I need to sspeak to Ardenai, and then to Ah'nora," Pythos replied, using the tone that was a smile. "Thee is no lesss tired than I, Gideon. Thee needss to bathe, and change thy bloody clothess, and find thysself ssome food. I sshall be along sshortly."

Gideon looked at the physician, then back to Ardenai, his hands suddenly nervous as they brushed imaginary bits of lint from the blanket. "I suppose I should," he said tentatively, "but I just hate to leave him, you know?"

"I do know," Pythos said softly. "I am going to leave Ah'nora in charge here, with very sspecific instructionss as to what sshe iss to do. More can sshe do, than either of uss, my young friend. Go ahead. I'll be along. I promisse."

Gideon nodded, rose, and bent to kiss the bloody scratch on Ardenai's forehead. "Please, don't go anywhere without me," he whispered. He wiped at his eyes and was letting himself quietly out the door when Ah'nora came down the dimly lit hall carrying a tray with several things on it, and a leather bag slung over one arm. She was dressed in the manner of her Amish neighbors, in a long-sleeved brown dress which brushed her ankles, and a creamy white muslin pinafore, her soft brown hair in a bun atop her head. It made her look...efficient. He smiled, held the door open for her, and then forced himself to close it.   She was a kind, competent, beautiful woman. Pythos had faith in her. Pythos loved Ardenai and would do nothing to harm him. Ah'nora loved Ardenai. It would be all right for Gideon to leave him. He would be all right. Things would be fine. The Declivian finally forced himself to point his toes down the hall and take a few steps.

He walked one door down and looked in on Io, who was being tended by Winslow Moonsgold. She looked like a discarded doll – her luxuriant hair dirty and tangled, her face marred with pain and sorrow. Winnie gave him a bright smile and a thumbs-up like it was just another day of stitches and upset tummies, and Gideon let himself back out again. There really wasn't one damned thing he could do, no matter how much he wanted to change that. He had become an observer. A hungry one. One that stank. *A little princcce musst not ssstink,* he told himself, and walked resolutely down to the bathing pools, chuckling softly to himself, though for the life of him, he didn't know what there was to laugh about.

Pythos' instructions to Ah'nora were brief and to the point, ending with, "Do anything, *anything,* thee musst to keep him ssafe, comfortable, and in mind of who he iss," the serpent hissed. Exhaustion was making him agitated, and slightly more difficult than usual to understand. "Do not let him ssleep too much. In deep ssleep can be losss as well as healing. Help him to eat ssomething. Help him put the child in her placce. Ssee that he rememberss that he iss Firstlord of Equuss, not a puling infant. For exsssample, if the ssight of thy presssented breasssts makess him want to sssuckle rather than have intercoursse with thee, thou art doing ssomething wrong. Change that. Indulge him. Ssee he ssstayss a man."

"I do understand," she said, and her voice had a bit of an edge to it, though she blushed uncomfortably. "Gideon explained things to me on the way back here, and I think he did a pretty good job. Why don't you let me see what I can do, Physician Pythos, and if I am not having enough success to suit you, we can discuss this further."

"I sshall take that as a disssmisssal," he said, flicked Ardenai gently with his tongue, and exited the room, leaving Ah'nora alone with the First-lord.

She looked at the closed door awhile, shaking her head, and turned with a chuckle to further organize the things on the tray. She had opened the chute to release more press-wood into the stove, and was watching the flames when a very rusty baritone said, "My dear and lovely Ah'nora," and she turned to see tired green eyes and the ghost of a smile from the Firstlord. "We do seem to take advantage of you, don't we?"

She came and sat next to him on the edge of the big, hand-carved bed, taking his hand into her lap and pushing his dark hair back from his face. "How are you feeling?" she asked, looking into his eyes and giving him a gentle smile that was all concern.

"Much better than Pythos thinks," he said, squeezing her hand. "You must pardon him for his unfeeling words, my dear. You are not an object to be used, and I ask your forgiveness."

"He loves thee, and I am thine, Firstlord," she replied, bending to kiss his forehead, "He is literally worried out of his mind. He delivered you from the womb of your mother. He delivered Io. Only a few weeks ago he married you to her, and oh, he was so happy! You should have seen him after you left on your wedding trip, laughing and dancing around on those short little legs of his, grabbing Teal for balance. And now Io lies near death, with her baby lost and maybe her fertility, and you..." She sighed and looked away a moment to regain herself. When she looked back, there were tears standing in Ardenai's eyes.

"I should have sent her away," he whispered. "I should have sent her away like I did you."

"She would not have gone, and you know it. She is Captain of the

Horse Guard of the Great House of Equus. You would have demeaned her by putting your marriage ahead of her responsibilities. She would have been incredibly angry with you."

"And now she's going to hate me anyway," he sighed. "I just want to be with her instead of in here. I don't know why Pythos had to separate us."

"Now I see what Pythos means," Ah'nora said in a gently scolding tone. "You are scaring him with the possibility that your daughter will take over your consciousness, and all of a sudden you sound like a child."

"Point taken, Mistress," snapped the Firstlord, and Ah'nora blushed, though her gaze didn't waver. Ardenai took a deep, steadying breath, and patted her hand in apology. "He has forgotten that controlling, comforting, teaching tiny, frightened children was my life for many, many years. I suppose that's good. It becomes tiresome when people always expect our very best from us. Some days, we are not capable of giving it." His face twisted with pain and he bit his lip, pulling his other hand across his middle.

"Did he give you something for pain?"

"No. He thought it best not to, how did he put it, distort my perception any more than it was already distorted by the presence of my daughter."

"I have some tea that will help with the cramping, but first we must get you swallowing properly again. Gideon says you can't keep water down?"

"Not even water. At least I couldn't a while ago."

"Water can be harder than you think to swallow. Let's try some small pieces of sugar melon. Crush them with your teeth a little, and let them slide down your throat. They're mostly water anyway, but this will be a little more substantial, and the sugar can be soothing to the stomach."

She gave him a small bite of the melon. He worked his jaw carefully, then swallowed and took a deep breath. "Better," he said, closing his eyes.

"Well, don't go to sleep on me just yet," she grinned. "A few more bites of this, and perhaps a couple sips of tea first."

"Trust me, I have no intention of going back to sleep until I get some answers," he said.

She used pillows to sit him up straighter, and they went about it slowly. Between bites, Ah'nora gently massaged his neck and shoulders to help him relax, and some of the tension in his jaw began to ebb away. "Pythos is concerned that with the baby being so young, her inability to swallow is keeping you from swallowing, as well," she said. "He is also concerned that she does not know how to breathe."

"He has always referred to me as his hatchling," Ardenai muttered, closing his eyes and relaxing into the pillows, "but after a hundred years he should at least give me credit for being able to out-think one."

"She's not giving you any trouble, then?"

"No. I don't think so. Right at the beginning, when I was getting Io's panic along with hers, it was a little scary, but she is...was...is...very tiny, and still very sleepy, poor little thing. Her mother must be devastated."

He squeezed his eyes shut for a few moments, gathering strength, and opened them again as the door crept open. Jilfan's scared, boyish face appeared around the corner. "Come," Ardenai said, and the boy shuffled in. "Sit."

The boy sat, shifting uncomfortably, sensing the blackness of the Firstlord's mood.

"Have you seen your mother?" asked Ardenai.

"Yes," Jilfan sighed. "They wouldn't let me stay. Doctor Moonsgold says she is resting. I told Pythos I would give her some of my blood. How are you?"

"Alive," Ardenai replied. "How are you?"

"Ashamed, I ran. You know that."

"No," Ardenai replied, glancing over at him in the lamplight. "I did not know. I have had other concerns. I was aware that you were not with your mother."

"Do you think she will forgive me?"

"I do not think she will blame you in the first place. She has seen grown men panic in battles that were planned. Surely a boy can run from an ambush."

"I had not thought myself a boy," Jilfan muttered.

"You were wrong. You are a boy," Ardenai said, gazing into the flames in the stove. "Because your assessment of yourself was in error, your expectations regarding your performance, were unrealistic."

"Not true," Jilfan said quietly. "I expected courage from myself because I have a collective history of courage in my family. I disappoint them. I disappoint myself. I have explained that to Teal and the others. I explain it to you, not because I expect your forgiveness, but so you will not believe your wife raised a coward – that your old friend, Abeyan, fosters cowardice. What I am, I am."

Ardenai sighed, pulling his eyes away from the fire to glance first at Ah'nora, who was pouring tea, then at Jilfan. "This has been a strange time, has it not? A time totally unlike what we are used to, and we are disappointed that we have not handled it well. We should be amazed that we have handled it at all."

Ah'nora brought the tea, offering a cup to Jilfan, who took it gratefully and thanked her, and then a cup to Ardenai. She stayed long enough to make sure he had a good hold on it, then excused herself, and slipped from the room to do other things for a bit.

Ardenai sipped slowly and carefully at his drink, noting that it was medicinal instead of the usual, fragrant orange peel and cinnamon which Jilfan had been given. He blew on it a little, and adjusted the warm cup in his hands. "I did not see you run away today, but I did see other things. I saw people who knew what they were doing – Konik, Teal, your mother – Daleth and Tarpan. Then I saw those of us who were trying to do what we thought best despite being out of our element. But mostly, one man's actions stand out in my mind." He sighed, leaning his head back against the pillows. "This man, I would have sworn I knew well," he said. "As you know Jilfan, or think you do, so I know him. And yet, I saw him kill a man today, not out of duty as one would kill an enemy of the state, but in fury, and in hatred, and he gloated in the face of death. I heard this man – this diplomat who has represented Equus at the opening of whole new worlds – this man to whom parents entrust their babes – I heard him scream in anger. I felt him use his strength for immoral and unreasonable purposes, and I wondered, could he have done what he had to do, without the anger? Was it him believing himself to be something he is not, who caused the lady to lie as she does, with her baby dead?"

There was a silence. Then Jilfan asked, "Why was there a settled woman on a field of battle?"

"Something she will wrestle with the rest of her life. Was it misjudgment on her part, or someone else's? Perhaps, she was counting on her husband to protect her, which he did not." Ardenai sighed. "Jilfan, this is not simple. To try and make it so, is unrealistic. This was mounted and accomplished with the necessity of great confusion and emotion. It must be evaluated in the same manner or we are making irrational and unlike comparisons. Do you understand?"

"Yes," he said quietly, looking into his cup. "I understand at least that it is neither logical nor simple. May I then also assume that the conclusions I draw, and the decisions I make may be emotional?"

"I know mine will be. I have discovered, though, that emotion can be a harsh master, and sinister. I would ask that you be gentle with yourself, and do not shoulder more of the responsibility than is your portion. Most of it – all of it, actually – is mine. I have been lying here these hours, and with the clarity of hindsight, I have seen a dozen ways, a hundred, a thousand I could have accomplished this without the loss of life."

"Name one," Jilfan demanded softly, and dared to meet Ardenai's eyes. Ardenai glared at him a moment, then snorted softly and looked away. "Take your own advice, Dragonhorse. Do not shoulder more than is yours to carry, nor too soon, before you can straighten up under it. Do you know where I have been, besides weeping in the horse barn?"

"No," Ardenai replied, and he was beginning to smile. "Tell me."

"I have been sitting in the straw with she who leads the prayers of Equus, listening to her agonize over the possibility that what happened was her fault. Now I hear it from you. If my mother lives, I shall hear it from her."

"Io will live," Ardenai said quietly. "I have told her she has to. We both know she would not dare cross me."

"Do not grieve," Jilfan whispered, his hand closing over Ardenai's forearm. "It is unnecessary, and inappropriate. Your wife yet lives."

"And for her I do not grieve quite so much," Ardenai replied. "But for the one perfectly innocent person involved in all this. Our daughter. Your sister."

Jilfan shook his head, having no words with which to respond. Ardenai could smell the dregs of the tea in the boy's cup, orange peel and cinnamon, and remembered this night he had spoken of, when they would get together and celebrate their victory. How naive to assume it could be had at no cost. This night, when they would announce to their friends that they were expecting a baby daughter. He felt tears on his face, and realized that part of him would weep forever. "Jilfan," he said, wiping at his eyes and shaking his head to clear it, "I need a boon of thee."

"Of course," the boy responded, and rose from where he was sitting.

"Go find Teal, Tarpan and Daleth, Keats, Moonsgold, Gideon and Marion. Let Pythos sleep. And find Kehailan. Tell them I wish to speak with all of them in here in thirty minutes. Can you do that?"

"Yes, Ardenai Firstlord, I can do that," Jilfan said, and was gone.

The Equi pulled his knees up, wrapped his arms around them, and slumped forward. Almost, the conversation had been too much for him. He was hungry, but too tired to want anything, and, truth be told, too weak to look for anything which Ah'nora might have left. He was half dozing when a pair of large, strong hands closed over his shoulders and someone kissed the top of his head.

"I am very, very sorry about your baby," Gideon whispered close to Ardenai's ear, and gave him another gentle kiss. He sat down beside the Equi, holding a small bowl with a spoon resting in it. "This is warm buckwheat cereal with honey in it. Ah'nora wants you to try it."

"Well," Ardenai said, "I have two choices here. I can eat this, and probably throw it up, or I can just throw it against the wall and be done with it."

"Remember what you told that slaver? You told him you won me in a poker game. I say what the hell, gamble. Eat it. At least if it stays down you'll feel like you've accomplished one thing today."

Ardenai looked at Gideon out of the corner of his eye. Gideon looked back and gave the Equi a gentle elbow. "Might find you a nicccce Declivian tree toad insssstead," he hissed.

Ardenai burst out laughing, and even as he laughed two big tears ran down his cheeks. "Oh, Gideon," he managed, wiping his face with the palms of his hands for what seemed the hundredth time, "Oh, Gideon, what a mess. What a kraaling mess this is."

"How many people have you asked?" Gideon retorted. "Equus lives. You live, and Sarkhan is dead. Isn't that what this was all about in the first place? I'll bet if you'd admit it, you haven't asked anybody. Oh, you've talked to Keats – medicine's answer to the insufferable ass. And I saw Jilfan come out of your room, so I assume you've talked to a panic stricken thirteen-year-old. He started sweating the second those men rode out of the trees, and within two minutes his perception was one hundred percent gone. He stayed, because his horse stayed. I say that not in contempt, but in realization. Save his heart; give him a computator. Io, who could tell you what really happened was doing one thing, and one thing only, that most proper task of trying to save your daughter. Those two agonized female minds are the only other things you've touched. You want to know what happened out there? Me too. Eat your cereal and then I'll go get Teal. Flaying yourself with introspection will avail you nothing."

Ardenai looked at him in amazement, and not for the first time. Amazing young man. "Who are you, really?" he asked. "What incarnation of pure intellect? And how do you manage to get inside my head like you do?"

"I love you too much to be afraid of what I'll find, so I just crawl in through your eyes," Gideon chuckled. "Please eat some of that. You are all the positive things I've never had. You are critic, teacher, and friend. You are father, mother, Paraclete, sibling. I ask instead, who sent you to me? El'Shadai heard my prayer for someone, one someone, to take the place of all the people I would never have. Ardenai, I will never marry. I do not function. Not as husband, not as father. What you did by accident, or so rumor has it, I can only dream of doing. What you had for a few moments in your daughter, have now in Kehailan, and will have again, many, many times over, I'll never have at all, even once. Can you understand?"

Ardenai nodded, ate what he could, and handed the bowl back to Gideon. "I hope you are planning a career in teaching, or in the diplomatic corps," he said. He studied the boy for a moment, nodded, half to himself, and went on speaking. "It is what thy father wishes for thee, though thy grandsire will try to make a farmer of thee. We are about to be visited by our companions. Open the door, and gather some cushions, will you?"

Gideon was glad of the immediate task; it gave him time to process the words, *thy father, thy grandsire.* Had he heard it right? Was Ardenai so tired and grief stricken that he was speaking out of his head? Was Pythos' worst fear coming to pass? Had the baby taken over Ardenai's conscious mind? *Thy father. Thy grandsire.* Though they might be a mistaken tune, their refrain rang sweetly in his head as he hurried to arrange the room.

As he opened the door, Teal's voice, usually as graceful and airborne as his name implied, fell heavily on their ears as he came down the hall. "You're a Terren. You cannot possibly understand the grief in Ardenai's mind just now. We Equi treasure our young. To us, the loss of a child is the ultimate tragedy."

"That, was not a child," Keats said reasonably. "It was a thumbnail sized glob of cells. Ardenai hardly gave Junior here the time of day for most of his adult life. It's a ludicrous reaction for a man of his stature."

"Now, Hadrian, nobody's going to agree with that," Marion said. "The story you're bringing up, and which I think you're vastly overstating, has two sides and two participants. The wee one had no say."

"A very human reaction, and one I'd expect from you, Marion. You're a sentimental slob. But from Ardenai? Given the momentous events of the day, and his part in them – for Godssake, he literally cut Sarkhan's heart in half with that knife!"

"It was his daughter," Kehailan said. "We Equi sense our children, their sex, their personalities, within seconds of conception. That baby was as much herself today as she will be a hundred years from now."

"Ludicrous," Keats snapped.

"No," Teal said hotly. "It is not. The knowledge she would have gained, that part of her was not there. But who she was, the spirit she was granted upon conception, entered with Ardenai to grow with Io." He realized the door was open, and dropped his voice. Keats did not.

"Alright, who was she?" Keats drawled, "What was she like?"

"A beauty," came Ardenai's voice. "Gentlemen, do come in. I'm sorry to have to meet with you from the depths of this bed, but since my muscles have turned to water and my legs have declared themselves sovereign islands, this is how it must be."

"We are sorry if we have disturbed you with our conversation, Beloved," Teal said, kissing Ardenai lingeringly on the forehead before seating himself on the floor near the fire. "We were having a philosophical discussion."

"About my daughter."

"Yes," Teal smiled. "Not many men are as fortunate as you have been. Will you tell us about her?"

"Of course," Ardenai nodded, and motioned Moonsgold, who had opened the adjoining door, to sit. "Leave it open. We will be quiet about this." He closed his eyes and let himself relax a moment, then opened them and said, "She would have been attractive, and pleasant of nature. Her capacity to learn was good, to discern, excellent. She had big eyes like Io, but green, like mine. Dark hair. A classic Equi female. She would have had neither her mother's diminutive stature, nor delicate features, though she was graced with her father's ears and her mother's nose. She would have been tall. Able, nearly, to look her brothers in the eye. Slender, long legged, like her father. More like me than Io, both in physical appearance and personality, but comelier of features, and more refined. A tragic loss to my home world, my household, and my heart."

"Pardon me for intruding on the moment," Keats said, "but how do you know all that? Or do you just want to know it."

"I know," Ardenai replied, tapping his forehead, "Because I have my daughter's entat, her living essence, I suppose you would call it; that part of her which would have been her thinking and feeling mind. And, from the coordination problems I'm having at the moment, I think she's trying to assert her right-handed motor skills, as well. She and I will share my mind from this day forward, though she will ultimately find her place mostly in my subconscious."

"May the change be a pleasant one," Tarpan said. "And uplifting. It is most certainly unique."

"Because she has learned so little, my capacity has been greatly expanded," Ardenai said. "Through her, I can better serve my people, and she will have purpose, as she was meant to."

"And do we know whose arrow struck her mother?" Gideon asked.

"Sarkhan's," Daleth replied. "It was his first arrow which struck her, and it was not meant for her, but for you, Gideon, as you rode to save Ah'krill. As you leaned over your horse's neck to clear Ardenai, the arrow passed behind you and struck the captain. Sarkhan nocked another bolt and hit Konik as he turned around. In the moments following, he fell to the Firstlord's good left hand."

"That," Timothy McGill said, "The flight of that forearm blade, was the most spectacular throw I've ever seen. For the power behind it – the dust, the blood in your eyes – it went as true, no curve, no wobble, as it could possibly have gone. I have known you through Kee for many years, Firstlord, and because I know what you have tried to accomplish as a diplomat and educator, I hesitate to compliment you as a fighter. Nevertheless, I do so. If it is inappropriate, forgive me."

"Well spoken," Tarpan said. "I add my commendation. You did well. Your manipulation of Sarkhan at the outset, is what won the day. By Sarkhan's pledge to the honor of the Wind Warriors, Konik was *bound* to do what he did. Because you showed Konik mercy, he was *able* to do what he did."

"Mercy?" Moonsgold echoed.

"Of course," Teal said. "Konik was watching Sarkhan, not Ardenai. He wasn't planning to win, or even to fight past pretense. Ardenai could have killed him at any moment, but he chose not to. He did what a scholar would do, he observed, and by observing, he saved the day."

"By offering himsself without hesssitation, even in a ssituation he knew logically he wass not equipped to handle, he ssaved our Io, and wass rewarded with the esssence of hiss child," Pythos hissed from the doorway where he stood with Ah'nora, taking in the room with a collective glare. "What a sshame that he iss sso crazed when it comess to matterss of hiss health that hiss nursse cannot even leave to refressh hersself and eat ssome dinner, without him filling the room with warriorss and talk of war, when he sshould be filling hiss head with meditation and ssleep."

"Sir Pent is upon us, flee for your lives," Ardenai muttered, and the old physician writhed with displeasure.

"Thee knows how I desspise that nickname!"

"Of course I do. That is why I use it. That is why I gave it to you, and will see to it that my sons continue it ..." Ardenai trailed off, and the good humor faded from his eyes.

"Ssuddenly sso ssad?" Pythos asked, coiling gracefully onto the floor near the fire.

"I am High Equi. In all probability I will outlive Kehailan and Gideon both, perhaps even Jilfan. Not a pleasant thought for a father to have." Ardenai stopped, shook his head and looked at the others in the room with some puzzlement. "Forgive me. That was an odd thing to say, wasn't it?"

"It wass...feminine," Pythos said with what passed for a wicked smile. "There iss yet a ssmall, red-gold moth fluttering at the cornerss of thy mind, and for all time, the little caterpillar will munch away at thy highly touted massculinity."

"Do not gloat," Ardenai said firmly. "You could as well have been the companion of her entat, and indeed already share your mind with many just like her."

"Yess, but I am both a male, and a female to begin with, sso I do not find it dissquieting."

"You're what?" Keats exclaimed, and Pythos hissed with delight.

"Again hiss mind topplesss from the narrow sshelf where he sstoress it! Come, Doctor Keatss, Come, Doctor Moonssgold, let uss check on our patientss, and I will let thee assk me quesstionss. And as for thee, Ardenai Firsstlord, thiss meeting could have waited upon thy sstrength a little. Assk what thee musst to allow thysself to ssleep, and then do sso, or ssteps will be taken to ssee that thee ssleeps – on my termss."

Pythos uncurled off the floor, gestured ahead of himself toward the door, and they would have exited, but Ardenai's voice stayed them. "Physician, I would at least know, before you leave us, the condition of the wounded."

The old serpent turned back with a gracious nod. "As thee wisshes, Firsstlord. Legate Konik losst a great deal of blood, and hiss breasst-bone wass broken, pusshed from the back through the flessh of his chesst, which tore the mussle and exposssed the bone. He iss not yet conssciouss, but I have every reasson to think he will recover, thankss to Doctor Keatss. The lady Io will quite possibly need repair work done when we return to Equuss, but sshe, too, hass a very good chancce of recovery given enough time and willpower."

"Thank you," Ardenai murmured, and the doctor took his leave, flashing a brief but meaningful glare at Teal and the others who lingered behind.

"There were three Telenir deaths," Teal said. "Sarkhan, the sniper Konik dispatched, and one other, who would have put an arrow in your back. Him, I killed myself. The others, finding themselves against overwhelming odds, surrendered their weapons."

"Where did all that cavalry come from?" Ardenai murmured. "The earth shook, the trees came alive; they seemed to rise from the very dust."

Teal chuckled. "Many, many Equi live here, Dragonhorse. They inhabit hold and keep, cot and countryside. Your wife sent word to them that the militia was needed. She drilled with them at night to re-sharpen their skills, and set them in reserve. Because we had no way of knowing how this would go, and because she wanted to take no chances with the conflagration escalating, or with some of Sarkhan's forces escaping to infiltrate South Hold and the surrounding area, she stationed them on the perimeter in a series of ever-larger concentric circles. It was the tightest circle which rode to our aid in those moments of battle."

"I see," Ardenai mused, one corner of his mouth turning up in a smile. "My wife is more cunning than even I imagined her to be. She knew I'd object. She knew I'd insist on a level playing field. So tell me, have our prisoners said anything? Are they Telenir, or are they Equi? This was far too easy. This was a distraction, not a battle. Sarkhan may have thought he knew who he was and what his purpose was, but he did not. My mother is absolutely right in her thinking. He was, quite simply, drooling mad. The danger lies elsewhere, and it may well be watching what goes on here. Tell me what you know."

"What I know," Teal said quietly, "is that Ah'nora summoned us here to help soothe your thoughts, no more. We promised we would not stay long. Strategy is for another day, brother mine."

The Firstlord looked puzzled. "Ah'nora summoned you?"

"Yes," Tarpan replied. "And then Jilfan summoned us, as well. Apparently you and Ah'nora shared a common thought, Ardenai."

"Yes, we did," Ardenai said, and smiled, holding out a hand to the young woman. "And we share more than that." When she had come to sit next to him, he said, "In the days before Sarkhan's arrival, when things were unsettled and it seemed a possibility that the Firstlord of Equus might perish on the field of honor, it was decided that a High Equi prince should be conceived as a hedge against the loss of those genes. Our dear and beautiful Ah'nora was approached, and graciously consented to bear me a son, though she had no time to prepare herself, and little time to consider the consequences. If indeed this has been a time of heroes, in the actions of this woman, I offer you yet another."

She blushed, and momentarily dropped her head, then raised it, and smiled at the room with proud and shining eyes as they hailed her. Ardenai, looking at her in profile, realized how strong she was, and how truly beautiful. A worthy woman. And he wondered, if he had known her better, sooner, would he have chosen her over Io to be his Primuxori? Was this then to be his fate, to lust after every attractive woman he met – to want to bed – to impregnate every woman he met? Was this what it meant to be The Thirteenth Dragonhorse?

"Have you decided what you will name the child?" he asked, mentally giving himself a shake.

"I have two names which please me," she said. "Krush, for your father, or Rustem, for mine. I cannot choose."

"Then you need another babe added to your womb before it is too late. Twin foals for the Firstlord," Kehailan said, rising with a wink. "Sire, we will take our leave so you may rest. If anything changes, if anything develops, we will waken you. You have my word."

His voice was cheerful, but Ardenai sensed the terrible pain in his words, the knowledge that he was to be replaced over and over and over, that the joy of many sons would cast him forever in the shadows. He wanted to comfort him, to tell him that his suppositions were not true, but he was too tired, and tired, too, of having to constantly reassure Kehailan as though he were a Creppia Nonage babe. *I can only prepare a place for him and tell him it is there. I cannot make him believe me, nor can I make him take it.*

When they had all gone and he was alone with Ah'nora, he allowed himself to relax against the pillows – really relax – and contemplate her as she moved gracefully about, gathering up cushions and putting the room to rights. As tired as he was, there was a tugging in his loins which told him he wanted her – not just the emotional and physical release of ejaculation – but her, as a person. Right now, he could enjoy being in bed with her, face to face with her, kissing her lips and caressing her breasts, and speaking softly of intimate things. To his amused edification, it was a comforting thought. It comforted him to know that this young woman who carried his son had been more than a means to an end. That, had she been chosen as Firstwife, he could have learned to love her. But, he sighed, letting his eyes close, it was self-willed, quirky little Io whom he had chosen. It was fragile, intelligent Io whom he loved. And, as he drifted off to sleep, it was his beautiful, beloved Io for whom he wept silent, desperate tears.

CHAPTER NINETEEN

I think you should leave immediately," Ardenai said. "It has been three days. By now this affair is common Alliance knowledge. It does us no good in allowing too much time for rumor, nor does it benefit the Great House of Equus to be without a leader in the Council."

"I agree," Eletsky replied, looking around the breakfast table. "If we leave by high sun today we can be back on board Belesprit by late tomorrow night."

"And what of us?" Teal asked, "And of you, Ardenai?"

"I will stay here awhile," the Firstlord replied. "Io has not awakened since she was injured, nor has Konik. It will be many days, perhaps weeks before they can make the journey to the CAC. Pythos, I will keep here with me, and Gideon. Tarpan and his squad, also. The rest of you are much needed at home, or back on board your ship."

"What would you have us do?" Teal asked.

"You, Teal, I would have as Captain of the Horse Guard." He acknowledged the look which crossed his brother-in-law's face with a raised hand and an understanding nod. "I know your heart lies in your duties as Master of Horse, and there is none better. But you know my wife's mind in these affairs better than I do, and it is you who can best convey and convince, so I must ask you to double up on your duties. When Io is herself again, we shall consult her wishes insofar as we can." Teal gave him a gracious nod, and Ardenai smiled. "Thank you. I must also ask you to see to our guests, our greater household, and the more pressing affairs of the family until I return. Oh yes, and the computator code which will free Josephus's ship so he can go back to work. Remind me to give that to you. Will you do these things?"

"Of course," he smiled.

"And Jilfan, to you I entrust my mother." Ardenai closed his eyes and shifted back in his chair, the angle of his body and the set of his jaw making it painfully obvious that he was not rested. "To all of you, I would commend my stepson. Pythos says the blood transfusion Jilfan gave his mother has strengthened her chances for survival."

"We thank you," Kehailan said. "May your sacrifice be returned to you in the life of your mother."

"Thank you," the boy replied, and his face was imperiously digni-fied. "I will do as you ask, Firstlord." It made Ardenai smile. Twice, Arde-nai had said to him that he might refer to the Firstlord as his father, the first time, he had politely demurred. The second time he had pointedly refused. He said he was the son of Salerno, and while he was honored, he was not swayed. The boy was strong inside, and Ardenai had a feeling he was going to be trouble, perhaps in a small way, perhaps in a big way, but he was going to be trouble. Ah well, better to be trouble than to be nothing at all, as Krush would say.

"Kehailan, my son, I would have you as our representative in this before the Alliance – you and Timothy. Though both of you are young, I think your cool heads best for the task. Lay to rest what rumors you can. Take the crys-tels Tim made with the hand-cranks, and show people the truth." He paused with a self-deprecating chuckle. "At least show them the facts." Kehailan gave him a curt nod and the ghost of a smile.

"Marion Eletsky, I would suggest the SGA give Sarkhan's nest a good shaking to see what falls out. Teal, Ah'krill, do the same for the Great Council. Though we think not, Sarkhan may indeed be the weak arm of an otherwise powerful foe. Even if he isn't, he has made a wondrous distraction for them – a time in which to burrow deeper under our collective skin. Give it a good scratching, just in case. To Konik's family and those who sought peace, I have given sanctuary. Seek them out, and ascertain their desires. Assure them that Konik is in good hands, and that he will be returned to them. Oonah, begin sending messages to the Telenir and to anyone else who is listening, telling them exactly what has happened, and offering to confabulate. Use your judgment as to what you say, and run it by Marion, just in case."

She nodded and flashed him one of her beautiful smiles. "I'll do my best," she said.

"And what of me," Keats said from down the table. "I am, like the Telenir, your prisoner."

Ardenai fixed him in his gaze.

"I have also decided to serve as your judge, which is my right. I have a very specific sentence picked out for you, which I will discuss with you before you leave. If you carry it out, to the letter and to the best of your ability, Hadrian Keats will indeed be dead, and Dennis Strathmore will find himself a graduate of SGAU-Med, and an officer in the SGA – or vice versa. You may keep whichever name suits you best. Where you will find yourself assigned, I cannot guarantee, but you will have no criminal record."

"You can do that?" Keats breathed, and his hands were shaking.

"Yes. I can do that." Again his eyes closed and he pressed his fingers against his forehead in an effort to think over the pain in his skull. Ah'krill said his name rather sharply and his eyes came open. "Sorry," he said. "I find myself flagging mentally this morning. What have you to say, Ah'krill?"

"That you are flagging mentally," she responded. While her tone was not unkind, it bore a certain firmness with brought the color up in Ardenai's face. "It comes from weeping all night at the bedside of one who apparently knows more of duty than does her husband. You are sending others to do that which is your responsibility as Firstlord of Equus. I am but High Priestess. You command the political entity which is now the outward face of Equus. You allow yourself to be turned by grief and emotional weakness away from your duties and into a state unbecoming your people, and your station. Your unwillingness to leave causes me to question your willingness to lead."

Every face at the table looked startled – Equi and Terren alike – and

Ardenai took a deep uneven breath, as though something hurt inside. "Mother," he said calmly, "It is not that I am unwilling to leave here and do my duty. I am unwilling to leave here and risk Io's life in two days of primitive travel to reach the ship. To leave without her, is unthinkable."

"Is it? Why? Pythos can care for her."

"Of course he can. That is beside the point. I accepted the armbands of Equus. I have gone to all manner of effort to protect and honor what they stand for. I took Ah'riodin as my Primuxori. I can do no less for her. What sort of man would I be if I honor my nation and dishonor my wife?"

"It is not dishonor to put the concerns of eleven worlds above the needs of one couple, Ardenai."

"Of course, you are correct," the Firstlord sighed. "I see that I won't convince you there's any kind of rationality to my decision. Indeed, there probably isn't. But I know what it is like to be injured, and to have someone there who loves you. Just to hear their voice, feel the touch of their hand, can mean the difference between life and death. I have ignored my own needs in an effort to serve Equus. I will not ignore the needs of my wife in an effort to serve your whim. What would she think if she awoke and found me gone?"

"She would think what I would like to," Ah'krill replied icily, "that you are the Thirteenth Dragonhorse, honoring your duty to your people."

"And so I would be," Ardenai said, and that half-smile crossed his face. "But she will not find it so. She will find her husband beside her. Do not think I am backing away from a confrontation to stay here. I have done my duty in this. In doing so, I have lost my daughter, and my wife may yet die. If you can prove to me that Equus needs a figurehead more than Io needs her husband, I will go. Otherwise, I stay."

"Ardenai, this is appalling," Ah'krill said quietly. "Think of the example you set for your companions; for all of Equus."

"Can you not let this go, Woman? All of Equus is not here!" the Firstlord exclaimed, trembling with anger. "As for the rest of you, Teal, would you leave your wife? Tarpan, would you leave yours?"

"A very unfair question," Ah'krill said, "Which of us do they cater to, their High Priestess, or their political ruler? You put those whom you call friends, in a very hard place."

The flush of anger drained from Ardenai's face, he and drew breath to make apologies, but his kinsman's slow, gentle tenor cut in. "Personally, I would see to my wife's needs. You are right, of course, the question was indiscreet, and under ordinary circumstances I would not approve. But, of the man asking the question, and his motive for doing so, I approve, always. It is unkind of you, Ah'krill, to take a man who has absorbed the essence of a girl child, who is exhausted and grief-stricken, yet still trying to do his best, and push him into asking such a thing."

"Your wife is the sister of the Firstlord of Equus ..." Ah'krill began, but Ardenai put his hands up, exhaling sharply in displeasure.

"Stop. Please. And the rest of you, forgive us our infighting. Kehai-lan, you especially, forgive me. You have put up with so much. My actions in no way reflect the teachings, or the wishes of my people. Teal is right. I am exhausted and grief-stricken. My mother is right. The fear of losing my wife has caused me to lose my wits as well. You will be repaid for what you are now suffering at my hands. When this is all over, and I am walking serenely in the halls of the Great House speaking with my colleagues, step from the shadows and look as if you are about to mention this. The price I will pay for your silence will keep you comfortable for the rest of your life."

"Sounds fair to me," Marion said with a smile. "You see, we realize far better than you think, what you're going through. What may be a terrible job of handling it for you, is far better than any of us could hope to do under the same circumstances. We will do what we can to help simplify this time for you. Let me know what ships you have and where you need your people. Anything you need, just say the word. We are your friends, and we are here to help you."

"Thank you," Ardenai nodded. "Again you come to my rescue, Marion. I am racking up a debt I cannot repay. As to ships and men and where they need to be, Teal, Tarpan and Daleth know best. I have not concerned myself a great deal with how everyone got here."

He stood up, dismissed the group, and beckoned to Eletsky and Teal.

"I would speak to you," he said, and stepped to one side. "Again, I ask your forgiveness. I sat...all night...." Ardenai pushed his fist against his mouth and stood for a few moments with his eyes closed. "Pythos holds out very little hope for Io. When I try to touch her thoughts she shrinks away from me, and I do not know why. Please, just get the boy out of here, lest he see his mother die. Get Ah'krill out of here. I cannot take the scrutiny. I'm ready to start screaming, and if I do, I want to do it with some privacy. In thirty-two days – exactly one half season – I will walk into the Great Council Chamber of Equus, either with my wife, or alone, but I will be there to assume my duties."

"I shall see that it is known," Teal said. "What else can we do?"

"You can drop Doctor Keats on Declivis, at a place Doctor Moonsgold will tell you about. He is going to do some research for me, and learn certain techniques. I'll speak to him here in a minute. Do we have a horse transport in orbit?"

"I think so," Teal frowned. "Yes, I'm sure we do. Shall I take it?"

"No. I want it left here for Tarpan to take. I'm going to use Kadeth at Canyon keep for a couple of years, and I know Gideon will be pleased to have Tolbeth, as well. I want you to go with Marion on Belesprit. They have the best facilities for incarcerating our prisoners. If it suits your plan, take Jilfan and my mother, as well, if Captain Eletsky will be so kind?"

"The honor is all mine," the captain drawled, and flashed his white teeth in a most charming smile.

When the others had cleared the kitchen, Ardenai beckoned Hadrian Keats back in and sat him down. "This is your sentence," he said. "Make no mistake, I will know if you do not go where I tell you, and if you do not do as I say."

"Of that I have no doubt," Keats muttered, and eyed the Equi First-lord with more than a tinge of his old dislike.

"You will be going to Declivis for the foreseeable future, to an institute on the island continent of Dorset. It is called Materia Medica, perhaps you've heard of it?"

The doctor shook his head. At the word, Declivis, his look had hardened, and his expression was closed. Ardenai chose to ignore the pout, and went on with what he was saying. "They do a great deal of research there into sexually transmitted disease, and how it affects the body and its organs. They have also been leaders in the research needed to restore function and generative power to those so affected. I've heard it said they have some near-miraculous procedures they're perfecting. I want you to lend them a hand in their research, and in turn, I want you to learn what they have to teach you. If you need tools or technology, you are to let me know, and I will see that you get anything you need."

"Oh, I get it," Keats said. "This is about fixing Gideon. The day his pecker stands up and spurts little towheaded, fox-eyed grandkids for you, I walk, don't I?"

"Um hm," Ardenai nodded. "At that point, it will be your choice to stay, or go."

"Now tell me something, just to satisfy my curiosity, okay?"

"Ask."

"Why aren't you sending me off to research how to repair the damage done to your wife by that crossbow bolt?"

Ardenai did not rise to the bait. "Pythos says the physical damage isn't all that bad, and he knows how to make those repairs better than anyone alive."

Keats began to chuckle under his breath, and his face was unpleasant. "But he can't fix Gideon, or he won't fix Gideon?"

Ardenai gave Hadrian a look which caused the laughter to die in his throat. "I am giving you a chance to redeem yourself," he said quietly. "If you'd prefer, I can snap your neck. No one will question my actions. I can do a partial mind-wipe in less than a minute and you will cease to exist as you – only your skills will remain. I can send you to a Caspian prison to tread water. I can leave you here to practice medicine as they did on Terren a few thousand years ago. Or, you can go to a modern research facility and be part of an excellent research team. They're not on the galactic medical map yet, but you just might be the man to change that. If Gideon benefits in the process, what's the harm?"

I see your point," Keats said, rising from the table. "Rest assured, Firstlord, I will do my best. On that, you have my word." He got as far as the door and turned back. "I do hope...Io gets better. I'll be in touch once I get settled in."

Later, when everyone was preparing to depart, and Ah'krill was sitting for a bit with Io, Kehailan took Ardenai aside, put his arms around his father and said, "I love you, more than anything. No matter what happens, know that you have my abiding admiration for you, and my abiding faith in your ability."

"Thank you," Ardenai said, and laid his head against the side of Kehailan's neck, breathing in the familiar scent of him. "I wish I could find the words to convince you of how much you mean to me."

"Don't try," Kehailan said. "Not now. Turn your thoughts to your wife and leave them there until such time as they are no longer needed, or will no longer help. Only then will you rest. I must go. They're waiting for me."

"I know. Thank you for your help in all of this, Kee. Please, take care of Jilfan as best you can, and if you see Abeyan, tell him...I am deeply sorry. Come, let us find Ah'krill and get you on your way."

They walked arm in arm, first to Io's room to fetch the High Priestess, and then out to where the entourage waited. "My thoughts will be with you as you explain a military contingent complete with prisoners and corpses to the Calumet Port Authority," Ardenai said to Eletsky. He spent a moment with each of them, thanking them personally, then stepped back, said, "Ahimsa, I wish thee peace," and with the ancient gesture, put the entourage in motion.

They made the loop in front of the house at a brisk trot, war bells jingling on the primary squad. Teal gave him a nod as he passed, and a slow, jungle green wink. Ardenai watched their passage down the long, tree lined access road. No dust today. Last night's rain had settled it. Nasty footing for a fight. How careful the planning, how quick the battle, how painful the aftermath. Ardenai sighed.

"Need a hug?" Gideon asked at his elbow, and Ardenai shook his head.

"Thank you, no. I need to get a grip on myself; my thoughts, my reactions, my vocabulary. I need to make myself think, period. My mind won't even finish a sentence. How can a man talk to himself if he can't finish a sentence, I ask you?"

"You're going to have to sleep," Gideon said. "I know you don't want to, but you saw what happened this morning because you didn't have the mental reserves to control your tongue and your temper."

"I made a fool of myself."

"Given your usual level of grace, yes, you did. Could have been worse, though."

"Yes. I could have behaved as Nargawerlders do – or Declivians."

"Horrors! Not those cesspit Declivians! Can I interest you in an early lunch, or a sssnack, perhaps? I see something rustling in the shrubbery over there."

Ardenai chuckled softly and turned with a shake of his head back toward the kitchen door. "Gideon," he asked, "how do you keep your per-spective?"

"Easy. I have none to lose. I have not risked my life, my family and my sanity to save my world. My daughter is not dead. I have not, while still grieving for my first wife, realized I love my second wife, only to face losing her, too. I have neither embarrassed my son, nor myself in my own expec-tations, nor are my standards for behavior as relentless as yours. My only perspective lies in the framework of serving you, and being your friend." Gideon opened the door for Ardenai and together they walked into the warm, fragrant kitchen, with its shining woodwork and chuffing iron cook stove. "I don't mean to harp, but please eat something. You look a hundred years old, and you've been shaking like a leaf all morning."

"I am a hundred years old," Ardenai smiled. "And I'm still young, for me. Now how do I look?"

"Like you're holding on to your self-control with the bloody nubs of your fingers. Why don't you go snooze with Io. I'll bring you something in a few minutes."

"Thank you," Ardenai nodded. He walked to the kitchen door, then turned and looked at the youth. "Gideon, I know you consider my mental state beyond credence, but I tell you this. You have saved not only my life, but my sanity. What has been accomplished, has been your doing as surely as mine."

Again he turned, and walked slowly toward the flared spokes of the bedroom wings. How much he wanted to be with Io, and how he dreaded going in there. Dreaded it. He clenched his teeth, making himself reach for the handle, making himself open the door, making himself look at her, so pale against the white sheets – her beautiful hair, dusty and tangled, escaping the braid which held it.

Ardenai sat beside her on the edge of the bed, took her hand and pressed it against his lips as he gazed down at her. On impulse, almost as if he were unaware of what he was doing, he unfastened her braid, gently spread her hair out around her face, and began to groom it with the karpah shell brush from the dressing table. "Well, Fledermaus, our guests, our children, are on their way, and we have our privacy. You know, I think sharing that privacy with them has given us a bit better understanding of one another, don't you?"

He wrapped a strand of her hair around his finger, as Ah'ree had done, then pulled his finger out, watching the long, obedient curl forming itself across her shoulder and breast. "Of course, of all of us, you have the least need to understand, because your innate sense of the balance between beings is so excellent. What an advisor on galactic affairs you are. A touchstone to the hearts of many worlds, and to mine, in particular.

"You should have been there to see what transpired between my mother and me after breakfast this morning. High comedy with all the stock characters, and I, of course, played the idiot. In a dozen ways I told her, 'I love my wife,' and I realize, I have never told you. Anyway, I became more and more irrational until Teal finally shut me up. He's gone now, along with our prisoners and the corpses we created, back to Equus to await our arrival, to tell my mother and my sister that I may yet make it home for dinner, and to tell them that I will be bringing a second, beautiful wife home with me. How fortunate can one man get?"

He was silent awhile, then spoke again, softly. "And you," he said, still running the brush in long strokes through the curls in his hand, "what have you to say for yourself, sulking there behind the chair in my study, hm? So the other children tell you there are no females in the Equi Horse Guard – that it is unrealistic to think of such things. So what? If you do not want your dreams assailed, don't share them, but don't give them up. Come, sit here with me. Tell me what you think about the wondrous order of things. Tell me, if you could be anything you wanted, what would it be? Remember what you told me, lip sticking out to here? 'A man. I wish to be a man, like you, and Kehailan, and my father.'

"That was the superior position in your mind, and yet how firmly you controlled every man you ever touched, including me, and Kehailan, and your father. And then, always the determined one, you married. Far too young you were, and we were dismayed. As usual, it availed us nothing. Of Salerno, I can say little, and your years together, because things changed little from where I stood. You pursued the career you had chosen, Salerno pursued his. You were on one side of the galaxy, he on another. To see you... settled with child, was a shock for me. To know that you had been with a man. I think it is a universal truth among civilized people that we cannot imagine our parents or our children in sexual situations, perhaps because at those times we are so frighteningly vulnerable."

Ardenai sighed, put the brush back on the dressing table and stood looking out the window, remembering the first time he'd ever made love to Ah'ree. Their wedding night. Terrifying. Highly amusing. He had been so nervous, so afraid of frightening her or hurting her, and his mind had abandoned him, leaving him fumbling and flustered. "Forgive me, Ah'ree. You'd think I'd never..." the flash of her eyes had stopped the comment, and everything else for a few minutes, and he'd spluttered his way through an explanation of how Equi heat cycles were dealt with on Equus among Equi. All quite proper, but very different from the way things were done on Terren. Not that he'd been in heat. He'd hastened to assure her of that, lest she fear for her safety with him. "We are different, Ah'ree, and you must change your thinking if you hope to be comfortable here with us." She had smiled, and kissed his mouth, and let her robe slide slowly to the floor. It was she, who had been in heat.

"And what do you suppose your father will think when he finds out about us? If it is difficult to imagine your family in sexual situations, try coping with the fact that a trusted old friend – key words being trusted, and old – has seduced your young daughter. No, I take back the word, seduction, and will defend my right to do so. Even I am not so guilt-ridden as to forget who seduced whom amongst the meadow flowers, you little pouncer."

Ardenai stroked Io's cheek with the back of his fingers, eyes, despite his best efforts, slowly beginning to fill with more tears than he knew he had left. "Why, in the ten tribute worlds of Equus, did you think I didn't want you to bear me little fruit-bat babies who would run screaming through the halls of the Great House? I would have welcomed them, and the noise, and the craziness and now it's all gone, isn't it? We have lost our baby, and I have lost you. I touch your thoughts to pull you close to help me grieve for her, and you pull away until now I am afraid to touch you at all – afraid you will recede beyond recall. I have lost you, too, and I don't understand why. I just...please...I love you so much, and I want you back." He knelt beside the bed, laid his head in his arms, and wept in utter, helpless exhaustion.

"Are you trying to ruin my skin?"

Ardenai's head snapped up so hard his neck cracked. "Io!" he gasped, wiping at his eyes and nose and praying he wasn't hallucinating. Her eyes came drowsily open, and she rubbed at her face like a child after a nap.

"This is the second salt-water bath you've given me today."

"It has been three days, Io, and it's about the tenth salt-water bath I've given you," Ardenai replied, catching her hand as she stroked his cheek. "You frightened me."

"I frightened me, too," she whispered. "I ..." her eyes filled with tears, and she caught her breath, wincing in pain.

"Hush. If not for your sake, then mine. I've had all the terror I can handle in the last few days," he said, kissing her hand as he spoke. "Nearly lost both my girls."

Io looked puzzled and Ardenai tapped his forehead with an index finger. "You...have her?" Io whispered. "You have her?"

Ardenai nodded. "I have both of you, and I want to keep it that way. Your eyes tell me you're in pain. Let me find Pythos."

Io frowned. "You don't have far to look. Pythos is right here."

Ardenai glanced briefly to each side, and felt himself going cold all over. "No, Io. Pythos is not here. Close your eyes. Rest."

"Ardenai, Pythos is right beside you – about to touch your left shoulder," Io said. She pointed...and Ardenai looked over his shoulder... and there was nothing there. No one. "Ardenai!" she cried in alarm.

"Io, don't get up!" he said sharply, "you're pale as death!" Then he fell and rolled, end over end, into the suffocating darkness.

▲ ▲ ▲ ▲ ▲ ▲ ▲

Moonsgold drove the buggy all that warm afternoon with Keats smoldering in silence beside him until he could stand it no more. "What?" he said at last. "What the hell have I done to you now, Hadrian? I've smelled burning flesh mile after mile, and I'm sick and tired of it."

Keats brought his head around in slow motion, and fixed the Declivian in a beady-eyed stare. "This was your idea, wasn't it? You put him up to this, didn't you? You couldn't stand the fact that I was Chief Medical Officer aboard the SGA's newest Science vessel – flagship for the entire Seventh Galactic Science Contingent – and that you were a secondary physician, so you arranged for my comeuppance. Well, it's a dandy, let me tell you. I hope you're happy, you split-chinned sonofabitch."

"Damned right," Moonsgold retorted. "Absolutely. I already had a job - but it was only head of the Science Wing, and any slouch can do that. I said to myself, I said, 'Winnie, old brick, let's see if we can get Hadrian Keats in a whole hell of a lot of trouble, so we can have his job, too.' Not that I have time to even do mine like it should be done, but I didn't let that stop me. Not for a minute. I decided to make it look like you'd stolen somebody's identity way back when, and gone to medical school on somebody else's credit. Then, here's the best part, I got Ardenai, Firstlord of Equus, and one of the most powerful telepaths in the Alliance, to pretend like he'd read your mind, so you'd confess to all of this and he'd send you to Declivis to research venereal disease as your punishment. El'Shadai, I'm good."

They glared at each other for a few moments, and then Keats looked away to stare at the buggy wheel. There was a light spot on it, and he could see it flashing by as the wheel spun, seeming to spread like spilled paint to encompass the entire rim. "It just seems damned convenient," he said after a few minutes.

"Now that, it does," Moonsgold agreed. "Convenient for you, at least. Have you thought of all the places he could have sent you?"

"Please, don't you rattle them off, too. Everybody's told me what a lucky son-of-a-gun I am. Why don't I feel lucky?"

"Because it wasn't your choice," Moonsgold said. "Because you're not in control. Because your voice isn't the loudest one in the room for a change. For pity's sake, Hadrian, he could have locked you up! Instead he's sending you to a place where there's some truly exciting research going on – a place where you get to be part of a research team. You even said he'd promised technological support. How much better than that does it have to get for you? Technically, you're a criminal, yet you're being given a plum assignment. I'd shut up, if I were you."

"And how did he find out about this, MedicusMedicus, or whatever the hell it's called?"

"It did come up in conversation early on," Moonsgold admitted, focusing on the road in front of them, "but it came up in conjunction with Gideon, not you. I told him about the place for the boy's sake, not as a place to send you for punishment. Declivis is my home, after all. I don't exactly consider it the hell-hole of the galaxy, and I don't think Ardenai does, either. It's pretty. You'll like it there. They have four seasons on Dorset. Spring can be windy, and the summers are a little on the muggy-buggy side, but the autumns can be really quite nice, and the winter skiing is just..."

"Aw, shut up," Keats muttered.

"Boys, boys," Eletsky chuckled as he trotted by. He moved to the head of the line, reining his horse in to keep pace with Teal's. "Decided yet how you want to work things?"

"Um...yes," Teal replied, and it was obvious Marion had broken his train of thought.

"Sorry. I missed the faraway look in your eye."

"No need to apologize. Best I get on with the business at hand and quit brooding."

Eletsky studied the big, soft-spoken Equi. Handsome, like his brother-in-law. They might have been blood relatives, had the Equi not been so careful about that kind of thing. But then Ardenai and Ah'din weren't really brother and sister, were they? Interesting possibility to consider. "Brooding about what, or may I ask?"

"This place. What went on here. I used to look forward to coming here with the squads and the recruits. Now, maybe not so much." He sighed and shook his head. "In answer to your question, yes. I have decided how best things will work. In large part, we'll go with Ardenai's idea. But Ah'krill says her own ship circles above us, and that woman, I do not want to travel with at this juncture. So, into her ship, we will place Jilfan, Ah'krill, and her retinue, and hurry them home to Equus. I'll ask the AEW to provide escort through each sector, just in case. Ardenai forgot, and so did I, that Konik must have a clipper in orbit, so Daleth and I will take that to drop Doctor Keats off on Declivis. If you have room, we can send the squad of Horse Guard with you, the horses can be held near the CAC to ride home with Tarpan, and we can leave Ardenai the clipper which Kehailan and Oonah Pongo brought, which should amuse him, since it's the one he lost on Hector. We may find more ships in orbit yet – the ones that brought the rest of the Telenir and their mounts. Those, I'm not counting on."

"We will check them out as we leave," Eletsky smiled. "Teal, may I ask you something?"

"Certainly," he said, cocking his head as he turned it in that characteristic Equi attitude of listening.

"Are you, and should I, be worried about Ardenai?"

"Should you? Probably not. Am I? Not really. But I do hurt for him. What happened here, no matter what it may have solved on the larger stage, was not winning – not for him. He's struggling mightily with that."

Marion looked around at the beautiful, wild countryside, and tried again to put all the pieces of this together. "Tell me," he said after a bit, "you have served with Io in battle, haven't you?"

"Yes. She's a brilliant strategist."

"So I hear. Why then, was she the first one hit? There just was not that much action overall."

"You know the answer to that, Marion, and so does Ardi. She was worrying about her husband when she should have been watching herself. If she dies ..." he shook his head and stopped the thought. "It grows late. Let's ride on ahead a bit and select a campsite for the night, shall we?"

▲ ▲ ▲ ▲ ▲ ▲ ▲

Ardenai's eyes flew open and he sobbed for air, even as the oxygen seared his lungs. He was bathed in clammy sweat and desperately sick to his stomach. It was dark. Still dark, and painfully cold. He moved his eyes without moving his head – wanting to see this suffocating terror which sat on his chest – wanting to roll out from under it if he could. But what if he fell again? Started rolling again? Fell from where? Where was he? How had he gotten here? Where had he been? Why was it dark? Why did he hurt like this, like he'd been beaten for no reason, squeezed and crushed? Why was he being held against his will? How could he escape when he couldn't understand? How could he scream if his throat wouldn't open? He groaned, deep in his middle, desperate to hear himself make a sound, to ascertain that he was awake, or even alive. Gentle fingers touched his cheek and forehead.

"Shhhhh." The familiar hiss. The touch of that comforting tongue – familiar mind – drawing him up to see where he was. "Thee iss all right. Do not be afraid. It iss over. Thee iss awake. Look around." There was a moment's pause. "Ardenai, Beloved, open thosse eyes and look around. Take a breath. Think about it, and make thysself take a breath."

Something pushed hard on his chest. He took in a rush of air as though he was nearly drowned, and realized he could breathe. His eyes, which he'd thought were already open, opened again, and he sagged in a retching, sweat-soaked heap against the pillows. There was a fire burning. Gideon was lighting a lamp. He could smell cinnamon and orange peel. He moved his left arm to the side. Nothing. With another gasp he sat up to look, then collapsed into Pythos' arms, gagging dryly and sobbing with the effort.

"Sshe's not here," Pythos said, and his fingers moved to quiet the hysteria in Ardenai's eyes. "Shhhhh, Ssave thy sstrength. Thee has had a very trying afternoon. Here, drink a little ssomething."

Ardenai sipped at the warm liquid, then closed his eyes and tried to think. Nothing happened. He opened his eyes and tried to sit up. Nothing happened. "Pythos," he managed, not really recognizing the voice or the fear in it, "I was talking to Io. I know I was. She was here!"

"Shhhhh. Be calm. What happened?"

Again the Firstlord closed his eyes. "I don't know," he said at last.
"Think."

"I can't!" he gasped, terror again squeezing at his throat. "I can't!"

"Yess, thee can. Think," the physician insisted, still holding Ardenai close in his arms. "What happened when thee wass talking to Io?"

"She looked to be in pain, so I said...I would find you. And she said, you were here, and she pointed."

"And wass I here?"

"She started to get out of bed, and I heard her saying my name..."

"Ardenai, stop. Listen only to my voice. Wass I here?"

"No! But Io's face...changed...to that color Sarkhan was when I looked at him last night. She's dead!" he cried. "Eladeus, she's dead!" He gagged, and panted for air.

"Shhhhh," Pythos soothed, using his fingers to quiet Ardenai's mind without influencing his thoughts. "Look again, Beloved. Thee iss talking to Io. Sshe ssayss I am here. Am I?"

"No," Ardenai groaned. "Pythos, just leave me. I wish to be alone."

"Why does thee wissh to be alone?"

"I don't know!" Ardenai said through his teeth.

"Yess, thee doess! Think. Listen only to my voice, and think!"

"Think. Funny word. Say it a few times and it ceases to have meaning. About, is another one. No meaning at all when you consider it."

"Good. Why doess thee wissh to be alone, my hatchling?"

"Because I do not wish to answer your questions."

"Why?"

"My head hurts, terribly, and my eyes, and if I could throw up I'd feel better. Please, I just want to go back to sleep and know nothing. I'm not ready...to know anything." He cocked his head to one side, and looked genuinely puzzled. "Uhhh..."

"Now it begins to ssink into thy tiny mammalian brain, doess it not? Good. I sshall explain it later. Here thee iss. All our guessstss are gone. Thee iss sstanding in the kitchen with Gideon. He asskss if thee iss hungry, and thee ssayss no. He ssayss he'll bring thee ssomething. Thee ssayss thank you. Thee tellss him how much he meanss to thee, and that'ss good. That feelss good insside. But now thee hass to walk down the hall, and open thiss door, and facce Io. Iss sshe alive, iss sshe dead? When thee finally openss the door, what doess thee ssee?"

Ardenai swallowed hard. "I see Io, lying in the bed."

"Iss sshe alive?"

"I do not know," Ardenai whispered. "I'll die without her! Pythos, I'm afraid."

"Don't be afraid. You will not die. Look. Iss sshe alive? Just look. Get it over with."

"Yes," Ardenai whispered, and exhaled sharply. "Yes. She is alive."

"How does thee know thiss?"

"She is breathing. I touch her. She is warm. I...brush her hair. I talk to her."

"You're ssure sshe'ss alive?"

"Positive."

"Abssolutely?"

"Absolutely."

"Good!" the Physician hissed. "Now, DON'T CRY. The lasst thing thee needss to do iss get down on thy kneess and cry ssome more. Insstead, give her a gentle kisss, walk around the bed, and lie besside her. Thee is about to ssleep and know nothing. But firsst, thee needs a cover. Ssit up and reach for the ssleeping robe at the end of the bed. Now, before thee lies down again, look around the room. Iss Io all right besside thee?"

"Yes."

"Doess the sstove need tending?"

"No."

"Every lasst thing iss as it sshould be?"

"Yes."

"Iss thee sstill looking?"

"Um hm."

"What elsse doess thee ssee of import?"

Ardenai swallowed hard, squeezing his eyes shut – slogging through the hardening muck in his brain.

"Io iss here. Io iss alive. Am I here?"

There was a long pause, then a lightening of the Firstlord's features. "Yes," he said wonderingly. "Yes, you are. Curled up beside the fire. How long have you been there?"

"Ssince before thee walked in," Pythos said, and flicked the exhausted Firstlord with his tongue.

"Then Io...was right." Ardenai drew a deep breath, rubbed at his burning eyes, and his voice grew surer of itself. "You were behind me. You were there all the time. I remember talking to my wife. I remember what I said. I remember thinking about Ah'ree. But I do not remember you. Why don't I remember you?" He flipped his hands. "When did I … lose touch?"

"About three dayss ago," the old dragon hissed. "I am the one who told thee thy wife was dead, remember? I am the one who took her, pried her from thy arms, who made thee let go of her body."

The tears in Ardenai's eyes sparkled in the firelight as he nodded. "I remember you telling me Ah'ree was dead. In my dreams, I have struggled against that voice."

"A pronouncement thee abssolutely did not think thee could sstand to hear again."

"I have dreaded the possibility."

"Enough to eliminate it from thy mind. A very logical sself-defensse mechanissm, especially for a tiny child, except that thee eliminated me with it." Pythos took a glass of dark liquid from the table beside the bed, lifted Ardenai back into a semi-sitting position and helped him with the drink. "It will ssoothe thy throat and thy sstomach. Take a little more. Good." Pythos eased him back down on the pillows, and gave him an extra flick of the tongue on his cheek. "When Io ssaid I wass there, and thee couldn't ssee me, thee panicked becausse thee thought sshe wass going into the delirium before death. In truth, it was thysself who wass having the delussion."

"So..." Ardenai drew a deep breath to steady himself, still trying to place himself in reality. "Is my wife all right? Is Io alive?"

Pythos motioned to Gideon, who went into the next room, leaving the door ajar, then he turned back to the Firstlord, and his eyes hardened. "O' Godlike and all-knowing Ah'krill Ardenai Morning Sstar, Firsstlord of Equus, Wissest of the Wisse, the nexsst time ssomeone older and wissser yet, tellss thee to be cognizant of danger, besst heed him. The nexsst time ssome-one older and wissser sslitherss up besside thee and tellss thee to have a little recreational ssex to reasssure thy body that it iss adult and that it iss male, besst heed him, yess? The nexsst time ssomeone older and wissser tells thee that the entity to which thee hass given ssanctuary CANNOT THINK AND THEREFORE CANNOT REASSON, besst heed him!"

Ardenai flushed uncomfortably at Pythos' caustic tone, and his eyes were embarrassed. "Oh," he breathed, and made a sharp sound of exaspera-tion, "the baby. That's why it was dark and I couldn't breathe and so on and so forth. That's why I haven't been able to do anything but cry."

"Correct," the serpent hissed, still speaking with some annoyance, now that the danger was over. "Thee busied thy arrogant little sself attempt-ing to out-think her, when, as I told thee, sshe is not capable of thought. Sshe iss too rudimentary to do anything but react, which iss why thy sself-touted ability to out-think even the most immature Creppia Nonage sstudent, gained thee nothing but a falsse ssensse of ssecurity. Sshe could well have killed thee, Dragonhorsse, and then who would comfort this lovely one?"

There, in Gideon's arms, was Io. This time she had her arms around his neck, her head on his breast, and Ardenai could see that she was smiling drowsily at him, not dead. Not dead. Of course she wasn't dead.

Gideon tucked Io in bed next to Ardenai, and Pythos said, "Jusst a ssafety precaution, moving the lady."

"Which is his polite way of telling you, you had a wow of a case of the DT's this afternoon," Gideon said. "I was scared. You're a big man, and a strong man. You're hell to hold when you're crazy."

Ardenai just shuddered. If Gideon had been wrong, or exaggerating, Pythos would have corrected him. Pythos said nothing. "Please forgive me," he whispered. "I am so sorry to have been such a fool. I am so sorry to have caused trouble and raised fear in those I love most."

"We forgive thee," Pythos hissed. "Now, forgive thysself. Resst a bit, and when thy sstomach hass ssettled, I sshall help thee out of that uni-form and take thee for a nicce sscrubbing. Right now, it iss my turn. Come,

Gideon, let uss leave the old wedded couple alone. You, are about to get your firsst lessson in how to oil a ssea sserpent."

"Gideon," Ardenai said, crooking a finger, and Pythos hissed,

"You amazssse me! You do! Sso weak and battered thee cannot ssit up, yet thee findss the sstrength to put thiss child up to missschief!"

Ardenai, already half asleep, looked puzzled, then amused. "Ah yes, that. I was going to thank the boy, but this will serve as well. When the old lizard goes to sleep, as he invariably does, oil the bottoms of his feet and then startle him. I only did it once, when I was six. I do remember it, though. Most entertaining."

"I ssee it iss time to tell tales out of sschool," Pythos hissed, motioning Gideon to walk in front of him. "Very well. I have ssome of my own. Let me tell thee firsst, though, that after oiling the bottomss of 'the old lizard's feet,' he couldn't ssit down for a week."

"They seem to be getting along well," Io noted, in the tone of someone having Hesychgyre breakfast in bed.

"Um hm. And they will continue to do so, though they got a bit of a rough start." The Firstlord got his elbow under him, and rolled on the pillows to look at Io. "And you, Firstwife, are you getting along well? We, too, seem to have gotten off to a rough start, but things will get better. I know they will."

She sighed, and gave him just the ghost of a smile. "Do you really think so?"

"It is both my thought, and my prayer," Ardenai replied, hitching onto his side to take her hand and press it to his lips. "As long as you are alive, Fledermaus, I have all the hope in the world."

CHAPTER TWENTY

Ardenai stood at the window watching Io and Gideon walk slowly arm in arm in the late afternoon sunshine. "It pleases me that they are fond of one another," he said. He accepted a glass of wine from Pythos, nodded his thanks, and sat on the wide mahogany sill overlooking the gardens. "He comforts her, I think, where I cannot."

"Give her time," Pythos said, resting his hand on the Firstlord's shoulder. "Woundsss heal sslowly here. Sshe musst deal with the pain of natural healing, and with a dissfiguring sscar to remind her of what sshe conssiderss a terrible misssjudgment on her part, and with the feeling that thy needss are not being adequately met."

Ardenai snorted humorlessly. "My needs, as you so euphemistically put it, burned themselves out rather quickly in the heat of emotional upheaval. Having sex with a woman, is about the last thing on my mind just now."

"Doess sshe know thiss?"

Ardenai shrugged, eyes far away as he chewed his lower lip a moment or two in contemplation. "I have told her. She has heard. Whether she has listened, and what she believes, I don't know. I do know she grieves for the child, and she fears that the loss of fertility will be permanent. I have tried to tell her that even her life is more than I dared hope for, and that no matter what the outcome, having her is enough. But she fears the worst, and, I think, just now she dwells on it."

"Her fertility is part of her sself. It iss of tremendous importancce to her, and, thee knowss, it will be of import to thy mother, as well."

"Oh yes," the Firstlord rejoined sarcastically, "My dam expects the mare in the hitch which draws the wagon of State to be fecund. She found time to bring that up to me before she left. Well, my wife was injured and her baby lost, trying to protect that woman, and she needs to remember that." Ardenai stood up from the window and turned to face the physician. "I have been doing some thinking, having been more or less my own captive audience these last several days." He brought up an index finger and shook it, studying the floor as he paced, forming his words thoughtfully, "From what I know of the biology of hominoids, it would be impossible to actually teach a sperm much of anything, or to carry it, untrammeled for half a millennium or so, but fertilized ova..." the mottled green eyes came up and met the physician's, "would be storable, and teachable. I was formed, not just from the body of Kehailan, but from a female, as well. I may have been implanted into Ah'krill, but she is not my mother. I do not share her DNA. Please tell me I'm right in this. Please tell me I'm not actually related to that pillar of dogmatic arrogance."

The old doctor writhed in a hissing chuckle, and flicked his tongue at the Firstlord. "Thee may well be correct in thy thinking, but ssince only we and the High Priestess know the truth of thy concception, the truth will be of little conssequencce, exccept to comfort thysself with disstancce. And thy disrespect sshe will ssensse, and sso will others. It iss beneath thee. Besst lose it before it becomess habit, Hatchling."

Ardenai snorted and turned back again to the window.

Nervous as a lithoped, Pythos thought. *Full of energy better burned off physically, than mentally.* "Perhapss thee sshould take Kadeth out for ssome exerccisse thiss evening," he suggested.

"In the morning," Ardenai said, dismissing the idea with an absent wave. "I'm going to speak again with Konik here in a few minutes." That worried, deep thinking look crossed his face. "That one puzzles me, Pythos. I almost understand, and yet I don't. I'm still trying to figure out whether he has some ties to, some love for our world, or his own, for that matter, having never been there, or whether this is all just a matter of doing the honorable thing, completely detached from any end."

"And now the honorable thing, includess death?"

"I'm afraid so. I'm not comfortable leaving him alone, which means his privacy is constantly being violated."

"Gideon tellss me thee claimss to be a gambling man. Take a rissk," the doctor suggested.

A smile crossed the Firstlord's face, and he gestured toward the window, and the pair of young people who were again on their way. "Of all the bets I've made, and of all the prizes I hope to win, having those two be whole again, to be able to make generative choices, is the desire of my heart."

"I meant with Konik," Pythos chuckled. "Thy betss are incredibly well hedged when it comess to thy wife, and the child of thy heart."

"I knew what you meant," Ardenai smiled. "Do you think Hadrian Keats will actually do what I sent him to do, then?"

"Abssolutely, I do. I think once his fragile ego iss mended, he will rather enjoy hiss work, not that he will ever admit it to thee. Hass thee told Gideon where thee ssent the good doctor, and for what purposse?"

Ardenai glanced up, and then away, which was answer enough. "I'd prefer he didn't know. When the time comes for him to make a choice about his procreative abilities, I want it to be a choice, not an obligation based on the efforts of others on his behalf. I told Keats the same thing. This has to be research for its own sake, not just a means to an end for one young man."

"He won't ssee it that way, and neither will Gideon; thee knowss that."

"I do," Ardenai chuckled, "but allow me to entertain my delusions for a bit. I'm going to go speak with Konik. Will I see you at dinner?"

The old doctor nodded, and Ardenai gave him a stiff, respectful bow as he exited the room and headed down the spoke which housed the legate's chambers. He stood a moment in front of the door and composed his thoughts before knocking and entering. Tarpan looked up from where he was reading in a chair by the window, and beyond him – listless, angry – still grey-faced with pain, Konik looked up as well.

"You appear much better today," Ardenai said.

"Hardly comforting to one who wishes death," Konik replied. "How can I persuade you?"

"You can't," Ardenai replied, sitting beside him. "I need to persuade you, instead."

"I am Telenir, Ardenai Firstlord, not Equi," Konik said.

He had one of the gentlest, most resonant voices Ardenai had ever heard – a voice that made him want to relax and go to sleep. How could a man with a voice like that be in any way evil? Ardenai shook his head without meaning to, answering his own mental query.

"I admire you, your people, your way of life, but it was never meant to be mine," Konik continued. "I was bred and raised up by my grandsire to be a creature of duty. I saw my duty. I tried. I failed. Sarkhan is dead and his forces scattering to the four winds by now. What good does it do to extend my life long enough to face a tribunal? It only brings shame to my family. Better that I should die now, and with honor."

"Hopefully, prolonging it does more good than ending it, Nik. Whether you are Telenir or not, remember that you are also an Equi senator, and you have served our worlds long and well. It is not my intention to torment you, but rather to understand your thinking in this. Enlighten me. Convince me you are of no worth, and I shall grant your request for death. I'll kill you myself."

"How easily you say it," Konik snorted. "It has been my experience that men who would kill so easily do not pace the halls every night begging Eladeus to forgive them for taking a life."

Ardenai looked startled, then defensive. "It is not my experience that those who truly plan to overthrow a government, spend most of their lives serving it first, and then offer up their own life to save it."

Konik adjusted himself in the bed, gasping with the effort of using his arms to straighten himself. "This discussion avails us nothing, and you do not call this torment?"

"No," Ardenai snapped, "I do not. A week ago, two weeks ago, I would have apologized. Today, no. Each day you ask me to do something completely irrational and give me not one rational reason for doing so. Are you so afraid of your life and your people, that death is better than facing them, Wind Warrior? Does Ah'davan mean so little to you?"

Konik winced, but smelled the bait and left it. "Has it occurred to you, Firstlord, that I may have cost my government the planet Equus?"

"Not for one minute," Ardenai replied, pouncing out of the chair and striding to the window. "Sarkhan would never have left this place alive, not you, nor your men, and you know it. The plan itself may have been brilliantly conceived in ages past, but nearly impossible to execute, and easily foiled this day and age."

"You underestimate yourself," Konik said. "Few would have seen through it until it was too late. We have so many in place." He sighed. "Had so many in place. So many years and lives wasted on this...nonsense."

The man was opening up at last and the Firstlord's face was alive with curiosity. "What were all these people going to do, exactly? Certainly there were not enough of them to rise up in violence."

"No," Konik said with a rueful smile. "They had lines to say. All of them the same. That was all."

"Oh, of course," Ardenai said slowly, and nodded with understanding. "We support Sarkhan's claim to be Firstlord of Equus."

"Exactly. As I said, you underestimate yourself. What you saw, what you guessed at, what you risked, and the way you chose to play the game even yet astounds me."

"I am honored," Ardenai said with a gracious nod, "though I did not work alone. I had Pythos, and Teal, and, of course, my wife."

Konik's face softened instantly. "And how is the lady feeling by now?"

"Better," Ardenai sighed. "Physically, at least."

Konik matched his sigh. "Not for anything, would I have wished her hurt, Ardenai."

"You didn't want anybody hurt, Nik. I know that, and so do you if you'd just let up on yourself. Neither of us wanted anybody hurt. The fact that both of you are alive, seems a sign to me from the Wisdom Giver that this might yet be mended between our peoples. I admire you and your perception of honor. Your life is my gain, and my government's. I will pin you to the wall, or the bed, and harangue you for as long as it takes to convince you of my peaceful intent regarding you, personally, and the Telenir."

"Of that, I need no convincing," Konik sighed. "Let us palaver; what harm can it do? Indeed, 'How many ages hence shall this our lofty scene be acted over in states unborn and accents yet unknown.' That's what they sent us forth with, you know. Those lines, millennia ago, or so they tell me. Little did they know that those unknown accents would become our own, that unborn state something many of us…nearly all of us…came to believe was unnecessary, and undesirable. Equus, does not need to change. It is the Telenir, who need to change. That thought, and others like it, make me a traitor to my cause, and useless to you as a bargaining chip."

"I think it early yet to establish comparative value, Nik. And I am going to try as Firstlord never to bargain with human lives. Now, I must ask if you consider diplomatic overtures a serious possibility, or do you simply consider me a serious fool?"

"Ardenai, I have seen you attempt things only a fool would do. I have seen you risk the fate of your world and the Alliance on a whole string of insane and illogical actions. And yet, in those actions you have appeared wise, and noble. If you are a fool, you have raised it to an art form. Overtures to the Telenir would be no more insane than anything else you've done lately."

Ardenai chuckled. "Let me think about that a minute. I think you said it might be worth the risk?"

"I might have said that, insofar as I know the Telenir, which is precious little to none at all."

"I know one thing. In order to make the risk acceptable on anyone's part, there is much I must learn of your planet, its people, your government and its function, your goals as a race, your inner strife and outward strength. This, only you can teach me. Will you do it?"

Konik was silent and his eyes thoughtful for some time. "Another risk. A great risk. A gamble, for that is the word foremost in your mind just now. I have never been a gambling man, Ardenai Firstlord, which is why I was a decent soldier."

"Ah'ria Konik Nokota, you are lying through your teeth. No man in his right mind, soldier or otherwise, would have taken the risks you did on that parade ground unless he was a gambler of the highest order. You risked your very life to defend a vow of honor, made to an enemy, by a man who had no plans to keep that vow. Sarkhan sent you out there to die, yet you honored him."

"I honored the vow and not the man," Konik smiled.

"You honored me, and the world we share," Ardenai said quietly, "and I thank you. I would be further honored if you would choose to aid me in my quest for peace between our people. But I understand the necessity of thought, as well. I know you have more than just yourself to consider in this." He read Konik's troubled blue eyes, and went on in a gentler tone. "I do wish I had word of your family, but I don't. Of course, I don't have word of mine, either. Let us assume things have gone well in our absence."

"Let us at least hope and pray so," Konik added.

Ardenai's brow twisted with concern. "You don't think...I don't have any idea how radical the Telenir faction is on Equus...they wouldn't have harmed your family, would they? They think you a prisoner of war, not a traitor."

"I am a prisoner of war, not a traitor," Konik replied. "I just don't know which alliance is where." He turned his face pointedly away from Ardenai and looked out the arched casement and into the gardens and the forest beyond. "It is a convoluted tale we spin. We've been here so long, we've become Equi. There was always this lofty goal of infiltrating and overthrowing the government of Equus, which existed outside the realm of everyday existence, and we spoke of it from time to time in abstract terms. But for many of us, even the generations before us, it had ceased to be reality. Indeed, we were drafting a plan to present to the government of the Wind Warriors, seeking a petition of peace. Since that isn't exactly what they had in mind, we were being cautious, trying to appeal to their...our sense of pride and honor as a people, trying to point out that the Equi think the same way, but exemplify the traits in a different manner. Most of us thought this the best way to solve the problem."

"Except for Sarkhan."

"Except for Sarkhan, his brother Sardure and his father, Sareman-no," Konik nodded. "And a few dozen others who were hard core – my grandfather among them. When the rest of us tried to reason with Sarkhan, he threatened to bring down the Wind Warriors upon us Telenir who were serving on Equus, to make examples of us. He told Saremanno and Sardure, and people died. It frightened many of the Telenir who had families, and they ceased to take up voice in the cause of peace. They were more afraid of the Wind Warriors than they were of the Equi government officials who might discover their traitorous activities."

"Have any of you ever been to Telenir, or even met, pardon the term, a real Telenir?"

"It has always been considered an extremely risky trip. Only Sarkhan has actually gone, and his family before him. His was the family designat-ed to rule nearly three thousand years ago. He, it is...was, who trumpeted the royal bloodline of Kabardin, who, according to Sarkhan was the father of the modern Telenir, which should have told me something right there. They were both mad, murdering bastards. It was funny, really," Konik said, though his eyes were hostile, "Sarkhan never married. The Wind Warriors would not send him a royal bride, and he refused to set his head against any but a royal consort. She who would rule beside him. So he remained single. As far as I know, he is the last of his line unless he has a wife on Telenir. If so, she's a very lonely woman."

"What about Sardure?"

"Ah yes, that one. I guess the line isn't quite dead, is it? Equally crazy, but totally out of favor with the family these last months. What he may know of the Wind Warriors..." Konik exhaled sharply, pulled his eyes from the window, and looked at Ardenai. "I will teach you what I know, but it will be precious little. Sarkhan became so afraid of having his power usurped, that it has been years since he's shared anything of any real import – just ranting – no policies, no useful information. His family was the only one who could actually make contact with the homeworld, you know. We only knew we were Telenir because we had been raised to be so. There are times I wonder if he ever contacted anybody on Telenir. If he was ever the designated seed, or if we had long since been abandoned by the government who sent us, and we were being manipulated by one, corrupt and pretty much insane family. Now that, would be truly funny, and it would make more sense than anything else."

Ardenai refrained from mentioning that he'd had those same thoughts. "Perhaps as a people you have collective memories – most especially the elders – and perhaps they will choose to share them with me, and with you, as we seek to shift the focus of your mission from one of conquest to one of diplomacy."

Konik's head cocked slightly as he contemplated what the Firstlord had said, and what he had implied. "They will have little choice but to tell you what they know," he said.

"They will have a choice," Ardenai said firmly, and parked his hip on the window ledge. "They are, each of them, bred and born citizens of Equus. They have not raised their hand against another citizen, nor done anything of a criminal nature, nor have you. They are free, and will remain free, under the protection of the government which has always protected them, and which they have served. You, too, are free, my friend."

Both Konik and Tarpan looked amazed, and Konik said, "I know soldiering is not your iron suit, but even you could not have missed the fact that I rode in here with every intention of killing you, or of seeing you killed."

"If you live another hundred and fifty years, and we are debating this upon our death-beds, you will not convince me of that, Senator. You saved my mother's life, and you saved mine, and I am firmly convinced that if it had come down to it, you'd have killed Sarkhan yourself to prevent the spread of his madness to an ordered world government. You have served

your Affined World as a senator. You have served on the agricultural council, and the antiquities council. You are an excellent polo player, a brilliant
test pilot and a fine mechanical engineer. Equus needs you. I need you. I
will give you time, and your freedom. It is difficult to think with someone
always watching you. Consider yourself a guest, a friend of the family, as
you have always been. Do no more than Pythos says you may do, for he is
both caring and perceptive."

Ardenai motioned to Tarpan, walked to the door, then paused and
turned back to Konik. "Forgive me," he said. "I have assumed what your
needs are, based on what mine would be. Do you wish to be alone, or would
you prefer company?"

"I prefer the option, thank you."

"Are you able to manage yourself in and out of there without undue
discomfort?"

"Yes," Konik smiled, and it was genuine, lighting his muscular face
and brilliant eyes. "I will be fine. Do not concern yourself."

"I shall have Gideon or Tarpan check in on you later. Perhaps you
will join us walking wounded for a little supper later on."

Konik nodded, and Ardenai quietly shut the door. "I don't know
whether or not that was wise," he said, answering the question on Tarpan's
face, "but the man is useless in his present state, both to us and to himself. If
we are to gain him, we must risk him, as well. He is an honorable man. He is
also an Equi, or I miss my guess. He will do the honorable thing."

"Agreed," the younger man nodded. They walked down the hall and
out into the garden before Tarpan spoke again. "Much have you learned here
of the nature of war," he said, glancing at Ardenai's profile. "Not all of it has
been pleasant, but war seldom is. It has changed you. Hurt you, deepened
you, softened you, I think, though not in a negative sense. You seem less
sure of yourself, though no less sure of your purpose. You seem younger,
somehow, than you did on Equus. You look younger, though your eyes are
old, and sadder than they once were."

"And you're telling me this because?" Ardenai grinned.

"Because if you're trying to hide it you are not succeeding."

"Should I be trying to hide it?" Ardenai asked, slowing his pace and linking his arm through Tarpan's. "Is it disturbing you somehow? Am I going to be an embarrassment to Equus and her people? Is this because of my pathetic performance on the parade grounds the other day? "

"More than one question at a time confuses the little ones, Ardenai Teacher," Tarpan replied with a chuckle. "Nothing about you disturbs me, nor will it disquiet those of your people who have truly lived. Those who have not, those who expect a stereotype, and who are stereotypical in and of themselves..."

"Will be given pause," Ardenai finished. "Their unpredictable leader, and his elfin Primuxori and his golden-eyed companion." He stopped abruptly and looked at Tarpan. "Do I need to tell you how deeply aware I am of the uncharacteristic image I'm going to present? I'm a little too evolved, or devolved even for seven hundred years, even without the pythons." He extended his arms and wiggled his fingers to make them ripple. "One of the reasons I chose to restore these is because they represent the ability to shed the old and expand into the new; the eternal constant of the need to change and grow.

"When I left Equus all those ages of the soul ago, I considered myself a typical Equi. Maybe even the stereotypical Equi of whom you spoke. And now," he sighed, "I pause, and I ask myself, if I am typical, are all Equi capable of this kind of metamorphosis, and if I'm not typical enough, does it truly serve the best interests of the Equi worlds for me to take the reins of government? The Firstlord is supposed to be a typical Equi, is he not?"

"And does anyone answer you?" Tarpan asked in quiet amusement.

"Of course. Why talk to yourself if you're not going to get any answers? I answer me, and all the different mes talk at once, then whichever one is strongest at the moment wins out, and I listen to what he has to say. And yet, when I ask how best I may serve my government, I fall silent inside, unable to determine whether I am hitting a stone wall or falling into an endless void."

"Perhaps the true unknown and unknowable is before thee."

"And behind me and all around me. I'd hoped, at some point, to leave uncertainty behind and go back to existence as I knew it."

"That door has shut. That Ardenai – my beloved teacher – is no more. He has been discarded as the pupal stage of a higher purpose, as a snake sheds his skin. The Ardenai which emerged from the dust of that battlefield, is not a typical Equi, but a true Equi. He belongs to that high strung, highly curious, risk-taking faction of Equi who are empire builders, world shakers, peace makers and rulers. The sort of Equi which any Equi with spirit desires to be. I see an Equi honed to the razor sharp cutting edge of absolute power. If you were sure, absolutely sure of yourself, your self-control, your ability to handle that power…Eladeus have mercy on us. You would be a dictator such as the galaxy has never seen. And I am convinced that what you are, and what you feel, you were bred to for that very reason. That means, you are a typical citizen and a typical Dragonhorse. Ahimsa, serve in peace, my leader."

Ardenai burst out laughing, and gave Tarpan a gentle cuff for his insolence. Then he linked his arm back through Tarpan's and began to walk again, his boots crunching through the first of the lazily tumbling leaves. "Odd, isn't it?" he asked in that deep, serene, beautifully dictioned voice of his. "This place? At times it seems almost tropical, and at other times harsh and cold. Today it is Oporens, but tomorrow, perhaps it will be Enalios again. One never knows." Again he was silent, walking slowly enough not to drag Tarpan, who was shorter legged. "Tell me," he said at last, "how is it that you youngsters seem to know more and see more clearly than those of us who have grown sharper of profile and longer of tooth? I don't remember ever having had that advantage."

"You didn't," Tarpan shrugged. "We have someone to look up to that you didn't have. The young men who council you, have your reflection to augment their ability."

Ardenai chuckled, but without humor. "The young men who admire me, didn't pay close attention to that battle a couple weeks back. The second hostilities actually began, I was worse than useless. I had no idea how to stay out of everyone's way. Teal killed a man who was going to shoot me in the back, because I didn't have the sense to look behind me. An arrow shot by a dying man, coming at a snail's pace and meant for my mother, managed to wobble into my path and I welcomed it, first with my arm-band, then with my forehead. I felt like I needed eyes in the back of my head."

Tarpan stopped and stared at him. "Are you trying to tell me, Ardenai Teacher, that you do not have eyes in the back of your head? You will never convince me. I never got away with a single thing in your classes, not Creppia Nonage, not Music History. And believe me, I tried. If ever a man had eyes in the back of his head, it is thee."

"You're laughing at me. I'm stung to the quick."

"I'm laughing at your need to be perfect in every way at every moment in every situation. Teal killed a man who was going to shoot you in the back, because it was Teal's job to kill anyone who tried to shoot you in the back. That's what military strategy is, a series of scenarios, of contingencies with theoretical solutions for each. You were assigned one task – kill Sarkhan. You killed Sarkhan, quickly and efficiently. I know that gives you no pleasure, but it was your assigned job on that warground, and you performed it. In that sense, you were perfect."

"Thank you," Ardenai laughed. "In that case, I'll stop while I'm ahead, and give up the business of being a warrior. It has caused me to spend much too much time in bed, and not nearly enough time in the saddle. Tomorrow morning, I think, we shall go with your squad and Gideon, and visit the cleomitite mines of Baal-Beeroth, and our friend, Mister Thatcher, yes?"

Tarpan nodded. "What about our friend, Legate Senator Konik?"

"He, like every other male I know, is drawn to the lady Io, and she to him. We will let them rest awhile in Pythos' tender care. Let them grant one another their own unique blend of diplomatic immunity unbothered by the brisk tattoo of war bells on cantering hocks."

Io, was not pleased. She understood, but she was not pleased. Her eyes said so in their coolness, and the way her teeth held her jaw closed.

"Please do not think I'm trying to aggravate you," her husband said, warming his hands at the fire in their bedchamber. "It is simply the most expeditious way of doing things just now. Very soon we must prepare to leave for Equus. Before we can do that we must know where we stand with Konik. And as for me, I will not leave here with those mines still operating. I have not forgotten the filth and the darkness, the desperate thirst and the endless pain. I was there but a short time. Perhaps there are men who have suffered much longer, and no less unjustly. I cannot leave it alone."

"Nor would I ask you to," Io replied, knees drawn up in the big bed. "I'm aggravated because I can't go and I want to. I smell like this house and this bed when I'd rather smell like horses and leather. I'm aggravated because I know you'll do fine without me, and perhaps better, which is just as well."

"Not true," Ardenai said, coming to sit next to her on the edge of the bed. He took her hand, kissed it, and held it against his breast. "I hope you are not making plans to retire, either in particular or in general. I will, if I must, forbid thee to do so. I need thee helping me hold the reins of government."

Io dropped her eyes and slowly, without anger, she pulled her hand away from his. "How long do you suppose we will skirt the issue before we finally discuss it?" she asked. "Every word of every conversation must be so carefully planned, and still the innuendo creeps in or is read in. Ardenai, we are strangers. The relationship we had is gone. Everything is ruined."

"And which of us do you no longer love?" Ardenai asked gently. "Is it me, or is it you? Io, this cannot be allowed to fester and spread its poison. If you blame me for what happened, say so. If you blame yourself, say so. Let's at least talk. I have loved you since the day you were born. To see you in pain, pains me."

"It is not my wish to cause you pain, Firstlord, but I do so," she sighed, and her eyes began to mist. "I have always done so, and the transgressions seem to grow worse with the passing years."

"Practice makes perfect," Ardenai smiled, but he hurt for the pain in her eyes. "I do not suppose it has crossed your iron-clad mind that we lost our daughter no more accidentally than we gained her?"

"I kept that which was not meant to be passed. I could have shut her out, I think. Instead of diving in that cold water a second time and welcoming her, I could have gotten out, and tried to push her back, but I didn't. If I hadn't been pregnant in the first place, there would have been none of this grief, none of this pain, nothing to be lost from this. I am ashamed. I was selfish, and I am ashamed."

"How could you have been truly open to me and not to her, as well? If I had not told you ten thousand times over the years what a pest you were..." He exhaled sharply and took up her hand again. "Listen to me. The settling was an accident, yes, an accident on my part, not yours, but it was certainly not a mistake. She was a gift, Io. Something not planned for, but willingly received, as is proper with gifts. I've been given no say at all in this, and you're assuming I didn't want that little girl. For thirty years and more you have been cajoling me into and out of all kinds of outrageous stuff. When did you give up on it? From the second you knew you were settled, you started apologizing for that little life inside you. Just because I was startled, doesn't mean I was annoyed. Surely you could sense that, Io. If I didn't want her, I wouldn't have saved what I could of her. Pythos was far more capable of that than I, but I did want her, however much of her was left. I wanted her, and the part of her that is now me, or vice versa, is hurt by your attitude. When did you decide I wouldn't accept your settling? When did you decide someone, you or I, must be made the villain in this?"

"I had no time to decide anything. Perhaps that is what's wrong. Perhaps because I wanted her for the wrong reasons, and had no time to change my mind, her death is a terrible loss."

Ardenai nodded slightly, watching her face in the firelight, the tears glowing in amber streaks as they spilled unchecked and seemingly unnoticed. "Tell me," he said softly, "tell me what the reasons were that were so wrong you cannot forgive yourself?"

Again she pulled her hand away, this time to wad it up with the other in her lap, twisting them as though she were washing away dirt. "I just...I wanted to prove to you that I could really, truly be a wife to you. Not just a toy, or an advisor, or a convenient way of getting out of marrying Ah'nis, but a real wife, with all the trimmings. Oh, that sounds so stupid and shallow and dishonorable when I say it. I promised you I would be your friend and your Primuxori and leave Ah'ree's memory as your wife alone, and an hour or so later I see my opportunity and make a liar out of myself. I truly did want to replace her you know. I truly wanted to be the one who made you forget Ah'ree."

"Horrors, girl, what a thing to admit!" Ardenai exclaimed, and she started a little. "That you wanted to be a wife to me? And a good one? That you wanted to so fulfill me I would let go of Ah'ree's memory and take up my life again? You're admitting that you wanted to make me a happy and fulfilled husband and father, and yourself a wife and mother of equal fulfillment in the bargain? That's truly disgusting, and it's certainly not what marriage is supposed to be all about. Once you get things fixed, and you're fecund, I certainly hope such a thing will never, ever cross your pouncing little Papilli mind again. You must promise."

Io looked up from the blanket and into Ardenai's laughing eyes – and she sniffed – and threw her arms around his neck, losing her grief in his kisses and the strength of his embrace.

"I love thee, Lady Io," Ardenai murmured, kissing her hair. "I am in love with thee, beloved wife. None other would I have but thee were I offered all the women on all the Equi worlds. Promise me that if you can, you'll bear me half a dozen little fruit bat babies to terrorize and scandalize my mother and the entire palace. Most important, promise that, no matter what happens, you will never leave me. I would die of boredom in a week."

"Perhaps better than what I'll get you into," she laughed, still crying. "Fruit bat babies and all."

"Better with a bang than a whimper, as my wife would say – and some OE poet I cannot seem to recall. That reminds me, Konik quoted Julius Caesar today. Well, he quoted Shakespeare's Caesar, and Macbeth, as well. A man of some depth, Konik. Light him with your beautiful smile and peer inside for me, will you? I do count on you for such things, such gentle diplomacy."

She nodded against his shoulder, sniffed again – endearingly as ever, and drew a deep, sobbing breath. "I love you," she said. "I will never leave thee, my sire. My teacher. My husband. My friend."

"I love you," he replied, "And I forgive you for cutting your hair off."

She curled in his arms to sleep that night, as she had in babyhood, and Ardenai lay with his chin on top of her head and listened to her even breathing, and felt the firmness and the warmth of her, and began looking forward with her rather than back.

CHAPTER TWENTY-ONE

A time for rethinking many things," Ardenai said. "A time for seeking out those areas in which I have been an observer and not a participant, and adjusting my perception."

"You seem this morning somehow more ready for such tasks," Gideon smiled, and Ardenai nodded. They rode easily at the back of the squad in a slow, ground-eating canter which had already put many miles between them and the stud at South Hold.

Ardenai jerked his chin forward in a pointing motion, and Gideon looked in time to see Tarpan reach over and pat the forearm of the girl beside him. "See," Ardenai said quietly, "the good my wife has done by her stubbornness? Today Tarpan shares the beauty of the countryside with she who is his wife. There were no women in the Equi Horse Guard before Io. Never had there been. She changed all that, and it was not an easy task. Abeyan indulged her in many ways, but at that point he drew a very hard line. She was his. The cavalry was his. The decision was his. And it was, no. She fought him all the way to the Great Council of Equus, and she won. Not emotionally, nor charmingly as you might imagine, but logically and legally."

"And you helped her," Gideon grinned. "She told me so."

"I encouraged her to follow her very best inclination," Ardenai amended. "I in no way abetted defiance for its own sake, nor would I. The girl is a splendid rider, archer, fighter, and thinker. She is fearless without ruthlessness, cautious without cowardice. She was a splendid candidate for her chosen field of endeavor, had worked very hard to accomplish it, and I upheld her right to be considered."

"Yet when Kehailan did the same thing, you opposed him. Rather bitterly, so I hear. Why is that?"

""Kehailan was different," Ardenai sighed, looking at other things. "He grew up displeased by everything Equus had to offer, everything I had to offer, and he was all too willing to share those feelings with me, day after day, year after year. He was the only child his mother would ever have, and, understandably, she wanted him to stay close. He refused and I felt he was shaking us off like dust from his boots. I was..."

"Hurt." Gideon supplied.

"Yes."

"Are you still hurt?"

"I still miss him," Ardenai said, looking again at Gideon and smiling, noting how easily he sat in his saddle, how his tan showed against the pale wealth of his hair and sky blue tunic. The boy was filling out. Even his voice was stronger and deeper. "I miss walking and talking and working with him on a daily basis. But, I am convinced that, for him, he made the right decision."

"And now that you rule Equus, you may order him home if you wish."

Ardenai laughed, and reined his horse lightly around a large puddle in the road. "You do not know Kehailan very well yet, Gideon. I may rule Equus, but I certainly do not rule that young man. I have known all sorts of stubborn individuals in my lifetime – stupid, tenacious, fierce, admirable – all sorts. Kehailan, exemplifies the apex of that particular trait. To order him home," Ardenai shook his head and laughed again. "Ah, Gideon, he would either defy me openly or hate me privately. What have I then accomplished?"

"Nothing," Gideon replied, and he seemed suddenly pensive. "It's just that ruling seems such a lonely occupation. I would not have you lonely."

A sliver of ice jabbed at the base of the Firstlord's spine. "Have you decided then not to join me on Equus?"

"Did I say that?"

"No," Ardenai snapped, "but you implied it."

"No, you inferred it," Gideon corrected, and even though he glared, Ardenai recognized the boy's academic accomplishments. "The only thing I meant to imply, Firstlord, is my pain at knowing I am neither truly an Equi, nor truly your son. I assumed I would be largely excluded from public life for those reasons."

Ardenai heaved a huge sigh of relief, unaware that he'd been holding his breath, and he felt Kadeth relax again beneath him. "You were wrong," he replied, "on all counts, I might add. I depend on your council and shall keep you beside me. I am having a little stool, brightly painted, made that you might sit at my feet, and a costume with a ruffled collar, and a cap and bells."

"Gee, thanks," Gideon laughed, unsure where the conversation was going. Ardenai had a strange, almost fierce look in his eyes, and Gideon couldn't help but wonder if he'd actually angered the man.

"As to not being truly Equi," Ardenai said, raking his hair back and using both hands to clip it in place as Kadeth cantered along, "any Equi will tell you it is a state of mind, not blue blood and multi-chambered ears. However, if you desire multi-chambered ears, you may ask Pythos for some."

"I'd rather be able to tuck my poor, naked penis," Gideon said, straight-faced. "But I want to be able to do what Kadeth does, and tuck it all the way in so it's a real phallus. I find having the head protruding just that little bit makes it seem like you can't quite finish the job, you know? Maybe we could find a dead pony and I could have his … you know."

"That is not the discussion we're having right now, young man," Ardenai said, and his eyes laughed in a face that was dead serious. "As to not truly being my son...again, you are wrong. Along with the instruction sheets for your little stool and your cap and bells, I sent back to Equus all the needed documentation to make you legally and bindingly mine. You *are* my son. As surely as if you had sprung from my not quite retractable phallus, you belong to me. Thou art become Ardenai Gideon Morning Star, Prince of the Great House of Equus. I thought perhaps you would prefer my name to your dam's."

Tolbeth came to an abrupt halt, and Ardenai reined in as well, turned Kadeth to face Gideon, and sat waiting – not scrutinizing, not evaluating – just waiting in easy silence. Gideon looked back at him, his golden eyes swimming with tears, nothing registering on his face. Then he blinked, and the tears spilled, and instead of knuckling them away in embarrassment, he caught them with his fingers, looked at them, touched them with his tongue, savoring each one, lost in his own thoughts. He sat thus a long minute or two, then drew a breath to steady himself, nodded deeply and graciously toward the Firstlord and said, "Equus honors me. With my mind and my heart will I serve thee always, my father."

"I am content," Ardenai smiled, returned the nod, and wheeled his horse to catch up with the others.

That evening after they had eaten and each walked apart as was the Equi custom, Ardenai felt Gideon's arm slip though his and they paced in silence, stride matching stride, breathing in the night damp fragrances of grass and lichens and looking up at the stars. "Soon, but not soon enough for me," Ardenai murmured, "we shall look up to the stars and the seven moons of home, you and I. And Io. We shall walk as a whole family with your grandparents, your uncle and his family, discussing the wondrous order of things, and tasting the night."

"El'Shadai be praised for his mercy. All of us have lived to see that day."

"Indeed."

"Ardenai...Sire..."

"Yes?" What a fine, straight profile the young man had, even in this light. How easy to feel that surge of pride. Gideon, son of Ardenai. Eladeus was indeed most merciful and giving.

"Why?"

"Pythos tells me I must cease to feel conversations and begin again to hear them. Why what?"

"Why me? I didn't even have to ask."

"Kehailan did not ask, either. I wanted him. I wanted you. If I'd asked you to be joined to me as my son, or put you in the position of asking me, it might have unduly influenced your decision to stay with me. I didn't want to do that to you. Kehailan was mine, yet he chose to leave. I could do no less for the younger of my sons."

"Would you please just stop walking for a minute?" Gideon asked with some annoyance, and Ardenai did so, chuckling to himself. Then Gideon took the Firstlord's arm and turned him until they faced one another. "I have a father. A real father. A dad of my very own. Thank you. So much! All right," he said abruptly, "I want my hug. Can I have my hug now, please?"

"Yes," Ardenai whispered, and took Gideon in his arms and held him tight and said, "I love thee, my son. Thank you for my life, and for being a part of my life."

▲ ▲ ▲ ▲ ▲ ▲ ▲

"Dragonhorse?" Gideon said from the doorway, and Ardenai looked up from his paperwork. "The Elder Authorities are here to speak with you."

"Thank you. Show them in, and then sit here beside me. I would have you learn from this."

Gideon nodded, disappeared, and Ardenai turned his eyes on Thatcher, seated to his left at the side of the big desk, a stack of files in front of him. "Still wondering if this is a joke?" the Equi asked evenly.

Thatcher looked at the files, then at his fingernails and finally at Ardenai. He'd looked up from his desk and seen them standing there – the two of them – filling the doorway and projecting that absolute power into the room, felt the terror of recognizing those almond-shaped eyes, the downturned mouth and those damned snake tattoos, all at the same time. God! Then, he'd recognized the arm-bands.

The boy, he'd recognized at once as Reed, but the raven haired Equi nobleman – what a shock. God, what a shock. To know he had whipped and kicked into unconsciousness a man who ruled half the galaxy, who was even bigger and uglier as an Equi than he'd been as a – whatever the hell kind of mongrel he'd been posing as. To know he'd sold that man to someone, God only knew who....

"Ah'riodin. She commands the Horse Guard of the Great House of Equus."

And some giggling queer who was probably – "Teal, Master of Horse, and my kinsman. And you remember my younger son, Gideon."

Oh yes. Kicked him in the balls at least once. Doomed. Doomed.

Ardenai hadn't laid a hand on him. Didn't need to. Thatcher had stepped aside, opened his files, closed his mouth and the mines. The men sat now, resting, eating a good meal. Waiting, like Thatcher. Ardenai had not swooped in as an avenging angel and released them all. No, not him. He was making Thatcher account for each and every man. Which were truly convicts, which were slaves? Flying papers, please. Internment papers, please. Bills of sale, please. Ah, one for a Mister Grayson, sold as a stud to one Jezzra Beor. He'd keep that particular sales slip for his wife. Oh, had he failed to mention that the Captain was also his wife? She looked a little different without the wig and the fake jaw and the weird eyes, but it was the same person. Quite the little comedienne. Deadly if provoked, but otherwise cuddly and amusing. She would enjoy this particular memento. "Death certificates, please."

Junior certainly didn't look like Daddy, and yet he did. He acted like him and sounded like him and their minds kind of thought together in shorthand. Doomed. God, he'd kicked Ardenai repeatedly in the kidneys just for the morbid curiosity of seeing if he'd piss blue blood. He had, too, nearly fainted doing it. At the time, it had been funny to hear a big man squeak like that. Blue? Then how come the boy had red blood?

"His mother had red blood. Next file, please."

"I am Ardenai Firstlord of Equus."

Yes, you are. And you're an ugly sonofabitch, too - cold and ugly.

"My son Gideon, and Mister Thatcher, no first name apparent. Gentlemen, please be seated."

Ask him for some authority to be here. Ask him what gives him the right to come looming in here and rob Calumet of a valuable export like cleomitite.

It didn't matter. Nobody asked. Didn't have to. Thorough bastard. Long winded to a fault. Cold. Ugly. Thorough. Relentless. Three days Thatcher sat in that chair and accounted for every man who had faced the hell of the mines in the last five years. Beyond that, there had been another superintendent. No files, no memories, no headstones.

Ardenai had finished with Thatcher and gone on to the Calumet Elder Authorities. These men were being shipped in under their noses, right under their noses, with practically no substantiating paperwork and no follow-up whatsoever. "An explanation, if you please. It will give you some practice for when you explain it to the Seventh Galactic Alliance." Oh yes, he would be bringing in Alliance mediators and Alliance personnel to protect the interests of his government. One needed to guard one's reputation, and the Equi had a reputation for being just and merciful, did they not? Of course. Hell, he was his government, and they knew it, skinny, goat bearded, psalm singing old farts. Half of them paid to look the other way and the other half blind. He, of course knew all this...somehow.

Not a pleasant week. Not at all. Ardenai walked out when the Seventh Galactic Alliance officials walked in. Briefed them, turned over his notes and just walked out. He and Junior had to get home to the little woman and then back to Equus. Things to do, you know. If an efficiency expert was needed to get things going again as a legitimate operation with paid employees and decent working conditions, he could provide one. As a matter of fact, he'd go ahead and send one along. Knew just the man for the job.

"Mister Thatcher," he'd nodded. That was all. Turned on his heel and left, the arrogant sonofabitch. He did have a whip scar on the side of his neck. A nice one. Hopefully his kidneys still hurt.

CHAPTER TWENTY-TWO

D id you ache when you were there?" Gideon asked, and Ardenai nodded.

"Every place Thatcher had kicked me, the hand he ground his boot heel into, and every place that whip had touched me." Ardenai sighed, lighting his eyes to ease the mood. "I think it was the dampness, and our collective imaginations. Are you still in pain?"

"No," Gideon smiled. "I'm fine, thanks."

"Ready then to face the eyes and ears of the Great House of Equus, my son?"

Gideon nodded, but the color drained from his face. Now, only hours away from Equus, he was beginning to panic. Not just his mind, but his blood and his bladder as well, and he knew the sort of decorum his father would expect. Even Io was quiet and reserved. She was elegant, fragile as Menorquin sea crystal, silent as her namesake. She stood now behind Ardenai, slender hands resting protectively on his shoulders, looking forward as he was to the stars of home.

Ardenai reached up and caught her hand where it rested on his right shoulder, bringing it to his lips. "It has been a long journey for you, Fledermaus. Are you tired?"

"No," she replied, and smiled. "I'm too excited to be tired."

"Then tomorrow will come," Ardenai chided, still holding her hand, "and you will think differently."

"Think, perhaps. Feel, no. I'm excited. My son is waiting. My father is waiting!"

"Ah, yes. My old friend."

"Ardenai, are you really nervous about what my father will say?"

"What he will say, and what he will do. Yes. What could be done to get you dishonored or killed I have brought upon you. Your father trusted me, and I valued that trust. Now, it may be gone and our friendship with it."

"Well, just see that you don't make the first hostile move," Gideon said absently, running his hands along the clipper's polished railings and glancing nervously out the front screen. "You can do such a thing without realizing it, sometimes. Give the man a chance to say what's on his mind. He loves his daughter. He has the right to be afraid for her. Fear can lead to an emotion closely resembling anger which, in reality, is relief."

"Are you quite through?" Ardenai drawled. "If you are..."

"This is the Seventh Galactic Alliance Ship Belesprit, calling Imperial Equi Clipper Dominus. IEC Dominus, are you hearing?"

In the time it took Ardenai to respond and greet Oonah Pongo, Gideon's stomach had tied itself in a knot and crawled most of the way up his throat. He forced himself to sit up straight and veil his expression. He felt it just for an instant, the barest flick of a green-gold eye before the screen brightened. "We have been sent by the Seventh Galactic Alliance to serve as your escort," Marion smiled. "Welcome home, Ardenai Firstlord. You, and your companions."

"Thank you," Ardenai smiled. "Ahimsa. I wish thee peace. You honor us with your presence."

"But will I honor Equus with mine?" Gideon said through his teeth.

"We have four hours before we enter orbit around Equus," Eletsky was saying, "and we'd like to bring you on board for a brief tour and a visit, give you a chance to stretch your legs a bit before the next round of festivities."

"That sounds good," Ardenai said. "I have people here who need to run off some steam before they have to face their adoring public."

"I have people here, as well," Marion said cryptically. "We'll just suck you right up into the shunt deck, if that's all right with you."

Ardenai nodded, cut power to the clipper, and Gideon watched in wonder as they were tractored slowly upward, through huge doors which retracted to allow the fifty foot clipper to pass with ease, and into a gleaming white space at least six storeys tall and larger than the parade grounds at South Hold Stud. The door to the clipper hissed open, the honor guard outside snapped to attention, and Ardenai said, "We might as well practice. I'll step out and then reach back for Io, like so. Now you, Gideon."

The Declivian stepped out, hooked his toe on something, he never could figure out what, and would have gone sprawling if Konik hadn't caught him from behind and set him on his feet again.

"It's okay," Marion laughed, "A bad dress rehearsal always makes for a good performance. Do come in and be comfortable for a bit. We have time for a celebratory glass of Teal's good Viridian wine. Physician Pythos, Senator Konik, right this way, please." He made a bow and a sweeping gesture that was both graceful and slightly humorous without being in the least disrespectful. They found themselves surrounded by Winslow Moonsgold, Timothy McGill, and Oonah Pongo, and Gideon found himself walking with Kehailan.

"This is Bonfire Dannis," Kehailan was saying. "Bonfire, this is my brother, Gideon. Bonfire is a Phyllan, and one of the best navigators in the SGA. She's also second in command. And this is Amir Cohen. He's Demetrian. He's our chief of Onboard Technologies...."

Ardenai, too, was nodding politely through the introductions, though his attention had been drawn off to one side, where a group of small children stood, round-eyed, watching the proceedings with their teacher. Amir's eyes followed the Firstlord's, and he muttered apologetically, "They've been studying all the named Dragonhorses this term. I hope you don't mind. This is an incredible thrill for them."

"It's a thrill for me, too," Ardenai chuckled. "I haven't seen anybody that short in ages. May I go and say hello, or will I scare them to death?"

"We don't expect you to take your valuable time," Amir began, but Ardenai was already on his way over to the children.

"Well, there he goes," Kehailan said to no one in particular. "Kiss him good-bye."

"We'll just wait a minute for him," Marion began, and Io laughed.

"We won't wait for him, because he's not going to wait for us. We no longer exist. Watch."

Ardenai nodded politely to the teacher, asked if he could speak to the children and lowered himself onto his boot heels to contemplate the young man front and center. "Hello there. I'm Ardenai. I'm Commander Kee's father. Who might you be?"

"I'm Yuthef Cohen," he said soberly. "Ith that an Equi cavaowy unifom, Thir?"

"No. This is the uniform of the Horse Guard of the Great House of Equus. The cavalry tunics are black with seven silver chevrons stacked on the right breast, and Horse Guard uniforms are silver green with six silver chevrons all in a row, because..."

"...because, when there is no Dragonhorse, which is most of the time, the Horse Guard protects the priestesses, and their color is silver green," said the pert little girl next to Yussef. "You knew that, you silly."

"Yeth," the little boy said, "I did. I'm justh nervoth."

"Why?" she asked, smiling at Ardenai. "You look like a very nice person to me."

"She doesn't know, does she?" Ardenai said very quietly, with a wink at Yussef.

"She thinkth you'wuh who you thaid you aw," he replied soberly.

"And so I am. Did Commander Kee tell you I'm a teacher?"

The little boy nodded and glanced toward the waiting group of adults. "You bwought the faiwy-wady with you. The pwetty haiwed wady from the Wything Cewemony. I appwethiated the hortheth and the big dwums."

"That's my wife. That's Io." He read the child's face and bit back laughter. "She's not Commander Kehailan's mother, though. Kehailan's mother died. Io is my second wife."

By this time the little girl was twitching with enthusiasm and the need to speak. "My name is Reynalda. I have all my teeth. We've been studying Equus, because this is the year of the Firstlord's rising. We have lots of neat stuff in our room. Want to come see?"

"I'd like that, if it's all right with your teacher." He looked up and got a nod from the young Equi.

"I became a teacher because of you," he said quietly, smiling down at the Firstlord. "You probably don't remember me," he added shyly, "but I was in your creppia nonage class for just one year. I'm ..."

"Orlov, right?" Ardenai laughed, and rose to embrace him. "I thought you looked familiar."

"Yes, Ardenai Firstlord. How did you remember?"

"Your teacher was exceptionally good at cutting things out and assembling them," Ardenai said to the children. "He made wonderful models of things."

"He still does," Reynalda said, and reached for Ardenai's hand. "Come on, we'll show you the ones he helped us make."

He left without a backward glance, and Io nodded after him. "Told you," she said. "He'll regain consciousness in a few minutes and realize what he's done, but he won't really care. He needs to relax a bit, and for him, children are better than wine."

Gideon looked at the others and said, "Would you mind if I followed them? Ardenai loves children more than anything else in this world, and I've never seen him with any. I'm sorry. Does that make it sound like a trip to the viewseum?"

"It is a trip to the viewseum," Kehailan chuckled. "Come on, I'll take you. It's easier than trying to tell you where to turn."

"Physician Pythos," said Moonsgold, gesturing toward the bay doors, "let me show you our medical facilities. I'm kind of filling in right now until we get a new Ship's Physician, or a new head of the science wing, one of the two."

Oonah Pongo slipped her arm through Io's and said, "Let me show you the ship, or would you rather have a glass of wine or a nice cup of tea?

How are you feeling? You look wonderful."

Marion turned to Konik and said, "Which leaves you and me, Senator Konik. Walk with me, will you?" The man nodded curtly and followed Eletsky through the bay doors and down a wide corridor. He wondered if Marion had something unpleasant in store, or if he was just the designated babysitter. Apparently everyone else had an assignment.

Marion stopped, opened a door, and nodded Konik inside. Three women, two men, and two small children stood up as one and turned their direction. "Addie!" Konik exclaimed, and ran to take her in his arms. "Ah'nia, Ah'rika! Eladeus be praised, I've been so worried!" Marion let the door close with himself on the outside, grinned, and strode off in the direction of Orlov's classroom.

He was nearly to his destination when he spotted Gideon, leaning against the bulkhead with his arms folded, staring out into the passing starscape. His face wore no expression, but the slight hunch of his body said he was uncomfortable. Marion cruised up beside him, slowing down so as not to startle the boy, and said quietly, "I thought you were going to watch Dad and the kids for a bit."

Gideon turned to look at him. "How do all of you know that he adopted me?" he asked. "Did he tell you in advance or something?"

"He sent the papers with me, and told me to tell everybody once they were filed. That way you wouldn't be a complete surprise."

"I kind of thought that," Gideon sighed. "He's worried about me, isn't he? I mean, worried that nobody will accept me?"

Marion's bright face softened with sudden understanding. "He loves you like life itself, Boy. Like he loves Kee, and Io, and Equus. It wouldn't matter a bit to him whether they all loved you, or none of them loved you. The reason he wanted it shared, is so that you didn't have ten thousand people walk up to you and ask if the rumor about Ardenai adopting you was true. This way, he walks into the Great Council, introduces Io as his wife and you as his son, and it's just a formality. There's no need to dwell on it. He can move right on to other things, and remove you from the direct scrutiny of the public eye until you're more comfortable."

"Captain Eletsky, I'm afraid I'm never going to be comfortable," the boy gulped. "The closer we get to this, the more scared I get. I fell out of the clipper here, what am I going to do there? What was I thinking? For the love of El'Shadai, Ardenai is the mighty ruler of many worlds, and I am the snot-nosed, uneducated whelp of a Declivian whore! This can't be happening to me. None of this can be happening to me!"

"Have you ever eaten ice cream?" Marion asked abruptly, and Gideon blinked at him.

"What?"

"Have you ever eaten ice cream?"

"I've never even heard of it," Gideon scowled.

"Time you did," Marion replied, and linked his arm through Gideon's.

"What can it help?" Gideon mumbled, and Marion did his best impression of Amir Cohen.

"What can it hurt? Things will be fine. Just relax."

Io said the same thing, and Ardenai, but Gideon was still so nervous that his teeth were chattering, his hands shaking so badly he couldn't fasten the frogs on his snow white tunic. Ardenai finally brushed the boy's hands aside and began to work the fasteners. "Gideon, if you say that one more time, I swear, I will carry you off this clipper ass-end up like a sack of wheat. You will honor Equus by your presence, simply because of who you are. You will not disgrace me, because, after what you have done for me, there is nothing you could do that would disgrace me."

"Shouldn't you be landing this thing?" Gideon squeaked.

"We're in a tractor beam, being lowered very, very slowly to the landing pad. If we were not, I suppose my son would step naked onto Equi soil, yes? But as it is, I can dress him."

"He used to dress me," Io confided, leaning into Gideon. "He does a fine job. You'll look wonderful, I promise."

"I'm terrified," Gideon whispered. "I really am. I loved the ice cream, but it didn't help, and now I'm afraid it's going to make me puke. I'm terrified."

Ardenai could see it was true. "Why?" he asked gently.

"I don't know, my father. If I disgrace you..."

"Oh, please," Ardenai chuckled, "don't try putting this off on me. I know thee much too well to be deceived. There. Now we will add a three quarter length cape to help hide your trembling knees." He swung the maroon cape over Gideon's shoulders and fastened the frog in the front. "A true son of Equus thou art, and mine," he said, and gave Gideon's shoulders a squeeze. He turned Gideon to look in the reflector, and the boy, despite his nerves, had to admit, he looked every inch a prince – sleeveless tunic and flowing cape, black riding tights and high black boots – his long hair, pale against the dark cape, blunt cut and flowing past his shoulders.

Io stood beside him in an ankle-length, sleeveless dress of pure white shimmer which was belted with a golden dragonhorse, a long, silver green cape cascading from the shoulders, and Ardenai... "What are you wearing?" Gideon asked, noting Ardenai's simple, silver-green Horse Guard tunic.

"I'm wearing exactly what I left in," Ardenai said. "Right down to the hair clasp. Less hair in the braid, but that can't be helped just yet." He stretched out his arms, and gave them a twist from side to side. "The gold collar, the bracelets, the circlet, which gives me a headache by the way, the forearm knives, and a summer uniform. The gold doesn't exactly go with the silver chevrons, but the less change they see, the better they'll like it." He scrutinized the green and gold pythons coiling down his arms, their snouts resting just past his wrists, barely touching the backs of his hands. "You watch, within a month everyone who is fashion conscious will be wearing snakes to all the formal occasions."

"Don't hold your breath," Io giggled, and just then there was the gentle bump of landing on the ground rather than in space dock.

They moved forward, and there was a hiss as the clipper's door came open. Again Gideon rehearsed it mentally, mopped at his brow with the back of his hand and felt the caress of Pythos' sympathetic tongue against his cheek. Konik's encouraging hand rested momentarily on Gideon's shoulder. "I'm scared too," he whispered, and Gideon smiled in spite of himself.

Ardenai ducked slightly to get his six foot six inch frame through the opening...two, three, four, reached back with his right hand for Io... two, three, four...what was that incredible sound? Five, six...Gideon stepped out into the warm, windswept sunlight of Equus, and the roar of tens of thousands of onlookers.

He was stunned. The city was huge. It stretched, gleaming white, for miles in every direction, dotted with trees and green belts. They must be elevated here. On a hill. No – a cliff. They were in an immense, elegantly paved courtyard slightly below the roofline and to one side of a massive building, blinding white in the sun, the likes of which Gideon had never seen. It appeared to be carved from the native stone of the mountain on which it stood. Below them, spilling first in a curve to the right, then back to the left, and right again, tier after tier of graceful plazas flowed down the cliff's face to meet the confluence of broad avenues below. As far as the eye could see, those avenues teemed with cheering citizens.

His legs moved him automatically away from the clipper toward the crowd on the plazas below them. By now Pythos and Konik would have exited behind him. He felt a slight vacuum, and realized the clipper had been lifted out of the way. His father and Io were proceeding forward to a spot where a group of people waited, some of whom he recognized. Teal and Daleth, Tarpan and Kehailan, and a class of a dozen or so extremely sober creppia nonage students.

Ardenai and Io came to the edge of the parapet and stopped. Teal stepped up beside Io, Konik to their outside. Pythos stood beside Ardenai, then motioned Gideon up beside him, and Kehailan stepped up on Gideon's other side. If it hadn't been for the curve of balustrade atop the parapet, it would have been an alarming drop, as the steps flowed off to their left and down, arcing back to the right before touching the next plaza. The boy was still looking discreetly about, amazed by the architecture and the scope of the setting, when he realized the crowd had quieted.

Ardenai stood slightly forward of the rest of them, and a tiny boy approached him, holding out a single flower.

"Hello, Ardenai Teacher," he smiled, and the Firstlord smiled back.

"Hello, Mahruss," Ardenai replied. "You've grown these last seasons."

"Yes," the child responded, pleased. He glanced to one side in response to a hiss, and recovered his mission. "All these flowers," he gestured to the large bouquets which lined the balustrade on both sides, "represent each student you have touched in the years you have taught. The sun flowers are us...I mean, your creppia nonage students. We picked them ourselves yesterday," he added, in what was obviously an ad lib. The crowd chuckled fondly, and Gideon realized they could clearly hear every word that was being said. He looked for microphones, but none were in immediate evidence.

The balustrade itself is a microphone, Pythos conveyed, and Gideon smiled, giving him the briefest nod of thanks. It registered with him, that when Pythos was communicating telepathically, there was no hiss in his sibilant consonants, and the thought made him smile a little more yet. A thought? All praise to El'Shadai, he could think. And he hadn't fallen out of the clipper. Life was good.

"The Oporens lupine is for all, I mean each, of your Lycee students, and the golden field lilies represent the students you taught who have died. There aren't many of those. And this flower is for you," he said formally, thrusting it out from his chest to arm's length in a motion resembling a military salute. "It represents the whole of us as a people. Welcome home. We're glad you're safe." There was another hiss and the little one cocked his head a moment while something was whispered in his ear. He nodded, and looked a little abashed. "I was supposed to say, greetings, Ardenai Firstlord, not Ardenai Teacher. But we're still glad you're home safe and here's still your flower."

Ardenai squatted on his boot heels to take it from him, took both his little hands, and gave him a lingering kiss on the forehead. "I'll be in to see all of you soon," he whispered, though he might as well have said it at the

SHOWANDAH S. TERRILL 409

top of his lungs. It made Gideon very glad not to have gas on his stomach.

There was a roar of applause as Mahruss stepped back. The First-lord straightened up, and turned to the multitudes below him, making the ancient gesture of greeting.

"Ahimsa, I wish thee peace," he said, and smiled. "I am so glad to be safe at home, feeling the warm sun of Equus on my shoulders, and your love and good wishes around me. I would not be here, and safe, if it were not for the people beside me, each of them coming to my aid, even saving my life, when I could not do it for myself. You know this beautiful one as the Captain of our Horse Guard, and my friend of many years. She is represent-ed by one of the sun flowers in these bouquets, here, as well as by one of the lupines, as is often the case, I think. Though I still cannot believe my luck, she is now my wife, and your Primuxori." There was a roar of approval from the crowd, and Ardenai kissed the tip of one of her ears. "We hope someday to add a couple sun flowers of our own to those vases," he chuckled, and add-ed laughter to the applause as he tucked Mahruss' flower behind his wife's ear. When it had died down he continued. "You also know Teal, Master of Horse, currently also Captain of the Horse Guard, and my kinsman, who saved my life on the wargrounds of Calumet, and Physician Pythos, who saved Io's life, and my sanity. It is in his honor that I wear these beautiful and ancient chain tattoos upon my arms. Daleth and Tarpan left Equus at my side, went ahead of me, and returned with me. My son, Kehailan, and his companions aboard the SGAS Belesprit, were invaluable Paracletes in this amazing adventure we have had. When there is time, I'll tell you all about it, I promise. The young man to Kehailan's left, is Gideon, who saved my life before he knew who I was, and who has stayed with me every step of the way. I recognized in him the very best qualities of an Equi citizen, and I have bound him to me as a son, and to you as a prince of the Great House." Again there was a mighty cheer, and Gideon felt himself flaming with em-barrassment, the very pavers seeming to vibrate beneath him from the sound and movement of the incredibly huge crowd.

"We have entered a new era of understanding with the Telenir," Ardenai said. "We know now for certain that they are more than a legend. We have among us a most extraordinary man, Senator Ah'ria Konik Nokota, from Anguine II. He and his family have served Equus all their days. Senator Konik is also Legate Konik, and a Wind Warrior." There was a rushing murmur, and Ardenai talked over it. "He has agreed to help us bridge the gap between our people and theirs, our world and theirs. We were met on a field of honor, and it was with the greatest honor that he acted, on behalf of both worlds. He is our first dual citizen, I think, and one who comports himself exceedingly well. He has agreed to lead a delegation to Telenir to petition for peace, and when I know more about that, I will tell you. Know this, he saved my life, and the life of High Priestess Ah'krill, and if for no other reasons than those, he will always be one of our most honored citizens.

"What I left here to do, I have done, though not alone, and not without trials. I am both more and less than the man who left here, though no less an Equi citizen, and no more glad to be back on Equi soil than I have ever been. It is good to be home. It is good to breathe the air of my homeworld once again. It is good to see all of you. I will serve you with all my heart."

He stepped back, nodded deeply at the cheers of the people, and turned left, proceeding with Io and the rest down a flight of steps carved from the face of the cliff and easily the span of ten mounted horsemen. Indeed, on each step they descended and facing crosswise on the step, stood one mounted member of the Horse Guard, many who had served with the Firstlord and Io on Calumet. On the opposite side of the step stood a softly chanting priestess, swinging a copper thurible, and the smell of horses and incense mingled together in the late morning air.

Gideon glanced to one side and realized that Kehailan was still beside him, strikingly handsome in the full dress blues of the Seventh Galactic Alliance, and that Teal was walking with Pythos and Konik. "Glad you're here," he said, knowing it was truly a whisper amid the cheers of the crowd, "I hate being terrified alone."

"You are still terrified alone, since I am not afraid," Kehailan smiled.

He looked calmly into the thronging, cheering thousands below and veiled his twinkling black eyes, though his strong hand squeezed Gideon's forearm.

There was the sudden thunder of Equi ceremonial drums, and for a full minute, their throbbing, complex rhythms were all one could hear. The crowd was utterly silent. Then a single gong sounded. Deep throated, echoing in the clear, dry air. With a sensation that made the hair stand up on his arms and the back of his neck, Gideon could hear the hollow ringing of Ardenai's boot heels as he entered the Great House of Equus.

CHAPTER TWENTY-THREE

T

he companions proceeded down a short, very high, very wide hall and turned right into an alabaster chamber elegantly hewn from living rock, that stretched up and away forever in all directions. Gideon had to force himself to look only as far as his peripheral vision would take him, and keep his mouth shut, when he wanted to crane his neck and gape. "This is the Hall of Ceremonies," Kehailan said in the barest whisper and right against Gideon's ear, and it felt as though every assembled dignitary from a hundred worlds had heard it, too. "When we refer to the Great House of Equus, this is what personifies it. When the Great Council meets in public session, this is where it's held."

First, they walked a short distance to their right, to the outside end of the great hall, where Ah'krill sat on a six-tiered rostrum, surrounded by dozens of priestesses, all in pure white and pale green. The high priestess herself was resplendent with cleomitites and emeralds, which flashed in gold settings about her neck, wrists, and fingers. She stood, inscrutable, watching them approach. There was a tall, blonde priestess standing beside and slightly above her. A woman with a beautiful, haughty face. Gideon saw his father's shoulders jerk slightly in recognition, or maybe annoyance, then he nodded to the woman before turning to his mother. He bowed respectfully and said, "As I promised, I am here. I am ready."

"A man of thy word. Take the place which is now thine, Ardenai Firstlord, and thy retinue with thee," she said, and gestured with a heavily bejeweled hand to the opposite end of the hall where an immense and ancient tapestry emblazoned with the seal of the Great House of Equus, hung in the center of the room. She struck the gong next to her, and there commenced a throbbing of ceremonial drums which put Gideon's heart in his throat.

They walked, accompanied by the drums and the cheers for what seemed to Gideon an eternity, the length of the impossibly long chamber, while the flags of Equus and the affined worlds dipped respectfully at Ardenai's passage and the huge tapestry folded slowly up and away, revealing their destination. They stopped, all seven of them, maintaining their spacing, and from the corner of his right eye Gideon could see people he recognized. Jilfan, a tall, sober man beside him who was probably Abeyan. All the senior officers from Belesprit, Marion and Winslow both giving the young man a subtle thumbs-up amid the applause.

There was no throne, per se, but another identical and elegantly curving rostrum, this one rising in seven tiers, seven seats in the lowest tier, nine in the second, eleven in the third, and so on, for a total of ninety-one arm-chairs. These were plushly upholstered in maroon wool, while the ones at Ah'krill's end were pale silver-green. Those along both sides in the lower level, were upholstered in pale blue.

There was a boulevard-width passage to either side of the rostrum, just like at the opposite end, and a pair of high and elegant archways which lead...somewhere. Gideon couldn't tell. The ones at the other end, led to daylight. These, led into darkness.

The two rostrums were much shorter in width than the banks of seats they formed ends for, and they differed in shape, but were no grander in design, Gideon decided. It was all grand, the sky-high palace in a flickernick tale, with gleaming floors and banks of flags, and huge pillars wrapped with the colors of the Great House of Equus and her affined worlds.

Kehailan was seated immediately to his father's left hand with Konik beside him, Gideon to Io's right with Teal and Pythos beside him, and they sat there four solid hours. Gideon had ample time to do some math, scribing subtly with one index finger against the thick, upholstered arm of his chair to help him keep track of the numbers.

Seven tiers of seats to each side of them in the long banks, two hundred and ten feet at least to the tier with an expanse at each end. Eighty-four plushly padded armchairs, each with its own writing surface in each row. Room for five hundred and eighty-eight people on each side; ninety-one more in the section they occupied, another seventy-two for the priestesses. That made ... he wished he had a scriber ... one thousand three hundred and thirty-nine chairs plus the public galleries, which stretched forever away above the tiers of dignitaries. Room for twenty thousand, thirty thousand, and yet room to spare. And every seat was filled, he was sure of it. Huge place – superb acoustics – and a million things to look at, tens of thousands of visible faces and still, after a while, Gideon wanted to squirm. His stomach growled. He'd been too nervous to eat earlier, and now he was hungry, which wasn't helping.

Ardenai, at least, got to get up and pace. He walked from one end of the rostrum to the other – one end of the Great Council to the other – addressing whomever questioned him. Not all Equi here this day, but representatives from the affined worlds, the many worlds of the Seventh Galactic Alliance, and the United Galactic Alliance, as well. Much to be explained, and many questions to be answered on a multiplicity of levels. Gracious and thorough, patient and lucid, the Thirteenth Dragonhorse responded. Yes, he was well, thanks to Pythos. Firstwife Ah'riodin and Senator Konik were also healed, though not yet strong. A fact which must be considered in the length of these proceedings.

"Commendable," Abeyan said, his face and voice an open challenge, "keeping alive so valuable and volatile a prisoner as Ah'ria Konik Nokota."

"Perhaps you missed what I said outside," Ardenai responded pleasantly. "Senator Konik is not a prisoner, nor his family, nor any Telenir who is also an Equi citizen, so far as I know." There was a buzz in the council chamber which could have been response to either the words between the two men, or the heat which flashed between them. "Senator Konik is a free man and a loyal Equi, as well as a loyal Telenir. He is capable of honor and of sacrifice to the cause of peace. When the time comes, he has agreed to escort my personal envoy to the Wind Warriors with an overture of friendship from Equus, and if the Alliance wishes, from them, as well."

Again a murmur arose. Louder this time, accompanied by nods and smiles from the off-worlders. "And who among us is equal to such a challenge?" Abeyan asked, looking around him with a palms-up gesture of question. "Surely you do not plan to leave your duties again so soon, Firstlord?"

"No, not I," Ardenai replied, ignoring the obvious jab. "Many are equal, but I have come to realize that some are more ideally suited. The Telenir have many of our traits, yes, but they are a war-like people, as well. I have yet much to learn before any delegation leaves this planet, but I am thinking that when the time comes I will send someone who understands and appreciates that kind of strategic thinking."

"Again you speak of many," Abeyan said. "Me, of course. Master of Horse Teal ..."

"Teal, perhaps, though I do not think it will be so," Ardenai responded. "No. I speak of one in particular, Kinsman. Someone of whom we have spoken often as a person brave without recklessness, merry without foolishness." Ardenai paused and turned to face the center dais. "Someone whose charm may succeed where diplomacy has failed." Utter silence. Almost, no one breathed, but their collective gaze turned with the movement of the Firstlord's hand. "Most reluctantly, I am thinking Equus will be represented before the Wind Warriors by Primuxori Ah'riodin, wife and warrior that she is."

Abeyan exploded in anger. "If you cannot kill her one way, do it another, is that it, Dragonhorse? You force her into a marriage that is tantamount to incest, impregnate her, and cause her to lose my granddaughter by your inept foolishness, then propose sending her, a female who is little more than a child herself, off to certain death so you can marry a fecund mare!"

"Master Captain Abeyan, your speech borders treason!" Ah'krill said sharply, and her voice sounded like she was beside them though her face was so far away as to be nearly unrecognizable. Ardenai's hand came up to silence her.

"It is not treason to love one's child," he said quietly. "I knew how he would feel, because it is how I would feel under the same circumstances.

My only regret is that we could not have had this conversation in private where it belongs."

"Do not use creppia nonage tactics to mollify me," Abeyan snarled, and at that point, Io stood up.

The hall was instantly hushed, for her eyes were blazing with tears and anger. She did not ask to speak, she simply stared at her father until his mouth closed, and then said, "I am an Equi, young in years but well able to make my own choices. I have long advised and am now Firstwife to your Liege Lord, whom I have loved all my life. I know what he wishes in these matters. I also know he does not wish me to go at all. Nevertheless, I have spent many days with Konik, and I trust him. Before I leave here I hope to understand equally well the wishes of the Telenir government. I was injured by my own inattentiveness, and my husband has suffered no less deeply than I because of it. The price has been paid and the matter will not be discussed here or anywhere else. I can choose to stay home and mourn the death of our daughter, or I can represent my government in a matter of great importance. My husband considers me capable in this, and I am honored. I choose to go forward, and it is I, who choose. The Dragonhorse was somewhat less than enthusiastic."

"For purely selfish reasons," Ardenai added softly, having arrived at her side. He took her hands and pressed them between his own to calm her. "One does not part willingly with such a treasure. At the same time I realize I can make no more open handed gesture on the part of my government and myself than the sending of one so precious to me. It pleases me to offer so costly a sacrifice on the altar of peace."

"Abraham Lincoln," Oonah said in a voice meant only for Captain Eletsky, but the dimples deepened slightly in Ardenai's cheeks, even as he kissed the palms of his wife's hands, and nodded to her to be seated.

Io returned the nod and sat back down, still shaking with emotion. Gideon's hand came to rest over hers and he whispered, "Nice going. Maybe they'll decide to take this brawl outside and we can sneak off for a bite of supper, since they didn't offer us lunch."

"Are you hungry again?" she scowled, turning slightly to look at him.

"Again? You mean in this lifetime? Yes, I am, and now you've set dear old Dad off on a tangent that may last another four hours."

"Just remember, that chair is a lot more comfortable than your little painted stool is going to be," Io smirked. She was silent for a few moments, then whispered, "Gideon, did I embarrass Ardenai?"

"The fact that you made him so proud he nearly made love to you on the spot? That probably embarrassed him. It was a little obvious that he's crazy about you. What...who, I mean, sorry...is the...entity speaking?"

Io looked, then inclined her head back toward Gideon. "That is Mal-Dor. In the Equi council he represents the parasectra of Kohath Zadok, five planets which are part of the constellation group we know as Mydrus. His kinsman ValDem represents them in the SGA chambers. Eloquent, the both of them. Slightly too concerned with Kohath Zadok as the center of all that matters, but intelligent, and if persuaded, reasonable."

"Seems a tad hot just now."

"Your sire cut off the nearest and richest cleomitite supply, and the Kohathis are very fond of their precious gems, as you can see."

"And when it is restored," MalDor bellowed, "what will be our cost, I ask you?"

"Less to you than to the men who have been slaving there, Ambassador. Might I suggest if you are concerned with the efficiency of the mines at Bal-Beeroth, you send some of your people to help with the reorganization? I was going to ask you in private to do that, but now will do as well. Your people are miners of great renown. The Alliance and Equus would welcome and value your expertise."

"And Kohath Zadok would welcome the absence of your meddling," MalDor muttered, looking down to study the opulent rings on his hands. He became aware of a sudden, ominous silence, and looked back up into the fixed gaze of the Dragonhorse. "Yes Firstlord?"

"Did it ever, even once occur to you, who are among the chiefest of buyers, to inspect those mines? To make sure your goods are coming from an acceptable source? That is part of your responsibility as a buyer, you know. Monstrosities like this thrive because of people like you, who are concerned only with the product and the price. I think I will request more specifically that you turn your hand to the rehabilitation of those mines."

By now MalDor was quaking just a little. "Yes, Firstlord. I will send..."

"You, MalDor," he said quietly, almost gently. "I believe it will refresh your mind as to what it means to organize, and rethink for the good of those less fortunate than you. I will look forward to your reports."

"As you wish," MalDor said with a slight bow, and sat back down with a deep sigh of relief.

Gideon leaned into Io. "Can he do that?"

"What?"

"Send MalDor to Calumet against his will?"

Io turned her head on her neck to look straight at Gideon. "Do you still not understand who he is and what he can do?"

Hush you two. Ardenai wiggled his fingers very slightly behind his back, but in their direction, and said, "Since we have been thus sidetracked, are there any questions at all as to where Equus stands on the subject of slavery, or the oppression of living things in general?" He raised a quizzical eyebrow and waited. It was quiet. "Is there anything I may clarify for any of you without leaving the present arena of discussion?" Again, there was silence.

"Thank you, Firstlord, for your graciousness in this matter and over these last hours," said Ambassador Sta'dan of Corvus. "We rejoice in your safe return, and welcome your wisdom in these proceedings." He crossed his elbows to slap his upper arms in the way of Corvi applause, and the chamber was filled with various noises and shouts as the others joined in.

Ardenai nodded deeply, once in each direction, once to his mother, and returned to his seat. "I hope this is over for a day or two," he said through his teeth.

"Are you tired?" Io asked, her hand closing over his bare forearm. It was cool in the depths of the Great House, and she wondered if he was getting chilled.

"I am concerned that you are. I would wish for our companions and our keep."

Granted. Ah'krill raised her hand and said, "Our Firstlord has been in conference across five sectors for the last sixteen days in a row. We shall allow him time to rest from his journey and visit his keep and his family, and all of us, most especially our keeplords, must see to the harvest. This date, we shall celebrate from now on as an Equi holiday, as it marks the day of the safe return of the Arms of Eladeus Incarnate, and the dawning of a new era." Ardenai's sigh of relief was short lived."For those who wish to question him further, the Firstlord will be available in the royal apartments from the twentieth hour until the penult hour tonight, and then he is to be given time to see to his keep and his harvest. You are dismissed."

Ardenai took Io's arm and walked with her into the corridor which led to the private sections of the old palace, their companions following behind them. "I was hoping to go home tonight," he said softly, and Io could sense the disappointment in his voice.

"Soon, Beloved," she said, patting his arm, and he stopped to catch her face in his large, capable hands. He was still smiling down at her, thinking about how good a kiss would taste, when Kehailan walked up in the company of Marion, and the rest of Belesprit's bridge crew.

"I have already been here for some time," he explained, "so my apartments are feeling a little more livable. We're heading that way, and I was wondering if my brother could join us awhile?" He turned and included the younger man in the conversation. "If you would like to come with us."

"Thank you," Gideon smiled, glancing at Ardenai and Io. "I think these two would welcome some privacy after two Equi weeks in the air."

Ardenai nodded. "Only if you are comfortable going with your brother."

"Tarpan and Daleth will be there," Kehailan said, "and perhaps Jilfan will join us." He felt the atmosphere stiffen and quickly added, "He has been most attentive to Ah'krill's wishes, and she has come to depend on him for many things. I am sure that when he is free he will seek your company."

"Thank you," Io smiled, but she was drooping noticeably, and Ardenai led her away toward the lift which led upward to their apartments. "Before we actually had to face them, apartments that haven't been occupied for half a millennium or more, didn't sound quite so intimidating," she said, leaning her head on his upper arm as they walked. "Now the thought is not nearly as pleasant."

Ardenai, too, had been looking forward to sleeping in his big bed at Canyon keep, where they could open the floor to ceiling casements and allow the fragrant night wind and the sound of the river to sweep through their slumber. "Well," he said, trying to smile, "Think of it this way, Io. It's solid rock. What could be wrong?"

"Don't ask," she sighed, and the image of a cave, with beds and furniture hacked out of stone, filled both their minds as they stepped into the elevator which rose a thousand hands or more on the outside of the cliff. They stepped off the lift and stopped in the wide cross corridor, looking at the immense, darkened archway in front of them and to their left. The first of the royal apartments. The most ancient apartments of the Firstlord and his Primuxori. Their eyes moved up the full fifty-four hands of the height of the massive double doors, then across the thirty-six hands of their width, then they looked slowly at each other. "Ardi," Io said softly, "Do you know who you are?"

"You've already asked that question today," he replied, scarcely above a whisper, and chuckled humorlessly as he stared up at the intricately carved entryway. "Do you know who you are?"

He could hear Kehailan and the others coming up behind them from one of the side corridors, and the normalcy of their approach was comforting. Steadying. "What I have figured out is that I am a fortunate new husband with a most charming and intelligent wife," he said, and to Io's delight he swept her up in his arms. "Over the threshold with thee, my bride and on to a whole new set of challenges."

Io put her arms around his neck, kissing him thoroughly even by newlywed standards, and they heard Gideon say, "In answer to your question, Kehailan, don't bother asking. They have other plans."

"Obviously," Kehailan gasped, hiking his brows, and Ardenai realized his apprehension was making him indiscreet, even for this relative privacy.

He chose not to embarrass his wife by acting penitent. He laughed instead, saying, "You shall receive no apologies from me. In this section of the palace there are only those who know us best just now, and the thought of going into an apartment, unoccupied for century upon century, is most disquieting. We find solace in that which is familiar."

"Don't despair just yet," Oonah Pongo laughed, and Kehailan nodded.

"Sire, we have had the benefit of being here for several days, and in that time the apartment before you was opened, cleaned, and furnished for your occupancy. Since Oonah and I were already here, we let ourselves in and made some suggestions. You are welcome to make changes, of course, but we did hope to make it a little more welcoming than it was." Kehailan pushed in on the great doors, and as they swung silently open he bowed with a flourish in Ardenai's direction. "Do go in. Be comfortable. If you would care to join us later, you are welcome to do so. We'll be right next door."

"Thank you," Ardenai smiled, stepped inside with Io still in his arms, and the door swung silently shut behind them. Slowly, he let Io down to stand beside him, and together they surveyed the interior. "My, my," he said at last, and Io burst into a fit of her wonderful laughter.

"A space created from the ancient times of more opulent monarchs," she said.

"The appropriate word escapes me."

"Probably not, snug?"

"Definitely not. Nor cozy, even as shunt-bays go. I think perhaps, excessive?"

"Well, it is certainly beautiful, and clean," Io said. "It has some bright touches."

"Probably Oonah's, or Kee's. And the sun flowers and lupines are here, as well. That's nice. Makes it smell fresh."

"And we'll get our exercise. We could dance."

"We could play polo," Ardenai snorted.

"It will be cool in the summer."

"Oh yes, count on that. And frigid in the winter."

"Perhaps not. The floors are warm, probably from the hot springs in the cliff behind us"

He looked down and realized she had taken off her sandals and was standing barefooted. "This is a good thing. The ancient architects were wise indeed."

"The wall hangings are most gracious."

"Agreed, and the stonework is superb. It dates to the time of the old palace itself. This should have been turned into a museum thousands of years ago. Timeless, this stone. Intimidating, in that timelessness. Reminding us we were not always modest and conservative as a people."

"Reminding us how transitory we are as living beings," she added. "This looks a little like one of the pleasure domes the Papilli manufacture and lease out. I like it."

"You, are a pouncer," Ardenai laughed, "I'm shocked to think you would have any knowledge whatsoever of pleasure domes." He felt a tug in his loins, and realized, hungry and tired as he was, how much he wanted to set his head against her, to forget all about the business of the day and lose himself in her.

"Ardenai?" He looked down at her, hoping she hadn't read his lascivious thoughts. "How do they plumb solid rock do you suppose?"

"Why, I don't suppose they do," he said, working himself up to a tease. He knew his wife's lavage habits by now, and they could be demanding, even by female standards.

"Then where do you suppose it is?"

"It?"

"Yes," she said with some annoyance, "It. Doesn't this place come with a map, or a directory, or an owner's manual? I've been sitting for the whole afternoon, and I need IT. NOW."

"Oh. Well then, let's think about this a minute. I do believe this part of the structure, and by that I mean the royal apartments, the apartments of the Eloi, and so on, covers well over five hundred thousand square feet on the ground floor. That would make it a rectangle at least a thousand feet long and five hundred feet deep – wide – right? I think that's what the history books tell us." He began to survey the place at length, pointing first one way then the other as he spoke. "I'm doing this in feet rather than hands, now, because it's easier to figure large amounts in terms of twelve inches rather than four, so try to keep up. There are six royal apartments, and they take up the whole length of this top level, if my history classes serve me right. This is the biggest of them, but we can't really assume it's twice as big, so let's assume fifty percent or so, and we'll have to allow for the thickness of the walls, which can't be counted into the size of the apartment, surely. Now, if the walls are eighteen hands, or six feet, thick, and considering that our apartments corner on the opposing precipice from where water could logically be brought in for purposes of bathing and flushing...actually that's rather nice, because it means we have windows on two sides rather than one, but it is going to be a sprint. I'm thinking," he pointed, "way over thataway someplace – toward the outside wall. Better get your little legs moving."

"You, are a miserable pain in the ass!" Io snapped, punched him in the gut with her fist, and stomped off toward the upper levels, leaving Ardenai howling with mirth in the middle of the entry.

When he'd quit laughing he took the time to do some exploring of his own. It was opulent, but hardly a shunt-bay. It was airy and open, the privacy of the huge windows guarded by the precipice on which they cornered. The tiles in the central entresol gleamed like mirrors, reflecting the plants, and a small fountain added the restful sound of water which the Equi so highly prized. To one side of the formal sitting and dining areas there was a relatively cozy step-down corner where a pair of friction fires danced in a huge fireplace. There were thick, long haired rugs, soft pillows, and an octagonal lounge, upholstered in wool forming a horseshoe around a table in front of the fireplace. *Nice*, he thought, turning around.

A wrapping of four very wide steps down to the right, and Ardenai found what would be his private conference room, The Firstwife's study, and the family dining room as well. Up a level from the main hearth he found four sleeping chambers for family, three at one end, a larger one at the other, and an ornate, centralized bathing pool. There was a sweeping balcony over-looking the city, with exterior stairs leading to the top of the hill on which they'd landed. He found his study, and a beautiful and well-kept library for his personal use. The third level up, yielded several elegant and commodi-ous guest chambers, each with its own small lavage, and access to the park just above them.

Going back down a level, and entering the sleeping chamber which was largest and closest to his study, he found his wife. She had removed her cape and dress and tumbled in her underbodice and briefcloth onto the heavily curtained bed, where she lay spread-eagle, her head on several pil-lows, gazing out the casements at the huge trees and the highest rooftops of the city.

Ardenai had unstrapped his forearm knives and was laying them on the dresser when Io said, "Come here, you," and patted the bed next to her, "I would beg a boon of thee."

She slid over, and Ardenai stepped up onto the sleeping platform and stretched his length with a sigh beside her. "How may I serve thee, my wife?" he asked.

Io rolled languidly onto one elbow and bent to flick his earlobe with her tongue. "At the risk of shocking you..."

"But dear, the children are right next door," Ardenai teased, easing over to face her.

"And the walls are six feet thick, remember? Are you tired of me already?"

"Concerned about you," Ardenai replied, and his eyes had ceased to smile. "Pythos has said nothing to me regarding such activities."

"I asked him not to. You had enough on your mind, and it's only been three or four days since he said we might resume intimacy without worry. This has really been the first opportunity to mention it."

"You wouldn't be fabricating such a report to get your own way, would you?" Ardenai smiled.

"Set your head against mine if you wish and look deeper than my desire for thee," Io retorted. "Decide for yourself if it is a fabrication." Tired, this one. As much in need of distraction as he was.

"I shall set my head against thee, but only to see how best to please thee," he murmured, and her fingers unfastened the frogs which held his tunic.

She leaned across him to bite gently at his nipples, and he groaned softly with pleasure as he felt his phallus begin to slide from its sheath. "A moment to get rid of the extraneous bits," he said, and stood up to remove his clothing, the circlet of gold around his head, and the heavy gold collar and bracelets. When he was naked, he lifted her to her feet and unfastened her garments, allowing them to fall to the floor as he bent to lick and suckle her breasts. He took a step down off the platform and repeated the process without the need to bend his back at such an angle. She tasted so good – warm and fragrant – and she trembled against him as he stroked her with his hands and his extended phallus.

She took it in her hands, and rubbed its head between her legs, allowing it to extend behind her while she bit his nipples, relishing his need for movement as though he were already inside her. She pulled him up beside her, then stepped down where he had been, and took the dripping wet head of his organ into her mouth, enjoying the sweet taste of the semen and the sweetness of knowing he couldn't resist her. She rubbed the head of his phallus against the roof of her mouth, sucking gently as she pushed the shaft between her lips with one hand, enjoying his moans and the jerking of his body.

He pulled her up to kiss her, long and deep, one hand behind her head, one hand stroking his phallus, rubbing it against her opening. "Which way?" he gasped, "Quickly," and she turned from him and positioned herself on the edge of the bed, presenting to him in traditional fashion. He leaned across her, groaning, fumbling, shaking with the need to penetrate her, and yet he entered a little at a time, without pushing hard, making sure she could take his length without pain. When she pushed up with a hoarse cry of pleasure and set herself full against him, he pushed back, gasping, setting his teeth against her neck, stroking her breasts as he thrust in, her cries compelling his own as they climaxed.

He rested across her back for a few moments, then murmured in her ear, "Am I hurting you?"

"Absolutely not," she replied.

"May I remain then a bit longer?" he asked. She groaned and moved against him in reply, and he began to thrust again, three deep strokes, three shallow, three deep, then he pushed full and stroked no more, quivering as he released without movement or sound – allowing himself to feel the strength of her contractions – allowing them to draw forth his release while he listened to her cries – like a wild animal in a bestiary foreign but fascinating.

He withdrew his phallus, still rigid, and pulled her gently backward off the bed. Then he turned her to face him, took her in his arms, and placed her on her back on the luxurious bedclothes. "I would have thee again," he said, "but face to face, if you can take my weight."

She held up her arms to him and he laid astraddle of her, suckling her breasts, nuzzling at her neck, his fingers exploring her primary iris, as if trying to make love to all of her at once. "I like that," she whispered, pushing her head back into the pillows, and he suckled her, pinching gently at her anterior clitoridis until she cried out with pleasure, and he could feel the surge of her body around his fingers. Quickly, he mounted her, and released without penetrating fully, keeping his weight on his elbows.

"I fear my weight and my size against your tender belly," he said, almost apologetically.

"I'm fine," she smiled, running a finger down the dimple in his cheek. It was childlike in his dignified adult face, and endearing. "Let's see how it goes, and if I feel any pain at all, I promise I'll say so immediately, and we can go to that priapic bench I see there, set to overlook the city. How nice."

"Would you prefer that now?"

"I would prefer thy tongue in my mouth just now," she said, and he arched himself to oblige her, groaning as she pinched his nipples, and ran her hands in long strokes down his sides and his flanks. She braced her feet to separate her legs further, and Ardenai could feel her hand touching the shaft of his phallus where he entered her.

She touched his mind and filled his thoughts with fierce images of putting a baby in her belly, and of holding her, sweat-slick on the birthing stool, aroused by her groans and screams as she spread herself and pushed in a gush of liquid, the baby's head hard and round as it slid out of her, his head hard and round as it slid in, gushing liquid, and on her birthing heat he would push himself inside her, and fill her with his get, and put another baby in her. He became aware that he was ejaculating, and that she was crying out, but he didn't know if it was with pleasure or pain, and he realized that if she'd asked him to stop, he hadn't heard her. The second he could, he put his hands down and picked himself up to look at her, concern filling his eyes, but she gave him a languid, slightly come-hither smile, and said, "That was very nice, thank you. A little abrupt, but nice."

"Coming, or going?" he queried, and she laughed and tucked a stray black lock back into his braid.

"Both. But I am a happy woman. Much more relaxed. Did you like the image I gave you?"

"Let us just say you are married to a happy man," he murmured, kissing her lips, her neck, and the point of her shoulder.

He rolled to bring her above him so she could cool off, and she smiled down at him – tumbled hair and burned cheeks and swollen lips – and murmured, "I wish thee to know that I love thee," and the tears brimmed in her eyes as she flattened out to kiss him. "Thou art life to me. All passionate and all uplifting."

"Don't," Ardenai groaned. "Please. Do not tell me how much you love me, and cause me to love you more, and then blackmail me into sending you to find the Telenir."

"It never occurred to me," she whispered, biting gently at his neck.

"It most assuredly did. Ouch! Little beast. That will not change the way I think on the matter. No, no, don't laugh! Now see what you have done? These bedclothes are probably a thousand years old or more, and...." he paused, exasperated. "You never listen to me, do you? And you're never going to."

"I do so listen to you," Io said later, and Ardenai looked up from the beautiful, six foot floor harp which had been his sire's – Kehailan Firstlord of Equus, the Twelfth Dragonhorse.

"Peace," he murmured, closed his eyes and went back to his music, enjoying the fire and the feel of a full stomach. They had descended from their bath to find dinner laid for them in warming trays on an elegantly set table complete with candles and fine cloth. It had made them glance with amusement at one another, and speculate as to who, and how many, and when, and how much they'd heard. And they realized that here, their private lives might not be so private as they would like and were used to.

There was a bell to which Io responded, assuming it was someone come to clear the dishes, and Abeyan's voice said, "I trust I have not come as you are retiring?"

"No," Io replied, and by then Ardenai was standing up. "We finished dinner shortly ago and were resting our meal. Please come in, Sire."

There was no hug, no warmth in Abeyan's eyes. Never in all the years Ardenai had watched those two had he seen such coolness. It hurt him, knowing he was the cause. It also left him momentarily awkward and tongue tied, a condition alien to his nature and experience. He gestured to a seat on one angle of the deep couch by the fire and sat opposite. Io stood looking at them both, then smiled at her father and sat down close to Ardenai, tucking her bare feet under her, and leaning against his muslin robed shoulder.

"So," Abeyan said, "You have chosen."

"I have chosen to marry a friend," She responded. "That does not exclude you, does it? He is my husband. You are my sire. There is no competition between those roles." Abeyan said nothing. "Not a very rational response to the situation, this silence," Io said. "You two were as brothers. I love you both."

"One does not marry his niece," Abeyan growled. "It is immoral and unclean, and no amount of power and public adoration can change that fact."

"It is a fact," Ardenai said quietly, "but it is not a reality. Io and I are not related, and you know it."

"Is it only blood which forms relationships?" Abeyan demanded. "Then how came we to be as brothers?"

"Through mutual trust and affection, and a common set of goals," Ardenai replied. "And uppermost, the goal of Io's well-being. You know this, too. Things have not changed."

"How can you sit there and say that?" Abeyan asked angrily, and his eyes blazed with frustration. "Look at her, her neck welted and red where thou hast bitten her in coitus, you filthy, perverted bastard! If I could, I would kill you! And you say things have not changed? Does this mean you have done this to her since childhood? If so, the penalty is death!" His fists were knotted, and he leaned forward with bared teeth, his upper lip curling in hatred.

"You have lost your senses!" Ardenai exclaimed, half expecting the man to come off the couch at him. He sat forward in a posture which was subtly more defensive, and at the same time more intimate. "Abeyan, this is not a logical reaction. You stand in the stirrups of my words and ride away from reason. When I said things had not changed, I meant only that I love Io no less now than I did when she was a baby. I love her differently, but not any less. And if you think she's the only one with love bites, I'd be happy to show you mine. The woman bites like an angry mare and calls it nibbling. Trust me, I'm not any less surprised than you to find myself in love with such a savage as this, but I am. Deeply, and forever. And that, too, will never change. Our keeping ceremony is tomorrow. Come see if she will have me of her own accord. It is your privilege."

Io patted his hand, and tried smiling again at her father, though Ardenai could feel her trembling slightly against him. "Sire," she said, "please listen to us. I know you only want to protect me because of your love for me, but this attitude of yours is foolish and immature. I am a grown woman with a son who will soon be a young man himself. I am capable of choosing, and choosing well. I was alone, and free to do that. Ardenai was alone, and free to choose. I knew, even before Ah'ree's death, that I could very easily fall in love with Ardenai. See, even he looks surprised, though I've told him this a dozen times. He still has this jaded image of himself as the old family friend, exciting though he is sexually, and charismatic in the extreme. I have been in love with him my whole adult life, burned for him and wanted his children, my whole adult life. You know what sort of man he is – kind, gentle, intelligent and powerful. I consider him quite a catch. I am happy. Be happy for me, as I was happy for you when you married your young Ah'kra."

"Daughter," Abeyan said, and Ardenai was relieved to hear a normal tone come out of him, "When I married Ah'kra, she was considerably older than you are now, and I was younger than Ardenai. You are not yet to the age when most Equi women marry for even the first time. You are in many ways still an adolescent, with adolescent views."

"Now that, is nonsense," Io laughed. "Equi women marry late because they have tremendously long life spans and they can afford the luxury of waiting. That does not mean they need all that time to grow up. I am blessed with Papilli blood. I am aging more rapidly than my thoroughbred counterparts, and I was sexually mature far younger than they."

"You are not aging fast enough to make up for sixty-five years, Io!"

Ardenai winced involuntarily. He was tired, and perturbed by the tack of the conversation. "Your father is right, of course," he muttered. "There is an age difference. One that may grow more pronounced as time goes on, but..."

"DAMN!" Io exploded, bounding to her feet. She was no less tired, and no more pleased than he was, and she read his admission as betrayal. "Precious Equus, Ardi! I thought you were on my side! I know there's an age difference! What do you think I am, an idiot? I also know how old you're likely to be when you die, and if I'm lucky, I might be still doddering around when that time comes. If I am, I'll throw myself onto the pyre with thee, and consider my life well lived! And tell me, what does age have to do with anything? Do you think I desire you only for the passion of your body? If I did, would I choose to go look for the Telenir with Nik? No! I would stay home in your bed and at your beck and call! You are my friend! My companion in intellectual pursuits! I desire you because of who you are and have been!"

"Do you realize you're yelling at your sire's commanding officer in front of your sire, who is your commanding officer?" Ardenai asked, pinching the corners of his mouth between thumb and forefinger, admiring the cobalt flash of her irises even as he resisted the urge to stand up and swat her butt.

"You see?" she exclaimed, no more quietly than before, "You see the things you care about? Protocol, in the face of heartbreak! And you think I'm immature? At least I have the common sense to be dismayed when I ought!"

Ardenai turned to Abeyan with a gesture of apology. "Please forgive my wife. She's tired. She forgets her position as Firstwife. You are right, of course. The fact that she bore a child as a child, makes her no less a child now, does it?"

"As you have so keenly observed, Firstlord, that is no child," Abeyan sighed. "And pandering to my temper will not make it so. That is a very mature, and very calculating young woman. One who assumes if she can be abrasive enough to offend our sensibilities we will form an alliance against her, thus reuniting ourselves."

"Another possibility," Ardenai nodded, turning his gaze to the slender figure near the fire. "She is as manipulative and scheming as she is beautiful. She weaves her web and casts it, and woe to him who is caught. He is caught forever. The shape of the web may change, but never its power to hold."

Io stepped stiff-backed from the hearth and nodded icily in Ardenai's direction. "Firstlord, forgive my outburst. It was unbefitting my surroundings, my lord you, and my station. May I serve you and your guest in any way before I retire?"

"No, thank you," Ardenai replied. "You may bid your father goodnight and take yourself to bed. You are exhausted, and your health will not yet tolerate such depleting. I will speak to my Senior Field Officer alone."

Ardenai discreetly excused himself for a few minutes so Io and Abeyan could be alone, and when he returned with a bottle of wine and two glasses, Abeyan was by himself at the fire. "Will you sit with me?" Ardenai asked. Abeyan nodded, and they passed the shank of the evening in quiet conversation, much as they had done for many years.

Gideon came in and was introduced, though Jilfan never put in an appearance. "Are we to have problems from him, also?" Ardenai asked, gesturing Gideon into a spot on the couch. "Was he with Kehailan?"

"Not there, either, Sire. It is said that he rarely leaves Ah'krill's side, nor does he wish to. They have found one another and are content in the finding. Master Abeyan?"

"So I hear. A good match, Ardenai."

"Not mine, but theirs. I am pleased. I trust Io will be, as well."

Abeyan flexed his hands back and studied his cuticles. "It is also said Jilfan believes there is no room for him in the life of the man who married his mother."

Ardenai looked concerned. "Have I given him that impression?" he asked, as much of himself as the others. "Truth be told, I hardly know him. I hardly knew his sire past creppia nonage, nor his paternal grandparents. The boy and I are strangers. I have made overtures, but he's having none of it so far."

"Too," Abeyan said, "You have Gideon, whom you have adopted, and upon whom you dote as shamelessly as ever I doted on Io. There is one difference. I had only Io. I had no one else to try to work into that special relationship. No one to wound by inadvertent exclusion. I see pain in your eyes, Ardenai, and I would not have it there. You have done nothing wrong, nor has Gideon. You bring out the best in one another, or so the stories go, and that is a most enviable circumstance."

"Forgive me, Gideon, but I am appalled to be so transparent," Ardenai murmured, and rose to stand by the fire, stretching his hands to the warmth.

"Do not misread yourself," Abeyan said. "Remember, I have the collective senses of the Horse Guard and the entire Equi cavalry at my fingertips. I see with many eyes, hear with many ears, evaluate from many perceptions. Many days have I spent with you on Calumet without ever having left my apartments."

"Then you know that a lot of Jilfan's problem stems from what he sees as his own inadequacies," Gideon began, then paused, studying his father's face. Abeyan was right, there was pain in Ardenai's eyes. The near physical pain of exhaustion. He'd pushed himself, sleeping little, all the way from Calumet. Always, he'd seemed to be in pourparler with one person or another, either face to face or by SGA conferencing, meeting in transit with those whose territories they passed through on their journey, until his voice was raspy and his throat was sore. Tonight, he swallowed with difficulty, and he was cold, Gideon could sense it. It had grown much too late to be sitting in a muslin robe and bare feet, especially in this mausoleum.

"What are you thinking?" Ardenai asked, and Gideon realized he'd stopped speaking in mid-thought.

"Only that Jilfan needs time to find himself as a person of merit, and an adequate space in which to do it. I think you should both make yourselves available, and let him come to you. He has friends, and a mother to talk with. And two older brothers. He'll be all right."

"His paternal grandparents raised him very strictly, when Io was not around. It may not be so simple as you think for him to relax with himself,"

Abeyan said.

"He's Io's son. He has Io's genes," Gideon smiled, as if that said everything. He slapped his knees and stood up to warm himself. "Tea, anyone? Sire, a heavier robe?"

Ardenai nodded, but Abeyan declined and took his leave of them. When Ardenai returned from showing him out, there were two steaming mugs of tea on the center table, a heavy woolen robe draped over Gideon's arm, and a pair of knee high moccasins, lined with shearling wool, warming by the fire. "Here," the boy said and held up the robe for Ardenai to shrug into. "The blue matches the tops of your ears. Why did you sit there and let yourself get so chilled?"

"Too intent on maintaining civilities, I suppose," Ardenai replied, accepting the moccasins and sliding into them with a sigh of pleasure. "Until a few minutes ago, I actually felt a little too warm. Thank you for this, and the tea. Where did you find the kitchen?"

Gideon pointed. "Around there, close to the family dining room. That whole wall opens up under the middle part of the upper level staircase. You mean you haven't eaten yet? These people need to take better care of you."

"They brought dinner in. Io said there was no kitchen in here."

"There isn't. There's just that thing that spits food and eats dishes, like on the clipper, only bigger."

"Yes. A kitchen. Or what passes for one in apartments such as these, where people are assumed to be too busy to cook, and where there is a central kitchen in the building."

"Oh. In that case, the kitchen is next to the little dining room, just like at Kehailan's, which is why I know where it is. More or less the same chambers, apparently, though this one is larger and more opulent. Slightly to the cold and echo-y side, I might add, just like his."

"I'm trying to think of it as historic," Ardenai chuckled. "Pleasant evening?"

"Very. After two weeks on a clipper with four adults, all of whom want me to excel as a scholar, an evening of relative mindlessness was delightful. I'm sorry yours wasn't so good. You mentioned a struggle to maintain the peace. Did you manage?"

"By the bloody nubs of my fingers, yes. We have established an uneasy truce, no more. For a while the conversation would flow, and then we would look at one another, and we were strangers, mutually trespassing on one another's most valued property."

"Io is not property, Sire. She is a person."

Ardenai glared at him through the steam from his tea. "You choose at this point to become insensitive to implication?"

"Of course not. I see the trespass; you into his life to take his daughter, he back to make you feel guilty. But because Io is a person, and has made her decision, you must leave her out of it. That is what I meant by her not being property. You do not walk back and forth over her, but over each other. I am sorry. I know you have dreaded this possibility."

"This is perhaps a wound which time must heal," Ardenai said. He rested his elbows on his knees, his chin in his upturned palms, and contemplated the intricate grain in the wood of the central table. "Fascinating, this new vantage point of mine. As an ambassador from Equus, I saw only the good points of my world – expounded only those – believed them. Now, I look down through the veneer which protects us from the scrutiny of others, and I see fear, anger, jealousy, pettiness. Because it is expressed in civil tones does not make it civility. I fear we have worked long and hard as a race, and in some ways accomplished very little. Perhaps we should not have chosen to move backward. Perhaps a stable, immovable base, no matter how comforting, is counterproductive, inexpedient to true, unbridled progress."

"Isn't that kind of the definition of civilization?" Gideon asked, stretching out on the lush wool carpet in front of the hearth to toast his backside. "That need to recognize both the strong points and the weak ones, and try to get them more balanced?"

"Is it? Gideon, civilization is found in relationships. Do you know what makes you so warm, and so wise? That which is loosely called humanity. Your innate ability to feel and to care and to project yourself into the position of others."

"Exactly those things which make you the leader you are, my friend. Are you saying your people do not have these qualities?"

Ardenai shook his head slowly from side to side. "I...no. I'm not sure what I'm saying, because I'm not sure what I'm feeling. It's probably just this whole thing with Abeyan, and the coolness I'm feeling from Ah'krill."

"Then let me tell you what I felt, and saw, my first day as an Equi citizen, in my hours sitting in the chambers of the Great Council. I feel wisdom here, and a deep, serene sort of kindness which is giving, not lending in nature. I see a world of people who adore you, and who would follow you anywhere, so you'd best be careful where you lead them. You speak of the ability to project oneself into the position of others? I can do it, and not very well, with one person at a time. You are clear headed enough to do it for a whole world. You object to anger and jealousy expressed in civil tones? I have seen it expressed with guns, knives, fists, open palms, penises, and spit. The Equi way is better. It is not perfect, maybe, but of enviable maturity, nevertheless. I, for one, am glad to be here."

Ardenai was quiet for a long time – eyes closed – only the occasional shifting of his fingers indicating that he was awake. "So," he said at last. "Thus endeth my first day as the absolute ruler of all Equus. Why does that sound so kraaling funny? I'm more worried about whether there are dental picks in the lavage than I am about the impression I made on the Great Council."

"Face it, Dad. You're no despot," Gideon laughed. "Fortunately, Equus doesn't need one. Probably wouldn't tolerate one for very long, despite what history tells us. That's where Sarkhan made his mistake, in thinking she would. He approached the whole campaign from the wrong angle, or so says Konik. You, are what Equus needs. Someone to listen, to arbitrate, to nudge here and pull back there, step in when necessary, step back the rest of the time, and to be there always, as a father should be. As you are now doing for me."

"And as my sire has always done for me," Ardenai said firmly, rising from the couch and extending his hand to Gideon. "Up. Off the floor and off to bed with you, young man. Tomorrow you shall meet the ultimate keeplord and his gentle wife. Tomorrow, all praise to the Wisdom Giver, we shall be truly home."

CHAPTER TWENTY-FOUR

T his is an awful thing to admit not knowing," Gideon said as they were eating a hurried breakfast, "but where exactly are we?" He reached for another piece of cheese-stuffed toast, and gestured out the large, steeply vaulted casement to his left with it before bringing it to his mouth. "And don't say, Equus, because I can see you getting ready to do that. I honestly don't know what continent we're on, or the name of the city we're in. You've always just said, 'The Great House,' or 'The Great Council,' but the city must have a name as well."

"You do know there are three continents, right?" Kehailan asked, looking over his coffee.

"Um hm. Andal, Benacus, and Viridia, plus the large island chain known as Achernar, which is where most of the serpent people live."

"Correct," Ardenai said.

"Plus we have two big ice caps, one at the top and one at the bottom," Io put in. "And you're pronouncing the mid-continent wrong. The emphasis goes on the first syllable. BEN -uh - kus, not Ben - AHH - kus."

"Benacus," Gideon repeated, and got a nod of approval from Io. "Is that where we are?"

"No," Ardenai said, biting into a peach and leaning over his plate to catch the juice. He swallowed and said, "We're on the most ancient continent of Viridia, not far from the westernmost tip, close to the sea, and smack on the equator. Not that it won't snow here. It does, and it will. Even though we get considerable heat in the summers, it gets chilly everywhere, because we are a cool planet. As we go home today we will be traveling inland nearly to the center of the continent, and then north to the sea again."

"Same sea?"

"Correct," his father said. "The Viridian Sea. Here, we are on the straits of Viridia. When we get to my father's keeps, we will be on the North Viridian Sea. If we went the other way, we'd be on the South Viridian Sea." Ardenai wiped his hands on his napkin and dabbed at his chin. "At least we got home in time for the late peaches. The city we are in is called Thura, or The City of The Great House of Equus. It is our planetary capital. There are three continental capitals, and the island capital of Achernar, plus capital cities for each of the regions on each of the continents. We do need to finish up, or we're going to miss our tube."

"I wish I was coming along," Kehailan said, "but duty calls. We need to get back to SeGAS-5 and pick up a science team for the Vandaval system. Something about studying a gas giant. I have arranged for the time we will need as a family at Mountain hold, and if nothing else, I'll meet you there." He rose from the table, kissed Io, embraced his father and Gideon, and strode out.

"Gee, Dad," Gideon said, staring after him. "He looks really spruce. I wanna be a space-man, too."

"Believe me, little fella, you are," Ardenai chuckled, and made shooing motions toward the door. "We do need to go."

Io hung back a little, and Ardenai's strong arm came around her waist as he propelled her toward the door. "He knows where to find us if he chooses to come," he said quietly in her ear, kissing its tip as he did so, and she nodded sadly. They looked up and down the long, wide hall before stepping into the lift, but Jilfan was nowhere to be seen.

Io sighed but said nothing, and as they exited through one of the side doors of the Great House and into the awakening streets of Thura, her mood lifted and she began pointing things out to Gideon as they walked. The rising sun was slanting onto the broad, white-cobbled avenues, brushing them to gold with its long, slim fingers of light, and Gideon thought he had never seen anything so beautiful and clean.

"This is such a huge city," he said, "surely people don't walk everywhere, but I don't see any conveyances of any kind. Do the people ride horses, or what? I don't see any horse...sign."

"Horses are for parks and countryside," Io chuckled. "We ride them in the city only on state occasions, like yesterday. And we do walk a great deal. It's one of our national pass-times. As you can see by the numbers of runners and joggers out this morning, that, too, is a favored exercise. As to actual conveyances, most of the market carts stay to the back alleys unless they are street vendors. There are tracks up from the tube system for them to travel on. We almost never see a vehicle of any kind on the avenues."

"And as for the manner in which the people themselves travel if they wish to go any distance, or if they choose not to walk to someplace closer by, you're about to be introduced to one of the ancient wonders of Equus," Ardenai smiled. He nodded to a woman who greeted them, and gestured toward a stone archway between two buildings. "Right this way."

They entered a tunnel, though that's not what it seemed to be. It was too light and airy, and considerably much too large for a tunnel, but it sloped gently down, and as Gideon looked past the people and the many greetings, he realized that a wide center section of the floor was moving, half in each direction, and that many of the people were whizzing in both directions at the pace of a fast trot. To their far left, he could see market carts, loaded with fresh produce and other goods, moving briskly along tracks which also moved in both directions. Another three or four minutes' walk put them in the center of a hub from which other tunnels extended, each with a number above it.

"Districts," Ardenai explained, pointing toward one with his chin and steering Io in that direction. "We decided long ago that if our world was going to have breathable air and drinkable water, we were going to have to do away with the combustion engine, which we did. Most of our power is geothermal, as our world is volcanically very active, and we are blessed with a superfluity of exceptionally hot, highly pressurized water. We also use a great deal of wind and solar power. We use the ocean waves and currents to power factories, city lights, all kinds of things. And this," he said as they approached the platform, "is what generates the fire in our fireplaces at the Great House. It's a precursor of time whip technology. This is an older, slower version. It was designed by a friction engineer named Balearic, to honor the rising of the Eighth Dragonhorse, which, much to his surprise, turned out to be him. Anyway, it's been around about thirty-five hundred years, but it's extremely efficient, as you will see. It works like a slingshot, using the power of the planet's rotational force. You do realize we're spinning extremely fast, over a thousand miles an hour?"

"Um hm," Gideon said, trying to look everywhere at once. There was a soft hiss, a breath of hot air, and where nothing had been a moment before, a gleaming silver tube with a pointed nose sat waiting. It was behind a very heavy pane of something clear, and represented everything Gideon had ever imagined when he'd pictured far-away planets and alien ways of life.

After ten seconds of something that sounded like a huge fan blowing the pane shot upward and disappeared, and the whole side of the thing opened up without making a sound. It was empty. There were rows of comfortable seats – reclining armchairs with footrests which faced each other across a wide aisle, and they entered with everyone else and sat down.

"Just made it," Ardenai said. "But just is good enough."

"There are cargo carriers, also," Io explained, "and horse haulers. This one is just for passengers. Some people find it a little disconcerting when it first starts. It feels like it's leaning back and launching itself, but the feeling passes quickly."

"How do the horses like it?" Gideon asked uneasily. "And where's Pythos? When did we lose Pythos? I haven't seen him or Teal since we left the Great Council yesterday." Gideon sounded a little alarmed, and Ardenai realized how new everything was for him, and how intimidated he must be feeling.

"I'm guessing that even as we speak Pythos is already sprawled in the branches of the biggest of the myrianotus trees in our garden," he chuckled. "I had to stay last night to accept visitors. He didn't. He and Teal both went straight to Ah'din's kitchen for dinner. We'll see them here in a bit."

"They got there that fast?" Gideon scowled. "Didn't you say we're going nearly halfway across the continent?"

"Um hm, in your terms, thirty-two hundred and seventy-two miles," Ardenai said. "And we'll have to change tubes once."

Despite the Firstlord's long, split-sleeved tunic and lack of any other ornamentation, people were making polite note of him behind their hands, and it was embarrassing Ardenai, which amused Gideon. On how many worlds could the planetary leader go about his business untrammeled by security or pageantry? Not on Declivis, for sure, and that was still Gideon's only measure of the universe.

Io engaged herself in conversation with the woman sitting next to her, and Ardenai leaned his chair back and closed his eyes. He looked comfortable, and Gideon was tempted to do the same thing, but there was a soft, building noise – not quite a whine – but a sound as though something with incredible tensile strength were being stretched to the breaking point. Ardenai's hand closed over his, and for the space of five seconds Gideon felt as though his intestines were being whirled around the inside of his ribcage like water being swung overhead in a bucket – first one way, then the other.

The sound stopped, Gideon's guts slopped into the center of his body, and he sagged and exclaimed, "OH HELL, OH SHIT! Oh...I mean golly gee whiz, that was an unpleasant little surprise, Dad. You couldn't have told me just a bit about what to expect?"

"Doesn't pay to tense up," Ardenai drawled, and his eyes were twinkling with mischief. "Really, it doesn't. Do you feel better?"

"Than what?" he shuddered, still wondering if he'd wet his pants. "Surely they don't do that to horses. It would scare them to death. Surely pregnant women don't ride this thing? Please tell me the ones for getting around the city don't do this!"

Ardenai fought back his laughter and worked on a concerned, parental look. "The locals are much, much slower. This is a long-distance express," he said comfortingly. "Equi anatomy is slightly different from yours. We're a little better anchored inside. On the way back we'll put a binder on you, and you won't feel the slingshot so much. As to the horses, those transports are considerably slower also."

"Forget the binder. Remind me to nicker next time," Gideon muttered, and began to look around. "We're outside!" he exclaimed. "I didn't realize this whole vehicle was a big window. It looked solid."

"It is solid, and we're not outside," said the girl who had come to sit across from Gideon. She had long, thick auburn hair pulled back in a clip at the crown of her head, and those green Equi eyes, and a nice, even smile. "I'm Ah'brianne," she said. "Timor Ah'brianne Ah'mae. You must be Ardenai Gideon Morning Star."

"What makes you think that?" he asked, half teasing, "and what do you mean, we're not outside?"

"I'm assuming you're Gideon because you're sitting between the Firstwife and the Firstlord of Equus, who was my creppia nonage teacher and is still my neighbor. Hello, Ardenai Teacher," she smiled, and for the first time there was a hint of shyness.

"Hello, Ah'brianne, it's good to see you," Ardenai grinned, and leaned back again in his chair, closing his eyes.

"Come, sit with me, so we don't holler back and forth and disturb your parents," she said.

His parents? The notion was startling enough to make Gideon jump a little and color in the face as he glanced at Io, seeing if she was offended. She just gave him a bland look and made a little motion with her hand that said, well, get over there, so he went. He settled himself, realizing there was no longer any sense of motion at all. "What do you mean, we're not outside?" he said again.

"We're seeing the outside," she explained, "It's being projected in here, but we're actually several hundred hands under the surface of Equus. Of course it's not all of the outside, because we're moving so fast it would just be a blur. The satellite imaging is far enough ahead of us that we can enjoy the view."

"Just how fast are we moving, or do I want to know?" Gideon asked.

"Oh, not very fast after being in space, like you were," Ah'brianne replied wistfully. "At top speed we'll only go seven and a half transonics, or about fifty-seven hundred miles an hour. You were going times-light! What did it feel like?"

"Well, the takeoff was a lot smoother," Gideon muttered. "Other than that, it felt like we were at a standstill, just like this does. Doesn't this thing produce an awful lot of heat from the friction? How can it go that fast on the ground...in the ground?"

"The tunnel is super-cooled, and the friction is transferred to heat and power generation," Ah'brianne shrugged. "It's ancient technology, but it works, and it would be expensive, disruptive, and unnecessary to upgrade to something more modern."

He poked a finger ceilingward, "Do you have roads up there?"

"Of course we do," she laughed, and Gideon realized she was pretty in a freshly-scrubbed woodsy sort of a way. He remembered Ardenai's story of how he'd met Ah'ree, and how he'd realized what a pretty girl she was. "Do you think we ride horseback through an endless wilderness to get from place to place?" she asked with this ... *tone* in her voice, and Gideon realized that while she might be pretty, she was brassy, and bossy, too, probably.

"I have no idea what to think. This is my first full day on Equus," Gideon replied. "Tell me about Viridia."

"Sure," she said, removing her sandals and tucking her feet up beside her on the seat. "Viridia is the oldest settled continent. The Serpents settled the islands, of course, but as far as hominoids go, Viridia bears the oldest life-signs. We're," she paused to convert, "fifty-seven hundred and nineteen miles West to East, and fourteen hundred and ten miles North to South, so we're long and narrow. We're mostly rolling grasslands, steep canyons, and rocky outcrops, reasonably high hills, but not many high mountains. Only three major ranges, two on the western half of the continent, and then kind of a spine that runs down parts of the center, but it's not as high as the others. Only about three thousand feet. What else?"

"Cities, towns, industries?"

Ah'brianne shook her head. "Viridia is a continent of keeps. Most of the industry is on Andal, or, more precisely, *under* Andal. Here, we raise horses, and crops like perennial alcibus and phaselus, mazea, chenopodium quinoa, and einkorn, which are all staples of our diet. And all kinds of fruit and nuts, except for ice-pomes." She thought a moment. "We do raise regular varieties of pomes, though. As a rule it doesn't get cold enough long enough here for most varieties of ice-pomes. They come from Benacus, as a rule. But we raise lots of soft fruit, like blood fruit, sundrops, rhax vines, prunes, peaches and dragon's eyes. Nuts, like ammons, klavis, and rugostum. And of course oranges, lemons and verdanbutters to the far south closest to Achernar. The Equi couldn't survive a day without their oranges. We flavor everything with them. Sun flowers, too. Hundreds of thousands of acres of sun flowers. We'll be coming up on them soon, so watch the monitors. It's late Enalios, so early harvest is getting underway."

She gestured toward the images, giving Gideon a split second to wonder if she'd ever stop talking about the first question, so he could ask her another, and if she'd get it answered before they got to their destination. The thought made him chuckle inside. "You'll get to see the big harvesters working as we go by. And they'll be working on our own keeps, as well. Anyway, there are five major cities on Viridia, four of them on the seacoast. One to the far west, that's Thura, where we just came from. Two on the south coast, one on the east coast, and one in the middle, that's Pomonar, the regional capital, where we'll change tubes."

Gideon heard himself groan, and flushed with embarrassment. "It's a local, and it has a section for horses, so it's considerably slower," Ah'brianne said quickly, sensing his discomfort. "We'll be there in just a few minutes. Look, those are vineyards – Rhax vines – those are for wine. We're neighbors, you know."

"I heard you telling Ardenai. How close are you?"

"No more than four furlongs or so. About half a mile. We tend to measure the older keeps in terms of furlongs."

"You're close," Gideon said. "I pictured the keeps as being huge,

Sea keep and Canyon keep both. I guess they're not."

"Oh, but they are, over four hundred furlongs to a long side, and two hundred...look, the sun flowers!" They watched the red and gold fields, spreading in all directions like paint spilled on a bright green carpet.

"Amazing," Gideon murmured. "What do you use them for?"

"Everything," the girl said. "We make oil out of the seeds, eat them whole, make flour out of them, grind them to cook with, along with other seeds and nuts, and the residue becomes animal fodder."

"You have domestic animals other than horses?"

"We have sheep for wool, milk and cheese, quite a few goats, and some llamas and alpacas, as well, imported from the high places of Calumet and Terren," Ah'brianne grinned. "Actually wool growing is a bigger industry on Benacus than it is here, at least the more exotic, higher elevation creatures. And we have some dogs imported from Calumet or Demeter. Big ones, mostly, for herding and protecting the livestock, but they have to be spayed or neutered before they can be brought onto the planet, lest they become feral and upset the ecology.

"That's because we don't have any native dogs of any kind, which I think is strange. We have horses and sheep, and wild kine and all kinds of what we call protopeds and you call...pants, or something like that, why not dogs? Some keeps use them, some keeps don't. The dogs, I mean. We have lithopeds, too. That's what we call the smallest protopeds..." she made claws and a meowing sound, and gave him a quizzical look. "Like in the house and the barn?"

"Cats?" The term she'd used registered. "Is that what you meant?"

"Yes. Protopeds – panthers, not pants," she giggled. "Cats – peds. And as I said, there are sheep, because we wear a lot of wool, and we Equi do love cheese, though many people stick strictly to products made from grains or vegetables. Anyway, as I was saying about the nature of keeps..." she slowed down momentarily, and gave him another quizzical look, "am I boring you?"

"Absolutely not. Please go on," Gideon urged, smiling politely. The rate at which she could talk, the way she could spread her thoughts all over the place and still keep track of all of them was amazing. He was both fascinated and impressed, and highly amused.

"Most of the keeps are rectangles, or something close, so in many cases there's a point where four keeps come together. It was and still is, traditional for the four keeplords to build their homes in that area, keep naves, as they're called, so that in case of emergency, one has neighbors. Your sire and his sire live exceptionally close, just a furlong or so apart. That's about an eighth of a mile. Mostly because that's how the thermal pools distributed themselves in this area, which determined to a great extent where the most ancient dwellings were constructed. And too, because those two keeps, plus the third, which will probably be yours when you marry, by the way, and the fourth, which we lease from them, have been held as one huge keep in their family for many statute generations, so there's no easement boundary."

"Seems like you could get around pretty fast to get help if you needed it," Gideon observed, indicating the tube.

"We have huge storms here, Gideon. Terrifying storms, sometimes. The kind of storm that can bat an Equi flyer right out of the air. The tubes may cease to function for days at a time. It's rare, but it does happen at least once every cold season. It's good to have neighbors, like Krush and Ah'rane, and Ardenai and Ah'ree..." she caught herself too late, and glanced in the Firstlord's direction to see if he'd heard her. If he had, it wasn't apparent. He was talking to the man next to him about the quality of horseshoes, and the comparative merits of the new membium alloy the Anguines were so excited about. Io, too, was engaged in conversation. "I'm sorry," she whispered, "Like Ardenai and Io. And of course Teal and Ah'din. They're just the most wonderful people of all. They're my fostering parents. In case I ever lost mine they would raise me as their own."

"I'm confused. Who has the fourth keep?" Gideon asked, and Ah'brianne pointed with her chin. "Your sire. And his sire," she said. "When I said those keeps had been in your family for many ages, I meant it. Keeps can't be broken down, or split up, and they do not change hands unless the entire family dies out. That's what I meant by the keep that would be yours. Huge holdings between the two of them, and not all here, I might add. Upland keep could be Ah'din and Teal's, but they're happier being with Ardenai, and Kehailan's certainly no keeplord. He's suspicious of anything with more legs than he has."

"What if the keeplord doesn't have any family members who want to farm? Then what?"

"Some lucky family gets to use it, like us," she grinned.

Gideon looked puzzled. "I thought there wasn't any..." he shook his head and dug in his mind for the right way to phrase this. "I didn't think anybody on Equus had any more than anybody else on Equus."

"You would be both right and wrong," she twinkled. "We could have a keep of our own somewhere far away, but we wanted to be here, close to where my parents grew up, and one of your grandsire's keeps was available. It is perfect for what my parents do, and when it was offered they gladly accepted."

"I see," he nodded. "What about everybody else on the planet?"

"No one has to be hungry. There is no lack of education, or health care, or access to services. Every citizen has the opportunity to become what he wants to be, and every citizen is warm, and fed, and well-schooled. Every citizen has time off to travel, or engage in hobbies. We all have that. But we have people who value different things, and whose needs are simple by choice. We also have people who are slothful, or stupid, unambitious or just unwell. That kind of thing can't be legislated, you know. There are ample opportunities to succeed, but it's not a requirement of citizenship, luckily."

There was that tone of voice again. Was she being sarcastic with him, and if so, why? Why luckily? Did he strike her as slothful or stupid? Before he could open his mouth she went on speaking.

"But remember, we also have a Royal House, The Great House of Equus. Before your sire was Firstlord, he was a prince, like his sire before him. Like you are now. You will have opportunities for acquisition which may pass others by. But that's okay," she hastened to add, seeing his discomfort. "On Equus, those of the Great House are not the idle rich. They work harder than any of us, and more is expected of them. Your sire being a prime example."

"I'm not sure if this is a rude question to ask," Gideon said, "so please tell me if it is, so I'll know." She nodded. "Is your sire a prince?"

"Yes. And it's a fine question. My great-great grandsire and his wife on my father's side were farmers on Calumet. They moved here when my great grandsire was a schoolboy. My sire is an agricultural specialist. My mother is a master weaver, like Ah'din. We're here."

"What?" Gideon gasped, "Already? Oh, is this thing going to go through any kind of a reverse...whiplash performance, because if it is, I've got to grab something," *like my liver*, he added under his breath.

"No. Look at the walls, Gideon. We're here. We're stopped. Come on." She linked her arm through his and pulled him along with the other passengers getting off, greeting with nods and laughter those she knew, which seemed to be most of them. "We're in Pomonar, which is our major central city, and our regional capital. It's also the largest city on Viridia outside Thura. I think I told you that. Sometimes on the weekends we get together and come here for concerts or plays or other entertainments. You're welcome to come with us."

"Who is us?" Gideon queried, pulling his hips around a lady with a large market basket, and bumping Ah'brianne in the process. "Sorry," he murmured, but she only giggled and tightened her grip on him.

"Young people from the keeps in the area, and from our village. Colts our age. It's not anything the Firstlord's son would bring embarrassment by doing. Does that worry you? Being the Firstlord's son, knowing what kind of an example you have to set? Knowing that everybody's judging your every move? It would worry me a lot, I'm afraid."

"It wasn't bothering me until now," Gideon winced. "Where are we, is this our tube?"

"Yes. This is platform two. This tube will take us to the little village of Falconstones, on the coast, and after that we'll travel inland, on land, or above land, to be more accurate. You'll actually get to look around."

This tube was larger across, obviously built to trundle things as well as people, and the seating was not so luxurious, but it was comfortable, rather like the old atom powered buses Gideon had ridden as a small boy. He looked around for Ardenai and Io, and caught a nod from the Firstlord as he and Io settled further back on the tube. There was a rush like a roller coaster, but no more, and they were once again underway. Ah'brianne pointed out things as they passed – or seemed to pass – Gideon corrected his thought. Rolling fields, huge orchards, more sun flowers, and horses everywhere. The most beautiful horses Gideon had ever seen in his life. There were huge horses, pulling farm machinery, like he'd seen on Calumet. He saw children on ponies, and horses being worked over fences and in arenas and round pens. They passed several farms, green and sweet-looking with lots of grass and long, low barns built of stone, with heavy sod roofs. Ah'brianne said they were small dairies, though he saw no sheep, and she said it was probably milking time. Within minutes, she said, "We're here," and Gideon could feel the tube glide to a stop.

When they exited, even before he could see it, Gideon could smell the sea. He'd only seen it once in his life, at a distance, when he and Ardenai had been sold to the slavers on Hector. Now, he hurried up to the surface and looked around, breathing in the salt air, hearing the cry of the sea birds, and savoring the breeze. Ah'brianne was chattering away, and despite her kindness, it was beginning to grate on Gideon's nerves. The person he really wanted to share this moment with, was his sire. He began looking around, trying to figure out how to escape with a modicum of grace.

Are you in distress? Came Ardenai's query. *You look rather wild in the eyes.*

His father's voice startled him a little, but they'd been practicing, so Gideon squeezed his eyes shut and concentrated. *C a n   y o u   h e a r   m e?*

Perfectly well. No need to shout. What's the matter?

It's this girl. She's very nice, but she's asked me to go to town with her and the other young people our own age. Ardenai, I've never been a child, or a young person my own age. I wouldn't have any idea what to do or how to act. She's asked me if I want to go riding with her. I told her I didn't have a horse, but that doesn't seem to dissuade her. What does she want from me?

She just wants to be friends. She's a very nice person from a very nice family, and you have nothing to fear from her. Nevertheless, if her chatter is becoming irksome, I shall rescue thee.

Please, yes. Thank you.

"Gideon," came Ardenai's unmistakable baritone, "attend, if you please, my son."

He turned toward the sound, and gave his sire a wave. "I must go," he said. "It was nice to meet you. I hope we'll see each other again some time."

"I'm right next door at Lea keep," she grinned, gave his arm a little pat and vanished into the Hoplegyr crowd of market-goers.

Gideon trotted over to where Ardenai and Io were leaning against a pipe railing, looking down into the sea, and leaned with them, contemplating the surge of water below. "Amazing," he breathed. "I thought there would be beaches and big, crashing waves."

"There are," said the Firstlord, "behind that outcropping and stretching away east of us there are two white sand beaches, complete with breakers. A very popular holiday destination when the weather's hot. This is just a deep, sheltered cove, which makes it nice for a marina, where we tie our boats. See the one the color of wine with the diagonal gold stripes on its bow, and the tall mast? That one belongs to our family. Are you ready to go on to the keep, or would you rather feel the sand between your toes first?"

Gideon looked longingly in the direction of the sand, but he said, "There are beaches near Thura. You have been away from your home and family for a very long time. Let's go on."

Ardenai nodded and smiled. "Thank you," he said. He turned back to Io, putting an arm around her shoulder and bending to kiss her softly on the cheek. "What's the matter Fledermaus? You're very quiet this morning."

She shrugged dismissively. "I just have a lot on my mind that we haven't talked through, I guess. But there will be time for that later. Right now, let's get you home."

Ardenai took a deep breath and began to comprehend. "It's your home, too, and my parents, are going to be so happy to have you in the family."

"Unlike my sire?"

"I didn't mean that. My parents have always loved you as a person, Io. The fact that you are now my wife, only adds to their affection. Come on, let's get the flyer."

It was an odd feeling, and it settled on the three of them despite their best efforts – that sense that they were suddenly a cobbled-together family, and that the man who had left alone as a Creppia Nonage teacher one Drasterigyre morning, was returning as the Firstlord of Equus, the Arms of Eladeus Incarnate, the Thirteenth Dragonhorse; bringing a new wife, and a new son, and pretty much a whole new dimension of life to the quietude of Canyon keep.

They got the sporty little Equi flyer from the place Ardenai had left it that fateful day, lifted off, and headed west, down the coast. "That was the village of Falconstones, by the way," he said into the thickening silence. "It's called that because the sea falcons nest in great numbers on those sea stacks just off the marina. They make a real mess of the boats, but they were there first, so there they stay."

"Ah'brianne told me that," Gideon sighed, and it made Ardenai chuckle.

"Talked holes in your hide, did she? She's just trying to make you feel at home. You should have heard this one talk when she was that age. Well, maybe a little younger. Papilli grow up fast. "

Gideon's face twisted with the question. "Just exactly how old is Ah'brianne, anyway?"

"Don't focus on age," Ardenai advised, "it'll throw you. Remember that we Equi don't figure age exactly as you do, and that we take much longer to get from puberty to maturity than Declivians do, and accept the fact that Ah'brianne is just about where you are in the growing up process."

He deftly piloted the craft inland, crossing over a large estuary filled with birds. "This is where Canyon keep begins," he said. "Its long side goes east along the coast, the short side goes south, so Falconstones is very close to our northeast corner. Lea keep lies beside it, sharing its long side, extending the short side further south, inland, following the river. Sea keep goes west along the coast and north from the central nave, where the four keeplords' homes are. Upland keep goes west and south, lying beside Sea keep to the south. Right now we're cutting diagonally across Canyon keep from northeast to southwest."

"Um hm." Gideon did some mental mapmaking. "Got it. I think. We're traveling more or less south, away from the sea. Therefore, the sea is to the north of us, Lea keep is to the south of us, which means it's in front of us and to our left. Falconstones is east of us and back north to our left, and your sire is west of us to our right. Right?"

"Right. Go to the head of the class," Ardenai chuckled, and Gideon flushed with pleasure.

They were following a wide gorge with rather shallow but precipitous sides in which Gideon could see caves, both large and small, and a verdant, heavily treed bottom through which ran a wide river of leisurely pace. The canyon rose to a steep, narrow mouth with a silver tongue of a waterfall spilling out of it, and beyond it, still climbing away, rolled the endless prairies of Viridia. From this vantage point it looked as though all of those prairies might drain down this graceful throat into the welcoming paunch of the sea. It was spectacular, and Gideon pictured himself riding a horse across that green expanse, and swimming in that river, and exploring in the caves, and wondering if – just maybe – he could make some friends his own age. He'd never known anyone, not a single person, his own age. If he had, he couldn't remember.

Where the canyon flared out into a series of huge rock outcrops, in an area dotted with evergreen and deciduous trees, several large structures could be seen. Gideon guessed they were barns and stables, some free-standing, some seeming to be part of the rocks themselves, or set into caves. There was a neat collection of stone cottages, each with its own garden, and there were corrals, round pens, and training arenas of various sizes, including what appeared to be a hunt course and a polo field. This, put Squire Fidel's holdings to shame, and for some odd reason, the thought delighted Gideon.

As they skimmed low over the main house, Pythos' sleepy voice murmured, *We are all at your house, Beloved,* and Ardenai swung momentarily east to the other side of the river before lowering the craft again and setting it gently in a large, semi-circular courtyard where five people stood waiting. Gideon recognized two of them: Teal, and Jilfan.

Io clapped her hands with delight, and as her laughter rippled out of the open flyer, Krush's boomed in.

"Well, it's about time you two sparring partners got together!" he laughed, hurrying toward them, "and I see the new baby's already up off the floor and ready to do a day's work in the fields! Welcome home, all of you!" By that time Ardenai was out of the flyer and in his father's arms, and Jilfan and Ah'din were hugging Io, and Gideon stepped out to find himself being held at arm's length by one of the most beautiful women he'd ever seen in his life. "And you, Ardenai Gideon Morning Star, are so very welcome here!" she said, and embraced him with such tenderness that it brought tears to his eyes. He knew who she was, of course; she looked just like her son, but she said it anyway. "I am your grandmother, Ah'rane."

"Thank you," he whispered. "I am so blessed to be here."

"Give me that boy!" Krush demanded, and Gideon found himself released by Ah'rane and squeezed until his bones cracked by a good looking man slightly shorter and more wiry than Ardenai, whose hair was turning silver, and whose grip was absolutely phenomenal. He was again held at arm's length and studied. "Welcome home, Gideon," he said in a voice which carried laughter just beneath the surface. "Your uncle Teal thinks the world and all of you. I need to sneak off and hug that new daughter-in-law of mine, but I'll be back for you."

He turned with amazing quickness and swept Io off her feet and into his arms with a shout of laughter. "You finally got him!" he crowed. "I knew you would! I'm so glad. You're going to be so good for him! And how are you feeling, little one? Am I roughing you up too much?"

Gideon watched Ardenai smile and walk slowly into his mother's arms as if savoring every step of the experience, and an arm came around his shoulder. "I need to hug you, as well," said the soft, shy voice, and Gideon looked into the third pair of beautiful, jungle green eyes. "I'm Ah'din. We're so very happy to have you join our family."

"Indeed," said a familiar voice, and Teal was hugging him, too. At that point it really hit him. Teal, Master of Horse, warrior extraordinaire, was his uncle.

"Thank you," Gideon said, and realized it would do for his entire vocabulary. "Thank you."

Ardenai sighed deeply and relaxed in his mother's embrace, lips against her neck, enjoying the familiar fragrance of her skin and hair. "I have a question I need to ask you," he said, and his eyes twinkled mischievously as he pulled back to look at her. "People are saying I'm adopted. Am I adopted?"

"Don't be silly. Of course you're not adopted," his mother said, and burst into peals of the merriest laughter Gideon had ever heard. It was like music, and he was enchanted. "Who would tell thee such an outrageous thing, Ardi?"

"Oh, I have missed you so much," Ardenai laughed. He held her back to feast his eyes on her. "I'm sorry for any alarm I've caused you, Mother. I would have gotten word to you had I been able to."

"You're forgetting that Josephus was here. He told us quite a bit of the story," she said, and took his face in her hands. "Still, it's the last time I'm sending a shopping list with you, young man. Are you in good health? You're thin, and your face…feels very hot. Ardi, you're running a fever."

He took her hands, pressed them together, and kissed them. "I'm in good health. The hard exercise has done me good. I'm going to get Pythos to spend some time sanding and priming on me here soon. I'm eating like a horse, and," he chuckled and looked abashed, "I lost that list someplace. I'm sorry. It's probably in the clothes I was wearing. I lost those, too. All told, it was rather a rough day in the city for me. People did bad things to me without even asking."

"I got that impression from the cosmoscope," she said with a smile and a shudder. "But after all, you found a fine wife, and a beautiful son, and most important, you found your way home. Now, I need to go welcome your new bride to the family before your father mauls her completely to death. Are you home for a bit?"

"Yes. Go on. I'll keep your spot for you." He patted his chest, and his mother walked away with a gentle laugh to embrace Io.

"Welcome home," Ah'din said, and Ardenai caught her up with a laugh of pure joy.

"Precious Equus! I am so glad to be home! My beautiful sister." He stopped speaking suddenly, and took a deep breath, and fought back sudden tears. It was over. This part was over, the loneliness was past.

She, too, took his face in her hands and looked worried. "Mother is right, Ardi. You have a fever."

"It's just the excitement of being home, nothing more," he laughed. He put one arm around his sister, one arm around Gideon, and together they walked through the fragrant gardens and up a series of sweeping shallow steps and broad patios to the big front door. "We must stop here," he said. "I have a duty to perform." As the words came out of his mouth the door opened, and in the doorway stood Abeyan.

Ardenai was visibly startled, then relieved, and he smiled at his old friend. "I'm glad you're here," he said. "Io will be so happy."

When Io drew abreast with Jilfan and Krush, Ardenai bowed formally to her, and held out his hand. "Wife," he said, "this is the home I offer thee, and these the family. Will you have me?"

"I will have thee," she responded, beaming at her father, and Ardenai took her in his arms and kissed her thoroughly.

As was tradition he led her to each room, then into their bedroom, accompanied by the family, who paused in the doorway. "We are home," he said, seating her gently on the huge, hand carved mahogany bed. "Mother, will you and Abeyan attend us, please?"

"We will attend thee," they responded, and stepped into the room with the couple, closing the door behind them.

Ardenai took a deep breath to steady himself, then swallowed his embarrassment, stood before his wife and undressed, one piece of clothing at a time, starting with his tunic and ending with his briefcloth. Then he extended his phallus from its sheath, so she could ascertain his length and girth. She nodded. She unfastened the frogs which held the top of her robe and exposed her breasts to him, then dropped her undergarments, but not the robe itself, and nodded again. "I am thine," she said. He took her hands, kissed them as he had at their marriage ceremony, and led her to the priapic bench where he had led Ah'ree on their wedding night. "What is mine, I give thee," she said. She raised the back of her robe, knelt, and presented for him.

"What is mine, you may have," he replied. He focused on her, the shape of her, the ripeness, and grew hard, his semen beginning to drip, providing added moisture with which to penetrate. He laid himself along her back, took his phallus in one hand, using his fingers as a depth gauge, and mounted her slowly and carefully, knowing this would be good practice for that time when she was heavy with child, or when he was mounting a woman who had never been with a man. When he was fully inserted he pushed gently, and she braced her elbows and pushed up toward him, moaning with pleasure, her motions demanding more. He straightened up then, and caught her thighs, and pulled her back, and up, so the entry was more direct, and she cried out with pleasure at the position, and he groaned, and lifted a little more, bringing his legs closer together and driving his phallus into her, feeling keenly the strong waves as she peaked, and with equal keenness, Abeyan's eyes from a few feet away. She was enjoying having him watch, Ardenai could sense it. He held himself until she was well satisfied, then lowered her and let himself release. As he began to ejaculate he withdrew, pushed her robe up further, and finished by ejecting his semen onto the small of her back and her buttocks, indicating to Abeyan that he was able to control himself, even in the heat of passion.

When he'd stopped shuddering, and dropped his head to breath a space, Ah'rane came over with a damp towel, fragrant with pineapple sage, and wiped the mottled blue, viscid material away. She spoke so quietly to Io that neither man heard, then said, "I am satisfied with this coupling," and left the room.

From his seat at the main hearth of the huge hub which formed the living areas of the house, Gideon saw her depart with the towel in her hand, and cocked an eyebrow in the direction of Teal and Krush. "What's that all about, or do I want to know?"

"The father of the bride, and the mother of the groom, watch the couple have sexual intercourse..." Krush began, and Gideon writhed in his chair.

"Eww, El'Shadai, that's just barbaric!" he squeaked, clapping his hands to his cheeks.

"Only if you consider sexual intercourse something to be ashamed of, or to be hidden away," Krush said, and was quiet as Teal's thoughts momentarily touched his own. "It's a cultural thing," he went on, "Probably comes from watching horses all the time," he grinned at Gideon. "As a rule, we do keep our love lives private."

"I know it sounds intrusive, but it's a very old tradition," Teal chuckled. "It allows the father to make sure his daughter is not being hurt, and it allows the mother, who is assumed to be an experienced lover, to give her son advice about how to be gentler, or more effective. It really makes sense if you think about it."

"But they were both with trainers growing up, and they've been married for over a season now, certainly long enough to have figured out what's right and what's wrong with their technique."

"It wouldn't matter if they'd been married for years," Krush said. "When they have intercourse in their home for the first time, they are supervised. I'm pretty sure more than a few couples forgo this, but because Ardenai is Firstlord, he knows sooner or later it will be questioned. He wants everything in place to please Ah'krill and her ilk."

"Did you go through this?" Gideon asked, flipping a hand toward the bedroom and looking into Krush's open, good humored face.

"Absolutely," he said. "And Teal had me standing in front of him, as well, and that was on their wedding night. Their very first time. I was comforted to know that he would never hurt my daughter, that his training was sufficient."

"So where's Abeyan?"

"He probably wants to see Ardi sweat," Krush chuckled. "He's not very happy about the age difference, or so he says. I think he's grasping enough that the thought of anyone taking anything he considers his, is abhorrent to him." He looked over his shoulder to see where Jilfan was, and turned back when he heard laughter from the kitchen area of the hub. "Forgive me. It is not my place to assume the thoughts of another. This may go on for a while, and they'll want to rest a bit and freshen up. Why don't you and your uncle and I go walk about a bit and familiarize you with things?"

"I'd like that," the boy smiled, rising from the chair, and he realized he was nearly as tall as his grandsire. It made him proud, as though they were really related, and then it made him feel foolish. "If you could just show me the lavage first, I'd appreciate it," he murmured.

"Let me show you your room," Teal said. "Ah'din's been fussing over it. Sire, if you would please tell my wife where we're going?"

Krush nodded and got to his feet, taking his heavy pottery mug with him in the direction of the kitchen, and Teal gestured Gideon through one of the archways which flanked the fireplace. "This house is so wide in the front. It has that wide front porch," Gideon said, "does it still have eight spokes like the one at South Hold?"

Teal looked at him, eyes lighting with pleasure. "You are just going to love being a part of this house!" he said enthusiastically. "This house is huge – built to shelter an extended family – ancient in design, dating to the Equi Awakening. The original Equi sunburst.   Instead of having eight spokes with knobs on the end, this house has seven big fins and a central hub like a windmill. Picture one in your mind, then set it flat on the ground, remove the fin in front of you, and push the others back to form a slightly obtuse angle. Can you see that in your mind?"

"Maybe I could if I knew what an obtuse angle was," Gideon muttered, slightly embarrassed.

"Look," Teal said. He put his hands together so his thumbs were on top and just the tips of his fingers touched. "If I close this, by bringing my palms closer together, I'm creating an acute angle, less than ninety degrees. If I push it the other way from ninety degrees, but not back to a straight line, I'm creating an obtuse angle."

"Got it," Gideon said.

"Can you see the shape now?" Teal asked, forming it with his hands.

"I think so, yes," he grinned. "Thanks."

"You're welcome. If you're still shaky on it, we'll grab a flyer and go up for a bird's perspective. Come. Ah'din and I debated a bit about which room should be yours. We weren't sure which view you'd like best, but we decided on the one facing north. It makes the room a bit cool, but there's a fireplace, and the floors and walls throughout the house are thermal, so if you just turn that blue valve in the lavage, you can heat your room to your liking. The trees and the river are beautiful from here, plus you can see the horses if you lean a bit."

Gideon wanted to laugh, and jump up and down and clap his hands like a child, not so much because he had a room to call his own, but because this busy man and his equally busy wife had cared enough about him – Gideon – to fuss over choosing a room for him. Little did they know, he'd have been content to curl by the fire the rest of his life. Or maybe they did know. Gideon smiled at Teal and blushed with the thought.

Teal opened the door and ushered Gideon into a room which had a pleasing series of gently angling walls. "Part of a fin," Gideon said, mostly to himself, and Teal nodded and smiled. The V shaped back wall was devoted to casements, with seats and bookcases full of books under the shorter ones in the center. Flanking them were two more casements which were the width of a door and stretched from floor to ceiling. A door-height piece of glass in each of these opened out into the gardens and the woods and river beyond. All the casements were the same shape, rising with straight sides, then tapering in almost to a point, like the roof of a tall, slender house.

Huge Equi pines stood outside, and Gideon could hear the wind gently soughing through them on its way in from the sea. There was a big, wonderfully eccentric bed molded into one corner and extending like a fan into the room. It had a bowed footboard made of heavy wood which gleamed a deep, burnished red, and it was clothed with soft, cream colored sheets, a creamy wool comforter, and a scattering of fluffy pillows in various sizes and colors. Near the small fireplace, there was an arm chair with blue wool upholstery and a green woolen lap robe tossed over one arm. There was a long, rather shallow desk with a reading lamp, a closet with hanging space and shelves, and behind the fireplace, a small lavage with a basin, a water closet, and a one person waterfall. "It's perfect," Gideon said. "This is all mine? I'd be happy to share it. It's so big."

"It's all yours, though you share this fin of the house with your brother, and your cousin, Criollo, who is my son. You'll meet him here someday soon," Teal said. "And there's a snug little room for Jilfan, if he wants it. He gestured out through the open casement. "Let's walk around the house and meet your grandsire. I think he'll expect us to do that. I'll wait outside for you."

Gideon relieved himself at leisure, partly because it felt good, and partly because he wanted time to absorb what was happening. He was home. Not in a walk-up, two room, cold water flat with a single, fly-specked window, where he slept on the floor behind the couch, and listened to his mother having sex and fighting with a different man every night, but in a house of white stone, with beautiful gardens, and trees and horses. A house where there was enough room for him, and enough food, and more than enough affection. He had a father who loved him, and grandparents who were amazing people, and Teal was now his kinsman. He had a room all his own, and an education to be had for the asking. He'd even met a girl who seemed to like him. Not that being a girl mattered, he told himself. She was his age, and she liked him. And...she was a girl.

He thought about what Ardenai and Io were doing in their chambers at this moment, and looked down at himself, giving his organ a little shake, and wondering what it would be like to have it grow rigid enough to insert into someone else – knowing he should desire that – wanting to desire that, for all the good it would do him. There was a distant memory of pain, and a child's screams for help which were never answered, and with a cold gasp he fastened his pants, dashed water on his hands and face, and nearly ran from the lavage to Teal's side.

"You needn't have hurried," Teal smiled, but he read fear in the boy's eyes, and put an arm around him as they walked. "Out here somewhere," he said as they passed through one of the autumn gardens, "Yes, there." He pointed up into a tree with the spreading branch habit of a Calumet syca-more, but the bark and leaves of a blanched aspen, "If you look closely, you will see your friendly serpent physician, robes and dignity cast aside. Taking the long rest he has so richly earned."

Gideon could see him – barely – green among the green leaves, twined about a limb which slanted slightly upward. His arms dangled limply, stubby legs hanging to either side of the branch, head twisted at an odd angle. He looked perfectly comfortable. Actually, he looked dead as a door hinge, but Gideon didn't say so for fear Pythos wasn't as asleep as he seemed.

Krush hailed them and they stepped up their pace, walking toward the river bridge and a set of long, low stables with gleaming white slabschist sides and thick roofs which were alive and growing. Were all the roofs like that? Gideon turned around and looked back up the slope to the main house. It blended so perfectly into its surroundings he almost couldn't see it, and they were only a hundred yards away. When he focused on it, that roof was alive, also. With a thrill which ran up his spine he realized this house was a living thing, carved from the native alabaster eons ago, and rooted to this spot for eternity. "Amazing," he said, and the two men with him laughed and nodded.

Across the river and another two hundred yards had them walking the packed earth of the horse complex. It reminded Gideon again of South Hold, of the parade grounds, and momentarily, of death.

"Now I know your father will want you to have a horse," Krush said, leading the way into one of the stables. "So I thought you might like to take a look at a few in advance." He gestured toward a stall with a large paddock behind, "We have Ethelred the Bold. What do you think?" Gideon looked over the stall door and laughed. Ethelred was asleep, and no taller than Gideon's waist. He was ancient and moth-eaten, his lips and ears slack with contentment. "He was Io's when she was a babe. Like Io, he can be a little wild at times. Might be a little too much horse for you just yet."

They walked further on, and Krush gestured again. "This is Pavil, one of Ardi's polo ponies. He's not quite finished, but he'll make a nice mount."

Pavil was big and black, and while he was beautiful, he was not inviting. "Really, I don't need a horse," Gideon said, though every bone in his body belied his words.

"We'll find you one, don't you fret," his grandsire said. "Let's just keep looking."

He met Teal's favorite horse, Duffy, a black and white spotted gelding with pale blue eyes and a sweet face, and Ah'din's palomino gelding, Aurelian. Ah'rane's roan mare, Spreckles, Criollo's tall paint, Bimini, and Krush's silver stallion, Beckett, who was absolutely beautiful. Even Io's little copper mare, Eubie, which Krush had brought from the stables of the Great House as a welcome home surprise.

"Then we have this one," Krush said, crimping a grin. "She just got here last night. See what you think, and if you like her, she's yours."

Gideon looked into the long, sunny paddock beyond the stall, and shouted with joy. "Tolbeth? It's Tolbeth!" he exclaimed. "It's Tolbeth!" He hugged Krush, hugged Teal, vaulted the stall door, and ran to his mare, calling her name as she jogged toward him, nickering in reply.

"Brushes are in the maroon boxes," Krush called after him.

"Your saddle's in the tack room at the end of this run," Teal added. "She could use some exercise."

The boy waved absently, but whether he'd comprehended or not was anybody's guess. "I do like that boy," Krush said. "Make a keeplord out of that one."

"As your son said you would," Teal chuckled. He sobered and added, "Shall we go back to the house and see if Abeyan's taken his hand off the throttle yet?"

He had. Finally. Ardenai sprawled bonelessly beside Io on the big bed, stale and sweating, but loathe to get up and go to the effort of bathing. "You must be half-cooked in that robe," he said to the ceiling.

"No. I'm cooked. Period."

"We could have taken it off."

"And have him see that scar on my belly? He'd be wearing your phallus as a belt by now, with your teeth for clasps. Besides, it was pleasant. It made me feel virginal."

"I'm glad. The rest of this ceased to be pleasant early on, wouldn't you say?"

"No, I enjoyed it, and it didn't go on nearly as long as I would have liked it to," Io said, and Ardenai could hear the smile in her voice. "I think my sire enjoyed it, as well, and I was happy to give him that pleasure. I think he was being you, remembering my mother. She was a little thing, too. But you would know that better than I."

"Yes," Ardenai said. "And you may well be right." He shifted, and caught his breath.

"Are you all right?"

"I ache all over," he admitted, and added a chuckle. "I considered myself quite the athlete, now I don't know. I wasn't worth much this morning."

"You seemed a little flushed earlier," Io said. "After spending two weeks in a pressurized atmosphere, conferencing with everybody and their kin, and then having to deal with the stress and the humidity, I'm not surprised you're a little out of form."

There was a gentle tap on the door, and when Io said, "Come in," a serving cart of hot tea and chilled fruit appeared, and then Ah'rane's smiling face. "Oh, you angel," Io breathed, and got up to help her while Ardenai pulled a sleeveless muslin robe over his head and got up on the other side of the bed.

He stood a few seconds, realizing he was a little woozy, and then managed a smile for his mother as he came to give her a kiss. "Thanks for the help," he said. "I wish you'd stayed."

"If I'd stayed, there would have been a fight," she said ominously. "Please, have a snack and then sleep until lunch time. I'll call you with time enough to bathe."

"Absolutely not," Ardenai said, kissing her hair in passing. "I came home to see my family and to enjoy our keep and our gardens. I can't do that from my bed, no matter how inviting it may seem. Besides, this is our Keep Day. It's a day to celebrate, not slumber. I'm just going to take a quick bath, and I'll join you ladies on the patio in a few minutes, if that's suitable."

"Marginally," his mother said dryly, "but we'll let it pass." The tea tray rolled on out into the garden, and Ardenai headed for the bathing pool. Io said that when he was done and could keep his mother company, she'd indulge, as well. Not that she needed it, mind you.

He only needed to freshen up a little, he told himself, dropping his robe and wading in. The water did feel good. He'd been too warm, but now he felt a little too cool, and the heat from the thermals was comforting as he settled into it. Part of him felt...fussy, and he searched his mind, trying to ascertain where his little Ah'leah might be. He dropped to clean himself, and when he looked, his groin and the tops of his thighs were covered with tiny red bumps, tender to the touch. "Friction burns," he chuckled. "That's a first. Or is it a heat rash? In either case a little mazea starch will fix it."

He could have slept and enjoyed it, but he forced himself to get dressed and join the females. That was where Krush and Teal found them. They were joined by Ah'din and Jilfan, and, after her bath, Io, as well, accompanied by Abeyan. The conversation was animated and filled with laughter, and after a while the noise began to wear on Ardenai. He excused himself for a bit and wandered apart through the gardens, then down along the river, and finally out to the stables. Why was he so dratted sleepy? He rubbed fitfully at his stiffening neck and shook his head to clear it.

Kadeth seemed more than ready for some exercise, so he saddled up and rode out with half a mind to find Gideon and Tolbeth. He passed down the side of the thundering waterfall, marveling at it, as always, and settling into the joy of being home. Home on Equus. Home at Canyon keep. Home with his parents, his wife, and his sons. His son, singular, he corrected himself. Jilfan did not want to be Ardenai's son, and did not want to be thought of as such. Ardenai reminded himself to respect that.

He got as far as the sun-warmed ledges and tall green grass along the river, turned Kadeth out to graze, and succumbed to the urge to close his eyes, just for a few minutes. If Gideon had gone this way, he had to come back this way, Ardenai reasoned. This was the wagon track coming up out of the canyon on this side of the river. He'd stop to observe the waterfall, because that's the kind of person Gideon was. He'd see Kadeth, and be over. Simple. Ardenai stretched out with a sigh and was instantly asleep.

He awoke to the sound of Io's persistent voice. "Ardenai, can you hear me?"

"Of course I can hear you," he said irritably, "you're right in my ear."

"You're going to get a bee sting if you're not careful. There's a nest under this ledge."

"There's always been a bee's nest under this ledge. We haven't been stung yet, have we?" There was something about the sound of Io's voice that was disconcerting. What was it? He felt her come and sit astride him, bouncing up and down on him as if he were a cushion. "Ouch, that hurts," he said groggily. "How many times do I have to tell you that? You can ruin a person's insides that way."

"Well, it can't be helped, because you have to get up, and I'm getting you up," she said. Ardenai pried his eyes open to discover it was late afternoon, and that Io was sitting astraddle of him, her hair going in twenty-seven different directions, eyes wide with excitement, the gaps in her teeth making her sound a bit like Pythos.

Something clicked into place, and Ardenai sat bolt upright, grasping the child's arms to keep her from toppling off the boulder and into the river. "Io, is that you?" he squinted, frowning. His head hurt like kraa, and he couldn't remember for the life of him how he'd gotten here.

"No, it's the blood fruit girl of ancient Thura," she quavered, making fangs and claws. "Of course it's me, silly. Ah'ree says you need to wake up so we can go home. There's school tomorrow."

Ardenai felt his mouth go slack. "Ah'ree," he breathed. "Where?"

"Right here," a warm voice chuckled, and Ardenai turned his head and looked into the laughing brown eyes of his beloved wife. "I thought I'd add my persuasive talents to the cause."

"Ree," he said softly, and his eyes filled with tears of joy and relief. He reached and caught her hand, pulling her to him, and she was as solid as the rock upon which they sat. She was real. "Oh, Precious Equus, I have had the wildest dream of my entire life. Was I asleep long?"

"An hour or so," she said, kissing his cheek. "You must have really been tired, and you're half-baked from the sun. What did you dream about?"

"Well," he shook his head and laughed, "I dreamed I became The Thirteenth Dragonhorse."

"Really?" she exclaimed, letting her eyes grow wide. "However did you fit it into your schedule?"

"It became my schedule."

"What else?"

"I fled through the stars, pursued by the Telenir."

"You're teaching that in class again, aren't you? It always gives you nightmares," Ah'ree said, tossing a pebble into the river. "So, did you escape?"

"I did. Yes. I was aided by a blond haired young Declivian, and Io was the Captain of the Horse Guard." he paused and shook his head. "It's all too bizarre."

"And what about me?" she grinned, cocking her head to smile into his eyes, "was I in your dream?"

He swallowed hard and looked away from her into the river. "You were dead, Ree, and nothing mattered. I just went through the motions, nothing more."

She patted his hand and then took it into her lap, rubbing his arm as she studied his face. "And did you marry Io?"

Ardenai jumped like she'd stuck him. "How did you know that?" he demanded.

"Well, you promised you would, remember? Yesterday? We were out in the gardens."

"Ah...yes. You know, I'll bet that's what set this whole thing off, that silly promise to Io. Because in my dream, she brought it up to me." He sighed, and stretched, and caught his wife in his arms. "I'm so glad that's over and I'm just a teacher again. Are we ready to go home, my love?"

"I think so," she grinned, and he got to his feet and pulled her up beside him.

"Where's the child? Why in the ten tribute worlds of Equus would I ever be insane enough to marry that marauding little beast? And I suppose we'll have to shake the bushes for Pythos? Where did he get to?"

CHAPTER TWENTY-FIVE

"I'm right here, Gideon," the old physician hissed, hurrying up beside him. "Wass he unconssciouss when thee found him?"

"Not exactly, but he wasn't conscious, either. He was really disoriented, and he had no idea who I was. I think he was delirious. I really do. I didn't want to leave him, so I tried to send Tolbeth back to get help, but she doesn't know where home is yet, and neither does Kadeth. We have to go! Now!"

"Thiss issn't Calumet, Gideon. Teal and Krush have already gone. Ssee, the flyer iss not there."

"Why didn't you go with them?" the boy demanded, tears standing in his eyes.

"They were gone by the time Io woke me. Thee ssounded a general alarm when thee rode up here. Thee can't exsspect people not to be alarmed, now can thee?"

"I'm sorry," Gideon managed. "I just thought this whole damned thing was over. I was so happy that things were going to be all right."

"Thingss will sstill be all right," Pythos hissed, flicking his tongue against Gideon's cheek. "I could usse thy help, though. Go put Tolbeth in her sstall, and then help me carry some thingss, pleasse." Gideon nodded, ran to his horse, and was cantering down the hill as the Equi flyer soared into sight. It slowed and dropped into Gideon's path, and instead of going to the stables, he headed back toward the mouth of the canyon, presumably to get Kadeth. "Good," Pythos said. "Ssomething for him to do."

The flyer landed on the patio behind Ardenai's wing of the house, and Pythos hurried that direction. By the time he arrived, Ardenai was stretched on the bed, and Krush was easing his boots off while Io tucked a blanket around him.

"Let me ssee him," Pythos said quietly, and the others stepped aside and let him make a quick, cursory examination. "He will be better off in the ssmall thermal room besside the pools, I think. All of my thingss are there, and I can do a more thorough analysis." He picked the Firstlord up with surprising ease and toddled at a good pace through the house with him, Io running ahead to make sure the bed had linens, as it was seldom used except when someone was ill, or in labor, or in need of extra warmth for some reason. It was one of the serpent's favorite winter places to sleep, and he placed Ardenai on the bed and looked around, making sure everything was as it should be.

This room had no windows, and was of rough, native stone, the rest of the house having been constructed around and above these boulders and the thermal pools which bubbled out of them on the other side of the wall. There was a high rock ledge from which fragrant herbs grew, bending down into the room, and above it a roof casement which provided light and additional warmth. There was a bed, a table, a comfortable chair, and in the corner a birthing stool, a stored baby box, and a priapic bench. As always, the room was immaculate, and very warm. Pythos dropped his robes onto the floor, and began very carefully removing the Firstlord's clothing.

The removing of Ardenai's shirt revealed sides and armpits covered with tiny red blisters, and the serpent began to hiss under his breath. He unfastened Ardenai's trousers and looked at the blistered flesh which spread from his belly, under his briefcloth to the tops of his thighs. Pythos waggled his head and gave Teal a hooded look. "Io," he said, "I need thee to go to thy chamberss, and bring me everything Ardenai hass worn ssince your arrival here, clean or not. And anything he might have brought with him. Take thy time, and leave nothing out." He waited until she was gone, then turned back to his examination. "Thiss iss Ah'krill'ss doing," he muttered, and the others standing around the bed added puzzlement to their worry. "Sshe'ss given Ah'leah cradle bumpss."

"Isn't that a baby disease, and a fairly innocuous one?" Krush asked, face lined with worry as he contemplated his son.

"Issn't Ah'leah a baby?" the old dragon responded. "I have to hand it to her. Thiss iss brilliant."

"Why would she do that?" Teal frowned. "What difference would it make? And why did you send Io off on some..." The serpent cut him off.

"It would make a differencce if Ah'leah had to be removed to ssave the Firstlord. Cradle bumps don't usually bother children too much, but they can be fatal in adultss."

"She wants the baby?" Teal whispered, and his eyes changed shape as he considered the ramifications. "She wants their baby, their little priestess, and she's willing to kill her son to get her embryonic granddaughter? I don't believe that of her."

Krush groaned, and the serpent said, "Not time for that, yet. He may fight thiss off on his own. Go, and let me ssee what I can do to make him more comfortable. Krush, thee and Teal, keep Gideon and your wives calm. And sstay closse. I may need thee in a russsh."

Io returned with a small pile of clothing, and Pythos gestured her into the chair, where she curled and contemplated him, her face a mask of misery. He stood a minute or two, looking up through the roof casement, then lay down beside the Firstlord, taking him in his arms as he coiled around him and set his forehead against Ardenai's.

In a warm, moist place, lighted only by the steady thrumming of a great heart, two beings spoke of the wondrous order of things. *Beloved, is thee there?* Asked the first.

Yes, came the boy's voice. *I am here, my mother.*

And how art thou this fine morning?

I am well. What are we going to study today? Are we going to do more with universal computations? I have enjoyed those lessons very much.

Not today.

Ancient languages, then?

No.

Celestial Navigation?

Not that, either, Beloved. Today we are going to talk about life, and death.

Why?

Because tonight I will place thee in the womb of she who will one day be called thy mother. She is Ah'krill, High Priestess of Equus.

But you are my mother. You are my father.

Today. Tomorrow, others will assume my titles.

And why are you doing this?

Because it is time for thee to be born, and to take thy human form.

I am happy here with you. I do not wish to leave you.

We will never be separated, thee and I. When thee is born, I will be the first thing thee sees, I promise, and I will be with thee thy entire life.

And then what?

I will be the last thing thee sees before thy body dies, and together we will continue our journey, as we are doing now - only we will be pure energy and bright light and all-encompassing compassion.

Why can't we do that now?

Because it is thy fate to be Firstlord of Equus. It is what the Wisdom Giver has willed for thee. This thee must do in the shape of a man. The world is a beautiful place. Thee will like it here, and while thou art here, thee will be able to remember nothing else.

Oh. There was a long pause. *Why is that?*

Because it is best. It helps one focus on one's tasks.

My mother, if becoming a man causes me to forget you, I will think I am alone. That frightens me.

On the deepest level, where things matter most, thee will never forget me, and I will always be there for thee, to keep thee safe, and informed, and on thy intellectual toes.

Toes. Will I have feet, then?

Yes. And a better sense of what is literal and what is figurative. It is nearly time, Beloved. Is thee ready for the next part of our adventure?

I am ready to do what you say I must, came the sad reply.

A sense of movement, and then of floating again, and terrible loss – of consciousness and self. A new heartbeat – different in rhythm and strength. A different pump. And singing, a different voice, and of growing, and seeing toes...and fingers. Arms and legs, of beginning to sense things, a second, beating heart.

And suffocating pain and being pushed, hard, thrust out in a rush of water...squeezed amid screams. And light...such light...and the last scream … and the first, searing breath of air, and...Pythos.

Thee does remember, then?

As you said I would, my father. My oldest and dearest friend.

Is thee able to think in the present at all?

I do not know when that is.

Can thee sense what is happening?

No. Not really. I think I might be sick.

How old are you, Beloved?

I do not know. Very old, I think. Many hundreds of years.

How old is the body of the man?

That, I do not know. It fails. There is fire in the head, and in the chest. *It burns away around me.*

Art thou alone?

There was a long pause. *No. There is a child here with me. She is* sick, too.

What can thee tell me about her?

Her name is...Ah'leah. She says she was supposed to be the next High Priestess of Equus. But something went wrong. She should have died then, but did not. She does not want to be here with me. With us. She is angry. No. Not angry, but...disappointed. She is sick. She wants to live, or to die, but not to be here. Why does that make me so sad?

Because thee has tried very hard to save her. She would have been born as thy daughter.

But you said Ah'ree could have only one child. I think even Kehai-

lan was too much for her.

Ardenai sat bolt upright, smelling the smoke, feeling the heat of the fire. "Ree!" he cried, "Ree, wake up! The house is on fire!"

Together they stumbled out of bed and raced for the door. Ardenai put the back of his hand against it and jerked back. It was red hot. He ran for the window, hearing Ree screaming for her baby. He hit the casement with his shoulder, his full body weight slamming behind it. The glass crumbled and he grabbed Ah'ree and dove through into the brief coolness of the night. "Stay here!" he commanded, and ran along the outside of the wall to the casement he knew was Kehailan's room. He touched it, and it was cool. He grabbed a large stone from the rockery near the fountain and slammed it into the glass – and again – and it yielded passage to him. The noise had made the baby cry, and made him easier to find as the room filled with smoke. Out of the crib, a blanket over his face, and back out the window with the flames behind them and into Ah'ree's arms.

"I must go back!" Ardenai cried. "We've left one!"

"No," Ah'ree said. "No, Ardenai. We only have the one."

Do not go back. Stay where it is cool and thou art safe. Doest thou hear me. Do not go back!

"There is another. Another son! Can't you hear him? Can't you hear him screaming? We've left one of our children!" And he turned, and ran back into the flames.

"I've losst hiss thoughtss. Io, get Teal, now," Pythos demanded, and she ran to the main hearth where the rest of the family sat waiting.

"Pythos wants you," she said, pointing to her kinsman, and he rose and hurried away. "He's delirious," she said simply, and followed Teal back to the thermal room.

When she got there, Pythos was starting a fluid pump. "He'ss burning up," he hissed, wrapping Ardenai's forearm tightly with the first wide band of enterodermal jacerei. Pythos inflated the device, activating the jets of cool water, and Ardenai jumped, and moaned softly with pain, but did not awaken. "Bring me ssome cool, wet towelss, four of them."

"Where's Teal? Didn't he come in here as I asked him to?"

"I find I cannot touch the high priestess with my thoughts, so I have sent Teal to fetch her. I fear only sshe can fixss thiss, cursse her."

"That fast? He was right ahead of me. And..." she looked puzzled, and more than a little alarmed. "What can Ah'krill do? Why are you cursing her? Is there something I should know?"

Pythos ignored all but the first question. "How long doess it take to ssay, 'Get Ah'krill here, one way or another'?" He snapped. "He came in one door and went out the other without ever sslowing down. A most efficc-cient man." Io took the hint and retreated to do his bidding, moving through the rough opening between the thermal room and the bathing pools to fetch cold water and a stack of towels for him. Pythos wrapped Ardenai's other forearm with a second wide band, and Io, returning with a pitcher and basin, winced as the skin of her husband's hand turned white, then purple under the high pressure, before regaining its normal color. Pythos repeated the process with even bigger bands around each of Ardenai's thighs, and turned the pump on full. He pulled back the sheet and took the head of Ardenai's phallus in his hand, extending it enough to insert a catheter tube.

"I'll give you exactly one hour to stop that, you evil woman."

"You make me evil," Ah'ree smiled, biting playfully at his chin as she stroked his phallus. "Please, Ardi, let's have another baby. Think of how much fun it would be. Luna is pregnant. They could grow up together. Maybe they'd even get married, if we have a boy." She slid astraddle of him on the big bed, and he could feel her heat beginning to build, feel the wetness of her opening as she sat up and guided him into her, pushing her-self down onto his phallus and swaying seductively back and forth. "I don't care whether it's a boy or a girl. You could just let yourself go." She leaned forward – a tall woman – and allowed her full breasts to brush, first one and then the other, against his lips. "Please," she groaned, "Please." She said it faster, and faster, and then she was crying out, and he was grinding his teeth because she'd ambushed him without a skin, and he had to think – so hard, work so hard – because he, too, was in heat, and generative and he didn't trust her to protect herself, so great was her desire for another child.

She sensed it, and her eyes grew hurt, and then hard, and she glared down at him. "I will not risk thee," he said softly, reaching up to take her upper arms. "I will not risk thee. You are my life, Ah'ree. Please try to understand." The anger in her eyes cooled, and it felt so good...to be cool. He laughed with her and she batted water at him and swam a short distance away, calling for Io.

"She gets so far away sometimes," Ah'ree said. "I can barely see her."

"That means she can barely see us, then, doesn't it?" Ardenai whispered, gliding over to join her and standing waist deep on the sandy bottom. He pulled Ah'ree close to him to kiss her, sliding the fingers of one hand under her sarong to fondle her anterior clitoridis as he pushed the top down far enough to expose her breasts. "Your nipples are hard, and you're already wet," he teased, nuzzling her. "I think we need to be planning a little getaway very soon." She made to push him away, then relented and walked up the bank, casting him a long, voluptuous look as she dropped with a splash to her hands and knees in the shallows and presented up to him.

There was a splash of water on the floor of the thermal room and another scream from Ah'ree. Ardenai held her naked body close against his, their sweat mingling as Ah'ree fought to bring this new life into the world. "The head iss pressenting," Pythos hissed, and she spread her legs a little further apart and crouched a little more, elbows and forearms resting on the smooth mahogany of the birthing stool, hands gripping the uprights as generations of Ardenai's family before her had done. Ardenai tightened his grip under her breasts and felt the strong contractions which seemed to flow like tidal waves through her entire body. She was making deep, guttural sounds – grunts and screams and shrieks, and her head pounded against his chest, back and back and back in terrible pain that had gone on for hours. "Once more," Pythos said, and she threw her head back and screamed as though she had an arrow in her belly – and Pythos was holding a tiny baby up for them to see.

"She survived it," Ardenai said to no one in particular. "She took an arrow in the belly and still brought forth a child – and wants another of my get." It seemed an uncaring, chauvinistic thing to say, and it made him feel masculine. He needed to feel masculine. It was expected of him, though he couldn't remember why.

He sat upright in bed and moved the sheet to contemplate an erection which would put another babe in her womb, in the womb of all Equus. The people standing around him – a room full – a throng, applauded and nodded their approval of this phallic monolith. It was pulsing and wet and urgent, and he made no attempt to touch it, or stop it, but pulled his knees up and spread his legs apart and watched it, feeling the deep pleasure of urinating, or ejaculating, not caring that he had no control over it. It felt so good. He groaned with pleasure at its release – watching it spray across the bedclothes and up the walls onto the ceiling.

Pythos wet another towel, twisted the excess water out of it and put it back across the Firstlord's pelvis, then checked the catheter and nodded. "Liquid iss moving through him at a good rate. Hiss temperature iss down a little for the time being, and he'ss sstopped thrashing. Thiss might be a good time for Krush and Ah'rane to sspend ssome time with him, yess?" He lifted the towel off Ardenai's other thigh, and dipped it in cool water. "Well, is thee going, Child?"

Io nodded and went numbly forth to get them, wondering if this was a dream of some kind, terrified by his pain and his delirium – terrified that each lunge, each gasp would be his last, that he was going to have a stroke from the terrible heat – annoyed that Pythos thought his parents needed this quiet time with him more than she did.

But they were so grateful, thanked her so profusely as they hurried to Ardenai's side, that she felt small and predatory. Her people were butterflies, not spiders; lovers of the light, not the darkness. Lovers of sociality, not solitude. She smiled, and put her arm around Gideon as Krush had put an arm around Ah'din. "I'm sure you were included in this," she said, walking him back down the ramp which led to the most ancient, subterranean wing of the house.

Gideon did no more than touch Ardenai to ascertain that he was breathing, and then went to lean against the warm stone of the wall, unable to stand the pain he could hear rattling in the Firstlord's throat, unable to look at the spots where the fluid pump was driving tiny, painful jets of water through his skin into his twitching body. Ardenai's arm jerked a little, the pump sputtered, and Ardenai grunted with the pain and lay gasping.

"Get up!" Thatcher snarled, aiming another booted kick at the small of the Equi's back. "I said GET UP, you sonofabitch!"

Ardenai lay panting, eyes glazed with pain and suffocation. He got his elbows to lock, his knees under him, and held that position, gasping, bright spots swimming in front of his eyes, blood pounding in the front of his face. "I cannot survive without water," he said through his teeth. "I will die...of thirst... and your money will be wasted."

"You're lucky I don't have to piss, or I'd give you water, you ugly bastard. Now get up! Before I lay you wide open."

Ardenai staggered the rest of the way to his feet, catching himself on the handle of the ore cart. He pushed it forward, but as it moved, his legs did not, and he measured his length on the tracks. "Damn you!" Thatcher cried in frustration, "Feel the bite of this for inspiration!" and he brought the whip down with all his might across the Firstlord's back. His tunic split and his flesh with it – a deep, bloody furrow from the side of his neck to the middle of his back.

Thatcher unchained him from the cart and dragged him off the tracks, kicking and cuffing, and left him there to bleed. Ardenai moved his head slightly, and set his lips against his shoulder where the blood was running down from his neck, grateful for the lash and the moisture it brought.

"There," Pythos said softly, "that will keep him from jerking away from the pump. He hass no ssensse of paralyssiss," he added, noting Ah'rane's look. "He jusst doessn't remember that he hass musscless in thosse placcess. It'ss not frightening for him, I promisse thee. I have ssimply removed the musscle memory for the time being – as though he were an infant."

She took his hand and held it without moving his arm, and stroked the sweat-soaked black tendrils off his cheeks and forehead, and stared into his face, willing him back to life. Willing him to know that she was there, and that he was home where he belonged.

"And here he iss," Pythos had said, placing the baby in her arms.

"He's really ours?" Krush had asked in wonder, pushing the blanket back to contemplate the infant. "He's going to be our son?"

"Yess," Pythos had said quietly. "He is never to be told he iss not thine own. He iss from a blind mating. A princcce of the Great House, as thou art a princcce, Krush, and ass thou art a princccess, Ah'rane. He iss of the mosst anccient and high blood. This is the one you have prepared for these long months. If you are still willing, I will give thee ssomething to sstart thy milk flowing for him, and no one will know he iss not thine own flesh."

They had looked at each other, and the baby had looked at both of them, and the three of them had looked at Pythos. "Oh, yes. We are more than willing," Krush had smiled, hugging his family close, and Ah'rane had nodded.

Within hours she had been able to hold him, warm and sleepy in her arms and give him suck, and he had stared up at her with huge, green-gold eyes, and almost, he seemed to smile and recognize her. "This is a very pleasant sensation, to have milk pulled from my breasts," she had said to Krush. "It is sexually stimulating, and wonderfully satisfying all at the same time. Not that I do not enjoy your attentions, as well."

"I would not presume to compete with such a master," Krush had chuckled. "Have you noticed, he looks just like you?" He had kissed her cheek, then slowly, awe in his handsome young face, he had kissed her full breast, and the cheek of his son, feeling the pull of his muscles as he nursed. "He looks just like you. I would like to name him for your grandsire, if you will permit it."

"Yes," Ah'rane had smiled, "I'd like that. And you, little one? How do you like the name, Ardenai? Thou shalt be Ah'rane Ardenai Krush."

"You will never convince me those two are not related," Gideon said, still leaning against the wall, and he turned his head to contemplate the serpent's profile. "If she's not his mother, she's his sister, or some very close kin. I'd stake my life on it."

The serpent's head turned very slowly until yellow eyes met gold. "Thou art a precociouss brat. Sso tell me, if Ah'rane be hiss ssisster, what doess that make Ah'din, being sshe is Ah'rane'ss daughter?"

"His niece?" Gideon shrugged. "I do not know how it was done, only that it was done, probably by you – and carefully – and over a very long period of time, or I miss my guess."

"Thee thinkss me capable of a great deal," Pythos said softly, "though whether or not it iss a compliment, I cannot assscertain."

"It is a compliment, though a fearful one," Gideon said, and went back to the main hearth, where Krush and Abeyan sat drinking tea and staring into the night, willing Ah'krill to come, wondering if Teal, who had left hours before to seek her on Andal, was having any luck finding her.

"I swear, if she's had anything to do with this..." Krush began, and his fists knotted on the arms of his chair. He looked at Abeyan, who was a strong supporter of Ah'krill, and bit off the rest of his statement. "Hasn't the man been through enough grief already?"

Abeyan cocked his head slightly and murmured, "Ah'krill has ears in thy house, Krush. My grandson has become her closest companion since the incident which nearly cost my daughter her life."

"And you still blame Ardenai for that, don't you?" Krush growled. "I can hear it in your tone."

"It was his misjudgment that caused her to be hit," Abeyan said. "I have analyzed the statements which were made after."

"It was not my sire's misjudgment," Gideon said firmly. "Your pardon, Master Abeyan, but I was there. I saw. Ardenai Firstlord did only what he was supposed to do. We were in very close quarters, dust was obscuring the wargrounds, and Sarkhan was practicing treachery. Io was struck because Tolbeth and I blocked her view of Sarkhan. I'm sure of it."

"That is the story I heard, and I do not believe it," Abeyan said. "If

Sarkhan were shooting at you, a tall youth on a horse fifteen hands at the shoulder, he would not have hit a smaller person, riding a smaller horse, low on the body."

"Maybe the bolt was meant, not for me, but for Ah'krill." Gideon said, "but...then it would have killed Tolbeth. I've thought, too, that it might have been meant for Konik, and that when he raised his arms to put Ah'krill across my saddle, the arrow passed, somehow. I just can't figure out how it missed the horse."

"Or the bolt didn't come from Sarkhan in the first place, but from a traitor within the ranks of Equus," Abeyan said, leaning forward.

"It was Sarkhan's bolt," a voice said, and Teal came into the room from the direction of the thermal pools. "It was the first meant for Konik. The pull on his crossbow was set too high for him and he was trying to compensate, which is how Io was hit and Konik survived. He was a lousy shot. Period." Teal was grey-faced with exhaustion, and he leaned heavily against the back of one of the lounges, though he did not sit. "Ah'krill is here. I would suggest we attend her and her ministrations and take this up again at another time." He turned without further comment to retrace his steps, and the others followed him.

Ah'krill and Pythos were eyeing each other, one on either side of the narrow bed, two Akoliti attending in the shadows, and it was obvious that words had been spoken. "Thiss iss not the time for animossity, but later, when we can do it correctly," Pythos hissed venomously. "Right now, thy sson, the Firsstlord of Equuss, iss lossing ground againsst the fever hiss daughter hass, in ssome sstrange manner contracted. Though it painss me to do thiss, I musst allow thee to take the child lesst sshe kill him, and Equus losse the Thirteenth Dragonhorse."

"You're going to let her take our baby? To keep?" Io exclaimed, rising from her chair. "Why didn't you tell me that? I thought you wanted her to help us, not rob us! I'm the baby's mother! I'm strong. I could give refuge to the child."

Pythos shook his head sadly and flicked her with his tongue. "Thee could not, beautiful one.   Thee doess not have the telepathic capability necesssary to physsically remove her. I cannot focusss on her and thy huss- band at the ssame time. It musst be Ah'krill."

"Be comforted," the priestess said. "The child was meant for the Eloi. She was among those who competed for the coveted position of High Priestess. Failing that, she should have died, but did not. She was not spilled at Mountain hold as she should have been. It was a tragic fluke that she was given animation at all. I take back what was mine in the first place, and was never meant to be yours at all."

Io's eyes grew large, then changed shape, and her mouth came open to speak.

"Not now!" Gideon said sharply. "For the love of El'Shadai, not now! Look at my sire, and the pain which tears him limb from limb – the fe- ver which cooks his body and his brains – and stop your damned, petty bick- ering, all of you! I care about one thing and one thing only, and so should you, if you are loyal Equi. You should care about him, there in that bed. The rest of us – all the rest of us – young, old, born, unborn, are expendable. He, is not. Fix him first, then fix each other any way you like! I'll referee!"

"Damn, I do like that boy," Krush chuckled. "He's a nail right out of the old horseshoe." As he spoke he stepped forward and took Gideon by the shoulders and hauled him back from his aggressive stance in the center of the room, kissing him soundly in the process. Ah'rane took Io in her arms and walked her over to stand between herself and Abeyan, and Teal walked slowly to drop his head against Ah'din's.

"I sshall do what I can to help our Firsstlord undersstand what iss happening, and to put it in perssspective. You take the child, Ah'krill, and nothing elsse! I will know if thee tresssspassesss. Are we agreed?"

The priestess looked a little surprised, then gave him a single, curt nod. "You misjudge me. Of course I agree." She held out her hands to the serpent and he leaned across the bed toward her, taking her hands and setting his flat head against her forehead. They stood in this manner for several minutes, then moved as one to set their heads, one against each temple of the

Firstlord. They took his hands, and each other's.

Ardenai awoke with the morning sun welcome in his face, and the need to relieve himself uppermost in his mind. He slipped from the bed so as not to disturb Ah'ree, and went into the lavage. He was grateful that she still slept. She'd had a troublous night, full of pain and confusion, and it broke his heart to see her so. Perhaps if she slept awhile she'd feel better, and he could carry her out into the gardens so she could enjoy the spring flowers and the ducks. There were some tender shoots in the vegetable beds. He would tempt her with those, as well. She had grown so thin, the illness slowly wasting away her body, though her spirit remained as beautiful and serene as ever.

He returned to the edge of the bed and sat beside her to study her in the first rays of morning. She looked so peaceful. Too...peaceful. He reached to stroke her face, to waken her, and she was cold. He jerked his hand back, then put his palms against her temples. There was no pulse. Ardenai groaned like he'd been knifed, and sprang up, grabbing her with both hands and gathering her fiercely against him. "PYTHOS!" he screamed, "PYTHOS! FOR THE LOVE OF ELADEUS, COME QUICKLY!"

"I am here," came the quiet voice. "Do not dessspair."

"She's dead!" he sobbed. "Ah'ree is dead! You must do something!"

"There iss nothing I can do," he said, putting his arms around both of them, huge tears rolling down the length of his body. "I cannot ssave her. I can only weep with thee for her losss."

"I can't let her go! I said I'd be responsible!" Ardenai exclaimed, and he began to shake all over, realizing he was in two places at once – In two dimensions – that two were being taken and not just the one.

There was a sudden warmth, and light, and a floating peace, and in it a voice that was Ah'ree's but not, said, *Do not mourn for me, and do not hold me against my will. I go where I was meant to go, to do what I was meant to do, but thee always will I love. Thee always will I love, my father.*

"No," Ardenai cried, "Oh, please...no ..." but the voice was gone, and the presence was gone. There came a vacuous relief that was physical, and a growing emptiness in his heart that was overwhelming. "Oh, Ah'ree, take me with you," he cried, "please take me with you."

"I can't do that. I have to go now," Ah'ree said sadly, and Ardenai felt her warmth and her essence slipping through his hands.

"Please, don't go," he whispered.

"Pythos says I must," she smiled, brushing his cheek with one hand. Almost, he couldn't feel her touch. "But before I go, I must ask you, do you love Io? Are you happy married to Io?"

"Yes," Ardenai sighed. "Crazy as it sounds, I am. I adore her more every day. But..."

"No buts. No apologies. No more looking back. I am happy for thee. I was not meant to fill your life as memory only. I have given you my whole being, my whole devotion for the span that was granted me. Now you must do that for Io for the span granted her. Be happy, Beloved. You two think of me, and with joy, and try to stay out of each other's hair, will you?" There was a last ripple of warmth, and then nothing at all. He collapsed, sobbing hysterically, and Pythos pried the corpse from his arms, and placed it on the bed.

"I have her," Ah'krill said, staggering back a little, and it was Gideon who stepped forward to steady her. "She's...I don't...feel very well."

"We have a place for you to rest and refresh yourself," Jilfan said, stepping from the doorway to her other side, and between the two of them they walked the High Priestess from the room, her attendants following close behind.

"You and I will chat later," Pythos shot after her, then turned back to Ardenai, who lay shuddering and sobbing. Quickly he released the jacerei bands from the Firstlord's arms and lifted him into a more elevated position, padding him in place with pillows which Ah'din hastened to bring him. "Come to me now, Beloved. Hide thyself in my breast, and be comforted," he said gently, and flicked his tongue against the feverish cheeks.

Ardenai's eyes, burned black with fever, came wearily open, and his hand moved in Io's direction when he focused on her. She came to him, and took it, pressing it to her lips and wetting it with her tears. He swallowed hard and squeezed his eyes shut, trying to think. "I have lost ..." they opened, filled with grief and dismay. He bit his cracked and bleeding lips and regained his composure. "I...Io, I've lost...I can't find Ah'leah anywhere. I think...she went with...Ah'ree? But that makes no sense. I think she told me...she wasn't meant to..."

"Ah'krill took her," Io said, trying without success to hide the angry frustration in her voice.

The man looked totally bewildered. "Why ...?"

"As you said, Husband. Ah'krill says she was never meant to be ours, and surely she was never meant to share a consciousness with you. You did your best, I know that, but I suppose it's best this way. This is the second time that the child has nearly killed you, Beloved, because you can't seem to focus on her enough to ascertain what she needs, as opposed to what you need. So now that's moot, isn't it? She is truly gone, and you can go back to being...whatever!" Io turned and ran sobbing from the room, and Ardenai's face crumpled with despair.

"She's right, isn't she? But what was I to do, Pythos? Your skill was...needed to save Io." He rubbed at his forehead in frustration, wincing at the monumental headache. "I cared more for my wife than my daughter. I chose the right person to save my wife, and the wrong person to save my daughter. But who else was there? What in the name of Eladeus did she expect me to do?"

"The only other choicce thee had, was Ah'krill. Thee knowss that."

"Is she right? Did I not focus ...?" he shook his head and drew a ragged breath. "No need to answer. We both know the truth. I was focused on my own affairs. Which is how Io came to cut her hair off, and how... my daughter came to be lost from us altogether. I thought of Equus and of myself only."

He took a deep breath and exhaled sharply, realizing with terrible guilt and effervescing joy that he felt more stable, more focused, more whole, than he had since that day on the wargrounds of Calumet. "I did want her," he added weakly. "There was just so much going on, and she rattled around in my head like she was trying to get out all the time, and it was so hard to focus over her...crying ...."

Krush came to the other side of the bed, and took Ardenai's hand. "Ardi," he said, "look at me, son. Now hear me. I want you to consider the possibility that Ah'krill is right about this. I know there's some thought that she went about this the wrong way." He paused, realizing too late that he'd slipped. It registered in the flushed countenance of his son, and the annoyed exhalation of his wife.

"Explain," the Firstlord said, and even in his state, it compelled response.

"This was going to come out sooner or later, and you're not going to like it one kraaling bit, but..."

"I think sshe gave Ah'leah cradle bumpss," Pythos hissed. "Until I can assscertain whether or not I am correct, I would like the matter dropped. Pleasse." He fixed Krush with one rolling golden eye, and the keeplord gave him a curt nod of acquiescence.

"As you wish," he said, but his eyes were on his son. "You're a man, Ardenai. A male of the species through and through. You're the Firstlord of Equus. The Dragonhorse! Look at your arms. You have more titles than the average god, and a planet to run – eleven planets to run. I know you feel terrible about the babe, but you had too many responsibilities to Equus to take the time for feminine introspection and you know it. And you don't have any more time now than you did then, and you'll have even less in the future, so whipping yourself is foolish. The child was meant to be a priestess. Now, she will be. She's better off, and so are you. There, I've said my say. Now please, rest and get your strength back." He stood up, kissed Ardenai tenderly on the forehead, and went to make peace with his wife.

"We'll talk in a minute," Ah'rane said, patting his arm, and she took her turn sitting beside Ardenai. "I know you think Io is angry at you for losing the babe. She's not. She's angry at herself for losing the baby, and there's nothing you can do to fix that. You need to rest, and get yourself well again. You're still very sick, and it's hard to think when you're sick. Now, it's been a long night, and I think we could all use a good breakfast, so I'm going to go cook, while Ah'din and Teal take a nap, because Teal had to chase Ah'krill all over two continents to get her here, and he looks hard ridden."

"And I'm going to go feed horses," Krush said, smiling at Ardenai. "And maybe I'll take that golden-eyed son of yours. What a find! He's a natural with the horses, and with people, too. Anyway, I'm going. You rest yourself. It's coming harvest season you know. We need you out there on the harvesters, keeplord Ardenai."

Ardenai tried for a smile as they left, but a wave of nausea kept it from sticking, and he turned his face away lest his parents worry even more. He let his head fall back against the pillows, and Pythos realized he was panting for breath, and very hot. "We have yet a way to go," he said quietly. "Much as I hate to do thiss to thee, I am going to ressset thosse Jacerei. I sshall numb thy armss thiss time, and ssing thee a ssweet lullaby about tassty tree toadss and ssucculent woodratss and ssucking eggss on a warm Ompha-ss morning."

"I'll pay you not to do that," Ardenai mumbled. He gagged, but there was nothing in his stomach, and a flick of Pythos' comforting tongue quieted the need to vomit. "I thought once you had cradle bumps, you couldn't...get them again," he said, managing to sound annoyed. "I know I had these way back."

"Indeed," the old doctor nodded. "Remember, though, thee doessn't have them. Ah'leah had them."

"That makes no sense," Ardenai sighed. He was so tired, groaning softly with every breath he took, and shaking his head fitfully from side to side with the heat building up in the pillows. "I don't suppose I could actually have water to drink?"

"Not without me wearing it," Pythos chuckled. "Thou art uncomfortably dry?"

"Yes."

"Perhapss a juiccy piece of ssweet fruit to ssuck on?"

"Anything," Ardenai managed.

Pythos disappeared, and shortly brought him bits of icy cold sugar melon, fresh from the garden, and laved his mouth with unguent to soothe the fever blisters. With the cool sweetness of the fruit to allay his thirst, and cold towels across his groin and thighs to ease his discomfort, he began to drift.

He heard Krush say quietly, "Go, my friend, have something to eat and rest yourself a bit," and his father came to sit beside him, as Pythos glided out of the room.

Ardenai felt his father's hand cover his, and he opened his eyes and gave him a fleeting smile. "I think having these was more fun the first time around," he said.

"I think you and Teal had them together," Krush replied. "Abeyan cried for days because his mother wouldn't let him play with you two. And both of you were more spotted than sick, and you rampaged around your bedroom for a week until all three mothers were thoroughly fed up and distracted. That was a very long time ago."

"Yes," Ardenai murmured. "A very long time."

Krush sensed his melancholy. "Are you ready to hear something funny?" he asked, and Ardenai nodded. "We just got a message from Kehailan. I brought it to read. It says, 'Ahimsa, I wish peace to all of you, and wish I were there to share the pleasure and deep contentment your homecoming must bring you. I am sending this to let you know that there has been an outbreak of cradle bumps on board. Winnie says Declivians don't usually get them, but I wanted to let you know, as I doubt Gideon has been properly inoculated, and I would not want to see him get sick. We are experiencing some amazing sights out here, and I will be most anxious to share them with you. Please take care of yourselves, and of one another until we meet again. Kehailan.'"

That same message was circulating at the breakfast table, and Gideon cast a look in Pythos' direction. "How does this fit with your theory?" he asked. Ah'krill still slept with Jilfan in attendance. Io and Abeyan were nowhere to be seen. Only Ah'rane was there with them, and she, too, looked interested in the reply.

"How, I assk thee, doess it change my theory?" Pythos responded, taking fruit from the tray which Gideon passed him.

"Well," Gideon said, giving it some thought. "When you said you thought Ah'krill had given my sire cradle bumps, I assumed you thought that one or more of the children at the welcoming ceremony had been infected. Someone on board Belesprit is a little more farfetched, isn't it?"

"Frankly, I think the whole thing is a little farfetched, if you'll forgive me saying so," Ah'rane added, smiling at Pythos and pouring more juice for Gideon.

"Thee cannot concceive of any dam rissking her sson'ss life, can thee, lovely one?"

"Yes, I can, if the prize was great enough. But taking a single child, no matter what she was supposed to be, at the risk of rendering the Thirteenth Dragonhorse sterile from fever and thus losing this line of the Great House, is just not an acceptable risk. It's not a big enough prize. Now that's a woman's perspective, but I think it's valid." Pythos had started a little at her words, and Ah'rane gave him a worried knot of a smile. "You haven't thought about the sterility issue yet, have you?"

Pythos didn't answer. He tipped his head back, staring at the ceiling while he mashed fruit in his toothless mouth and swallowed, flicking his tongue with pleasure. "What if, by acquiring the child, one could gain accesss to the thoughtss of the Firsstlord, as well?" he asked, turning his head slightly to focus on Ah'rane.

The woman pulled her brows together in thought, just like Ardenai. She looked, just like Ardenai. It was uncanny. Gideon couldn't help thinking what an exceptional way that would be to hide a Firstlord from whomever might want to harm him – to have him look exactly like one of his parents – but how had it been accomplished?

"I didn't think the babe had access to her sire's thoughts, so much as she had access to his processes," Ah'rane said slowly. "Which would mean she took precious little information away with her. Certainly she wasn't sophisticated enough to be able to ascertain which thoughts were of value, was she?"

"No. I'm ssure thee iss correct in thy thinking," Pythos said. "But what if thee had a beloved wife whose telepathic abilitiess were not ssufficcient to vissit the child on her own, and ccertainly a conssiderate granddam would offer ssuch visssitation, would sshe not? Then, to ssoothe thy wife, thee would vissit her thysself, would thee not, sso that thee could report her good health to her biological mother?"

"I thought," Gideon interjected, "Ardenai was one of the most powerful telepaths on Equus. He's going to know if she tries to pick his brain, isn't he? Besides, he's powerful enough that he has nothing to fear from her. He's going to tell her whatever it is she wants to know, anyway. He has no worries about reprisals."

"I do not know whether the two of thee are sssoothing me, or annoying me," Pythos hissed. "Let uss ssee...let uss jusst ssee what our high priestesss ssayss when sshe arissess, sshall we?"

"Assuming she survives my daughter-in-law," Ah'rane chuckled. "Where is that one, do you suppose, and where is her father?"

Abeyan had taken his leave quietly, holding both Io's hands in his and telling her how sorry he was for the ills which had befallen her of late. He placed no blame, and kept innuendo from his voice, saying there would be time enough for meaningful discussion when things were back on an even keel. As affairs stood, with both the Firstlord and the High Priestess away from the Great House, and the Firstlord likely to be gone for some time, he felt his presence was needed in the council chambers. Rumors did have a way of spreading, no matter how secretive one tried to be, and someone who could tell the straight story and allay fears, was needed there. Io had nodded, and thanked him profusely for coming. She'd put her arms around him and held him tight for a few moments, grateful beyond words for the arms which tightened around her in reply.

He'd taken her face in his hands, then, and fixed her in his gaze, and said, "You are married to one of the most powerful men in the galaxy, and of your own free will. If you do anything, say anything, to dishonor him, or your relationship, you dishonor Equus. Remember that." Then he'd kissed her forehead, and within moments the little Equi Flyer had skimmed out of sight over the treetops and down the canyon toward the sea.

She felt so lost. More so than she'd ever felt in her life – and alienated from everything and everybody. She didn't want to see Ardenai for fear, not of what she'd see, but of what she'd think when she saw him. She knew she would never feel the same devotion to him again. Never even love him again. How easily he had let their baby go to that woman. How puzzled he had looked to find her gone, as if she were a piece of tack gone missing, or a misplaced cup of tea. And everybody was going to side with him. Everybody was going to say she was overreacting. And what was he going to think of her, and the way she'd acted, reacted, in front of Ah'krill, and her father, and his parents? As for Ah'krill, the thought of seeing her any time soon, twisted in Io's guts like a rope pulled taut enough to strangle. The thought of that woman and her cold, haughty gaze and her jewels and fine clothing, and the tone of her voice when she said she'd only taken what was hers in the first place made Io's fists ball up.

And Pythos – who was supposedly her friend and physician, who had helped her win Ardenai's heart, had not helped her save her own daughter. She knew what he was thinking. She was Papilli. A little corrective surgery and she'd be popping out little curly haired babes with never a thought for the one she'd lost. No. Not lost. Worse. Ah'leah had been stolen! Ardenai had let her be stolen. At this moment she wasn't even sure she wanted the surgery. She knew she never wanted the Firstlord to touch her again. The only thing that sounded inviting was leaving with Konik for the realm of the Wind Warriors, which, hopefully, was far, far away somewhere.

Her father's words came back to haunt her. If she dishonored her husband, or their relationship, by doing anything or saying anything, she dishonored Equus. She was Primuxori, and the Captain of the Horse Guard of the Great House of Equus. How she wished the latter were all she was. How she wished she had died with honor on that warground, and Ardenai had married Ah'nora or Ah'nis, or somebody and been miserable. The thought of him grieving for her, crying for her as he had for Ah'ree, was pleasant, and she enjoyed it momentarily before tasting the bitterness in her throat. She sighed and dusted her hands together, wondering as she did so what she thought she was brushing away, then combed her hair with her fingers, and went to check on her husband.

Krush was sitting beside him, speaking softly, and when Io got close enough she realized he was reminding Ardenai of all the crazed things he'd done as a boy. Telling him he'd known from the outset who he was, and who he was destined to become. The second he'd realized how much he looked like Ah'rane, he'd known. Io wondered about that as she settled herself in the easy chair. Krush heard the rustling, and turned to smile at her. "Would you like some time alone with him?" he asked.

"No, she smiled, "you're fine. I'm sure he's enjoying the sound of your voice. I'll just sit here, if that's all right with you."

Krush looked puzzled by the statement. "Of course it's all right with me," he smiled. "Have you eaten, though? Have you had some rest?"

"Yes," she lied. "I'm fine."

"You're sure you don't want to be alone?"

"I'm sure."

"Probably wouldn't know what to say to him anyway," Krush said, almost to himself, and returned to his reminiscences.

It startled Io, and made her feel transparent, somehow. Krush had never said anything about having any particularly well developed telepathic abilities, but then again, neither had his son. Both self-effacing men, more likely to laugh at themselves than to brag. Was she wearing her bitterness on her face? She was tempted to go look in a reflector, just to see.

Ardenai shifted in the bed, she could see the restless movement of his legs, and she heard him ask, "Where's...Pythos?"

"Having some breakfast, by now I would imagine. He just sprinted by the window in hot pursuit of a marchling. Do you have need of him?"

"No," Ardenai sighed. "I just wanted to ask him some things, that's all."

"Like what?"

"Oh, I don't know. Like, why did he let Ah'krill take Ah'leah without asking me first?"

"Ardi, she was killing you. You weren't conscious enough to ask."

"You think she was doing that on purpose? The babe was sick. She couldn't help that."

"Do I need to give you the old, 'You are Equus, and you've risked enough' lecture? Because I can, and I certainly will," Krush said, sponging gently at Ardenai's face with cool water. "You need to relax and stop upsetting yourself. Do you think you're the only father who has ever lost a daughter? Are you the only couple who has ever lost a child? People lose children every day, to disease, to accidents; not just fetuses, but children who are established in the home and the heart. You at least got to know her a little. Most men don't have that luxury with an unborn. Their wives grieve, and they have no idea how to react, because they haven't possessed that fetus, that little life. You got to do that. Consider yourself blessed to have met her, lucky to have survived the experience, and let it go. It will bring you nothing but grief and anger and bitterness, and what good will any of them do? Will they make you better able to serve Equus?"

"No," Ardenai murmured.

"Then please, son, don't do with this babe what you did with Ah'ree, and let her death take over your life until it seems to your family like you're dead, too, We've missed you these last two and a half years, Ardi, and we want you back." Ardenai took a ragged breath and closed his eyes, and Krush was quick in repentance. "I'm sorry. That was a thoughtless thing to say when you're so sick."

"It would be less thoughtless when I'm not sick?" Ardenai asked, trying manfully to chuckle. "It's alright. Gideon told me the same thing awhile back. It just...I had a family again. A wife, and a baby on the way, and it meant so much to me. More than what went on that day. Our 'win' over the Telenir. What a joke that was. And I made a mess of it, just like I made a mess of raising Kehailan, a mess of saving Ah'leah. I'm a creppia nonage teacher. You'd think I could do a better job with my own children, wouldn't you?"

"You're not any worse than the rest of us," Krush smiled, listening to the fever ramble in Ardenai's voice, "just a little higher profile all of a sudden." He laid his hand against his son's cheek, then pulled the sheet back, and took the towels one by one, dipping them in cool water, wringing them out, and replacing them on Ardenai's blistered flesh. "Does this hurt?"

"No, I don't think so," Ardenai said. "Burns a little, maybe, like blisters will do."

"Would you like some fruit, or some slivered ice to suck on?"

"No, really, I'm fine. You should go get some rest. Harvest is starting, it's time to be bringing in the horses for medicating, and here you sit, having to deal with me rather than me helping you, as it should be. I didn't really feel well when I got up yesterday morning. Or whatever day it was."

"Yesterday."

"Is that all?" he murmured. It feels so long ago." He cleared his throat and forced a smile. "I'm a little foggy. I should have thought about the possibilities and stayed where I was."

"You're right. You should have realized immediately that your unborn daughter, who was supposed to be absorbing nicely into your subconscious, except that she really didn't want to be absorbed in the first place, had cradle bumps, and that's why you felt a little off. Just stop, will you? You feel like shit, you look like shit, you can't think worth shit, and you're lying there using what little strength you have to berate yourself. You're smarter than that. Now act like it."

"Yes sir," Ardenai sighed, and resisted the urge to burst out laughing – or maybe crying. Something was definitely trying to get out. "Make me a crys-tel of that, will you? 'You're smarter than that. Now act like it.' I'll play it like a little mantra a couple times a day after my obligatory prayers."

"Happy to," Krush snorted. He caught movement in the doorway, and realized Ah'krill was standing there. "She who is High Priestess is here," he said formally. "I'm going to take your wife and go have a nice cup of something hot. We'll be back in a few minutes."

"Io is here?" Ardenai grimaced. "Why didn't you say so?"

"Of course she's here. I assumed you'd assume." He turned to the young woman and held out his hand. "Let's go make some coffee, shall we?" he said. He nodded and smiled in Ah'krill's direction without really looking at her, and piloted Io out of the room, keeping himself between his daughter-in-law and the other woman.

"Please," Ardenai said, gesturing toward the chair at the bedside, then vaguely at the room, "sit wherever is most comfortable. How are you feeling by now?"

"I'm fine," Ah'krill smiled. "Fortunately I was inoculated recently for a whole battery of things. I suppose cradle bumps was one of them."

Ardenai felt a little prickle run along his spine. "Why did you have yourself inoculated?"

"I had that exploratory visit to Lebonath Jas, remember? You were asked to accompany us, but Ah'ree had been in death such a short time, and you were not feeling up to traveling so far. It was a primitive, even savage place in many ways, and in desperate need. I would recommend further, more intimate contact in the future." She caught the look in his eye, and stopped her comment. "I assume all of us who went were inoculated, Dragonhorse, not just me."

"A wise precaution," he murmured.

"I did not come in here to work you up," she said, and her eyes seemed sad. "I only wanted to see how you were feeling. You're feverish, and your lips look as though talking is painful. I should go."

"Not yet," he said. "Tell me, how is my daughter this morning?"

"Sleeping, with the other little priestesses."

"There are others?"

"Two more," Ah'krill said, and didn't wait for his next, obvious question. "One is the daughter of an akolyte. The mother died in childbirth, and the babe died the next day, despite all we could do. The other is the child I conceived not long after I had you. I wanted a babe to replace you, to fill up that empty space, though I knew it probably wasn't a very good idea. I convinced an old friend of mine to marry me. He was a confirmed bachelor and busy on other worlds most of the time. He obliged me, and settled me, and considered his job done. But my womb was not as strong as it should have been, and when I began to grow heavy, it tore, and the babe was lost – all but her essence."

"I'm sorry," Ardenai said. "Does Pythos know you have them?"

"Does he need to?" Ah'krill asked coolly."He is your physician, not mine."

"No. It is not his...he does not need to know."

"He thinks I made you sick. He thinks I risked your life to gain your daughter. Why would he think that? Why would I do that?"

"I honestly do not know," Ardenai said, then closed his eyes and took a deep breath, shifting a little in an attempt to get comfortable. Ah'krill rose from her chair and lifted him, resting his head on her upper arm. She flipped the sweat-soaked pillow to the dry side, and adjusted it under his neck and shoulders. "Thank you," he said. "That feels better."

"Dragonhorse, tell me the truth. Do you think me capable of this? Of making you so very ill?"

He studied her for a long moment, then closed his eyes and shook his head slowly. "No. I do not. But you are my mother. You gave me life. I cannot conceive of you taking it back from me. You would have to be evil indeed before I would see it."

"Let your wife point it out to you," Ah'krill muttered. "Just remind them, I did not come here of my own accord. I came because Pythos sent for me, because Teal said you were frighteningly ill. I took the child because Pythos asked me to. Touching your mind, trying to find your daughter in there, was like being in a burning house. She was terrified, and so was I."

"I did not want that for her, or you. I don't really remember much. Lots of vivid images that aren't attached to anything. And then she was just…gone."

"She's right here," Ah'krill said soothingly. "You may visit her any time you like, though she will become very hard to identify, as she would have had she stayed with you and eventually become a part of your subconscious mind. But for a while, while the pain and the loss are still fresh, you may yet identify her and be comforted. I know Io would have trouble, as she is not overly telepathic, but you are always welcome."

"Thank you," Ardenai said. He heard movement, and cocked his head to look down the short, rough passage to the bathing pools. Pythos was sprawled, half in and half out of the hottest pool, and Gideon was working him over with scrubsand. He seemed asleep, but Ardenai knew better, just as he knew the timing of this bath was not serendipitous. "Surely you must be hungry," Ardenai began, and instantly Ah'din appeared in the doorway.

"Please come have some breakfast, or perhaps by now, some lunch," she said, smiling at Ah'krill, and the priestess rose with a gracious nod as Ah'din continued. "We have not formally met, Priestess. I am Ardenai's sister, and the wife of Teal. I am Ah'din."

"Thy family has been most gracious to me, and I am pleased to meet thee," she said, and bent to give the Firstlord a kiss on the temple. "And you, get some rest. You have duties to perform." He nodded, gave her a slight smile, and she was gone.

In that moment, a bright yellow eyeball gleamed out of a green, hooded lid, and Pythos' thoughts touched him. *A most interesting conversation, hatchling.*

Ardenai huffed a little with annoyance. *You might simply have joined us, rather than eavesdropping, my good snake.*

Oh, thee knows how mixing the company sometimes changes the gist of a conversation.

Are you still thinking she tried to kill me?

I never thought she tried to kill thee, my child. Only make thee sick unto oblivion. Would thee have yielded the child otherwise?

You're wrong about her, Pythos.

I am not. Thee has too much of the milk of human kindness in thy veins, Firsstlord. I can only hope thee also still has the finest seed of Equus in thy loins.

What?

This fever may have parboiled thy progeny, my friend. Then what?

You think I'm planning to use my phallus as a measure of justice? I can still rule. Actually, I think it would be rather funny, myself. They might actually have to accept me for my mind rather than my sexual prowess. What a joke. I hate that part. I really do. I'd welcome being shed of it.

Thee has responsibilities of a reproductive nature, and a generative phallus will be of more use to thee than that smart mouth.

Well, then. Can you...insert a needle or something into my primary testes and draw material for a sperm count? He shuddered a little at the thought. He didn't like needles very much, and the thought of one in that particular spot, was not pleasant.

Thee could simply ejaculate for me. It would be faster, and far less painful.

I'm not generative.

Thee is generative.

I'm not generative. I'm ejaculating half a dozen times at the most during any given encounter. That's not enough to activate my primary testes. And when is this dragonhorse finally going to wear completely off?

It is not. One ejaculation, ten ejaculations. In heat, not so in heat, but never out of heat. Thee is generative at all times now.

"PYTHOS, GET YOUR SCALY GREEN ASS IN HERE!" Ardenai bellowed, and Gideon looked up in alarm.

"Is he in pain?"

"Yess, in a manner of sspeaking. I thank thee for the sscrub, hatchling. I sshall claim my oiling of thee another time. Right now I musst tend thy ssire."

"Should I come with you? Does he need my help?"

"Delirium takess many formss. Best ssteer clear of thiss awhile, and advisse otherss to do likewisse," the serpent hissed, removed himself with reluctance from the hot water and warm sand, and toddled into the thermal room, pulling on his robe as he went. "Yess, Firsstlord, wissest of the wisse, O' mosst intuitive one. How may I sserve thee?"

The outburst had left Ardenai panting, raw throated, and he lay spread-eagle on the bed, trying to cool himself. Pythos pulled back the sheet and changed the towels, then flicked Ardenai with his long tongue, chuckling with fond amusement. "Here, hatchling, put a piecce of ssugar melon in thy mouth. It will help thee get thy voicce back sso thee can sshout ssome more."

Ardenai crushed the melon against the roof of his mouth, allowing the juice to trickle onto his tongue and down his parched throat. After a minute he said, "You make me crazed. You know this, of course. Explain yourself, Lizard."

"As thee wisshes. As a ssea dragon, I have no asss, insstead I…"

Ardenai jerked up a hand. "I am in no mood, Sir Pent."

"Very well. It iss my theory, that sshe kept thee after the counccil ssession, had thee hold audiencce rather than coming home, becausse sshe asssumed that the adult onsset of cradle bumpss would have the ssame incubation period as an infant or ssmall child. Sshe wass there with thee, sshe and her physsician. I wass here, an hour away. It wass perfect. When thee did not get immediately ssick, sshe asssumed that sshe had failed in her attempt, and went off on legitimate bussinesss. Off to that religiouss retreat that made her ssssso kraaling hard to find."

"You really are bound and determined to unearth conspiracy in this, aren't you? Well, it's all fascinating, but that's not what I meant, and you know it. I don't want to hear about your anatomy, or your conspiracy theories. Tell me about this newest verse in our hymn to propagation? I'm generative?"

"Thee didn't notice? I think thy wife did."

"I assumed that was residual."

"Yess, in a manner of sspeaking. But it wass not ssingular in nature. Nor iss the fact that thee iss sstill jusst a little warm in the loinss."

The Equi gave him a look which mingled resignation and dismay in equal portions. "Wonderful. Not only am I generative all the time, which lets out any possibility of recreational sex, but I'm in heat all the time? How am I going to think?"

"Doesst thee think with thy phalluss, Firsstlord?" the serpent hissed. "Thee can sstill usse thy brain. If thee checks, thee will find they are ssepa-rate organss."

Ardenai did not react, though he nodded acknowledgment of the well-placed sarcasm. "So tell me, what made you think this would be easier on me if you sprang it in a series of annoying little hops? What in kraa did you do to me that night in the cave, Pythos? What did Ah'krill do to me with those potions of hers? I want to know. Now, if you please."

"All thee needed to do, wass assk thy humble sservant," Pythos re-plied, and seated himself beside the Firstlord. "Thee never thinkss to assk. Not a good trait in a sstatessman of thy sstature." He reached for the plate of sugar melon, taking a piece for himself, and then holding a piece out for Ardenai.

"I stand chastised," Ardenai muttered. He paused a moment and let the juice moisten his mouth. "Please tell me what you did to me."

"Nothing."

"Please tell me what Ah'krill did to me."

"Nothing," Pythos hissed, and began his snaky chuckle.

"Well now I know ever so much more than I did. Thank you. If you did nothing, and Ah'krill did nothing then why…?" he trailed off and flipped his hands, palms up, in a question, being careful not to put tension on the jacerei bands.

"If thee had not rissen to be Firsstlord, if thee had been, ssay, sship-wrecked on ssome unknown planet ssomewhere, with only thy creppias for company, thiss exact ssame ssequencce of physsical changess would sstill have taken placce. Thiss iss not happening to thee becausse ssomeone iss caussing it to happen, but becausse it iss bred into thee. All Firstlordss risse on their hundredth birthing day, becausse sshortly thereafter, thosse mech-anissmss which were bred into them and their ilk, kick in, and they do kick hard. Thee hass had ample opportunity to obsserve thiss." He reached for another piece of melon and gummed it with a hiss of pleasure. "The ssug-ar melonss are esspeccially ssucculent thiss year. I hope they sstore well. Ssometimess they do, and ssometimess they don't. It iss all dependent upon the sseasson, one asssumess. I wonder what Sssegens and First Enalios were like thiss year?"

"And you didn't tell me? We're not talking about sugar melons, now, or the weather, or your lack of an ass, in case you wondered."

"I repeat, thee didn't assk. Thee musst learn to assk quesstionss about thesse thingss, rather than asssuming. Would thee like more melon? And then thee musst ssleep, becausse thee iss sstill very ssick. Doess thee sstill ache all over?"

"Yes, I would, and yes, I do," Ardenai replied, and gave the physi-cian a brief, painful smile. "Physician Pythos, what else can I expect from this new incarnation?"

"Physsically? Thiss iss the worsst of it. Thee will be slightly more eassily aroussed than thee wass before, which iss already pleassing thy lit-tle Papilli wife, and each heat ccycle will be a Dragonhorsse, unlesss we can pacccify it. Mountain hold hass thosse faccilitiess, which iss why thee needss to get thysself there ssoon. Thee will find thy interesst in femaless heightened, but not uncontrollably sso. As I think of other thingss, I sshall tell thee. Iss thee sstill feeling the urge to vomit?"

At the mention of Io, Ardenai's eyes had ceased to smile, and he took a deep breath and pushed his head back against the pillow. "All of a sudden, yes. We are to have problems, are we not? My little Papilli wife and I? She blames me, and rightly so, for the loss of the child, but also I think for most everything else that's wrong with her life right now."

"Conssider that either sshe hass been ssick, or thee hass been ssick, ssince nearly the day thee wass married. Sshe lovess thee, though sshe iss no longer quite sso infatuated, and that'ss good. Sshe loved thee beyond reasson. Sshe ssaw thee as the ideal man. There'ss nothing like marriage and intimacy to clear one'ss vission about ssuch thingss, or sso I am told. Sshe doess not realize thiss iss what iss happening, that the two of thee are leveling off – thee falling more in love with her, and sshe finding hersself sslightly lesss wild about thee. Sshe iss sseeking answerss in circumsstancces, and trying to regain her father'ss favor. Give her time. If thee musst, forcce her to comply with thy dessiress, ssexual or otherwisse. Do not allow her to alienate hersself from thee."

Ardenai snorted voicelessly and stared up into the vining herbs for a few moments before looking again at Pythos. "I will not force her, sexually or otherwise. It's beginning to feel like we've done nothing but fight since we got married. That first day, the day we wed, we conceived our daughter, and we had her to plan for, and Sarkhan to plan for, and now that we have neither of those things, perhaps...we have nothing at all. I do know I'm off balance by having her madly in love with me one minute and hating my very soul the next. My son, who is not yet seventeen, is more mature than my wife, and suddenly, I'm sick and tired of it. If she wants to go to Telenir with Konik, she's got my blessing."

He pounded his head against the pillow once for emphasis. It was all he could manage. And let his eyes shut, aching all over, and beginning to itch like fire, nauseous, weak, worried, guilty, frustrated to know he had duties, so many duties which needed tending while he lay sick unto death with a baby's disease, and unaware that his wife had turned from the doorway in dismay. She set aside the tray of tea and the favored tidbits she'd prepared for him as an apology, and crept silently back to their chambers.

CHAPTER TWENTY-SIX

It was such a beautiful autumn day, Gideon had to remind himself that he was working. He also reminded himself that here it was not autumn, but the beginning of Oporens, and that when it was over, October would be gone. Nevertheless, the drifting leaves were familiar, the dry grass, the crispness in the air, and he was happier than he'd ever been in his life.

He and Tolbeth were jogging along beside his grandsire and Beckett, up on the canyon's rim, searching for stray horses. They all needed to be brought in for their semi-annual medications, and not all of them had been found yet. Twice already today they'd returned to the keep nave with horses, three the first time, seven the second. Krush had said there was a big bay mare with a blue roan colt at her side, who was particularly good at avoiding capture, and this was her usual territory. If she could be found, they'd call it a day.

They'd talked about all kinds of things while they rode: the coming winter months, poetry, what you'd most likely think about if you were a duck, Ardenai's artistic accomplishments, computators, vegetable gardening, and the concept of a personal deity. Like Ardenai, Krush was easy to talk to. During the Firstlord's illness it was Krush who had taken over Gideon's lessons for the most part, and Gideon had quickly come to adore the man nearly as much as he adored Ardenai. They'd gone outside for their science lessons, to study plants and their habits while they gardened and harvested and walked in the meadows and woods. They'd observed rocks and their properties, water and its movement relative to the movement of the planet. As part of that lesson, Krush had taken him deep under the house at Sea keep, to the thermal fusion, or fundere chamber. There, Gideon had gotten his first lessons on thermal dynamism, and a basic idea of how the hot water which bubbled up at a high boil, could be used against itself to increase its temperature by two and a half times or more. Then, they'd gone upstairs again, and into the fragrant kitchen, where Krush and Ah'rane had demonstrated how the huge old cookstove worked, how the top and the ovens were regulated by the injection of hot and cold water in the necessary proportions to maintain an even temperature. The culmination of the lesson had been a wonderful cake, redolent with honey and spices, and topped with fresh, wild azure berries – the first of the season.

They had doctored horses together, and Gideon learned the nature of wounds, and how to treat them. He learned more about the ancient dwellings they occupied, the houses and barns, the towns, the ancient cities, old beyond anything he could conceive of, in a civilization older than he could comprehend, with a population seemingly unchanged for millennia, yet ever-changing and ever-advancing globally and intergalactically. On the surface it seemed paradoxical, but like most things Equi, there was a simple, patient, far-seeing explanation.

As Gideon understood it, the Equi had found themselves astride a runaway economy, with cities getting bigger, education becoming less respected, the air and water becoming increasingly polluted. They studied their history and discovered that time when the population was not straining the resources of their world, when education was at its best, crime at its lowest, mental stability the norm, and had slowly backed into it, sparing no effort and no expense to see that it remained for all time a place where the most people would be the most safe, secure, comfortable and creative.

They had chosen to be a rural, agricultural society, and on the surface they had not changed for thousands upon thousands of years, and nobody minded that. They had done away with internal combustion engines, nuclear fission, and many of the material things they had come to consider necessities, improving education, and most important, voluntarily reducing their population through the careful breeding programs of the Great House of Equus. Having accomplished the transformation of their world, they set their minds to the tasks of galactic peace and internal stability. It had made them serene, content without satisfaction, endlessly curious, and incredibly powerful.

What they wished to learn, they found in books, and in study, in contact, and experimentation, in meditation, and schooling. School, they took very seriously, and they spent a very long time there – Twenty-one years of compulsory education – from age five when they toddled off to Creppia Nonage, to age twenty-six, when they finished Final Form. Then, there was Lycee. And if you were a prince of the Great House, or a princess of the Great House, you went. Another four years, at least. Ardenai, Teal, Krush – had gone for ten. Any Equi could go – the high Equi, had to go.

Gideon sighed. He had not a prayer of catching up enough to actually go to school with people his own age. And he'd be expected to go to Lycee until he was thirty, like everybody else, and while they'd still be youngsters, he'd be a grown man, with other things on his mind. He smiled to himself, wondering what, exactly that would be. It wouldn't be a wife and family, that much was sure. He knew he would always want to be close to his father, but he was also falling in love with this place – with the notion of being a breeding and bloodlines specialist like his grandsire.

He wondered a little uneasily if he'd also be expected to spend time with a sexual trainer. He didn't have heat cycles, so he didn't need to learn how to control them, but the thought of such intrusiveness was unpleasant, and put him in mind of the conversation he'd had with Pythos that first day – to remove the brands, not to remove the brands. The family was used to them, or too polite to mention them, but would he always be bathing with family? And whom else would he want to bathe with? Nobody. With whom did he wish to train? Nobody. And what part of him could be trained, anyway? He wanted no part of sex, which was just not going to be considered healthy, especially as the son of the Thirteenth Dragonhorse, and then, when he refused training, would his affliction be made public, and would he be pitied, or just laughed at, or considered unworthy to be a son of Ardenai Firstlord?

"You're not brooding about your sire, are you?" Krush asked, responding to the sigh. "He's a little weak in the knees just yet, but he's going to be fine."

"I know that," Gideon said. And it was true. Ardenai was better. The last two nights he'd even been at the table for dinner, and had spent a short while visiting afterward – sitting up, looking reasonably comfortable and bright-eyed.

Early this morning Gideon had found him in the east-facing gardens. He had been dressed in loose trousers and an old, paint-spattered tunic and jacket, Ah'ree's two ducks quacking companionably about his feet. He'd been working in watercolors, painting the Viridian sunrise with a talent which had astounded the boy.

"It gives me something to do as therapy until I can be more productive," he'd said, and smiled at Gideon. His lips were soft and full again, nearly healed of the terrible cracks and blisters which had accompanied the fever, though his forearms still bore the bruises left by the jacerei bands.

"Well, I think it's stunning," Gideon had remarked. "If you're doing it only to pass the time, you can give it to me when you're done. Or to your mother," he'd added, feeling greedy. "I'm sure she'd love one of your paintings."

"My mother's house – I assume we're talking about Ah'rane, not Ah'krill – is so full of my paintings she'd take another only to be polite."

"Those are yours?" Gideon had gasped. "That huge one of the running horses…is yours?"

"Mmmmm," Ardenai had responded, but his eyes were on the sunrise, and Gideon had bid him a good morning and gone on to find his grandsire. They'd talk about painting later. Ardenai's attention span was still short and so was his temper. Gideon didn't want to tempt it.

"Io and Teal should be coming home today," Krush said, trying to start up a conversation. He'd been watching the boy out of the corner of his eye, and whether Gideon would admit it or not, he was a little broody. "And I believe tomorrow the elder contingent of our resident Telenir, along with Senator Konik, will be meeting here, since your sire is not yet strong enough to go to them. That should be interesting to sit in on, and I'm sure there are many who will think so. I hope it's warm enough for everyone to be outdoors, or we'll be crowded, I'm afraid. Ah'din and your granddam are already preparing food for the occasion."

"I hope they don't wear him out," Gideon said, remembering to look around for that mare and her babe. "A little over a week ago he was nearly dead, and I just...I wish he'd give himself time to really rest. I think Pythos is worried about him."

"Neh. If he thought Ardenai wasn't up for having a palaver here, he'd have said so, and not just to Ardi. He knows one broom-straw won't sweep a room, especially if the room doesn't want to be swept."

"I suppose you're right," Gideon nodded. "I hope having Io home to entertain him will keep my sire a little more relaxed. Not necessarily in *that* sense of the word," Gideon hastened to add, and it made Krush want to snicker. The boy was such a prude. He knew there was a very sad story that went with it, and he was worried about this new and precious grandson, but on the surface it was amusing, especially the expression on the handsome young face. "He's just been unsettled, or unhappy, with her away. I know she has duties to the Great House, but she also has duties to my sire."

"That's what we're here for," Krush chuckled. "To take care of Ardenai. But I do hope you're right. Ardi's been short tempered and distracted. I keep telling myself that it's the misery of getting over an adult case of cradle bumps, but I think it's more than that."

"I think they had a fight. I think something was said that sent Io to Thura with a kink in her cinch," Gideon muttered, and Krush burst out laughing.

"Now you're starting to sound like me. Don't do that around your grandmother or she'll lie down and die of despair. And don't worry about Io and Ardi. They've been fighting for thirty-five years. It doesn't seem to get in the way of their love for each other."

"They've got a lot more to fight about these days," Gideon said, and

Krush reined his horse to a halt and really looked at Gideon.

"Boy, what is on your mind? You sound like the world's oldest cynic."

Gideon looked intently to one side, pretending to search for the mare as he spoke. "It's...my birthing day is coming up, and I was hoping... oh, I don't know. I really don't."

"Is that what's bothering you, everybody being here for your birthing day? Is number seventeen a big one for Declivians?"

"Not that I know of," Gideon chuckled. "Truth be told, I've never been to a birthing day celebration, or had one of my own. I only know when my birthing day is, and how old I am, because I got hold of my birth certificate in order to alter it to get my flying papers."

"Well, on Equus we celebrate birthing days," Krush said, swinging off his horse to look over the rim of the canyon. "Excuse me while I water the vegetation. On Equus, when it's your birthing day, you get to choose anything you want for breakfast. And you get to choose a little excursion someplace, because that's what we do by way of a gift, we take the birthing day person wherever he or she wants to go, within reason. If your birthing day falls on a work day, you get taken where you want to go at week's end, Hesychgyre, or Hiergyre, or Hormigyre. Or maybe all three if you've chosen to travel and things work out. Have you thought of a place you'd like to see? We'll go for your birthing day."

Gideon felt the color rising in his cheeks. "I...if my sire is feeling well enough in another week...I know we have to think of him first, but...I have never been to the seashore. I would like to go to the sea and walk in the sand and taste the salt water and see the breakers up close." He took a deep breath and added even more to what seemed an enormous request. "And...I'd like a picnic. I've never been on a picnic, either. I'd like a picnic at the shore. Is that too much?"

Krush got back on his horse and reached over to slap Gideon on the thigh. "Done," he said. "It's an embarrassingly modest request. And when we get home, we'll eat sweet cakes and pudding. That's the part I like best."

Gideon had been looking over the canyon's rim and into the river valley below. He thought he'd seen movement, and now he was sure of it. Horses moving upriver. Two or three singles, mares with late foals and what appeared to be a bay mare with a blue colt. "There," Gideon said, pointing. "What do you see?"

"There she is," Krush chuckled, and by then they could see the rider, coming behind them. "Looks like Ah'brianne's got her in with some of their stock. Good. Go on down there and help her get her horses home, then put this halter on Windymere, and bring her home. Can you do that?"

"I...where...what are you going to do?" Gideon stammered.

"Go back to the main house and help my herdsmen doctor horses, I would assume," Krush said, giving him a raised eyebrow. "Or maybe I'll go run one of the harvesters, or one of the balers, or one of the barn shuttles or help with the canning and freezing. Are you worried that I'll have nothing to do, or have I asked you to do something that's beyond your capabilities?"

"No Sir," Gideon replied, the color high in his face.

"Glad to hear it. Now, ride back a bit with me, and I'll show you the way down to the canyon floor. When you get down there, don't ride straight up on her or you'll part the horses. Then you'll have to round them up again." Krush turned Beckett back toward home and glanced over his shoulder at the reluctant boy behind him. "Well, come on," he said, and looked forward again before Gideon could see his smile. He hated seeing the fear in Gideon's eyes, but he reminded himself that the boy needed a life of his own, and that such a life required friends, peers, to make it complete.

They jogged back in silence to the place where a single Equi pine leaned south from the prevailing winds, marking a trail which dropped off the rim of the canyon and switched back to the broad valley below. It was slightly too steep and too narrow for Gideon's comfort, but Tolbeth gave it a quick study, and headed on down at a good pace, tempted by the smell of green grass and water, and the calls of other horses drifting up.

Most of the way down Ah'brianne passed under them on a big black gelding, and Gideon called to her, aided by Tolbeth's greeting. She looked up and waved, and slowed her pace a little to wait for them. They hit the bottom in a scrabble of fissle stone, and slowly cantered the distance it took to catch up to her.

"My Grandfather sent me to get Windymere and her colt," he said, reining in beside her.

"And here I thought you were coming to keep me company," the girl grinned. She really was an impudent little thing. Well, not so little. Like most Equi women she was tall and slender. She spoke to her horse to get him moving again and turned to Gideon. "How is your sire?"

"Better," Gideon said. He started to ask her how she knew that he was sick and then remembered that his father was Firstlord of Equus. Everybody knew he was sick. It still seemed odd to him. Nobody ever appeared to be watching a cosmoscope, yet the Equi were exceptionally well informed.

Fascinating things, Equi cosmoscopes. They just appeared on command, projecting themselves across the wall. No. More suspended themselves in front of a wall, the sound coming from no place, an image so sharp it was three dimensional. One could watch the news, or cultural events, or use it as an educational tool. Ah'din had showed him how to activate the one in his room, and how to access the atlases and galactic encyclopedias. How to set worlds spinning in front of his fascinated eyes.

"I hate it when you ramble on so," Ah'brianne snorted, looking at Gideon and shaking her long, auburn braid.

"Hm?"

"I asked how your sire was doing, and you said 'better.' Better than what? Better than dead, better than average?"

"Better than he was," Gideon said, and gave her an apologetic smile. "He's up, if not around. He's not strong yet, but he's better."

"Good," she smiled, and made a throwing motion with her left hand to move the herd dog further away from the horses.

"I miss dogs," Gideon said, almost to himself. "They make nice companions, I think."

"I like them too," Ah'brianne said. "Sawkus," she jerked her chin toward the big, lion colored dog who was padding along at a distance on huge paws, "is getting old, so we just got a new puppy – so Sawkus can train him. If you come to the nave with me you can meet him. He's cute."

"My Grandsire instructed me to go with and help you," Gideon said.

"Otherwise you wouldn't come, right?"

"I...no. I mean, yes. I'd like to meet your new puppy," Gideon managed.

"Do I scare you, or what?" Ah'brianne asked, and the tilt of her head, and the way the sun picked up the color in her cheeks, made Gideon chuckle.

"You do. You scare me half to death," he admitted, then wondered at his own honesty. It was too late to take back the comment, so he took a deep breath and forged ahead with his thoughts. "Not because you're a girl, or even because you're you. It's just that I've never been around other kids much."

She gave him a quizzical look. "Other what? What's that word you just used?"

"Kids?"

She laughed. "That's what we call baby goats."

"But you used a word the day I met you. You said, colts, I think, which was funny to me, because I'd never heard it applied to young hu-mans...hominoids, you know."

"So, on Declivis, colts are called kids?"

"If they're really people and not goats they are," Gideon grinned. "I don't know what they call goats. I've never even met a goat." They laughed.

"And you've never been around kids your own age? You didn't have a brother or a sister?"

"No," Gideon said, and he could feel his smile beginning to freeze into unnatural lines. This was a conversation he didn't want to have. He moved to counter. "Do you have a sibling?"

"I have an older brother, Merens. I made him crazy, like Io made Kehailan crazy, or so Merens tells me. He still can't believe Ardenai would marry her. She's beautiful, but I guess she has quite the temper." Ah'brianne glanced at Gideon and looked embarrassed. "Sorry. Just neighbor-hood gossip. There's no malice meant in it. We'll bear left here, over this slumped spot in the canyon's rim. That's the shortest path to my house. If it was warmer we could stop and go for a swim before we left the river, but it was chilly last night, and the water's probably down a few degrees today. Besides, the breeze is a little cool for wanting to be naked and wet, don't you think? We could probably wrestle Windymere into her halter at this point, if you want. She's tired enough to be cooperative. Your house is just a few furlongs over there through those trees."

"I...want to see your new puppy," Gideon said shyly, and Ah'brianne smiled and nodded.

"Right this way."

They concentrated on getting their mounts and the horses they were driving over the steep spot, and when they'd leveled off again on higher ground, Ah'brianne took time to study Gideon's horse. "I don't remember seeing your mare before. She's really pretty."

"Thank you," Gideon smiled, giving the sweet-faced bay a pat on the neck. "She was my horse on Calumet. My father had her brought here for me as a surprise. He brought the stallion he was riding there, as well. This is Tolbeth."

"This is Grendith," the girl said, patting the tall black. "He's been my horse since I was a little girl." She sighed, and the pats turned to a gentle stroking. "I suppose sooner or later I'll have to start training a new horse to take his place, but I really don't want to think about it. What was life like on Declivis?"

The transition was abrupt and momentarily startling. Gideon had to think. He didn't want to lie, but he didn't want to go into detail, or have her ask a lot of questions. From the way she could talk, he knew she could ask questions faster than he could concoct mild deception, and his father had taught him that lies were always a trap. "I guess if you come from a good home, and are given some opportunities, life on Declivis can be pretty good, or so I hear. The planet is really overcrowded, and the air quality is bad almost everywhere. It's kind of like a big, sprawling, smoky city, at least where I grew up."

"It doesn't sound very nice," she said, not looking at him. "For you, either."

"No. It wasn't. I ran away when I was fourteen and went to Demeter. That's where I met Ardenai."

"Can you tell me about your adventures with him?" she asked, eyes lighting up with anticipation.

"I don't know," he said, looking embarrassed. "I haven't asked my sire which stories I can share, or if there are any I shouldn't. If you'll give me time to ask him, so I'm sure I'm not overstepping my bounds, I'd enjoy telling you about some of the places we saw and the things we did."

"Of course," she said. "That's very discreet of you. Are you going to go back to the Great House with him when he goes?"

That, too, gave Gideon pause. He'd never considered that he had the option, though when she mentioned it, he knew he did. "I'm sure I will."

"Have you been enrolled in school yet?"

"No. My sire's been teaching me, and my grandsire, and others from time to time, like Teal, and my granddam, and Pythos. Do you know Pythos?"

"He's my doctor," the girl smiled. "He delivered me from the womb of my mother. He's delivered most of the foals around here. The human foals at least. So you're not enrolled in school?"

"Again, I do not know what my father's wishes will be," Gideon said, looking at other things. It was a beautiful ride across the uplands. "Amazing view," he said, and pointed south and slightly west of their position. "Do I see the river way off in the distance?"

"Yes. This is the Little Sister. It runs for nearly half the width of the continent. Along with its siblings it drains this part of the north slope of the plains. It forms three branches about fifty miles on the other side of Lea keep, so it's considerably slower coming through here. The Big sister is farthest east, and can be a very rough piece of water. Logically enough, Middle

Sister is in the middle. Little sister is farthest west."

"Does it form the border between Lea keep and Upland keep, as well as Canyon keep and Sea keep?"

"Um hm. Fortunately it's quiet most of the time, and stays to its bed. You know," she said a little hesitantly, as though she were putting some thought into what she was going to say for once, "when you go to school here, you can learn whatever you need to, no matter how old you are. It's nice to have company, and friends to socialize with, and enough people around you to play team sports. It's really a very pleasant experience."

Gideon looked at her with some annoyance. She was the most persistent thing he'd ever been around in his life. Of course until now the only female he'd ever been around for very long was his mother. Men's minds were more well-ordered – except for Tarkelians. Theirs were slightly on the vacant side. More like women's minds, or what he'd been led to believe were women's minds.

Ah'din and Ah'rane were certainly not insubstantial. Ah'rane was a Friction-Analysis Engineer. That had come out in the course of learning how the big old cookstove worked. Ah'din was a medical doctor with a Secundoctora in Medicinal Herbs. She was a Master Weaver, and she dabbled in textile design, on top of everything else she did. Gideon smiled, and stroked the sleeve of the beautiful tunic she'd made him.

Io, was a military strategist, and a much respected one, at an age when some Equi had just left Lycee. Maybe he just hadn't been around enough women yet to find the mien. It was a possibility. And Io? There was an interesting thought. She obviously hadn't gone to Lycee for as long as everybody else, or she wouldn't have been in the cavalry long enough to have made it into the Horse Guard, much less into the top position. He'd have to ask her about that when she got home. Maybe if you grew up faster, you got through with things faster. It only made sense.

"I didn't mean to offend you," Ah'brianne said softly, and her hand brushed his forearm. "I just don't want you to feel like an outsider. You're not, you know. This is your home now, and you have a perfect right to all the privileges and benefits of Equi citizenship. Not getting an education when you're a child, doesn't mean you can't ever have one. And it doesn't mean you have to be isolated by the embarrassment of not being right where everybody else is in their learning, that's all."

He turned, and let his gold eyes bore a hole in her until her mouth closed and she dropped her eyes from his face. Then he said, "What makes you think I don't have an education? Do I seem stupid to you?"

"Stupid, no. What you seem, is rude," she snapped. "If you ran away from home at fourteen you were still little. You still had twelve years of school left to go. You're a lot more than fourteen now, so you've been out of school awhile. Getting back into something when you've been away, can be hard, especially when you're surrounded by strangers and a strange system. Why does that bother you so much?"

"I'm sorry," Gideon said, and moved his eyes away, dropping the confrontation. "I guess I didn't get off to a very good start. Not in my first life, and not in this one, either. It is not my intention to give offense. I find myself the son of the Firstlord of Equus, whom I adore, but I was absolutely, completely alone up until Ardenai found me. I'd never had a friend, or anyone who took an interest in me. Now, all of a sudden, everybody's taking an interest in me, and I'm feeling the pressure. I know it's well intentioned. I know it's me and not you...not them. It's just tiring to be...somebody, rather than nobody. Does that make any sense?"

"I guess so," she said, still slightly offended. She smiled, but only with her mouth, and her body language was stiff and indifferent.

"Where I come from, on Declivis, you're only required to go to school for eight years, from age six, to fourteen, and that isn't enforced. If your mother has other things for you to do, nobody comes around and knocks on your door to see why you're not getting an education. You do what you can. You listen, you observe, you get your hands on books whenever you can, and sometimes you meet people who are willing to teach you things, and talk to you about concepts, ideas, rather than just things, or people. But Declivis has a whole, hidden population – a whole bunch of people living under the floorboards of civilized society, and it's a hell of a long way up to the light."

"Look up," she said softly. "You made it. You're here."

He chuckled and nodded, and when he looked at her, there were tears shining in her eyes, and he wondered why, but he didn't ask her. He took a deep breath, and patted his willing horse, and looked for a bit at other things until his head cleared. "That first day I met you, you were on the tube coming from Thura," he said finally. "That was on a Hoplegyre, which is like our Friday, I think. That's a day when young people are usually in school. Please explain to me how school works."

"Sure," she said, again moving the dog with her hand. "We go to school on Equus for five of the eight days, Humilgyre through Hoplegyre, but because your father had returned home, and all Equus was rejoicing, school was released a day early. I was coming from Thura, because that's where I've chosen to go to school. I serve the Great House as a page. Right now I'm aiding MalDor, of Kohath Zadok, and it's fascinating for me. Criollo goes to Thura as well. Since your sire is Firstlord, maybe you..." She thought better of the comment, and broke off.

"But today is a schooling day, is it not? And here you are."

"It is Oporens High Harvest. Most of us are keeplings. We are need-ed to get the season's work done before the storms hit, and they're supposed to be early this year. We school with our parents in the evenings, and we go on one day of each week to pick up our lessons and turn in our homework, and to ask Master Breton about any questions we may have. When the season turns, we will all go back to schooling as usual."

"In Thura?" Gideon asked.

"Falconstones for the younger ones, and for those of the older ones who choose not to serve or study within The Great House. Those of us who do serve as pages, or who have a particular thing we want to study, go to Thura. Some of us stay in dormitories in the Great House during the week especially those of us who serve, but we can always come home if we want."

"And how do you get there? It seems a far piece to travel."

"Each keep gathers its keeplings, and flies them to a central spot, which happens to be Sea keep for our area, and everybody piles in together and goes to Falconstones, and from there to the tube. It only takes an hour or so all told."

"And what if the weather's bad? Or gets bad? How do you get the little ones home?"

"Sometimes we don't. Often in the season of Aellaeno they have to stay at school, but there is a big kitchen, and dormitories for everybody. It's kind of fun, because it's different, and the teachers have things for them to do in the evening. They dance, or sing, or play games or put on plays, and they all have some personal items there so they are comfortable. Our parents know we're safe when we're at school. It's fine."

"And when my sire was a creppia nonage teacher, did he stay there with you when you were little?"

"Absolutely. If the storm was bad enough, and loud enough that the little ones were afraid, he'd make a big, soft nest on the floor, and all of us would sleep in it together, with him in the middle and us all over him. I don't know how much sleep he got, but it was really fun for the rest of us."

"It does sound like fun," Gideon agreed. "All of you, divided by age of course, stayed in the same place?"

"Um hm. It's all very well thought out, and proper by Equi standards."

"I'm sure it is," Gideon smiled. "Is that where you live?"

"Yes," she said. "This is Lea keep. Look familiar?"

It did. It was much like both Canyon keep and Sea keep in the way it was laid out, taking advantage of the protection which various rock faces provided, graced with huge Equi pines, and the company of the Little Sister, though here she kept her distance. At Canyon keep the house was separated from the barns by water, because Krush's father, and Krush's grandfather, had decided to combine work sites for the stock, and had pretty much stopped using the stone barns and stables of Canyon keep. Now they were used as an overflow facility, and Teal used them for storing his excellent wines.

At Lea keep, everything was on the east side of the river, and seemed much more compact, partly because the walking distances were shorter, and partly because Lea keep had no hunt course, and no polo field. "That's because we don't raise horses as our primary function," the girl explained. "We have horses for pleasure. My sire plays polo, too, but he uses the polo grounds at Sea keep. And we have some horses for work. But mainly, my mother has some very exotic, long haired sheep and goats, and my sire is a farmer. We raise hay and grain for the main stables of the Horse Guard in Thura. Have you been there yet?"

Gideon shook his head. "I was only in Thura a few hours," he said ruefully, "and I haven't seen anything except the inside of the Great House, and the street leading to the tube station."

"The stables are amazing, and huge! I'll take you there – oh, hey, don't you take off on me, Windymere!" she said, and focused on getting the horses corralled.

The main house looked much the same as the other two Gideon had been in, as did the barns and stables, and both were a hive of activity. People were hurrying to and fro, emptying trundlers loaded with hay into huge lofts, doctoring horses and piteously bleating sheep, storing some grain and mazea, and loading the rest onto transport shuttles.

Ah'brianne herded the horses into a round pen near the closest stable, and hailed a man with surprisingly red hair, who was just coming around the corner of one of the hay barns. "That is my sire," she said, dismounting to close the gate behind the horses. "Come on, I'll introduce you."

Timor was a pleasant man, more quiet than his daughter, but quick with a smile and a welcome for Gideon, and tumbling awkwardly around his feet, was a wooly puppy with huge paws, an impossibly long red tongue, and brown eyes which popped comically out from under his wiry bangs. The young people put their horses up to rest for a bit, and with Sawkus and the puppy in tow, they went up to the house to meet Ah'brianne's mother.

Like most Equi women she was tall, slender, and lovely, with coloring which reminded Gideon of Ah'nora, and an easy way of speech which mirrored her daughter's. Gideon was given no time to feel awkward, and certainly no reason to feel hungry. He was stuffed full of crusty flat bread, warm from the oven, dressed with hot, spiced negrolea oil, cheese, and slices of broiled vegetables, and when he'd answered all of Ah'mae's questions, and she'd gone back to putting up the season's harvest with the women who were helping her, he and Ah'brianne were allowed to retire to the sunny side of the house to play with the pup.

He didn't have a name yet, and they spent awhile thinking some up, each a little sillier than the last, and they laughed at his antics, and his sharp teeth, and his playful puppy growls, and Gideon realized that he was comfortable. He was in unfamiliar territory, but he was comfortable, because Ah'brianne was there. He also realized that Timor Ah'brianne Ah'mae, was both intelligent, and pretty, and that being around her might not be such a chore as he had first imagined.

Ardenai had set aside the painting of the sunrise, opened the valve to the irrigation channel which ran from the river into the expansive gardens, and was sketching the ducks. They were busy snorkeling in the water being laid on the herb beds, and they were so genuinely happy to be thus occupied, that it made him laugh. "I need to learn to enjoy my job as much as you enjoy yours," he said to them, and leaned back in his chair to rest his eyes and relax a bit.

The remains of the breakfast Ah'din had brought him were still at his elbow, and he sipped his tea and munched on a flat-wrap. His sister made amazing flat-wraps. Rolled with a filling of sautéed mushrooms, seeds and vegetables, they stayed fresh all day, even in a saddlebag. But for breakfast she drizzled their insides with honey from her own hives, then stuffed them with sweet spices, chopped nuts, fruit and soft, white cheese before rolling them and serving them, still warm from the griddle. He had missed them, even dreamed of them a time or two. Now, he closed his eyes, and turned his face to the sun, and savored every bite – every sensation of being in familiar gardens in a familiar chair, surrounded by familiar sounds and fragrances. He was home. He was centered. He could let himself rest.

He turned his mind inward and examined himself. Nothing ached. Nothing burned. Nothing itched. He could sense that he was a little agitated, a little short tempered, but that was because of Io's abrupt and largely unexplained departure, and because Pythos kept nagging at him to get his sperm count done, and he wasn't ready to do that just yet. Soon. But not yet. Either he was generative or he wasn't. A day or two probably wouldn't change that. His thought processes seemed lucid enough. He felt pretty sharp, mentally. His recall was quick. His tongue seemed to once again be moving at a normal speed, the words he said made sense. His coordination had returned to normal, along with his extreme left-handedness.

Emotionally, he felt more stable than he had for a while, and he was reasonably sure that could be attributed to his daughter's absence. He let himself think about it briefly, but he forbad any twinge of guilt. He had visited Ah'leah briefly before Ah'krill returned to Thura, and was comforted by her presence and the fact that she seemed content. Pythos had raised kraa with him for setting his head against his mother's, but he felt none the worse for the experience, and truth be told, he actually felt better, knowing the little one was secure and would have purpose within the ranks of the Eloi.

He stretched with his arms up and behind him, first to crack his back, then to flex his shoulders in their sockets. He didn't feel like running a foot race, or trotting up river to the spot where he usually swam and flinging himself into the water, or seeing if he could hunt somebody up for a little one on one polo match, but he did feel like he could put one foot in front of the other and get where he was going. He felt like in another day or two he could go to the barns and put in some work. In a few days, he'd be putting in his fair share.

He put the last of the flat-wrap in his mouth, chewed it slowly, and washed it down with the last of his tea. It put him in mind of Ah'nora's wonderful cooking, and he wondered how she was feeling these days, if the baby had moved for the first time. Probably it was too soon, but still, he needed to contact her, to let her know he was thinking of her and her gift to the Great House. He wanted to be there for the birth of his son, and wondered if that was going to bother his wife. Perhaps, with luck, she'd be settled into another pregnancy by then, and wouldn't be hurt by the thought of him holding another on the birthing stool.

He heard the plaintive, questioning quack, realized he was being contemplated at very close range by two sets of reproachful duck eyes, and sat up to search his plate for some suitable crumbs. Ah'din, who thought of everything, had included a small bowl of stale crackers, which, Ardenai assumed with a chuckle, were not for him. He leaned forward and held out a cracker, first to one duck, then the other, and laughed again at their delight in simple things. He sketched them there, with their heads cocked questioningly to the side, blue-grey feathers gleaming in the late morning sunshine, waddling busily about discussing crackers and bugs, stopping occasionally to scratch their chins with a flat, clawed foot and look to him for more treats.

"Ardi, those are precious!" said his sister's soft, laughing voice, and she came from behind him to take the sketch pad in her hand. "I love the way you've turned these on here in all directions. You don't usually do whimsy."

"Not like you do," he chuckled. He patted the arm of his chair and she sat, sketch pad still in her hand.

"Do you have plans for these?" she asked, casting him a mischievous smile and a calculating green eye.

"Why, do you?"

"These would be delightful on fabric. Fat grey ducks on a tan or black background? They'd work well on most any background, even lighter grey."

"Well, just in case this Firstlord thing doesn't work out, I suppose I'd better let you have those. I can work on commission and at least feed my growing family."

Ah'din let the sketch pad rest on her lap, and put her left arm around her brother. "Are you happy?" she asked, leaning to kiss his thick, dark hair. "Things have happened so fast for you. You've had so many wild adventures, and changed so much, done such wild things."

"Name one," he chuckled, seeing an opening to avoid the original question, the one for which he had no answer.

"Defeating a Telenir lord in hand to hand combat comes immediately to mind," she said. "And the whole thing with becoming Firstlord of Equus is pretty amazing, though not surprising, really."

"You're joking, right?" Ardenai grimaced, squinting up at her.

"No. I assumed the Firstlord would be you, or Teal, I really did. After all, the rising is announced in a framework of five years, and this is the fourth year. How many High Equi princes were turning one hundred in the time that's left? Our sire has known for years that you would be rising, or so he says now."

"His rationale being?"

"He says it's because you look so much like Mother. What are the odds of a fosterling looking so much like his dam? Of course I never knew you were a fosterling, and I'm not sure anybody else did, either, so I didn't think anything about you being a reflection of our mother. I look like our mother, too. But I look a little bit like our sire, as well. You don't."

"So tell me," Ardenai chuckled, tipping her off the arm of the chair and into his arms, "What is your theory, baby sister?"

"I think, what your golden-eyed son thinks, that Ah'rane is your sister. Let me up, unless you want to be tickled." Ardenai sat up a little straighter, and let her sit up as well. She got up from his lap, and assumed a seat in the chair close by, noting that he seemed a little shocked and wondering if she should have said anything. "It's just something we bantered around during supper one night. Pythos could tell the tale if he chose, which of course he doesn't. Besides, you would need a common parent, and we know Ah'krill didn't give birth to mother before she gave birth to you. Is this upsetting you? I didn't mean to annoy you with silly-talk."

"What makes you think I'm annoyed," Ardenai grinned. "I'm intrigued, that's all. You didn't say what I expected you to say when I asked the original question, and so this is all new territory."

"The question about naming wild things you'd done?" He nodded, and his sister's eyes narrowed in speculation. "Oh. You were expecting me to say that marrying Ah'riodin was the craziest thing you could possibly have done."

"Um hm. I had my defense all prepared."

"Why do you need a defense, Ardi?" Ah'din leaned forward in her chair, rested her hands on her thighs, and fixed him in her gaze. She looked a little put out with him, and he winced inside. Having Ah'din put out with you, could be quietly…very painful. "Just because you think it was the craziest thing you could have done, doesn't mean that I do, or that anybody else does, for that matter. Now you listen to me, and pay attention for once. Io, is a beautiful, brilliant woman whom you've known for years. I think you're an amazing catch as husbands go, but as wives go I think Io's every bit as desirable as you are. Given that you are now the Thirteenth Dragonhorse, with all that implies in song and legend, you couldn't possibly have done anything smarter than marrying a woman who's got Papilli blood. She's going to be up to you, and for you, anytime, anywhere. The fact that she's younger, gives you the advantage of her stamina, and you may need it, not just sexually, but diplomatically, as well."

She took a deep breath and sat back up again, folding her arms. "You two have always fought, and you're always going to fight, because you're both hard-headed and opinionated and strong willed and too smart for your own good. That doesn't mean you're not the perfect couple. You are. If you could spend fifty years dealing with Ah'ree, who was frail and moody and completely dependent on you, you can certainly deal with Io, who is strong and temperamental, who needs you like a mare needs lace underwear, and who loves you with all her heart."

Ardenai made a fending motion and hunched his shoulders in submission. "I take it you know why she blew out of here like a small and silent storm?" he asked. Ah'din gave him a blank look. Whether it was genuine or contrived he didn't know, but he knew he wasn't going to get through it. He sighed, and dropped his eyes to the expectant ducks. "I'm all out of crackers, ladies. You'll have to settle for bugs."

"That's what you need to add to these sketches," his sister said, picking up the pad, "bugs." She handed the pad to him, gathered up the breakfast dishes, gave him a peck on the temple, and went back into the house, leaving Ardenai wondering whether she was miffed at him or not.

She was probably missing Teal, who had been home far too little for far too long. It was time to give the man a rest. The Firstlord had been contemplating his advisory staff, and Teal was at the top of the list, right next to Pythos. His kinsman loved his position as Master of Horse, but perhaps he could be convinced to set it aside, at least for a while. He'd mentioned more than once that he'd enjoy seeing his wife grow heavy with another child, perhaps a daughter this time, and that would turn his thoughts and desires to Canyon keep. From here, the Great House of Equus was little more than an hour away.

The Firstlord smiled, cocking a dark eyebrow after his sister, and began sketching bugs. An advisory staff of eight, he thought, nine being an uneven number with the addition of himself. No deadlocks. The next bug, looked remarkably like Krush Ah'din Teal, and it made him laugh out loud.

Ardenai was sitting in the afternoon shade afforded by the sprawling myrianotus tree on the patio which overlooked the river, when a movement up and to the north shifted his gaze from the list of possible advisors, to the Equi flyer gliding down to settle in the courtyard below him. He set the tablet aside with all good intentions of leaping out of his chair and running down there. He got as far as sliding forward in the chair, and found himself frozen with indecision. He watched Io and Teal get out of the flyer, watched Ah'din run from the front door to embrace her husband, saw Io look around, then up at him. He gritted his teeth and pushed himself the rest of the way out of his chair, forcing a smile as he forced his legs to move toward her.

She walked a few steps toward him, and then stopped. Her eyes shifted left and right in consideration of her options, and Ardenai realized with a lump in his throat that she wasn't sure she wanted to go to him. For the first time in her life, she wasn't sure of him. Before she could sit up, she'd held her arms up to him. She'd crawled to him, toddled to him, run to him, walked beside him to become his bride, presented herself to him as his lover...and she wasn't sure of him? The very thought of it made him weak in the knees. It made him angry, even as it broke his heart. He felt his mouth come open, but no words came out. He shook his head, and touched her with his eyes before moving slowly forward. She dropped her head and walked in his direction, not in joy, but in obedience. He could see it in the way she carried herself.

When they were close enough that he didn't have to shout to be heard, he sucked in a big gulp of air, threw away the words he'd practiced, and managed in an awkward rush, "Io, I do love you. Whatever I said, whatever I did to hurt you, I'm so very sorry. Please forgive me."

She looked up at him and her eyes filled with tears. "I love you, too. Whatever I did to make you feel guilty, whatever I felt inside myself that I took out on you, I'm so very sorry. Please forgive me."

"Come here," he said, and folded her in his arms, holding her tight and pressing her head to his chest, kissing her hair and the tips of her elegant ears, thinking about how he wanted to phrase the thoughts and emotions milling around in his brain. Half of him was still thinking about that list of advisors. He really wanted to run a couple of them past his wife, but he knew that wouldn't do at all just now, if he valued his love life. He kissed her again and murmured, "Why did you leave so suddenly? I know you must have given me a reason, but I wasn't thinking very well."

"Neither was I," she sighed, speaking to him without moving her head from the comfort of his chest. "There was this ugly part of me that felt like you'd let your mother take our baby without a fight. I'm sorry, I know that's a terrible thing to say. I know how sick you were, and how sick Ah'leah was making you. I just felt so helpless, and after Ah'krill made that comment about taking back what was meant to be hers...I hated her. I was frustrated, and you were the easiest one to take it out on."

"Have you changed your mind now, about what happened?"

"About Ah'krill, not yet," she muttered, "but I'm working on it. And

Teal made me see what an amazing thing you'd done by taking Ah'leah in the first place, and how it demonstrated your love for me, and for any children we might ever have. He pointed out how much you'd gone through because of her, and how much you were willing to go through in the future, just to keep her consciousness alive for me."

"And for me," the Firstlord amended, kissing her hair.

"I know that," she whispered. "I just needed time to think, and somebody to yell at me. Teal did that perspicaciously and thoroughly. I spent some time with the Horse Guard, and reviewing some cavalry maneuvers, and I went to Achernar for a day – to the Centrum Medea." At that point she looked up at him, waiting for a reaction.

He took her chin on his index finger and looked into her eyes. "Why? Pythos was right here."

"Pythos was not who I wanted to see," she said. "I wanted to see a stranger. Someone who could make me feel good about myself, or bad about myself and my chances of having another baby – because I was me, not the wife of the Firstlord."

"And what did you find out?" he asked. Not waiting for an answer he said, "Let's walk a bit, shall we? At least to a comfortable place to sit out of the sun."

She nodded, slipped her arm through his, and walked beside him, her boots clicking on the stone pavers in a slow, deliberate cadence. "They said that the Papilli reproductive system is amazingly regenerative. Apparently everything about Papilli systems is pretty amazing. It makes me wonder why my mother died. Not that I'm blaming Pythos, I'm not. I just wonder. Anyway, I only went for a consultation, but they removed some scar tissue, trimmed things up a bit, smoothed over the scar, and sent me on my way without keeping me."

Her tone was noncommittal, and Ardenai wondered what he was supposed to say next. "That sounds like wonderful news to me," he ventured. "I was worried that if you chose to pursue this, you'd have to go through some complicated and time consuming surgeries. So, when can you...we ...I'm sure not for a while, but..."

"About three seasons," she said, rescuing him. "I am to go in at the turning of Omphas to make sure everything is strong enough to sustain a settling, and to have my tubes untied so that settling can occur."

"If that is what you wish," he said. She was being so vague. She had wanted babies so much, and now he felt like it was the farthest thing from her mind. Like she couldn't care less whether she ever settled or not. Maybe he'd pushed her too far, somehow, and she'd decided she didn't want any of his get. No little fruit-bat babies to terrorize the royal apartments. He realized that the thought of them being childless bothered him. "I hope it is," he added. "But I will understand if you want your freedom to pursue other things. A babe certainly ties you down to his or her schedule."

"Yes," she said, seeming a little puzzled. "I'm more worried about the other women whom you were to settle than I am about me. I mean, I have an excuse if we need one, but what about the others?"

"Stop," Ardenai frowned. "Sit." He pointed to the low rock wall which ran freeform under the myrianotus trees. She sat, and he sat beside her. He shook his head back and forth a couple of times to try to generate an intelligent question, and ended up saying, "What are you talking about?"

Io looked at him with a small crease between her eyebrows. "Are you pretending like nothing is wrong, or am I missing something?"

"One of us is missing something, that's for sure," he muttered. "Tell me what you're thinking."

"I'm thinking," she said, "that if you're not generative..."

"What makes you think I'm not generative?"

She looked at him, round eyed. "I thought...I heard as I was leaving the Centrum..." she looked at his expression, trying to read it, then flipped her hands up and blurted, "Nine-tenths of the population of Equus fears that you're sterile because of the fever – and not just the people who gossip – everybody."

"Why would they think that?" Ardenai grimaced. "I haven't even been tested yet."

"Why not?" she demanded. "Do you know how quickly people jump to conclusions about something like this?"

"Do you know how little I care?" he retorted. "I wanted to wait until you were here."

"I'm sorry," she said contritely. "I assumed you could just..." she made an apologetic little shrug and the slightest of gestures that made him smile in spite of his annoyance.

"I *can* just..." he repeated the gesture, then reached and took her hands in his. "But whether that's how it's done or not, you're my wife. You're the one I care about when it comes to a family, Io. Those other women are a duty. You, are the one I want a baby underfoot with. If we get bad news, you deserve to hear it with me. If we get good news, you deserve to be here to celebrate with me. I waited for you."

She exhaled with a whoosh of relief, and squeezed his hands. "I'm so sorry I paid attention to rumor. It just seemed so well founded. Not really like a rumor at all."

"Becausse it sstarted within the Eloi for ssome sstrange, sstrange reasson," came the familiar, laconic hiss, and both Io and Ardenai peered up into the shadowing leaves to see Pythos, draped over one of the branches above their heads.

"You heard it?" Ardenai demanded, "And you said nothing?"

"I ssaid ssomething sseveral timess without resssponding to rumor. Mentioning the common conccern would sscarcely have made thee any sss- weeter. As it wass, thee told me to sstop hisssing like a big, green teapot, and find mysself a placce to ssleep until thy wife got home. Here I am."

"Oh yes, so I did," Ardenai replied, looking apologetic. "And you, have you no shame when it comes to eavesdropping?"

"None," Pythos replied. "I'm a worm of the worsst kind. I have no moralssss at all. If I had not losst the ability to breathe fire sssometime back, I'd sstill be devouring the occasssional maiden insstead of ssucking up ssugar melonss and sstealing duck eggsss. Thy wife iss here. Let usss get on with thiss, now. Perhapss I can yet do ssome damage control before that meeting on the morrow."

He began sinuously unwinding himself from the branch, and Ardenai turned to Io, giving her an apologetic smile as he kissed the palms of her hands. "I'd planned on dinner by candlelight first, and perhaps a stroll beside the river to apologize for hurting you, and disappointing you as the sire of our first daughter."

"Enough. Don't mention the little priestess again," Io said, and just for a moment her eyes flashed. She took a bit deeper breath, drew herself up to her full stature, which brought the top of her head and the tips of her ears nearly to Ardenai's collarbone, and became businesslike. "We can still have dinner by candlelight, and stroll by the river to celebrate, afterward, but I do think Pythos is right. The sooner this thing can be put to rest one way or another, the better off Equus will be."

"Tell me," the Firstlord grinned, realizing how completely he loved her and relishing it enough to forget discretion, "if you thought I was sterile, why did you pursue your own fertility?" He realized it might be something he didn't want an answer to, or something that would anger his elfin bride, but it was out, and he tried not to cringe or look challenging as he stood up and turned to offer his hand.

"Why do you think I did it?" she said with an evil smile. She had him. His ears pinned tight, and he looked thoroughly uncomfortable, which made her giggle. "First of all, I didn't hear about your 'condition' until I was leaving the centrum. But I did think that if Teal would be so kind as to oblige us, or perhaps our friend Tarpan – maybe even Nik – someone we could trust with your secret, that if I was having babies we'd be able to blame the females for not being fecund, at least for a while. It sounds chipped, but it was a plan. I'm just hoping we don't need it."

"Me, too," Ardenai nodded. They walked toward their apartments in silence, Pythos trailing shortly behind. "What is your pleasure in this, my wife? You may take an active part, or you may keep me company, or you may absent yourself all together. Physician Pythos, what is needed of me, aside from the obvious?"

"We sshall need to empty thy ancillaries firsst, and tesst their con-tentss, and then thy primariess."

"Empty them?" Ardenai grimaced. "Empty? Really?"

"If posssible," the physician replied.

"I think," Io said, preceding him through the open casement door, "You're going to need all the help you can get."

The part of Ardenai which could stand aside and observe, admitted freely that his wife was incredibly accomplished at the art of arousal and love making. The way she undressed herself, and him, the sensitivity with which she touched and fondled, suckled and bit, knowing when to be gentle, knowing when to add a little pain to the mix – knowing just when to add stimulation to bring him to a peak with the least amount of effort on his part. An amazing woman. A woman to lose oneself in, to consume like the fresh-est, sweetest fruit – to immerse oneself in, like warm, flowing water – time after time after time. Fantasy after fantasy.

The afternoon sun had turned across their bed, its angle adding only the slightest warmth, but bathing them with color and lighting her hair to flame as they spent themselves. They rested in one another's arms awhile, only vaguely aware that Pythos was close by, their mission pleasantly in the background of their exploration.

When Ardenai could do no more, Pythos beckoned to Io, and she took some deep breaths to tighten up before stepping off the sleeping plat-form. "I'll meet you in the baths," she said, kissed his chest, gave him a friendly little pat, and followed Pythos into the adjoining room.

Ardenai was amazed. He was warm, and flushed with blood from the exercise, but he wasn't sweating, and he wasn't exhausted. His legs were a little tight, but that was all. Even as he thought that this might be be-cause his sexual prowess was increasing, he was shaking his head and laugh-ing. He knew where the credit lay. Io had once again gotten him through a situation which, had he been left to his own machinations, would have been miserable at best, and would quite probably have required intervention by Pythos and one or more of his potions. "Ugh," he said aloud, and huffed with relief as he rolled off the bed and onto his feet.

He shrugged into a robe and headed for the bathing pools. Just now a swim sounded good, but he knew that once he cooled off and that river water hit him, he'd regret his impulsiveness. He took the shortcut across the courtyard, dropped his robe beside the coolest of the pools, and slid into the water with a deep sigh of relief. He rested his arms across boulders smoothed by ten generations of his family, and turned his face up to the westering sun.

What would he do, he wondered, if he had lost his generative capabilities? What would that mean for him, and for Equus? He thought back to his illness, and the terrible heat, and the cool towels which had felt so good across his thighs and his abdomen. Surely if all those tiny lives had been in danger he would have sensed it, wouldn't he? He nodded to himself. He'd have known. He was fine.

It dawned on him as he sank toward slumber, that his wife, who put any trainer, any hetaera he'd ever been with to shame, had come from right here, under his roof. Oh, she'd lived with her father the rare times he was home, but largely, Io had come from this spot. Most of what she knew, he or Ah'ree had taught her. Where, then, had this incredible sexual talent come from? Not from him. Certainly not from Ah'ree, bless her spirit. Was this inherent? Was it in the genes? He wondered how to ask her that. He drowsed, searching his mind for her childhood, looking for telltale signs of sexual aptitude, or budding promiscuity. There were none. He was a teacher. He'd have recognized them in a heartbeat. So, where, and when, and with whom?

He snorted and choked as his face nodded into the water, and pulled himself back up into more of a sitting position. Thinking about Io as a tot, set him thinking about babes in general, the one they'd lost, and the ones they might have, either by his own seed, or Teal's. What if they had another daughter? Would she inherit her mother's...skills, and if so, at what point; because he needed to be building fortifications of some kind.

He realized he'd dozed again when he felt Io snuggling against him with no memory of her having come into the pool. "Hi," he whispered, kissing her hair. "Being with you this afternoon, was...the word escapes me. Amazing, isn't good enough. I learned a great deal. Thank you."

"You're a very good student," she murmured, resting her head in the hollow of his shoulder. "I wanted to keep your mind on pleasure and off business as much as possible. I hope I didn't shock you."

"But you did," he chuckled. "At least once or twice. I lived to enjoy it, very much. Where did you go to school for that?"

"You were never with a male trainer?" she asked in a disbelieving tone. "Surely you must have been. You were trained to have sexual intercourse with males, weren't you?"

"Certainly, I was," he responded, "I'm not a mannerless lout. But this was very different, and I'm not sure what a male trainer has to do with it. I just wondered where you'd been trained in such a fashion."

She looked puzzled. "No place. I mean, when you love someone enough, you just want to do things like that with them, don't you?"

Ardenai thought about that. "I don't believe it ever crossed my mind. I suppose you're right, and I did enjoy it, and I will again, but I'm not sure the average Equi, or whomever else we're talking about, thinks quite like that. We don't have that kind of imagination."

"Oh, that wasn't imagination. I have some things that fit that category, though. I'll share them with you when you're stronger. Did you enjoy that birthing stool image I sent you that first night in our apartments at the Great House? It's Papilli tradition for the father to ejaculate onto the child as it's being born, to welcome and bless it with fertility and a love for the sensual aspects of life. I think it's a beautiful thing to do, don't you? I'd like you to do that with our babes. I wonder if my father did that for me, to honor my mother."

She snuggled around a little, and yawned, and he just shook his head and stared down at her, not sure whether he should be excited, or apprehensive. He was definitely not going to scream and run, which was his first inclination, nor was he going to mention that he'd been standing with Abeyan when Io was born, and that Abeyan had done nothing more than laugh, cry and gag a little.

"I suppose Pythos will be along with our results presently?" Ardenai said, shaking off some rather vivid images. "In the meantime we can let our negative imaginations have their way with us, or we can come up with some contingencies. I've been thinking about what you said regarding Teal and Tarpan, maybe Nik, and I would prefer Teal, if you..."

"Oh, that's right," she said sleepily, "he says to tell you you're fine. Pythos says, I mean. Both your ancillaries and your primaries are functioning as they should." He let out a huge groan and slid down in the water, inadvertently dunking his bride, who sputtered and spit and dunked him back. "Now my hair's wet," she groused. "Did you mean to do that? I'll have to go to the supper table with wet hair."

"And my hair's wet, too. See what a bad temper accomplishes?"

She gave him an appraising eye. "This seems a little like foreplay. Are you ready to go again? We can practice making babies for the Great House of Equus."

Ardenai laughed in spite of his dismay. "Mistress, no. I'm not even remotely ready. Are you able to think of other things than reproduction, because if you are, I'm trying to come up with a list of personal advisors, and I could use your help."

"You really should settle some female as soon as possible, you know. Nothing puts a rumor to rest like evidence to the contrary," she observed. "Can we move to one of the warmer pools, please?"

He obliged her, wading out and moving indoors to the warmest of the bathing pools and dropping his robe to settle in again before saying anything. Io drifted toward the stack of fresh linens near the water's edge, and reached for a towel before turning back.

"I'm sure Pythos has already thought of that. Since Priestess Ah'nis was standing with my mother the other day, I expect she will be my first challenge. Though not for a while, I hope. I need a little tuck-time first. Could we not talk about sex for a few minutes? Will you help me with my list?"

"Who's on it so far?" she asked, wringing her hair into the pool.

She wrapped the towel around her head like a turban and sat in the shallows across from him, reaching for scrub-sand and branches of foaming rosemary which were in a basket on the ledge beside her. "Come here, I'll give you a bath."

He floated over and turned to have his back scrubbed. "You, of course, and Pythos, and Teal. I want eight. I'm thinking seriously of asking Oonah Pongo if she will take a leave of absence from the SGA and join us, or maybe Winslow Moonsgold. I do like him, though Oonah's expertise as a protocol officer would come in very handy, and when you put Pythos and Moonsgold together you get utter hysteria. At best I'd like Marion Eletsky, but I have other plans for him, and for Kehailan, as well. Ordinarily, I'd want your father on there, but I do think that's just too many relatives."

"Have you thought about Senator Konik?" she asked, rinsing his back and applying scrub-sand to his armbands and the scar tissue surrounding them. "You really should see somebody, Landais, probably, about getting rid of the divot Sarkhan put in your armband. A little heat would do it."

Ardenai just nodded and tried not to wince at the thought. "Yes, I have thought about Konik. I haven't decided whether or not to ask him. If I bind him too closely to myself as an Equi, he may lose his value as a Telenir. I think I'd like to see how our initial attempt at contact goes, first."

"Good thinking," she said. She floated around in front of him, and he took rosemary and scrub-sand, and began scribing gentle little circles on her back. "Be careful whom you choose, lest you cause jealousy amongst the affined worlds. The Menorquins are the oldest of our allies, followed by the Amberians. Maybe you should consider someone from one of those worlds."

"Of course," he said, bending to kiss her where neck met shoulder. "I didn't realize you had another side to your neck," he chuckled. "It's really very pretty. You should wear your hair up more often."

"Are we talking about your advisors, or are we back to foreplay?" she asked turning her profile toward him. Really a beautiful woman. How had he gone for so long with her right under his nose, and not noticed she was a woman?

"It makes me wonder what else is right under my nose that I'm not noticing," he said aloud, and she just rolled her eyes and sighed.

"We need to get out and get dressed," she said. "Pythos wants Equus to get a look at you for this evening's newscast. You get to tell everybody that you're not sterile, though just how you'll phrase it is a mystery to me."

"And you were going to tell me this, when?" he scowled, standing up and shaking water out of his hair.

"In time to think about it," she replied in a casual tone, "but not far enough in advance to angst over it. You did enough of that over the speech you gave to the people your first day back. I've laid your clothes out for you, and Ah'din will braid your hair, though I think you might consider cutting it short again. It was very attractive. It would be much easier to take care of, and you could set yet another trend, to go with the snake tattoos, you know. Pythos expects you in the west gardens in forty-five minutes for the broadcast."

"My life is not my own," the Firstlord muttered, snapping a towel around his waist and reaching for his robe, "my life is just not my own."

"It could be worse," she called after him. "You could be a Lebonathi, and have to ride around in a transparent dynamium bubble all the time, because everybody who wants your job is trying to kill you, or so the rumor goes. We know for sure the Tarkelians get shot at."

"Point taken," came the Firstlord's irate and retreating baritone. He added something that sounded like, 'You're joining me for this,' so Io decided she'd better get out and do something with a couple pounds of curly, wet hair. She put it into a loose three strand overbraid, and tucked it under itself in man-fashion – so the back of her neck showed, then put on a long-sleeved tunic and riding tights, and, as intimation she knew would be appreciated, she tucked a small, wild sun flower behind one ear.

"It was excellent," Krush said, gesturing with the spoon in his hand. "Very well done. Understated, but unmistakable. I think you were right to put rumor to rest as soon as you could." He reached for the beaker of hot, azure berry syrup, and poured a little more on his crisp slices of toasted mazea.

"Glad you approve," Ardenai smiled. "And you, Teal, what did you think?"

"You spoke to 'unfounded and unappreciated rumor,' and I liked that," he said, passing a steaming bowl of tiny sautéed tomatoes. "I think if Pythos is right and this did come from the Eloi, they will know you are displeased, and they may think twice before doing anything like this again."

"Why did they do it in the first place, is what I want to know," Gideon said, putting down his sticks to take a long drink of rhax juice. "What would the benefit be to having Equus think you were...you know."

"It has to do with power," Ardenai said, leaning back with his tea.

"Power? I thought you were the absolute, undisputed ruler of Equus," the boy persisted.

"If I choose to function as such, I most assuredly am. I could have all the Eloi taken into custody and questioned, starting with Ah'ti, who hates my very innards. I could figure out very quickly who started this, and I could get a thousand opinions as to why it was done. I'm choosing not to. This one I'm going to let go by, but as I said last night, this will not happen again without repercussions. It does our people no good to be unsure of the Great House, and it does us no good to be unsure of each other." He set his cup back on the table and reached for another flat-wrap. "We didn't see much of you last evening, young man, and what in the ten tribute worlds of Equus happened to your hands? You look like you met a mothering kel on the trail."

"I met Ah'brianne's new puppy," he grinned. "He's adorable. All feet and tongue."

"And milk teeth," Ah'rane threw in with a chuckle. "Ah'mae said they were getting another dog. Sawkus is getting older, and they need the help, what with the kel population, and the cerastaper population both on the rise around here. We've always had protopeds to contend with, and it would be a tragedy if Ah'mae lost those beautiful woollies of hers."

"Gee, maybe we should have a dog, too," Gideon said, resisting the urge to hug his grandmother for making an opening for him. She had said she would, saying in the same breath that she wouldn't advocate. Krush had never been much of a one for dogs around the place. "If there are to be babes here soon." he grimaced a little. He didn't want the conversation veering off before he was through with it. "Or maybe not so soon, but it takes a puppy awhile to learn his or her responsibilities, and a dog would make a good guardian for the...for whatever children. Even the herdsmen have children, and we have no dog at all anyplace." He took a breath and actually thought about what Ah'rane had said, and his smile faded. "What are kels and...Certus...that other thing you mentioned?"

"Kel, in the ancient language, means claw," Ah'din said. "Kels are huge, hairy mammals with great, long claws and teeth. They aren't usually aggressive, but if they're hungry, or they're cornered, they can be deadly. And we do have reports of them moving out of the solitudes toward us. Usually the sign of a bad winter coming."

"They look very much like the ancient sport bears of Declivis," Krush added, biting into an extra crispy slice of fried mazea. It turned out to be hotter than he'd expected it to be, and he paused, and sucked in some cool air to soothe his tongue and the roof of his mouth, and waved at his son to continue.

Ardenai took up the instruction. "Cerastapers are wild Equi boars. They have ten inch tusks in their lower jaw, horns on their heads, and horns on their front shoulders. They can grow to be the size of Ethelred the Bold, and they can be nasty, deadly creatures."

"And there are really kels, and cerastapers around here?"

"Oh yes," Krush muttered. "And why Timor thinks something the size of a dog could defend anything against one is beyond me. A dog wouldn't make two bites for a kel, and a cerastaper would just horn him into the next keep. Dogs are better for carrying off shoes and digging holes and chasing what they're not supposed to chase, than they are protecting anybody against anything."

"I'm sure you're right," Gideon sighed, and lowered his eyes to his cereal bowl.

"What else did you and Ah'brianne talk about?" Io asked, patting his thigh under the table.

"Oh, just stuff, I guess. I met her parents, and they seem very nice. And she told me that there's a schoolmaster at the Great House, Master Breton. He tutors the students who are serving as pages. They spend two hours together every school night. She invited me to come and sit in."

"And will you?" Teal asked.

"I was thinking about it," Gideon said with an offhand shrug.

"Well, let me recommend Master Breton," Teal smiled. "He's tough, but he has a wonderful, lucid way of explaining things, and I'm sure he'd give your education a leg up. You ought to try it, just for the experience."

"Was he your teacher?" Gideon asked, looking surprised. "He's been there that long?"

"Ancients that your father and I are," Teal laughed. "Yes, he was."

"It gets more unbelievable yet," Ah'rane said soberly. "He was there when I was a page. Back when we still carried clubs to school to fight off barbarians in the streets."

"That's how I met your grandmother," Krush said fondly, "at club wielding class. Good old CWC. Over the years it was shortened until it just became, the club. 'Let's go to the club,' we'd say, and that's what we'd mean. And there she was one night, wearing that fresh kel skin, with his teeth hanging around her neck and a cerastaper tusk in her hair. Oh, I was in love. I just whacked her over the head, and dragged her home with me."

"And then they had me," Ardenai said, then held up one finger. "Oops. No. They didn't have me, did they? Where did you get me?"

"We found you under a rock," Krush said, and at the same time Ah'rane said, "An eagle dropped you on his way over."

"The sslithery-ssnake brought thee in hiss big, green ssack," Pythos hissed, smacking down another piece of fruit. "Actually, I'd sstolen thee from a young mother of the Great Housse, and wass carrying thee off for my ssupper, when it ssuddenly occurred to me that I might be able to barter thee for ssomething truly delectable, like a wood rat. Sso I sstopped at the cottage of a humble farmer and hiss lovely young wife ..."

"Who just happened to look exactly like my sire," Gideon added dryly.

"My sstory, if thee pleasses," the serpent said blandly. "And I ass-ked them if they would pay me one wood rat every time all sseven moonss appeared together in the ssky for the nexxt hundred yearss in exchange for thiss beautiful little boy, and they agreed. It iss the truth, Gideon. Ssuch iss the sstuff of legendss." He popped another piece of fruit in his mouth and received a round of applause for his tale.

He nodded graciously and cocked his head in Gideon's direction. "We had besst be getting sstarted if thee wantss to be finisshed by the time the conferencce beginss, Hatchling."

Ardenai looked concerned, or at least interested. "How much damage did that puppy's teeth do, yesterday? Or is it any of my business?"

Pythos looked to Gideon, who smiled uncomfortably and said, "I've asked Pythos to – how did my sire put this – do a little sanding and priming. Oh, and Ah'brianne has asked me if I'd like to go to a concert next Hesst-ee..." He smiled, and tried again. "Hess-chee-gyre evening in Pomonar. I told her I would ask thee, my father."

Ardenai cocked a dark eyebrow and crimped a grin. "How late will you be, and where will you sleep?"

"I believe the concert is over at the twenty-third hour, and wherever you are sleeping, is where I will sleep, as well. If you are here, I will come here. If you are at the Great House, I will return to Thura."

"You may come here without me," Ardenai chuckled. "This is your home."

"No," Gideon said quietly. "My place is with thee, Mister Grayson, watching thy back, and carrying thy knapsack."

"As thee wishes, Mister Gideon. You have my permission. Go with thy physician, and then get ready for the conference. I would have thee sit in, at least for the morning. The afternoon, belongs to your grandsire and the harvesting machinery. Tomorrow, we *all* belong to your grandsire and the harvesting machinery."

They watched Gideon exit with Pythos and Io said softly, "I think perhaps the young lady is changing Gideon's outlook on things."

"Not too quickly, I hope," Ardenai replied. "There are many ways in which one may be overwhelmed, and some look more inviting than others. In any case you find yourself overwhelmed, and then, it is too late."

"Your son is a young man of rare good sense," Krush said sternly. "Give him a little more rein. I said it with Kehailan, I'll say it with Gideon. I'll say it with the next one, and the next. You're too strict. You have wonderful sons. Enjoy them. I must go. I need to talk to Timor about something, and then I, too, would like to sit in on this conference, which means I must cease to look like a humble farmer. I see the chernai are here with furnishings for today's pourparler. Have you any preference in their setting, Dragonhorse?"

"I will see to this, Sire," said Teal, nodding with deep respect to his father-in-law. "Make thyself ready."

Krush caught his face and kissed his forehead in passing. "I am blessed with a wonderful family," he said, heading for the front door and his own house. "Now if only there were more grandchildren. Ah'din, thank you for breakfast. Ah'rane, lovely young wife of humble farmer, attend, if you please."

"We'll see you children in a bit," she laughed, kissing the top of Ardenai's head and giving Io a pat on the shoulder, before hugging Ah'din and hurrying after her husband, who was whistling himself away to the ancient tune of the Wind Warriors.

"And this day we shall meet them," Ardenai said quietly. Picking up his sire's tune he sang softly,

"'Ghostly horsemen, riding by,

Pallid death on hooves of night.'

What will they be like, I wonder?   In any event, I must go and prepare. Teal, may I speak with thee first a moment?"

From the corner of his eye he saw Io give Ah'din a subtle thumbs-
up, and resisted the urge to laugh, even as he turned to glare at her. "I can
do things myself, you know," he said, and paused a moment, and sent up a
prayer, thanking the Creator Spirit that he didn't have to. "I would beg a
most great boon of thee, my trusted friend, away from these scheming wom-
en," Ardenai said, winked at his wife, and bowed his kinsman through the
archway to the main hearth.

▲ ▲ ▲ ▲ ▲ ▲ ▲

"If there is anything else we need to ask, to explore, to clarify in
this first meeting, it escapes me," Ardenai said, catching the circlet with its
seven chevrons into the tuck of his braid and reaching for the first of the gold
bracelets. "We shall forgo the forearm knives, I think. They don't exactly
smack of hospitality, and this is our home."

"And you did kill their arrogating Firstlord with one of them,"
Io chuckled, and immediately regretted the grimace of pain it caused. "I
shouldn't have said that," she murmured, six years old again, squirming under Ardenai Teacher's look of strained but infinite patience. She concentrated on trying to hide the tips of her ears under her hair while she recovered her
adulthood and present status. "Anyway, we had best get out there," she said
briskly. "Ah'krill's shunt will be here any minute." She looked at her husband in the reflector, and was not encouraged by the lines in his handsome
face. "Are you feeling good enough to do this, beloved? You've only been
out of bed a few days."

He silenced her with a smile and kissed the tips of her ears, which
had promptly reasserted themselves above her mass of curls. "I'm well on
the road to recovery. Remind me not to get drawn into the dancing and I'll
be just fine. This won't be all that long a palaver. We'll get acquainted, and
get comfortable and talk a bit, and then spend time eating and visiting. Can

you imagine what stories they'll have to tell? We'll be wishing they'd stay longer. Krush is so excited he can hardly stand it."

"Him, I'm not worried about," Io muttered. She took a deep breath and said, "Truth be told, I'm more worried about your dam and my sire and some of the other senators you invited than I am about the Telenir. The Telenir will come as a delegation. They'll go as a delegation. The others, may linger like a bad pot of phaselus, despite what Krush or any of the rest of us can do."

"Charming image," he chuckled. He finished rubbing the water marks off his armbands and bent to kiss his elfin consort. "Please see to the greeting of our guests. I want a word with Teal, and I'll be out to join you."

Io's eyebrows knit with worry. "He did say yes, didn't he? He did say he'd be on the advisory council?"

"Yes," Ardenai soothed. "Please do as I ask and see to our guests, Fledermaus, and for heaven's sake, quit clucking."

She nodded obediently, fastened her long cape with its gold dragonhorse clasp, gave herself a quick last appraisal, and went toward the area flagged for the landing of shuntcraft, waving to Gideon and Pythos as she hurried across the freshly washed pavers. She wondered how the morning's procedure had gone, and resisted the urge to turn aside and ask.

Ardenai left his chambers and strode toward the big central hub of the house, calling for his kinsman. He ran into Teal just coming out of the wing he shared with Ah'din, and seized him, steering him into the kitchen and away from the distraction of the first shunt's landing. "May I speak with you a minute?"

"Of course," Teal frowned. "Is everything all right? Are you well enough to do this?"

"*Et tu?*" Ardenai snorted. "I'm fine. I just wanted to make sure you haven't changed your mind. I would have you introduced today as one of my advisors, but I know how much you love your position as Master of Horse, and I'm beginning to feel like I popped this on you."

"I love being Master of Horse. I'm actually enjoying being Captain of the Horse Guard, but I love you more. I will join you. I said I would, and on that matter I have not changed my mind." He sucked his cheeks and glanced sideways at his sober kinsman. "Besides, the thought of having all that power makes me feel quite mad. How easily I could become another Sarkhan."

Ardenai scowled at his brother-in-law. "You're not going to regret this haste?"

"Oh, probably, from time to time, but that is the nature of politics, and of kinship, is it not? If you are content to have me serve thee, Dragon-horse, I am content to do so." Teal flashed his good-looking grin, and Ardenai pulled him into a quick, back slapping embrace.

"Thank you," he said. "I shall try to make it worth your while."

"Just try to make it through this without collapsing," Teal muttered, and steered him out through the front door and around the corner of the house into the bustle of the gardens.

"I was right in having this here rather than at the Great House, wasn't I?" Ardenai asked, and Teal's arm came around his shoulder as they walked.

"You're fussing like an old mare with a new foal, Ardi. You know perfectly well it's best that you don't travel right now, and the Great House, while beautiful and symbolic, can be intimidating. I think it was kind of you to invite them here, to your home. It certainly demonstrates a willingness to be friends, or at least allies."

"Actually, it's our home," Ardenai corrected, and glanced at the tall, handsome man striding beside him – as tall, more powerfully built than the Firstlord himself – and, in Ardenai's studied opinion, at least as worthy of the office. Right now, he wished it had gone so. "Now that I am Firstlord, I worry that our private lives may suffer. I would understand if you took your wife and went to Upland keep just to get away from the hubbub."

"Would you like me to take my wife and move to Upland keep? No hard feelings if you do."

Ardenai looked stricken, and Teal pursed his lips in annoyance. The man just was not well enough recovered from his illness for this. Every minor vexation was a shock, every twist in the thread of conversation a Gordian knot. But would he postpone this? Would he rest like he was supposed to? Of course not. He was Ardenai Firstlord of Equus, the Thirteenth Dragonhorse, and the hardest head on the planet. "Forget I mentioned it," Teal said, and his hand closed more tightly on the Firstlord's shoulder. "You couldn't survive a day without your sister's flatwraps, and you and I both know it. Besides..." he thought a moment and discarded what he was going to say about Ardenai's duties holding him in the planetary capital, or, like many of his predecessors on some faraway planet that needed subduing. Ardenai loved his home. He didn't need to be reminded that he'd be gone a good deal of the time. "Besides, Upland keep already sits empty, awaiting whichever one of our children desires it. Ah'din and I are happy here, and we'll need to stick together as an extended family, or Sea keep, as well as Upland, will go to wrack and ruin, despite all Krush can do. He needs us, and as he gets older, he will need us and our sons even more. Most of all, we must consider Krush and Ah'rane. She will need our wives and our daughters. We are bound to this place, and to those good people. Of all our sacred duties, the greatest is to the land and to our elders, you know that."

"Yes," Ardenai agreed. "To the land, and the children who will grow up here in this beautiful place."

They paused a moment to survey the activities, and Teal added quietly, "You have done exactly the right thing. Look about you. Look at this commanding scene that you have engineered. Trust yourself as much as the rest of us trust you."

It was, indeed, impressive. The dragonhorse of Equus raced across the brilliant sun of the Equi flag, while maroon banners emblazoned with the seven chevrons of the Firstlord fluttered in the late morning breeze. A huge round table of finest Calumet mahogany sat gleaming in the center of the largest courtyard, with comfortable chairs arranged around it for the twelve Telenir they were expecting, as well as the eight Equi representing the Great House, the two Seventh Galactic Alliance representatives, and the two senators representing the affined worlds – a total of twenty-four to be present at table – but all of Equus was invited. The table's seemingly solid surface was imbued with voice projection molecules, just like the balustrades at the Great House, needing only to be activated to project what was being said, not only to the audience, but to anyone who chose to watch by cosmoscope. The image, too, was being sent, bounced off several imagers set discreetly at different levels about the garden. A canopy had been set high above to protect the participants from the brightness of the sun off the tabletop as well as any Oporens squalls which might blow up from the sea to bring a brief drizzle, and several dozen seats had been arrayed out from the table for various pages, family members and observers.

The musicians from the Great House were beginning to play, and Ardenai strolled over to greet them, humming the traditional ballad they were warming up with. Perhaps he'd get a chance to sit in with them a bit later on. That was an inviting thought. He'd had no time for any of his instruments since he'd been sick, and it would be good to make music again.

He was diverted by hails from several of the ambassadors from the affined worlds, and was changing directions to greet them when Dominus came gliding up the canyon and settled onto her landing pods. Ardenai growled softly, half to himself, and half to his kinsman, who rolled his eyes in sympathy. "I'll take care of the ambassadors," Teal murmured, and hastened away.

"No time at all to enjoy the music," Ardenai sighed, and strode resolutely forward, hands extended, to greet Ah'krill and her retinue. The Firstlord veiled his thoughts, took her heavily bejeweled hands in his own, and bowed respectfully over them. "Mother," he said, and received a gracious nod. Interested, but devoid of any real warmth.

"Firstlord," she replied respectfully. "I trust you are recovering from your ordeal." It was not a question, it was an expectation. She smiled ever so slightly and added, "We are pleased to hear that the generative capabilities of the Thirteenth Dragonhorse have not been compromised. We trust they will soon be demonstrated to the enrichment of the Great House."

Their eyes met for an uncomfortable moment and Ardenai realized for the dozenth time, the hundredth, that he would never be able to think of this woman as his mother. His dam was Ah'rane, wife of Krush. She of the unadorned, hard-working hands – she who had given him suck as an infant, and succor for all of his hundred years. This woman, was a political opponent, perhaps even an enemy. Most certainly worthy of respect, but not someone he could love on a personal basis.

How sad, he thought, to discover that the High Priestess of Equus was his birth mother and have it be nothing more than a mild annoyance. He wondered with some amusement if she felt the same way. The cocking of her finely chiseled head and the slow blinking of her draconian eyes told him she just might.

The fact that she was accompanied by priestess Ah'nis – very tall, very blonde, and exceedingly chilly – reminded him with all the delicacy of a bludgeon that, despite her words on Calumet, his mother wasn't pleased with his choice of a mate. It was Ah'nis who had been his mother's choice for him, and he knew mating with her would be inevitable.

From the look on her face, Ah'nis was no more pleased with the prospect than he was, but like Ardenai, she, too, served at the pleasure of the Great House. She would grit her teeth and with her usual stare of longsuffering arrogance she would dutifully allow him to mount her, and dutifully bear him children, purebred, High Equi princes and princesses; Ah'krill would see to it. She'd probably sit in on the mating to make sure Ardenai did what was expected of him. And he would do his duty as Firstlord, though the thought of touching the woman made him cringe a little inside. He knew he'd have to mate many times over to perpetuate the line of the Great House, and he'd been hoping fervently that Ah'nis wouldn't be first. With her appearance here this morning, that hope was beginning to fade.

He glanced at her, but she was watching the SGA shuttle land, and didn't catch the look. Perhaps when she was in heat he'd find her a little more attractive. In any case, he knew Ah'krill was going to fawn over those children, and she'd let him know in a dozen different ways, some more annoying than others, that these were the purest of the pure, the noblest, the most worthy, and they'd be insufferable because of it. His mouth twitched at the corners, thinking about Io, and the little fruit bat babies she'd promised him; the ones who were going to wreak havoc in the royal apartments of the Great House. He bowed again, partly to break his chain of thought lest Ah'krill tune into it, and partly to dismiss the women, who were growing restive under his scrutiny.

Jilfan, who was beside Ah'krill as usual, nodded politely to the First-lord, then walked Ah'krill to a seat at the table. He found a place for Ah'nis and himself under the myrianotus tree and sat obliquely studying Ardenai while appearing to look at everything else. Ardenai wondered if the boy, always so solicitous to Ah'krill, had taken time to speak to his own dam. Another gulf to be bridged. Another skill to be learned, being a stepfather to someone who didn't want a stepfather. Ardenai chuckled humorlessly and turned back to his duties as host.

Gideon caught his eye with a smile and a wave, and Ardenai's spirits rose as they always did at the sight of him. The boy was escorting Marion Eletsky and Oonah Pongo, and with them, was Kehailan. "All three of my sons here today," the Firstlord said aloud to no one in particular. "The one born to me, the one chosen, and the one my wife bore, who doesn't want a thing to do with me." Ardenai went with a smile to embrace them before turning to greet Abeyan, who had Io on his arm.

They, at least, seemed to have made their peace with one another. It was awkward, Ardenai thought, suddenly having one's lifelong chum as a father-in-law. It was awkward to go from teaching tiny children one minute, to being the absolute ruler of the most powerful planet in the SGA the next. It did leave one quite...what was the word he wanted, baffled? Breathless? That was it, breathless. Ardenai drew in the air he lacked and squared his shoulders. Any weakness on his part would be observable, and noted. One thing he did not wish to convey to the various factions at this meeting, was weakness.

Soon, he promised himself, he could sit down and take a cool drink of water to steady himself without being obvious. Teal had been right. His mother Ah'rane had been right, and his father, and his sister, his wife and Gideon. He really wasn't up for this. But Nik would be. He could lead the conversation, and Ardenai could sit back and look sage and hope everybody else was comprehending better than he was, and then he'd apologize to his family when nobody was around, and admit they'd been correct, and pick their collective brains for anything he'd missed, and then go back to sleep for a couple of days. The musicians began to play, and Ardenai smiled to himself and nodded. An auspicious day for Equus – a new day of peace and understanding.

The Imperial Equi Clipper Regence, carrying the Telenir delegation was the last to glide up the canyon and settle on its pods next to the SGA vessel. It was Commander of the Secondary Squads Tarpan, who stepped out, and offered his hand to the elderly gentleman who alighted first, followed by three women, two younger men, an old couple who looked thoroughly confused and more than a little hostile, a young couple, and last, a stunningly beautiful, very frail, middle-aged woman. Ardenai recognized her immediately as Ah'davan, Konik's wife.

He knew Konik had married his sexual trainer, a woman more than fifty years his senior. He was completely and publicly devoted to her, which added to his image of the perfect Equi nobleman. That thought, juxtaposed with the image of Konik as Telenir, made Ardenai chuckle. He paused a moment, waiting for Konik to appear. He did not, and the questioning expression on Ah'davan's face as she searched the crowd, sent a chill of premonition up the Firstlord's spine.

He shot Teal a look and a thought, Teal gave Marion a subtle punch in the thigh, and in a moment one of them stood on either side of the Firstlord. "Welcome to my home," he said, approaching the first gentleman with a cordial nod and the ancient gesture of greeting. "Ahimsa, I wish thee peace. Pardon so abrupt a question on so historic an occasion, but where is Senator Konik? I was looking forward to his company in this. He is not ill, I hope."

Ah'davan's face went from puzzled to pale in a heartbeat, and she brushed past the others to stand in front of Ardenai. "He is not here? He said he got a message from you to join him here a day early. He should be here!"

Ardenai's eyes widened, and he gave his head a brief shake. "Ah'davan, I sent no such message." She swayed with shock and he reached quickly and caught her by the elbows to steady her. "Did you see this message? Did any of you?" he asked, including all of them. "Who brought it? How did he get it?"

"I don't know!" she moaned, and began to sob.

By then Io was beside her, offering her a hug and a place to sit, and Ardenai dropped his voice under the rising cacophony of questions and speculation. "Tarpan, I want all these people put under my personal protection immediately. You need, all of you, to tell Tarpan exactly who is in your family, and where they are right now. We need to secure your personal safety before we pursue this any further. Master Abeyan, attend if you would be so kind."

When the Master of Cavalry was close beside him, Ardenai hissed, "Get everybody out of here and back to the Great House, now. Personally escort my mother and deposit her in her chambers with a guard at the door."

Abeyan cocked his head and studied the Firstlord's face. "You fear for her, or you suspect her?"

"Yes," Ardenai replied. "Please get her out of here now, and leave Jilfan with Krush. If someone is going to try to pick us off, I want the child out of the middle of it."

Abeyan nodded, spun on his heel, and hurried over to Ah'krill. Ardenai didn't want to focus enough to actually figure out what was being said, but he gathered it was both confusing and unpleasant. Rather than going to her shunt, Ah'krill swept toward him, and her eyes were hard when she spoke.

"How can you suspect me of treachery when it is the leader of the Wind Warriors who is missing?" she demanded. "It is he whom you should suspect. He's probably sitting on one of these rocks or up in one of these trees, getting ready to throw bolts at us all."

"Be consoled," Ardenai replied, glancing sideways at Abeyan, who shrugged and looked puzzled, indicating he had said nothing. "I am most concerned for your safety, and you will go."

"I wish to remain," she said firmly. "I want to hear this story they tell, to decide for myself if there is treachery afoot."

Ardenai returned the gaze, took her firmly by the left elbow, and steered her away from the ears of the Telenir. "I do not have time, and will not make time, to argue with you, Priestess. You disobeyed me once, and came to Calumet when I asked you not to. The results were disastrous. You know it and I know it. Now, go to your shunt and go home, and when I look for you, I expect to find you EXACTLY where I've sent you. Master Abeyan, please see to my mother's comfort, if not to her wishes. Carefully screen anyone she sees, lest they bring further danger upon her most holy person."

"Yes, Firstlord," Abeyan said, took her opposite elbow, and propelled her away.

Ardenai returned to his Telenir guests with a palms up gesture of frustration and apology. "I am so sorry this is happening," he said. "Is there something more I can do? Is there something I am missing, something I should know?"

The elderly gentleman who had first alighted gave Ardenai a tight knot of a smile and shook his white head slowly from side to side. "I fear that those of us who spoke of peace, will die a lonely and dishonorable death. Those of us who spoke not at all, will simply disappear, and those of us who failed in our treason, will be executed, and there is nothing you can do to stop it. We were foolish, all of us, to think that a mission of conquest could be turned into one of diplomacy, simply because a handful of diplomatic people willed it. We have failed, not because we failed to kill you, but because we failed to pay attention. None of us, not a one, not even Sarkhan's own parents," he jerked his chin at the elderly couple clinging to one another nearest the shunt, "knows how to communicate with the Wind Warriors, I'm sure of it, though Saremanno claims he can. Sardure claims it as well, but we have seen no proof, and he refused to come today. We cannot tell them what we are doing, what our motives are, what our thinking is. They see only betrayal."

"See from where?' Marion asked, opening his arms to the sky. "If they can see, they can hear. It only makes sense. Something is going on here that we do not understand, and obviously it's closer to us than we ever suspected." He glanced at Ardenai, and saw him nodding in agreement.

"Things are not what they seem," Ardenai said simply. "I am sorry for what has befallen you. It is my earnest desire that nothing worse yet comes upon you. Please, place yourselves in Tarpan's capable hands. My wife will assist you as well. Let us gather what you need, and make you as comfortable as we can. Sir..."

"I am Taki."

Ardenai nodded in respect of his age. "Taki, how many of you are there? Have you a firm count?"

The old man shook his head. "Nothing about this was ever firm. All was nebulous. All was mystery." He sighed. "As far as I know, there were eight hundred and sixty-three of us. Now, apparently, there are eight hundred and fifty-nine. Some have gone into hiding, some left Equus after the failed coup. How many can be accounted for I do not know."

"I have no intention of taking from you anything which you have earned. None of you. Not lands, nor goods, though for the time being, I must take your freedom. I have a few places in mind which will hold your numbers, and in safety. I must split you up to protect you properly until we can figure out what's happening. Do not allow yourselves to be separated from your loved ones, as that is not our intent. Stay calm, hold out hope, and hold up prayer."

He gestured his wife to one side and murmured, "These, who were the delegation, take with their families and such personal goods as are most precious to them to Mountain hold."

Io looked astonished, then whispered, "Mountain hold has been closed since the Twelfth Dragonhorse died."

Ardenai raised a black eyebrow and murmured, "Open it. You're a smart girl. And the fewer people who know, the better. Marion Eletsky is correct, something's very wrong here. It's been wrong from the very start. I just hope when we find Nik he's still in one piece and breathing."

Within an hour they were standing alone – Ardenai, Teal, Pythos, Marion and Oonah, Gideon and Kehailan. Krush had taken a rather sullen Jilfan in to keep Ah'din company, and Io had quickly changed clothes and gone with Tarpan. The other shunts had left with their human cargo. Even the table was gone, and the graceful canopy with its seven silver chevrons and maroon banners. The music had ended as quickly as it had begun, and Ardenai had not gotten a chance to play.

"Rather an unpleasant turn of events, given the effort that went into these preparations," Teal groused, looking around the abandoned gardens.

"Doesst thee get the ssensse that thee iss in danger here?" asked the physician, flicking his long tongue into the uneasy salt air blowing in on the wind, and rolling a hooded yellow eye in the Firstlord's direction.

"No, Pythos, I don't," Ardenai replied. He was standing with his palms up, head back, eyes closed. "I'm not getting a sense of anything. Not a thing, and it's not for lack of trying. It's as if someone just dreamed this. Are you sensing anything?"

"No," the old dragon hissed, and narrowed his eyes to slits. "There iss nothing. There iss not enough."

Teal shook his head and folded his arms across his broad chest. "You know," he said unwillingly, "there is the possibility that Ah'krill is right, Ardi. Konik could have staged this. He could be headed for Telenir. He could be watching and laughing. He could be thinking absolutely anything, doing absolutely anything. He told us a dozen times, 'I am a loyal Wind Warrior.' Maybe we should have believed him."

Ardenai dropped his arms and turned with an exasperated sigh. "He also told us a dozen times he was a loyal Equi. No. He is not the instigator. I spent a little time with Ah'davan's thoughts earlier, just as a precaution. She's genuinely terrified for him. She doesn't have a clue where he is. He never hinted to her in any way that this might be going to happen, and he had no reason not to."

"Of course he did," Kehailan said. "He had you. Nobody knows better than he does what a powerful telepath you are. He's not going to tell his wife something that's going to pop into the front of her mind the second he goes missing. He may love her very much, but he may also love the Wind Warriors. I think Teal may be right."

"No," Ardenai said. "Ah'davan has...what your mother had." He shuddered momentarily, remembering the disease which had taken Ah'ree from him. "All Konik could think about was getting home to her. Being with her. He would not shock her in such a manner, and he would never leave her."

A sudden thought struck Marion Eletsky, and he reached into the inner pocket of his dress uniform jacket, saying, "Speaking of shock, in all the excitement, and then all the confusion I forgot that Moonsgold sent this for you, Ardenai." He extracted an envelope and handed it to the Firstlord. "He said it was a bit of a shocker."

Ardenai opened it, read it – scowled, not with anger but with puzzlement – read it again and muttered, "As if this wasn't confusing enough as it is." There was a pause while he glanced over the two sheets again. One was figures, one was findings. "Those samples we sent with Doctor Moonsgold, blood, tissue and bone from Konik, Sarkhan and the others? He tested them. Had several other people test them."

"And?" Marion said, edging closer to get a look.

"And," Ardenai grimaced, "They are Equi, and Anguine. Nothing more."

"Not unexpected," Teal said. "It has long been suspected that the Telenir may be close relatives."

Ardenai released the corner of his bottom lip from his teeth and handed the papers to Teal. "No," he said again. "They are from this homeworld – back at least a hundred generations. Konik may have lived on Anguine II, but he was born here. There is not a single planetary adaptation in a single one of his chromosomes. None of the rest ever left Equus or her two sister planets – ever. They are Equi, just like us. The farthest Sarkhan ever traveled, is Calumet."

Kehailan's face was a complete blank for several moments and his words, when they came, were spoken with great effort. "So…what does that mean? No Telenir? No…planet somewhere in the great unknown? Have we gone through all of this for nothing?"

Ardenai just stood shaking his head, staring at the pavers as though trying to read something in the ancient stones. "It is beginning to rain," he said at last. "If we are cold and hungry none of this will make any sense. Not that it will anyway, but my sister and my mother have been cooking for two days, we might as well go in and enjoy it."

He turned momentarily south, toward the vast grasslands of Viridia, and stared at something only he could see. "I hoped, I really did, that the foolish games had ended with the death of Sarkhan on the wargrounds of Calumet, and that this would begin a new era of diplomacy and peace. I was wrong. It seems we have yet another puzzle to solve, and somehow I don't think it's the one we thought it was at all. This is an enigma, like Nik himself, and we have got to find him."

Kehailan's eyes swept the familiar surroundings, and there was an uneasiness in his action. "We still don't know *who*, apparently, but *where*, is suddenly gaining an alarming clarity."

As they ducked in out of the rain, Marion chuckled humorlessly and said, "One of the most famous quotes from Old Earth, long before we were Terren and a tribute world of Equus, goes like this: 'We have seen the enemy, and he is us.' Could that be the case?"

"It could," Ardenai sighed. "Right now anything is possible. We prepared for this for a very long time, and in most ways we were right. We did head off a usurpation of some kind…I think…and we have made a good start. Every bit of information adds to the solving of this puzzle. I am confident we will solve it."

"Do they know, I wonder?" Oonah said quietly, sipping her tea and looking around the table, "the ones we saw today – the old people – the old gentleman who spoke. Do they really know they are Equi, or do they really think they are Wind Warriors?"

"What I'm wondering," Ardenai mused, leaning back in his chair and staring into the depths of his wine glass, "is if they're both. Or neither. And where is Nik, because every fiber of my being tells me he is in terrible trouble right now, and it has everything to do with being Telenir and nothing to do with being Equi. Who is the third party in this? Who benefits, and how?"

CHAPTER TWENTY-SEVEN

G ideon snugged the soft wool of the comforter closer around his shoulder and winced at the high pitched howl of the wind in the huge Equi pines outside his bedroom window. The last of the moons had gone down and the sun had not yet begun to rise, but it didn't sound much like weather for a birthing day celebration. He sighed. He'd been looking forward to this more than he wanted to admit. Not that anybody would be in much of a mood to celebrate, least of all his sire.

He pulled himself up onto one elbow and cocked his head to listen, wondering if the wind was as cold as it sounded. Except for the wind, the ancient house was silent. Only the slight warmth of the alabaster walls told him that water flowed through them, through the floors, heating the structure as it had for thousands of years. Canyon keep. Home. He had a home, and a family. What else could possibly matter more than that? He smiled. He could always go to the beach another time. He flopped back down for a bit, but there was no sleep in him. It was his birthing day! Today, here, people would remember that. He didn't think he could wait to hear it the first time.

Again he listened, straining his ears for any sound of his father. Was he home safe in bed, or was he out in this? Perhaps pressing matters had kept him at the Great House. He could be pacing back and forth like a big, graceful protoped, debating even yet with MalDor over the issue of cleomitite mining on Calumet. Or maybe he'd agreed to a meeting with the delegation from Lebonath Jas that had appeared out of nowhere three days ago. Gideon had been at the Great House for their arrival. Interesting looking people, with their pallid skins and their large, colorless eyes and pale hair. Backward and uncouth, but fascinating. They were secretive in the extreme, spoke rudely, and, Gideon thought, the ones he'd gotten close to didn't smell all that good, either. They seemed to be nocturnal, so meeting at night would be the courteous thing to do. His father, ever courtly and gentle of spirit, would honor them in such a manner. Their unexpected arrival in the midst of the furor over the Telenir and the disappearance of Konik, had given Ardenai even more to think about. Certainly, he was not here in his bed at Canyon keep.

Gideon sighed again. The ruler of eleven worlds was not to be expected at the birthing day party of an adopted boy – the castoff son of a Declivian whore – who had managed to attach himself to a powerful and magnanimous prince. What was he thinking to imagine that Ardenai would come? He rubbed at the soft edges of his blanket, just to make sure he wasn't dreaming the whole thing, to make sure he wasn't huddled under a thin rag on the dirty wood floor of his mother's two room flat, where he'd be stumbled over by his drunken dam, or kicked awake to fetch for her or her current bed mate. Or sleeping in his bunk on Squire Fidel's plantation on Demeter, where he'd be cuffed awake, or pissed on as a joke while he slept. He grinned, remembering the fate of the last man who'd decided to urinate on him while he was asleep. That unfortunate soul had run afoul of the big stranger who'd turned out to be the Thirteenth Dragonhorse. How much fun it would be to walk back into that bunkhouse – today – with his father.

Gideon rolled his head ever so slightly to the right, playing the game of daring himself to look. The tall, powerful figure of Grayson was not in the top bunk next to him. There was no bunk next to him. He was in his own comfortable bed, which snuggled into the corner of his spacious room like a big, soft wedge of Ah'din's homemade cream pie, its intricately carved head and footboards seeming a friendly fence, keeping out the bad things which had haunted his young life.

Gideon flipped the covers aside and got out of bed. It was foolish to lie here and let these fantasies and speculations eat at him. He'd go peek into his father's room. If he went outside, he could look in through the windows. That way he'd know how cold the wind was, and he'd know if Ardenai was going to be home to help him celebrate his birthing day.

Even as he thought it, he felt a little petty. He told himself again that there were more important things afoot than celebrating. A week's frantic search had turned up no sign of Konik. Ardenai had employed every man, every mind, every strategy at his disposal, including reinforcements from the Seventh Galactic Alliance, and come up completely empty. Finally, he'd had to put the search into the hands of others and return to the affairs of the Great House, and of his own harvest.

The boy wrapped himself in a heavy woolen robe, wiggled his feet into lined, knee-high moccasins, and opened the door which led onto the main patio of the north garden. He hunched his shoulders against the wind and stood there a moment – long enough to realize that it wasn't all that cold. The breath of the Creator Spirit always sounded frigid as it whipped through the pine boughs. He should have remembered that.

He smiled to himself and hurried across the sand-colored pavers toward his sire's wing of the house, giving the sky a brief glance to ascertain that there were no clouds to rain on his celebration. The season was fast changing. More rain was a possibility. The huge harvesters ran day and night, their lights just visible on the hills past the barns, trying to finish ahead of the imminent and sometimes terrible storms. The old people who told the weather said this winter was going to be long and cold.

There were no clouds, only the last of the Equi moons, sinking on the western horizon, pulling a few faint stars along behind. He slipped up to the bank of casements on the northwest side of his father's bedchambers and peeked in. It was utterly black. He closed his eyes for a few moments to allow his pupils to dilate, and looked again. Not a chance. He couldn't see a thing. He huffed with annoyance and was rethinking his strategy when an amused baritone touched his thoughts.

Did you really think I would miss my son's first birthing day party?

Gideon jumped. *I...Sire, I didn't mean to...I mean, no...I...*

Organize your thoughts, Gideon. What did you not mean to do?

Gideon now felt very foolish indeed, standing outside Ardenai's bedroom window in the small hours of the morning like a lovesick suitor.

He took a deep breath and brought his thoughts to the forefront, suppressing his emotions and realizing he was still very sleepy. *Sire, forgive me. I did not mean to waken you, nor to make you think that I didn't think you'd be home for my birthing day, or to make you think that I thought it was important enough that you ought to be, you know. And I didn't mean to intrude on anything you and Io might be...doing. Is she home, by the way?*

Mmmmm. Tucked into her accustomed spot beneath my chin - and very warm and cuddly she is, too. I love you, son. Blessed birthing day. Now go back to bed and let us sleep, will you?

"Of course," the boy murmured aloud, turning away, then added, *Did you find him?*

Not yet. But Equus is just so big. The galaxy is just so big. Nik will be found in good time. Go to bed before you get chilled, and I wake myself the rest of the way, and both of us start the day on an unhappy note.

Gideon hugged himself as he trotted back to his room. Ardenai was home. The business of finding Konik had not been greater than the business of being home for his son's birthing day. The business of the Great House of Equus, the Kohathis, the Lebonathi, had not been greater than the business of being home for his son's birthing day.

Hubris is not a particularly endearing trait, came the stern thought, and Gideon realized with a twinge of fear just how powerfully invasive his father could be if the mood took him

"Sorry," he said aloud, and crawled back into his warm, soft bed.

The next time he awoke the room was full of daylight, and his bed was alive! Something was wriggling under the comforter, over his toes and feet and legs, something which tickled and scratched and made little chuffing sounds like a tiny steam engine. Gideon's eyes flew open and he went up on his elbows with a squawk and a giggle, expecting to find his aunt's lithoped under the covers with him, probably in pursuit of a spinklemaus, brought as a prize from the barn. Mikilosh occasionally did things like that.

Instead of Mikilosh, he found himself looking into the laughing face of someone he didn't know. A young man roughly his own age, who said,

"Blessed birthing day. I'm your cousin, Criollo."

Before Gideon could acknowledge the introduction, there was another scrambling, this time up the center of his chest, and a black button nose on a pointed muzzle, and two bright brown eyes in a light brown, foxy face, poked out from under the covers at him.

Gideon crowed with delight and seized the intruder. "What are you?" he exclaimed, hoisting the little creature up to examine it. It was a dog. A tiny, wiggling dog, with a freckled belly, short, rakishly floppy ears, and an amazingly long, frantic tongue.

"He's a miniature Caspian terrier," Criollo said, sitting down on the edge of the bed. "He's just about as big as he's going to get, because of course you can't bring a dog onto Equus until it's been neutered or spayed, and they have to be two seasons old to do that, but what's there is all dog. I hope you like him."

"Oh, I do," Gideon breathed, holding the pup just out of tongue's reach, and stroking the sleek, spotted coat with one admiring hand. "Thank you...I'm Gideon," he began, remembering his manners, and Criollo burst out laughing. He sounded exactly like his sire.

"I'm glad, because if you're not Gideon, I've given your puppy to somebody else."

Gideon pulled the pup under his chin and arched a questioning eyebrow. "I love the dog, of course, but how...I mean," he glanced around and lowered his voice a little despite the fact that they were obviously alone, "I don't think my grandsire wanted me to have a dog, because he thinks they're kind of useless, even the big ones, and he thought it might start an unfortunate fad of some kind if the son of the Firstlord had a dog, you know, since they're not native to the planet, or upset Ah'krill if I took it to Thura with me, and now here you are."

"With a dog. Yes. Well, what can you expect from a cousin in his third year of final form, after all? Colts that age can be so heedless and impulsive. It was a whim. Your sire and grandsire will disapprove, no doubt, but being polite, and for the sake of family relations, they'll let you keep the little rascal, though my mother's fat, spoiled lithoped is going to be scandal-ized."

"Oh," Gideon said, and a slow smile crossed his face as he snuggled the gently snoring pup. "But who told you I wanted a dog?"

"One of the family nickered in somebody's ear," Criollo grinned. "I am but the agent of delivery. Would you like me to take him so you can get bathed and dressed?"

Gideon started to hand him over, then hesitated and tucked him back under his chin. "I could just put him here on my bed. All of a sudden he's sound asleep."

"Don't delude yourself," Criollo advised. "He's been my compan-ion for two days now, and I can tell you this, he's saving himself. If he wakes up and there's no supervision, there will be chaos. Here, I'll sit with him and wait for you."

"Thanks," Gideon said, and reluctantly handed over his prize.

A dog. He had a dog of his very own. He couldn't bathe fast enough, barely had the patience to properly comb his hair for want of holding that dog. A series of short yips told him the pup was awake once again, and he heard Criollo's laugh as he stepped out of the small lavage in his room and started rummaging for something to put on.

"You could have gone to the main pools," his cousin said. "You had plenty of time before breakfast."

"We bathed for over an hour last night," Gideon replied, and it was true. At High Harvest, when they all spent long days in the fields, hauling hay, running harvesters, tending horses from dawn until dark, or putting up food for the winter in the huge kitchen of Canyon keep, a long evening soak was especially welcome. They'd laugh, and discuss the day, and drink some of Teal's fine wine, or cinnamon orange tea, and groom one another while they chatted and snoozed in the big thermal pools beneath the house.

"The family is waiting for us," Criollo said, and handed Gideon his puppy. "That's a beautiful painting of the sunrise there on your wall. One of your Sire's, I assume?"

"Yes, one of Ardenai's," Gideon smiled. "He painted it while he was recovering from his illness and gave it to me as a birthing day gift." His sire. He belonged to someone. He wondered if the novelty of that thought would ever wear off. He doubted it very much.

Gideon took time to study his companion as they walked toward the kitchen. He could see both Teal and Ah'din in Criollo's features, and when Criollo looked back at him and grinned, his eyes sparkled with mischief, just like his grandsire's. Gideon couldn't help wondering if they'd be friends – maybe even best friends, like Ardenai and Teal.

The puppy wiggled in his arms, wanting down, and Gideon was suddenly keenly aware of who waited in the kitchen. Teal, who had recently begun advising Ardenai on top of being Master of Horse and Captain of the Horse guard, and who valued his quiet times at home. Ah'din, who never seemed to sit still, and who would be less than pleased with a puppy underfoot and into her weaving baskets. His sire, who carried the weight of an ancient government on his shoulders with Io beside him. If they'd come for breakfast as they often did, there would also be Krush, who thought dogs were good for nothing but chewing up shoes and tack, Ah'rane, who had said quietly but firmly that she would not advocate for a dog in this house. And yet someone had nickered in Criollo's ear. Who? Gideon sighed and snuggled the puppy close under his chin. This could be a very short acquisition.

"You're squashing your dog," Criollo observed, and gave the faltering Gideon a gentle push into the fragrant, sunlit kitchen.

They were all there – his whole family – even Pythos, who had temporarily given up residence in the myrianotus tree for the occasion, and Kehailan, still in his SGA uniform. When the two boys walked in, all conversation ceased abruptly.

"What in the ten tribute worlds of Equus is that thing with the birthing day boy?" Krush asked, pointing at the puppy, who was peeking out between Gideon's encircling fingers.

"That's my son," Teal said. "You remember him. Home from Oporens Academy on Anguine II? Has the room next to Gideon's?"

"The other thing," Krush amended, poker faced.

"Well, it's too small to be a horse," Teal said blandly. "Definitely not a horse. Which is a good thing. The women in this family object to having horses in here under usual circumstances, though there has been the occasional foal by the cookstove for a bit."

"Tiny even for a pony," Ah'din added. "Too quiet for a duck."

"Too small for a dog," Ah'rane chuckled, "so that whole argument's laid to rest."

"About the right ssize for a wood rat, and it lookss tassty enough," Pythos hissed, flicking his long tongue in the pup's direction. "Doesst thee have planss for it?"

"Too small for a lithoped," Io said, winking at the boys as she set flatwraps on the table.

"Not the right shape for a spinklemaus," Ardenai smiled, "though it has those beady eyes that spinkles have. Please, tell us. We're intrigued. Did you catch it under the bed, or did old fat Mikilosh drag it in and spit it up on your comforter?"

"Old fat Mikilosh has caught more spinkles and rats than you have, brother dear," Ah'din snapped, quick in the defense of her beloved ped, and her brother burst out laughing.

"Of that I have no doubt," he managed, and caught her hand to kiss it as she brushed past him. "I've never been much of a rat catcher, much to my chagrin."

Ah'din shot him a look, then a smile, and turned back to the boys. "Tell us, Gideon, what have you there?"

"It's a dog," Gideon squeaked. "It's a..." he glanced at Criollo, visualizing those first minutes in the bedroom, "miniature...something terrier."

"Caspian," Kehailan added helpfully, and all eyes turned to him. "What? Because I know what kind of dog it is, I'm behind this?"

"That, and because you don't have to live here, yes." Ardenai growled softly, but his eyes were twinkling.

Kehailan snorted. "I also know that it was originally bred tiny like that to keep rats out of the prisons on Caspia, and that Ah'brianne's old dog, Sawkus, is a Newland Potiffur mix developed on Declivis as a herding breed about four hundred years ago." He paused and colored just a bit, realizing that his enthusiasm had become unmistakable. "I'm rather fond of dogs, that's all."

"And you wanted your little brother to have one," Ardenai said flatly.

Kehailan just pursed his lips and arched his brows.

"I could...give him back," Gideon whispered, beginning to turn in his cousin's direction.

"Oh no, I don't want him." Criollo said, backing away. "I'm just the delivering agent, remember? Turn him loose in the hay barn. He's bred for the express purpose of catching tiny pests. Supposedly he's a ratter to match any ped." He gave his mother a nervous glance. "Not my choice of words, just purported prowess."

"Not so hasty," Krush admonished, wagging a finger. "Here, let me examine the beast. Careful now, I don't want to get my arm taken off."

Gideon handed him over, and Krush held the little fellow in his cupped hands to examine him. "You," he said softly, dropping his head close to the pup's foxy little face, "are absolutely adorable. Probably useless, but adorable. None of us will be able to top this. The rest of the day will be details. Here, take your dog. Blessed birthing day, Grandson."

The table exploded with laughter and applause, which sent the pup wiggling out of Gideon's grasp and bounding deer-like around the room over various objects at an amazing rate of speed and with an athletic grace which brought more than one admiring nod.

"Let him run," Krush advised, and pulled out a chair for Gideon before turning to embrace Criollo. "Who set you on the path of a puppy if not Kehailan?"

Criollo just shrugged his shoulders. "I'll never tell," he said, and turned his good-looking grin toward his uncle. "Ardenai Firstlord, congratulations on your marriage to the lovely former Captain of the Horse Guard. Lovely former Captain, blessings on your marriage to my favorite, albeit only, uncle."

Io gave him a gracious nod and said, "We have been told that we are not a very likely couple, but we are nonetheless a happy one, and we thank you for your felicitations."

"Sire," Kehailan said, impatient to get back to the subject at hand, "We were discussing the ramifications of the Lebonathi delegation."

"A conversation for another time," Ardenai smiled. "Perhaps this evening at the main fire. For now, we give ourselves over to the celebration of Gideon's birthing day."

"As you wish," Kehailan acquiesced. "Gideon, what is your outing to be?"

"The shore," he sighed. "I've never been to the shore."

"And we're picnicking," Ah'rane said, "so you had best lose that uniform for the day, and put on something more casual, Tactical Wing Commander Ah'ree Kehailan Ardenai."

Kehailan nodded and smiled, his black eyes flashing with affection for his granddam. The thought of the shore was not a particularly inviting one, but he would go to please her, and his father. Perhaps he could steal some of Ardenai's time to further discuss the Lebonathi delegation, and what their arrival on the doorstep of Equus might mean to the political stability of this particular spatial extension.

It was well known that Lebonath Jas and Lebonath Tras were more than a little xenophobic, and it was unprecedented for them to send a delegation anywhere for any reason. Nobody knew a single thing about them, but speculation was rampant that they were seeking an alliance, and perhaps the opportunity to join the SGA. Ah'krill had visited there with a delegation about two years ago. Had it been that long? Longer? His sire had been invited. Perhaps he should have made himself put aside his grief and go, Kehailan thought, passing a steaming platter of mazea cakes and helping himself to one of them as it went by. He realized his father was watching him out of the corner of one eye, and tried not to look as frustrated as he felt at the moment.

He put aside his speculations as best he could, and focused on his family. It was unusual for him to be home so much. Now that Ardenai was Firstlord, Kehailan's responsibilities to Equus would increase exponentially, and Marion Eletsky seemed to know that. It was surprising, really, mostly to Kehailan. He'd always considered himself an outsider, someone of mixed blood who was a prince of the Great House only because his father was of royal blood. Now, here he was in the thick of things and rather pleased to be so. Occasionally of late he'd speculated about where that might lead someday. What he might find himself doing.

▲ ▲ ▲ ▲ ▲ ▲ ▲

"Kee, look up!" Ardenai called from the hayloft, and a bale of sweet-smelling hay dropped at his feet. Kehailan waved and grinned, popped the cords of twisted straw which held the bale together, and began tossing thick flakes of the stuff to the eager horses which lined the aisle. Krush and Gideon were feeding from the other end of the huge barn, Criollo and Teal putting out the grain, and Kehailan found himself enjoying the activity. His dislike of the agrarian lifestyle was legend, and he wondered as he took in the sounds and smells of the early morning and the horses, if he might just be changing as he got a little older.

He had long ago made it clear he wanted nothing to do with the keeping of horses, nor did he want to be a keeplord. He did not want to play polo, deliver foals on a cold Omphas morning, or walk behind a pony-plow in the family garden. He had no desire to harvest grain or look for stray animals in the middle of the night. But now, somehow, things seemed smoother, as though all the shaking and stirring of late had finally homogenized the diverse elements of Kehailan's life into something which flowed together and seemed richer than it had, and sweeter.

A soft muzzle brushed his forearm and he dropped the hay into Tolbeth's manger before stopping a moment to stroke her soft, bay shoulder. "You're welcome," he smiled.

There was a sudden movement in the doorway, and a bounding of brown and white that set even gentle Tolbeth's eyes bulging with alarm.

She was jerking up a warning hoof when Kehailan snatched up the pup and stepped back out of the stall with him. "You'd best be careful, young man," he said, offering the tiny dog up for Tolbeth to sniff over the door, "You'll be a small smear on a very large wall." The mare stuck out her nose until her head was nearly parallel to the floor, snorted a couple of times in what was obviously contempt, and went back to her breakfast. "You have some confidences to win, and it'll take some time," Kehailan advised. He stroked the puppy under its chin with one finger, and set it back on the floor.

In a moment Gideon was beside him, looking concerned, then relieved when he saw the dog. "Thanks. I suppose I ought to give him a name so I can call him," he grinned.

"A good idea. We can work on that at the shore," Kehailan smiled, and realized with a flood of relief that he no longer resented Gideon, that he had grown to admire, and then to love this sincere and intelligent young man. "Come on, little brother, the sun is long since up and the tide is going out. The women will be packed and waiting for us."

They went shoulder to shoulder toward the house at Canyon keep, and Ardenai watched them with a deep sense of pleasure, and relief no less than Kehailan's. "I do think my sons are growing rather fond of one another," he said to his father, and Krush nodded.

"And a fine brace they are. Our wives are waiting for us. Teal, are you coming, and where is Criollo? I'm not used to having my whole family at home all at once."

It was novel, and delightful, and they piled into the little flyers with much laughter and high spirits. They'd talked about riding the horses down to the beach, but it was two hours or more by that mode, and they'd opted instead to take the Equi flyers, which would get them there quickly and optimize Gideon's first experience at the shore. If Kehailan suspected that they'd done it partially so that he wouldn't have to ride a horse all that way, he kept it to himself, and there wasn't really any evidence that it had been a factor in their decision-making.

The day was warm and beautiful despite the season, and the flyers swept low over the waterfall and followed the river down the wide, steep-sided canyon which led to the sea. The grass was gold with the kiss of first frosts, the deciduous trees beginning to release their leaves to the ground's embrace. Caves dotted the sides of the canyon on both sides, and as they meandered from side to side they talked about the different ones, and the adventures to be had there, and of some of the ancient paintings which were to be found inside.

The tang of the salt grew sharper, and with a slight bend to the northeast, it sprang into view. Marshes, then a long, white sand beach, split by the Little Sister's rush to the great waters of the North Viridian. Falcons rose crying from the sea stacks and spiraled into the air as the flyers circled down and settled on the east side of the river, and fifty yards or so back on the sand. "Is this a good spot?" Ardenai asked, "or would you rather go to the beach at Falconstones? We could get out the boat and go sailing."

"This is wonderful," Gideon breathed, stepping out of the flyer and onto the beach. "This is perfect. Thank you so much." He put the puppy down beside him, and sat in the warming sand to remove his boots and socks. In an instant, he was littered with sand as the pup began to dig, spinning in a circle and throwing sand indiscriminately in all directions in his quest for something only he was privy to. The rest of the family carried blankets, food and supplies to a vantage point close to both the river and the breakers, and spread themselves out to enjoy the day.

It was Pythos who lingered behind, observing Gideon, who did not move when the others did. He sat where he had first landed, slowly running his fingers through the temperate, alabaster sand and watching it trickle from his palm onto his knees. The old dragon toddled over on his short, powerful legs and coiled beside the boy, waiting, saying nothing. When Gideon finally looked up, there was wonder in his golden eyes.

"Who am I," he said at last and softly, "that I should deserve this?"

"Deserve what?" Pythos hissed, opening one bulging yellow eye to more than a slit.

"This," the Declivian gestured, taking in the beach and himself with a sweep of his hand. "I am wearing clothes that have never belonged to anybody else but me. Even the boots. My sire had these boots made for me, and Ah'din made me this tunic with her own hands. As busy as she is, she made this for me. I have a warm bed to sleep in at night, with a lavage that is not only indoors, but all mine. I have enough to eat at every single meal. I have a place to bathe. I have the unspeakable luxury of pets. I have a horse of my own and a dog of my own. Pythos, I have a family, and I really think they love me, at least they say they do. I have a father, grandparents, an aunt and an uncle, even a cousin and a big brother. And I have you, so I have the best of medical care. We are all gathered here to celebrate my birthing day. Mine. I just...I can't fathom what I've done to deserve such riches."

"Thee iss a child of the Wisdom Giver. That iss enough."

"Then why do others who revere the Wisdom Giver, have so much less?"

The serpent turned his frond-like hands upward in a questioning gesture and made the noise that Gideon had come to recognize as a chuckle of bemusement. "Thee asskss very hard quesstionss, young princcce. Thiss one knowss only that with much richnesss, comess much ressponssibility. Perhapss, becausse thee took up a heavy burden of ressponssibility without being assked, thou art rewarded in kind."

"And your help when I was in direst need was more than I could ever have imagined you giving," Ardenai said, coming up to sit quietly on the other side of Gideon.

"That was the catalyst, then?" Gideon asked, turning to Ardenai.

Ardenai stared out to sea for a bit before answering. "No," he said at last. "You, the force of your personality on a day to day, routine basis, the depth of your desire to succeed, made what you did a very natural extension of who you are. The fact that you saved me was an act of heroism. The fact that you stayed with me from that moment on, sharing the danger, the pain, the unknown, the fear, that was the act of a kinsman, a brother. Now I will tell you something I haven't told you before. I loved you from the time I met you. Had you not come with me at the outset, when all was said and done, and the fighting was over, I would have gone back to Demeter for you. You didn't need to do one, single thing beyond the everyday, to make me love you. Eladeus willed that we should be together."

Gideon sighed, and a weight he didn't know he'd been carrying, lifted from his heart. He put his hand on Ardenai's updrawn knee, and set his forehead momentarily against the broad shoulder. "As surely as if I were the seed of your body, you have given me life," he said softly, "and I thank you."

The sleek little flyer in whose shade they were sitting chimed softly as its proximity beacon sensed another vessel, and Gideon tensed as a rather large shuntcraft glided up the canyon and settled close by. What if it were Ah'krill?

"It's not," Ardenai said flatly, as though the boy had spoken aloud. "She hasn't said one word to me in a week, and I don't suppose she will for a while yet. I wounded her pride by sending her back to the Great House with Abeyan. I angered her by separating her from Jilfan. She will remain aloof until she needs something of me."

"I hope you're right," Gideon muttered, and stood up, brushing the sand off his trousers with his hands. "I don't recognize this shunt. It's not Equi, is it?"

"No," Ardenai chuckled, realizing whose it was.

Just then the door slid open and a familiar figure filled the doorway. "Josephus!" Gideon exclaimed, and ran to help his father's old friend get down the steps and onto the sand.

Ardenai hurried up behind him, extending his hands. "Ahimsa, I wish thee peace!" he said. "What brings you?"

"Just a short layover," Josephus chuckled, tucking one of them under each massive arm. "I have a few hours, so I thought I'd stop by the house and say hello, and they told me you was all down here, so anyways, here I am. Here, here, what's this dancing about our feet all in a dither?"

The pup had arrived, dripping mud from the river and all smiles, bearing a dead spinklemaus in his jaws. "This is my dog," Gideon said proudly. "Criollo, my cousin, gave him to me for my birthing day."

Josephus let his eyes get wide. "So it's today is it? That mystical, wonderful seventeenth year is upon you, is it? Well, that's pretty amazing that I should arrive on such a momentous occasion. I do hope I'm in time for some of your auntie's honey cake. And there's the old dragon hisself. Pythos, it's good to see you."

"Thee iss mosst welcome, friend of my friend," Pythos hissed, and the four of them made their way across the sand, with the pup bounding proudly ahead with his trophy.

Josephus kicked his boots off, settled his bulk in the warm sand, and gladly accepted a drink and a sweet cake. "Hope I'm not wearing out my welcome, beings as I was here for some time just shortly ago," he said, nodding to Ah'din and Ah'rane.

"Never," Ah'din laughed. "Anyone who can thread a floor loom as well as you can has a permanent welcome at my hearth."

"Good to know," Josephus grinned. "Boy seems to be working real well into the family."

The conversation turned that direction, and Ardenai was content to stretch out beside Kehailan on the sand and listen, and soak up the last of the season's warm sunshine.

The last shunt to arrive brought Timor, his wife Ah'mae, and Ah'bri-anne, who, Gideon thought, seemed just a little too happy to see Criollo. On the other hand, she seemed no less happy to see him, and she adored the puppy. They had brought their own puppy, Rhorus, who was huge, but no older than Gideon's pup, and the two dogs romped happily, unaware of the comic picture they presented.

"You didn't bring Sawkus?" Gideon asked, walking beside her in the wet sand at the waves' edge.

"Sawkus was delighted to be rid of him for the day," Ah'brianne chuckled, and her bright eyes flashed with sunlight as she smiled at him.

The puppy flew by, then stopped abruptly and began to dig at the water's edge, making exuberant chuffing noises, and shoving his little terrier nose eye-deep into the rapidly growing hole.

Gideon watched him for a bit, and his looked softened to a memory which stood in his golden eyes and caused Ah'brianne to ask, "What are you thinking?"

Gideon looked momentarily startled, then chuckled and shook his head. "I don't have many happy memories of being little," he said quietly, "but there was this place not too far from where I lived, and I would go there sometimes. The Museum of Transportation. They had all kinds of things in there that traveled on the land, and under and over it, and they had trains from our planet, and others, as well." He sighed with pleasure at the memory. "They even had a replica of an ancient model train that had been a children's toy. It was black, and on its side it said, Lionel, in big gold letters, and it made little chuffing noises, just like he's doing. I wanted that little train more than anything else in the world."

"Only now he's more choking and gagging," Criollo observed. "I think he's probably inhaled a bit too much sand."

"Lionel," Gideon said again, scooping up the puppy and wiping his face with the corner of his shirt, "Lionel. I like that. You move just like that little train used to, and I've wanted a dog more than I ever wanted that toy."

"Here's to Lionel," Criollo said with a solemn wink. 'Let's hope he's easy to...train."

There was a communal groan, but the name was decided on, and the puppy was released back to tumble with Rhorus.

They spent the day feasting on bulging flatwraps, crisp vegetables, fruit and sweets, and laughing and running on the beach playing scoops, which didn't sound like a game that required skill and agility, but of course it did. They played old against the young, boys against the girls, with Pythos and Josephus serving as audience. During a quiet time, they sat and listened while Pythos told them the story of the ancient city of Destrier, long buried in the desert sands of Viridia. His hissing, sibilant tones, coupled with the cool breeze blowing off the Viridian Sea, made the hair stand up on the back of Gideon's neck, and he shivered with delight at the tale. He'd never had anybody take time to tell him a ghost story before.

Josephus added a tale or two of his own, as well as the interstellar gossip surrounding the arrival of the Lebonathi delegation. When the adults seemed fairly settled into that particular conversation, Criollo and Gideon forded the chilly river with Ah'brianne and headed west down the beach.

The young people spoke of school, and of returning to the Great House. That meant Gideon would have not just one friend in school there, but two, and it strengthened his determination to go. His father and grand-father, his whole family, had been tutoring him at length for seasons, and his confidence was on the rise. Before Ah'brianne left that afternoon she exacted a promise from him to attend at least a few of old Master Breton's classes, and Gideon agreed.

Ardenai and Io, too, strolled together and spoke of the need to return to the Capital, and Ardenai's eyes were sad as he gazed out toward the setting sun. "I always hate to leave this place," he said, bending to kiss the top of his wife's head. They stopped, and sat in the sand, and watched the sun go down without speaking further. "Still, I suppose we must," he sighed, and Io nodded.

"We'll be back in just a few days," she said, patting his arm, "and we do have that meeting with the Lebonathis on Scoligyre nightfall. I'm look-ing forward to that, aren't you? Who are these fascinating people, exactly, and why have they come so far to see you?"

"Good questions," Ardenai smiled, rose to his feet, and pulled her up beside him. "I would like you to stay with me for a while, at least until we see what the delegates want of us. Others can continue the search for Nik in the meantime."

Io nodded her assent and pulled his hand over her shoulder, stroking his fingers as they strolled back toward the rest of the family, by now pack-ing things up and stuffing them into the flyers. "It's cooling off rapidly," she observed, walking a little closer to her husband to share his warmth. "We are moving into Oporens. Perhaps that's good. Things will feel less hectic when harvest is over."

"Yes," Ardenai nodded, but his mind was not on the harvest; it was elsewhere – on the affairs of the Great House, the sudden disappearance of an honorable man, and the mysterious delegation from Lebonath Jas. "We need to go," he said. "We'll miss our train."

THE ELEVEN PLANETS OF THE AFFINED EQUI WORLDS (AEW)

Equus
Menorquin
Corvus
Amberia
Demeter
Anguine Prime
Anguine II
Papillia
Phylla
Calumet
Terren

CHARACTER LIST
(Alphabetically)

Abeyan, Equi – Master of Cavalry, father of Ah'riodin

Ah'brianne, Equi – daughter of Timor and Ah'mae. Fostering daughter of Teal and Ah'din

Ah'dara, Calumet Equi – Mentioned as a possible bride for Ardenai

Ah'davan, Equi – (Addie) Beloved wife of Konik

Ah'din, Equi – Sister of Ardenai, wife of Teal, Mother of Criollo, Daughter of Krush and Ah'rane

Ah'keena, Equi – Member of the Horse Guard, bride of Tarpan

Ah'kra, Anguine Equi – Second wife of Abeyan, Master of Cavalry

Ah'krill, Equi – High Priestess of Equus. Ardenai's birth mother

Ah'leah, Equi/Papilli – Infant daughter of Ah'riodin and Ardenai, lost before birth

Ah'mae, Equi – Friend and neighbor of Ah'din, wife of Timor

Ah'nia, Equi – One of Konik's twin daughters, grown, with a family of her own

Ah'nis, Equi – Priestess. Of Ah'krill's inner circle, and Ah'krill's choice as a wife for Ardenai

Ah'nora, Calumet Equi – Manages the house at South hold. Mentioned as a bride for Ardenai

Ah'pia, Equi – Member of the Horse Guard. Mentioned as a bride for Ardenai

Ah'rane, Equi – Friction Analysis Engineer. Ardenai's foster mother, wife of Krush

Ah'ree, Equi/Terrasian – Ardenai's late first wife

Ah'rika, Equi – One of Konik's twin daughters, grown, with a family of her own

Ah'riodin, Equi/Papilli – (Io) Captain of the Horse Guard of the Great House of Equus. Primuxori.

Ah'ti, Equi – On the Education Council. Mentioned as a possible wife for Ardenai

Ardenai, Equi – (Mister Grayson) Who rises to be the 13th Dragonhorse

Catrio, Equi – Member of the Horse Guard

Cohen, Amir, Demetrian Mix – Chief of Onboard Technologies, Belesprit. Father of Yussef

Cohen, Yussef, Demetrian cross – small son of Amir Cohen

Criollo, Equi – In his last year of Final Form. Son of Teal and Ah'din, Nephew of Ardenai

Daleth, Equi – Standard Bearer, Horse Guard

Dannis, Bonfire, Phyllan – Navigator and Second in Command, SGASV Belesprit

De Los Angeles, Adjutant, Equi – Chief Investigator in charge of SEGAS Seven

Eletsky, Marion, Terren – Captain, SGASV Belesprit, friend of Kehailan and Ardenai

Gideon, Declivian/Terren/Coronian cross – (Reed) Sixteen-year-old boy who befriends Ardenai

Jilfan, Equi/Papilli – Twelve-year-old son of Ah'riodin by her late husband, Salerno

Josephus, Terren – Captain of "The Grand Old Rust Bucket," who rescues Ardenai and Gideon

Kabardin, Equi – The Ninth Dragonhorse. The supposed father of the "True line of Dragonhorses"

Kais, Theseus, Hectorian/Coronian – Who Konik hires to transport Ardenai's clipper

Keats, Hadrian, Terren (Dennis Strathmore) – Chief Medical Officer, SGASV Belesprit

Kehailan, Equi/Terrasian – (Kee) Wing Commander, SGASV Belesprit, Ardenai's son

Konik (Ah'ria Konik Nokota) Equi – Senator from Anguine II, Telenir Legate, husband of Ah'davan

Krush, Equi – Ardenai's foster father. Husband of Ah'rane, father of Ah'din

Landais, Equi – Master Farrier, friend of Ardenai and Teal

Luna, Papilli/Equi – Late mother of Ah'riodin, late wife of Abeyan

Mahruss, Equi – A member of Ardenai's Creppia Nonage class of five and six-year-olds

MalDor, Kohathi – Represents the Parasectra of Kohath Zadok on the Great Council

Markis, Tarkelian – Works for Squire Fidel

Master Breton, Equi – Ancient Master of Education for the Great House of Equus

McGill, Timothy, Demetrian/Terren – Chief Botanist aboard Belesprit, friend of Kehailan

Merens, Equi – Older brother of Ah'brianne

Moonsgold, Winslow, Declivian mix – (Winnie) Head of the Science Wing, SGASV Belesprit

Orlov Teacher, Equi – Teacher of six and seven-year-olds aboard Belesprit

Pongo, Oona, Terren – Communications Officer, SGASV Belesprit

Pythos, Achernarean – Of the ancient line of Sea Dragon Physicians. Ardenai's personal physician

Reynalda, Corvi/Terren – small girl aboard Belesprit

Salerno, Equi – Late husband of Ah'riodin, father of Jilfan

Sardure, Telenir – Brother of Sarkhan, whose place was taken by Konik

Saremanno, Telenir – Father of Sarkhan and Sardure

Sarkhan, Telenir– Senator, Telenir. Pretender to the title of Dragonhorse

Seglawi, Equi – Captain of Arms, Horse Guard

Squire Fidel, Demetrian cross – Plantation owner on Demeter, where Grayson meets Gideon.

Sta'dan, Corvi – Ambassador to Equus from Corvus

Taki, Telenir – Telenir elder who represents the delegation pleading for peace

Tarpan, Equi – Commander of the Secondary Squads, Equi Cavalry, Horse Guard Division

Teal, Equi – Master of Horse, friend of Ardenai, married to Ah'din, father of Criollo

Thatcher, Calumet/Hectorian – Boss of the cleomitite mine

Timor, Equi – Neighbor to Ardenai, Krush and Teal, father of Ah'brianne, husband of Ah'mae

ValDem, Kohathi – Represents Kohath Zadok in the Seventh Galactic Alliance Chambers

OTHER NAMES OF IMPORT

Eladeus – the Equi name for the Creator Spirit

El'Shadai – the Declivian name for the Creator Spirit

THE ANCIENT LINES OF THE GREAT HOUSE

Equine – From which most of the Dragonhorses have come, including Ardenai

Waterfowl – More ancient than Equine. Teal is from this line

Aviarium – More ancient yet. Represented mostly by the ancient beings of Mountain hold

Arboranthus – An early line which has fallen into obscurity, but is still represented

Achernarean – Represented by the venerable and powerful sea dragons

HOW EQUI NAMES WORK

A woman carries her father's name first, then her given name, then her mother's name. For example: Ah'din was Krush Ah'din Ah'rane before her marriage to Teal, at which time she took his given name to become Krush Ah'din Teal.

A man carries his mother's name first, then his given name, then his father's name. This does not change when he marries. Hence Ardenai was Ah'rane Ardenai Krush. When he rose to become Dragonhorse his name became Ah'krill Ardenai Morning Star. Morning Star being the designate of all the named Dragonhorses.

Ah' prefaces nearly all women's names. It is an ancient designate meaning, "lady, woman or female."

ABOUT THE AUTHOR

Showandah S. Terrill is an award winning speaker and storyteller, as well as a lifelong writer and equestrian. Steeped in Native American culture, she was raised as the only child of an itinerant cowhand on sprawling ranches in Southern California during the turbulent 1960's.

She is currently writing two extended series: the epic science-fiction *Dragonhorse Chronicles* and the fictional autobiographical *Peter Aarons'* novels.

CPSIA information can be obtained
at www.ICGtesting.com
Printed in the USA
BVHW031010291020
592124BV00015B/295/J